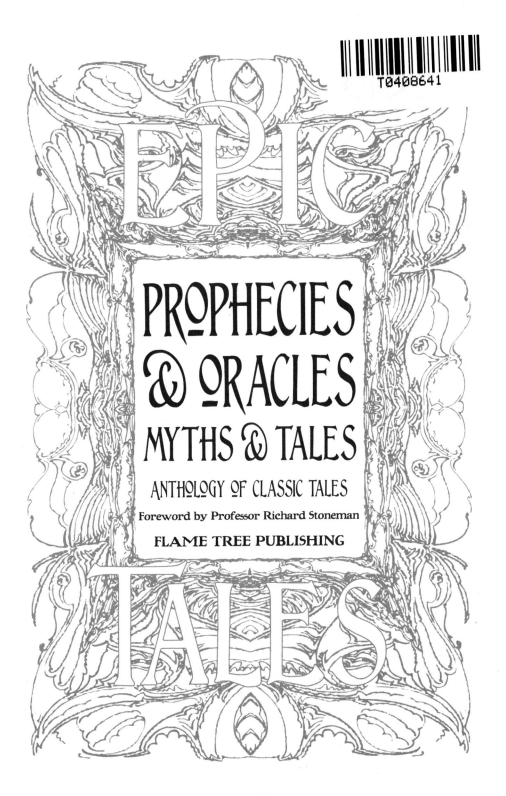

PROPHECIES & ORACLES MYTHS & TALES

ANTHOLOGY OF CLASSIC TALES

Foreword by Professor Richard Stoneman

FLAME TREE PUBLISHING

This is a FLAME TREE Book

Publisher & Creative Director: Nick Wells
Editorial Director: Catherine Taylor
Project Editor: Jemma North
Special thanks to Michael Kerrigan and Claire Gault

FLAME TREE PUBLISHING
6 Melbray Mews, Fulham,
London SW6 3NS, United Kingdom
www.flametreepublishing.com

First published 2025

Copyright © 2025 Flame Tree Publishing Ltd

25 27 29 28 26
1 3 5 7 9 10 8 6 4 2

ISBN: 978-1-83562-290-2
Special ISBN: 978-1-83562-675-7

All rights reserved. No part of this publication may be reproduced, stored in a
retrieval system, or transmitted in any form or by any means, electronic,
mechanical, photocopying, recording or otherwise, without the prior written
permission of the publisher.

The cover image is created by Flame Tree Studio based on artwork by
Slava Gerj, Gabor Ruszkai and Adwo. Internal decorations are courtesy
Shutterstock.com and the following artists: Jeremy Show, Agnieszka Karpinska,
and Karlionau (story headers), Media Guru.

Publisher's Note: Due to the historical nature of the classic text, we're aware
that there may be some language used which has the potential to cause offence
to the modern reader. However, wishing overall to preserve the integrity of the
text, rather than imposing contemporary sensibilities, we have left it unaltered.
A copy of the CIP data for this book is available from the British Library.

Printed and bound in China

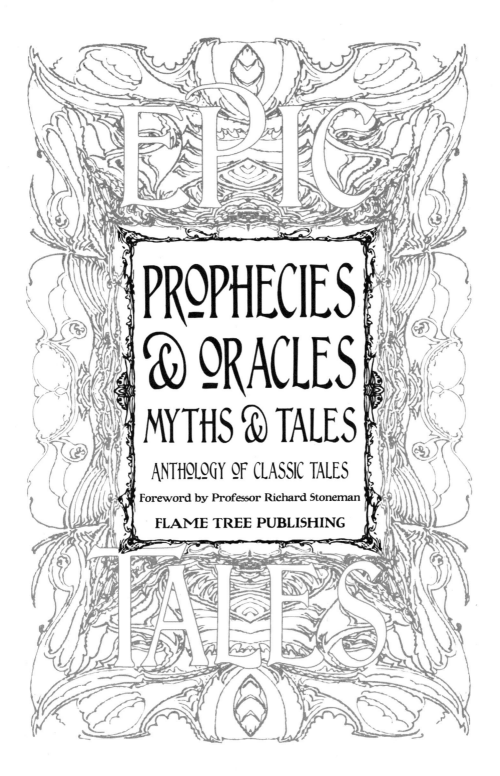

EPIC

PROPHECIES & ORACLES
MYTHS & TALES

ANTHOLOGY OF CLASSIC TALES

Foreword by Professor Richard Stoneman

FLAME TREE PUBLISHING

TALES

Contents

Foreword 12

Publisher's Note 13

Prophecies & Oracles in Myth & Folklore: Introduction

The Spirits' Message 14

An Anticlimactic Outcome 14

Oracular Ambiguity 15

Open to Interpretation 15

A Symbolic Logic 16

Beauty and Birthright 16

A Moral Dimension 17

Marked Men 18

Role Models? 18

Reality Check 19

Folly and Fire 20

Disaster on the Horizon

Introduction 24

The Loves of Apollo 25
(From Greek mythology)

How the Argonauts Sailed to Colchis 27
(From Greek mythology)

Trojan Victories 37
(From Greek mythology)

The Death of Achilles 41
(From Greek mythology)

Icarus and Daedalus 47
(From Greek mythology)

CONTENTS

Letter LXXXIII to Sura 48
(From Roman folktales)

Tyr's Sword 50
(From Norse mythology)

Ragnarok 52
(From Norse mythology)

The Story of Grímur, Who Killed Skeljúngur 55
(From Icelandic folktales)

The Prince Who Insisted on Possessing the Moon.. 63
(From the Congo and Central Africa)

Kwege and Bahati 67
(From the Zaramo Peoples, Tanzania)

The Road to Heaven 69
(From the Rongo-speaking peoples, Mozambique)

Horse Cursed by Sun 71
(From South Africa)

The Constable 71
(From Chinese mythology)

The Reward of a Benevolent Life 74
(From Chinese mythology)

Tobikawa Imitates a Tengu 80
(From Japanese mythology)

Chrysanthemum-Old-Man 80
(From Japanese mythology)

An End to the Exile 81
(From Indian mythology)

Katcha and the Devil 83
(From Czech folktales)

The Banshee of the Mac Carthys 87
(From Irish mythology)

A PROMISING PATH AHEAD

Introduction 96

Vidar 97
(From Norse mythology)

5

PROPHECIES & ORACLES: MYTHS & TALES

The Sultan's Snake-child 98
(From the Swahili-speaking peoples, East Africa)

The Orphan Boy and the Magic Stone 101
(From Southern Nigeria, West Africa)

How a Girl Reached the Land of the Ghosts
and Came Back.. 103
(From the Changa peoples, Tanzania)

The Chief and the Tigers................................... 104
(From Lesotho, Southern Africa)

The Gift of Corn... 106
(From Native American mythology)

Ojeeg Annung, or The Summer Maker.................... 108
(From Native American mythology)

The White Hare of Inaba................................... 111
(From Japanese mythology)

The Man Who Went to Seek His Fortune 112
(From Indian mythology)

Yama and Sivitri.. 114
(From Indian mythology)

The Rose-Beauty 120
(From Turkish folktales)

THE CHOSEN ONES

Introduction.. 124

The Labour of Hercules 125
(From Greek mythology)

The Stealing of Helen.. 134
(From Greek mythology)

The Young Thief... 142
(From the Swahili-speaking peoples, East Africa)

The Physician's Son and the King of the Snakes 145
(From Zanzibar, Tanzanian coast)

Sudika-Mbambi the Invincible 151
(From the Bantu-speaking peoples, Angola)

CONTENTS

Morena-y-a-Letsatsi, or the Sun Chief 154
(From Lesotho, Southern Africa)

Tau-wau-chee-hezkaw, or The White Feather 158
(From Native American mythology)

Tulla, the Hiding Nook of the Snake 161
(From Aztec mythology)

The Stolen Child 164
(From Inca mythology)

The Divine Messengers 168
(From Japanese mythology)

The Temple to the God of War 170
(From Korean folktales)

The Story of Saiáwush 172
(From Persian mythology)

The Ram with the Golden Fleece 196
(From Serebian folktales)

He Whom God Helps No One Can Harm 200
(From Serbian folktales)

The Cattle-Raid of Cualnge 202
(From Irish mythology)

How Fin Went to the Kingdom of the Big Men 205
(From Irish mythology)

The Prophecies of Merlin, and the Birth of
Arthur 209

The Fourth Branch of the Mabinogi 214
(From Celtic mythology)

The Birth of Cúchulainn 225
(From Celtic mythology)

Briar-Rose 227
(From German fairy tales)

The Devil with the Three Golden Hairs 229
(From German fairy tales

Oracles, Seers & Sages

Introduction 234

Oedipus 235
(From Greek mythology)

Themis 237
(From Greek mythology)

The Norns' Web 238
(From Norse mythology)

The Story of Nornagesta 239
(From Norse mythology)

Hermod 241
(From Norse mythology)

King Kitamba kia Shiba (and the
Kingdom of Death) 242
(From the Mbundu peoples, Angola)

Piqua 243
(From Native American mythology)

The Spirits of the Yellow River 250
(From Chinese mythology)

The Vengeance of the Goddess 253
(From Chinese mythology)

The Mysterious Buddhist Robe 259
(From Chinese mythology)

In the Palace of the Sea God 269
(From Japanese mythology)

Fate 270
(From Serbian folktales)

The Flaming Horse 275
(From Czech fairy tales)

The Three Fates 279
(From Macedonian folktales)

How Cobbler Ahmet Became the
Chief Astrologer 283
(From Turkish folktales)

CONTENTS

The Beresford Ghost 286
(From Irish mythology)

The Terrible Head 291
(From Scottish fairy tales)

The Seer's Death 297
(From Scottish mythology)

The Tale of Taliesin 299
(From Celtic mythology)

The Curse of the Fires and of the Shadows 318
(From Celtic mythology)

CLAIRVOYANT VISIONS & DREAMS

Introduction 322

Balder and the Mistletoe 323
(From Norse mythology)

Ryangombe and Binego 327
(From the Banyawanda people, Rwanda)

Berossus's Account of the Deluge 329
(From Babylon and Sumer mythology)

Nebuchadnezzar 330
(From Babylon and Sumer mythology)

Iosco, or The Prairie Boys' Visit to the Sun
and the Moon 332
(From Native American mythology)

The Undying Head 338
(From Native American mythology)

The Shepherd and the Daughter of the Sun 346
(From Inca mythology)

The Vision of Yupanqui 349
(From Inca mythology)

Benten-of-the-Birth-Water 349
(From Japanese mythology)

Dutiful Daughter 351
(From Korean folktales)

PROPHECIES & ORACLES: MYTHS & TALES

The Dream of the King's Son.................................359
(From Serbian folktales)

Water of Youth, Water of Life,

and Water of Death.................................362
(From Russian mythology)

The Three Dreams.................................366
(From Hungarian mythology)

The Dream of Maxen Wledig.................................369
(From Welsh folktales)

Seaforth's Dream.................................374
(From Scottish mythology)

The Conflagration.................................375
(From French fairy tales)

ORIGIN PROPHECIES

Introduction.................................380

Ion.................................381
(From Greek mythology)

The Story of the Drummer and the Alligators.....382
(From Southern Nigeria, West Africa)

Why Dead People are Buried.................................385
(From Southern Nigeria, West Africa)

How Kimyera Became King of Uganda.................................386
(From Uganda, East Africa)

The Legend of the Leopardess and Her Two Servants,

Dog and Jackal.................................396
(From the Congo, Central Africa)

The Elephant and the Lion.................................404
(From the Congo, Central Africa)

The First of the Rattlesnakes.................................407
(From Native American mythology)

The Gods of the Azteca.................................410
(From Aztec mythology)

Manco Capac Founds Cuzco.................................412
(From Inca mythology)

The Prophecy of Chilam Balam and the
Story of Antonio Martinez 413
(From Mayan mythology)

The Origin of the Deity Fehuluni 415
(From Polynesian mythology)

The Twelve Brothers 417
(From German fairy tales)

BIOGRAPHIES & TEXT SOURCES 421

Foreword

PEOPLE ALL OVER the world, from time immemorial, have wanted to have insight into the future: to know what is going to happen, and to receive guidance on what they should do. 'What sort of person will this child be?', 'If I marry X, will it turn out well for me?' The past spreads out before us like a broad landscape, but the future, in the ancient Greek conception, is behind us and therefore invisible. We should like to be able to turn our heads, just a little, and see into the future. The gods, it is supposed, have 360-degree vision, and so people have devised various ways of communicating with the gods to get their guidance. The ancient Babylonians, followed by the Greeks and Romans, developed various sophisticated quasi-scientific procedures for achieving this. These included the casting of horoscopes, based on astronomical observations, and extispicy, or the examination of the entrails of sacrificed animals. (Plato remarked how strange it was that the gods chose to inscribe their messages to humans on the livers of oxen.) In ancient China predictions and guidance were read by experts from the cracks created when turtle carapaces were heated by fire.

The Greeks developed techniques for making the gods speak. The oracle at Delphi, as Heraclitus wrote, neither reveals nor conceals, but gives a sign. But Apollo replied to his questioners through the medium of an 'inspired' or 'raving' prophetess, whose works were relayed to the inquirers by priests who expressed them in finely composed hexameter verses. Classic tales concerning the Pythia's responses appear in Herodotus's *Histories*, such as the advice to the Athenians to 'trust in their wooden walls', which the wise statesman Themistocles rightly interpreted as referring not to a stockade, but to the fleet of wood-built triremes, with which the Persians were defeated at Salamis.

But many decision-making procedures were and are much simpler than this, both in the classical world and elsewhere. The Zande people of Africa seek yes-or-no answers to questions, mostly about decisions, by feeding poison to chickens and observing whether they die or survive. Other lucky-dip types of inquiry include the numerous tomb oracles of southern Turkey, such as that at Olympus, where in the early centuries AD consultants would choose a lucky number corresponding to one of a set of 24 hexameter verses inscribed on a tomb wall, on the lines of 'You will love to see the offspring of lawful marriage' and 'Phoebus says clearly "Wait, friend".'

Predictions and prophecies play a role in folktales from many parts of the world. The Delphic oracle foretold that Oedipus would grow up to kill his father and marry his mother: despite his parents' evasive action in exposing him to die, he was rescued and unwittingly did exactly what the oracle had foretold. The Irish hero Cú Chulainn had life of fame and eventual death foretold at his birth. The Scandinavian god Baldur was guaranteed invulnerability by all the plants of earth except the mistletoe which thought itself too insignificant to need to swear. The appearance of the goddess Eris (Strife) at the wedding of Peleus and Thetis ensured that their son, Achilles, would meet with misfortune; and Thetis's attempt to make him invulnerable by dipping him in the River Styx left him vulnerable at the ankle. The evil stepmother in the tale of Snow White receives forbidding answers from her magic speaking mirror, which inflame her jealousy and cause her to seek the girl's death.

Prophecies and predictions are frequent plot-movers in folk tales. Oedipus (above) is a good example. In the story of Cupid and Psyche, first told in Latin by Apuleius in the second century AD, Psyche's father consults the Delphic oracle on how to secure her marriage, and later a stone tower speaks to explain to her how to visit the Underworld for guidance (as both Odysseus and Heracles in myth visited the Underworld).

It was normal in classical antiquity to consult an oracle before founding a city. Alexander the Great, according to legend, did so before founding Alexandria, and took the opportunity to ask the god Sarapis when and how he was going to die: the prophecy regarding Alexandria predicted flourishing commercial success but the king was warned that it was better for a man not to know the day of his death. The Inca people consulted oracles before the foundation of the city of Cuzco.

For philosophers in Greece and Rome, the reliability of prophecies of the future raised intriguing questions about fate and determinism: if all the future was predetermined, where did that leave human choice? For the characters of traditional tales, they seemed to be caught in unavoidable destiny. The popularity of newspaper horoscopes, astrology and fortune-telling today suggests that many people still sense that they are not, as they believe they should be, free. No Chinese restaurant opens without professional consultation regarding its Feng Shui (mainly a geomantic interpretation of its relation to Air and Water). So the ancient folktales continue to speak to the denizens of a supposedly scientific age.

Professor Richard Stoneman
Honorary visiting professor at the University of Exeter

Publisher's Note

PROPHECIES have always been a powerful element of folklore and storytelling, fulfilling the need to seek answers. These stories tell of predictions and decision-making processes across the world, from the Delphic oracle to Ragnarök in Norse mythology. They are a mix of myths, legends, folklore and fairy tales – exploring the many ways oracles and fortune-tellers feature in tales of prediction.

We must remind the reader that, as tales from mythology and folklore are principally derived from an oral storytelling tradition, their written representation depends on the transcription, translation and interpretation by those who heard them and first put them to paper, and also on whether they are recently re-told versions or more directly sourced from original first-hand accounts. The stories in this book are a mixture, and you can learn more about the sources and authors at the back of the book. Due to the historical nature of such texts, we're aware that there may be some language used which has the potential to cause offence to the modern reader. However, wishing to preserve the overall integrity of the writing, rather than imposing contemporary sensibilities, we have left it largely unaltered.

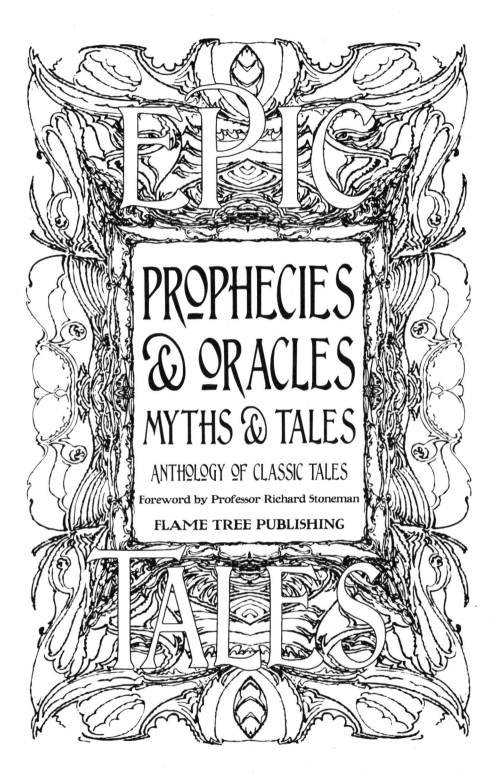
EPIC
PROPHECIES & ORACLES
MYTHS & TALES
ANTHOLOGY OF CLASSIC TALES

Foreword by Professor Richard Stoneman

FLAME TREE PUBLISHING

TALES

Prophecies & Oracles in Myth & Folklore

Introduction

IN 1846, with their survival at stake, South Africa's Xhosa made another stand against the British in what history has recorded as the Seventh Cape Frontier War. It went the same way as the previous six: Bantu military technology couldn't match that of a modern European power and the Xhosa had to surrender still more of their precious grazing land. By 1854, British farming families were being settled on the veld. The Xhosa were then further afflicted by two years of calamitous crop failure and cattle disease.

The Spirits' Message

At this point, a war-orphaned fifteen-year-old girl named Nongqawuse made a prophecy to transform her people's fortunes. The message she proclaimed, apparently given to her by three mystic beings she'd met down by the river bank, spread like wildfire. The three figures were, they'd assured her, ancestral spirits who had come to entrust her with a sacred task. The Xhosa must systematically kill their cattle, destroy their grain stores and let their fields lie fallow. A fearful sacrifice but, they promised, from this ground zero, renewal would come. A red sun would rise in the west, and great prodigies would appear. Storms would rage and spirit warriors would return from the world beyond to help the living Xhosa drive the invaders out. This great day of vengeance and salvation would dawn on 18 February, 1857.

The hesitancy of a minority was quickly overborne by the enthusiasm of the mass of Xhosa who saw this as a clear call to arms. Hundreds of thousands of cattle were killed, the carcases piled high, the carrion stench mingling with the acrid smell of burning crops as the Xhosa's entire sustenance went up in smoke. Despite their hunger, they felt no fear, and it was with an ecstatic sense of anticipation that, in the early hours of 18 February, they waited, eyes fixed on the western horizon as the first light stole over the veld, only to find the rays creeping across the landscape from behind them, where the sun was rising on its accustomed eastern side. Of the vast and vengeful ancestor-army – there was no sign.

An Anticlimactic Outcome

So much for their victory over the British. Instead, in the weeks and months that followed, as whole families slowly starved, the Xhosa had to beg the invader for food handouts. Some

75,000 are estimated to have died. As in Ireland a decade earlier, famine meant much more than hunger and death: a whole society was shattered, a culture swept away.

As for the hapless Nongqawuse, she had to flee for her safety. After a period in British detention, she spent the rest of her life in exile on a remote farm in the Eastern Cape. Her story may be seen to illustrate one important point: prophecies need not necessarily be true. Sometimes because purported prophets are opportunistic frauds; more often – and more interestingly – because, like Nongqawuse, they are deluded by visions they really want to be true.

Oracular Ambiguity

Some inexactitude surrounds the definition of an 'oracle', used interchangeably of a person – essentially a prophet; a predictor of the future – and the prediction such a person makes. And sometimes too for the place from which they make it. History's most celebrated oracle was at Delphi, in central Greece – and, in the Greek imagination, the centre of the world. This status was underlined by the presence of a rock, supposedly set down by the god Zeus, to mark the *omphalos* or 'navel' of the earth. A temple was built on this sacred site.

Pythia, the temple priestess, was supposedly the mouthpiece of Apollo, god of the sun, music and dance, but also of truth and prophecy. Pythia was a title rather than a name, held by a series of high priestesses. On appointed days in summer, when it seemed natural that the sun god would be in residence, she stepped forth attended by priests to perform purification rituals. Only when these were completed did she voice her prophecies, standing above a natural cleft in the rock which gave the impression that she was delivering messages from the earth itself.

Open to Interpretation

It is unclear what form her pronouncements took. There is, however, some suggestion that she entered a trance during which she came out with a screed of what to uninitiated hearers sounded like nonsense, only for this to be interpreted by special priests. (It has indeed been suggested that gaseous emissions from the chasm beneath her feet may have helped intensify her prophetic trance.) Prophets naturally expressed themselves in high-flown, poetic language. Like Nongqawuse they were dealing in the stuff of dream, of yearning. Often, though, they talked in semi-comprehensible babble which (it was believed) could only be interpreted by a select few.

This on the one hand enhanced their hearers' sense that they were imparting privileged and sacred wisdom; on the other, it opened the way to cynical abuse. Even now, we can't say with certainty that the sixteenth-century French astrologer Nostradamus was a fraud, but the obscurity of his language and the obliqueness of his claims undoubtedly made it easy for later admirers to credit him with predictions he didn't directly make.

The so-called 'Scottish Nostradamus', Coinneach Odhar or the 'Brahan Seer', also wrote elliptically, though some have claimed to find predictions of everything from the Battle of Culloden to the discovery of North Sea oil in his convoluted texts. His tragic end may be read as a neat illustration of the openness of narrative to interpretation. Attached to the household of the Earl of Seaforth at Brahan Castle, on the Black Isle, in the Highlands, he's said to have made unhelpful hints about the paternity of some of the children there – including those of Lady Seaforth herself. It isn't even known whether he made his remarks in cryptic, 'prophetic' mode or as banal innuendos. Either way, the Lady of Brahan was not amused. Some accounts say that she had the offending Seer burned at the stake; others that she had him pitched into a barrel of boiling tar.

A Symbolic Logic

Why were the Xhosa so ready to follow such a suicidal strategy? A lack of more rational, realistic options was evidently a factor. But so too, surely, was a powerful sense that, outlandish as it was, Nongqawuse's vision struck some sort of chord in the collective imagination of a proud people facing ruin. At some important level it rang true psychologically; satisfied some need in the Xhosa to have their worth acknowledged, to feel recognized.

Perverse as it sounds (as it very much was, indeed) for the Xhosa to destroy their livelihood, this kind of scorched-earth strategy has often appealed to those in desperate straits. It isn't difficult to understand the appeal of a purgative destruction of the status quo, a clean slate and a wholly new fresh start. For similar reasons, the thought of the sun rising in the west – though scientifically absurd – has a certain poetic logic. The Xhosa felt that what was needed was an event of all but unthinkable magnitude – and one that, more specifically, would seem to turn time right around. History had not been on their side for decades now. It's not hard to see why they'd have wanted to see the sun – the natural clock of their days and calendar of their years – being thrown into reverse.

That their ancestors might return to rescue them made sense to a people who had always religiously revered their forebears. With their whole identity under threat, they naturally looked for help to those who had given them their life and bequeathed them both their possessions and their culture. While we quite properly see prophecy as a prediction of the future, it can also be a projection of the past. However hopelessly lacking Nongqawuse's vision may have been in real-world credibility, it convinced the Xhosa because, symbolically, it restored an age-old order in which they had been the lords of their own lands.

Beauty and Birthright

We see a comparable logic acted out in the Turkish Tale of 'The Rose Beauty'. This story starts with a wayward young princess who, growing impatient at her older sisters' failure to find husbands and marry, demands of her father that she be allowed to jump the informal queue. Increasingly angered by her badgering, her father hands all three young women bows and arrows and tells them to fire them off. They'll marry whoever's living where their arrows land. The younger girl is rewarded for her impatience by being compelled to 'marry down' dramatically after her arrow lands on a woodcutter's cabin in the forest. Fairy tale isn't realist fiction, so we never do hear how the woodcutter feels about being hitched to a woman wed to him as a punishment for her impetuousness and impertinent pride. We are told, however, that she bitterly laments her lot. Largely, in fairness, for the sake of the baby she soon has.

Fortunately, three fairies smile over Rose Beauty when she's born and promise to protect her as she grows. Her beauty will be beyond all normal girlish loveliness: '"Instead of tears, pearls shall she shed," says the first fairy. "When she smiles, roses shall blossom," says the second. "Wherever her foot falls shall grass spring up!," says the third.'

These blessings are, of course, marks of the deeper reality that will ultimately trump her poverty and disadvantage: this is a woodcutter's daughter of royal blood.

And so, over time, this reality will prevail, the prince falling in love with Rose Beauty when the fairies introduce her to him in a dream. Not that her destiny will be fulfilled that easily: a wicked schemer on the palace staff practises against Rose Beauty and pushes her own daughter in her place. Quite literally: seeing that the girl has a slight resemblance to Rose Beauty, she builds on it so determinedly that she's able to persuade the ingenuous prince that her daughter is really his dream-girl. Eventually, in her path to royal mother-in-law status she will go so far as to contrive Rose Beauty's death.

She and her daughter are left in possession of the field. The prince puts aside his doubts and marries the false Rose Beauty. But the rightful order will restore itself, the real Rose Beauty assuming the role of the Xhosa's ancestral warriors, returning from the dead to save the day. Her spirit visits the prince in another dream and reveals the truth. He goes to her grave, where his love brings her back to life; the usurping mother and daughter are expelled from court and Rose Beauty and her prince live happily ever after. Glowing prospects for the future, then, but Rose Beauty's sufferings, we see, have had to be endured in expiation of a sin from the past: her mother's disregard for her duties as a daughter.

A Moral Dimension

Sometimes it's the old-established moral order that must be restored. We see that in the Japanese story of 'The White Hare of Inaba'. Here, present-day evil is embodied in the generally unseemly conduct of the eighty royal princes and, more specifically, their bullying of their youngest brother. They treat him as a lowly servant and the story's action begins with them forcing him to trudge behind them carrying their heavy baggage on their travels. They are going to Inaba to pay their suit to the Princess of Yakami – the man who marries her will reign over the whole country. The princes, stupid and selfish, quarrel constantly over who is the most eminent, and who will rule. It doesn't occur to them that their youngest brother has any hope.

Fortunately he doesn't have to hear their squabbling. He's toiling some way behind them, weighed down by his burden, when he finds a furless white hare shivering wretchedly on a hillside. Despite his plight, he's clearly a cunning creature. Wishing to cross over from the Oki Islands to the Honshu mainland, he asks the local crocodiles to place themselves in line. He wants to carry out a census of their numbers. He'd then hop across from back to scaly back across the water, until he reached the last one, whose reptilian owner arches up and snaps off all his fur in a single bite as he jumps over. Smart as he is, the hare is sufficiently decent that he doesn't doubt the word of a purportedly kindly stranger, so had been vulnerable to the vile cruelty of the older princes.

They had found him shivering there, he tells the youngest prince, and advised him to bathe in the sea, then climb the highest mountain he could find to let the wind dry off the water. It would, they swore, be soothing. Cruel advice, of course, because the salt water makes his naked skin itch and the biting mountain wind exacerbates his discomfort. The young prince, appalled at the pain he's in, bids him bathe in fresh water then roll upon the ground to dry. Doing this, the hare immediately feels better. He tells the boy that he'll have his reward:

> *"Those eighty wicked and cruel brothers of yours," said he, "shall never win the Princess of Inaba. It is you who shall marry her and reign over the country."*

Marked Men

This young Prince's character was exemplary, but the White Hare's prophecy was prompted by a specific action of his in which his qualities were manifested. Sometimes, however, mythic prophecies relate directly to the person: certain individuals are designated special from their birth. The Persian hero Saiáwush is one such figure. He was, according to the royal astrologers' calculations, 'of wonderful promise', marked out for virtue and 'future renown'. His father, Shah Kaús, gives him an education worthy of such a splendid outcome, placing him under the tutelage of the holy warrior Rostem. That noble champion trains him up in everything from martial skills and statesmanship to hunting and etiquette. His deeds of daring and chivalry are recounted in the tenth-century epic, the *Shahnameh*.

In Ireland, Finn Mac Cumhal is born with a more ambivalent destiny. On the one hand, the son of Cumhal, chief of the Fianna, a company of warriors, the High King's bodyguard, he has the noblest possible birth and is marked out to do great things. On the other, he's precariously placed, being born just after his father Chief Cumhal's death at a time when his former rivals are circling in hopes of winning influence with the King. Finn's mother, Murna, fears for his safety:

> *She gave him to a Druidess and another wise woman of Cumhal's household, and bade them take him away and rear him as best they could. So they took him into the wild woods on the Slieve Bloom Mountains, and there they trained him to hunt and fish and to throw the spear, and he grew strong.*

Role Models?

The Japanese White Hare's protégé-prince and Persian Saiáwush are both striking in their virtue, but we should be careful of reading too much into this. We expect our heroes to be good, and so by and large did early storytellers, but they didn't necessarily place this front and centre in quite the way that we might do. And certainly not as emphatically as the great collectors of the late nineteenth and early twentieth centuries, working at what was generally a moralistic time. "The good ended happily, and the bad unhappily. That is what Fiction means," says Oscar Wilde's Miss Prism. (*The Importance of Being Earnest*, II, i.)) The focus in Finn Mac Cumhal's upbringing, we've seen, was on fresh air, physical fitness, warlike skills and courage. Such moral instruction as he received centred on his need to be able to conduct himself in accordance with his noble destiny. A matter of decorum, then, more than morality as such. Notions of right and wrong are, of course, by no means absent from the old mythologies, but we can't simply assume that they're present – or that they correspond entirely with our own.

At times, indeed, a cheerful amorality prevails, so it certainly seems to in the stories of the Inca of Peru with regard to their empire's founder and first king. Manco Capac is acknowledged to have been a brutal and cruel man. He hailed from the northern Andes, a region in which, in the remotest past (actually, it's believed by scholars, not that long ago; some time around the thirteenth century), there was a considerable amount of political volatility and conflict. Many groups were dislodged from long-established homelands and set to wander. It seems that, severed from their older traditions by their recent history of displacement, they attributed this to the destruction of the world in a great flood, the *uñu pachacuti* ('water that overturns the land').

One such *ayllu* or extended family, the Inca, eventually arrived on the *altiplano* – the long, high plateau snaking down the centre of the Andes range. Claiming to be the children of the creator-god Viracocha Pachayachachi, they travelled across country, carrying with them the precious *Indi* – a stylized eagle figure, worked in gold. (A reminder that, in addition to all its other uses, the word 'oracle' can apply to objects: this ornate bird, its supposed utterances interpreted by priests who were always in attendance, was to be the most important source of sacred wisdom to the Inca.) For a time, they settled in a place called Tampo-tocco. Manco Capac having emerged as the toughest and cruellest of the group, he married his sister Mama Occlo and they became the Inca king and queen. A generation or so later, they pushed on. They appear to have been still haunted by the fear of seeing their civilizations obliterated and their lives, with those of their children, lost by the advent of a new and maybe even more destructive flood.

Finally, though, they arrived in a broad, green valley. Cresting a hill here, 'they saw a rainbow, which the natives call *huanacauri*.'

> *Holding it to be a fortunate sign, Manco Capac said: "Take this for a sign*
> *that the world will not be destroyed by water."*

Here, then, the Inca built their capital, Cuzco. Here, for several centuries till their defeat by the Spanish, Manco Capac's successors reigned as Inca emperors, counselled daily by the wisdom afforded them by the eagle *Indi*.

Reality Check

The prophetic style, we've seen, is typically at least poetic and in some cases impossibly obscure. Appropriate enough for a form of language that's supposed to reflect what are often lurid truths. Sometimes, though, the prophet can paradoxically be the one who delivers the dash-of-cold-water common sense that's needed to correct the folly of deluded normal thinkers. This is what happens in the story of the 'Prince who Insisted on Possessing the Moon'. In this tale, from Basoko, by the river in what is now the Democratic Republic of the Congo, a great and powerful ruler spoils his son, so much so that, as the young prince boasts, his father will deny him nothing, "I have only to ask, and it is given unto me."

His friends hear him with awed attention, but one is bold enough to sound a note of scepticism. "It is true, prince," he concedes:

> *"Your father has been very good to you. He is a mighty king, and he is*
> *as generous as he is great. Still, I know of one thing that he cannot give*
> *you – and it is certain that you will never possess it."*

That thing is, of course, the moon. The prince is naturally annoyed at this put-down but too foolish smilingly to admit defeat. Instead, he goes to his still more foolish father who allows himself to be persuaded that if he builds a tower high enough, he'll be able to secure the moon.

> *Then it was proclaimed throughout the wide lands of the Bandimba*
> *that all the people should be gathered together to proceed at once with*

the work of obtaining the moon for the king's son. And the forest was cut down, and while some of the workmen squared the trees, others cut deep holes in the ground, to make a broad and sure base for the lower scaffold; and the boys made thousands of rope coils to lash the timbers together, out of bark, fibre of palm, and tough grass; and the girls, big and little, hoed up the ground and planted the cassava shrubs and cuttings from the banana and the plantain, and sowed the corn; and the women kneaded the bread and cooked the greens, and roasted green bananas for food for the workmen.

Folly and Fire

The construction of the tower becomes the task of the entire nation. All other activities are put aside. Progress is certainly made. In two months, we're told, the tower is "so lofty that the top could not be seen with the naked eye." Finally, it's high enough and, climbing triumphantly to the top (a journey of twenty days), the king gives the order to his engineer to pull at the moon to bring it down. Its silvery surface turns out to be hot, though, and quickly sets the wooden tower alight, the flames licking up to touch the moon itself:

A large portion of it tumbled to the earth, and its glowing hot materials ran over the ground like a great river of fire, so that most of the country of the Bandimba was burnt to ashes. On those who were not smothered by the smoke, nor burnt by the fire, and who fled from before the burning river, the effect was very wonderful. Such of them as were grown up, male and female, were converted into gorillas, and all the children into different kinds of long-tailed monkeys.

The king and his son had both been killed in the inferno they had caused.

The prophet here was the boy who quietly tried to check the prince's vanity, calling him back to the realities of the world. His counsel, as wise as Nongqawuse's, was deluded.It hadn't been what his listeners had wanted to hear. Ultimately, perhaps, a prophet is only as reliable as his or her audience: it's up to us how seriously their words are taken. To read these stories is to be reminded of how closely common sense and folly can be related – and how widely, how spectacularly they can diverge.

But it's also to learn something important about how we read, what we go to stories for and just how they beguile us. For prophecies are foregone conclusions; oracles open up narrative avenues whilst simultaneously foreclosing them. Tales of the expected, it might be said. Of course there will be switchback twists and turns along the way – not to say complete surprises when predictions prove unfounded. But the overarching principle of the prophetic narrative, the source of the satisfaction it brings us, is the sense it gives us ultimately of a universal order clicking into place. Included here are prophecies of warning ('Disaster on the Horizon') and more upbeat predictions ('A Promising Path Ahead') too. Some individuals ('The Chosen Ones') are marked out from the beginning for outstanding destinies; some 'Origin Prophecies' preordain the way things are going to be, in the world at large or in a given place or society. Sometimes our interest is going to lie more in the prophet than in the prophecy: such stories are gathered in the section 'Oracles, Seers and Sages'. And then there are those tales in which it's the texture of the prophecy as a visionary experience that's most at issue, as in the 'Clairvoyant Visions and Dreams' collected here. Taken together, the stories in this book provide an enthralling introduction to the world of prophecy and the force it's wielded at the deepest level in our lives.

Disaster on the Horizon

Introduction

HUANGHE, CHINA'S YELLOW RIVER, has been a boon of immeasurable value to the country. Its waters and its fertile silt have sustained civilization for centuries, millennia indeed. But it's also been the country's curse, its frequent floods overwhelming lands and sweeping villages away and claiming countless lives in just about every generation. "For many hundreds of years," we're told, fresh inundations have been heralded by the appearance of monsters – "sometimes in the shape of dragons, at others in that of cattle and horses." The wise will heed such signs and make offerings to appease these spirits and also to thank those benign creatures – those frogs, lizards and water snakes which are the souls of worthy mortals who died in the effort to build up the river dams. Every now and then, a man is arrogant enough to scorn the spirits. One wealthy man built a high stone wall, confident that it would protect his home. As the waves rose around him, he tried to quell them with cannon shot but to no avail. Finally, his terrified neighbours forced him to do appropriate honour to the spirits and the floodwaters abated just in time. The moral of this story – as it is of so many here – is that we ignore prophetic warnings at our peril.

The Loves of Apollo

HIS FIRST LOVE was Daphne (daughter of Peneus, the river god), who was so averse to marriage that she entreated her father to allow her to lead a life of celibacy, and devote herself to the chase, which she loved to the exclusion of all other pursuits. But one day, soon after his victory over the Python, Apollo happened to see Eros bending his bow, and proud of his own superior strength and skill, he laughed at the efforts of the little archer, saying that such a weapon was more suited to the one who had just killed the terrible serpent. Eros angrily replied that his arrow should pierce the heart of the mocker himself, and flying off to the summit of Mount Parnassus, he drew from his quiver two darts of different workmanship – one of gold, which had the effect of inspiring love; the other of lead, which created aversion. Taking aim at Apollo, he pierced his breast with the golden shaft, whilst the leaden one he discharged into the bosom of the beautiful Daphne. The son of Leto instantly felt the most ardent affection for the nymph, who, on her part, evinced the greatest dislike towards her divine lover, and, at his approach, fled from him like a hunted deer. He called upon her in the most endearing accents to stay, but she still sped on, until at length, becoming faint with fatigue, and fearing that she was about to succumb, she called upon the gods to come to her aid. Hardly had she uttered her prayer before a heavy torpor seized her limbs, and just as Apollo threw out his arms to embrace her, she became transformed into a laurel-bush. He sorrowfully crowned his head with its leaves, and declared, that in memory of his love, it should henceforth remain evergreen, and be held sacred to him.

He next sought the love of Marpessa, the daughter of Evenus; but though her father approved his suit, the maiden preferred a youth named Idas, who contrived to carry her off in a winged chariot which he had procured from Poseidon. Apollo pursued the fugitives, whom he quickly overtook, and forcibly seizing the bride, refused to resign her. Zeus then interfered, and declared that Marpessa herself must decide which of her lovers should claim her as his wife. After due reflection she accepted Idas as her husband, judiciously concluding that although the attractions of the divine Apollo were superior to those of her lover, it would be wiser to unite herself to a mortal, who, growing old with herself, would be less likely to forsake her, when advancing years should rob her of her charms.

Cassandra, daughter of Priam, king of Troy, was another object of the love of Apollo. She feigned to return his affection, and promised to marry him, provided he would confer upon her the gift of prophecy; but having received the boon she desired, the treacherous maiden refused to comply with the conditions upon which it had been granted. Incensed at her breach of faith, Apollo, unable to recall the gift he had bestowed, rendered it useless by causing her predictions to fail in obtaining credence. Cassandra became famous in history for her prophetic powers, but her prophecies were never believed. For instance, she warned her brother Paris that if he brought back a wife from Greece he would cause the destruction of his father's house and kingdom; she also warned the Trojans not to admit the wooden horse within the walls of the city, and foretold to Agamemnon all the disasters which afterwards befell him.

Apollo afterwards married Coronis, a nymph of Larissa, and thought himself happy in the possession of her faithful love; but once more he was doomed to disappointment, for one day his favourite bird, the crow, flew to him with the intelligence that his wife had transferred her affections to a youth of Haemonia. Apollo, burning with rage, instantly destroyed her with one of his death-bringing darts. Too late he repented of his rashness, for she had been tenderly beloved by him, and he would fain have recalled her to life; but, although he exerted all his healing powers, his efforts were in vain. He punished the crow for its garrulity by changing the colour of its plumage from pure white to intense black, and forbade it to fly any longer among the other birds.

Coronis left an infant son named Asclepius, who afterwards became god of medicine. His powers were so extraordinary that he could not only cure the sick, but could even restore the dead to life. At last Hades complained to Zeus that the number of shades conducted to his dominions was daily decreasing, and the great ruler of Olympus, fearing that mankind, thus protected against sickness and death, would be able to defy the gods themselves, killed Asclepius with one of his thunderbolts. The loss of his highly gifted son so exasperated Apollo that, being unable to vent his anger on Zeus, he destroyed the Cyclops, who had forged the fatal thunderbolts. For this offence, Apollo would have been banished by Zeus to Tartarus, but at the earnest intercession of Leto he partially relented, and contented himself with depriving him of all power and dignity, and imposing on him a temporary servitude in the house of Admetus, king of Thessaly. Apollo faithfully served his royal master for nine years in the humble capacity of a shepherd, and was treated by him with every kindness and consideration. During the period of his service the king sought the hand of Alcestis, the beautiful daughter of Pelias, son of Poseidon; but her father declared that he would only resign her to the suitor who should succeed in yoking a lion and a wild boar to his chariot. By the aid of his divine herdsman, Admetus accomplished this difficult task, and gained his bride. Nor was this the only favour which the king received from the exiled god, for Apollo obtained from the Fates the gift of immortality for his benefactor, on condition that when his last hour approached, some member of his own family should be willing to die in his stead. When the fatal hour arrived, and Admetus felt that he was at the point of death, he implored his aged parents to yield to him their few remaining days. But 'life is sweet' even to old age, and they both refused to make the sacrifice demanded of them. Alcestis, however, who had secretly devoted herself to death for her husband, was seized with a mortal sickness, which kept pace with his rapid recovery. The devoted wife breathed her last in the arms of Admetus, and he had just consigned her to the tomb, when Heracles chanced to come to the palace. Admetus held the rites of hospitality so sacred, that he at first kept silence with regard to his great bereavement; but as soon as his friend heard what had occurred, he bravely descended into the tomb, and when death came to claim his prey, he exerted his marvellous strength, and held him in his arms, until he promised to restore the beautiful and heroic queen to the bosom of her family.

Whilst pursuing the peaceful life of a shepherd, Apollo formed a strong friendship with two youths named Hyacinthus and Cyparissus, but the great favour shown to them by the god did not suffice to shield them from misfortune. The former was one day throwing the discus with Apollo, when, running too eagerly to take up the one thrown by the god, he was struck on the head with it and killed on the spot. Apollo was overcome with grief at the sad end of his young favourite, but being unable to restore him to life, he changed him into the flower called after him the Hyacinth. Cyparissus had the misfortune to kill by accident one of Apollo's favourite stags, which so preyed on his mind that he gradually pined away, and died of a broken heart. He was transformed by the god into a cypress-tree, which owes its name to this story.

How the Argonauts Sailed to Colchis

AND WHAT HAPPENED NEXT, whether it be true or not, stands written in ancient songs. And grand old songs they are, written in grand old rolling verse; and they call them the Songs of Orpheus, or the Orphics, to this day. And they tell how the heroes came to Aphetai, across the bay, and waited for the south-west wind, and chose themselves a captain from their crew: and how all called for Heracles, because he was the strongest and most huge; but Heracles refused, and called for Jason, because he was the wisest of them all. So Jason was chosen captain; and Orpheus heaped a pile of wood, and slew a bull, and offered it to Hera, and called all the heroes to stand round, each man's head crowned with olive, and to strike their swords into the bull. Then he filled a golden goblet with the bull's blood, and with wheaten flour, and honey, and wine, and the bitter salt-sea water, and bade the heroes taste. So each tasted the goblet, and passed it round, and vowed an awful vow: and they vowed before the sun, and the night, and the blue-haired sea who shakes the land, to stand by Jason faithfully in the adventure of the golden fleece; and whosoever shrank back, or disobeyed, or turned traitor to his vow, then justice should minister against him, and the Erinnues who track guilty men.

Then Jason lighted the pile, and burnt the carcase of the bull; and they went to their ship and sailed eastward, like men who have a work to do; and the place from which they went was called Aphetai, the sailing place, from that day forth. Three thousand years and more they sailed away, into the unknown Eastern seas; and great nations have come and gone since then, and many a storm has swept the earth; and many a mighty armament, to which *Argo* would be but one small boat; English and French, Turkish and Russian, have sailed those waters since; yet the fame of that small *Argo* lives for ever, and her name is become a proverb among men.

So they sailed past the Isle of Sciathos, with the Cape of Sepius on their left, and turned to the northward toward Pelion, up the long Magnesian shore. On their right hand was the open sea, and on their left old Pelion rose, while the clouds crawled round his dark pine-forests, and his caps of summer snow. And their hearts yearned for the dear old mountain, as they thought of pleasant days gone by, and of the sports of their boyhood, and their hunting, and their schooling in the cave beneath the cliff. And at last Peleus spoke, "Let us land here, friends, and climb the dear old hill once more. We are going on a fearful journey; who knows if we shall see Pelion again? Let us go up to Cheiron our master, and ask his blessing ere we start. And I have a boy, too, with him, whom he trains as he trained me once – the son whom Thetis brought me, the silver-footed lady of the sea, whom I caught in the cave, and tamed her, though she changed her shape seven times. For she changed, as I held her, into water, and to vapour, and to burning flame, and to a rock, and to a black-maned lion, and to a tall and stately tree. But I held her and held her ever, till she took her own shape again, and led her to my father's house, and won her for my bride. And all the rulers of Olympus came to our wedding, and the heavens and the earth rejoiced together, when an immortal wedded mortal man. And now let me see my son; for it is not often I shall see him upon earth: famous he will be, but short-lived, and die in the flower of youth."

So Tiphys the helmsman steered them to the shore under the crags of Pelion; and they went up through the dark pine forests towards the centaur's cave.

And they came into the misty hall, beneath the snow-crowned crag; and saw the great Centaur lying, with his huge limbs spread upon the rock; and beside him stood Achilles, the child whom no steel could wound, and played upon his harp right sweetly, while Cheiron watched and smiled.

Then Cheiron leapt up and welcomed them, and kissed them every one, and set a feast before them of swine's flesh, and venison, and good wine; and young Achilles served them, and carried the golden goblet round. And after supper all the heroes clapped their hands, and called on Orpheus to sing; but he refused, and said, "How can I, who am the younger, sing before our ancient host?" So they called on Cheiron to sing, and Achilles brought him his harp; and he began a wondrous song; a famous story of old time, of the fight between the centaurs and the Lapithai, which you may still see carved in stone. He sang how his brothers came to ruin by their folly, when they were mad with wine; and how they and the heroes fought, with fists, and teeth, and the goblets from which they drank; and how they tore up the pine-trees in their fury, and hurled great crags of stone, while the mountains thundered with the battle, and the land was wasted far and wide; till the Lapithai drove them from their home in the rich Thessalian plains to the lonely glens of Pindus, leaving Cheiron all alone. And the heroes praised his song right heartily; for some of them had helped in that great fight.

Then Orpheus took the lyre, and sang of chaos, and the making of the wondrous world, and how all things sprang from love, who could not live alone in the Abyss. And as he sang, his voice rose from the cave, above the crags, and through the treetops, and the glens of oak and pine. And the trees bowed their heads when they heard it, and the grey rocks cracked and rang, and the forest beasts crept near to listen, and the birds forsook their nests and hovered round. And old Cheiron claps his hands together, and beat his hoofs upon the ground, for wonder at that magic song.

Then Peleus kissed his boy, and wept over him, and they went down to the ship; and Cheiron came down with them, weeping, and kissed them one by one, and blest them, and promised to them great renown. And the heroes wept when they left him, till their great hearts could weep no more; for he was kind and just and pious, and wiser than all beasts and men. Then he went up to a cliff, and prayed for them, that they might come home safe and well; while the heroes rowed away, and watched him standing on his cliff above the sea, with his great hands raised toward heaven, and his white locks waving in the wind; and they strained their eyes to watch him to the last, for they felt that they should look on him no more.

So they rowed on over the long swell of the sea, past Olympus, the seat of the immortals, and past the wooded bays of Athos, and Samothrace the sacred isle; and they came past Lemnos to the Hellespont, and through the narrow strait of Abydos, and so on into the Propontis, which we call Marmora now. And there they met with Cyzicus, ruling in Asia over the Dolions, who, the songs say, was the son of Aeneas, of whom you will hear many a tale some day. For Homer tells us how he fought at Troy, and Virgil how he sailed away and founded Rome; and men believed until late years that from him sprang our old British kings. Now Cyzicus, the songs say, welcomed the heroes, for his father had been one of Cheiron's scholars; so he welcomed them,

DISASTER ON THE HORIZON

and feasted them, and stored their ship with corn and wine, and cloaks and rugs, the songs say, and shirts, of which no doubt they stood in need.

But at night, while they lay sleeping, came down on them terrible men, who lived with the bears in the mountains, like Titans or giants in shape; for each of them had six arms, and they fought with young firs and pines. But Heracles killed them all before morn with his deadly poisoned arrows; but among them, in the darkness, he slew Cyzicus the kindly prince.

Then they got to their ship and to their oars, and Tiphys bade them cast off the hawsers and go to sea. But as he spoke a whirlwind came, and spun the *Argo* round, and twisted the hawsers together, so that no man could loose them. Then Tiphys dropped the rudder from his hand, and cried, "This comes from the Gods above." But Jason went forward, and asked counsel of the magic bough.

Then the magic bough spoke, and answered, "This is because you have slain Cyzicus your friend. You must appease his soul, or you will never leave this shore."

Jason went back sadly, and told the heroes what he had heard. And they leapt on shore, and searched till dawn; and at dawn they found the body, all rolled in dust and blood, among the corpses of those monstrous beasts. And they wept over their kind host, and laid him on a fair bed, and heaped a huge mound over him, and offered black sheep at his tomb, and Orpheus sang a magic song to him, that his spirit might have rest. And then they held games at the tomb, after the custom of those times, and Jason gave prizes to each winner. To Ancaeus he gave a golden cup, for he wrestled best of all; and to Heracles a silver one, for he was the strongest of all; and to Castor, who rode best, a golden crest; and Polydeuces the boxer had a rich carpet, and to Orpheus for his song a sandal with golden wings. But Jason himself was the best of all the archers, and the Minuai crowned him with an olive crown; and so, the songs say, the soul of good Cyzicus was appeased and the heroes went on their way in peace.

But when Cyzicus's wife heard that he was dead she died likewise of grief; and her tears became a fountain of clear water, which flows the whole year round.

Then they rowed away, the songs say, along the Mysian shore, and past the mouth of Rhindacus, till they found a pleasant bay, sheltered by the long ridges of Arganthus, and by high walls of basalt rock. And there they ran the ship ashore upon the yellow sand, and furled the sail, and took the mast down, and lashed it in its crutch. And next they let down the ladder, and went ashore to sport and rest.

And there Heracles went away into the woods, bow in hand, to hunt wild deer; and Hylas the fair boy slipt away after him, and followed him by stealth, until he lost himself among the glens, and sat down weary to rest himself by the side of a lake; and there the water nymphs came up to look at him, and loved him, and carried him down under the lake to be their playfellow, for ever happy and young. And Heracles sought for him in vain, shouting his name till all the mountains rang; but Hylas never heard him, far down under the sparkling lake. So while Heracles wandered searching for him, a fair breeze sprang up, and Heracles was nowhere to be found; and the *Argo* sailed away, and Heracles was left behind, and never saw the noble Phasian stream.

Then the Minuai came to a doleful land, where Amycus the giant ruled, and cared nothing for the laws of Zeus, but challenged all strangers to box with him, and those whom he conquered he slew. But Polydeuces the boxer struck him a harder blow than he ever felt before, and slew him; and the Minuai went on up the Bosphorus, till they came to the city of Phineus, the fierce Bithynian king; for Zetes and Calais bade Jason land there, because they had a work to do.

And they went up from the shore toward the city, through forests white with snow; and Phineus came out to meet them with a lean and woful face, and said, "Welcome, gallant heroes, to the land of bitter blasts, the land of cold and misery; yet I will feast you as best I can." And he led them in, and set meat before them; but before they could put their hands to their mouths, down came two fearful monsters, the like of whom man never saw; for they had the faces and the hair of fair maidens, but the wings and claws of hawks; and they snatched the meat from off the table, and flew shrieking out above the roofs.

Then Phineus beat his breast and cried, "These are the Harpies, whose names are the Whirlwind and the Swift, the daughters of Wonder and of the Amber-nymph, and they rob us night and day. They carried off the daughters of Pandareus, whom all the Gods had blest; for Aphrodite fed them on Olympus with honey and milk and wine; and Hera gave them beauty and wisdom, and Athene skill in all the arts; but when they came to their wedding, the Harpies snatched them both away, and gave them to be slaves to the Erinnues, and live in horror all their days. And now they haunt me, and my people, and the Bosphorus, with fearful storms; and sweep away our food from off our tables, so that we starve in spite of all our wealth."

Then up rose Zetes and Calais, the winged sons of the North-wind, and said, "Do you not know us, Phineus, and these wings which grow upon our backs?" And Phineus hid his face in terror; but he answered not a word.

"Because you have been a traitor, Phineus, the Harpies haunt you night and day. Where is Cleopatra our sister, your wife, whom you keep in prison? And where are her two children, whom you blinded in your rage, at the bidding of an evil woman, and cast them out upon the rocks? Swear to us that you will right our sister, and cast out that wicked woman; and then we will free you from your plague, and drive the whirlwind maidens to the south; but if not, we will put out your eyes, as you put out the eyes of your own sons."

Then Phineus swore an oath to them, and drove out the wicked woman; and Jason took those two poor children, and cured their eyes with magic herbs.

But Zetes and Calais rose up sadly and said, "Farewell now, heroes all; farewell, our dear companions, with whom we played on Pelion in old times; for a fate is laid upon us, and our day is come at last, in which we must hunt the whirlwinds over land and sea for ever; and if we catch them they die, and if not, we die ourselves."

At that all the heroes wept; but the two young men sprang up, and aloft into the air after the Harpies, and the battle of the winds began.

The heroes trembled in silence as they heard the shrieking of the blasts; while the palace rocked and all the city, and great stones were torn from the crags, and the forest pines were hurled earthward, north and south and east and west, and the Bosphorus boiled white with foam, and the clouds were dashed against the cliffs.

But at last the battle ended, and the Harpies fled screaming toward the south, and the sons of the North-wind rushed after them, and brought clear sunshine where they passed. For many a league they followed them, over all the isles of the Cyclades, and away to the south-west across Hellas, till they came to the Ionian Sea, and there they fell upon the Echinades, at the mouth of the Achelous; and those isles were called the Whirlwind Isles for many a hundred years. But what became of Zetes and Calais I know not, for the heroes never saw them again: and some say that Heracles met them, and quarrelled with them, and slew them with his arrows; and some say that they fell down from weariness and the heat of the summer sun, and that the Sun-god buried them among the Cyclades, in the pleasant Isle of Tenos; and for many hundred years their grave was shown there, and over it a pillar, which turned to every wind. But those dark storms and whirlwinds haunt the Bosphorus until this day.

DISASTER ON THE HORIZON

But the Argonauts went eastward, and out into the open sea, which we now call the Black Sea, but it was called the Euxine then. No Hellen had ever crossed it, and all feared that dreadful sea, and its rocks, and shoals, and fogs, and bitter freezing storms; and they told strange stories of it, some false and some half-true, how it stretched northward to the ends of the earth, and the sluggish Putrid Sea, and the everlasting night, and the regions of the dead. So the heroes trembled, for all their courage, as they came into that wild Black Sea, and saw it stretching out before them, without a shore, as far as the eye could see.

And first Orpheus spoke, and warned them, "We shall come now to the wandering blue rocks; my mother warned me of them, Calliope, the immortal muse."

And soon they saw the blue rocks shining like spires and castles of grey glass, while an ice-cold wind blew from them and chilled all the heroes' hearts. And as they neared they could see them heaving, as they rolled upon the long sea-waves, crashing and grinding together, till the roar went up to heaven. The sea sprang up in spouts between them, and swept round them in white sheets of foam; but their heads swung nodding high in air, while the wind whistled shrill among the crags.

The heroes' hearts sank within them, and they lay upon their oars in fear; but Orpheus called to Tiphys the helmsman, "Between them we must pass; so look ahead for an opening, and be brave, for Hera is with us."

But Tiphys the cunning helmsman stood silent, clenching his teeth, till he saw a heron come flying mast-high toward the rocks, and hover awhile before them, as if looking for a passage through. Then he cried, "Hera has sent us a pilot; let us follow the cunning bird."

Then the heron flapped to and fro a moment, till he saw a hidden gap, and into it he rushed like an arrow, while the heroes watched what would befall.

And the blue rocks clashed together as the bird fled swiftly through; but they struck but a feather from his tail, and then rebounded apart at the shock.

Then Tiphys cheered the heroes, and they shouted; and the oars bent like withes beneath their strokes as they rushed between those toppling ice-crags and the cold blue lips of death. And ere the rocks could meet again they had passed them, and were safe out in the open sea.

And after that they sailed on wearily along the Asian coast, by the Black Cape and Thyneis, where the hot stream of Thymbris falls into the sea, and Sangarius, whose waters float on the Euxine, till they came to Wolf the river, and to Wolf the kindly king. And there died two brave heroes, Idmon and Tiphys the wise helmsman: one died of an evil sickness, and one a wild boar slew. So the heroes heaped a mound above them, and set upon it an oar on high, and left them there to sleep together, on the far-off Lycian shore. But Idas killed the boar, and avenged Tiphys; and Ancaios took the rudder and was helmsman, and steered them on toward the east.

And they went on past Sinope, and many a mighty river's mouth, and past many a barbarous tribe, and the cities of the Amazons, the warlike women of the East, till all night they heard the clank of anvils and the roar of furnace-blasts, and the forge-fires shone like sparks through the darkness in the mountain glens aloft; for they were come to the shores of the Chalybes, the smiths who never tire, but serve Ares the cruel War-god, forging weapons day and night.

And at day-dawn they looked eastward, and midway between the sea and the sky they saw white snow-peaks hanging, glittering sharp and bright above the clouds. And they knew that they were come to Caucasus, at the end of all the earth: Caucasus the highest of all mountains, the father of the rivers of the East. On his peak lies chained the Titan, while a vulture tears his heart; and at his feet are piled dark forests round the magic Colchian land.

And they rowed three days to the eastward, while Caucasus rose higher hour by hour, till they saw the dark stream of Phasis rushing headlong to the sea, and, shining above the tree-tops, the golden roofs of King Aeetes, the child of the Sun.

Then out spoke Ancaios the helmsman, "We are come to our goal at last, for there are the roofs of Aeetes, and the woods where all poisons grow; but who can tell us where among them is hid the golden fleece? Many a toil must we bear ere we find it, and bring it home to Greece."

But Jason cheered the heroes, for his heart was high and bold; and he said, "I will go alone up to Aeetes, though he be the child of the Sun, and win him with soft words. Better so than to go altogether, and to come to blows at once."

But the Minuai would not stay behind, so they rowed boldly up the stream.

And a dream came to Aeetes, and filled his heart with fear. He thought he saw a shining star, which fell into his daughter's lap; and that Medea his daughter took it gladly, and carried it to the river-side, and cast it in, and there the whirling river bore it down, and out into the Euxine Sea.

Then he leapt up in fear, and bade his servants bring his chariot, that he might go down to the river-side and appease the nymphs, and the heroes whose spirits haunt the bank. So he went down in his golden chariot, and his daughters by his side, Medea the fair witch-maiden, and Chalciope, who had been Phrixus's wife, and behind him a crowd of servants and soldiers, for he was a rich and mighty prince.

And as he drove down by the reedy river he saw *Argo* sliding up beneath the bank, and many a hero in her, like Immortals for beauty and for strength, as their weapons glittered round them in the level morning sunlight, through the white mist of the stream. But Jason was the noblest of all; for Hera, who loved him, gave him beauty and tallness and terrible manhood.

And when they came near together and looked into each other's eyes the heroes were awed before Aeetes as he shone in his chariot, like his father the glorious Sun; for his robes were of rich gold tissue, and the rays of his diadem flashed fire; and in his hand he bore a jewelled sceptre, which glittered like the stars; and sternly he looked at them under his brows, and sternly he spoke and loud:

"Who are you, and what want you here, that you come to the shore of Cutaia? Do you take no account of my rule, nor of my people the Colchians who serve me, who never tired yet in the battle, and know well how to face an invader?"

And the heroes sat silent awhile before the face of that ancient king. But Hera the awful goddess put courage into Jason's heart, and he rose and shouted loudly in answer, "We are no pirates nor lawless men. We come not to plunder and to ravage, or carry away slaves from your land; but my uncle, the son of Poseidon, Pelias the Minuan king, he it is who has set me on a quest to bring home the golden fleece. And these too, my bold comrades, they are no nameless men; for some are the sons of Immortals, and some of heroes far renowned. And we too never tire in battle, and know well how to give blows and to take: yet we wish to be guests at your table: it will be better so for both."

Then Aeetes' race rushed up like a whirlwind, and his eyes flashed fire as he heard; but he crushed his anger down in his breast, and spoke mildly a cunning speech –

"If you will fight for the fleece with my Colchians, then many a man must die. But do you indeed expect to win from me the fleece in fight? So few you are that if you be worsted I can load your ship with your corpses. But if you will be ruled by me, you will find it better far to choose the best man among you, and let him fulfil the labours which I demand. Then I will give him the golden fleece for a prize and a glory to you all."

So saying, he turned his horses and drove back in silence to the town. And the Minuai sat silent with sorrow, and longed for Heracles and his strength; for there was no facing the thousands of the Colchians and the fearful chance of war.

But Chalciope, Phrixus's widow, went weeping to the town; for she remembered her Minuan husband, and all the pleasures of her youth, while she watched the fair faces of his kinsmen, and their long locks of golden hair. And she whispered to Medea her sister, "Why should all these brave men die? Why does not my father give them up the fleece, that my husband's spirit may have rest?"

And Medea's heart pitied the heroes, and Jason most of all; and she answered, "Our father is stern and terrible, and who can win the golden fleece?"

But Chalciope said, "These men are not like our men; there is nothing which they cannot dare nor do."

And Medea thought of Jason and his brave countenance, and said, "If there was one among them who knew no fear, I could show him how to win the fleece."

So in the dusk of evening they went down to the river-side, Chalciope and Medea the witch-maiden, and Argus, Phrixus's son. And Argus the boy crept forward, among the beds of reeds, till he came where the heroes were sleeping, on the thwarts of the ship, beneath the bank, while Jason kept ward on shore, and leant upon his lance full of thought. And the boy came to Jason, and said:

"I am the son of Phrixus, your Cousin; and Chalciope my mother waits for you, to talk about the golden fleece."

Then Jason went boldly with the boy, and found the two princesses standing; and when Chalciope saw him she wept, and took his hands, and cried: "O cousin of my beloved, go home before you die!"

"It would be base to go home now, fair princess, and to have sailed all these seas in vain." Then both the princesses besought him; but Jason said, "It is too late."

"But you know not," said Medea, "what he must do who would win the fleece. He must tame the two brazen-footed bulls, who breathe devouring flame; and with them he must plough ere nightfall four acres in the field of Ares; and he must sow them with serpents' teeth, of which each tooth springs up into an armed man. Then he must fight with all those warriors; and little will it profit him to conquer them, for the fleece is guarded by a serpent, more huge than any mountain pine; and over his body you must step if you would reach the golden fleece."

Then Jason laughed bitterly. "Unjustly is that fleece kept here, and by an unjust and lawless king; and unjustly shall I die in my youth, for I will attempt it ere another sun be set."

Then Medea trembled, and said, "No mortal man can reach that fleece unless I guide him through. For round it, beyond the river, is a wall full nine ells high, with lofty towers and buttresses, and mighty gates of threefold brass; and over the gates the wall is arched, with golden battlements above. And over the gateway sits Brimo, the wild witch-huntress of the woods, brandishing a pine-torch in her hands, while her mad hounds howl around. No man dare meet her or look on her, but only I her priestess, and she watches far and wide lest any stranger should come near."

"No wall so high but it may be climbed at last, and no wood so thick but it may be crawled through; no serpent so wary but he may be charmed, or witch-queen so fierce but spells may soothe her; and I may yet win the golden fleece, if a wise maiden help bold men."

And he looked at Medea cunningly, and held her with his glittering eye, till she blushed and trembled, and said:

"Who can face the fire of the bulls' breath, and fight ten thousand armed men?"

"He whom you help," said Jason, flattering her, "for your fame is spread over all the earth. Are you not the queen of all enchantresses, wiser even than your sister Circe, in her fairy island in the West?"

"Would that I were with my sister Circe in her fairy island in the West, far away from sore temptation and thoughts which tear the heart! But if it must be so – for why should you die? – I have an ointment here; I made it from the magic ice-flower which sprang from Prometheus's wound, above the clouds on Caucasus, in the dreary fields of snow. Anoint yourself with that, and you shall have in you seven men's strength; and anoint your shield with it, and neither fire nor sword can harm you. But what you begin you must end before sunset, for its virtue lasts only one day. And anoint your helmet with it before you sow the serpents' teeth; and when the sons of earth spring up, cast your helmet among their ranks, and the deadly crop of the War-god's field will mow itself, and perish."

Then Jason fell on his knees before her, and thanked her and kissed her hands; and she gave him the vase of ointment, and fled trembling through the reeds. And Jason told his comrades what had happened, and showed them the box of ointment; and all rejoiced but Idas, and he grew mad with envy.

And at sunrise Jason went and bathed, and anointed himself from head to foot, and his shield, and his helmet, and his weapons, and bade his comrades try the spell. So they tried to bend his lance, but it stood like an iron bar; and Idas in spite hewed at it with his sword, but the blade flew to splinters in his face. Then they hurled their lances at his shield, but the spear-points turned like lead; and Caineus tried to throw him, but he never stirred a foot; and Polydeuces struck him with his fist a blow which would have killed an ox, but Jason only smiled, and the heroes danced about him with delight; and he leapt, and ran, and shouted in the joy of that enormous strength, till the sun rose, and it was time to go and to claim Aeetes' promise.

So he sent up Telamon and Aithalides to tell Aeetes that he was ready for the fight; and they went up among the marble walls, and beneath the roofs of gold, and stood in Aeetes' hall, while he grew pale with rage.

"Fulfil your promise to us, child of the blazing Sun. Give us the serpents' teeth, and let loose the fiery bulls; for we have found a champion among us who can win the golden fleece."

And Aeetes bit his lips, for he fancied that they had fled away by night: but he could not go back from his promise; so he gave them the serpents' teeth.

Then he called for his chariot and his horses, and sent heralds through all the town; and all the people went out with him to the dreadful War-god's field.

And there Aeetes sat upon his throne, with his warriors on each hand, thousands and tens of thousands, clothed from head to foot in steel chain-mail. And the people and the women crowded to every window and bank and wall; while the Minuai stood together, a mere handful in the midst of that great host.

And Chalciope was there and Argus, trembling, and Medea, wrapped closely in her veil; but Aeetes did not know that she was muttering cunning spells between her lips.

Then Jason cried, "Fulfil your promise, and let your fiery bulls come forth."

Then Aeetes bade open the gates, and the magic bulls leapt out. Their brazen hoofs rang upon the ground, and their nostrils sent out sheets of flame, as they rushed with lowered heads upon Jason; but he never flinched a step. The flame of their breath swept round him, but it singed not a hair of his head; and the bulls stopped short and trembled when Medea began her spell.

DISASTER ON THE HORIZON

Then Jason sprang upon the nearest and seized him by the horn; and up and down they wrestled, till the bull fell grovelling on his knees; for the heart of the brute died within him, and his mighty limbs were loosed, beneath the steadfast eye of that dark witch-maiden and the magic whisper of her lips.

So both the bulls were tamed and yoked; and Jason bound them to the plough, and goaded them onward with his lance till he had ploughed the sacred field.

And all the Minuai shouted; but Aeetes bit his lips with rage, for the half of Jason's work was over, and the sun was yet high in heaven.

Then he took the serpents' teeth and sowed them, and waited what would befall. But Medea looked at him and at his helmet, lest he should forget the lesson she had taught.

And every furrow heaved and bubbled, and out of every clod arose a man. Out of the earth they rose by thousands, each clad from head to foot in steel, and drew their swords and rushed on Jason, where he stood in the midst alone.

Then the Minuai grew pale with fear for him; but Aeetes laughed a bitter laugh. "See! If I had not warriors enough already round me, I could call them out of the bosom of the earth."

But Jason snatched off his helmet, and hurled it into the thickest of the throng. And blind madness came upon them, suspicion, hate, and fear; and one cried to his fellow, "Thou didst strike me!" and another, "Thou art Jason; thou shalt die!"

So fury seized those earth-born phantoms, and each turned his hand against the rest; and they fought and were never weary, till they all lay dead upon the ground. Then the magic furrows opened, and the kind earth took them home into her breast and the grass grew up all green again above them, and Jason's work was done.

Then the Minuai rose and shouted, till Prometheus heard them from his crag. And Jason cried, "Lead me to the fleece this moment, before the sun goes down."

But Aeetes thought, "He has conquered the bulls, and sown and reaped the deadly crop. Who is this who is proof against all magic? He may kill the serpent yet."

So he delayed, and sat taking counsel with his princes till the sun went down and all was dark. Then he bade a herald cry, "Every man to his home for tonight. Tomorrow we will meet these heroes, and speak about the golden fleece."

Then he turned and looked at Medea. "This is your doing, false witch-maid! You have helped these yellow-haired strangers, and brought shame upon your father and yourself!"

Medea shrank and trembled, and her face grew pale with fear; and Aeetes knew that she was guilty, and whispered, "If they win the fleece, you die!"

But the Minuai marched toward their ship, growling like lions cheated of their prey; for they saw that Aeetes meant to mock them, and to cheat them out of all their toil. And Oileus said, "Let us go to the grove together, and take the fleece by force."

And Idas the rash cried, "Let us draw lots who shall go in first; for, while the dragon is devouring one, the rest can slay him and carry off the fleece in peace." But Jason held them back, though he praised them; for he hoped for Medea's help.

And after a while Medea came trembling, and wept a long while before she spoke. And at last –

"My end is come, and I must die; for my father has found out that I have helped you. You he would kill if he dared; but he will not harm you, because you have been his guests. Go then, go, and remember poor Medea when you are far away across the sea."

But all the heroes cried: "If you die, we die with you; for without you we cannot win the fleece, and home we will not go without it, but fall here fighting to the last man."

35

"You need not die," said Jason. "Flee home with us across the sea. Show us first how to win the fleece; for you can do it. Why else are you the priestess of the grove? Show us but how to win the fleece, and come with us, and you shall be my queen, and rule over the rich princes of the Minuai, in Iolcos by the sea."

And all the heroes pressed round, and vowed to her that she should be their queen.

Medea wept, and shuddered, and hid her face in her hands; for her heart yearned after her sisters and her playfellows, and the home where she was brought up as a child. But at last she looked up at Jason, and spoke between her sobs:

"Must I leave my home and my people, to wander with strangers across the sea? The lot is cast, and I must endure it. I will show you how to win the golden fleece. Bring up your ship to the wood-side, and moor her there against the bank; and let Jason come up at midnight, and one brave comrade with him, and meet me beneath the wall."

Then all the heroes cried together, "I will go!" "and I!" "and I!"

And Idas the rash grew mad with envy; for he longed to be foremost in all things. But Medea calmed them, and said, "Orpheus shall go with Jason, and bring his magic harp; for I hear of him that he is the king of all minstrels, and can charm all things on earth."

And Orpheus laughed for joy, and clapped his hands, because the choice had fallen on him; for in those days poets and singers were as bold warriors as the best.

So at midnight they went up the bank, and found Medea; and beside came Absyrtus her young brother, leading a yearling lamb.

Then Medea brought them to a thicket beside the War-god's gate; and there she bade Jason dig a ditch, and kill the lamb, and leave it there, and strew on it magic herbs and honey from the honeycomb.

Then sprang up through the earth, with the red fire flashing before her, Brimo the wild witch-huntress, while her mad hounds howled around. She had one head like a horse's, and another like a ravening hound's, and another like a hissing snake's, and a sword in either hand. And she leapt into the ditch with her hounds, and they ate and drank their fill, while Jason and Orpheus trembled, and Medea hid her eyes. And at last the witch-queen vanished, and fled with her hounds into the woods; and the bars of the gates fell down, and the brazen doors flew wide, and Medea and the heroes ran forward and hurried through the poison wood, among the dark stems of the mighty beeches, guided by the gleam of the golden fleece, until they saw it hanging on one vast tree in the midst. And Jason would have sprung to seize it; but Medea held him back, and pointed, shuddering, to the tree-foot, where the mighty serpent lay, coiled in and out among the roots, with a body like a mountain pine. His coils stretched many a fathom, spangled with bronze and gold; and half of him they could see, but no more, for the rest lay in the darkness far beyond.

And when he saw them coming he lifted up his head, and watched them with his small bright eyes, and flashed his forked tongue, and roared like the fire among the woodlands, till the forest tossed and groaned. For his cries shook the trees from leaf to root, and swept over the long reaches of the river, and over Aeetes' hall, and woke the sleepers in the city, till mothers clasped their children in their fear.

But Medea called gently to him, and he stretched out his long spotted neck, and licked her hand, and looked up in her face, as if to ask for food. Then she made a sign to Orpheus, and he began his magic song.

And as he sung, the forest grew calm again, and the leaves on every tree hung still; and the serpent's head sank down, and his brazen coils grew limp, and his glittering eyes closed lazily, till he breathed as gently as a child, while Orpheus called to pleasant Slumber, who gives peace to men, and beasts, and waves.

Then Jason leapt forward warily, and stepped across that mighty snake, and tore the fleece from off the tree-trunk; and the four rushed down the garden, to the bank where the *Argo* lay.

There was a silence for a moment, while Jason held the golden fleece on high. Then he cried, "Go now, good *Argo*, swift and steady, if ever you would see Pelion more."

And she went, as the heroes drove her, grim and silent all, with muffled oars, till the pine-wood bent like willow in their hands, and stout *Argo* groaned beneath their strokes.

On and on, beneath the dewy darkness, they fled swiftly down the swirling stream; underneath black walls, and temples, and the castles of the princes of the East; past sluice-mouths, and fragrant gardens, and groves of all strange fruits; past marshes where fat kine lay sleeping, and long beds of whispering reeds; till they heard the merry music of the surge upon the bar, as it tumbled in the moonlight all alone.

Into the surge they rushed, and *Argo* leapt the breakers like a horse; for she knew the time was come to show her mettle, and win honour for the heroes and herself.

Into the surge they rushed, and *Argo* leapt the breakers like a horse, till the heroes stopped all panting, each man upon his oar, as she slid into the still broad sea.

Then Orpheus took his harp and sang a paean, till the heroes' hearts rose high again; and they rowed on stoutly and steadfastly, away into the darkness of the West.

Trojan Victories

THE WAR MIGHT NOW have ended, but an evil and foolish thought came to Pandarus, a prince of Ida, who fought for the Trojans. He chose to shoot an arrow at Menelaus, contrary to the sworn vows of peace, and the arrow pierced the breastplate of Menelaus through the place where the clasped plates meet, and drew his blood. Then Agamemnon, who loved his brother dearly, began to lament, saying that, if he died, the army would all go home and Trojans would dance on the grave of Menelaus.

"Do not alarm all our army," said Menelaus, "the arrow has done me little harm"; and so it proved, for the surgeon easily drew the arrow out of the wound.

Then Agamemnon hastened here and there, bidding the Greeks arm and attack the Trojans, who would certainly be defeated, for they had broken the oaths of peace. But with his usual insolence he chose to accuse Odysseus and Diomede of cowardice, though Diomede was as brave as any man, and Odysseus had just prevented the whole army from launching their ships and going home. Odysseus answered him with spirit, but Diomede said nothing at the moment; later he spoke his mind. He leaped from his chariot, and all the chiefs leaped down and advanced in line, the chariots following them, while the spearmen and bowmen followed the chariots. The Trojan army advanced, all shouting in their different languages, but the Greeks came on silently. Then the two front lines clashed, shield against shield, and the noise was like the roaring of many flooded torrents among the hills. When a man fell he who had slain him tried to strip off his armour, and his friends fought over his body to save the dead from this dishonour.

Odysseus fought above a wounded friend, and drove his spear through head and helmet of a Trojan prince, and everywhere men were falling beneath spears and arrows and heavy stones which the warriors threw. Here Menelaus speared the man who built the ships with which Paris had sailed to Greece; and the dust rose like a cloud, and a mist went up from the fighting men, while Diomede stormed across the plain like a river in flood, leaving dead bodies behind him as the river leaves boughs of trees and grass to mark its course. Pandarus wounded Diomede with an arrow, but Diomede slew him, and the Trojans were being driven in flight, when Sarpedon and Hector turned and hurled themselves on the Greeks; and even Diomede shuddered when Hector came on, and charged at Odysseus, who was slaying Trojans as he went, and the battle swayed this way and that, and the arrows fell like rain.

But Hector was sent into the city to bid the women pray to the goddess Athene for help, and he went to the house of Paris, whom Helen was imploring to go and fight like a man, saying: "Would that the winds had wafted me away, and the tides drowned me, shameless that I am, before these things came to pass!"

Then Hector went to see his dear wife, Andromache, whose father had been slain by Achilles early in the siege, and he found her and her nurse carrying her little boy, Hector's son, and like a star upon her bosom lay his beautiful and shining golden head. Now, while Helen urged Paris to go into the fight, Andromache prayed Hector to stay with her in the town, and fight no more lest he should be slain and leave her a widow, and the boy an orphan, with none to protect him.

"The army," she said, "should come back within the walls, where they had so long been safe, not fight in the open plain."

But Hector answered that he would never shrink from battle, "yet I know this in my heart, the day shall come for holy Troy to be laid low, and Priam and the people of Priam. But this and my own death do not trouble me so much as the thought of you, when you shall be carried as a slave to Greece, to spin at another woman's bidding, and bear water from a Grecian well. May the heaped up earth of my tomb cover me ere I hear thy cries and the tale of thy captivity."

Then Hector stretched out his hands to his little boy, but the child was afraid when he saw the great glittering helmet of his father and the nodding horsehair crest. So Hector laid his helmet on the ground and dandled the child in his arms, and tried to comfort his wife, and said good-bye for the last time, for he never came back to Troy alive. He went on his way back to the battle, and Paris went with him, in glorious armour, and soon they were slaying the princes of the Greeks.

The battle raged till nightfall, and in the night the Greeks and Trojans burned their dead; and the Greeks made a trench and wall round their camp, which they needed for safety now that the Trojans came from their town and fought in the open plain.

Next day the Trojans were so successful that they did not retreat behind their walls at night, but lit great fires on the plain: a thousand fires, with fifty men taking supper round each of them, and drinking their wine to the music of flutes. But the Greeks were much discouraged, and Agamemnon called the whole army together, and proposed that they should launch their ships in the night and sail away home.

Then Diomede stood up, and said: "You called me a coward lately. You are the coward! Sail away if you are afraid to remain here, but all the rest of us will fight till we take Troy town."

38

DISASTER ON THE HORIZON

Then all shouted in praise of Diomede, and Nestor advised them to send five hundred young men, under his own son, Thrasymedes, to watch the Trojans, and guard the new wall and the ditch, in case the Trojans attacked them in the darkness. Next Nestor counselled Agamemnon to send Odysseus and Ajax to Achilles, and promise to give back Briseis, and rich presents of gold, and beg pardon for his insolence. If Achilles would be friends again with Agamemnon, and fight as he used to fight, the Trojans would soon be driven back into the town.

Agamemnon was very ready to beg pardon, for he feared that the whole army would be defeated, and cut off from their ships, and killed or kept as slaves. So Odysseus and Ajax and the old tutor of Achilles, Phoenix, went to Achilles and argued with him, praying him to accept the rich presents, and help the Greeks. But Achilles answered that he did not believe a word that Agamemnon said; Agamemnon had always hated him, and always would hate him. No; he would not cease to be angry, he would sail away next day with all his men, and he advised the rest to come with him.

"Why be so fierce?" said tall Ajax, who seldom spoke. "Why make so much trouble about one girl? We offer you seven girls, and plenty of other gifts."

Then Achilles said that he would not sail away next day, but he would not fight till the Trojans tried to burn his own ships, and there he thought that Hector would find work enough to do. This was the most that Achilles would promise, and all the Greeks were silent when Odysseus delivered his message. But Diomede arose and said that, with or without Achilles, fight they must; and all men, heavy at heart, went to sleep in their huts or in the open air at their doors.

Agamemnon was much too anxious to sleep. He saw the glow of the thousand fires of the Trojans in the dark, and heard their merry flutes, and he groaned and pulled out his long hair by handfuls. When he was tired of crying and groaning and tearing his hair, he thought that he would go for advice to old Nestor. He threw a lion skin, the coverlet of his bed, over his shoulder, took his spear, went out and met Menelaus – for he, too, could not sleep – and Menelaus proposed to send a spy among the Trojans, if any man were brave enough to go, for the Trojan camp was all alight with fires, and the adventure was dangerous. Therefore the two wakened Nestor and the other chiefs, who came just as they were, wrapped in the fur coverlets of their beds, without any armour. First they visited the five hundred young men set to watch the wall, and then they crossed the ditch and sat down outside and considered what might be done. 'Will nobody go as a spy among the Trojans?' said Nestor; he meant would none of the young men go. Diomede said that he would take the risk if any other man would share it with him, and, if he might choose a companion, he would take Odysseus.

"Come, then, let us be going," said Odysseus, "for the night is late, and the dawn is near."

As these two chiefs had no armour on, they borrowed shields and leather caps from the young men of the guard, for leather would not shine as bronze helmets shine in the firelight. The cap lent to Odysseus was strengthened outside with rows of boars' tusks. Many of these tusks, shaped for this purpose, have been found, with swords and armour, in a tomb in Mycenae, the town of Agamemnon. This cap which was lent to Odysseus had once been stolen by his grandfather, Autolycus, who was a Master Thief, and he gave it as a present to a friend, and so, through several hands, it had come to young Meriones of Crete, one of the five hundred guards, who now lent it to Odysseus. So the two princes set forth in the dark, so dark it was that though they heard a heron cry, they could not see it as it flew away.

While Odysseus and Diomede stole through the night silently, like two wolves among the bodies of dead men, the Trojan leaders met and considered what they ought to do. They did not know whether the Greeks had set sentinels and outposts, as usual, to give warning if the enemy were approaching; or whether they were too weary to keep a good watch; or whether perhaps they were getting ready their ships to sail homewards in the dawn. So Hector offered a reward to any man who would creep through the night and spy on the Greeks; he said he would give the spy the two best horses in the Greek camp.

Now among the Trojans there was a young man named Dolon, the son of a rich father, and he was the only boy in a family of five sisters. He was ugly, but a very swift runner, and he cared for horses more than for anything else in the world. Dolon arose and said, "If you will swear to give me the horses and chariot of Achilles, son of Peleus, I will steal to the hut of Agamemnon and listen and find out whether the Greeks mean to fight or flee."

Hector swore to give these horses, which were the best in the world, to Dolon, so he took his bow and threw a grey wolf's hide over his shoulders, and ran towards the ships of the Greeks.

Now Odysseus saw Dolon as he came, and said to Diomede, "Let us suffer him to pass us, and then do you keep driving him with your spear towards the ships, and away from Troy."

So Odysseus and Diomede lay down among the dead men who had fallen in the battle, and Dolon ran on past them towards the Greeks. Then they rose and chased him as two greyhounds course a hare, and, when Dolon was near the sentinels, Diomede cried "Stand, or I will slay you with my spear!" and he threw his spear just over Dolon's shoulder. So Dolon stood still, green with fear, and with his teeth chattering. When the two came up, he cried, and said that his father was a rich man, who would pay much gold, and bronze, and iron for his ransom.

Odysseus said, "Take heart, and put death out of your mind, and tell us what you are doing here."

Dolon said that Hector had promised him the horses of Achilles if he would go and spy on the Greeks.

"You set your hopes high," said Odysseus, "for the horses of Achilles are not earthly steeds, but divine; a gift of the Gods, and Achilles alone can drive them. But, tell me, do the Trojans keep good watch, and where is Hector with his horses?" for Odysseus thought that it would be a great adventure to drive away the horses of Hector.

"Hector is with the chiefs, holding council at the tomb of Ilus," said Dolon; "but no regular guard is set. The people of Troy, indeed, are round their watch fires, for they have to think of the safety of their wives and children; but the allies from far lands keep no watch, for their wives and children are safe at home." Then he told where all the different peoples who fought for Priam had their stations; but, said he, "if you want to steal horses, the best are those of Rhesus, King of the Thracians, who has only joined us tonight. He and his men are asleep at the furthest end of the line, and his horses are the best and greatest that ever I saw: tall, white as snow, and swift as the wind, and his chariot is adorned with gold and silver, and golden is his armour. Now take me prisoner to the ships, or bind me and leave me here while you go and try whether I have told you truth or lies."

"No," said Diomede, "if I spare your life you may come spying again," and he drew his sword and smote off the head of Dolon. They hid his cap and bow and spear where they could find them easily, and marked the spot, and went through the night to the dark camp of King Rhesus, who had no watch-fire and no guards. Then Diomede silently stabbed each sleeping man to the heart, and Odysseus seized the dead by the feet and threw them aside lest they should frighten the horses, which had never been in battle, and would shy if they were led over the bodies of dead men. Last of all Diomede killed King Rhesus, and Odysseus led forth his horses, beating them with his bow, for he had forgotten to take the whip from the chariot. Then Odysseus and Diomede leaped on the backs of the horses, as they had not time to bring away the chariot, and they galloped to the ships, stopping to pick up the spear, and bow, and cap of Dolon. They rode to the princes, who welcomed them, and all laughed for glee when they saw the white horses and heard that King Rhesus was dead, for they guessed that all his army would now go home to Thrace. This they must have done, for we never hear of them in the battles that followed, so Odysseus and Diomede deprived the Trojans of thousands of men. The other princes went to bed in good spirits, but Odysseus and Diomede took a swim in the sea, and then went into hot baths, and so to breakfast, for rosy-fingered Dawn was coming up the sky.

The Death of Achilles

ODYSSEUS THOUGHT MUCH and often of Helen, without whose kindness he could not have saved the Greeks by stealing the Luck of Troy. He saw that, though she remained as beautiful as when the princes all sought her hand, she was most unhappy, knowing herself to be the cause of so much misery, and fearing what the future might bring. Odysseus told nobody about the secret which she had let fall, the coming of the Amazons.

The Amazons were a race of warlike maids, who lived far away on the banks of the river Thermodon. They had fought against Troy in former times, and one of the great hill-graves on the plain of Troy covered the ashes of an Amazon, swift-footed Myrine. People believed that they were the daughters of the God of War, and they were reckoned equal in battle to the bravest men. Their young Queen, Penthesilea, had two reasons for coming to fight at Troy: one was her ambition to win renown, and the other her sleepless sorrow for having accidentally killed her sister, Hippolyte, when hunting. The spear which she threw at a stag struck Hippolyte and slew her, and Penthesilea cared no longer for her own life, and desired to fall gloriously in battle. So Penthesilea and her bodyguard of twelve Amazons set forth from the wide streams of Thermodon, and rode into Troy. The story says that they did not drive in chariots, like all the Greek and Trojan chiefs, but rode horses, which must have been the manner of their country.

Penthesilea was the tallest and most beautiful of the Amazons, and shone among her twelve maidens like the moon among the stars, or the bright Dawn among the Hours which follow her chariot wheels. The Trojans rejoiced when they beheld her, for she looked both terrible and beautiful, with a frown on her brow, and fair shining eyes, and a blush on her cheeks. To the Trojans she came like Iris, the Rainbow, after a storm, and they gathered round her cheering, and throwing flowers and kissing her stirrup, as the people of Orleans welcomed Joan of Arc when she came to deliver them. Even Priam was glad, as is a man long blind, when he has been healed, and again looks upon the light of the sun. Priam held a great feast, and gave to Penthesilea many beautiful gifts: cups of gold, and embroideries, and a sword with a hilt of silver, and she vowed that she would slay Achilles. But when Andromache, the wife of Hector, heard her she said within herself, "Ah, unhappy girl, what is this boast of thine! Thou hast not the strength to fight the unconquerable son of Peleus, for if Hector could not slay him, what chance hast thou? But the piled-up earth covers Hector!"

In the morning Penthesilea sprang up from sleep and put on her glorious armour, with spear in hand, and sword at side, and bow and quiver hung behind her back, and her great shield covering her side from neck to stirrup, and mounted her horse, and galloped to the plain. Beside her charged the twelve maidens of her bodyguard, and all the company of Hector's brothers and kinsfolk. These headed the Trojan lines, and they rushed towards the ships of the Greeks.

Then the Greeks asked each other, "Who is this that leads the Trojans as Hector led them, surely some God rides in the van of the charioteers!"

Odysseus could have told them who the new leader of the Trojans was, but it seems that he had not the heart to fight against women, for his name is not mentioned in this day's battle. So the two lines clashed, and the plain of Troy ran red with blood, for Penthesilea slew Molios, and Persinoos, and Eilissos, and Antiphates, and Lernos high of heart, and Hippalmos of the loud war cry, and Haemonides, and strong Elasippus, while her maidens Derinoe and Clonie slew each a chief of the Greeks. But Clonie fell beneath the spear of Podarkes, whose hand Penthesilea cut off with the sword, while Idomeneus speared the Amazon Bremousa, and Meriones of Crete slew Evadre, and Diomede killed Alcibie and Derimacheia in close fight with the sword, so the company of the Twelve were thinned, the bodyguard of Penthesilea.

The Trojans and Greeks kept slaying each other, but Penthesilea avenged her maidens, driving the ranks of Greece as a lioness drives the cattle on the hills, for they could not stand before her.

Then she shouted, "Dogs! Today shall you pay for the sorrows of Priam! Where is Diomede, where is Achilles, where is Ajax, that, men say, are your bravest? Will none of them stand before my spear?"

Then she charged again, at the head of the Household of Priam, brothers and kinsmen of Hector, and where they came the Greeks fell like yellow leaves before the wind of autumn. The white horse that Penthesilea rode, a gift from the wife of the North Wind, flashed like lightning through a dark cloud among the companies of the Greeks, and the chariots that followed the charge of the Amazon rocked as they swept over the bodies of the slain. Then the old Trojans, watching from the walls, cried: "This is no mortal maiden but a Goddess, and today she will burn the ships of the Greeks, and they will all perish in Troyland, and see Greece never more again."

Now it so was that Ajax and Achilles had not heard the din and the cry of war, for both had gone to weep over the great new grave of Patroclus. Penthesilea and the Trojans had driven back the Greeks within their ditch, and they were hiding here and there among the ships, and torches were blazing in men's hands to burn the ships, as in the day of the valour of Hector: when Ajax heard the din of battle, and called to Achilles to make speed towards the ships.

So they ran swiftly to their huts, and armed themselves, and Ajax fell smiting and slaying upon the Trojans, but Achilles slew five of the bodyguard of Penthesilea. She, beholding her maidens fallen, rode straight against Ajax and Achilles, like a dove defying two falcons, and cast her spear, but it fell back blunted from the glorious shield that the God had made for the son of Peleus.

Then she threw another spear at Ajax, crying, "I am the daughter of the God of War," but his armour kept out the spear, and he and Achilles laughed aloud.

Ajax paid no more heed to the Amazon, but rushed against the Trojan men; while Achilles raised the heavy spear that none but he could throw, and drove it down through breastplate and breast of Penthesilea, yet still her hand grasped her sword-hilt. But, ere she could draw her sword, Achilles speared her horse, and horse and rider fell, and died in their fall.

There lay fair Penthesilea in the dust, like a tall poplar tree that the wind has overthrown, and her helmet fell, and the Greeks who gathered round marvelled to see her lie so beautiful in death, like Artemis, the Goddess of the Woods, when she sleeps alone, weary with hunting on the hills. Then the heart of Achilles was pierced with pity and sorrow, thinking how she might have been his wife in his own country, had he spared her, but he was never to see pleasant Phthia, his native land, again. So Achilles stood and wept over Penthesilea dead.

Now the Greeks, in pity and sorrow, held their hands, and did not pursue the Trojans who had fled, nor did they strip the armour from Penthesilea and her twelve maidens, but laid the bodies on biers, and sent them back in peace to Priam. Then the Trojans burned Penthesilea in the midst of her dead maidens, on a great pile of dry wood, and placed their ashes in a golden casket, and buried them all in the great hill-grave of Laomedon, an ancient king of Troy, while the Greeks with lamentation buried them whom the Amazon had slain.

The old men of Troy and the chiefs now held a council, and Priam said that they must not yet despair, for, if they had lost many of their bravest warriors, many of the Greeks had also fallen. Their best plan was to fight only with arrows from the walls and towers, till King Memnon came to their rescue with a great army of Aethiopes. Now Memnon was the son of the bright Dawn, a beautiful Goddess who had loved and married a mortal man, Tithonus. She had asked Zeus, the chief of the Gods, to make her lover immortal, and her prayer was granted. Tithonus could not die, but he began to grow grey, and then white haired, with a long white beard, and very weak, till nothing of him seemed to be left but his voice, always feebly chattering like the grasshoppers on a summer day.

Memnon was the most beautiful of men, except Paris and Achilles, and his home was in a country that borders on the land of sunrising. There he was reared by the lily maidens called Hesperides, till he came to his full strength, and commanded the whole army of the Aethiopes. For their arrival Priam wished to wait, but Polydamas advised that the Trojans should give back Helen to the Greeks, with jewels twice as valuable as those which she had brought from the house of Menelaus. Then Paris was very angry, and said that Polydamas was a coward, for it was little to Paris that Troy should be taken and burned in a month if for a month he could keep Helen of the fair hands.

At length Memnon came, leading a great army of men who had nothing white about them but the teeth, so fiercely the sun burned on them in their own country. The Trojans had all the more hopes of Memnon because, on his long journey from the land of sunrising, and the river Oceanus that girdles the round world, he had been obliged to cross the country of the Solymi. Now the Solymi were the fiercest of men and rose up against Memnon, but he and his army fought them for a whole day, and defeated them, and drove them to the hills. When Memnon came, Priam gave him a great cup of gold, full of wine to the brim, and Memnon drank the wine at one draught. But he did not make great boasts of what he could do, like poor Penthesilea.

"For," said he, "whether I am a good man at arms will be known in battle, where the strength of men is tried. So now let us turn to sleep, for to wake and drink wine all through the night is an ill beginning of war."

Then Priam praised his wisdom, and all men betook them to bed, but the bright Dawn rose unwillingly next day, to throw light on the battle where her son was to risk his life. Then Memnon led out the dark clouds of his men into the plain, and the Greeks foreboded evil when they saw so great a new army of fresh and unwearied warriors, but Achilles, leading them in his shining armour, gave them courage. Memnon fell upon the left wing of the Greeks, and on the men of Nestor, and first he slew Ereuthus, and then attacked Nestor's young son, Antilochus, who, now that Patroclus had fallen, was the dearest friend of Achilles. On him Memnon leaped, like a lion on a kid, but Antilochus lifted a huge stone from the plain, a pillar that had been set on the tomb of some great warrior long ago, and the stone smote full on the helmet of Memnon, who reeled beneath the stroke. But Memnon seized his heavy spear, and drove it through shield and corselet of Antilochus, even into his heart, and he fell and died beneath his father's eyes.

Then Nestor in great sorrow and anger strode across the body of Antilochus and called to his other son, Thrasymedes, "Come and drive afar this man that has slain thy brother, for if fear be in thy heart thou art no son of mine, nor of the race of Periclymenus, who stood up in battle even against the strong man Heracles!"

But Memnon was too strong for Thrasymedes, and drove him off, while old Nestor himself charged sword in hand, though Memnon bade him begone, for he was not minded to strike so aged a man, and Nestor drew back, for he was weak with age. Then Memnon and his army charged the Greeks, slaying and stripping the dead. But Nestor had mounted his chariot and driven to Achilles, weeping, and imploring him to come swiftly and save the body of Antilochus, and he sped to meet Memnon, who lifted a great stone, the landmark of a field, and drove it against the shield of the son of Peleus. But Achilles was not shaken by the blow; he ran forward, and wounded Memnon over the rim of his shield. Yet wounded as he was Memnon fought on and struck his spear through the arm of Achilles, for the Greeks fought with no sleeves of bronze to protect their arms.

Then Achilles drew his great sword, and flew on Memnon, and with sword strokes they lashed at each other on shield and helmet, and the long horsehair crests of the helmets were shorn off, and flew down the wind, and their shields rang terribly beneath the sword strokes. They thrust at each others' throats between shield and visor of the helmet, they smote at knee, and thrust at breast, and the armour rang about their bodies, and the dust from beneath their feet rose up in a cloud around them, like mist round the falls of a great river in flood. So they fought, neither of them yielding a step, till Achilles made so rapid a thrust that Memnon could not parry it, and the bronze sword passed clean through his body beneath the breastbone, and he fell, and his armour clashed as he fell.

Then Achilles, wounded as he was and weak from loss of blood, did not stay to strip the golden armour of Memnon, but shouted his war cry, and pressed on, for he hoped to enter the gate of Troy with the fleeing Trojans, and all the Greeks followed after him. So they pursued, slaying as they went, and the Scaean gate was choked with the crowd of men, pursuing and pursued. In that hour would the Greeks have entered Troy, and burned the city, and taken the women captive, but Paris stood on the tower above the gate, and in his mind was anger for the death of his brother Hector. He tried the string of his bow, and found it frayed, for all day he had showered his arrows on the Greeks; so he chose a new bowstring, and fitted it, and strung the bow, and chose an arrow from his quiver, and aimed at the ankle of Achilles, where it was bare beneath the greave, or leg-guard of metal, that the God had fashioned for him. Through the ankle flew the arrow,

DISASTER ON THE HORIZON

and Achilles wheeled round, weak as he was, and stumbled, and fell, and the armour that the God had wrought was defiled with dust and blood.

Then Achilles rose again, and cried: "What coward has smitten me with a secret arrow from afar? Let him stand forth and meet me with sword and spear!"

So speaking he seized the shaft with his strong hands and tore it out of the wound, and much blood gushed, and darkness came over his eyes. Yet he staggered forward, striking blindly, and smote Orythaon, a dear friend of Hector, through the helmet, and others he smote, but now his force failed him, and he leaned on his spear, and cried his war cry, and said, "Cowards of Troy, ye shall not all escape my spear, dying as I am."

But as he spoke he fell, and all his armour rang around him, yet the Trojans stood apart and watched; and as hunters watch a dying lion not daring to go nigh him, so the Trojans stood in fear till Achilles drew his latest breath. Then from the wall the Trojan women raised a great cry of joy over him who had slain the noble Hector: and thus was fulfilled the prophecy of Hector, that Achilles should fall in the Scaean gateway, by the hand of Paris.

Then the best of the Trojans rushed forth from the gate to seize the body of Achilles, and his glorious armour, but the Greeks were as eager to carry the body to the ships that it might have due burial. Round the dead Achilles men fought long and sore, and both sides were mixed, Greeks and Trojans, so that men dared not shoot arrows from the walls of Troy lest they should kill their own friends. Paris, and Aeneas, and Glaucus, who had been the friend of Sarpedon, led the Trojans, and Ajax and Odysseus led the Greeks, for we are not told that Agamemnon was fighting in this great battle of the war. Now as angry wild bees flock round a man who is taking their honeycombs, so the Trojans gathered round Ajax, striving to stab him, but he set his great shield in front, and smote and slew all that came within reach of his spear. Odysseus, too, struck down many, and though a spear was thrown and pierced his leg near the knee he stood firm, protecting the body of Achilles. At last Odysseus caught the body of Achilles by the hands, and heaved it upon his back, and so limped towards the ships, but Ajax and the men of Ajax followed, turning round if ever the Trojans ventured to come near, and charging into the midst of them. Thus very slowly they bore the dead Achilles across the plain, through the bodies of the fallen and the blood, till they met Nestor in his chariot and placed Achilles therein, and swiftly Nestor drove to the ships.

There the women, weeping, washed Achilles' comely body, and laid him on a bier with a great white mantle over him, and all the women lamented and sang dirges, and the first was Briseis, who loved Achilles better than her own country, and her father, and her brothers whom he had slain in war. The Greek princes, too, stood round the body, weeping and cutting off their long locks of yellow hair, a token of grief and an offering to the dead.

Men say that forth from the sea came Thetis of the silver feet, the mother of Achilles, with her ladies, the deathless maidens of the waters. They rose up from their glassy chambers below the sea, moving on, many and beautiful, like the waves on a summer day, and their sweet song echoed along the shores, and fear came upon the Greeks. Then they would have fled, but Nestor cried: "Hold, flee not, young lords of the Achaeans! Lo, she that comes from the sea is his mother, with the deathless maidens of the waters, to look on the face of her dead son." Then the sea nymphs stood around the dead Achilles and clothed him in the garments of the Gods, fragrant raiment, and all the Nine Muses, one to the other replying with sweet voices, began their lament.

Next the Greeks made a great pile of dry wood, and laid Achilles on it, and set fire to it, till the flames had consumed his body except the white ashes. These they placed in a great golden cup and mingled with them the ashes of Patroclus, and above all they built a tomb like a hill, high on a headland above the sea, that men for all time may see it as they go sailing by, and may remember Achilles. Next they held in his honour foot races and chariot races, and other games, and Thetis gave splendid prizes. Last of all, when the games were ended, Thetis placed before the chiefs the glorious armour that the God had made for her son on the night after the slaying of Patroclus by Hector. "Let these arms be the prize of the best of the Greeks," she said, "and of him that saved the body of Achilles out of the hands of the Trojans."

Then stood up on one side Ajax and on the other Odysseus, for these two had rescued the body, and neither thought himself a worse warrior than the other. Both were the bravest of the brave, and if Ajax was the taller and stronger, and upheld the fight at the ships on the day of the valour of Hector; Odysseus had alone withstood the Trojans, and refused to retreat even when wounded, and his courage and cunning had won for the Greeks the Luck of Troy.

Therefore old Nestor arose and said: "This is a luckless day, when the best of the Greeks are rivals for such a prize. He who is not the winner will be heavy at heart, and will not stand firm by us in battle, as of old, and hence will come great loss to the Greeks. Who can be a just judge in this question, for some men will love Ajax better, and some will prefer Odysseus, and thus will arise disputes among ourselves. Lo! Have we not here among us many Trojan prisoners, waiting till their friends pay their ransom in cattle and gold and bronze and iron? These hate all the Greeks alike, and will favour neither Ajax nor Odysseus. Let *them* be the judges, and decide who is the best of the Greeks, and the man who has done most harm to the Trojans."

Agamemnon said that Nestor had spoken wisely. The Trojans were then made to sit as judges in the midst of the Assembly, and Ajax and Odysseus spoke, and told the stories of their own great deeds, of which we have heard already, but Ajax spoke roughly and discourteously, calling Odysseus a coward and a weakling.

"Perhaps the Trojans know," said Odysseus quietly, "whether they think that I deserve what Ajax has said about me, that I am a coward; and perhaps Ajax may remember that he did not find me so weak when we wrestled for a prize at the funeral of Patroclus."

Then the Trojans all with one voice said that Odysseus was the best man among the Greeks, and the most feared by them, both for his courage and his skill in stratagems of war. On this, the blood of Ajax flew into his face, and he stood silent and unmoving, and could not speak a word, till his friends came round him and led him away to his hut, and there he sat down and would not eat or drink, and the night fell.

Long he sat, musing in his mind, and then rose and put on all his armour, and seized a sword that Hector had given him one day when they two fought in a gentle passage of arms, and took courteous farewell of each other, and Ajax had given Hector a broad sword-belt, wrought with gold. This sword, Hector's gift, Ajax took, and went towards the hut of Odysseus, meaning to carve him limb from limb, for madness had come upon him in his great grief. Rushing through the night to slay Odysseus he fell upon the flock of sheep that the Greeks kept for their meat. And up and down among them he went, smiting blindly till the dawn came, and, lo! his senses returned to him, and he saw that he had not smitten Odysseus, but stood in a pool of blood among the sheep that he had slain. He could not endure the disgrace of his madness, and he fixed the sword, Hector's gift, with its hilt firmly in the ground, and went back a little way, and ran and fell upon the sword, which pierced his heart, and so died the great Ajax, choosing death before a dishonoured life.

Icarus and Daedalus

IN THE CITY OF ATHENS lived Daedalus, an inventor and artisan renowned across the world for his skill and genius. He loved nothing more than to create masterpieces of invention and wonder, except the recognition and admiration his talents won him. On fearing that his nephew and apprentice would one day surpass his lofty skills, Daedalus murdered the boy in cold blood. He and his family then fled to Crete. It was here that King Minos requested his service for a very special purpose.

The king had a monster living among his household, one that was cursed with insatiable, unnatural appetites. This miscreation was the Minotaur, the half-bull, half-human progeny of Minos's wife, Pasiphae. Pasiphae had been enchanted to fall in love with the bull of Poseidon. Her blood boiling in lust for the magnificent beast, Pasiphae demanded that Daedalus build her a contraption so that the bull could mount her. The resulting offspring was the atrocity that grew into the uncontrollable Minotaur. Seeking advice from the Delphic oracle, Minos was told to build a creation dense and elaborate enough to house the beast safely. For this, Minos needed Daedalus. Eager to test his skills, Daedalus accepted and, taking his son Icarus, he set off to Minos's palace to begin work on the Labyrinth, which would be his most extraordinary work.

The Labyrinth was an immense maze in the ground of Minos's palace. Daedalus used every method he could think of in the formation of his masterpiece; dead ends, winding passages, shadowy corners and pathways that never seemed to end, driving anyone trapped within to the very edge of insanity and beyond. So cunning was the Labyrinth that Daedalus himself was almost doomed among its dark and convoluted corridors. The complex twists and perplexing turns successfully trapped the Minotaur, who was kept contented by annual sacrifices of seven youths and seven maidens for him to hunt down and gorge upon at will.

But Minos did not react as Daedalus expected. Instead of showering him with praise and riches, the king was desperate to ensure that no one would ever discover the secret of the great Labyrinth. He trapped Daedalus and his son in a tall tower to ensure that the dark mystery of the Labyrinth would forever be protected. And so the days passed, but Minos would not release his prisoners. He even took the precaution of having the routes out of Crete by both land and sea guarded. But Daedalus was also crafty, as well as resourceful. The time came when he grew desperately weary of his enforced capture. Never forgetting that his beloved son had been imprisoned because of his ambition and love of fame, Daedalus plotted to win their freedom.

Daedalus began collecting the supplies they would need for their escape. Careful not to arouse suspicion in the king, he knew he would have to use natural objects where possible.

He also knew that Minos was watching the roads and sea, which left only one way for escape. They would have to fly.

Daedalus set to work making wings for himself and Icarus. Basing them on the natural curve of a bird's wing, he carefully bound together layers and layers of feathers with cord and sealed the binding with wax, without which the feathers would be pulled out of the cords during flight. He took the utmost care in his creation, placing the wings in order of size from smallest to largest. Finally, the instruments of freedom were ready. Trialling them, Daedalus strapped his wings in place and flapped his arms. The movement caught the wind and lifted him up into the air where he was able to hover above the ground.

Ecstatic with joy at the thought of their approaching freedom, Icarus – a tempestuous boy with little of his father's foresight – wanted immediately to set off for home. Tempering his son's eagerness, Daedalus again impressed upon Icarus how to get home safely. They had to avoid both the spray from the sea that would weigh down the wings and the heat from the sun, which would melt the wax securing the wings together.

Father and son took flight, leaving their tower of captivity forever. As they flew, Crete growing smaller behind them, both grew lighter at heart at the thought of home. Passing landmarks, ever hopeful that they would reach the shores of Athens, Daedalus's heart filled with heady pride at his construction. But he was overconfident. His invention – masterful as it was – was imperfect.

Icarus, his reckless boy, had inherited some of his father's ego. Feeling invincible, all warnings about how to fly safely flew from his mind. As the Aegean sea glittered beneath him, Icarus felt like a king up there in the heavens, so he flew higher and higher so as to fly among the gods. However the blazing sun caused the wax holding his precious wings together to melt. Desperately trying to regain control, Icarus swooped downwards to escape the sun's burning rays. But it was too late. Before his father could even make a move to help him, Icarus – with barely time to give his beloved father one final glance – plummeted to his death. Landing heavily in the deep, dark sea, Icarus breathed his last.

Wracked with grief, Daedalus was almost unable to complete his journey home, the sweet sensation of liberty forever tainted by his tragic loss. In homage to his son, and as a permanent reminder of the grief and loss caused by his pride and arrogance, Daedalus named the land nearest to Icarus's place of death Icaria, which it remains to this day.

Letter LXXXIII to Sura

THE PRESENT RECESS from business we are now enjoying affords you leisure to give, and me to receive, instruction. I am extremely desirous therefore to know whether you believe in the existence of ghosts, and that they have a real form, and are a sort of divinity, or only the visionary impressions of a terrified imagination. What particularly inclines me to believe in their existence is a story which I heard of Curtius Rufus. When he was in low circumstances and unknown in the world, he attended the governor of Africa into that province.

One evening, as he was walking in the public portico, there appeared to him the figure of a woman, of unusual size and of beauty more than human. And as he stood there, terrified and astonished, she told him she was the tutelary power that presided over Africa, and was come to inform him of the future events of his life: that he should go back to Rome, to enjoy high honours there, and return to that province invested with the proconsular dignity, and there should die. Every circumstance of this prediction actually came to pass. It is said further that upon his arrival at Carthage, as he was coming out of the ship, the same figure met him upon the shore. It is certain, at least, that being seized with a fit of illness, though there were no symptoms in his case that led those about him to despair, he instantly gave up all hope of recovery; judging, apparently, of the truth of the future part of the prediction by what had already been fulfilled, and of the approaching misfortune from his former prosperity. Now the following story, which I am going to tell you just as I heard it, is it not more terrible than the former, while quite as wonderful? There was at Athens a large and roomy house, which had a bad name, so that no one could live there. In the dead of the night a noise, resembling the clashing of iron, was frequently heard, which, if you listened more attentively, sounded like the rattling of chains, distant at first, but approaching nearer by degrees: immediately afterwards a spectre appeared in the form of an old man, of extremely emaciated and squalid appearance, with a long beard and dishevelled, hair, rattling the chains on his feet and hands.

The distressed occupants meanwhile passed their wakeful nights under the most dreadful terrors imaginable. This, as it broke their rest, ruined their health, and brought on distempers, their terror grew upon them, and death ensued. Even in the daytime, though the spirit did not appear, yet the impression remained so strong upon their imaginations that it still seemed before their eyes, and kept them in perpetual alarm.

Consequently the house was at length deserted, as being deemed absolutely uninhabitable; so that it was now entirely abandoned to the ghost. However, in hopes that some tenant might be found who was ignorant of this very alarming circumstance, a bill was put up, giving notice that it was either to be let or sold. It happened that Athenodorus the philosopher came to Athens at this time, and, reading the bill, enquired the price. The extraordinary cheapness raised his suspicion; nevertheless, when he heard the whole story, he was so far from being discouraged that he was more strongly inclined to hire it, and, in short, actually did so.

When it grew towards evening, he ordered a couch to be prepared for him in the front part of the house, and, after calling for a light, together with his pencil and tablets, directed all his people to retire. But that his mind might not, for want of employment, be open to the vain terrors of imaginary noises and spirits, he applied himself to writing with the utmost attention. The first part of the night passed in entire silence, as usual; at length a clanking of iron and rattling of chains was heard: however, he neither lifted up his eyes nor laid down his pen, but, in order to keep calm and collected, tried to pass the sounds off to himself as something else. The noise increased and advanced nearer, till it seemed at the door, and at last in the chamber. He looked up, saw, and recognized the ghost exactly as it had been described to him: it stood before him, beckoning with the finger, like a person who calls another. Athenodorus in reply made a sign with his hand that it should wait a little, and threw his eyes again upon his papers; the ghost then rattled its chains over the head of the philosopher, who looked up upon this, and seeing it beckoning as before, immediately arose, and, light in hand, followed it. The ghost slowly stalked along, as if encumbered with its chains, and, turning into the area of the house, suddenly vanished. Athenodorus, being thus deserted, made a mark with some grass and leaves on the spot where the spirit left him.

The next day he gave information to the magistrates, and advised them to order that spot to be dug up. This was accordingly done, and the skeleton of a man in chains was found there; for the body, having lain a considerable time in the ground, was putrefied and mouldered away from the fetters. The bones, being collected together, were publicly buried, and thus after the ghost was appeased by the proper ceremonies, the house was haunted no more. This story I believe upon the credit of others; what I am going to mention, I give you upon my own. I have a freedman named Marcus, who is by no means illiterate. One night, as he and his younger brother were lying together, he fancied he saw somebody upon his bed, who took out a pair of scissors, and cut off the hair from the top part of his own head, and in the morning, it appeared his hair was actually cut, and the clippings lay scattered about the floor.

A short time after this, an event of a similar nature contributed to give credit to the former story. A young lad of my family was sleeping in his apartment with the rest of his companions, when two persons clad in white came in, as he says, through the windows, cut off his hair as he lay, and then returned the same way they entered. The next morning it was found that this boy had been served just as the other, and there was the hair again, spread about the room. Nothing remarkable indeed followed these events, unless perhaps that I escaped a prosecution, in which, if Domitian (during whose reign this happened) had lived some time longer, I should certainly have been involved. For after the death of that emperor, articles of impeachment against me were found in his scrutoire, which had been exhibited by Carus. It may therefore be conjectured, since it is customary for persons under any public accusation to let their hair grow, this cutting off the hair of my servants was a sign I should escape the imminent danger that threatened me.

Let me desire you then to give this question your mature consideration. The subject deserves your examination; as, I trust, I am not myself altogether unworthy a participation in the abundance of your superior knowledge. And though you should, as usual, balance between two opinions, yet I hope you will lean more on one side than on the other, lest, whilst I consult you in order to have my doubt settled, you should dismiss me in the same suspense and indecision that occasioned you the present application. Farewell.

Tyr's Sword

TYR, TIU, OR ZIU was the son of Odin, and, according to different mythologists, his mother was Frigga, queen of the gods, or a beautiful giantess whose name is unknown, but who was a personification of the raging sea. He is the god of martial honour, and one of the twelve principal deities of Asgard. Although he appears to have had no special dwelling there, he was always welcome to Vingolf or Valhalla, and occupied one of the twelve thrones in the great council hall of Gladsheim.

As the God of courage and of war, Tyr was frequently invoked by the various nations of the North, who cried to him, as well as to Odin, to obtain victory. That he ranked next to Odin and Thor is proved by his name, Tiu, having been given to one of the days of the week, Tiu's day, which in modern English has become Tuesday. Under the name of Ziu, Tyr was the principal divinity of the Suabians, who originally called their capital, the modern Augsburg, Ziusburg. This people, venerating the god as they did, were wont to worship him under the emblem of a sword, his distinctive attribute, and in his honour held great sword dances, where various figures were performed. Sometimes the participants forming two long lines, crossed their swords, point upward, and challenged the boldest among their number to take a flying leap over them. At other times the warriors joined their sword points closely together in the shape of a rose or wheel, and when this figure was complete invited their chief to stand on the navel thus formed of flat, shining steel blades, and then they bore him upon it through the camp in triumph. The sword point was further considered so sacred that it became customary to register oaths upon it.

A distinctive feature of the worship of this god among the Franks and some other Northern nations was that the priests called Druids or Godi offered up human sacrifices upon his altars, generally cutting the bloody or spread-eagle upon their victims, that is to say, making a deep incision on either side of the backbone, turning the ribs thus loosened inside out, and tearing out the viscera through the opening thus made. Of course only prisoners of war were treated thus, and it was considered a point of honour with north European races to endure this torture without a moan. These sacrifices were made upon rude stone altars called dolmens, which can still be seen in Northern Europe. As Tyr was considered the patron god of the sword, it was deemed indispensable to engrave the sign or rune representing him upon the blade of every sword – an observance which the Edda enjoined upon all those who were desirous of obtaining victory.

Tyr was identical with the Saxon god Saxnot (from sax, a sword), and with Er, Heru, or Cheru, the chief divinity of the Cheruski, who also considered him god of the sun, and deemed his shining sword blade an emblem of its rays.

According to an ancient legend, Cheru's sword, which had been fashioned by the same dwarfs, sons of Ivald, who had also made Odin's spear, was held very sacred by his people, to whose care he had entrusted it, declaring that those who possessed it were sure to have the victory over their foes. But although carefully guarded in the temple, where it was hung so that it reflected the first beams of the morning sun, it suddenly and mysteriously disappeared one night. A Vala, druidess, or prophetess, consulted by the priests, revealed that the Norns had decreed that whoever wielded it would conquer the world and come to his death by it; but in spite of all entreaties she refused to tell who had taken it or where it might be found. Some time after this occurrence a tall and dignified stranger came to Cologne, where Vitellius, the Roman prefect, was feasting, and called him away from his beloved dainties. In the presence of the Roman soldiery he gave him the sword, telling him it would bring him glory and renown, and finally hailed him as emperor. The cry was taken up by the assembled legions, and Vitellius, without making any personal effort to secure the honour, found himself elected Emperor of Rome.

The new ruler, however, was so absorbed in indulging his taste for food and drink that he paid but little heed to the divine weapon. One day while leisurely making his way towards Rome he carelessly left it hanging in the antechamber to his pavilion. A German soldier seized this opportunity to substitute in its stead his own rusty blade, and the besotted emperor did not notice the exchange. When he arrived at Rome, he learned that the Eastern legions had named Vespasian emperor, and that he was even then on his way home to claim the throne.

Searching for the sacred weapon to defend his rights, Vitellius now discovered the theft, and, overcome by superstitious fears, did not even attempt to fight. He crawled away into a dark corner of his palace, whence he was ignominiously dragged by the enraged populace to the foot of the Capitoline Hill. There the prophecy was duly fulfilled, for the German soldier, who had joined the opposite faction, coming along at that moment, cut off Vitellius's head with the sacred sword.

The German soldier now changed from one legion to another, and travelled over many lands; but wherever he and his sword were found, victory was assured. After winning great honour and distinction, this man, having grown old, retired from active service to the banks of the Danube, where he secretly buried his treasured weapon, building his hut over its resting place to guard it as long as he might live. When he lay on his deathbed he was implored to reveal where he had hidden it, but he persistently refused to do so, saying that it would be found by the man who was destined to conquer the world, but that he would not be able to escape the curse. Years passed by. Wave after wave the tide of barbarian invasion swept over that part of the country, and last of all came the terrible Huns under the leadership of Attila, the 'Scourge of God'. As he passed along the river, he saw a peasant mournfully examining his cow's foot, which had been wounded by some sharp instrument hidden in the long grass, and when search was made the point of a buried sword was found sticking out of the soil.

Attila, seeing the beautiful workmanship and the fine state of preservation of this weapon, immediately exclaimed that it was Cheru's sword, and brandishing it above his head he announced that he would conquer the world. Battle after battle was fought by the Huns, who, according to the Sagas, were everywhere victorious, until Attila, weary of warfare, settled down in Hungary, taking to wife the beautiful Burgundian princess Ildico, whose father he had slain. This princess, resenting the murder of her kin and wishing to avenge it, took advantage of the king's state of intoxication upon his wedding night to secure possession of the divine sword, with which she slew him in his bed, once more fulfilling the prophecy uttered so many years before.

The magic sword again disappeared for a long time, to be unearthed once more, for the last time, by the Duke of Alva, Charles V's general, who shortly after won the victory of Mühlberg (1547). The Franks were wont to celebrate yearly martial games in honour of the sword; but it is said that when the heathen gods were renounced in favour of Christianity, the priests transferred many of their attributes to the saints, and that this sword became the property of the Archangel St. Michael, who has wielded it ever since.

Tyr, whose name was synonymous with bravery and wisdom, was also considered by the ancient Northern people to have the white-armed Valkyrs, Odin's attendants, at his command, and they thought that he it was who designated the warriors whom they should transfer to Valhalla to aid the gods on the last day.

Ragnarok

TOO LATE THE GODS REALIZED how evil was this spirit that had found a home among them, and too late they banished Loki to earth, where men, following the gods' example, listened to his teachings, and were corrupted by his sinister influence.

Seeing that crime was rampant, and all good banished from the earth, the gods realized that the prophecies uttered of old were about to be fulfilled, and that the shadow of Ragnarok, the twilight or dusk of the gods, was already upon them. Sol and Mani grew pale with affright, and drove their chariots tremblingly along their appointed paths, looking back with fear at the pursuing wolves which would shortly overtake and devour them; and as their smiles disappeared the earth grew sad and cold, and the terrible Fimbul-winter began. Then snow fell from the four points of the compass at once, the biting winds swept down from the north, and all the earth was covered with a thick layer of ice.

This severe winter lasted during three whole seasons without a break, and was followed by three others, equally severe, during which all cheer departed from the earth, and the crimes of men increased with fearful rapidity, whilst, in the general struggle for life, the last feelings of humanity and compassion disappeared.

In the dim recesses of the Ironwood the giantess Iarnsaxa or Angur-boda diligently fed the wolves Hati, Skoll, and Managarm, the progeny of Fenris, with the marrow of murderers' and adulterers' bones; and such was the prevalence of these vile crimes, that the well-nigh insatiable monsters were never short on food. They daily gained strength to pursue Sol and Mani, and finally overtook and devoured them, deluging the earth with blood from their dripping jaws.

At this terrible calamity the whole earth trembled and shook, the stars, affrighted, fell from their places, and Loki, Fenris, and Garm, renewing their efforts, rent their chains asunder and rushed forth to take their revenge. At the same moment the dragon Nidhug gnawed through the root of the ash Yggdrasil, which quivered to its topmost bough; the red cock Fialar, perched above Valhalla, loudly crowed an alarm, which was immediately echoed by Gullin-kambi, the rooster in Midgard, and by Hel's dark-red bird in Niflheim.

Heimdall, noting these ominous portents and hearing the cock's shrill cry, immediately put the Gjallarhorn to his lips and blew the long-expected blast, which was heard throughout the world. At the first sound of this rally Aesir and Einheriar sprang from their golden couches and sallied bravely out of the great hall, armed for the coming fray, and, mounting their impatient steeds, they galloped over the quivering rainbow bridge to the spacious field of Vigrid, where, as Vafthrudnir had predicted long before, the last battle was to take place.

The terrible Midgard snake Iormungandr had been aroused by the general disturbance, and with immense writhings and commotion, whereby the seas were lashed into huge waves such as had never before disturbed the deeps of ocean, he crawled out upon the land, and hastened to join the dread fray, in which he was to

One of the great waves, stirred up by Iormungandr's struggles, set afloat Nagilfar, the fatal ship, which was constructed entirely out of the nails of those dead folks whose relatives had failed, through the ages, in their duty, having neglected to pare the nails of the deceased, ere they were laid to rest. No sooner was this vessel afloat, than Loki boarded it with the fiery host from Muspellsheim, and steered it boldly over the stormy waters to the place of conflict.

This was not the only vessel bound for Vigrid, however, for out of a thick fog bank towards the north came another ship, steered by Hrym, in which were all the frost giants, armed to the teeth and eager for a conflict with the Aesir, whom they had always hated.

At the same time, Hel, the goddess of death, crept through a crevice in the earth out of her underground home, closely followed by the Hel-hound Garm, the malefactors of her cheerless realm, and the dragon Nidhug, which flew over the battlefield bearing corpses upon his wings.

As soon as he landed, Loki welcomed these reinforcements with joy, and placing himself at their head he marched with them to the fight.

Suddenly the skies were rent asunder, and through the fiery breach rode Surtr with his flaming sword, followed by his sons; and as they rode over the bridge Bifrost, with intent to storm Asgard, the glorious arch sank with a crash beneath their horses' tread.

The gods knew full well that their end was now near, and that their weakness and lack of foresight placed them under great disadvantages; for Odin had but one eye, Tyr but one hand, and Frey nothing but a stag's horn wherewith to defend himself, instead of his invincible sword. Nevertheless, the Aesir did not show any signs of despair, but, like true battle-gods of the North, they donned their richest attire, and gaily rode to the battlefield, determined to sell their lives as dearly as possible.

While they were mustering their forces, Odin once more rode down to the Urdar fountain, where, under the toppling Yggdrasil, the Norns sat with veiled faces and obstinately silent, their web lying torn at their feet. Once more the father of the gods whispered a mysterious communication to Mimir, after which he remounted Sleipnir and rejoined the waiting host.

The combatants were now assembled on Vigrid's broad plain. On one side were ranged the stern, calm faces of the Aesir, Vanir and Einheriar; while on the other were gathered the motley host of Surtr, the grim frost giants, the pale army of Hel, and Loki and his dread followers, Garm, Fenris, and Iormungandr, the two latter belching forth fire and smoke, and exhaling clouds of noxious, deathly vapours.

All the pent-up antagonism of ages was now let loose in a torrent of hate, each member of the opposing hosts fighting with grim determination, as did our ancestors of old, hand to hand and face to face. With a mighty shock, heard above the roar of battle which filled the universe, Odin and the Fenris wolf came into impetuous contact, while Thor attacked the Midgard snake, and Tyr came to grips with the dog Garm. Frey closed with Surtr, Heimdall with Loki, whom he had defeated once before, and the remainder of the gods and all the Einheriar engaged foes equally worthy of their courage. But, in spite of their daily preparation in the heavenly city, Valhalla's host was doomed to succumb, and Odin was amongst the first of the shining ones to be slain. Not even the high courage and mighty attributes of Allfather could withstand the tide of evil as personified in the Fenris wolf. At each succeeding moment of the struggle its colossal size assumed greater proportions, until finally its wide-open jaws embraced all the space between heaven and earth, and the foul monster rushed furiously upon the father of gods and engulfed him bodily within its horrid maw.

None of the gods could lend Allfather a helping hand at that critical moment, for it was a time of sore trial to all. Frey put forth heroic efforts, but Surtr's flashing sword now dealt him a death-stroke. In his struggle with the arch-enemy, Loki, Heimdall fared better, but his final conquest was dearly bought, for he, too, fell dead. The struggle between Tyr and Garm had the same tragic end, and Thor, after a most terrible encounter with the Midgard snake, and after slaying him with a stroke from Miolnir, staggered back.

Vidar now came rushing from a distant part of the plain to avenge the death of his mighty sire, and the doom foretold fell upon Fenris, whose lower jaw now felt the impress of that shoe which had been reserved for this day. At the same moment Vidar seized the monster's upper jaw with his hands, and with one terrible wrench tore him asunder.

The other gods who took part in the fray, and all the Einheriar having now perished, Surtr suddenly flung his fiery brands over heaven, earth, and the nine kingdoms of Hel.

The raging flames enveloped the massive stem of the world ash Yggdrasil, and reached the golden palaces of the gods, which were utterly consumed. The vegetation upon earth was likewise destroyed, and the fervent heat made all the waters seethe and boil.

The great conflagration raged fiercely until everything was consumed, when the earth, blackened and scarred, slowly sank beneath the boiling waves of the sea. Ragnarok had indeed come; the world tragedy was over, the divine actors were slain, and chaos seemed to have resumed its former sway. But as in a play, after the principals are slain and the curtain has fallen, the audience still looks for the favourites to appear and make their bow, so the ancient Northern races fancied that, all evil having perished in Surtr's flames, from the general ruin goodness would rise, to resume its sway over the earth, and that some of the gods would return to dwell in heaven for ever.

The Story of Grímur, Who Killed Skeljúngur

A CERTAIN MAN was named Kári, the son of Össur. He was the nephew of Hjálmúlfr, who had made himself possessor of Blönduhlíd, extending from the river Djúpadalsá to the river Nordurá, and who dwelt at Hjálmúlfsstadir, and is buried in the barrow called Ulfshaugur, south of the farm.

Kári came from Norway, in company with Hjálmúlfr, made himself possessor of the land between Nordurá and Merkigil, and dwelt at the farm called Flatatúga; whereupon he was named Túngukári.

He had a son, Thorgrímur, a strong and wise man, who married Ashildur, daughter of Thorbrandur, of Thorbrandsstadir, in Nordurárdalur, and with her he received the property belonging to the farm Silfrastadir, where he began his life as a farmer, and became very wealthy in flocks and herds.

Thorbrandur lived at Thorbrandsstadir, to a high age, and possessed, besides this farm, one called Haukagil. At the former of these he built the famous hall, so much spoken of in the Sagas, through which the highway ran, where there were tables of provisions always ready for every passer-by. Thorbrandur was buried on the other side of the river Nordurá, where a large mound was raised above him, in a place he had himself chosen, whence he could see over both Thorbrandsstadir and Haukagil.

Thorgrímur of Silfrastadir had a son by his wife, named Grímur, who was one of the handsomest and best-grown men in Skagafjördur. He had also a daughter, named Ingibjörg, who was both winsome and wise, and was looked upon as one of the chief ladies in all that neighbourhood.

Thorgrímur had large flocks, as his pasture-grounds were good, and was therefore in need of an active herdsman, if he wished all to go well with his sheep. Once it happened that a vessel from Norway came into the harbour of Kolbeinsá late in the summer. Thorgrímur, with many other farmers, rode down to the ship, the merchants of which had on board, besides other wares, a certain bondman named Skeljúngur. He was tall, strong, and of an indomitable temper.

Thorgrímur, being apprised by the merchants that this man was for sale, went to him and asked him for what work he was fit.

Skeljúngur answered, "Thralls are not fit for much. But in good weather I have not refused ere now to watch sheep, and if you will, I can do so still."

Thorgrímur said, "I will risk buying you if you will guard my sheep, which are numerous, and their pastures dangerous."

"Do as you like," answered Skeljúngur.

So the farmer purchased this bondman, and took him home to Silfrastadir, where he commenced his duties as herdsman towards the beginning of the winter, and Thorgrímur soon perceived that the man had the strength and courage of two, in everything he undertook.

Skeljúngur was very obedient to his master, but could not agree with the other men of the farm, and least of all with Grímur.

Amongst the servants at the farm was a bond-maid named Bóla, who was fiendishly evil-minded and malicious, insomuch that nobody could come to any understanding with her. Many fancied that her nature partook of that of the trolls; and her quarrels with Skeljúngur were so fierce and frequent, that the farmer had repeatedly to interfere between them.

At last, Bóla ran away from Silfrastadir in a fit of rage, and everyone was convinced that she had taken up her abode in a deep rocky gulf, near the farm. In this gulf there were three high waterfalls, as a little river ran through it. The approach to the two lower ones was difficult; to the uppermost one, under which Bóla was supposed to have taken up her abode in a cave, nearly impossible. From this place she infested the neighbourhood, part of which, with the gulf itself, was subsequently called by her name.

Once, early in the winter, Thorgrímur lost five of his best wethers from Skeljúngur's keeping, and it was suspected that Bóla had taken them. Skeljúngur became very cross at this, and wanted to find out whether she had taken them or not. But the farmer entreated him to run no such risk, assuring him that it would be far better to remain quiet. The man obeyed him, and, for the present, desisted from any search into the matter.

Next autumn eight wethers were lost from Skeljúngur's charge, who still did not endeavour to find them, as the farmer had begged him not to do so.

The third autumn ten more were lost, and then Skeljúngur became so enraged that he would not listen in the least to what the farmer said. So he ran off in a state of blind and mad rage, like that in which the warriors of old could fight their best, and hastened to the gulf, and over the waterfall into the cave; which leap has been since called "Skeljúngur's leap".

Now, after this, nothing distinct is known concerning his struggle with Bóla; but the story runs, that, after a fierce and long fight with her, he contrived to suffocate her in the deep pool beneath the fall. This done, Skeljúngur returned to the farm, and said that he fancied the stealing of his sheep would not be continued now; but Thorgrímur, far from pleased, held his peace.

People soon found that Skeljúngur's temper had become more diabolical than ever, since his struggle with Bóla, so that it became almost impossible to treat with him; but he still continued faithful and attached to his master, and so time passed quietly on.

Now we must return to Grímur, the son of Thorgrímur, who had lived with his father to manhood, and was now the most active of all his fellows.

One day Grímur came to his father, and said, "Advance me some money from my inheritance. I wish to travel hence and become acquainted with the customs of other countries; for to sit here at home like a girl will prove but a scanty advantage to me."

The farmer replied, "You shall not need to ask twice. I will give you money enough; but I have a foreboding that at some future time we shall need you here; and then you had better be at home than away; and I fear that you will have some great dangers to overcome."

Grímur answered, "I will run the risk;" and after this went on board a vessel belonging to some Norway merchants, with plenty of money for his travels. He took an affectionate leave of his father, and sailed away. But the ship had started very late, having been prevented from sailing by the Greenland ice, and when once at sea, was so hard tossed by storms, as to lose her way and be driven hither and thither all the rest of the summer. At the approach of the winter, they were, in a heavy snow-storm, carried near the shores of an unknown country, where there was no harbour, and where the coast was surrounded by cliffs. Here they were wrecked, and every life was lost, and all the merchandise swallowed by the waves; Grímur alone being able to swim to shore, where he wandered about forlorn and tired, not knowing whither to go, till he heard the sound of someone cutting wood near him. He went in that direction, and found a young and strongly built man, hewing wood with a large axe.

Grímur saluted this youth, who courteously received him, and asked him about his journey, and how he had come there.

Grímur answered, "I am an Icelander, by name Grímur. My ship, with all its merchandise and all my companions, has been wrecked, and all lost but myself. Tell me now, to what land I have been driven; who is its ruler? and whom do I now address?"

The other replied, "I am your namesake, for my name is also Grímur. You have come to the wildernesses of Greenland, a long way from the thickly inhabited districts; but my father's hut is not far hence. His name also is Grímur, and my mother's Thórhildur, and I have a sister, two years older than myself, named Ingibjörg. No one else lives in the house, nor have we many neighbours.

"Now, as matters stand, I think you can do no better than accompany me home to my father, appeal to his good feeling, and see what comes of it. And I suppose he will do better who aids you than he who is against you."

To this the Icelandic Grímur agreed, and the young men went towards the hut together.

The cottage was neat and strongly built, and the Greenland Grímur brought his namesake into the room where his father was sitting; an old man of noble aspect, hale for his age, and active in all his movements. His wife, an aged woman, was very neat in her dress, and imposing in her demeanour.

The old man saluted his son kindly, and said, "Who is the young fellow with you?"

His son replied, "He is an Icelander who has been wrecked on the shore, and has lost all his possessions. I beg you, my father, to help him, for he is an honourable and well-born youth."

His father said, "I was not curious concerning him, but as he has been driven to shore, to the compassion of his fellow creatures, take him with you, my son, we bid him welcome for the winter."

The young men thanked the farmer for his kindness, and from that time became, as it were, brothers. Ingibjörg was a noble and lovely maiden, and she and the Icelander became much attached to one another, at which no one wondered, as all were fond of him.

So the winter passed, until shortly before Christmas time, when it happened one day, that the brothers, while gathering driftwood on the shore, saw a monster in woman's form, with large and repulsive countenance, approaching them.

She addressed them with these words: "I must tell you, young men, that my mother Skráma, who lives in the mountains, invites you to her Christmas festivities, and is very anxious that you should accept her invitation."

The youths answered her only with curses, and spurned her invitation; whereupon she at once disappeared.

When they came home late in the evening, the old man asked them whether they had any news for him, but they said they had nothing new to relate to him. He continued, however. "I am sure that you have seen something unusual, and that you will not refuse to tell me the truth about it."

So they told him that they had seen the monster, and laughed to scorn her invitation; "for," they said, "what cared we for her?"

The old man answered, "It will not do for you to reject her invitation. And now, I will give you some useful information. In the mountains some way from here, is a valley with a cave in it, in which lives a trollwoman, Járngerdur by name, who is an awful and malignant creature. Her two daughters live with her, Skinnbrók and Skinnhetta, who are very dangerous to have to do with.

"Now, because I and Járngerdur have for long been opposed to one another, and I have always had the advantage, she will seek to take vengeance upon you, by her troll's arts. But it will not do for you two to go by yourselves to her, therefore I and my dog Grámúll will join your company. This Járngerdur is the worst troll of all the infernal tribe, and upon whomsoever her dying eyes shall fall, he will rot alive beneath their glare, in that very hour. Therefore we must make all possible preparations, and take every precaution, if we wish to escape from her alive."

The young men begged the old farmer to make for them every needful preparation, declaring that they trusted implicitly in his great experience.

On the morning of Christmas Eve they left the hut; had to reach the valley through heavy snowdrifts, and would have lost their way to it, had not the dog Grámúll found the path for them. In the evening they saw before them a large cave in some rocks, and following the narrow passage, came into it. There was a blazing fire in the cave, by which two young, monstrous, and hideous trollwomen were sitting.

The one, Skinnbrók, said to the other, Skinnhetta, "See! we shall not lie alone tonight, and tomorrow we will cut those young men up for our Christmas feast. But if this old Grímur can carry out his intentions, we shall all perish. I would that the old man could have some punishment for his curiosity in coming here against our will."

Then Grímur the Icelander went close to the fire and said: "Is the Christmas meal ready? and the table dressed?"

The sisters started at this, and sprang to their feet; and Skinnbrók ran towards Grímur the Icelander, to struggle with him, saying, "I suppose you will not consider yourself the worse treated if you embrace such a fine lady as myself, before the Christmas feast?"

Then they fought together with brute fury, and dashed one another from corner to corner of the cave. After a while the Icelander found that, troll as she was, she began to flag and lose her breath; then he tried to trip her up, and at last flung her down so that her neck was broken, and he left her dead, he himself being tired and bruised after the struggle.

Now Skinnhetta, in her turn, attacked Grímur the Greenlander, and they had a long and fierce fight, each trying to throw the other into the fire; but at last Grímur succeeded in lifting her up from the ground and hurling her, head foremost, into the boiling kettle, where he kept her till she died. After that he rested himself.

Meanwhile, the old troll-mother had attacked Grímur the father, and their struggle was a deadly one. When the brothers saw that their father began to lose strength, they set the dog

Grámúll upon the troll. The hound flew savagely at her, and tore her side so that her entrails were seen, and the dog rent them out. At this the troll fell down, and in dying fixed a horrible and ghastly glare upon Grámúll, till the dog rotted beneath her eyes, and crumbled to dust at her feet; and thus died Járngerdur and the dog that had slain her.

Then the men lighted a great fire outside the cave, and burned the bodies of the three trolls. They found over the bed of the old troll a spear, which was a great rarity; glittering as glass, and adorned with gold. After this they searched all through the cave, and found many good things and valuable; all of which they bound into bundles and took away with them, the old Grímur carrying the spear, and returned home.

Here Grímur the Icelander dwelt for a long time, beloved by them all, but by none more than by the daughter, Ingibjörg.

The story now returns to Iceland. It happened that the winter after Grímur's departure, a meeting was appointed at Hofmannaflöt. To this many of the strongest men in the country, and even the giants and the mountaineers, came to make trials of their strength in wrestling. There came also Lágálfur, the son of Litildrós. When he came from this meeting in the south, down the mountains to the Skagafjördur, he had to cross the River Nordurá, opposite to Silfrastadir. It was late in the day, and the snow drifted heavily, and just now Lágálfur saw a man of huge stature striding towards him along the bank of the river. The giant saluted Lágálfur, and asked him what news he had to tell. Lágálfur told him all the most important news, and asked with whom he was speaking.

The other answered: "I am Skeljúngur, and I come from my flocks. I dare say you are a great and strong man, but I am cold with standing over my sheep all day, and it would be good sport for us to wrestle a little, to warm ourselves."

Lágálfur replied: "I have for some time had good sport in wrestling with gallant men, but although you look like a rascal and a troll, I will not refuse to wrestle with you. Let each man look to himself."

Skeljúngur consented to this, and having thrown off their outer clothes, they began to wrestle. Lágálfur soon felt that Skeljúngur had the strength of two strong men, and that he must not spare his own strength against him. Now they wrestled with such fury that frozen stones started from the ground beneath their feet. When Lágálfur was tired of this undecided struggle, he tried to trip up his adversary, and a fit of blind madness and heroic fury seized them. At last Lágálfur lifted Skeljúngur by his hip and threw him so high that when he fell both his thighs were broken upon the frozen ground, and both his shoulders dislocated. Then his enemy set upon him with such rage that he left him at the point of death.

After this, Lágálfur went to the farm Silfrastadir, where all the people were already assembled in the family-room, and sang outside the window a verse, telling how he had fought with and subdued Skeljúngur.

"Quickly over the earth I ran,
And dealt with that rascally shepherd-man;
The strength-failing thrall himself brought it to be
That he should be dealt with so hardly by me.
The hair-brained fellow was beaten, and found
A good drubbing on the stony ground.
Skeljúngur scarcely will find him again
To watch his sheep and to guard the pen."

From this farm he went to another house, named Frostastödum, and stopped at that end of the house at which the farmer slept, where was a window through which he could see into the house. He saw the farmer sitting there, a grey-headed man, and heard him scolding his wife for having taken a handful of meal from the leather sack hanging in the roof over the farmer's head, and at last he struck her with his hand upon the cheek, so that she wept. Then Lágálfur thrust through the window the spear which he held in his hand, so as to cut the cords of the leather meal-bag, which fell down suddenly on the farmer's head, and sent him fainting to the ground. As soon as he saw that the farmer had recovered his senses, he retired from the window and sang:

"The meal-sack fell from the roof above
Upon the old man's pate,
And the beaten wife sat bewailing her fate
Till Lágálfur's spear avenged the sweet love."

Then Lágálfur went home, and henceforth is no more seen in our story, which returns now to Silfrastadir.

The farmer began to suspect something about Skeljúngur, when he heard Lágálfur sing at the window, and he supposed that the latter had left the herdsman unable to help himself. He therefore ordered his servants to search for Skeljúngur, but they could not find him, as the night was very dark. Early in the morning, the farmer started off with his men to search again for him. They discovered the place where Lágálfur and Skeljúngur had fought, by the trodden ground, and the stones which had been kicked up by their feet, but of the man himself they could find nothing.

After a little time people began to be aware that Skeljúngur did not lie quiet in death, and that he was a goblin, and now lived in the mountain close to Silfrastadir. And it became dangerous to pass through the valley, for he used to kill the horses of travellers, and their dogs, and mislead themselves. But Thorgrímur received the worst harm of all from him; for his herdsman was killed the following Christmas, and the same fatal thing took place till the third Christmas.

Now the story returns to Greenland again. Grímur the Icelander had lived there in all happiness with the good farmer and his family all this time. He had learnt many things, and excelled everybody in bravery and skill.

Once in the last spring the old farmer came to him and said to him, "This night I have seen many visions, and I suppose that your father is in hard need of you, for his herdsman has become a dangerous goblin, destroying his property and killing his servants, and I tell you that you are the only man capable of killing this monster. Now you shall make ready to return to Iceland, and I will give you a little ship for the voyage, in which Grímur, my son and Ingibjörg, my daughter, shall accompany you. I see that your lines of fate lie together, and on your arrival in Iceland, you will marry your sister Ingibjörg to my son Grímur. He will bring her hither, but will return again to Iceland, where they will rear their family. Your fortune, however, will lead you away from your native land; but in whatever company you move, you will always be the foremost and best. And now I will equip you for your journey as well as I can."

Grímur the Icelander thanked the old man for his kind gifts, and promised to follow his advice.

When the ice had disappeared, the young men prepared their vessel for their voyage, and the farmer gave them everything they required, of the best quality. To the Icelander he gave

DISASTER ON THE HORIZON

many rarities, and, among others, the troll's spear which they had found in the cave, and, as he delivered it into his hand, said, "I think this will wear through many a rough combat."

After this the old Grímur bade farewell to his children and to his future son-in-law, and wished them God-speed. So they weighed anchor and sailed away into the Greenland sea, and a long and rough passage they had, between the stormy weather and the ice, but at last they came safely into harbour in the mouth of the River Blanda, two days before Christmas.

The Icelander said, "I will ride as speedily as possible northwards to Silfrastadir, and I shall be none too early; but do you wait by the ship till my return."

So he procured two of the best riding-horses in the neighbourhood, and rode, dressed in glittering armour and carrying the troll's spear, along Blanda up through Vatnsskard. The snow had drifted, and the roads were heavy, but he rode so fast that, as the tale goes, one of his horses died in the middle of the journey, and the other by the wall of the grass-field of Silfrúnarstadir.

When he arrived there it was Christmas Eve, and the day far spent, and he went in to his father, who received him with great joy. Then he went to the family-room and threw off his riding-dress. He saw that all the people of the household looked sorrowful, and as he knew what was the cause of their sadness, he questioned them about Skeljúngur's habits. They told him that all night this goblin used to sit outside of the sleeping-room roof, kicking his heels into it, and that he was so dangerous, that no one dared go out after nightfall.

Grímur saw lying on the floor the fresh skin of the ox which had been killed for the Christmas feast, so he took it and cut out of it three strong ropes, and after that went out of the house, and directed his steps southward, carrying the spear in one hand, the ropes in the other, till he came to a mound called, after him, Grímshóll, where he found a stone standing on the south side, broad at the bottom and narrow at the top. Grímur went to it, and pierced three holes through it with his spear. Into these holes he put the three ropes, and made, by means of loops, three nooses, which could be drawn tight against the stone. This accomplished, he returned home, where a merry Christmas feast awaited him, for every one was glad of his return, and none more so than his father. As the night advanced, Grímur begged all the people to go to bed.

The servant men of the farm slept in a dormitory near the entrance, where there were many beds. Grímur lay down on the bed nearest the door, wrapped up in the fresh ox-skin from which he had cut the cords, and through the head of which he could see the door. One lamp was burning in the room, and Grímur told all the others to be neither afraid nor troubled if anyone should come unceremoniously into the house. Everyone, with silent dread, expected Skeljúngur, and thus, in perfect quiet, some part of the night was spent.

After midnight some one was heard to mount on to the house and ride astride of the dormitory roof, kicking his heels with such fury that every rafter cracked again.

Then this house-rider jumped down, and, coming to the door, kicked it open.

Skeljúngur (for it was he) rolled his horrible eyes round the room, till none of the men could move for fear. When he saw that there was a new sleeper in the room, he went up to the bed nearest the door and caught hold of the ox-skin, but Grímur held it so tight that the other could not move it. Finding this, the other pulled with all his strength; but Grímur put his foot against the wainscot, and pushed against him till he broke the wainscot down. Then in their struggle they arrived at the door; and Grímur, seeing that he could not resist Skeljúngur except by stratagem, lay on the skin and let the other drag him out, planting his feet, however, against everything that came in his way, and thus they came to the outer door. Skeljúngur

61

dragged the skin from the door across the field, in a southerly direction, but Grímur made the dragging as difficult for him as he could by planting his feet against every hillock and every stone that they passed. Active as the goblin was, he now began to be tired, and at last they came to Grímshóll.

By this time the night was far advanced towards dawn, and Grímur fought then and there more fiercely than ever, contriving finally to bind him to the stone by means of the nooses which he had prepared. Having securely fastened Skeljúngur to the rock, he went home in order to procure fire and fuel for burning him.

But when he came back he found that both Skeljungur and the stone had disappeared. He judged that the direction the goblin would have most probably taken with his load was a southerly one, down the slope of the mountain, so he followed that way. After a while he saw before him Skeljúngur dragging the great stone behind him with great difficulty. Then Grímur ran up to him and cut off his head, and, fetching the fire and fuel, burnt him there. After that he took his ashes to a well close by and threw them in, and, according to the current story, two fishes, covered with blue hair, sprung from them, and lived there until the Nordurá changed its course and swept over the well, when the fishes disappeared.

The stone, bound to which Skeljúngur lost his second life, is yet to be seen standing by the highway, sunk deep into the ground, and there is still one hole visible, which was pierced by the iron spear.

The poet Hjálmar Jónsson, who has written this story, asserts that he has seen, in his youth, two holes in the stone, the lower one of which was close to the surface of the earth. But this was forty years ago, and nobody can tell how large the stone may be.

On the spot where the goblin was burnt, was afterwards built a farm called Skeljúngsstadir, which is mentioned in Sturlúnga, for Eyólfur the Vehement rested there with his men when he attacked the Earl Gissur at Flugumýri.

Skeljúngshellir, or the cave of Skeljúngur, is also to be found in the adjacent mountain.

Now we will return to Grímur, who went home after this struggle very weary. Everybody in the farm thanked him with fair words for the riddance he had made, and everybody agreed that no one was his equal in all Skagafjördur. Now he told his father about his journey to Greenland, and mentioned all the conditions he had made with his Greenland friends, asking him frankly to consent to them, for that he had to thank those men for his preservation; nor, declared he, would his sister be better off with any husband than with Grímur the Greenlander.

Thorgrímur said that all their agreements should stand unbroken, "And my daughter," he continued, "shall go with your friend to Greenland, for I know that they will return and settle in Iceland to rear their family around them."

Grímur thanked his father for his kind answer, and his sister's departure from home was prepared for with all possible liberality, and both her father and brother accompanied her to the vessel lying in the mouth of the Blanda. Thorgrímur gave her a large number of gold and silver ornaments, and to Grímur the Greenlander a new body of sailors, sending also with him gifts for the old man in Greenland. Then they parted in affection, and when Thorgrímur kissed his daughter at farewell, he wept tears of fatherly love.

With a fair wind, Grímur the Greenlander and his bride sailed away.

Thorgrímur and his son rode northwards to Silfrastadir, taking with them Ingibjörg of Greenland, who was looked upon as very beautiful, and who made a right good wife; for, a short time after this, Grímur married her, and their marriage was a happy one. It was soon found that Grímur, after his struggle with the goblin, had become very irritable, and it was impossible for his neighbours to agree with him; so they induced him to go south, to Borgarfjördur, but having dwelt a short time there, he sailed from Iceland with his wife Ingibjörg, and settled in Sweden, where he raised up a family, and none of his descendants are known to have come to Iceland.

And where he dwelt he became celebrated for his bravery.

People say that Grímur the Greenlander returned to Iceland with his wife Ingibjörg, and settled at Skaga, between Skagafjörður and Húnaflóa.

His son was Thorgrímur, the Weatherwise, who lived at Keta.

His son was Grímur, who lived at Hafnir.

His son again was Grímur, who lived there after his father's death, at the time when Thorgerdur Kolka came from Hornstrandir and built the farm called Kolkunes, trusting herself to Grímur's honour.

The priest Eyólfur of Vellir mentions her in his "Antiquarian Transactions" as a benevolent woman, and one of great account, and says that at her death a miraculous earthquake took place, doing much damage, both at Skaga and at other places, and swallowing up Gullbrekka, with all its inhabitants and cattle.

And there is now a great slough where the farm formerly stood.

And thus ends the story of Grímur, who killed Skeljúngur.

The Prince Who Insisted on Possessing the Moon

THE COUNTRY NOW INHABITED BY THE BASOKO TRIBE was formerly known as Bandimba. A king called Bahanga was its sole ruler. He possessed a houseful of wives, but all his children were unfortunately of the female sex, which he considered to be a great grievance, and of which he frequently complained. His subjects, on the other hand, were blessed with more sons than daughters, and this fact increased the king's grief, and made him envy the meanest of his subjects.

One day, however, he married Bamana, the youngest daughter of his principal chief, and finally he became the father of a male child, and was very happy, and his people rejoiced in his happiness.

The prince grew up to be a marvel of strength and beauty, and his father doted on him so much, that he shared his power with the boy in a curious manner. The king reserved authority over all the married people, while the prince's subjects consisted of those not yet mated. It thus happened that the prince ruled over more people than his father, for the children were, of course, more numerous than the parents. But with all the honour conferred upon him the prince was not happy. The more he obtained, the more he wished to possess. His eyes had but to see a thing to make him desire its exclusive possession. Each day he preferred one or more requests to his father, and because of his great love for him, the king had not the heart to refuse anything to him. Indeed, he was persuaded to bestow so many gifts upon his son that he reserved scarcely anything for himself.

One day the prince was playing with the youth of his court, and after the sport retired to the shade of a tree to rest, and his companions sat down in a circle at a respectful distance from him. He then felt a gush of pride stealing over him as he thought of his great power, at the number and variety of his treasures, and he cried out boastfully that there never was a boy so great, so rich and so favoured by his father, as he had become. "My father," said he, "can deny me nothing. I have only to ask, and it is given unto me."

Then one little slender boy with a thin voice said, "It is true, prince. Your father has been very good to you. He is a mighty king, and he is as generous as he is great. Still, I know of one thing that he cannot give you – and it is certain that you will never possess it."

"What thing is that which I may not call my own, when I see it – and what is it that is not in the king's power to give me?" asked the prince, in a tone of annoyance.

"It is the moon," answered the little boy; "and you must confess yourself that it is beyond the king's power to give that to you."

"Do you doubt it?" asked the prince. "I say to you that I shall possess it, and I will go now and claim it from my father. I will not give him any peace until he gives it to me."

Now it so happens that such treasures as are already ours, we do not value so much as those which we have not yet got. So it was with this spoiled prince. The memory of the many gifts of his father faded from his mind, and their value was not to be compared with this new toy – the moon – which he had never thought of before and which he now so ardently coveted.

He found the king discussing important matters with the old men.

"Father," said he, "just now, while I was with my companions I was taunted because I did not have the moon among my toys, and it was said that it was beyond your power to give it to me. Now, prove this boy a liar, and procure the moon for me, that I may be able to show it to them, and glory in your gift."

"What is it you say, my son, you want the moon?" asked the astonished king.

"Yes. Do get it for me at once, won't you?"

"But, my child, the moon is a long way up. How shall we be ever able to reach it?"

"I don't know; but you have always been good to me, and you surely would not refuse me this favour, Father?"

"I fear, my own, that we will not be able to give you the moon."

"But, Father, I must have it; my life will not be worth living without it. How may I dare to again face my companions after my proud boast before them of your might and goodness? There was but one thing that yonder pert boy said I might not have, and that was the moon. Now my soul is bent upon possessing this moon, and you must obtain it for me or I shall die."

"Nay, my son, speak not of death. It is an ugly word, especially when connected with my prince and heir. Do you not know yet that I live only for your sake? Let your mind be at rest. I will collect all the wise men of the land together, and ask them to advise me. If they say that the moon can be reached and brought down to us, you shall have it."

Accordingly the great state drum was sounded for the general palaver, and a score of criers went through the towns beating their little drums as they went, and the messengers hastened all the wise men and elders to the presence of the king.

When all were assembled, the king announced his desire to know how the moon could be reached, and whether it could be shifted from its place in the sky and brought down to the earth, in order that he might give it to his only son the prince. If there was any wise man present who could inform him how this could be done, and would undertake to bring it to him, he would give the choicest of his daughters in marriage to him and endow him with great riches.

When the wise men heard this strange proposal, they were speechless with astonishment, as no one in the Basoko Land had ever heard of anybody mounting into the air higher than a tree, and to suppose that a person could ascend as high as the moon was, they thought, simple madness. Respect for the king, however, held them mute, though what their glances meant was very clear.

But while each man was yet looking at his neighbour in wonder, one of the wise men, who appeared to be about the youngest present, rose to his feet and said:

"Long life to the prince and to his father, the king! We have heard the words of our king, Bahanga, and they are good. I – even I – his slave, am able to reach the moon, and to do the king's pleasure, if the king's authority will assist me."

The confident air of the man, and the ring of assurance in his voice made the other wise men, who had been so ready to believe the king and prince mad, feel shame, and they turned their faces to him curiously, more than half willing to believe that after all the thing was possible. The king also lost his puzzled look, and appeared relieved.

"Say on. How may you be able to perform what you promise?"

"If it please the king," answered the man, boldly, "I will ascend from the top of the high mountain near the Cataract of Panga. But I shall first build a high scaffold on it, the base of which shall be as broad as the mountain top, and on that scaffold I will build another, and on the second I shall build a third, and so on and so on until my shoulder touches the moon."

"But is it possible to reach the moon in this manner?" asked the king doubtingly.

"Most certainly, if I were to erect a sufficient number of scaffolds, one above another, but it will require a vast quantity of timber, and a great army of workmen. If the king commands it, the work will be done."

"Be it so, then," said the king. "I place at your service every able-bodied man in the kingdom."

"Ah, but all the men in your kingdom are not sufficient, O king. All the grown-up men will be wanted to fell the trees, square the timber and bear it to the works; and every grown-up woman will be required to prepare the food for the workmen; and every boy must carry water to satisfy their thirst, and bark rope for the binding of the timbers; and every girl, big and little, must be sent to till the fields to raise cassava for food. Only in this manner can the prince obtain the moon as his toy."

"I say, then, let it be done as you think it ought to be done. All the men, women, and children in the kingdom I devote to this service, that my only son may enjoy what he desires."

Then it was proclaimed throughout the wide lands of the Bandimba that all the people should be gathered together to proceed at once with the work of obtaining the moon for the king's son. And the forest was cut down, and while some of the workmen squared the trees, others cut deep holes in the ground, to make a broad and sure base for the lower scaffold; and the boys made thousands of rope coils to lash the timbers together, out of bark, fibre of palm, and tough grass; and the girls, big and little, hoed up the ground and planted the cassava shrubs and cuttings from the banana and the plantain, and sowed the corn; and the women kneaded the bread and cooked the greens, and roasted green bananas for food for the workmen. And all the Bandimba people were made to slave hard every day in order that a spoiled boy might have the moon for his toy.

In a few days the first scaffolding stood up as high as the tallest trees, in a few weeks the structure had grown until it was many arrow-flights in height, in two months it was so lofty that the top could not be seen with the naked eye. The fame of the wonderful wooden tower that the Bandimba were building was carried far and wide; and the friendly nations round about sent messengers to see and report to them what mad thing the Bandimba were about, for rumour had spread so many contrary stories among people that strangers did not know what to believe. Some said it was true that all the Bandimba had become mad; but some of those who came to see with their own eyes, laughed, while others began to feel anxious. All, however, admired the bigness, and wondered at the height of the tower.

In the sixth month the top of the highest scaffold was so high that on the clearest day people could not see half-way up; and it was said to be so tall that the chief engineer could tell the day he would be able to touch the moon.

The work went on, and at last the engineer passed the word down that in a few days more it would be finished. Everybody believed him, and the nations round about sent more people to be present to witness the completion of the great tower, and to observe what would happen. In all the land, and the countries adjoining it, there was found only one wise man who foresaw, if the moon was shifted out of its place what damage would happen, and that probably all those foolish people in the vicinity of the tower would be destroyed. Fearing some terrible calamity, he proposed to depart from among the Bandimba before it should be too late. He then placed his family in a canoe, and, after storing it with sufficient provisions, he embarked, and in the night he floated down the river Aruwimi and into the big river, and continued his journey night and day as fast as the current would take him – far, far below any lands known to the Bandimba. A week later, after the flight of the wise man and his family, the chief engineer sent down word to the king that he was ready to take the moon down.

"It is well," replied the king from below. "I will ascend, that I may see how you set about it."

Within twenty days the king reached the summit of the tower, and, standing at last by the side of the engineer, he laid his hand upon the moon, and it felt exceedingly hot. Then he commanded the engineer to proceed to take it down. The man put a number of cool bark coils over his shoulder and tried to dislodge it; but, as it was firmly fixed, he used such a deal of force that he cracked it, and there was an explosion, the fire and sparks from which scorched him. The timber on which the king and his chiefs were standing began to burn, and many more bursting sounds were heard, and fire and melted rock ran down through the scaffolding in a steady stream, until all the woodwork was ablaze, and the flames soared upward among the uprights and trestles of the wood in one vast pile of fire; and every man, woman, and child was utterly consumed in a moment. And the heat was so great that it affected the moon, and a large portion of it tumbled to the earth, and its glowing hot materials ran over the ground like a great river of fire, so that most of the country of the Bandimba was burnt to ashes. On those who were not smothered by the smoke, nor burnt by the fire, and who fled from before the burning river, the effect was very wonderful. Such of them as were grown up, male and female, were converted into gorillas, and all the children into different kinds of long-tailed monkeys. After the engineer of the works, the first who died were the king and the prince whose folly had brought ruin on the land.

If you look at the moon when it is full, you may then see on a clear night a curious dark portion on its face, which often appears as though there were peaky mountains in it, and often the dark spots are like some kind of horned animals; and then again, you will often fancy that on the moon you see the outlines of a man's face, but those dark spots are only the holes made in the moon by the man who forced his shoulders through it. Now ever since that dreadful day when the moon burst and the Bandimba country was consumed, parents are not in the habit of granting children all they ask for, but only such things as their age and experience warn them are good for their little ones. And when little children will not be satisfied by such things, but fret and pester their parents to give them what they know will be harmful to them, then it is a custom with all wise people to take the rod to them, to drive out of their heads the wicked thoughts.

Kwege and Bahati

There was once upon a time a man who married a woman of the Uwingu clan (*uwingu* means 'sky') who was named Mulamuwingu, and whose brother, Muwingu, lived in her old home a day or two's journey from her husband's.

The couple had a son called Kwege, and lived happily enough till, in course of time, the husband died, leaving his wife with her son and a slave, Bahati, who had belonged to an old friend of theirs and had come to them on that friend's death.

Now the *tabu* of the Sky clan was rain – that is, rain must never be allowed to fall on anyone belonging to it; if this were to happen he or she would die.

One day when the weather looked threatening Mulamuwingu said, "My son Kwege, just go over to the garden and pick some gourds, so that I can cook them for our dinner." Kwege very rudely refused, and his mother rejoined, "I am afraid of my *mwidzilo* (*tabu*). If I go to the garden I shall die." Then Bahati, the slave, said, "I will go," and he went and gathered the gourds and brought them back.

Next day Kwege's mother again asked him to go to the garden, and again he refused. So she said, "Very well; I will go; but if I die it will be your fault." She set out, and when she reached the garden, which was a long way from any shelter, a great cloud gathered, and it began to rain. When the first drops touched her she fell down dead. Kwege had no dinner that evening, and when he found his mother did not come home either that day or the next (it does not seem to have entered into his head that he might go in search of her) he began to cry, saying, "Mother is dead! Mother is dead!" Then he called Bahati, and they set out to go to his uncle's village.

Now Kwege was a handsome lad, but Bahati was very ugly; and Kwege was well dressed, with plenty of cloth, while Bahati had only a bit of rag round his waist.

As they walked along Kwege said to Bahati, "When we come to a log lying across the path you must carry me over. If I step over it I shall die." For Kwege's *mwidzilo* was stepping over a log.

Bahati agreed, but when they came to a fallen tree he refused to lift Kwege over till he had given him a cloth. This went on every time they came to a log, till he had acquired everything Kwege was wearing, down to his leglets and his bead ornaments. And when they arrived at Muwingu's village and were welcomed by the people Bahati sat down on one of the mats brought out for them and told Kwege to sit on the bare ground. He introduced himself to Muwingu as his sister's son, and treated Kwege as his slave, suggesting, after a day or two, that he should be sent out to the rice fields to scare the birds. Kwege, in the ragged kilt which was the only thing Bahati had left him, went out to the fields, looked at the flocks of birds hovering over the rice, and then, sitting down under a tree, wept bitterly. Presently he began to sing:

"I, Kwege, weep, I weep!
And my crying is what the birds say.
Oh, you log, my tabu!
I cry in the speech of the birds.
They have taken my clothes,
They have taken my leglets,
They have taken my beads,
I am turned into Bahati.
Bahati is turned into Kwege.
I weep in the speech of the birds."

Now his dead parents had both been turned into birds. They came and perched on the tree above him, listening to his song, and said, *"Looo!* Muwingu has taken Bahati into his house and is treating him like a free man and Kwege, his nephew, as a slave! How can that be?"

Kwege heard what they said, and told his story. Then his father flapped one wing, and out fell a bundle of cloth; he flapped the other wing and brought out beads, leglets, and a little gourd full of oil. His mother, in the same way, produced a ready-cooked meal of rice and meat. When he had eaten they fetched water (by this time they had been turned back into human beings), washed him and oiled him, and then said, "Never mind the birds – let them eat Muwingu's rice, since he has sent you to scare them while he is treating Bahati as his son!" So they sat down, all three together, and talked till the sun went down.

On the way back Kwege hid all the cloth and beads that his parents had given him in the long grass, and put on his old rag again. But when he reached the house the family were surprised to see him looking so clean and glossy, as if he had just come from a bath, and cried out, "Where did you get this oil you have been rubbing yourself with? Did you run off and leave your work to go after it?" He did not want to say, "Mother gave it me," so he simply denied that he had been anointing himself.

Next day he went back to the rice field and sang his song again. The birds flew down at once, and, seeing him in the same miserable state as before, asked him what he had done with their gifts. He said they had been taken from him, thinking that, while he was about it, he might as well get all he could. They did not question his good faith, but supplied him afresh with everything, and, resuming their own forms, they sat by him while he ate.

Meanwhile Muwingu's son had taken it into his head to go and see how the supposed Bahati was getting on with his job – it is possible that he had begun to be suspicious of the man who called himself Kwege. What was his astonishment to see a good-looking youth, dressed in a clean cloth, with bead necklaces and all the usual ornaments, sitting between two people, whom he recognized as his father's dead sister and her husband. He was terrified, and ran back to tell his father that Kwege was Bahati and Bahati Kwege, and related what he had seen. Muwingu at once went with him to the rice field, and found that it was quite true. They hid and waited for Kwege to come home. Then, as he drew near the place where he had hidden his cloth, his uncle sprang out and seized him. He struggled to get away, but Muwingu pacified him, saying, "So you are my nephew Kwege after all, and that fellow is Bahati! Why did you not tell me before? Never mind; I shall kill him today." And kill him they did; and Kwege was installed in his rightful position. Muwingu made a great feast, inviting all his neighbours, to celebrate the occasion. "Here ends my story," says the narrator.

The Road to Heaven

THERE WAS ONCE A GIRL who was sent by her mother to fetch water from the river. On the way, talking and laughing with her companions, she dropped her earthen jar and broke it. "Oh, what shall I do now?" she cried, in great distress, for these large jars are not so easily replaced, and she knew there would be trouble awaiting her on her return. She exclaimed, "*Bukali bwa ngoti!* Oh, that I had a rope!" and, looking up, sure enough she saw a rope uncoiling itself from a cloud. She seized it and climbed, and soon found herself in the country above the sky, which appeared to be not unlike the one she had left.

There was what looked like a ruined village not far off, and an old woman sitting among the ruins called to her, "Come here, child! Where are you going?" Being well brought up and accustomed to treat her elders with politeness, she answered at once, and told her story. The old woman told her to go on, and if she found an ant creeping into her ear to let it alone. "It will not hurt you, and will tell you what you have to do in this strange country, and how to answer the chiefs when they question you."

The girl walked on, and in a little while found a black ant crawling up her leg, which went on till it reached her ear. She checked the instinctive impulse to take it out, and went on till she saw the pointed roofs of a village, surrounded by the usual thorn hedge. As she drew near she heard a tiny whisper: "Do not go in; sit down here." She sat down near the gateway. Presently some grave old men, dressed in white, shining bark-cloth, came out and asked her where she had come from and what she wanted. She answered modestly and respectfully, and told them she had come to look for a baby. The elders said, "Very good; come this way." They took her to a hut where some women were at work. One of them gave her a *shirondo* basket, and told her to go to the garden and get some of the new season's mealies. She showed no surprise at this unexpected request, but obeyed at once, and (following the directions of the ant in her ear) pulled up only one stalk at a time, and arranged the cobs carefully in the basket, so as not to waste any space.

When she returned the women praised her for performing her task so quickly and well, and then told her first to grind the corn and then to make porridge. Again instructed by the ant, she put aside a few grains before grinding, and, when she was stirring the porridge, threw these grains in whole, which, it seems, is a peculiar fashion in the cooking of the Heaven-dwellers. They were quite satisfied with the way in which the girl had done her work, and gave her a place to sleep in. Next morning the elders came to fetch her, and conducted her to a handsome house, within which a number of infants were laid out on the ground, those on one side wrapped in red cloth, on the other in white. Being told to choose, she was about to pick up one of the red bundles, when the ant whispered, "Take a white one," and she did so. The old men gave her a quantity of fine cloth and beads, as much as she could carry in addition to the baby, and sent her on her way home. She reached her village without difficulty, and found that everyone was out, as her mother and the other women were at work in the gardens. She went into the hut, and hid herself and the baby in the inner enclosure. When the others returned from the fields, towards evening, the mother sent her younger daughter on ahead to put on the cooking pots. The girl went in and stirred the fire; as the flames leapt up she saw the treasures her sister had brought home, and, not knowing how they had come there, she was frightened, and ran back to tell her mother and aunts. They all hurried in, and found the girl they had thought lost, with a beautiful baby and a stock of cloth to last a lifetime. They listened to her story in great astonishment; but the younger sister was seized with envy, and wanted to set off at once for that fortunate spot. She was a rude, wilful creature, and her sister, knowing her character, tried to dissuade her, or, at any rate, to give her some guidance for the road. But she refused to listen. "You went off without being told anything by anybody, and I shall go without listening to anyone's advice."

Accordingly when called by the old woman she refused to stop, and even spoke insultingly; whereupon the crone said, "Go on, then! When you return this way you will be dead!" "Who will kill me, then?" retorted the girl, and went on her way. When the ant tried to get into her ear she shook her head and screamed with impatience, refusing to listen when it tried to persuade her. So the ant took itself off in dudgeon.

In the same way she gave a rude answer to the village elders when they asked her why she had come, and when requested to gather mealies she pulled up the stalks right and left, and simply ravaged the garden. Having refused to profit by the ant's warnings, she did not know the right way to prepare the meal or make the porridge, and, in any case, did the work carelessly. When taken to the house where the babies were stored she at once stretched out her hand to seize a red-wrapped one; but immediately there was a tremendous explosion, and she was struck dead. "Heaven," we are told, gathered up her bones, made them into a bundle, and sent a man with them to her home. As he passed the place where she had met with the ant that insect called out, "Are you not coming back dead? You would be alive now if you had listened to advice!" Coming to the old woman's place among the ruins, the carrier heard her cry, "My daughter, haven't you died on account of your wicked heart?" So the man went on, and at last he dropped the bones just above her mother's hut. And her sister said, "She had a wicked heart, and that is why Heaven was angry with her."

Horse Cursed by Sun

IT IS SAID THAT ONCE Sun was on Earth, and caught Horse to ride it. But it was unable to bear his weight, and therefore Ox took the place of Horse, and carried Sun on its back. Since that time Horse is cursed in these words, because it could not carry Sun's weight:

"From today thou shalt have a (certain) time of dying.
This is thy curse, that thou hast a (certain) time of dying.
And day and night shalt thou eat,
But the desire of thy heart shall not be at rest,
Though thou grazest till morning and again until sunset.
Behold, this is the judgement which I pass upon thee,"

said Sun. Since that day Horse's (certain) time of dying commenced.

The Constable

IN A CITY in the neighbourhood of Kaiutschou there once lived a constable by the name of Dung. One day when he returned from a hunt after thieves the twilight had already begun to fall. So before he waded through the stream that flowed through the city he sat down on the bank, lit a pipe and took off his shoes. When he looked up, he suddenly saw a man in a red hat dressed as a constable crouching beside him.

Astonished, he inquired: "Who are you? Your clothes indicate that you are a member of our profession, but I have never yet seen you among the men of our local force. Tell me, pray, whence you come?"

The other answered: "I am weary, having come a long journey, and would like to enjoy a pipeful of tobacco in your company. I am sure you will not object to that."

Dung handed him a pipe and tobacco.

But the other constable said: "I do not need them. Just you keep on smoking. It is enough for me to enjoy the odour."

So they chatted a while together, and together waded through the stream. And gradually they became quite confidential and the stranger said: "I will be quite frank with you. I am the head constable of the Nether World, and am subject to the Lord of the Great Mountain. You yourself are a constable of reputation here in the Upper World. And, because of my skill, I have standing in the world below. Since we are so well suited to each other, I should like to enter into a bond of brotherhood with you."

Dung was agreeable and asked: "But what really brings you here?"

Said the other: "In your district there lives a certain Wang, who was formerly superintendent of the granaries, and at that time caused the death of an officer. This man has now accused him in the Nether World. The King of the Nether World cannot come to a decision in the case, and therefore has asked the Lord of the Great Mountain to settle it. The Lord of the Great Mountain has ordered that Wang's property and life be shortened. First his property is to be sequestered here in the Upper World, and then his soul is to be dragged to the nether one. I have been sent out by the Judge of the Dead to fetch him. Yet the established custom is, when someone is sent for, that the constable has first to report to the god of the city. The god of the city then issues a summons, and sends one of his own spirit constables to seize the soul and deliver it over to me. Only then may I take it away with me."

Dung asked him further particulars; but the other merely said: "Later on you will see it all for yourself."

When they reached the city Dung invited his colleague to stay at his home, and entertained him with wine and food. But the other only talked and touched neither the goblet nor the chopsticks.

Said Dung: "In my haste I could not find any better meal for you. I am afraid it is not good enough."

But his guest replied: "Oh no, I am already surfeited and satisfied! We spirits feed only on odours; in which respect we differ from men."

It was late at night before he set out to visit the temple of the city god.

No sooner did morning dawn than he reappeared to take farewell and said: "Now all is in order: I am off! In two years' time you will go to Taianfu, the city near the Great Mountain, and there we will meet again."

Dung began to feel ill at ease. A few days later, in fact, came the news that Wang had died. The district mandarin journeyed to the dead man's natal village in order to express his sympathy. Among his followers was Dung. The innkeeper there was a tenant of Wang's.

Dung asked the innkeeper: "Did anything out of the ordinary happen when Sir Wang died?"

"It was all very strange," he answered, "and my mother who had been very busy in his house, came home and fell into a violent fever. She was unconscious for a day and a night, and could hardly breathe. She came to on the very day when the news of Sir Wang's death was made public, and said: 'I have been to the Nether World and I met him there. He had chains about his neck and several devils were dragging him along. I asked him what he had done, but he said: 'I have no time to tell you now. When you return ask my wife and she will tell you all!'"

"And yesterday my mother went there and asked her. And Wang's wife told her with tears: 'My master was an official, but for a long time he did not make any head-way. He was superintendent of the granaries in Nanking, and in the same city was a high officer, with whom my master became very intimate. He always came to visit at our house and he and my master would talk and drink together. One day my master said to him: 'We administrative mandarins have a large salary and a good income besides. You are an officer, and have even reached the second step in rank, yet your salary is so small that you cannot possibly make it do. Have you any other income aside from it?' The officer replied: 'We are such good friends that I know I can speak openly to you. We officers are compelled to find some additional sources of revenue in order that our pockets may not be altogether empty. When we pay our men we make a small percentage of gains on the exchange; and we also carry more soldiers on our rosters than there actually are present. If we had to live on our salaries we would die of hunger!'

"'When my husband heard him say this he could not rid himself of the idea that by disclosing these criminal proceedings the State would be indebted to him, and that it would surely aid his plans for advancement. On the other hand, he reflected that it would not be right to abuse his friend's confidence. With these ideas in his mind he retired to his inner rooms. In the courtyard stood a round pavilion. Lost in heavy thought, he crossed his hands behind his back, and for a long time walked round and round the pavilion. Finally he said with a sigh: 'Charity begins at home; I will sacrifice my friend!' Then he drew up his report, in which the officer was indicted. An imperial order was issued, the matter was investigated, and the officer was condemned to death. My husband, however, was at once increased in rank, and from that time on advanced rapidly. And with the exception of myself no one ever knew anything of the matter.'"

"When my mother told them of her encounter with Wang in the Nether World, the whole family burst into loud weeping. Four tents full of Buddhist and Taoist priests were sent for, who fasted and read masses for thirty-five days in order that Wang might be delivered. Whole mountains of paper money, silk and straw figures were burned, and the ceremonies have not as yet come to an end."

When Dung heard this he was very much frightened.

Two years later he received an order to journey to Taianfu in order to arrest some robbers there. He thought to himself: 'My friend, the spirit, must be very powerful indeed, to have known about this trip so far in advance. I must inquire for him. Perhaps I will see him again.'

When he reached Taianfu he sought out an inn.

The inn-keeper received him with the words: "Are you Master Dung, and have you come from the bay of Kaiutschou?"

"I am the man," answered Dung, alarmed, "how do you happen to know me?"

The innkeeper replied: "The constable of the temple of the Great Mountain appeared to me last night and said: 'Tomorrow a man by the name of Dung who is a good friend of mine is coming from the bay of Kaiutschou!' And then he described your appearance and your clothes to me exactly, and told me to make careful note of them, and when you came to treat you with the greatest consideration, and to take no pay from you, since he would repay me lavishly. So when I saw you coming everything was exactly as my dreams had foretold, and I knew you at once. I have already prepared a quiet room for you, and beg that you will condescend to make yourself at ease."

Joyfully Dung followed him, and the innkeeper waited on him with the greatest consideration, and saw that he had great plenty to eat and to drink.

At midnight the spirit arrived. Without having opened the door, he stood by Dung's bedside, gave him his hand, and asked how things had gone with him since he had last seen him.

Dung answered all his questions and thanked him into the bargain for appearing to the inn-keeper in a dream.

He continued to live for some days at the inn. During the day he went walking on the Great Mountain and at night his friend came to visit him and talked with him, and at the same time asked him what had happened to Sir Wang.

"His sentence has already been spoken," answered the other. "This man pretended to be conscientious, and traitorously brought about the death of his friend. Of all sins there is no greater sin than this. As a punishment he will be sent forth again into the world as an animal." Then he added: "When you reach home you must take constant care of your health. Fate has allowed you seventy-eight years of mortal life. When your time is up I will come to fetch you myself. Then I will see that you obtain a place as constable in the Nether World, where we can always be together."

When he had said this, he disappeared.

The Reward of a Benevolent Life

ON THE BANKS of a river flowing through the prefecture of Tingchow, there stood a certain city of about ten thousand inhabitants. Among this mass of people there was a very fair sprinkling of well-to-do men, and perhaps half-a-dozen or so who might have been accounted really wealthy.

Amongst these latter was one particular individual named Chung, who had acquired the reputation of being exceedingly large-hearted and benevolently inclined to all those in distress. Anyone who was in want had but to appeal to Chung, and his immediate necessities would at once be relieved without any tedious investigation into the merits of his case. As may be inferred from this, Chung was an easy-going, good-natured man, who was more inclined to look kindly upon his fellow-men than to criticize them harshly for their follies or their crimes. Such a man has always been popular in this land of China.

Now the whole soul of Chung was centred upon his only son Keng. At the time when our story opens, this young fellow was growing up to manhood, and had proved himself to be possessed of no mean ability, for on the various occasions on which he had sat for examination before the Literary Chancellor, his papers had been of a very high order of merit.

The rumours of Chung's generosity had travelled further than he had ever dreamed of. Several reports of the noble deeds that he was constantly performing had reached the Immortals in the Western Heaven, and as these are profoundly concerned in the doings of mankind, steps were taken that Chung should not go unrewarded.

One day a fairy in the disguise of a bonze called upon him. He had always had a sincere liking for men of this class. He admired their devotion, and he was moved by their self-sacrifice in giving up home and kindred to spend their lives in the service of the gods and for the good of humanity.

No sooner, therefore, had the priest entered within his doors, than he received him with the greatest politeness and cordiality. The same evening he prepared a great dinner, to which a number of distinguished guests were invited, and a time of high festivity and rejoicing was prolonged into the early hours of the morning.

Next day Chung said to his guest, "I presume you have come round collecting for your temple. I need not assure you that I shall be most delighted to subscribe to anything that has to do with the uplifting of my fellow-men. My donation is ready whenever you wish to accept it."

The bonze, with a smile which lit up the whole of his countenance, replied that he had not come for the purpose of collecting subscriptions.

"I have come," he said, "to warn you about a far more important matter which affects you and your family. Before very long a great flood will take place in this district, and will sweep everything before it. It will be so sudden that men will not be able to take measures to preserve either their lives or their property – so instantaneous will be the rush of the mighty streams, like ocean floods, from the mountains you can see in the West. My advice to you is to commence at once the construction of boats to carry you and your most precious effects away. When the news first comes that the waters are rising, have them anchored in the creek that flows close by your doors; and when the crisis arrives, delay not a moment, but hurry on board and fly for your lives."

"But when will that be?" asked Chung anxiously.

"I may not tell you the precise day or hour," replied the bonze; "but when the eyes of the stone lions in the East Street of the city shed tears of blood, betake yourselves with all haste to the boats, and leave this doomed place behind you."

"But may I not tell the people of this approaching calamity?" asked Chung, whose tender heart was deeply wrung with distress at the idea of so many being overwhelmed in the coming flood.

"You can please yourself about that," answered the priest, "but no one will believe you. The people of this region are depraved and wicked, and your belief in my words will only cause them to laugh and jeer at you for your credulity."

"But shall I and my family escape with our lives?" finally enquired Chung.

"Yes, you will all escape," was the reply, "and in due time you will return to your home and your future life will be prosperous. But there is one thing," he continued, "about which I must entreat you to be exceedingly careful. As you are being carried down the stream by the great flood, be sure to rescue every living thing that you meet in distress upon the waters. You will not fail to be rewarded for so doing, as the creatures you save will repay you a thousandfold for any services you may render them. There is one thing more that I would solemnly warn you against. You will come across a man floating helplessly on the swiftly flowing tide. Have nothing to do with him. Leave him to his fate. If you try to save him, you will only bring sorrow upon your home."

As the priest was departing, Chung tried to press into his hand a considerable present of money, but he refused to accept it. He did not want money from him, he said. The gods had heard of his great love for men, and they had sent him to warn him so that he might escape the doom which would overtake his fellow-citizens.

After his departure Chung at once called the boat-builders who had their yards along the bank of the stream, and ordered ten large boats to be built with all possible speed. The news of this spread through the town, and when the reasons were asked and the reply was given that the boats were in anticipation of a mighty flood that would ere long devastate the entire region, everyone screamed with laughter; but Chung let them laugh.

For weeks and months he sent an old man to East Street to see if the eyes of the stone lions there had overflowed with bloody tears.

One day two pig-butchers enquired of this man how it was that every day he appeared and looked into the eyes of the lions. He explained that Chung had sent him, for a prophecy had come from the gods that when the eyes of the lions shed blood, the flood which was to destroy the city would be already madly rushing on its way.

On hearing this, these two butchers determined to play a practical joke. Next day, in readiness for the coming of the old man, they smeared the stone eyes with pigs' blood. No sooner had Chung's messenger caught sight of this than, with terror in his eyes, he fled along the streets to tell his master the dreadful news. By this time everything had been prepared, and Chung was only waiting for the appointed sign. The most valuable of his goods had already been packed in some of the boats, and now his wife and son and household servants all hurried down to the water's edge and embarked; and remembering the injunction of the priest that there should be no delay, Chung at once ordered the anchors to be raised, and the boatmen, as if for dear life, made for the larger stream outside.

Hardly had the vessels begun to move when the sun, which had been blazing in the sky, became clouded over. Soon a terrific storm of wind tore with the force of a hurricane across the land. By-and-by great drops of rain, the harbingers of the deluge which was to inundate the country, fell in heavy splashes. Ere long it seemed as though the great fountains in the heavens had burst out, for the floods came pouring down in one incessant torrent. The sides of the mountains became covered with ten thousand rills, which joined their forces lower down, and developed into veritable cataracts, rushing with fearful and noisy tumult to the plain below.

Before many hours had passed, the streams everywhere overflowed their banks, and ran riot amongst the villages, and flowed like a sea against the city. There was no resisting this watery foe, and before night fell vast multitudes had been drowned in the seething floods from which there was no escape.

Meanwhile, carried swiftly along by the swollen current, Chung's little fleet sped safely down the stream, drawing further and further away from the doomed city.

The river had risen many feet since they had started on their voyage, and as they were passing by a high peak, which had been undermined by the rush of waters hurling themselves against its base, the boats were put into great danger by the whirl and commotion of the foam-flecked river. Just as they escaped from being submerged, the party noticed a small monkey struggling in the water, and at once picked it up and took it on board.

Further on they passed a large branch of a tree, on which there was a crow's nest, with one young one in it. This, also, remembering the solemn injunction of the priest, they carefully took up and saved.

As they were rushing madly on down the tawny, swollen river, they were all struck with sudden excitement by seeing something struggling in the boiling waters. Looking at this object more attentively as they drew nearer to it, they perceived that it was a man, who seemed to be in great peril of his life.

Chung's tender heart was filled with sympathy, and he at once gave orders for the boatmen to go and rescue him. His wife, however, reminded him of the warning of the priest not to save any man on the river, as he would inevitably turn out to be an enemy, who would in time work his rescuer great wrong.

Chung replied that at such a time, when a human being was in extreme danger of being drowned, personal interests ought not to be considered at all. He had faithfully obeyed the command of the priest in saving animal life, but how much more valuable was a man than any of the lower orders of creation? "Whatever may happen," he said, "I cannot let this man drown before my eyes," and as the boat just then came alongside the swimmer, he was hauled into it and delivered from his peril.

After a few days, when the storm had abated and the river had gone down to its natural flow, Chung returned with his family to his home. To his immense surprise, he found that his house had not been damaged in the least. The gods who had saved his life had used their supernatural powers to preserve even his property from the ruin and devastation that had fallen upon the inhabitants of the city and of the surrounding plain.

Shortly after they had settled down again, Chung enquired of Lo-yung, the man whom he had saved from the flood, whether he would not like to return to his family and his home.

"I have no family left," he answered with a sad look on his face. "All the members of it were drowned in the great flood from which you delivered me. What little property we had was washed away by the wild rush of the streams that overflowed our farm. Let me stay with you," he begged, "and give me the opportunity, by the devoted service of my life, to repay you in some slight degree for what you have done in saving my life."

As he uttered these words his tears began to flow, and his features showed every sign of profound emotion. Always full of tenderness and compassion, Chung was profoundly moved by the tears and sobs of Lo-yung, and hastened to assure him that he need be under no concern with regard to his future. "You have lost all your relatives, it is true, but from today I shall recognize you as my son. I adopt you into my family and I give you my name."

Six months after this important matter had been settled, the city was placarded with proclamations from its Chief Mandarin. In these he informed the people that he had received a most urgent Edict from the Emperor stating that an official seal, which was in constant use in high transactions of the State, had in a most mysterious manner disappeared and could not be found. He was therefore directed to inform the people that whoever informed His Majesty where the seal was, so that it could be recovered, would receive a considerable reward and would also be made a high mandarin in the palace of the Emperor.

That very night, whilst Chung was sleeping, a fairy appeared to him in a dream. "The gods have sent me," he said, "to give you one more proof of the high regard in which they hold you for your devotion to your fellow-men. The Emperor has lost a valuable seal which he is most anxious to recover, and he has promised large and liberal rewards to the man who shows him where it may be found. I want to tell you where the seal is. It lies at the bottom of the crystal well in the grounds behind the palace. It was accidentally dropped in there by the Empress-Dowager, who has forgotten all about the circumstance, but who will recollect it the moment she is reminded of it. I want you to send your own son to the capital to claim the reward by telling where the seal is."

When Chung awoke in the morning, he told his wife the wonderful news of what had happened to him during the night, and began to make preparations for his son to start for the capital without delay, in order to secure the honours promised by the Emperor. His wife, however, was by no means reconciled to the idea of parting with her son, and strongly opposed his going.

"Why are you so set upon the honours of this life that you are willing to be separated from your only child, whom perhaps you may never be able to see again?" she asked her husband, with tears in her eyes. "You are a rich man, you are beloved of the gods, you have everything that money can buy in this flowery kingdom. Why not then be contented and cease to long after the dignities which the State can confer, but which can never give you any real happiness?"

Just at that moment Lo-yung came in, and hearing the wonderful story, and seeing the distress of the mother, he volunteered to take the place of her son and go to the capital in his stead.

"I have never yet had the chance," he said, "of showing my gratitude to my benefactor for having saved my life, and for the many favours he has showered upon me. I shall be glad to undertake this journey. I shall have an audience with His Majesty and will reveal to him the place where the seal lies hidden, and I shall then insist that all the honours he may be prepared to bestow on me shall be transferred to your son, to whom of right they naturally belong."

It was accordingly arranged that Lo-yung should take the place of Chung's son, and preparations were at once made for his journey to the capital. As he was saying goodbye to his benefactor, the latter whispered in his ear: "If you succeed in your enterprise and the Emperor makes you one of his royal officers, do not let ingratitude ever enter your heart, so that you may be tempted to forget us here, who will be thinking about you all the time you are away."

"Nothing of the kind can ever happen," exclaimed Lo-yung impetuously. "My gratitude to you is too firmly embedded within my heart ever to be uprooted from it."

On his arrival at the capital, he at once sought an interview with the Prime Minister, who, on hearing that a man wished to see him about a state matter of urgent importance, immediately admitted him to his presence. Lo-yung at once explained that he had come to reveal the place where the lost seal at that moment lay concealed. "I am perfectly ready to tell all I know about it," he said, "but if possible I should prefer to make it known to the Emperor himself in person."

"That can quickly be arranged," eagerly replied the Prime Minister, "for His Majesty is so anxious to obtain information about the seal, that he is prepared at any hour of the day or night to give an audience to anyone who can ease his mind on the subject."

In a few minutes a eunuch from the palace commanded the Prime Minister to come without delay to the Audience Hall and wait upon the Emperor. He was also to bring with him the person who said that he had an important communication to lay before the Throne.

When they arrived they found there not only the King, but also the Empress-Dowager, waiting to receive them. In obedience to a hasty command, Lo-yung told in a few words where the seal was, and how it happened to be there. As he went on with the story the face of the Empress lit up with wonder, whilst a pleasing smile overspread it, as she recognized the truth of what Lo-yung was saying.

"But tell me," said the Emperor, "how you get all your information and how it is that you have such an intimate acquaintance with what is going on in my palace?"

Lo-yung then described how the Immortals in the Western Heaven, deeply moved by the loving character of Chung, and wishing to reward him and bring honour to his family, had sent a fairy, who appeared to him in a dream and told him the secret of the seal.

"Your home," said the Emperor, "must indeed be celebrated for benevolent and loving deeds to men, since even the fairies come down from the far-off Heaven to express their approbation. In accordance with my royal promise, I now appoint you to a high official position that will enrich you for life, for I consider that it will be for the welfare of my kingdom to have a man from a home, which the gods delight to honour, to assist me in the management of my public affairs."

From the moment when the royal favour was bestowed on Lo-yung, it seemed as though every particle of gratitude and every kindly remembrance of Chung had vanished completely out of his heart. He cut himself off from the home he had left only a few days ago, as completely as though it had never existed.

Weeks and months went by, but no news came from him, and the heart of Chung was wrung with anguish, for he knew that Lo-yung's unnatural conduct would in the end bring retribution upon Lo-yung himself.

DISASTER ON THE HORIZON

At last he determined to send his son, Keng, to the capital to find out what had really become of Lo-yung. Attended by one of his household servants, the young man reached his journey's end in a few days. On enquiring at his inn about Lo-yung, he was informed that he was a mandarin of great distinction in the city, and was under the special protection of the Emperor, whose favourite he was.

Hearing this joyful news, Keng, followed by his servant, at once hastened to the residence of Lo-yung, and was lucky enough to meet him as he rode out on horseback from his magnificent yamen, attended by a long retinue of officers and attendants.

Running up to the side of his horse, Keng cried out joyfully, "Ah! my brother, what a joy to meet you once more! How glad I am to see you!"

To his astonishment, Lo-yung, with a frown upon his face, angrily exclaimed; "You common fellow, what do you mean by calling me your brother? I have no brother. You are an impostor, and you must be severely punished for daring to claim kinship with me."

Calling some of the lictors in his train, he ordered them to beat Keng, and then cast him into prison, and to give strict injunctions to the jailer to treat him as a dangerous criminal. Wounded and bleeding from the severe scourging he had received, and in a terrible state of exhaustion, poor Keng was dragged to the prison, where he was thrown into the deepest dungeon, and left to recover as best he might from the shock he had sustained.

His condition was indeed a pitiable one. Those who could have helped and comforted him were far away. He could expect no alleviation of his sorrows from the jailer, for the heart of the latter had naturally become hardened by having to deal with the criminal classes. Besides he had received precise orders from the Chief Mandarin, that this particular prisoner was to be treated as a danger to society. Even if he had been inclined to deal mercifully with him, he dared not disobey such definite and stringent commands as he had received from his superior.

The prison fare was only just enough to keep body and soul together. Keng had no money with which to bribe the jailer to give him a more generous diet, and there was no one to guarantee that any extra expenses which might be incurred would ever be refunded to him.

And then a miracle was wrought, and once more the fairies interfered, this time to save the life of the only son of the man whose fame for tenderness and compassion had reached the far-off Western Heaven.

One morning, as Keng lay weary and half-starved on the blackened heap of straw that served him as a bed in the corner of the prison, a monkey climbed up and clung to the narrow gratings through which the light penetrated into his room. In one of its hands it held a piece of pork which it kept offering to Keng. Very much surprised, he got up to take it, when to his delight he discovered that the monkey was the identical one which had been picked up by his father on the day of the great flood.

The same thing was repeated for several days in succession, and when the jailer asked for some explanation of these extraordinary proceedings, Keng gave him a detailed account of their wonderful deliverance by the fairies, the picking up of the monkey, and the rescue of Lo-yung, now the Chief Mandarin, who was keeping him confined in prison. "Ah!" muttered the jailer under his breath, "the lower animals know how to show gratitude, but men do not."

A few days after this another messenger of the gods came to give his aid to Keng. A number of crows gathered on a roof which overlooked the narrow slits through which the prisoner could catch a glimpse of the blue sky. One of them flew on to the ledge outside, and Keng immediately recognized it as the one which had been saved from the floating branch in the turbid river. He was overjoyed to see this bird, and besought the jailer to allow him to write

79

a letter to his father, telling him of his pitiful condition. This request was granted, and the document was tied to the leg of the crow, which flew away on its long flight to Chung with its important news.

Chung was greatly distressed when he read the letter that his son had written in prison, and with all the speed he could command, he travelled posthaste to the capital. When he arrived there he made various attempts to obtain an interview with Lo-yung, but all in vain. The mandarin had not sense enough to see that the threads of fate were slowly winding themselves around him, and would soon entangle him to his destruction.

Very unwillingly, therefore, because he still loved Lo-yung and would have saved him if possible, Chung entered an accusation against him before Fau-Kung, the famous criminal judge.

The result of the investigation was the condemnation of Lo-yung, whose execution speedily followed, whilst Keng was promoted to the very position that had been occupied by the man who had tried to work his ruin.

Tobikawa Imitates a Tengu

TOBIKAWA, AN EX-WRESTLER who lived in Matsue, spent his time in hunting and killing foxes. He did not believe in the various superstitions concerning this animal, and it was generally believed that his great strength made him immune from the witchcraft of foxes. However, there were some people of Matsue who prophesied that Tobikawa would come to an untimely end as the result of his daring deeds and disbelief in supernatural powers.

Tobikawa was extremely fond of practical jokes, and on one occasion he had the hardihood to imitate the general appearance of a *Tengu*, feathers, long nose, claws and all. Having thus disguised himself he climbed up into a tree belonging to a sacred grove. Presently the peasants observed him, and deeming the creature they saw to be a *Tengu*, they began to worship him and to place many offerings about the tree. Alas! the dismal prophecy came true, for while the merry Tobikawa was trying to imitate the acrobatic antics of a *Tengu*, he slipped from a branch and was killed.

Chrysanthemum-Old-Man

KIKUO ('CHRYSANTHEMUM-OLD-MAN') was the faithful retainer of Tsugaru. One day his lord's force was overthrown, and the castle and fine estates were taken away by the enemy; but fortunately Tsugaru and Kikuo were able to escape to the mountains.

Kikuo, knowing his master's love of flowers, especially that of the chrysanthemum, resolved to cultivate this flower to the best of his ability, and in so doing to lessen a little of his master's remorse and humiliation in exile.

His efforts pleased Tsugaru, but unfortunately that lord soon fell sick and died, and the faithful Kikuo wept over his master's grave. Then once more he returned to his work, and planted chrysanthemums about his master's tomb till he had made a border thirty yards broad, so that red, white, pink, yellow and bronze blossoms scented the air, to the wonder of all who chanced to come that way.

When Kikuo was about eighty-two he caught cold and was confined to his humble dwelling, where he suffered considerable pain.

One autumn night, when he knew those beloved flowers dedicated to his master were at their best, he saw in the verandah a number of young children. As he gazed upon them he realised that they were not the children of this world.

Two of these little ones drew near to Kikuo, and said: "We are the spirits of your chrysanthemums, and have come to tell you how sorry we are to find you ill. You have guarded and loved us with such care. There was a man in China, Hozo by name, who lived eight hundred years by drinking the dew from chrysanthemum blossoms. Gladly would we lengthen out your days, but, alas! the Gods ordain otherwise. Within thirty days you will die."

The old man expressed the wish that he might die in peace, and the regret that he must needs leave behind him all his chrysanthemums.

"Listen," said one of the ghostly children: "we have all loved you, Kikuo, for what you have done for us. When you die we shall die too." As soon as these words were spoken a puff of wind blew against the dwelling, and the spirits departed.

Kikuo grew worse instead of better, and on the thirtieth day he passed away. When visitors came to see the chrysanthemums he had planted, all had vanished. The villagers buried the old man near his master, and, thinking to please Kikuo, they planted chrysanthemums near his grave; but all died immediately they were put into the ground. Only grasses grow over the tombs now. The child-souls of the chrysanthemums chatter and sing and play with the spirit of Kikuo.

An End to the Exile

BEFORE THE PANDAVAS left the forest, Yudhishthira invoked the goddess Durga, giver of favours, saying: "Oh slayer of the Buffalo Asura, you are worshipped by the gods, for you are the protector of the three worlds. Chief of all deities, bless us. Grant us victory, and help us in our distress." The goddess heard Yudhishthira, and confirmed the promise of Dharma that the Pandava brothers and Draupadi would remain unrecognized during the last year of their exile.

Then the wanderers concealed their weapons in a tree, and went together towards the city of Virata so that they might hide themselves. According to the terms of their banishment, they would have to spend a further twelve years in the jungle if the Kauravas discovered their whereabouts.

The Pandavas found favour in the eyes of the king. Yudhishthira became his instructor in the art of playing with dice, because he was accustomed to lose heavily. Bhima was made chief cook. Arjuna taught dancing and music to the ladies of the harem. Nakula was given care of horses, and Sahadeva of cattle. The queen was drawn towards Draupadi, who offered to become a servant on condition that she should not have to wash the feet of anyone, or eat food left over after meals; and on these terms she was engaged. The queen feared that Draupadi's great beauty would attract lovers and cause strife; but the forlorn woman said that she was protected by five Gandharvas, and was without fear.

Bhima soon won renown for his matchless strength. At a great festival he overcame a wrestler from a far country who was named Jimúta, and he received many gifts. The king took great pride in him, and often took him to the apartments of the women, where he wrestled with caged tigers and lions and bears, slaying each one at will with a single blow. Indeed, all the brothers were well loved by the monarch because of their loyal services.

It happened that the queen's brother, Kichaka, a mighty warrior and commander of the royal army, was smitten with the beautiful Draupadi, and in time he sought to carry her away. But one night Bhima waited for him when he came stealthily towards Draupadi, and after a long struggle the strong Pandava killed him. Then Bhima broke all this prince's bones and rolled up his body into a ball of flesh.

Kichaka's kinsmen were horrified when they discovered what had happened, and they said: "No man has done this awful deed; the Gandharvas have taken vengeance." In their anger they seized Draupadi, intent on burning her on the pyre with the body of Kichaka; but Bhima disguised himself and went to her rescue. He scattered her tormentors in flight, killing many with a great tree which he had uprooted.

The king was terror-stricken, and spoke to the queen, who in turn asked Draupadi to leave Virata. But the wife of the Pandavas begged to remain in the royal service; and she said that her Gandharva protectors would serve the king in his greatest hour of peril, which, she foretold, was already near to him. So the queen supported her, and Draupadi stayed there.

Soon afterwards the King of Trigartis, hearing that mighty Kichaka was dead, plotted with the Kauravas at Indraprastha to attack the city of Virata in order to capture the kingdom. Duryodhana agreed to help him, so the King of Trigartis invaded the kingdom from the north, while the Kauravas marched against Virata from the south.

And so it came to pass that on the last day of the thirteenth year of the Pandavas' exile, the first raid took place from the north, and many cattle were carried off. Yudhishthira and Bhima, with Nakula and Sahadeva, offered to help when they heard that the King of Virata had been captured by his enemies. The Pandavas went off to rescue the monarch. They soon defeated the raiders and rescued their prisoner; they also seized the King of Trigartis, and forced him to submit to his rival before he was allowed to return to his own city.

Meanwhile the Kauravas had advanced from the south. Uttar, son of the King of Virata, went against them, with Arjuna as his charioteer. When the young man, however, saw his enemies, he wanted to flee, but his driver forced him to remain in the chariot.

Arjuna recovered his own weapons from the tree in which they were hidden. Then, fully armed, he rode against the Kauravas, who said: "If this is Arjuna, he and his brothers must go into exile for another twelve years."

Bhishma responded: "The thirteenth year of concealment is now ended." The Kauravas, however, persisted that Arjuna had appeared before the full time was spent.

Indra's great son advanced boldly. Suddenly he blew his celestial war shell, and all the Kauravas were stricken with fear. They fainted and lay on the field like they were sleeping. Arjuna refrained from killing them, instead he commanded Uttar to take possession of their royal attire. Then the great archer of the Pandavas returned to the city with the king's son.

Now when the monarch discovered how Arjuna had served him by warding off the attack of the Kauravas, he offered the brave Pandava his daughter, Uttara, for a bride; but Arjuna said: "Let her be given to my son."

It was then that the Pandava brothers revealed to the King of Virata who they were. All those who had assembled in the palace rejoiced and honoured them.

Many great kings came to the marriage of Abhimamju, son of Arjuna and Subhadra. Krishna came with his brother Balarama, and the King Drupada came with his son Dhrishtadyumna.

Now the King of Virata resolved to help Yudhishthira claim back his kingdom from the Kauravas, who continued to protest that their kinsmen had been discovered before the complete term of exile had ended.

Shakuni, the cunning gambler, and the vengeful Karna supported the proud and evil-hearted Duryodhana in refusing to make peace with the Pandava brothers, despite the warnings of the sages who sat around the Maharajah Dhritarashtra.

Katcha and the Devil

THERE WAS ONCE A WOMAN named Katcha who lived in a village where she owned her own cottage and garden. She had money besides but little good it did her because she was such an ill-tempered vixen that nobody, not even the poorest labourer, would marry her. Nobody would even work for her, no matter what she paid, for she couldn't open her mouth without scolding, and whenever she scolded she raised her shrill voice until you could hear it a mile away. The older she grew the worse she became until by the time she was forty she was as sour as vinegar.

Now as it always happens in a village, every Sunday afternoon there was a dance either at the burgomaster's, or at the tavern. As soon as the bagpipes sounded, the boys all crowded into the room and the girls gathered outside and looked in the windows. Katcha was always the first at the window. The music would strike up and the boys would beckon the girls to come in and dance, but no one ever beckoned Katcha. Even when she paid the piper no one ever asked her to dance. Yet she came Sunday after Sunday just the same.

One Sunday afternoon as she was hurrying to the tavern she thought to herself: "Here I am getting old and yet I've never once danced with a boy! Plague take it, today I'd dance with the devil if he asked me!"

She was in a fine rage by the time she reached the tavern, where she sat down near the stove and looked around to see what girls the boys had invited to dance.

Suddenly a stranger in hunter's green came in. He sat down at a table near Katcha and ordered drink. When the serving maid brought the beer, he reached over to Katcha and asked her to drink with him. At first she was much taken back at this attention, then she pursed her lips coyly and pretended to refuse, but finally she accepted.

When they had finished drinking, he pulled a ducat from his pocket, tossed it to the piper, and called out:

"Clear the floor, boys! This is for Katcha and me alone!"

The boys snickered and the girls giggled hiding behind each other and stuffing their aprons into their mouths so that Katcha wouldn't hear them laughing. But Katcha wasn't noticing them at all. Katcha was dancing with a fine young man! If the whole world had been laughing at her, Katcha wouldn't have cared.

The stranger danced with Katcha all afternoon and all evening. Not once did he dance with anyone else. He bought her marzipan and sweet drinks and, when the hour came to go home, he escorted her through the village.

"Ah," sighed Katcha when they reached her cottage and it was time to part, "I wish I could dance with you forever!"

"Very well," said the stranger. "Come with me."

"Where do you live?"

"Put your arm around my neck and I'll tell you."

Katcha put both arms about his neck and instantly the man changed into a devil and flew straight down to hell.

At the gates of hell he stopped and knocked.

His comrades came and opened the gates and when they saw that he was exhausted, they tried to take Katcha off his neck. But Katcha held on tight and nothing they could do or say would make her budge.

The devil finally had to appear before the Prince of Darkness himself with Katcha still glued to his neck.

"What's that thing you've got around your neck?" the prince asked.

So the devil told how as he was walking about on earth he had heard Katcha say she would dance with the devil himself if he asked her. "So I asked her to dance with me," the devil said. "Afterwards just to frighten her a little I brought her down to hell. And now she won't let go of me!"

"Serve you right, you dunce!" the prince said. "How often have I told you to use common sense when you go wandering around on earth! You might have known Katcha would never let go of a man once she had him!"

"I beg your Majesty to make her let go!" the poor devil implored.

"I will not!" said the prince. "You'll have to carry her back to earth yourself and get rid of her as best you can. Perhaps this will be a lesson to you."

So the devil, very tired and very cross, shambled back to earth with Katcha still clinging to his neck. He tried every way to get her off. He promised her wooded hills and rich meadows if she but let him go. He cajoled her, he cursed her, but all to no avail. Katcha still held on.

Breathless and discouraged he came at last to a meadow where a shepherd, wrapped in a great shaggy sheepskin coat, was tending his flocks. The devil transformed himself into an ordinary looking man so that the shepherd didn't recognize him.

"Hi, there," the shepherd said, "what's that you're carrying?"

"Don't ask me," the devil said with a sigh. "I'm so worn out I'm nearly dead. I was walking yonder not thinking of anything at all when along comes a woman and jumps on my back and won't let go. I'm trying to carry her to the nearest village to get rid of her there, but I don't believe I'm able. My legs are giving out."

The shepherd, who was a good-natured chap, said: "I tell you what: I'll help you. I can't leave my sheep long, but I'll carry her halfway."

"Oh," said the devil, "I'd be very grateful if you did!"

So the shepherd yelled at Katcha: "Hi, there, you! Catch hold of me!"

When Katcha saw that the shepherd was a handsome youth, she let go of the devil and leapt upon the shepherd's back, catching hold of the collar of his sheepskin coat.

Now the young shepherd soon found that the long shaggy coat and Katcha made a pretty heavy load for walking. In a few moments he was sick of his bargain and began casting about for some way of getting rid of Katcha.

Presently he came to a pond and he thought to himself that he'd like to throw her in. He wondered how he could do it. Perhaps he could manage it by throwing in his greatcoat with her. The coat was so loose that he thought he could slip out of it without Katcha's discovering what he was doing. Very cautiously he slipped out one arm. Katcha didn't move. He slipped out the other arm. Still Katcha didn't move. He unlooped the first button. Katcha noticed nothing. He unlooped the second button. Still Katcha noticed nothing. He unlooped the third button and kerplunk! he had pitched coat and Katcha and all into the middle of the pond!

When he got back to his sheep, the devil looked at him in amazement.

"Where's Katcha?" he gasped.

"Oh," the shepherd said, pointing over his shoulder with his thumb, "I decided to leave her up yonder in a pond."

"My dear friend," the devil cried, "I thank you! You have done me a great favour. If it hadn't been for you I might be carrying Katcha till doomsday. I'll never forget you and some time I'll reward you. As you don't know who it is you've helped, I must tell you I'm a devil."

With these words the devil vanished.

For a moment the shepherd was dazed. Then he laughed and said to himself: "Well, if they're all as stupid as he is, we ought to be able for them!"

The country where the shepherd lived was ruled over by a dissolute young duke who passed his days in riotous living and his nights in carousing. He gave over the affairs of state to two governors who were as bad as he. With extortionate taxes and unjust fines they robbed the people until the whole land was crying out against them.

Now one day for amusement the duke summoned an astrologer to court and ordered him to read in the planets the fate of himself and his two governors. When the astrologer had cast a horoscope for each of the three reprobates, he was greatly disturbed and tried to dissuade the duke from questioning him further.

"Such danger," he said, "threatens your life and the lives of your two governors that I fear to speak."

"Whatever it is," said the duke, "speak. But I warn you to speak the truth, for if what you say does not come to pass you will forfeit your life."

The astrologer bowed and said: "Hear then, oh Duke, what the planets foretell: Before the second quarter of the moon, on such and such a day, at such and such an hour, a devil will come and carry off the two governors. At the full of the moon on such and such a day, at such and such an hour, the same devil will come for your Highness and carry you off to hell."

The duke pretended to be unconcerned but in his heart he was deeply shaken. The voice of the astrologer sounded to him like the voice of judgement and for the first time conscience began to trouble him.

As for the governors, they couldn't eat a bite of food and were carried from the palace half dead with fright. They piled their ill-gotten wealth into wagons and rode away to their castles, where they barred all the doors and windows in order to keep the devil out.

The duke reformed. He gave up his evil ways and corrected the abuses of state in the hope of averting if possible his cruel fate.

The poor shepherd had no inkling of any of these things. He tended his flocks from day to day and never bothered his head about the happenings in the great world.

Suddenly one day the devil appeared before him and said: "I have come, my friend, to repay you for your kindness. When the moon is in its first quarter, I was to carry off the former governors of this land because they robbed the poor and gave the duke evil counsel. However, they're behaving themselves now so they're to be given another chance. But they don't know this. Now on such and such a day do you go to the first castle where a crowd of people will be assembled. When a cry goes up and the gates open and I come dragging out the governor, do you step up to me and say: 'What do you mean by this? Get out of here or there'll be trouble!' I'll pretend to be greatly frightened and make off. Then ask the governor to pay you two bags of gold, and if he haggles just threaten to call me back. After that go on to the castle of the second governor and do the same thing and demand the same pay. I warn you, though, be prudent with the money and use it only for good. When the moon is full, I'm to carry off the duke himself, for he was so wicked that he's to have no second chance. So don't try to save him, for if you do you'll pay for it with your own skin. Don't forget!"

The shepherd remembered carefully everything the devil told him. When the moon was in its first quarter he went to the first castle. A great crowd of people was gathered outside waiting to see the devil carry away the governor.

Suddenly there was a loud cry of despair, the gates of the castle opened, and there was the devil, as black as night, dragging out the governor. He, poor man, was half dead with fright.

The shepherd elbowed his way through the crowd, took the governor by the hand, and pushed the devil roughly aside.

"What do you mean by this?" he shouted. "Get out of here or there'll be trouble!"

Instantly the devil fled and the governor fell on his knees before the shepherd and kissed his hands and begged him to state what he wanted in reward. When the shepherd asked for two bags of gold, the governor ordered that they be given him without delay.

Then the shepherd went to the castle of the second governor and went through exactly the same performance.

It goes without saying that the duke soon heard of the shepherd, for he had been anxiously awaiting the fate of the two governors. At once he sent a wagon with four horses to fetch the shepherd to the palace and when the shepherd arrived he begged him piteously to rescue him likewise from the devil's clutches.

"Master," the shepherd answered, "I cannot promise you anything. I have to consider my own safety. You have been a great sinner, but if you really want to reform, if you really want to rule your people justly and kindly and wisely as becomes a true ruler, then indeed I will help you even if I have to suffer hellfire in your place."

The duke declared that with God's help he would mend his ways and the shepherd promised to come back on the fatal day.

With grief and dread the whole country awaited the coming of the full moon. In the first place the people had greeted the astrologer's prophecy with joy, but since the duke had reformed their feelings for him had changed.

Time sped fast as time does whether joy be coming or sorrow and all too soon the fatal day arrived.

Dressed in black and pale with fright, the duke sat expecting the arrival of the devil.

Suddenly the door flew open and the devil, black as night, stood before him. He paused a moment and then he said, politely:

"Your time has come, Lord Duke, and I am here to get you!"

Without a word the duke arose and followed the devil to the courtyard, which was filled with a great multitude of people.

At that moment the shepherd, all out of breath, came pushing his way through the crowd, and ran straight at the devil, shouting out:

"What do you mean by this? Get out of here or there'll be trouble!"

"What do you mean?" whispered the devil. "Don't you remember what I told you?"

"Hush!" the shepherd whispered back. "I don't care anything about the duke. This is to warn you! You know Katcha? She's alive and she's looking for you!"

The instant the devil heard the name of Katcha he turned and fled.

All the people cheered the shepherd, while the shepherd himself laughed in his sleeve to think that he had taken in the devil so easily.

As for the duke, he was so grateful to the shepherd that he made him his chief counsellor and loved him as a brother. And well he might, for the shepherd was a sensible man and always gave him sound advice.

The Banshee of the Mac Carthys

CHARLES MAC CARTHY was, in the year 1749, the only surviving son of a very numerous family. His father died when he was little more than twenty, leaving him the Mac Carthy estate, not much encumbered, considering that it was an Irish one. Charles was gay, handsome, unfettered either by poverty, a father, or guardians, and therefore was not, at the age of one-and-twenty, a pattern of regularity and virtue. In plain terms, he was an exceedingly dissipated – I fear I may say debauched, young man. His companions were, as may be supposed, of the higher classes of the youth in his neighbourhood, and, in general, of those whose fortunes were larger than his own, whose dispositions to pleasure were, therefore, under still less restrictions, and in whose example he found at once an incentive and an apology for his irregularities. Besides, Ireland, a place to this day not very remarkable for the coolness and steadiness of its youth, was then one of the cheapest countries in the world in most of those articles which money supplies for the indulgence of the passions. The odious exciseman – with his portentous book in one hand, his unrelenting pen held in the other, or stuck beneath his hat-band, and the ink-bottle ('black emblem of the informer') dangling from his waistcoat-button – went not then from ale-house to ale-house, denouncing all those patriotic dealers in spirits, who preferred selling whiskey, which had nothing to do with English laws (but to elude them), to retailing that poisonous liquor, which derived its name from the British 'Parliament' that compelled its circulation among a reluctant people. Or if the gauger – recording angel of the law – wrote down the peccadillo of a publican, he dropped a tear upon the word, and blotted it out forever! For, welcome to the tables of their hospitable neighbours, the guardians of the excise, where they existed at all, scrupled to abridge those luxuries which they freely shared; and thus the competition in the market between the smuggler, who incurred little hazard, and the personage who was named fair trader, who enjoyed little protection, made Ireland a land flowing, not merely with milk and honey, but with whiskey and wine. In the enjoyments supplied by these, and in the many kindred pleasures to which frail youth is but too prone, Charles Mac Carthy indulged to such a degree, that just about the time when he had completed his four-and-twentieth year, after a week of great excesses, he was seized with a violent fever, which, from its malignity, and the weakness of his frame, left scarcely a hope of his recovery. His mother, who had at first made many efforts to check his vices, and at last had been obliged to look on at his rapid progress to ruin in silent despair, watched day and night at his pillow. The anguish of parental feeling was blended with that still deeper misery which those only know who have striven hard to rear in virtue and piety a beloved and favourite child; have found him grow up all that their hearts could desire, until he reached manhood; and then, when their pride was highest, and their hopes almost ended in the fulfilment of their fondest expectations, have seen this idol of their affections plunge headlong into a course of reckless profligacy, and, after a rapid career of vice, hang upon the verge of eternity, without the leisure or the power of repentance. Fervently she prayed that, if his life could not be spared, at least the delirium, which continued with increasing violence from the first few hours of his disorder, might vanish before death, and leave enough of light and of calm for making his peace with offended Heaven. After several days, however, nature seemed quite exhausted, and he sunk into a state too like death to be mistaken for the repose of sleep. His face had that pale, glossy, marble look, which is in general so sure a symptom that life has left its tenement of clay. His eyes were closed and sunk; the lids having that compressed and stiffened appearance which seemed to indicate that some friendly hand had done its last office. The lips, half closed and perfectly ashy, discovered just so much of the teeth as to give to the features of death their most ghastly, but most impressive look. He lay upon his back, with his hands stretched beside him, quite motionless; and his distracted mother, after repeated trials, could discover not the least symptom of animation. The medical man who attended, having tried the usual modes for ascertaining the presence of life, declared at last his opinion that it was flown, and prepared to depart from the house of mourning. His horse was seen to come to the door. A crowd of people who were collected before the windows, or scattered in groups on the lawn in front, gathered around when the door opened. These were tenants, fosterers, and poor relations of the family, with others attracted by affection, or by that interest which partakes of curiosity, but is something more, and which collects the lower ranks round a house where a human being is in his passage to another world. They saw the professional man come out from the hall door and approach his horse; and while slowly, and with a melancholy air, he prepared to mount, they clustered round him with inquiring and wistful looks. Not a word was spoken, but their meaning could not be misunderstood; and the physician, when he had got into his saddle, and while the servant was still holding the bridle as if to delay him, and was looking anxiously at his face as if expecting that he would relieve the general suspense, shook his head, and said in a low voice, "It's all over,

James"; and moved slowly away. The moment he had spoken, the women present, who were very numerous, uttered a shrill cry, which, having been sustained for about half a minute, fell suddenly into a full, loud, continued, and discordant but plaintive wailing, above which occasionally were heard the deep sounds of a man's voice, sometimes in deep sobs, sometimes in more distinct exclamations of sorrow. This was Charles's foster-brother, who moved about the crowd, now clapping his hands, now rubbing them together in an agony of grief. The poor fellow had been Charles's playmate and companion when a boy, and afterwards his servant; had always been distinguished by his peculiar regard, and loved his young master as much, at least, as he did his own life.

When Mrs Mac Carthy became convinced that the blow was indeed struck, and that her beloved son was sent to his last account, even in the blossoms of his sin, she remained for some time gazing with fixedness upon his cold features; then, as if something had suddenly touched the string of her tenderest affections, tear after tear trickled down her cheeks, pale with anxiety and watching. Still she continued looking at her son, apparently unconscious that she was weeping, without once lifting her handkerchief to her eyes, until reminded of the sad duties which the custom of the country imposed upon her, by the crowd of females belonging to the better class of the peasantry, who now, crying audibly, nearly filled the apartment. She then withdrew, to give directions for the ceremony of waking, and for supplying the numerous visitors of all ranks with the refreshments usual on these melancholy occasions. Though her voice was scarcely heard, and though no one saw her but the servants and one or two old followers of the family, who assisted her in the necessary arrangements, everything was conducted with the greatest regularity; and though she made no effort to check her sorrows they never once suspended her attention, now more than ever required to preserve order in her household, which, in this season of calamity, but for her would have been all confusion.

The night was pretty far advanced; the boisterous lamentations which had prevailed during part of the day in and about the house had given place to a solemn and mournful stillness; and Mrs Mac Carthy, whose heart, notwithstanding her long fatigue and watching, was yet too sore for sleep, was kneeling in fervent prayer in a chamber adjoining that of her son. Suddenly her devotions were disturbed by an unusual noise, proceeding from the persons who were watching round the body. First there was a low murmur, then all was silent, as if the movements of those in the chamber were checked by a sudden panic, and then a loud cry of terror burst from all within. The door of the chamber was thrown open, and all who were not overturned in the press rushed wildly into the passage which led to the stairs, and into which Mrs Mac Carthy's room opened. Mrs Mac Carthy made her way through the crowd into her son's chamber, where she found him sitting up in the bed, and looking vacantly around, like one risen from the grave. The glare thrown upon his sunk features and thin lathy frame gave an unearthly horror to his whole aspect. Mrs Mac Carthy was a woman of some firmness; but she was a woman, and not quite free from the superstitions of her country. She dropped on her knees, and, clasping her hands, began to pray aloud. The form before her moved only its lips, and barely uttered, "Mother"; but though the pale lips moved, as if there was a design to finish the sentence, the tongue refused its office. Mrs Mac Carthy sprung forward, and catching the arm of her son, exclaimed, "Speak! In the name of God and His saints, speak! Are you alive?"

He turned to her slowly, and said, speaking still with apparent difficulty, "Yes, my mother, alive, and – but sit down and collect yourself; I have that to tell which will astonish you still more than what you have seen." He leaned back upon his pillow, and while his mother remained kneeling by the bedside, holding one of his hands clasped in hers, and gazing on him with the look of one who distrusted all her senses, he proceeded: "Do not interrupt me until I have done. I wish to speak while the excitement of returning life is upon me, as I know I shall soon need much repose. Of the commencement of my illness I have only a confused recollection; but within the last twelve hours I have been before the judgement-seat of God. Do not stare incredulously on me – 'tis as true as have been my crimes, and as, I trust, shall be repentance. I saw the awful Judge arrayed in all the terrors which invest him when mercy gives place to justice. The dreadful pomp of offended omnipotence, I saw – I remember. It is fixed here; printed on my brain in characters indelible; but it passeth human language. What I *can* describe I *will* – I may speak it briefly. It is enough to say, I was weighed in the balance, and found wanting. The irrevocable sentence was upon the point of being pronounced; the eye of my Almighty Judge, which had already glanced upon me, half spoke my doom; when I observed the guardian saint, to whom you so often directed my prayers when I was a child, looking at me with an expression of benevolence and compassion. I stretched forth my hands to him, and besought his intercession. I implored that one year, one month, might be given to me on earth to do penance and atonement for my transgressions. He threw himself at the feet of my Judge, and supplicated for mercy. Oh! Never – not if I should pass through ten thousand successive states of being – never, for eternity, shall I forget the horrors of that moment, when my fate hung suspended – when an instant was to decide whether torments unutterable were to be my portion for endless ages! But Justice suspended its decree, and Mercy spoke in accents of firmness, but mildness, 'Return to that world in which thou hast lived but to outrage the laws of Him who made that world and thee. Three years are given thee for repentance; when these are ended, thou shalt again stand here, to be saved or lost for ever.' I heard no more; I saw no more, until I awoke to life, the moment before you entered."

Charles's strength continued just long enough to finish these last words, and on uttering them he closed his eyes, and lay quite exhausted. His mother, though, as was before said, somewhat disposed to give credit to supernatural visitations, yet hesitated whether or not she should believe that, although awakened from a swoon which might have been the crisis of his disease, he was still under the influence of delirium. Repose, however, was at all events necessary, and she took immediate measures that he should enjoy it undisturbed. After some hours' sleep, he awoke refreshed, and thenceforward gradually but steadily recovered.

Still he persisted in his account of the vision, as he had at first related it; and his persuasion of its reality had an obvious and decided influence on his habits and conduct. He did not altogether abandon the society of his former associates, for his temper was not soured by his reformation; but he never joined in their excesses, and often endeavoured to reclaim them. How his pious exertions succeeded, I have never learnt; but of himself it is recorded that he was religious without ostentation, and temperate without austerity; giving a practical proof that vice may be exchanged for virtue, without the loss of respectability, popularity, or happiness.

Time rolled on, and long before the three years were ended the story of his vision was forgotten, or, when spoken of, was usually mentioned as an instance proving the folly of believing in such things. Charles's health, from the temperance and regularity of his habits, became more robust than ever. His friends, indeed, had often occasion to rally him upon a seriousness and abstractedness of demeanour, which grew upon him as he approached the completion of his seven-and-twentieth year, but for the most part his manner exhibited the same animation and cheerfulness for which he had always been remarkable. In company he evaded every endeavour to draw from him a distinct opinion on the subject of the supposed prediction; but among his own family it was well known that he still firmly believed it. However, when the day had nearly arrived on which the prophecy was, if at all, to be fulfilled, his whole appearance gave such promise of a long and healthy life, that he was persuaded by his friends to ask a large party to an entertainment at Spring House, to celebrate his birthday. But the occasion of this party, and the circumstances which attended it, will be best learned from a perusal of the following letters, which have been carefully preserved by some relations of his family. The first is from Mrs Mac Carthy to a lady, a very near connection and valued friend of her's, who lived in the county of Cork, at about fifty miles' distance from Spring House.

> *To Mrs Barry, Castle Barry.*
> *Spring House, Tuesday morning,*
> *October 15th, 1752.*
> *My Dearest Mary,*
> *I am afraid I am going to put your affection for your old friend and kinswoman to a severe trial. A two days' journey at this season, over bad roads and through a troubled country, it will indeed require friendship such as yours to persuade a sober woman to encounter. But the truth is, I have, or fancy I have, more than usual cause for wishing you near me. You know my son's story. I can't tell you how it is, but as next Sunday approaches, when the prediction of his dream, or vision, will be proved false or true, I feel a sickening of the heart, which I cannot suppress, but which your presence, my dear Mary, will soften, as it has done so many of my sorrows. My nephew, James Ryan, is to be married to Jane Osborne (who, you know, is my son's ward), and the bridal entertainment will take place here on Sunday next, though Charles pleaded hard to have it postponed for a day or two longer. Would to God – but no more of this till we meet. Do prevail upon yourself to leave your good man for one week, if his farming concerns will not admit of his accompanying you; and come to us, with the girls, as soon before Sunday as you can.*
> *Ever my dear Mary's attached cousin and friend,*
> *Ann Mac Carthy.*

Although this letter reached Castle Barry early on Wednesday, the messenger having travelled on foot over bog and moor, by paths impassable to horse or carriage, Mrs Barry, who at once determined on going, had so many arrangements to make for the regulation of her domestic affairs (which, in Ireland, among the middle orders of the gentry, fall soon into confusion when the mistress of the family is away), that she and her two young daughters were unable to leave until late on the morning of Friday. The eldest daughter remained to keep her father company, and superintend the concerns of the household. As the travellers were to journey in an open one-horse vehicle, called a jaunting-car (still used in Ireland), and as the roads, bad at all times, were rendered still worse by the heavy rains, it was their design to make two easy stages – to stop about midway the first night, and reach Spring House early on Saturday evening. This arrangement was now altered, as they found that from the lateness of their departure they could proceed, at the utmost, no farther than twenty miles on the first day; and they, therefore, purposed sleeping at the house of a Mr Bourke, a friend of theirs, who lived at somewhat less than that distance from Castle Barry. They reached Mr Bourke's in safety after a rather disagreeable ride. What befell them on their journey the next day to Spring House, and after their arrival there, is fully recounted in a letter from the second Miss Barry to her eldest sister.

Spring House, Sunday evening,
20th October 1752.
Dear Ellen,

As my mother's letter, which encloses this, will announce to you briefly the sad intelligence which I shall here relate more fully, I think it better to go regularly through the recital of the extraordinary events of the last two days.

The Bourkes kept us up so late on Friday night that yesterday was pretty far advanced before we could begin our journey, and the day closed when we were nearly fifteen miles distant from this place. The roads were excessively deep, from the heavy rains of the last week, and we proceeded so slowly that, at last, my mother resolved on passing the night at the house of Mr Bourke's brother (who lives about a quarter-of-a-mile off the road), and coming here to breakfast in the morning. The day had been windy and showery, and the sky looked fitful, gloomy, and uncertain. The moon was full, and at times shone clear and bright; at others it was wholly concealed behind the thick, black, and rugged masses of clouds that rolled rapidly along, and were every moment becoming larger, and collecting together as if gathering strength for a coming storm. The wind, which blew in our faces, whistled bleakly along the low hedges of the narrow road, on which we proceeded with difficulty from the number of deep sloughs, and which afforded not the least shelter, no plantation being within some miles of us. My mother, therefore, asked Leary, who drove the jaunting-car, how far we were from Mr Bourke's? "'Tis about ten spades from this to the cross, and we have then only to turn to the left into the avenue, ma'am." "Very well, Leary; turn up to Mr Bourke's as soon as you reach the cross roads." My mother had scarcely spoken these words, when a shriek, that made us thrill as if our very hearts were pierced by it, burst from the hedge to the right of our way. If it resembled anything earthly it seemed the cry of a female, struck by a sudden and mortal blow, and giving out her life in one long deep pang of expiring agony. "Heaven defend us!" exclaimed my mother. "Go you over the hedge, Leary, and save that woman, if she is not yet dead, while we run back to the hut we have just passed, and alarm the village near it." "Woman!" said Leary, beating the horse violently, while his voice trembled, "that's no woman; the sooner we get on, ma'am, the better"; and he continued his efforts to quicken the horse's pace. We saw nothing. The moon was hid. It was quite dark, and we had been for some time expecting a heavy fall of rain. But just as Leary had spoken, and had succeeded in making the horse trot briskly forward, we distinctly heard a loud clapping of hands, followed by a succession of screams, that seemed to denote the last excess of despair and anguish, and to issue from a person running forward inside the hedge, to keep pace with our progress. Still we saw nothing; until, when we were within about ten yards of the place where an avenue branched off to Mr Bourke's to the left, and the road turned to Spring House on the right, the moon started suddenly from behind a cloud, and enabled us to see, as plainly as I now see this paper, the figure of a tall, thin woman, with uncovered head, and long hair that floated round her shoulders, attired in something which seemed either a loose white cloak or a sheet thrown hastily about her. She stood on the corner hedge, where the road on which we were met that which leads to Spring House, with her face towards us, her left hand pointing to this place, and her right arm waving rapidly and violently as if to draw us on in that direction. The horse had stopped, apparently frightened at the sudden presence of the figure, which stood in the manner I have described, still uttering the same piercing cries, for about half a minute. It then leaped upon the road, disappeared from our view for one instant, and the next was seen standing upon a high wall a little way up the avenue on which we purposed going, still pointing towards the road to Spring House, but in an attitude of defiance and command, as if prepared to oppose our passage up the avenue. The figure was now quite silent, and its garments, which had before flown loosely in the wind, were closely wrapped around it. "Go on, Leary, to Spring House, in God's name!" said my mother; "whatever world it belongs to, we will provoke it no longer." "'Tis the Banshee, ma'am," said Leary; "and I would not, for what my life is worth, go anywhere this blessed night but to Spring House. But I'm afraid there's something bad going forward, or she would not send us there." So saying, he drove forward; and as we turned on the road to the right, the moon suddenly withdrew its light, and we saw the apparition no more; but we heard plainly a prolonged clapping of hands, gradually dying away, as if it issued from a person rapidly retreating. We proceeded as quickly as the badness of the roads and the fatigue of the poor animal that drew us would allow, and arrived here about eleven o'clock last night. The scene which awaited us you have learned from my mother's letter. To explain it fully, I must recount to you some of the transactions which took place here during the last week.

You are aware that Jane Osborne was to have been married this day to James Ryan, and that they and their friends have been here for the last week. On Tuesday last, the very day on the morning of which cousin Mac Carthy despatched the letter inviting us here, the whole of the company were walking about the grounds a little before dinner. It seems that an unfortunate creature, who had been seduced by James Ryan, was seen prowling in the neighbourhood in a moody, melancholy state for some days previous. He had separated from her for several months, and, they say, had provided for her rather handsomely; but she had been seduced by the promise of his marrying her; and the shame of her unhappy condition, uniting with disappointment and jealousy, had disordered her intellects. During the whole forenoon of this Tuesday she had been walking in the plantations near Spring House, with her cloak folded tight round her, the hood nearly covering her face; and she had avoided conversing with or even meeting any of the family.

Charles Mac Carthy, at the time I mentioned, was walking between James Ryan and another, at a little distance from the rest, on a gravel path, skirting a shrubbery. The whole party was thrown into the utmost consternation by the report of a pistol, fired from a thickly planted part of the shrubbery which Charles and his companions had just passed. He fell instantly, and it was found that he had been wounded in the leg. One of the party was a medical man. His assistance was immediately given, and, on examining, he declared that the injury was very slight, that no bone was broken, it was merely a flesh wound, and that it would certainly be well in a few days. "We shall know more by Sunday," said Charles, as he was carried to his chamber. His wound was immediately dressed, and so slight was the inconvenience which it gave that several of his friends spent a portion of the evening in his apartment.

On inquiry, it was found that the unlucky shot was fired by the poor girl I just mentioned. It was also manifest that she had aimed, not at Charles, but at the destroyer of her innocence and happiness, who was walking beside him. After a fruitless search for her through the grounds, she walked into the house of her own accord, laughing and dancing, and singing wildly, and every moment exclaiming that she had at last killed Mr Ryan. When she heard that it was Charles, and not Mr Ryan, who was shot, she fell into a violent fit, out of which, after working convulsively for some time, she sprung to the door, escaped from the crowd that pursued her, and could never be taken until last night, when she was brought here, perfectly frantic, a little before our arrival.

Charles's wound was thought of such little consequence that the preparations went forward, as usual, for the wedding entertainment on Sunday. But on Friday night he grew restless and feverish, and on Saturday (yesterday) morning felt so ill that it was deemed necessary to obtain additional medical advice. Two physicians and a surgeon met in consultation about twelve o'clock in the day, and the dreadful intelligence was announced, that unless a change, hardly hoped for, took place before night, death must happen within twenty-four hours after. The wound, it seems, had been too tightly bandaged, and otherwise injudiciously treated. The physicians were right in their anticipations. No favourable symptom appeared, and long before we reached Spring House every ray of hope had vanished. The scene we witnessed on our arrival would have wrung the heart of a demon. We heard briefly at the gate that Mr Charles was upon his death-bed. When we reached the house, the information was confirmed by the servant who opened the door. But just as we entered we were horrified by the most appalling screams issuing from the staircase. My mother thought she heard the voice of poor Mrs Mac Carthy, and sprung forward. We followed, and on ascending a few steps of the stairs, we found a young woman, in a state of frantic passion, struggling furiously with two men-servants, whose united strength was hardly sufficient to prevent her rushing upstairs over the body of Mrs Mac Carthy, who was lying in strong hysterics upon the steps. This, I afterwards discovered, was the unhappy girl I before described, who was attempting to gain access to Charles's room, to "get his forgiveness," as she said, "before he went away to accuse her for having killed him." This wild idea was mingled with another, which seemed to dispute with the former possession of her mind. In one sentence she called on Charles to forgive her, in the next she would denounce James Ryan as the murderer, both of Charles and her. At length she was torn away; and the last words I heard her scream were, "James Ryan, 'twas you killed him, and not I – 'twas you killed him, and not I."

Mrs Mac Carthy, on recovering, fell into the arms of my mother, whose presence seemed a great relief to her. She wept – the first tears, I was told, that she had shed since the fatal accident. She conducted us to Charles's room, who, she said, had desired to see us the moment of our arrival, as he found his end approaching, and wished to devote the last hours of his existence to uninterrupted prayer and meditation. We found him perfectly calm, resigned, and even cheerful. He spoke of the awful event which was at hand with courage and confidence, and treated it as a doom for which he had been preparing ever since his former remarkable illness, and which he never

94

once doubted was truly foretold to him. He bade us farewell with the air of one who was about to travel a short and easy journey; and we left him with impressions which, notwithstanding all their anguish, will, I trust, never entirely forsake us.

Poor Mrs Mac Carthy – but I am just called away. There seems a slight stir in the family; perhaps –

The above letter was never finished. The enclosure to which it more than once alludes told the sequel briefly, and it is all that I have further learned of the family of Mac Carthy. Before the sun had gone down upon Charles's seven-and-twentieth birthday, his soul had gone to render its last account to its Creator.

A Promising Path Ahead

Introduction

VIDAR THE SILENT, in Norse legend, is at once a hero and a force of nature. The child of the great god Odin and the beautiful giantess Grid, he is revered as a personification of the primeval forest, quiet and deep. But also respected as a warrior, and described in the *Poetic Edda* (a collection of narrative poems) as being 'tall, well-made, and handsome, clad in armour, girded with a broad-bladed sword'. He was certainly a fine figure of a man and it's really no surprise that the Norns – those mythic sisters who spun out mortals' destiny in lengths of thread – should have predicted great things for him. When Odin went to the Norns and asked them what his own prospects were, they warned him that he would one day be killed in battle by his enemies. But his son would fight alongside him, they assured him, and avenge him when he was gone. The idea of the 'Prophet of Doom' has become a cliché but prophecies can be full of promise too. The road may still be hard, the stories in this section show, but the outcome can be favourable; the right ending achieved.

Vidar

IT IS RELATED THAT ODIN once loved the beautiful giantess Grid, who dwelt in a cave in the desert, and that, wooing her, he prevailed upon her to become his wife. The offspring of this union between Odin (mind) and Grid (matter) was Vidar, a son as strong as he was taciturn, whom the ancients considered a personification of the primaeval forest or of the imperishable forces of Nature.

As the gods, through Heimdall, were intimately connected with the sea, they were also bound by close ties to the forests and Nature in general through Vidar, surnamed 'the silent', who was destined to survive their destruction and rule over a regenerated earth. This god had his habitation in Landvidi (the wide land), a palace decorated with green boughs and fresh flowers, situated in the midst of an impenetrable primaeval forest where reigned the deep silence and solitude which he loved.

This old Scandinavian conception of the silent Vidar is indeed very grand and poetical, and was inspired by the rugged Northern scenery. "Who has ever wandered through such forests, in a length of many miles, in a boundless expanse, without a path, without a goal, amid their monstrous shadows, their sacred gloom, without being filled with deep reverence for the sublime greatness of Nature above all human agency, without feeling the grandeur of the idea which forms the basis of Vidar's essence?"

Vidar is depicted as tall, well-made, and handsome, clad in armour, girded with a broad-bladed sword, and shod with a great iron or leather shoe. According to some mythologists, he owed this peculiar footgear to his mother Grid, who, knowing that he would be called upon to fight against fire on the last day, designed it as a protection against the fiery element, as her iron gauntlet had shielded Thor in his encounter with Geirrod. But other authorities state that this shoe was made of the leather scraps which Northern cobblers had either given or thrown away. As it was essential that the shoe should be large and strong enough to resist the Fenris wolf's sharp teeth at the last day, it was a matter of religious observance among Northern shoemakers to give away as many odds and ends of leather as possible.

When Vidar joined his peers in Valhalla, they welcomed him gaily, for they knew that his great strength would serve them well in their time of need. After they had lovingly regaled him with the golden mead, Allfather bade him follow to the Urdar fountain, where the Norns were ever busy weaving their web. Questioned by Odin concerning his future and Vidar's destiny, the three sisters answered oracularly; each uttering a sentence:

"Early begun."
"Further spun."
"One day done."

To these their mother, Wyrd, the primitive goddess of fate, added: "With joy once more won." These mysterious answers would have remained totally unintelligible had the goddess not gone on to explain that time progresses, that all must change, but that even if the father fell in the last battle, his son Vidar would be his avenger, and would live to rule over a regenerated world, after having conquered all his enemies.

As Wyrd spoke, the leaves of the world tree fluttered as if agitated by a breeze, the eagle on its topmost bough flapped its wings, and the serpent Nidhug for a moment suspended its work of destruction at the roots of the tree. Grid, joining the father and son, rejoiced with Odin when she heard that their son was destined to survive the older gods and to rule over the new heaven and earth.

Vidar, however, uttered not a word, but slowly wended his way back to his palace Landvidi, in the heart of the primaeval forest, and there, sitting upon his throne, he pondered long about eternity, futurity, and infinity. If he fathomed their secrets he never revealed them, for the ancients averred that he was "as silent as the grave" – a silence which indicated that no man knows what awaits him in the life to come.

Vidar was not only a personification of the imperishability of Nature, but he was also a symbol of resurrection and renewal, exhibiting the eternal truth that new shoots and blossoms will spring forth to replace those which have fallen into decay.

The shoe he wore was to be his defence against the wolf Fenris, who, having destroyed Odin, would direct his wrath against him, and open wide his terrible jaws to devour him. But the old Northmen declared that Vidar would brace the foot thus protected against the monster's lower jaw, and, seizing the upper, would struggle with him until he had rent him in twain.

As one shoe only is mentioned in the Vidar myths, some mythologists suppose that he had but one leg, and was the personification of a waterspout, which would rise suddenly on the last day to quench the wild fire personified by the terrible wolf Fenris.

The Sultan's Snake-child

ONCE UPON A TIME there was a sultan and his wazir, and those two men were very rich with much wealth, but neither had a son.

They took counsel together. "How will it be when we die? Who shall we leave all this wealth to and we are without children?"

The sultan said to the wazir, "We must go to a far country and look for some wise man who will tell us what to do."

So they went away, and wandered on and on for three years, till at last they met an old woman, bent with the weight of many years.

That woman said to them, "My grandsons, I know what you have come for."

Then she sank down to the bottom of a big lake, and when she came up again out of the water she brought in her hands two charms, which were two slimy roots; one for the sultan and one for the wazir. And she said, "Take these, and when you return home you will find that your wish has already been accomplished; but to these charms I give you there are conditions attached. When you arrive in your town, you must tell no man about it, and take heed that in the way you neither chirrup nor look back."

Then she shook her withered hand and said, "It has taken you three years to come; you will return in one month. Farewell."

Then the sultan and the wazir set off home.

In the way the wazir said, "Allah be praised that our wish has been granted." The sultan, forgetting the old woman's warning, chirruped, as much as to say, "I will believe when I see."

After one month they came to the gate of their town, and as they entered the cannons sounded and the news spread forth. "There is an heir in the palace of the sultan, and there is an heir in the house of the wazir."

The wazir returned to his house swiftly, and there he found a most beautiful boy.

The sultan came to the palace, and there he found a snake.

When he heard that the wazir had a lovely child he was very pleased, and he used to go every day to the wazir's house to see that child, but he told his people to throw that snake out of the palace.

Now there was a slave girl in the palace called Mizi, and when she saw them taking that snake to throw it in the river she said, "Give me that snake, that I may bring him up as my child."

So Mizi took that snake and wore him round her neck till he grew, and then she came to the sultan and said, "Build me a grass hut, that I may live there with my child, the snake."

So a hut was built for her, and she stayed there by herself with that snake. She took her cooking pots there, and cooked food for herself and the snake. Every day she fed that snake, and it grew and grew, till at last it filled up the whole hut.

Then that snake said to Mizi, "Go and tell the sultan that his little snake wants a stone house of seven storeys in which to live. He must look for craftsmen who are not afraid, to come and build the house, and what they ask must be given them."

So Mizi came and told those words to the sultan, and craftsmen who had no fear were sought for. They came and built a house of seven storeys in the space of seven days, and the wages they asked for were given them.

When the house was finished, they said, "Go and tell the little snake that the house is ready."

Then Mizi and the snake moved into that house and lived there, till one day the snake said to Mizi, "Go and look for a sage who will teach me learning, but he must be master of his heart and unafraid. He must come of his own free will."

So she went and sought a man of learning, but everyone she asked to come replied, "I am not going so as to be swallowed whole by that snake."

At last she found a sage who said, "I will go, for I see that Mizi lives with this snake and is not devoured, so why should I be eaten?"

So that professor came and taught the snake learning of every kind, and when he had finished he went to the Sultan and received the pay he asked for.

So the snake and Mizi lived together, till one day that snake said to her, "Now you must go and look for a wife for me; but she must come of her own free will, and what money she wants she must have."

So a wife for the snake was sought for in all the land, but none was found; all said, "Who wants to go and be swallowed whole by a big snake?"

Now in that country was a very poor man who had seven daughters. When the news came to them all refused, till the seventh and youngest was asked, and she replied, "We are very poor; I will go and be eaten by that snake. What matter?"

So that girl was taken and decked out with pearls and precious stones and clothes of silk, and then Mizi was called and told, "This is the wife of your master, the snake. Take her."

So Mizi took her and brought her to the snake, and he said, "Arrange everything for her comfort."

When night had come, Mizi slept with that girl till, when twelve o'clock came, that snake came out from inside his skin. He put on wooden sandals and went to the bathroom and made his ablutions. When he had finished washing he took his prayer mat and spread it out and prayed and read the Koran.

After that he came and sat near that girl and looked at her and said, "My wife is beautiful; she has beautiful eyes, lovely ears and long straight hair. Hhum! Poor me, who am a snake. Sleep, my beautiful wife."

Then he entered his skin again and slept.

Seven days passed in this way, and on the eighth Mizi said to that girl, "I will fasten a thread to your thumb; when I pull it open your eyes and look at him."

That night, at twelve o'clock, the snake came out of his skin, and then Mizi pulled the thread and that girl awoke and opened her eyes and saw a wondrously handsome Arab youth: in all that country there was no youth so handsome as that son of the Sultan.

The snake went to the bathroom and made his ablutions, and then returned and prayed and read the Koran.

At the time of the before dawn breezes he came and looked at his wife and then returned to his skin. When dawn came Mizi and that girl took counsel together, and then Mizi went to the Sultan and said to him, "Give me three tins of oil and ten maunds of firewood."

When she had got them she had them brought to the house.

Then she said to that girl, "Now we must dig a pit here in the other room."

So they dug a pit and put in it the firewood and then poured the oil over it.

That night they watched till after midnight. When the youth went to the bathroom they got up and seized on the skin and tried to drag it into the pit, but it was too heavy for them. So they exerted all their strength, till at last they managed to drag it into the pit. After that they set fire to the wood and the oil.

When its owner in the bathroom heard the skin crackling he ran in and said to Mizi, "What have you done, taking away my clothes to put in the fire?" Then he fell down, and did not regain consciousness till three o'clock next day, for that youth did not know the world outside of his skin.

When he recovered Mizi cooked porridge for him, and when he had eaten it he said to Mizi, "Go to the sultan and tell him to make offerings, nine shells full of alms; for the day after tomorrow I will go out."

So Mizi went with the news to the sultan, but he replied, "Go back and get eaten by that snake. We do not want any more of your folly; for you have taken the poor man's daughter and brought her to the snake, and she has already been swallowed up. Now you in your turn will be eaten, and today, I suppose, you have come to take leave of us."

Mizi returned and said to that youth, "He will not give the offering."

He replied, "Then leave him; he who has had no luck does not trust to luck. On Friday I will come forth by the power of Allah, alone."

When Friday came he decked his horse with pearls and precious stones and rode off to the mosque to pray amongst all the people; but the sultan did not know that it was his son.

Then Mizi came forth and trilled and shouted for joy, and told everyone in the mosque: "Look at me today, for it is today that my son, the snake, has come to life."

Many people thought that Mizi had gone mad. When the sultan had finished praying he came forth, and Mizi said to him, "Today my child has come forth."

The sultan said, "Peace be upon you;" and he followed that youth on his horse and knew that it was his son, and rejoiced greatly.

He said to his slaves, "Run to the palace, spread out diamonds and cushions, carpets and mats; do not leave anything of any value, but spread everything out."

Then was the wedding of that girl, the poor man's daughter, and the snake held with great festivity. So that snake and Mizi lived happily, and he loved her as if she had been his own mother. When he became sultan he gave the kingdom to her, he gave Mizi what spoke and what did not speak; it became her country, because she had nurtured that snake from its infancy until it became a full-grown man of wisdom.

The Orphan Boy and the Magic Stone

A CHIEF OF INDE NAMED INKITA had a son named Ayong Kita, whose mother had died at his birth.

The old chief was a hunter, and used to take his son out with him when he went into the bush. He used to do most of his hunting in the long grass which grows over nearly all the Inde country, and used to kill plenty of bush buck in the dry season.

In those days the people had no guns, so the chief had to shoot everything he got with his bow and arrows, which required a lot of skill.

When his little son was old enough, he gave him a small bow and some small arrows, and taught him how to shoot. The little boy was very quick at learning, and by continually practising on lizards and small birds, soon became expert in the use of his little bow, and could hit them almost every time he shot at them.

When the boy was ten years old his father died, and as he thus became the head of his father's house, and was in authority over all the slaves, they became very discontented, and made plans to kill him, so he ran away into the bush.

Having nothing to eat, he lived for several days on the nuts which fell from the palm trees. He was too young to kill any large animals, and only had his small bow and arrows, with which he killed a few squirrels, bush rats, and small birds, and so managed to live.

Now once at night, when he was sleeping in the hollow of a tree, he had a dream in which his father appeared, and told him where there was plenty of treasure buried in the earth, but, being a small boy, he was frightened, and did not go to the place.

One day, some time after the dream, having walked far and being very thirsty, he went to a lake, and was just going to drink, when he heard a hissing sound, and heard a voice tell him not to drink. Not seeing anyone, he was afraid, and ran away without drinking.

Early next morning, when he was out with his bow trying to shoot some small animal, he met an old woman with quite long hair. She was so ugly that he thought she must be a witch, so he tried to run, but she told him not to fear, as she wanted to help him and assist him to rule over his late father's house. She also told him that it was she who had called out to him at the lake not to drink, as there was a bad Ju Ju in the water which would have killed him. The old woman then took Ayong to a stream some little distance from the lake, and bending down, took out a small shining stone from the water, which she gave to him, at the same time telling him to go to the place which his father had advised him to visit in his dream. She then said, "When you get there you must dig, and you will find plenty of money; you must then go and buy two strong slaves, and when you have got them, you must take them into the forest, away from the town, and get them to build you a house with several rooms in it. You must then place the stone in one of the rooms, and whenever you want anything, all you have to do is to go into the room and tell the stone what you want, and your wishes will be at once gratified."

Ayong did as the old woman told him, and after much difficulty and danger bought the two slaves and built a house in the forest, taking great care of the precious stone, which he placed in an inside room. Then for some time, whenever he wanted anything, he used to go into the room and ask for a sufficient number of rods to buy what he wanted, and they were always brought at once.

This went on for many years, and Ayong grew up to be a man, and became very rich, and bought many slaves, having made friends with the Aro men, who in those days used to do a big traffic in slaves. After ten years had passed Ayong had quite a large town and many slaves, but one night the old woman appeared to him in a dream and told him that she thought that he was sufficiently wealthy, and that it was time for him to return the magic stone to the small stream from whence it came. But Ayong, although he was rich, wanted to rule his father's house and be a head chief for all the Inde country, so he sent for all the Ju Ju men in the country and two witch men, and marched with all his slaves to his father's town. Before he started he held a big palaver, and told them to point out any slave who had a bad heart, and who might kill him when he came to rule the country. Then the Ju Ju men consulted together, and pointed out fifty of the slaves who, they said, were witches, and would try to kill Ayong. He at once had them made prisoners, and tried them by the ordeal of Esere bean to see whether they were witches or not. As none of them could vomit the beans they all died, and were declared to be witches. He then had them buried at once. When the remainder of his slaves saw what had happened, they all came to him and begged his pardon, and promised to serve him faithfully. Although the fifty men were buried they could not rest, and troubled Ayong very much, and after a time he became very sick himself, so he sent again for the Ju Ju men, who told him that it was the witch men who, although they were dead and buried, had power to come out at night and used to suck Ayong's blood, which was the cause of his sickness. They then said, "We are only three Ju Ju men; you must get seven more of us, making the magic number of ten." When they came they dug up the bodies of the fifty witches, and found they were quite fresh. Then Ayong had big fires made, and burned them one after the other, and gave the Ju Ju men a big present. He soon after became quite well again, and took possession of his father's property, and ruled over all the country.

Ever since then, whenever anyone is accused of being a witch, they are tried by the ordeal of the poisonous Esere bean, and if they can vomit they do not die, and are declared innocent, but if they cannot do so, they die in great pain.

How a Girl Reached the Land of the Ghosts and Came Back

MARWE AND HER BROTHER were ordered by their parents to watch the bean-field and drive away the monkeys. They kept at their post for the greater part of the day, but as their mother had not given them any food to take with them they grew very hungry.

They dug up the burrows of the field-rats, caught some, made a fire, roasted their game, and ate it. Then, being thirsty, they went to a pool and drank. It was some distance off, and when they came back they found that the monkeys had descended on the bean-patch and stripped it bare. They were terribly frightened, and Marwe said, "Let's go and jump into the pool." But her brother thought it would be better to go home without being seen and listen to what their parents were saying. So they stole up to the hut and listened through a gap in the banana leaves of the thatch. Father and mother were both very angry. "What are we to do with such good-for-nothing creatures? Shall we beat them? Or shall we strangle them?" The children did not wait to hear any more, but rushed off to the pool. Marwe threw herself in, but her brother's courage failed him, and he ran back home and told the parents: "Marwe has gone into the pool." They went down at once, quite forgetting the hasty words provoked by the sudden discovery of their loss, and called again and again, "Marwe, come home! Never mind about the beans; we can plant the patch again!" But there was no answer. Day after day the father went down to the pool and called her – always in vain. Marwe had gone into the country of the ghosts.

You entered it at the bottom of the pool. Before she had gone very far she came to a hut, where an old woman lived, with a number of children. This old woman called her in and told her she might stay with her. Next day she sent her out with the others to gather firewood, but said, "You need not do anything. Let the others do the work." Marwe, however, did her part with the rest, and the same when they were sent out to cut grass or perform any other tasks. She was offered food from time to time, but always made some excuse for refusing it. (The living who reach the land of the dead can never leave it again if they eat while there.) So time went on, till one day she began to weary, and said to the other girls, "I should like to go home." The girls advised her to go and tell the old woman, which she did, and the old body had no objection, but asked her, "Shall I hit you with the cold or with the hot?" and Marwe asked to be hit with the cold.

The woman told her to dip her arms into a pot she had standing beside her. She did so, and drew them out covered with shining bangles. She was then told to dip her feet, and found her ankles adorned with fine brass and copper chains. Then the woman gave her a skin petticoat worked with beads, and said, "Your future husband is called Sawoye. It is he who will carry you home."

She went with her to the pool, rose to the surface and left her sitting on the bank. It happened that there was a famine in the land just then. Someone saw Marwe and ran to the village saying that there was a girl seated by the pool richly dressed and wearing the most beautiful ornaments, which no one else in the countryside could afford, the people having parted with all their valuables to the coast-traders in the time of scarcity. So the whole population turned out, with the chief at their head. They were filled with admiration of her beauty. They all greeted her most respectfully, and the chief wanted to carry her home; but she refused. Others offered, but she would listen to none till a certain man came along, who was known as Sawoye. Now Sawoye was disfigured by a disease from which he had suffered called *woye*, whence his name. As soon as she saw him Marwe said, "That is my husband." So he picked her up and carried her home and married her.

Sawoye soon lost his disfiguring skin disease and appeared as the handsomest man in the clan. With the old lady's bangles they bought a fine herd of cattle and built themselves the best house in the village. And they would have lived happy ever after if some of his neighbours had not envied him and plotted to kill him. They succeeded, but his faithful wife found means to revive him, and hid him in the inner compartment of the hut. Then, when the enemies came to divide the spoil and carry Marwe off to be given to the chief as his wife, Sawoye came out, fully armed, and killed them all. After which he and Marwe were left in peace.

The Chief and the Tigers

THERE LIVED LONG AGO a chief whose wife was beautiful as the morning sun. Dear was she to the heart of her lord, and great was his sorrow when she grew sick. Many doctors and wise women tried to cure her, but in vain. Worse and worse she grew, till the people said she would surely die, and the heart of the chief became as water within him.

One day, as the shadows grew long on the ground, an old, old man came slowly to the village, and asked to see the chief. "Morena (Master)," he said, "I have heard of your trouble, and have come to help you. Your wife is ill of a great sickness, and she will die unless you can get a tiger's heart with which to make medicine for her to drink. See, I have here a wonderful stone which will help you, and some medicine for you to drink. Now wrap yourself in a tiger-skin. The medicine will make you wise to understand and to speak their tongue; so shall they look upon you as a brother. When you have drunk the medicine, take the stone in your hand, and set out on your journey. When you come to the home of the tigers, you must live among them as one of themselves, until you can find yourself alone with one. Him must you quickly kill, and tear from his warm body his heart unbroken, and then, throwing away your tiger skin, you must flee to your home. The tigers will chase you, but when they come too near, you must throw down the stone in front of you and jump upon it, when it will become a great rock, from whose sides fire will dart forth, and burn any who try to climb it. Thus will you be saved from the power of the tigers, and your wife be restored to health."

Gratefully the chief did as the old man desired, and set off to seek the home of the tigers. Many days he wandered across the plains and over the mountains, into the unknown valleys beyond, and there he found those he sought. They greeted him joyfully, welcoming him as a brother; only one, a young tiger of great beauty, held back, and muttered, "This is no tiger but a man. He will bring misfortune upon us. Slay him, my brothers, ere it be too late;" but they heeded him not. Not many days had passed, when all the tigers scattered themselves over the valley, and the chief found himself alone with the angry young tiger. Watching him patiently, he soon found the opportunity he sought, and, hastily killing him, he tore the still warm heart from the lifeless body, and throwing off his disguise, set off towards his home.

On, on he went, and still no sign of the tigers, but, as the sun sank to rest, they appeared in the distance, and he knew they would soon overtake him. When they were so close behind him that he heard the angry snap of their teeth, he threw down the stone the old man had given him, and sprang on to it. Instantly it became a great rock, even as the old man had said. Up came the tigers, each striving to be the first to tear the heart out of the chief, even as he had torn out their brother's heart; but the first one that reached the rock, sprang back with a howl of agony, and rolled over on his side – dead. The others all drew up in alarm, and dared not approach the stone, but spent many hours in wandering round and round the rock, and grinding their teeth at the chief, who calmly watched them from his seat on the top of the rock.

Just before dawn the tigers, now thoroughly tired, lay down, and soon were fast asleep. Carefully, silently, the chief crawled down from the rock, which immediately became again a small stone. Taking the stone in his hand, and holding close the precious heart, which was to restore his wife to health, he fled like a deer towards his village, which he now saw in the plain below. Should he reach it before the tigers caught him? The perspiration streamed from his body, his ears rang with strange noises, and his breath came in great gasps, but still he hurried on. Presently he heard the tigers coming. There was no time even to look behind. He *must* reach the village before they overtook him. On, on, stumbling blindly over every obstacle, he staggered. How far away it still looked! Would his people *never* see him? Yes, at last he is seen. He can hear the shout of his men as they rush to help him, only a few more steps now, and he is safe. Bravely he totters on, then stumbles and falls helpless, exhausted, as his men arrive, and carry him in triumph into the village, while the tigers, baffled and furious, retreat to their home beyond the mountains.

With song and dance the people keep festival, for their chief has returned in safety, and his beautiful wife, restored to perfect health, sits smiling by his side, to receive the loving congratulations of old and young; but the old man came not to join the throng, nor was he ever seen in their land again. Quietly as he came, he had gone, leaving no sign behind him.

The Gift of Corn

LONG AGO, THERE LIVED A POOR INDIAN who dwelt with his wife and children in a tiny lodge in the heart of the forest. The family relied on hunting for their food, and although the father was never lacking in courage and skill, there were often times when he returned home without provisions, so that his wife and children had only the leaves on the trees to satisfy their hunger. The eldest son of the family, a boy of fourteen, had inherited the same kind and gentle disposition as his father, and as he watched the old man struggle to take care of them all, he longed only for the time when he would be able to help out in some way.

At last, the young boy reached the age of the great fast, when he was obliged to shut himself away without food, praying night and day to the Great Spirit in preparation for the coming of his spirit-guide and guardian through life. This solemn and sacred event demanded that he empty his mind and heart of every evil thought and he now began to meditate earnestly on the generosity of the Great Spirit who never ceased to provide mankind with everything good and wholesome. As he roamed the fields and mountains during the first few days of his retreat, he was deeply moved by the beauty of his surroundings, the glorious flowers, the succulent berries, and he felt the strong desire to make his own contribution to this remarkable world.

The young boy was well aware that both he and his family were deeply indebted to the Great Spirit, but at the same time, he began asking himself why it was that the divine ruler had not made it easier for them to find enough food to survive on.

"Perhaps if I pray very hard," the boy thought to himself, "the Great Spirit will reveal to me in a dream the means by which I can ease the hardship my family now suffers." And with that he lay down and kept to his bed for a full day and a night.

It was now the fifth day of his fast and the boy lay feeble with hunger, drifting in and out of sleep and hoping that some sort of vision would soon come to him. Suddenly the room in which he lay became filled with a dazzling light, out of which emerged a beautiful young man who moved gracefully towards him. The stranger's slender form was draped in a luxurious, satin robe of green and yellow, his complexion was the purest marble-white and on his head he wore an exotic plume of jade-green feathers. The boy was startled by the apparition, but the stranger's eyes conveyed the gentlest, warmest expression and his voice was as sweet as music as he spoke.

"The Great Spirit has been listening to your prayers," he said softly. "He understands how deeply you care for your family and he knows that you have always been a loyal and obedient child. For these reasons he has sent me to guide you in your pursuit and to ensure that your desire is fulfilled. Arise young warrior," added the beautiful stranger, "and prepare yourself to wrestle with me, for such is the wish of the Great Spirit."

Even though his limbs were weak from fasting, the young boy stood up courageously and did as the stranger commanded him. The struggle which followed was long and punishing and at length the boy began to grow faint. But just at this precise moment, the stranger called a halt to the conflict, promising to return on the following day when the boy had replenished his strength.

At exactly the same hour next morning, the celestial visitor reappeared and the two took up the fighting once more. As they battled on, the young boy felt his strength improve and his courage increase. He threw himself wholeheartedly into the struggle, wrestling fiercely with his visitor, until the latter was forced to cry out in pain.

"You have certainly proven your worth today," the stranger declared, "now it is my turn to rest before we begin our final trial. Tomorrow will be the seventh day of your fast," he continued, "and your father will bring you food to strengthen you. In the evening, you will wrestle with me and easily overcome me, for you have succeeded in winning the favour of the Great Spirit.

"As soon as I have fallen, you must strip me of my garments and bury me in the earth. Once a month, come and cover me with fresh soil and make certain that no weeds or grass are allowed to grow upon my grave. If you do all this, I shall return to life and I promise that you will see me again, splendidly clothed in a garment of green."

The stranger had no sooner spoken these words than he vanished into thin air, leaving his opponent to fathom the meaning of all that he had been told.

Shortly after dawn on the following day, the young boy's father filled a small basket with nourishing food and set off in search of his son. He was greatly relieved to see the boy again, but noticed that he had grown thin and frail.

"My son, you must eat something," he urged him. "You have fasted long enough and I feel certain that the Great Spirit does not require you to sacrifice your own life."

"Father," the boy replied, "please be patient with me until sundown, and at that hour I will happily partake of the meal you have brought me."

For the young boy was determined to prove his hero's strength without assistance, resolving to rely on his inner strength alone during the trial ahead.

Once again, at the usual hour, the stranger appeared and the contest was renewed as before. Though he had not eaten any of his father's food, or allowed even a drop of water to pass his lips, the boy felt invigorated and irrepressible. Fired by the need to achieve some great purpose, he lunged at his handsome opponent, pushing him violently against a rock in the ground. The stranger did not rise up again to challenge him and, as he bent over to examine him where he lay, the boy could find no trace of life in the handsome youth. A deep sadness and regret suddenly invaded his soul as he began digging the earth to bury the body and he swore to himself that he would tend the grave as lovingly as if it were that of his own mother.

Throughout the spring which followed, the boy never once allowed a day to slip past without visiting the burial place of his friend. He stooped and carefully weeded out the grass and carried fresh soil up the mountain to replace the old, just as he had vowed he would. By summertime, tiny green shoots began to appear in the earth, but because they so reminded the young boy of the feather plume his visitor always wore, he was loath to remove them and so they continued to rise in height as the months progressed.

The days and weeks passed by and during all of this time, the boy never once revealed to a single soul the purpose of his regular excursions up into the mountains. Then one day, he gingerly approached his father requesting that he follow him on his mysterious ramble. Though he was surprised and a little apprehensive, the old man agreed to accompany his son and soon they had reached the spot where the handsome stranger lay buried.

The sight which now greeted them was truly the most astonishing and gratifying they had ever witnessed. Overnight, the green shoots on the grave had broadened out into beautiful, graceful plants with velvet-soft foliage, each one bearing a generous golden cluster crowned by a majestic plume.

Leaping for joy, the young boy began shouting aloud: "It is my friend, the friend of my vision who promised he would return to me."

"It is Mondamin," (from the words *moedo*, meaning 'spirit' and *min*, meaning 'grain' or 'berry') replied his father, filled with admiration for his son. "It is the spirit grain the old ones have sometimes spoken of, the Indian corn which the Merciful Master has sent to nourish us because he is greatly pleased with you."

And the two began to gather the golden ears of corn, tearing away the green husks from the stalks as once the young boy had torn away the garments of his extraordinary wrestling companion.

From that day forward, the people no longer depended entirely on hunting and were blessed with beautiful fields of healthy grain which they harvested every year just as soon as the long hot summer had begun to fade into autumn.

Ojeeg Annung, or The Summer Maker

THERE LIVED A CELEBRATED HUNTER on the southern shores of Lake Superior, who was considered a Manito by some, for there was nothing but what he could accomplish. He lived off the path, in a wild, lonesome, place, with a wife whom he loved, and they were blessed with a son, who had attained his thirteenth year. The hunter's name was Ojeeg, or the Fisher, which is the name of an expert, sprightly little animal common to the region. He was so successful in the chase, that he seldom returned without bringing his wife and son a plentiful supply of venison, or other dainties of the woods. As hunting formed his constant occupation, his son began early to emulate his father in the same employment, and would take his bow and arrows, and exert his skill in trying to kill birds and squirrels. The greatest impediment he met with, was the coldness and severity of the climate. He often returned home, his little fingers benumbed with cold, and crying with vexation at his disappointment. Days, and months, and years passed away, but still the same perpetual depth of snow was seen, covering all the country as with a white cloak.

One day, after a fruitless trial of his forest skill, the little boy was returning homeward with a heavy heart, when he saw a small red squirrel gnawing the top of a pine bur. He had approached within a proper distance to shoot, when the squirrel sat up on its hind legs and thus addressed him:

"My grandchild, put up your arrows, and listen to what I have to tell you." The boy complied rather reluctantly, when the squirrel continued: "My son, I see you pass frequently, with your fingers benumbed with cold, and crying with vexation for not having killed any birds. Now, if you will follow my advice, we will see if you cannot accomplish your wishes. If you will strictly pursue my advice, we will have perpetual summer, and you will then have the pleasure of killing as many birds as you please; and I will also have something to eat, as I am now myself on the point of starvation.

"Listen to me. As soon as you get home you must commence crying. You must throw away your bow and arrows in discontent. If your mother asks you what is the matter, you must not answer her, but continue crying and sobbing. If she offers you anything to eat, you must push it away with apparent discontent, and continue crying. In the evening, when your father returns from hunting, he will inquire of your mother what is the matter with you. She will answer that you came home crying, and would not so much as mention the cause to her. All this while you must not leave off sobbing. At last your father will say, 'My son, why is this unnecessary grief? Tell me the cause. You know I am a spirit, and that nothing is impossible for me to perform.' You must then answer him, and say that you are sorry to see the snow continually on the ground, and ask him if he could not cause it to melt, so that we might have perpetual summer. Say it in a supplicating way, and tell him this is the cause of your grief. Your father will reply, 'It is very hard to accomplish your request, but for your sake, and for my love for you, I will use my utmost endeavours.' He will tell you to be still, and cease crying. He will try to bring summer with all its loveliness. You must then be quiet, and eat that which is set before you."

The squirrel ceased. The boy promised obedience to his advice, and departed. When he reached home, he did as he had been instructed, and all was exactly fulfilled, as it had been predicted by the squirrel.

Ojeeg told him that it was a great undertaking. He must first make a feast, and invite some of his friends to accompany him on a journey. Next day he had a bear roasted whole. All who had been invited to the feast came punctually to the appointment. There were the Otter, Beaver, Lynx, Badger, and Wolverine. After the feast, they arranged it among themselves to set out on the contemplated journey in three days. When the time arrived, the Fisher took leave of his wife and son, as he foresaw that it was for the last time. He and his companions travelled in company day after day, meeting with nothing but the ordinary incidents. On the twentieth day they arrived at the foot of a high mountain, where they saw the tracks of some person who had recently killed an animal, which they knew by the blood that marked the way. The Fisher told his friends that they ought to follow the track, and see if they could not procure something to eat. They followed it for some time; at last they arrived at a lodge, which had been hidden from their view by a hollow in the mountain. Ojeeg told his friends to be very sedate, and not to laugh on any account. The first object that they saw was a man standing at the door of the lodge, but of so deformed a shape that they could not possibly make out who or what sort of a man it could be. His head was enormously large; he had such a queer set of teeth, and no arms. They wondered how he could kill animals. But the secret was soon revealed. He was a great Manito. He invited them to pass the night, to which they consented.

He boiled his meat in a hollow vessel made of wood, and took it out of this singular kettle in some way unknown to his guests. He carefully gave each their portion to eat, but made so many odd movements that the Otter could not refrain from laughing, for he is the only one who is spoken of as a jester. The Manito looked at him with a terrible look, and then made a spring at him, and got on him to smother him, for that was his mode of killing animals. But the Otter, when he felt him on his neck, slipped his head back and made for the door, which he passed in safety; but went out with the curse of the Manito. The others passed the night, and they conversed on different subjects. The Manito told the Fisher that he would accomplish his object, but that it would probably cost him his life. He gave them his advice, directed them how to act, and described a certain road which they must follow, and they would thereby be led to the place of action.

They set off in the morning, and met their friend, the Otter, shivering with cold; but Ojeeg had taken care to bring along some of the meat that had been given him, which he presented to his friend. They pursued their way, and travelled twenty days more before they got to the place which the Manito had told them of. It was a most lofty mountain. They rested on its highest peak to fill their pipes and refresh themselves. Before smoking, they made the customary ceremony, pointing to the heavens, the four winds, the earth, and the zenith; in the mean time, speaking in a loud voice, addressed the Great Spirit, hoping that their object would be accomplished. They then commenced smoking.

They gazed on the sky in silent admiration and astonishment, for they were on so elevated a point, that it appeared to be only a short distance above their heads. After they had finished smoking, they prepared themselves. Ojeeg told the Otter to make the first attempt to try and make a hole in the sky. He consented with a grin. He made a leap, but fell down the hill stunned by the force of his fall; and the snow being moist, and falling on his back, he slid with velocity down the side of the mountain. When he found himself at the bottom, he thought to himself, it is the last time I make such another jump, so I will make the best of my way home. Then it was the turn of the Beaver, who made the attempt, but fell down senseless; then of the Lynx and Badger, who had no better success.

"Now," says Fisher to the Wolverine, "try your skill; your ancestors were celebrated for their activity, hardihood and perseverance, and I depend on you for success. Now make the attempt." He did so, but also without success. He leaped the second time, but now they could see that the sky was giving way to their repeated attempts. Mustering strength, he made the third leap, and went in. The Fisher nimbly followed him.

They found themselves in a beautiful plain, extending as far as the eye could reach, covered with flowers of a thousand different hues and fragrance. Here and there were clusters of tall, shady trees, separated by innumerable streams of the purest water, which wound around their courses under the cooling shades, and filled the plain with countless beautiful lakes, whose banks and bosom were covered with water-fowl, basking and sporting in the sun. The trees were alive with birds of different plumage, warbling their sweet notes, and delighted with perpetual spring.

The Fisher and his friend beheld very long lodges, and the celestial inhabitants amusing themselves at a distance. Words cannot express the beauty and charms of the place. The lodges were empty of inhabitants, but they saw them lined with mocuks of different sizes, filled with birds and fowls of different plumage. Ojeeg thought of his son, and immediately commenced cutting open the mocuks and letting out the birds, who descended in whole flocks through the opening which they had made. The warm air of those regions also rushed down through the opening, and spread its genial influence over the north.

When the celestial inhabitants saw the birds let loose, and the warm gales descending, they raised a shout like thunder, and ran for their lodges. But it was too late. Spring, summer, and autumn had gone; even perpetual summer had almost all gone; but they separated it with a blow, and only a part descended; but the ends were so mangled, that, wherever it prevails among the lower inhabitants, it is always sickly.

When the Wolverine heard the noise, he made for the opening and safely descended. Not so the Fisher. Anxious to fulfil his son's wishes, he continued to break open the mocuks. He was, at last, obliged to run also, but the opening was now closed by the inhabitants. He ran with all his might over the plains of heaven, and, it would appear, took a northerly direction. He saw his pursuers so close that he had to climb the first large tree he came to. They commenced shooting at him with their arrows, but without effect, for all his body was invulnerable except the space of about an inch near the tip of his tail. At last one of the arrows hit the spot, for he had in this chase assumed the shape of the Fisher after whom he was named.

He looked down from the tree, and saw some among his assailants with the totems of his ancestors. He claimed relationship, and told them to desist, which they only did at the approach of night. He then came down to try and find an opening in the celestial plain, by which he might descend to the earth. But he could find none. At last, becoming faint from the loss of blood from the wound on his tail, he laid himself down towards the north of the plain, and, stretching out his limbs, said, "I have fulfilled my promise to my son, though it has cost me my life; but I die satisfied in the idea that I have done so much good, not only for him, but for my fellow-beings. Hereafter I will be a sign to the inhabitants below for ages to come, who will venerate my name for having succeeded in procuring the varying seasons. They will now have from eight to ten moons without snow."

He was found dead next morning, but they left him as they found him, with the arrow sticking in his tail, as it can be plainly seen, at this time, in the heavens.

The White Hare of Inaba

IN ANCIENT DAYS there were eighty-one brothers, who were princes in Japan. With the exception of one brother they were quarrelsome fellows, and spent their time in showing all manner of petty jealousy, one toward the other. Each wanted to reign over the whole kingdom, and, in addition, each had the misfortune to wish to marry the Princess of Yakami, in Inaba. Although these eighty princes were at variance in most things, they were at one in persistently hating the brother who was gentle and peaceful in all his ways.

At length, after many angry words, the eighty brothers decided to go to Inaba in order to visit the Princess of Yakami, each brother fully resolved that he and he alone should be the successful suitor. The kind and gentle brother accompanied them, not, indeed, as a wooer of the fair princess, but as a servant who carried a large and heavy bag upon his back.

At last the eighty princes, who had left their much-wronged brother far behind, arrived at Cape Keta. They were about to continue their journey when they saw a white hare lying on the ground looking very miserable and entirely divested of fur.

The eighty princes, who were much amused by the sorry plight of the hare, said: "If you want your fur to grow again, bathe in the sea, and, when you have done so, run to the summit of a high mountain and allow the wind to blow upon you." With these words the eighty heartless princes proceeded on their way.

The hare at once went down to the sea, delighted at the prospect of regaining his handsome white fur. Having bathed, he ran up to the top of a mountain and lay down upon it; but he quickly perceived that the cold wind blowing on a skin recently immersed in salt water was beginning to crack and split. In addition to the humiliation of having no fur he now suffered considerable physical pain, and he realized that the eighty princes had shamefully deceived him.

While the hare was lying in pain upon the mountain the kind and gentle brother approached, slowly and labouriously, owing to the heavy bag he carried. When he saw the weeping hare he inquired how it was that the poor animal had met with such a misfortune.

"Please stop a moment," said the hare, "and I will tell you how it all happened. I wanted to cross from the Island of Oki to Cape Keta, so I said to the crocodiles: 'I should very much like to know how many crocodiles there are in the sea, and how many hares on land. Allow me first of all to count you.' And having said these words the crocodiles formed themselves into a long line, stretching from the Island of Oki to Cape Keta. I ran across their horny bodies, counting each as I passed. When I reached the last crocodile, I said: 'O foolish crocodiles, it doesn't matter to me how many there are of you in the sea, or how many hares on land! I only wanted you for a bridge in order that I might reach my destination.' Alas! my miserable boast cost me dear, for the last crocodile raised his head and snapped off all my fur!"

"Well," said the gentle brother, "I must say you were in the wrong and deserved to suffer for your folly. Is that the end of your story?"

"No," continued the hare. "I had no sooner suffered this indignity than the eighty princes came by, and lyingly told me that I might be cured by salt water and wind. Alas! Not knowing that they deceived me, I carried out their instructions, with the result that my body is cracked and extremely sore."

"Bathe in fresh water, my poor friend," said the good brother, "and when you have done so scatter the pollen of sedges upon the ground and roll yourself in it. This will indeed heal your sores and cause your fur to grow again."

The hare walked slowly to the river, bathed himself, and then rolled about in sedge pollen. He had no sooner done so than his skin healed and he was covered once more with a thick coat of fur.

The grateful hare ran back to his benefactor. "Those eighty wicked and cruel brothers of yours," said he, "shall never win the Princess of Inaba. It is you who shall marry her and reign over the country."

The hare's prophecy came true, for the eighty princes failed in their mission, while the brother who was good and kind to the white hare married the fair princess and became king of the country.

The Man Who Went to Seek His Fortune

THERE WAS ONCE a zemindar (landowner) or jhut who was very poor, and he had a brother who was very rich, but the rich brother never helped him at all and often reproached him for his poverty.

One day, the poor zemindar was determined to go out into the wide world to seek his fortune, and not to return until he had found it.

Having thus made up his mind he set out on his journey, and the first thing he came across was a king's palace, which was in the hands of carpenters and masons; but no sooner had they built it up on one side, than the other side fell down, so that the place was at all times under repairs, and caused its owner much expense and anxiety.

As the zemindar stood watching the place, the king came out, and asked him who he was, and where he was going; so he told him that it was to seek his fortune.

"Well, when you get to the place where you find it, will you think of me, and enquire the reason why my palace is constantly falling down?"

This the zemindar promised to do, and then continued on his journey.

The next place he arrived at was a river, and a turtle was on its bank. It asked him whither he was going, and he said: "To seek my fortune."

"Friend, remember me when it is found, and say that the poor turtle, although it lives in water, suffers from a severe burning sensation inwardly. Pray enquire the reason for this."

So the zemindar promised, and, as a reward, the turtle bore him across the river on its back.

After another long journey, when he was both hungry and footsore, the zemindar spied in the distance a most beautiful plum tree. It was the season for plums, so he determined to have a good feast of the fruit, plucked one of the largest and best, but it tasted so bitter that he quickly threw it away, and, turning to the tree in anger and disappointment, cursed it.

"You are fair to look at, but otherwise good for nothing," he cried bitterly.

"Alas!" replied the tree, "this is what all travellers say to me. Yet I cannot discover why my fruits are bitter. Will you, O traveller, find out for me in your travels, and bring me word?"

After leaving the plum tree, the zemindar went into a thick jungle, and in the midst of it found an old fakir fast asleep. He did not know that this holy man had slept for twelve years, and was just about to awake. While he stood there the old fakir opened his eyes, and saw him.

"Son, you have looked after me while I was asleep; who are you and where are you going?"

"I am going to seek my fortune, for I am a poor man."

"Go no further, but return the same way that you have come," said the old fakir.

"Before I go, will you tell me, O holy fakir, why a certain rajah's house is always falling down, though he is constantly rebuilding it?"

"The rajah has a daughter who is grown up but unmarried; when she is married the trouble will cease."

"A turtle is troubled with burning sensations inwardly, and would be glad to know the cause."

"The turtle is full of wisdom, but selfishly keeps all its knowledge to itself. Let it tell half it knows to another, and it will become quite well."

"There is a beautiful plum tree whose fruits are bitter to the taste. What is the cause of this?"

"There is hidden treasure at the root of the tree, and when this is removed, the fruit will be sweet," said the old fakir.

Then the zemindar thanked him, made a low salaam, and returned the same way he had come.

First he met the plum tree, and it at once enquired if he had found out why its fruit was bitter, and he told it the reason.

"It is yours to remove that cause, my friend, so dig quickly, and see what there is at my roots."

The zemindar did as he was bid, and found a box full of treasure – pearls, and gold and rubies – so he tied them in his blanket, and went on his way.

At the river his friend the turtle awaited him eagerly; so the zemindar explained everything, and the turtle said: "I will impart half the knowledge to you as a reward; stoop down and listen."

The man did as he was bid, and the creature imparted great wisdom to him in whispers.

After this he met the king, who said: "Well, traveller, what news? Have you found your fortune?"

"Yes, O King, and the cause of your trouble is, that, until your daughter is married, your house will continue to fall down."

"Will you marry her?" said the king.

The zemindar gladly consented, and the marriage took place with great pomp. After it he returned to his own home, and there his elder brother met him.

"You see, brother," said the zemindar, "that you said it was my fate to have but a seer of *atta* (flour) a day, but I have found my good fortune at last."

Yama and Sivitri

THERE WAS ONCE A PRINCESS in the country of Madra, and her name was Savitri. She was the gift of the goddess Gayatri, wife of Brahma, the self-created, who had heard the prayers and received the offerings of Aswapati, the childless king of Madra, when he practised austere penances so that he might have children of his own. The young woman grew to be beautiful; her eyes had burning splendour, and were as fair as lotus leaves; she had exceeding sweetness and grace.

It came to pass that Savitri looked with eyes of love at a youth named Satyavan 'the Truthful'. Although Satyavan lived in a hermitage, he was of royal birth. His father was a virtuous king, named Dyumatsena, who became blind, and was then deprived of his kingdom by an old enemy living nearby. The dethroned monarch retired to the forest with his faithful wife and his only son, who in time grew up to be a handsome youth.

When Savitri confessed her love to her father, the great sage Narada, who sat beside him, spoke and said: "The princess has done wrong in choosing this royal youth Satyavan for her husband. He is attractive and courageous, he is truthful and magnanimous and forgiving, he is modest and patient and without malice; he possesses every virtue. But he has one defect, and no other. He is to have a short life; it has been decreed that within a year from this day he must die; within a year Yama, god of the dead, will come for him."

The king turned to his daughter: "Savitri, you have heard the words of Narada. Therefore go and choose another lord for yourself, for the days of Satyavan are numbered."

The beautiful young woman said to her father the king: "The die is cast; it can fall only once; only once can a daughter be given away by her father; only once can a woman say, 'I am yours'. I have chosen my lord. Let his life be brief or be long, I must marry Satyavan."

Narada said: "Oh King, the heart of your daughter will not waver; she will not be turned away from the path she has chosen. Therefore I approve of the marriage of Savitri and Satyavan."

The king replied: "As you advise, so I must do, Narada, because you are my teacher. I cannot disobey."

Then Narada said: "Peace be with Savitri! I must go now. My blessing to all of you!"

Aswapati went to visit Dyumatsena in the forest, and his daughter went with him. Dyumatsena asked his visitors: "Why have you come here?"

Aswapati replied: "Royal sage, this is my beautiful daughter Savitri. Take her for your daughter-in-law."

Dyumatsena responded by saying: "I have lost my kingdom, and live here in the woods with my wife and my son. We live as ascetics and perform great penances. How will your daughter endure the hardships of a forest life?"

Aswapati answered: "My daughter well knows that joy and sorrow come and go and that nowhere is bliss assured. Therefore accept her from me."

Dyumatsena consented that his son should marry Savitri. Satyavan was happy because he was given a wife who had every accomplishment. Savitri also rejoiced because she obtained a husband after her own heart, and she took off her royal garments and ornaments and dressed herself in bark and red cloth.

So Savitri became a hermit woman. She honoured Satyavan's father and mother, and she gave joy to her husband with her sweet speeches, her skill at work, her subdued and even temper, and especially her love. She lived the life of the ascetics and practised every austerity. But she never forgot the dreadful prophecy of Narada the sage; his sad words were always present in her secret heart, and she counted the days as they went past.

Soon the time came when Satyavan must cast off his mortal body. When he had just four days to live, Savitri took the Tritatra vow of three nights of sleepless penance and fast.

Dyumatsena warned her of how hard this would be, but Savitri was determined not to break her vow. So Savitri began to fast. She grew pale and became wasted by her rigid penance. Three days passed, and then, believing that her husband would die the following day, Savitri spent a night of bitter anguish through all the dark and lonely hours.

As the sun rose on the fateful morning, she said to herself, "Today is the day." Her face was bloodless but brave; she prayed in silence and made offerings at the morning fire; then she stood before her father-in-law and her mother-in-law in reverent silence with joined hands, concentrating her senses. All the hermits of the forest blessed her and said: "May you never suffer widowhood."

Dyumatsena spoke to Savitri then, saying: "Now that your vow has been completed you may eat the morning meal."

But Savitri replied: "I will eat when the sun goes down."

Hearing her words Satyavan stood up, and taking his axe on his shoulder, turned towards the distant jungle to find fruits and herbs for his wife, whom he loved. He was strong and self-possessed.

Savitri spoke to him sweetly and said: "You must not go alone, my husband. It is my heart's desire to go with you. I cannot endure to be parted from you today."

Satyavan replied: "It is not for you to enter the dark jungle; the way is long and difficult, and you are weak on account of your severe penance. How can you walk so far on foot?"

Savitri laid her head on his chest and said: "I have not been made weary by my fast. Indeed I am now stronger than before. I will not feel tired when you are by my side. I have resolved to go with you: therefore do not seek to stand in the wat of my wish – the wish and the longing of a faithful wife to be with her lord."

Satyavan replied: "If it is your desire to accompany me I will allow it. But you must ask permission of my parents so that they do not find fault with me for taking you through the trackless jungle."

Then Savitri spoke to the blind sage and her husband's mother and said: "Satyavan is going towards the deep jungle to find fruits and herbs for me, and also fuel for the sacrificial fires. It is my heart's wish to go too, for today I cannot endure to be parted from him."

Dyumatsena said: "Since you have come to live with us in our hermitage you have not asked anything of us. So have your wish in this matter, but do not delay your husband in his duties."

Having received permission to leave the hermitage, Savitri turned towards the jungle with Satyavan, her beloved lord. Smiles covered her face, but her heart was torn with secret sadness.

Peacocks fluttered in the green woodland through which they walked together, and the sun shone in all its splendour in the blue heaven.

In a sweet voice Satyavan said: "How beautiful are the bright streams and the blossoming trees!"

The heart of Savitri was divided into two parts: with one she talked with her husband while she watched his face and followed his moods; with the other she awaited the dreaded coming of Yama, but she never uttered her fears. Birds sang sweetly in the forest, but sweeter to Savitri was the voice of her beloved. It was very dear to her to walk on in silence, listening to his words.

Satyavan gathered fruits and stored them in his basket. Then he began to cut down the branches of trees. The sun was hot and he perspired. Suddenly he felt weary and he said: "My head aches; my senses are confused and my limbs have grown weak. A sickness has seized me. My body seems to be pierced by a hundred darts. I would gladly lie down and rest, my beloved; I would gladly sleep even now."

Speechless and terror-stricken, the gentle Savitri wound her arms about her husband's body; she sat on the ground and she pillowed his head on her lap. Remembering the words of Narada, she knew that the dreaded hour had come; the very moment of death was at hand. Gently she held her husband's head with caressing hands; she kissed his panting lips; her heart was beating fast and loud. The forest grew dark and lonesome.

Suddenly an awful shape emerged from the shadows. He was of great stature; his clothing was blood-red; on his head he wore a gleaming crown; he had red eyes and was fearsome to look at; he carried a noose... The shape was Yama, God of Death. He stood in silence, and gazed at the sleeping Satyavan.

Savitri looked up, and when she saw that a celestial had come near, her heart trembled with misery and with fear. She laid her husband's head on the green grass and stood up quickly: then she spoke, saying, "Who are you, divine one, and what is your mission to me?"

Yama replied: "You do love your husband; you are endued also with ascetic merit. I will therefore speak with you. I am the Monarch of Death. The days of this man, your husband, are now spent, and I have come to bind him and take him away."

Savitri responded by saying: "Wise sages have told me that your messengers carry mortals away. Why, then, mighty King, have you come here yourself?"

Yama replied: "This prince is of spotless heart; his virtues are without number; he is, indeed, an ocean of accomplishments. It would not be fitting to send messengers for him, so I have come here myself."

The face of Satyavan had grown ashen. Yama cast his noose and tore out from the prince's body the soul-form, which was no larger than a man's thumb; it was tightly bound and subdued.

So Satyavan lost his life; he stopped breathing; his body became unsightly; it was robbed of its lustre and deprived of its power to move.

Yama fettered the soul with tightness, and turned abruptly towards the south; silently and speedily he went on his way. Savitri followed him. Her heart was drowned in grief. She could not desert her beloved lord. She followed Yama, the Monarch of Death.

Yama said to her: "Turn back, Savitri. Do not follow me. Perform the funeral rites of your lord. Your allegiance to Satyavan has now come to an end: you are free from all wifely duties. Dare not to proceed further on this path."

But Savitri answered: "I must follow my husband whether he is carried or whether he goes of his own will. I have undergone great penance. I have observed my vow, and I cannot be turned back... I have already walked with you seven paces, and the sages have declared that one who walks seven paces with another becomes a companion. I must converse with you, I must speak and you must listen... I have attained the perfect life on earth by performing my vows and by reason of my devotion to my lord. It is not right that you should part me from my husband now, and prevent me from attaining bliss by saying that my allegiance to him has ended and another mode of life is opened to me."

Yama responded: "Turn back now... Your words are wise and pleasing; therefore, before you go, you can ask a favour of me and I will grant it. Except the soul of Satyavan, I will give you whatever you desire."

Savitri said: "Because my husband's father became blind, he was deprived of his kingdom. Restore his eyesight, mighty One."

Yama agreed and said: "The wish is granted. I will restore the vision of your father-in-law... But you have now grown faint on this difficult journey. Turn back, therefore, and your weariness will pass away."

Savitri responded: "How can I be weary when I am with my husband? The fate of my husband will be my fate also; I will follow him even to the place where you carry him...Hear me, Mighty One, whose friendship I cherish! It is a blessed thing to see a celestial; still more blessed is it to converse with one; the friendship of a god must bear great fruit."

Yama replied: "Your wisdom delights my heart. Therefore you can ask of me a second favour, except the life of your husband, and it will be granted to you."

So Savitri said: "May my wise and saintly father-in-law regain the kingdom he has lost. May he once again become the protector of his people."

Yama replied: "The wish is granted. The king will return to his people and be their wise protector... Turn back now, princess; your desire is fulfilled."

To this Savitri said: "All people must obey your decrees; you take away life in accordance with divine ordinances and not of your own will. Therefore you are called Yama – he that rules by decrees. Hear my words, Divine One. It is the duty of celestials to love all creatures and to award them according to their merit. The wicked are without holiness and devotion, but the saintly protect all creatures and show mercy even to their enemies."

Yama responded by saying: "Your wise words are like water to a thirsty soul. Therefore ask of me a third favour, except your husband's life, and it will be granted to you."

Savitri said: "My father, King Aswapati, has no son. Grant that a hundred sons may be born to him."

Yama replied: "A hundred sons will be born to your royal father. Your wish is granted... Now turn back, princess; you cannot come any further. Long is the path you have already travelled."

But Savitri would not give up. She said: "I have followed my husband and the way has not seemed long. Indeed, my heart desires to go on much further. Hear my words, Yama, as you proceed on your journey. You are great and wise and powerful; you deal equally with all human creatures; you are the lord of justice... One cannot trust oneself as one can trust a celestial; therefore, one seeks to win the friendship of a celestial. It is proper that one who seeks the friendship of a celestial should make answer to his words."

Yama responded: "No mortal has ever spoken to me as you have spoken. Indeed your words are pleasing, princess. I will grant you a fourth wish, except your husband's life, before you go."

Savitri said: "May a century of sons be born to my husband and me so that our race may endure. Grant me this, the fourth favour, Mighty One."

Then Yama said: "I grant to you a century of sons, princess; they will be wise and powerful and your race will endure... Be without weariness now, and turn back; you have come too far already."

Savitri replied: "Those who are pious must practise eternal morality, Yama. The pious uphold the universe. The pious hold communion with the pious only, and are never weary; the pious do good to others without ever expecting any reward. A good deed done to the righteous is never thrown away; such an act does not entail loss of dignity nor is any interest impaired. Indeed, the doing of good is the chief office of the righteous, and the righteous therefore are the true protectors of all."

To this Yama said: "The more you speak, the more I respect you, princess. You, who are so deeply devoted to your husband, you can now ask of me some incomparable favour."

So Savitri said: "Mighty One, bestower of favours, you have already promised what cannot be fulfilled unless my husband is restored to me; you have promised me a century of sons. Therefore, I ask you, Yama, to give me back Satyavan, my beloved, my lord. Without him, I am like one who is dead; without him, I have no desire for happiness; without him I have no longing even for Heaven; I will have no desire to prosper if my lord is snatched away; I cannot live without Satyavan. You have promised me sons, Yama, yet you take away my husband from my arms. Hear me and grant this favour: Let Satyavan be restored to life so that your decree may be fulfilled."

Eventually Yama replied: "So be it. With cheerful heart I now unbind your husband. He is free... Disease cannot afflict him again and he will prosper. Together you will both have a long life; you will live for four hundred years; you will have a century of sons and they will be kings, and their sons will be kings too."

Yama, the Lord of Death, then departed. And Savitri returned to the forest where her husband's body lay cold and pale; she sat on the ground and pillowed his head on her lap. Then Satyavan was given back his life... He looked at Savitri with eyes of love; he was like one who had returned from a long journey in a strange land. He said: "My sleep was long; why did you not wake me, my beloved?... Where is that Dark One who dragged me away?"

Savitri replied: "Yama has come and gone, and you have slept long, resting your head on my lap, and are now refreshed, blessed one. If you can rise up, let us now leave because the night is already dark..."

Satyavan rose up refreshed and strong. He looked round about and saw that he was in the middle of the forest.

Then he said: "Oh fair one, I came here to gather fruit for you, and while I cut down branches from the trees a pain afflicted me. I grew faint, I sank to the ground, I laid my head on your lap and fell into a deep sleep even whilst you embraced me. Then it seemed to me that I was enveloped in darkness, and that I saw someone... Was this a vision or a reality?"

Savitri responded: "The darkness deepens... I will tell you everything tomorrow... Now let us find our parents. The beasts of the night are coming; I hear their awesome voices; they tread the forest in glee; the howl of the jackal makes my heart afraid."

Satyavan said: "Darkness has covered the forest with fear; we cannot find the path by which to return home."

So Savitri said: "I will gather sticks and make a fire and we will wait here until daylight comes."

Satyavan replied: "My sickness has gone and I would gladly see my parents again. I have never before spent a night away from the hermitage. My mother and father are old, and I am their crutch. They will be afflicted with sorrow because we have not returned."

Satyavan lifted up his arms and wept, but Savitri dried his tears and said: "I have performed penances, I have given away in charity, I have offered up sacrifices, I have never uttered a falsehood. May your parents be protected by virtue of the power which I have obtained, and may you, my husband, be protected too."

Satyavan replied: "Beautiful one, let us now return to the hermitage."

Savitri raised up her despairing husband. Then she placed his left arm on her right shoulder and wound her right arm around his body, and they walked on together... After some time the moon came out and shone on their path.

Meanwhile Dyumatsena, the father of Satyavan, had regained his sight, and he went with his wife to search for his lost son, but had to return to the hermitage in despair. The sages comforted the weeping parents and said: "Savitri has practised great austerities, and there can be no doubt that Satyavan is still alive."

Finally Satyavan and Savitri reached the hermitage, and their own hearts and the hearts of their parents were freed from sorrow.

Then Savitri told of all that had taken place, and the sages said: "Oh chaste and illustrious lady, you have rescued the race of Dyumatsena, the foremost of kings, from the ocean of darkness."

The following morning messengers came to Dyumatsena and told him that the king who had deprived him of his kingdom was now dead, having fallen by the hand of his chief minister. All the people clamoured for their legitimate ruler. "Chariots are waiting for you, king. Therefore return to your kingdom," said the messengers.

So the king was restored to his kingdom, in accordance with the favour Savitri had obtained from Yama. And in time sons were born to her father. The gentle Savitri, because of her great devotion, had raised the family of her husband and her own father from misery to high fortune. She was the rescuer of all; the bringer of happiness and prosperity... He who hears the story of Savitri will never endure misery again.

The Rose-Beauty

IN OLDEN TIMES, when the camel was a horse dealer, the mouse a barber, the cuckoo a tailor, the tortoise a baker, and the ass still a servant, there was a miller who had a black cat. Besides this miller, there was a Padishah who had three daughters, aged respectively forty, thirty, and twenty years. The eldest went to the youngest and made her write a letter to her father in these terms:

"Dear father, one of my sisters is forty, the other thirty, and they have not yet married. Take notice that I will not wait so long before I get a husband."

The Padishah, on reading the letter, sent for his daughters and thus addressed them: "Here are a bow and arrow for each of you; go and shoot, and wherever your arrows fall, there you will find your future husbands."

Taking the weapons from their father, the three maidens went forth. The eldest shot first, and her arrow fell in the palace of the vezir's son; she was accordingly united to him. The second daughter's arrow fell in the palace of the son of the Sheikh-ul-Islam, and him she got for a husband. When the youngest shot, however, her arrow fell into the hut of a woodcutter. "That doesn't count," cried everybody; and she shot again. The second time the arrow fell in the same spot; and a third attempt met no better success.

The shah was wrathful with his daughter on account of her letter, and exclaimed: "You foolish creature, that serves you right. Your elder sisters have waited patiently and are rewarded. You, the youngest, have dared to write me that impertinent letter: you are justly punished. Take your woodcutter and be off with you." So the poor girl left her father's palace to be the wife of the woodcutter.

In the course of time a beautiful baby girl was born to them. The woodcutter's wife bitterly lamented the fact that her child must have so poor a home, but even while she wept, three wonderful fairies stepped through the wall of the hut into the dismal room where the child lay. Standing by her cot, each in turn stretched out a hand over the sleeping infant.

Said the first fairy: "Rose-Beauty shall she be called; and instead of tears, pearls shall she shed."

Said the second fairy: "When she smiles, roses shall blossom." Said the third: "Wherever her foot falls shall grass spring up!" Then the three disappeared as they had come.

Years passed away. The child grew and attained her twelfth year, developing such loveliness as none had ever seen before. To gaze once upon her was to be filled with love for her. When she smiled roses blossomed; when she wept pearls fell from her eyes, and grass grew wherever her feet trod. The fame of her beauty spread far and wide.

The mother of a certain prince heard of Rose-Beauty and resolved that this maiden and no other should become her son's bride. She called her son to her and told him that in the town was a maiden who smiled roses, wept pearls, and under whose feet grass grew; he must see her.

The fairies had already shown the maid to the prince in a dream, and thus kindled in him the fire of love; but before his mother he was shy and refused to seek the object of his passion. The sultana therefore insisted, and finally ordered a lady of the palace to accompany him on his quest. They entered the hut, explained the purpose of their visit, and in the name of Allah demanded the maiden for the Shahzada. The poor people were overcome with joy at their good fortune; they promised their daughter, and commenced preparations for her departure.

Now this palace-dame had a daughter, who somewhat resembled the Rose-Beauty, and she was displeased that the prince should marry a poor girl instead of her own daughter. Accordingly she concocted a scheme to deceive the people and bring about the prince's marriage to her own child. On the wedding-day she gave the woodcutter's daughter salt food to eat, and took a jug of water and a large basket and put them in the bridal coach wherein the Rose-Beauty, herself, and her daughter were about to set out for the palace.

On the way the maiden, complaining of thirst, asked for a drink of water. The palace-dame answered: "I shall give you no water unless you give me an eye in exchange." Nearly dying of thirst, the maiden took out one of her eyes and gave it to the cruel woman for a drink of water.

As they proceeded the torments of thirst again overcame the poor maiden, and again she asked for water. "I will give you drink, but only in exchange for your other eye," answered the woman. So great was her agony that the victim yielded her other eye. No sooner had the woman got it in her possession than she took the now sightless Rose-Beauty, bound her in the basket, and had her carried to the top of a mountain.

The woman now hastened to the palace and presented her daughter, clad in a gorgeous wedding garment, to the prince, saying: "Here is your bride." The marriage was accordingly celebrated with great festivity; but when the prince came to lift his wife's veil he saw that she was not the one revealed to him in his dream. As, however, she resembled the dream bride somewhat, he held his peace.

The prince knew that the maiden of his dream wept pearls, smiled roses, and that the grass grew under her feet; from this one, however, came neither pearls, roses, nor grass. He suspected more than ever that he had been deceived, but "I will soon find out," he thought to himself, and spoke no word on the subject to anyone.

Meanwhile the poor Rose-Beauty on the mountaintop wept and moaned, pearls rolling down her cheeks from her sightless eye-sockets until the basket in which she lay bound was filled to overflowing. A scavenger at work on the road heard the sounds of grief and cried out in fear: "Who is that, a spirit or a fairy?" The maiden answered: "Neither a spirit nor a fairy, but a human being like yourself."

The scavenger, reassured, approached the basket, opened it, and saw the blind girl and the pearls she had shed. He took her home to his miserable hovel, and being alone in the world, adopted her as his own child. But the maiden constantly bemoaned the loss of her eyes, and as she was always weeping, the man now had nothing else to do but gather the pearls she shed and go out and sell them. Time rolled on. In the palace was merriment, in the scavenger's hovel grief and pain. One day as the Rose-Beauty was sitting at the door, she smiled at some pleasant recollection, and forthwith a rose appeared. Said the maiden to the scavenger: "Father, here is a rose; take it to the prince's palace and say thou hast a rose of a rare kind to sell. When the palace dame appears, say it cannot be sold for money, but for a human eye." The man took the rose, went to the palace and cried aloud: "A rose for sale; the only one of its kind in the world."

Indeed, it was not the season for roses. The palace-dame, hearing the scavenger's cry, resolved to buy the rose for her daughter, thinking that when the prince saw the flower in his wife's possession his suspicions would be set at rest. Calling the poor man aside, she inquired the price of the rose. "Money cannot buy it," replied the scavenger, "but I will part with it for a human eye." Hereupon the woman produced one of the Rose-Beauty's eyes and gave it in exchange for the rose. Carrying the flower immediately to her daughter, she fixed it in her hair, and when the prince saw her he began to fancy that she might after all be the maiden the fairies had showed him in his dream, though he was by no means sure. He consoled himself with the thought that soon the matter would be cleared up.

The old man took the eye and gave it to the Rose-Beauty. Praising Allah, she fixed it in its place, and had the joy of being able to see quite well once more. In her newfound happiness the maiden smiled so much that ere long there were quite a number of roses. One of these she gave to the scavenger that he might go with it to the palace and secure her remaining eye. Scarcely had he arrived at the palace than the woman saw him with the rose and thought to herself: "All is coming right; the prince is already beginning to love my daughter. I will buy this other rose, and as his love strengthens he will soon forget the woodcutter's child." She called the scavenger and demanded the rose, which the man said could only be sold on the same terms as the first. The woman willingly gave him the other eye and hastened with the flower to her daughter, while the old man went home with his prize.

The Rose-Beauty, now in possession of both her eyes, was even lovelier than before. As now she smilingly took her walks abroad, roses and grass transformed the barren hillside into a veritable Eden. One day while the maiden was walking in the neighbourhood, the palace-dame saw her and was dismayed. What would be her daughter's fate if the truth became known? She inquired for the scavenger's dwelling, hastened to him, and frightened the old man out of his wits by accusing him of harbouring a witch. In his fright he asked the woman what he should do. "Ask her about her talisman," she advised; "then I can soon settle the matter." So when the girl came in, the first thing her foster-father did was to ask her how it was that, being human, she could work such magic.

Suspecting no harm, she informed him that at her birth the fairies gave her a talisman whereby she could bring forth pearls, roses and grass as long as the talisman lived. "What is your talisman?" inquired the old man. "A young stag that lives on the mountain; when it dies I must die too," answered the maiden.

Next day the palace-dame came secretly to the scavenger, and learned from him what the talisman was. With this precious knowledge she hastened joyfully home, imparted the information to her daughter, and advised her to ask the prince for the stag. Without delay the young wife complained to her lord of indisposition, saying she must have the heart of a certain mountain stag to eat. The prince sent out his hunters, who ere long returned with the animal, slaughtered it and took out its heart, which was cooked for the pretended invalid.

At that same instant the Rose-Beauty also died. The scavenger buried her, and mourned for her long and sincerely.

Now in the stag's heart was a red coral, that escaped observation; and when the prince's wife was eating, it fell to the floor and rolled under the stairs.

A year later there was born to the prince a daughter who wept pearls, smiled roses, and under whose tiny feet grass grew. When the prince saw that his child was a Rose-Beauty, he easily persuaded himself that his wife was really the right one. But one night in a dream the Rose-Beauty appeared to him and said: "Oh, Prince, my own bridegroom, my soul is under the palace stairs, my body in the cemetery, thy daughter is my daughter, my talisman the little coral."

As soon as the Prince awoke he went to the stairs and searched for and found the coral. He carried it to his room and laid it on the table. When his little daughter came in she took up the coral, and hardly had her fingers touched it than both vanished. The three fairies conveyed the child to her mother, the Rose-Beauty, who, as the coral fell into her mouth, awakened to a new life.

The prince, in his restless state, went to the cemetery. Behold! There he found the Rose-Beauty of his dreams with his child in her arms. They cordially embraced, and as mother and daughter wept for joy, pearls streamed from the eyes of both; when they smiled roses blossomed, and grass sprang up wherever their feet touched.

The palace-dame and her daughter were severely punished, and the old scavenger was invited to live with the Rose-Beauty and the prince at their palace. The reunited lovers had a magnificent wedding feast and their happiness lasted forever.

THE CHOSEN ONES

Introduction

FROM ZANZIBAR COMES the story of 'The Physician's Son and the King of Snakes'. Its hero Hasseeboo struggles to find his niche in life. Attempts to train as a tailor, a silversmith and several other trades end in failure. A bid to follow his late father into medicine fares no better. His last resort is work with the woodcutters in the forest but he barely lasts a week there before he's distracted by a hole he finds full of honey. His workmates take the honey and then leave him to his fate at the bottom. Finding a crack in the wall, he enters what turns out to be the kingdom of the snakes, and forges a firm friendship with its king. The 'chosen ones' in folktales may be valiant warriors or handsome princes but they're as likely to be 'chosen' on more quirky lines. They may have extraordinary strengths and skills – the giants of Norse legend could construct mountains – but Hasseeboo's only superpower is generosity of heart. The ultimate hero, Hercules is compelled to carry out his famous 'labours' as a punishment for his pride. It is in his moral weakness that he's forced to find his strength.

The Labour of Hercules

Before the birth of Hercules, Jupiter had explained in the council of the gods that the first descendant of Perseus should be the ruler of all the others of his race. This honour was intended for the son of Perseus and Alcmene; but Juno was jealous and brought it about that Eurystheus, who was also a descendant of Perseus, should be born before Theseus. So Eurystheus became king in Mycene, and the later-born Hercules remained inferior to him.

Now Eurystheus watched with anxiety the rising fame of his young relative, and called his subject to him, demanding that he carry through certain great tasks or labours. When Hercules did not immediately obey, Jupiter himself sent word to him that he should fulfill his service to the King of Greece.

Nevertheless the hero son of a god could not make up his mind easily to render service to a mere mortal. So he travelled to Delphi and questioned the oracle as to what he should do. This was the answer:

> *The overlordship of Eurystheus will be qualified on condition that Hercules perform ten labours that Eurystheus shall assign him. When this is done, Hercules shall be numbered among the immortal gods.*

Hereupon Hercules fell into deep trouble. To serve a man of less importance than himself hurt his dignity and self-esteem; but Jupiter would not listen to his complaints.

The First Labour

The first labour that Eurystheus assigned to Hercules was to bring him the skin of the Nemean lion. This monster dwelt on the mountain of Peloponnesus, in the forest between Kleona and Nemea, and could be wounded by no weapons made of man. Some said he was the son of the giant Typhon and the snake Echidna; others that he had dropped down from the moon to the earth.

Hercules set out on his journey and came to Kleona, where a poor labourer, Molorchus, received him hospitably. He met the latter just as he was about to offer a sacrifice to Jupiter.

"Good man," said Hercules, "let the animal live thirty days longer; then, if I return, offer it to Jupiter, my deliverer, and if I do not return, offer it as a funeral sacrifice to me, the hero who has attained immortality."

So Hercules continued on his way, his quiver of arrows over his shoulder, his bow in one hand, and in the other a club made from the trunk of a wild olive tree which he had passed on Mount Helicon and pulled up by the roots. When he at last entered the Nemean wood, he looked carefully in every direction in order that he might catch sight of the monster lion before the lion should see him. It was midday, and nowhere could he discover any trace of the lion or any path that seemed to lead to his lair. He met no man in the field or in the forest: fear held them all shut up in their distant dwellings. The whole afternoon he wandered through the thick undergrowth, determined to test his strength just as soon as he should encounter the lion.

At last, toward evening, the monster came through the forest, returning from his trap in a deep fissure of the earth.

He was saturated with blood: head, mane and breast were reeking, and his great tongue was licking his jaws. The hero, who saw him coming long before he was near, took refuge in a thicket and waited until the lion approached; then with his arrow he shot him in the side. But the shot did not pierce his flesh; instead it flew back as if it had struck stone, and fell on the mossy earth.

Then the animal raised his bloody head; looked around in every direction, and in fierce anger showed his ugly teeth. Raising his head, he exposed his heart, and immediately Hercules let fly another arrow, hoping to pierce him through the lungs. Again the arrow did not enter the flesh, but fell at the feet of the monster.

Hercules took a third arrow, while the lion, casting his eyes to the side, watched him. His whole neck swelled with anger; he roared, and his back was bent like a bow. He sprang towards his enemy; but Hercules threw the arrow and cast off the lion skin in which he was clothed with the left hand, while with the right he swung his club over the head of the beast and gave him such a blow on the neck that, all ready to spring as the lion was, he fell back, and came to a stand on trembling legs, with shaking head. Before he could take another breath, Hercules was upon him.

Throwing down his bow and quiver, that he might be entirely unencumbered, he approached the animal from behind, threw his arm around his neck and strangled him. Then for a long time he sought in vain to strip the fallen animal of his hide. It yielded to no weapon or no stone. At last the idea occurred to him of tearing it with the animal's own claws, and this method immediately succeeded.

Later he prepared for himself a coat of mail out of the lion's skin, and from the neck, a new helmet; but for the present he was content to don his own costume and weapons, and with the lion's skin over his arm took his way back to Tirynth.

The Second Labour

The second labour consisted in destroying a hydra. This monster dwelt in the swamp of Lerna, but came occasionally over the country, destroying herds and laying waste the fields. The hydra was an enormous creature – a serpent with nine heads, of which eight were mortal and one immortal.

Hercules set out with high courage for this fight. He mounted his chariot, and his beloved nephew Iolaus, the son of his stepbrother Iphicles, who for a long time had been his inseparable companion, sat by his side, guiding the horses; and so they sped towards Lerna.

At last the hydra was visible on a hill by the springs of Amymone, where its lair was found. Here Iolaus left the horses stand. Hercules leaped from the chariot and sought with burning arrows to drive the many-headed serpent from its hiding place. It came forth hissing, its nine heads raised and swaying like the branches of a tree in a storm.

Undismayed, Hercules approached it, seized it, and held it fast. But the snake wrapped itself around one of his feet. Then he began with his sword to cut off its heads. But this looked like an endless task, for no sooner had he cut off one head than two grew in its place. At the same time an enormous crab came to the help of the hydra and began biting the hero's foot. Killing this with his club, he called to Iolaus for help.

The latter had lighted a torch, set fire to a portion of the nearby wood, and with brands therefrom touched the serpent's newly growing heads and prevented them from living. In this way the hero was at last master of the situation and was able to cut off even the head of the hydra that could not be killed. This he buried deep in the ground and rolled a heavy stone over the place. The body of the hydra he cut into half, dipping his arrows in the blood, which was poisonous.

From that time the wounds made by the arrows of Hercules were fatal.

The Third Labour

The third demand of Eurystheus was that Hercules bring to him alive the hind Cerynitis. This was a noble animal, with horns of gold and feet of iron. She lived on a hill in Arcadia, and was one of the five hinds which the goddess Diana had caught on her first hunt. This one, of all the five, was permitted to run loose again in the woods, for it was decreed by fate that Hercules should one day hunt her.

For a whole year Hercules pursued her; came at last to the river Ladon; and there captured the hind, not far from the city Oenon, on the mountains of Diana. But he knew of no way of becoming master of the animal without wounding her, so he lamed her with an arrow and then carried her over his shoulder through Arcadia.

Here he met Diana herself with Apollo, who scolded him for wishing to kill the animal that she had held sacred, and was about to take it from him.

"Impiety did not move me, great goddess," said Hercules in his own defence, "but only the direst necessity. How otherwise could I hold my own against Eurystheus?"

And thus he softened the anger of the goddess and brought the animal to Mycene.

The Fourth Labour

Then Hercules set out on his fourth undertaking. It consisted in bringing alive to Mycene a boar which, likewise sacred to Diana, was laying waste the country around the mountain of Erymanthus.

On his wanderings in search of this adventure he came to the dwelling of Pholus, the son of Silenus. Like all centaurs, Pholus was half man and half horse. He received his guest with hospitality and set before him grilled meat, while he himself ate raw. But Hercules, not satisfied with this, wished also to have something good to drink.

"Dear guest," said Pholus, "there is a cask in my cellar; but it belongs to all the centaurs jointly, and I hesitate to open it because I know how little they welcome guests."

"Open it with good courage," answered Hercules, "I promise to defend you against all displeasure."

As it happened, the cask of wine had been given to the centaurs by Bacchus, the god of wine, with the command that they should not open it until, after four centuries, Hercules should appear in their midst.

Pholus went to the cellar and opened the wonderful cask. But scarcely had he done so when the centaurs caught the perfume of the rare old wine, and, armed with stones and pine clubs, surrounded the cave of Pholus. The first who tried to force their way in Hercules drove back with brands he seized from the fire. The rest he pursued with bow and arrow, driving them back to Malea, where lived the good centaur, Chiron, Hercules's old friend. To him his brother centaurs had fled for protection.

But Hercules still continued shooting, and sent an arrow through the arm of an old centaur, which unhappily went quite through and fell on Chiron's knee, piercing the flesh. Then for the first time Hercules recognized his friend of former days, ran to him in great distress, pulled out the arrow, and lay healing ointment on the wound, as the wise Chiron himself had taught him. But the wound, filled with the poison of the hydra, could not be healed; so the centaur was carried into his cave. There he wished to die in the arms of his friend. Vain wish! The poor centaur had forgotten that he was immortal, and though wounded would not die.

Then Hercules with many tears bade farewell to his old teacher and promised to send to him, no matter at what price, the great deliverer, Death. And we know that he kept his word.

When Hercules from the pursuit of the other centaurs returned to the dwelling of Pholus he found him also dead. He had drawn the deadly arrow from the lifeless body of one centaur, and while he was wondering how so small a thing could do such great damage, the poisoned arrow slipped through his fingers and pierced his foot, killing him instantly. Hercules was very sad, and buried his body reverently beneath the mountain, which from that day was called Pholoë.

Then Hercules continued his hunt for the boar, drove him with cries out of the thick of the woods, pursued him into a deep snow field, bound the exhausted animal, and brought him, as he had been commanded, alive to Mycene.

The Fifth Labour

Thereupon King Eurystheus sent him upon the fifth labour, which was one little worthy of a hero. It was to clean the stables of Augeas in a single day.

Augeas was king in Elis and had great herds of cattle. These herds were kept, according to the custom, in a great inclosure before the palace. Three thousand cattle were housed there, and as the stables had not been cleaned for many years, so much manure had accumulated that it seemed an insult to ask Hercules to clean them in one day.

When the hero stepped before King Augeas and without telling him anything of the demands of Eurystheus, pledged himself to the task, the latter measured the noble form in the lion-skin and could hardly refrain from laughing when he thought of so worthy a warrior undertaking so menial a task. But he said to himself: "Necessity has driven many a brave man; perhaps this one wishes to enrich himself through me. That will help him little. I can promise him a large reward if he cleans out the stables, for he can in one day clear little enough." Then he spoke confidently:

"Listen, O stranger. If you clean all of my stables in one day, I will give over to you the tenth part of all my possessions in cattle."

Hercules accepted the offer, and the king expected to see him begin to shovel. But Hercules, after he had called the son of Augeas to witness the agreement, tore the foundations away from one side of the stables; directed to it by means of a canal the streams of Alpheus and Peneus that flowed near by; and let the waters carry away the filth through another opening. So he accomplished the menial work without stooping to anything unworthy of an immortal.

When Augeas learned that this work had been done in the service of Eurystheus, he refused the reward and said that he had not promised it; but he declared himself ready to have the question settled in court. When the judges were assembled, Phyleus, commanded by Hercules to appear, testified against his father, and explained how he had agreed to offer Hercules a reward. Augeas did not wait for the decision; he grew angry and commanded his son as well as the stranger to leave his kingdom instantly.

The Sixth Labour

Hercules now returned with new adventures to Eurystheus; but the latter would not give him credit for the task because Hercules had demanded a reward for his labour. He sent the hero forth upon a sixth adventure, commanding him to drive away the Stymphalides. These were monster birds of prey, as large as cranes, with iron feathers, beaks and claws. They lived on the banks of Lake Stymphalus in Arcadia, and had the power of using their feathers as arrows and piercing with their beaks even bronze coats of mail. Thus they brought destruction to both animals and men in all the surrounding country.

After a short journey Hercules, accustomed to wandering, arrived at the lake, which was thickly shaded by a wood. Into this wood a great flock of the birds had flown for fear of being robbed by wolves. The hero stood undecided when he saw the frightful crowd, not knowing how he could become master over so many enemies. Then he felt a light touch on his shoulder, and glancing behind him saw the tall figure of the goddess Minerva, who gave into his hands two mighty brass rattles made by Vulcan. Telling him to use these to drive away the Stymphalides, she disappeared.

Hercules mounted a hill near the lake, and began frightening the birds by the noise of the rattles. The Stymphalides could not endure the awful noise and flew, terrified, out of the forest. Then Hercules seized his bow and sent arrow after arrow in pursuit of them, shooting many as they flew. Those who were not killed left the lake and never returned.

The Seventh Labour

King Minos of Crete had promised Neptune (Poseidon), god of the sea, to offer to him whatever animal should first come up out of the water, for he declared he had no animal that was worthy for so high a sacrifice. Therefore the god caused a very beautiful ox to rise out of the sea. But the king was so taken with the noble appearance of the animal that he secretly placed it among his own herds and offered another to Neptune. Angered by this, the god had caused the animal to become mad, and it was bringing great destruction to the island of Crete. To capture this animal, master it, and bring it before Eurystheus was the seventh labour of Hercules.

When the hero came to Crete and with this intention stepped before Minos, the king was not a little pleased over the prospect of ridding the island of the bull, and he himself helped Hercules to capture the raging animal. Hercules approached the dreadful monster without fear, and so thoroughly did he master him that he rode home on the animal the whole way to the sea.

With this work Eurystheus was pleased, and after he had regarded the animal for a time with pleasure, set it free. No longer under Hercules's management, the ox became wild again, wandered through all Laconia and Arcadia, crossed over the isthmus to Marathon in Attica and devastated the country there as formerly on the island of Crete. Later it was given to the hero Theseus to become master over him.

The Eighth Labour

The eighth labour of Hercules was to bring the mares of the Thracian Diomede to Mycene. Diomede was a son of Mars and ruler of the Bistonians, a very warlike people. He had mares so wild and strong that they had to be fastened with iron chains. Their fodder was chiefly hay; but strangers who had the misfortune to come into the city were thrown before them, their flesh serving the animals as food.

When Hercules arrived the first thing he did was to seize the inhuman king himself and after he had overpowered the keepers, throw him before his own mares. With this food the animals were satisfied and Hercules was able to drive them to the sea.

But the Bistonians followed him with weapons, and Hercules was forced to turn and fight them. He gave the horses into the keeping of his beloved companion Abderus, the son of Mercury, and while Hercules was away the animals grew hungry again and devoured their keeper.

Hercules, returning, was greatly grieved over this loss, and later founded a city in honour of Abderus, naming it after his lost friend. For the present he was content to master the mares and drive them without further mishap to Eurystheus.

The latter consecrated the horses to Juno. Their descendants were very powerful, and the great king Alexander of Macedonia rode one of them.

The Ninth Labour

Returning from a long journey, the hero undertook an expedition against the Amazons in order to finish the ninth adventure and bring to King Eurystheus the sword belt of the Amazon Hippolyta.

The Amazons inhabited the region of the river Thermodon and were a race of strong women who followed the occupations of men. From their children they selected only such as were girls. United in an army, they waged great wars. Their queen, Hippolyta, wore, as a sign of her leadership, a girdle which the goddess of war had given her as a present.

Hercules gathered his warrior companions together into a ship, sailed after many adventures into the Black Sea and at last into the mouth of the river Thermodon, and the harbour of the Amazon city Themiscira. Here the queen of the Amazons met him.

The lordly appearance of the hero flattered her pride, and when she heard the object of his visit, she promised him the belt. But Juno, the relentless enemy of Hercules, assuming the form of an Amazon, mingled among the others and spread the news that a stranger was about to lead away their queen. Then the Amazons fought with the warriors of Hercules, and the best fighters of them attacked the hero and gave him a hard battle.

The first who began fighting with him was called, because of her swiftness, Aëlla, or Bride of the Wind; but she found in Hercules a swifter opponent, was forced to yield and was in her swift flight overtaken by him and vanquished. A second fell at the first attack; then Prothoë, the third, who had come off victor in seven duels, also fell. Hercules laid low eight others, among them three hunter companions of Diana, who, although formerly always certain with their weapons, today failed in their aim, and vainly covering themselves with their shields fell before the arrows of the hero. Even Alkippe fell, who had sworn to live her whole life unmarried: the vow she kept, but not her life.

After even Melanippe, the brave leader of the Amazons, was made captive, all the rest took to wild flight, and Hippolyta the queen handed over the sword belt which she had promised even before the fight. Hercules took it as ransom and set Melanippe free.

The Tenth Labour

When the hero laid the sword belt of Queen Hippolyta at the feet of Eurystheus, the latter gave him no rest, but sent him out immediately to procure the cattle of the giant Geryone. The latter dwelt on an island in the midst of the sea, and possessed a herd of beautiful red-brown cattle, which were guarded by another giant and a two-headed dog.

Geryone himself was enormous, had three bodies, three heads, six arms and six feet. No son of earth had ever measured his strength against him, and Hercules realized exactly how many preparations were necessary for this heavy undertaking. As everybody knew, Geryone's father, who bore the name 'Gold-Sword' because of his riches, was king of all Iberia (Spain). Besides Geryone he had three brave giant sons who fought for him; and each son had a mighty army of soldiers under his command. For these very reasons had Eurystheus given the task to Hercules, for he hoped that his hated existence would at last be ended in a war in such a country. Yet Hercules set out on this undertaking no more dismayed than on any previous expedition.

He gathered together his army on the island of Crete, which he had freed from wild animals, and landed first in Libya. Here he met the giant Antaeus, whose strength was renewed as often as he touched the earth. He also freed Libya of birds of prey; for he hated wild animals and wicked men because he saw in all of them the image of the overbearing and unjust lord whom he so long had served.

After long wandering through desert country he came at last to a fruitful land, through which great streams flowed. Here he founded a city of vast size, which he named Hecatompylos (City of a Hundred Gates). Then at last he reached the Atlantic Ocean and planted the two mighty pillars which bear his name.

The sun burned so fiercely that Hercules could bear it no longer; he raised his eyes to heaven and with raised bow threatened the sun-god. Apollo wondered at his courage and lent him for his further journeys the bark in which he himself was accustomed to lie from sunset to sunrise. In this Hercules sailed to Iberia.

Here he found the three sons of Gold-Sword with three great armies camping near each other; but he killed all the leaders and plundered the land. Then he sailed to the island Erythia, where Geryone dwelt with his herds.

As soon as the two-headed dog knew of his approach he sprang towards him; but Hercules struck him with his club and killed him. He killed also the giant herdsman who came to the help of the dog. Then he hurried away with the cattle.

But Geryone overtook him and there was a fierce struggle. Juno herself offered to assist the giant; but Hercules shot her with an arrow deep in the heart, and the goddess, wounded, fled. Even the threefold body of the giant which ran together in the region of the stomach, felt the might of the deadly arrows and was forced to yield.

With glorious adventures Hercules continued his way home, driving the cattle across country through Iberia and Italy. At Rhegium in lower Italy one of his oxen got away and swam across the strait to Sicily. Immediately Hercules drove the other cattle into the water and swam, holding one by the horns, to Sicily. Then the hero pursued his way without misfortune through Italy, Illyria and Thrace to Greece.

Hercules had now accomplished ten labours; but Eurystheus was still unsatisfied and there were two more tasks to be undertaken.

The Eleventh Labour

At the celebration of the marriage of Jupiter and Juno, when all the gods were bringing their wedding gifts to the happy pair, Mother Earth did not wish to be left out. So she caused to spring forth on the western borders of the great world-sea a many-branched tree full of golden apples. Four maidens called the Hesperides, daughters of Night, were the guardians of this sacred garden, and with them watched the hundred-headed dragon, Ladon, whose father was Phorkys, the parent of many monsters. Sleep came never to the eyes of this dragon and a fearful hissing sound warned one of his presence, for each of his hundred throats had a different voice. From this monster, so was the command of Eurystheus, should Hercules seize the golden apples.

The hero set out on his long and adventurous journey and placed himself in the hands of blind chance, for he did not know where the Hesperides dwelt.

He went first to Thessaly, where dwelt the giant Termerus, who with his skull knocked to death every traveller that he met; but on the mighty cranium of Hercules the head of the giant himself was split open.

Farther on the hero came upon another monster in his way – Cycnus, the son of Mars and Pyrene. He, when asked concerning the garden of the Hesperides, instead of answering, challenged the wanderer to a duel, and was beaten by Hercules. Then appeared Mars, the god of war himself, to avenge the death of his son; and Hercules was forced to fight with him. But Jupiter did not wish that his sons should shed blood, and sent his lightning bolt to separate the two.

Then Hercules continued his way through Illyria, hastened over the river Eridanus, and came to the nymphs of Jupiter and Themis, who dwelt on the banks of the stream. To these Hercules put his question.

"Go to the old river god Nereus," was their answer. "He is a seer and knows all things. Surprise him while he sleeps and bind him; then he will be forced to tell you the right way."

Hercules followed this advice and became master of the river god, although the latter, according to his custom, assumed many different forms. Hercules would not let him go until he had learned in what locality he could find the golden apples of the Hesperides.

Informed of this, he went on his way toward Libya and Egypt. Over the latter land ruled Busiris, the son of Neptune and Lysianassa. To him during the period of a nine-year famine a prophet had borne the oracular message that the land would again bear fruit if a stranger were sacrificed once a year to Jupiter. In gratitude Busiris made a beginning with the priest himself. Later he found great pleasure in the custom and killed all strangers who came to Egypt. So Hercules was seized and placed on the altar of Jupiter. But he broke the chains which bound him, and killed Busiris and his son and the priestly herald.

With many adventures the hero continued his way, set free, as has been told elsewhere, Prometheus, the Titan, who was bound to the Caucasus Mountains, and came at last to the place where Atlas stood carrying the weight of the heavens on his shoulders. Near him grew the tree which bore the golden apples of the Hesperides.

Prometheus had advised the hero not to attempt himself to make the robbery of the golden fruit, but to send Atlas on the errand. The giant offered to do this if Hercules would support the heavens while he went. This Hercules consented to do, and Atlas set out. He put the dragon to sleep, who lived beneath the tree and killed him. Then with a trick he got the better of the keepers, and returned happily to Hercules with the three apples which he had plucked.

"But," he said, "I have now found out how it feels to be relieved of the heavy burden of the heavens. I will not carry them any longer." Then he threw the apples down at the feet of the hero, and left him standing with the unaccustomed, awful weight upon his shoulders.

Hercules had to think of a trick in order to get away. "Let me," he said to the giant, "just make a coil of rope to bind around my head, so that the frightful weight will not cause my forehead to give way."

Atlas found this new demand reasonable, and consented to take over the burden again for a few minutes. But the deceiver was at last deceived, and Hercules picked up the apples from the ground and set out on his way back. He carried the apples to Eurystheus, who, since his object of getting rid of the hero had not been accomplished, gave them back to Hercules as a present. The latter laid them on the altar of Minerva; but the goddess, knowing that it was contrary to the divine wishes to carry away this sacred fruit, returned the apples to the garden of the Hesperides.

The Twelfth Labour

Instead of destroying his hated enemy the labours which Eurystheus had imposed upon Hercules had only strengthened the hero in the fame for which fate had selected him. He had become the protector of all the wronged upon earth, and the boldest adventurer among mortals.

But the last labour, he was to undertake in the region in which his hero strength – so the impious king hoped – would not accompany him. This was a fight with the dark powers of the Underworld. He was to bring forth from Hades Cerberus, the dog of Hell. This animal had three heads with frightful jaws, from which poison incessantly flowed. A dragon's tail hung from his body, and the hair of his head and of his back formed hissing, coiling serpents.

To prepare himself for this fearful journey Hercules went to the city of Eleusis, in Attic territory, where, from a wise priest, he received secret instruction in the things of the upper and lower world, and where also he received pardon for the murder of the centaur.

Then, with strength to meet the horrors of the Underworld, Hercules travelled on to Peloponnesus, and to the Laconian city of Taenarus, which contained the opening to the lower world. Here, accompanied by Mercury, he descended through a cleft in the earth, and came to the entrance of the city of King Pluto. The shades which sadly wandered back and forth before the gates of the city took flight as soon as they caught sight of flesh and blood in the form of a living man. Only the Gorgon Medusa and the spirit of Meleager remained. The former Hercules wished to overthrow with his sword, but Mercury touched him on the arm and told him that the souls of the departed were only empty shadow pictures and could not be wounded by mortal weapons.

With the soul of Meleager the hero chatted in friendly fashion, and received from him loving messages for the Upper World. Still nearer to the gates of Hades, Hercules caught sight of his friends Theseus and Pirithous. When both saw the friendly form of Hercules they stretched beseeching hands towards him, trembling with the hope that through his strength they might again reach the Upper World. Hercules grasped Theseus by the hand, freed him from his chains and raised him from the ground. A second attempt to free Pirithous did not succeed, for the ground opened beneath his feet.

At the gate of the City of the Dead stood King Pluto, and denied entrance to Hercules. But with an arrow the hero shot the god in the shoulder, so that he feared the mortal; and when Hercules then asked whether he might lead away the dog of Hades he did no longer oppose him. But he imposed the condition that Hercules should become master of Cerberus without using any weapons. So the hero set out, protected only with cuirass and the lion skin.

He found the dog camping near the dwelling of Acheron, and without paying any attention to the bellowing of the three heads, which was like the echo of fearful resounding thunder, he seized the dog by the legs, put his arms around his neck, and would not let him go, although the dragon tail of the animal bit him in the cheek.

He held the neck of Cerberus firm, and did not let go until he was really master of the monster. Then he raised it, and through another opening of Hades returned in happiness to his own country. When the dog of Hades saw the light of day he was afraid and began to spit poison, from which poisonous plants sprung up out of the earth. Hercules brought the monster in chains to Tirynth, and led it before the astonished Eurystheus, who could not believe his eyes.

Now at last the king doubted whether he could ever rid himself of the hated son of Jupiter. He yielded to his fate and dismissed the hero, who led the dog of Hades back to his owner in the lower world.

Thus Hercules after all his labours was at last set free from the service of Eurystheus, and returned to Thebes.

The Stealing of Helen

THIS HAPPY TIME did not last long, and Telemachus was still a baby, when war arose, so great and mighty and marvellous as had never been known in the world. Far across the sea that lies on the east of Greece, there dwelt the rich King Priam. His town was called Troy, or Ilios, and it stood on a hill near the seashore, where are the straits of Hellespont, between Europe and Asia; it was a great city surrounded by strong walls, and its ruins are still standing. The kings could make merchants who passed through the straits pay toll to them, and they had allies in Thrace, a part of Europe opposite Troy, and Priam was chief of all princes on his side of the sea, as Agamemnon was chief king in Greece. Priam had many beautiful things; he had a vine made of gold, with golden leaves and clusters, and he had the swiftest horses, and many strong and brave sons; the strongest and bravest was named Hector, and the youngest and most beautiful was named Paris.

There was a prophecy that Priam's wife would give birth to a burning torch, so, when Paris was born, Priam sent a servant to carry the baby into a wild wood on Mount Ida, and leave him to die or be eaten by wolves and wild cats. The servant left the child, but a shepherd found him, and brought him up as his own son. The boy became as beautiful for a boy as Helen was for a girl, and was the best runner, and hunter, and archer among the country people. He was loved by the beautiful Oenone, a nymph – that is, a kind of fairy – who dwelt in a cave among the woods of Ida. The Greeks and Trojans believed in these days that such fair nymphs haunted all beautiful woodland places, and the mountains, and wells, and had crystal palaces, like mermaids, beneath the waves of the sea. These fairies were not mischievous, but gentle and kind. Sometimes they married mortal men, and Oenone was the bride of Paris, and hoped to keep him for her own all the days of his life.

It was believed that she had the magical power of healing wounded men, however sorely they were hurt. Paris and Oenone lived most happily together in the forest; but one day, when the servants of Priam had driven off a beautiful bull that was in the herd of Paris, he left the hills to seek it, and came into the town of Troy. His mother, Hecuba, saw him, and looking at him closely, perceived that he wore a ring which she had tied round her baby's neck when he was taken away from her soon after his birth. Then Hecuba, beholding him so beautiful, and knowing him to be her son, wept for joy, and they all forgot the prophecy that he would be a burning torch of fire, and Priam gave him a house like those of his brothers, the Trojan princes.

The fame of beautiful Helen reached Troy, and Paris quite forgot unhappy Oenone, and must needs go to see Helen for himself. Perhaps he meant to try to win her for his wife, before her marriage. But sailing was little understood in these times, and the water was wide, and men were often driven for years out of their course, to Egypt, and Africa, and far away into the unknown seas, where fairies lived in enchanted islands, and cannibals dwelt in caves of the hills.

Paris came much too late to have a chance of marrying Helen; however, he was determined to see her, and he made his way to her palace beneath the mountain Taygetus, beside the clear swift river Eurotas. The servants came out of the hall when they heard the sound of wheels and horses' feet, and some of them took the horses to the stables, and tilted the chariots against the gateway, while others led Paris into the hall, which shone like the sun with gold and silver. Then Paris and his companions were led to the baths, where they were bathed, and clad in new clothes, mantles of white, and robes of purple, and next they were brought before King Menelaus, and he welcomed them kindly, and meat was set before them, and wine in cups of gold. While they were talking, Helen came forth from her fragrant chamber, like a Goddess, her maidens following her, and carrying for her an ivory distaff with violet-coloured wool, which she span as she sat, and heard Paris tell how far he had travelled to see her who was so famous for her beauty even in countries far away.

Then Paris knew that he had never seen, and never could see, a lady so lovely and gracious as Helen as she sat and span, while the red drops fell and vanished from the ruby called the Star; and Helen knew that among all the princes in the world there was none so beautiful as Paris. Now some say that Paris, by art magic, put on the appearance of Menelaus, and asked Helen to come sailing with him, and that she, thinking he was her husband, followed him, and he carried her across the wide waters of Troy, away from her lord and her one beautiful little daughter, the child Hermione. And others say that the Gods carried Helen herself off to Egypt, and that they made in her likeness a beautiful ghost, out of flowers and sunset clouds, whom Paris bore to Troy, and this they did to cause war between Greeks and Trojans. Another story is that Helen and her bower maiden and her jewels were seized by force, when Menelaus was out hunting. It is only certain that Paris and Helen did cross the seas together, and that Menelaus and little Hermione were left alone in the melancholy palace beside the Eurotas. Penelope, we know for certain, made no excuses for her beautiful cousin, but hated her as the cause of her own sorrows and of the deaths of thousands of men in war, for all the Greek princes were bound by their oath to fight for Menelaus against anyone who injured him and stole his wife away. But Helen was very unhappy in Troy, and blamed herself as bitterly as all the other women blamed her, and most of all Oenone, who had been the love of Paris. The men were much more kind to Helen, and were determined to fight to the death rather than lose the sight of her beauty among them.

The news of the dishonour done to Menelaus and to all the princes of Greece ran through the country like fire through a forest. East and west and south and north went the news: to kings in their castles on the hills, and beside the rivers and on cliffs above the sea. The cry came to ancient Nestor of the white beard at Pylos, Nestor who had reigned over two generations of men, who had fought against the wild folk of the hills, and remembered the strong Heracles, and Eurytus of the black bow that sang before the day of battle.

The cry came to black-bearded Agamemnon, in his strong town called 'golden Mycenae', because it was so rich; it came to the people in Thisbe, where the wild doves haunt; and it came to rocky Pytho, where is the sacred temple of Apollo and the maid who prophesies. It came to Ajax, the tallest and strongest of men, in his little isle of Salamis; and to Diomedes of the loud war cry, the bravest of warriors, who held Argos and Tiryns of the black walls of huge stones, that are still standing. The summons came to the western islands and to Odysseus in Ithaca, and even far south to the great island of Crete of the hundred cities, where Idomeneus ruled in Knossos; Idomeneus, whose ruined palace may still be seen with the throne of the king, and pictures painted on the walls, and the King's own draught-board of gold and silver, and hundreds of tablets of clay, on which are written the lists of royal treasures. Far north went the news to Pelasgian Argos, and Hellas, where the people of Peleus dwelt, the Myrmidons; but Peleus was too old to fight, and his boy, Achilles, dwelt far away, in the island of Scyros, dressed as a girl, among the daughters of King Lycomedes. To many another town and to a hundred islands went the bitter news of approaching war, for all princes knew that their honour and their oaths compelled them to gather their spearmen, and bowmen, and slingers from the fields and the fishing, and to make ready their ships, and meet King Agamemnon in the harbour of Aulis, and cross the wide sea to besiege Troy town.

Now the story is told that Odysseus was very unwilling to leave his island and his wife Penelope, and little Telemachus; while Penelope had no wish that he should pass into danger, and into the sight of Helen of the fair hands. So it is said that when two of the princes came to summon Odysseus, he pretended to be mad, and went ploughing the sea sand with oxen, and sowing the sand with salt. Then the prince Palamedes took the baby Telemachus from the arms of his nurse, Eurycleia, and laid him in the line of the furrow, where the ploughshare would strike him and kill him. But Odysseus turned the plough aside, and they cried that he was not mad, but sane, and he must keep his oath, and join the fleet at Aulis, a long voyage for him to sail, round the stormy southern Cape of Maleia.

Whether this tale be true or not, Odysseus did go, leading twelve black ships, with high beaks painted red at prow and stern. The ships had oars, and the warriors manned the oars, to row when there was no wind. There was a small raised deck at each end of the ships; on these decks men stood to fight with sword and spear when there was a battle at sea. Each ship had but one mast, with a broad lugger sail, and for anchors they had only heavy stones attached to cables. They generally landed at night, and slept on the shore of one of the many islands, when they could, for they greatly feared to sail out of sight of land.

The fleet consisted of more than a thousand ships, each with fifty warriors, so the army was of more than fifty thousand men. Agamemnon had a hundred ships, Diomedes had eighty, Nestor had ninety, the Cretans with Idomeneus, had eighty, Menelaus had sixty; but Ajax and Odysseus, who lived in small islands, had only twelve ships apiece. Yet Ajax was so brave and strong, and Odysseus so brave and wise, that they were ranked among the greatest chiefs and advisers of Agamemnon, with Menelaus, Diomedes, Idomeneus, Nestor, Menestheus of Athens, and two or three others. These chiefs were called the Council, and gave advice to Agamemnon, who was commander-in-chief. He was a brave fighter, but so anxious and fearful of losing the lives of his soldiers that Odysseus and Diomedes were often obliged to speak to him very severely. Agamemnon was also very insolent and greedy, though, when anybody stood up to him, he was ready to apologise, for fear the injured chief should renounce his service and take away his soldiers.

Nestor was much respected because he remained brave, though he was too old to be very useful in battle. He generally tried to make peace when the princes quarrelled with Agamemnon. He loved to tell long stories about his great deeds when he was young, and he wished the chiefs to fight in old-fashioned ways.

For instance, in his time the Greeks had fought in clan regiments, and the princely men had never dismounted in battle, but had fought in squadrons of chariots, but now the owners of chariots fought on foot, each man for himself, while his squire kept the chariot near him to escape on if he had to retreat. Nestor wished to go back to the good old way of chariot charges against the crowds of foot soldiers of the enemy. In short, he was a fine example of the old-fashioned soldier.

Ajax, though so very tall, strong, and brave, was rather stupid. He seldom spoke, but he was always ready to fight, and the last to retreat. Menelaus was weak of body, but as brave as the best, or more brave, for he had a keen sense of honour, and would attempt what he had not the strength to do. Diomedes and Odysseus were great friends, and always fought side by side, when they could, and helped each other in the most dangerous adventures.

These were the chiefs who led the great Greek armada from the harbour of Aulis. A long time had passed, after the flight of Helen, before the large fleet could be collected, and more time went by in the attempt to cross the sea to Troy. There were tempests that scattered the ships, so they were driven back to Aulis to refit; and they fought, as they went out again, with the peoples of unfriendly islands, and besieged their towns. What they wanted most of all was to have Achilles with them, for he was the leader of fifty ships and 2,500 men, and he had magical armour made, men said, for his father, by Hephaestus, the God of armour-making and smithy work.

At last the fleet came to the Isle of Scyros, where they suspected that Achilles was concealed. King Lycomedes received the chiefs kindly, and they saw all his beautiful daughters dancing and playing at ball, but Achilles was still so young and slim and so beautiful that they did not know him among the others. There was a prophecy that they could not take Troy without him, and yet they could not find him out. Then Odysseus had a plan. He blackened his eyebrows and beard and put on the dress of a Phoenician merchant. The Phoenicians were a people who lived near the Jews, and were of the same race, and spoke much the same language, but, unlike the Jews, who, at that time were farmers in Palestine, tilling the ground, and keeping flocks and herds, the Phoenicians were the greatest of traders and sailors, and stealers of slaves. They carried cargoes of beautiful cloths, and embroideries, and jewels of gold, and necklaces of amber, and sold these everywhere about the shores of Greece and the islands.

Odysseus then dressed himself like a Phoenician pedlar, with his pack on his back: he only took a stick in his hand, his long hair was turned up, and hidden under a red sailor's cap, and in this figure he came, stooping beneath his pack, into the courtyard of King Lycomedes. The girls heard that a pedlar had come, and out they all ran, Achilles with the rest, to watch the pedlar undo his pack. Each chose what she liked best: one took a wreath of gold; another a necklace of gold and amber; another earrings; a fourth a set of brooches, another a dress of embroidered scarlet cloth; another a veil; another a pair of bracelets; but at the bottom of the pack lay a great sword of bronze, the hilt studded with golden nails. Achilles seized the sword. "This is for me!" he said, and drew the sword from the gilded sheath, and made it whistle round his head.

"You are Achilles, Peleus's son!" said Odysseus; "and you are to be the chief warrior of the Achaeans," for the Greeks then called themselves Achaeans. Achilles was only too glad to hear these words, for he was quite tired of living among maidens. Odysseus led him into the hall where the chiefs were sitting at their wine, and Achilles was blushing like any girl.

"Here is the Queen of the Amazons," said Odysseus – for the Amazons were a race of warlike maidens – "or rather here is Achilles, Peleus's son, with sword in hand." Then they all took his hand, and welcomed him, and he was clothed in man's dress, with the sword by his side, and presently they sent him back with ten ships to his home.

There his mother, Thetis, of the silver feet, the goddess of the sea, wept over him, saying, "My child, thou hast the choice of a long and happy and peaceful life here with me, or of a brief time of war and undying renown. Never shall I see thee again in Argos if thy choice is for war."

But Achilles chose to die young, and to be famous as long as the world stands. So his father gave him fifty ships, with Patroclus, who was older than he, to be his friend, and with an old man, Phoenix, to advise him; and his mother gave him the glorious armour that the God had made for his father, and the heavy ashen spear that none but he could wield, and he sailed to join the host of the Achaeans, who all praised and thanked Odysseus that had found for them such a prince. For Achilles was the fiercest fighter of them all, and the swiftest-footed man, and the most courteous prince, and the gentlest with women and children, but he was proud and high of heart, and when he was angered his anger was terrible.

The Trojans would have had no chance against the Greeks if only the men of the city of Troy had fought to keep Helen of the fair hands. But they had allies, who spoke different languages, and came to fight for them both from Europe and from Asia. On the Trojan as well as on the Greek side were people called Pelasgians, who seem to have lived on both shores of the sea. There were Thracians, too, who dwelt much further north than Achilles, in Europe and beside the strait of Hellespont, where the narrow sea runs like a river. There were warriors of Lycia, led by Sarpedon and Glaucus; there were Carians, who spoke in a strange tongue; there were Mysians and men from Alybe, which was called 'the birthplace of silver', and many other peoples sent their armies, so that the war was between Eastern Europe, on one side, and Western Asia Minor on the other. The people of Egypt took no part in the war: the Greeks and islesmen used to come down in their ships and attack the Egyptians as the Danes used to invade England. You may see the warriors from the islands, with their horned helmets, in old Egyptian pictures.

The commander-in-chief, as we say now, of the Trojans was Hector, the son of Priam. He was thought a match for any one of the Greeks, and was brave and good. His brothers also were leaders, but Paris preferred to fight from a distance with bow and arrows. He and Pandarus, who dwelt on the slopes of Mount Ida, were the best archers in the Trojan army. The princes usually fought with heavy spears, which they threw at each other, and with swords, leaving archery to the common soldiers who had no armour of bronze. But Teucer, Meriones, and Odysseus were the best archers of the Achaeans. People called Dardanians were led by Aeneas, who was said to be the son of the most beautiful of the goddesses. These, with Sarpedon and Glaucus, were the most famous of the men who fought for Troy.

Troy was a strong town on a hill: Mount Ida lay behind it, and in front was a plain sloping to the sea shore. Through this plain ran two beautiful clear rivers, and there were scattered here and there what you would have taken for steep knolls, but they were really mounds piled up over the ashes of warriors who had died long ago. On these mounds sentinels used to stand and look across the water to give warning if the Greek fleet drew near, for the Trojans had heard that it was on its way. At last the fleet came in view, and the sea was black with ships, the oarsmen pulling with all their might for the honour of being the first to land. The race was won by the ship of the prince Protesilaus, who was first of all to leap on shore, but as he leaped he was struck to the heart by an arrow from the bow of Paris. This must have seemed a good omen to the Trojans, and to the Greeks evil, but we do not hear that the landing was resisted in great force, any more than that of Norman William was when he invaded England.

The Greeks drew up all their ships on shore, and the men camped in huts built in front of the ships. There was thus a long row of huts with the ships behind them, and in these huts the Greeks lived all through the ten years that the siege of Troy lasted. In these days they do not seem to have understood how to conduct a siege. You would have expected the Greeks to build towers and dig trenches all round Troy, and from the towers watch the roads, so that provisions might not be brought in from the country. This is called 'investing' a town, but the Greeks never invested Troy. Perhaps they had not men enough; at all events the place remained open, and cattle could always be driven in to feed the warriors and the women and children.

Moreover, the Greeks for long never seem to have tried to break down one of the gates, nor to scale the walls, which were very high, with ladders. On the other hand, the Trojans and allies never ventured to drive the Greeks into the sea; they commonly remained within the walls or skirmished just beneath them. The older men insisted on this way of fighting, in spite of Hector, who always wished to attack and storm the camp of the Greeks. Neither side had machines for throwing heavy stones, such as the Romans used later, and the most that the Greeks did was to follow Achilles and capture small neighbouring cities, and take the women for slaves, and drive the cattle. They got provisions and wine from the Phoenicians, who came in ships, and made much profit out of the war.

It was not till the tenth year that the war began in real earnest, and scarcely any of the chief leaders had fallen. Fever came upon the Greeks, and all day the camp was black with smoke, and all night shone with fire from the great piles of burning wood, on which the Greeks burned their dead, whose bones they then buried under hillocks of earth. Many of these hillocks are still standing on the plain of Troy. When the plague had raged for ten days, Achilles called an assembly of the whole army, to try to find out why the Gods were angry. They thought that the beautiful God Apollo (who took the Trojan side) was shooting invisible arrows at them from his silver bow, though fevers in armies are usually caused by dirt and drinking bad water. The great heat of the sun, too, may have helped to cause the disease; but we must tell the story as the Greeks told it themselves.

So Achilles spoke in the assembly, and proposed to ask some prophet why Apollo was angry. The chief prophet was Calchas. He rose and said that he would declare the truth if Achilles would promise to protect him from the anger of any prince whom the truth might offend.

Achilles knew well whom Calchas meant. Ten days before, a priest of Apollo had come to the camp and offered ransom for his daughter Chryseis, a beautiful girl, whom Achilles had taken prisoner, with many others, when he captured a small town. Chryseis had been given as a slave to Agamemnon, who always got the best of the plunder because he was chief king, whether he had taken part in the fighting or not. As a rule he did not. To Achilles had been given another girl, Briseis, of whom he was very fond. Now when Achilles had promised to protect Calchas, the prophet spoke out, and boldly said, what all men knew already, that Apollo caused the plague because Agamemnon would not return Chryseis, and had insulted her father, the priest of the God.

On hearing this, Agamemnon was very angry. He said that he would send Chryseis home, but that he would take Briseis away from Achilles. Then Achilles was drawing his great sword from the sheath to kill Agamemnon, but even in his anger he knew that this was wrong, so he merely called Agamemnon a greedy coward, 'with face of dog and heart of deer', and he swore that he and his men would fight no more against the Trojans. Old Nestor tried to make peace, and swords were not drawn, but Briseis was taken away from Achilles, and Odysseus put Chryseis on board of his ship and sailed away with her to her father's town, and gave her up to her father. Then her father prayed to Apollo that the plague might cease, and it did cease – when the Greeks had cleansed their camp, and purified themselves and cast their filth into the sea.

We know how fierce and brave Achilles was, and we may wonder that he did not challenge Agamemnon to fight a duel. But the Greeks never fought duels, and Agamemnon was believed to be chief king by right divine. Achilles went alone to the sea shore when his dear Briseis was led away, and he wept, and called to his mother, the silver-footed lady of the waters. Then she arose from the grey sea, like a mist, and sat down beside her son, and stroked his hair with her hand, and he told her all his sorrows. So she said that she would go up to the dwelling of the Gods, and pray Zeus, the chief of them all, to make the Trojans win a great battle, so that Agamemnon should feel his need of Achilles, and make amends for his insolence, and do him honour.

Thetis kept her promise, and Zeus gave his word that the Trojans should defeat the Greeks. That night Zeus sent a deceitful dream to Agamemnon. The dream took the shape of old Nestor, and said that Zeus would give him victory that day. While he was still asleep, Agamemnon was full of hope that he would instantly take Troy, but, when he woke, he seems not to have been nearly so confident, for in place of putting on his armour, and bidding the Greeks arm themselves, he merely dressed in his robe and mantle, took his sceptre, and went and told the chiefs about his dream. They did not feel much encouraged, so he said that he would try the temper of the army. He would call them together, and propose to return to Greece; but, if the soldiers took him at his word, the other chiefs were to stop them. This was a foolish plan, for the soldiers were wearying for beautiful Greece, and their homes, and wives and children. Therefore, when Agamemnon did as he had said, the whole army rose, like the sea under the west wind, and, with a shout, they rushed to the ships, while the dust blew in clouds from under their feet. Then they began to launch their ships, and it seems that the princes were carried away in the rush, and were as eager as the rest to go home.

But Odysseus only stood in sorrow and anger beside his ship, and never put hand to it, for he felt how disgraceful it was to run away. At last he threw down his mantle, which his herald Eurybates of Ithaca, a round-shouldered, brown, curly-haired man, picked up, and he ran to find Agamemnon, and took his sceptre, a gold-studded staff, like a marshal's baton, and he gently told the chiefs whom he met that they were doing a shameful thing; but he drove the common soldiers back to the place of meeting with the sceptre. They all returned, puzzled and chattering, but one lame, bandy-legged, bald, round-shouldered, impudent fellow, named Thersites, jumped up and made an insolent speech, insulting the princes, and advising the army to run away. Then Odysseus took him and beat him till the blood came, and he sat down, wiping away his tears, and looking so foolish that the whole army laughed at him, and cheered Odysseus when he and Nestor bade them arm and fight. Agamemnon still believed a good deal in his dream, and prayed that he might take Troy that very day, and kill Hector. Thus Odysseus alone saved the army from a cowardly retreat; but for him the ships would have been launched in an hour. But the Greeks armed and advanced in full force, all except Achilles and his friend Patroclus with their two or three thousand men. The Trojans also took heart, knowing that Achilles would not fight, and the armies approached each other. Paris himself, with two spears and a bow, and without armour, walked into the space between the hosts, and challenged any Greek prince to single combat. Menelaus, whose wife Paris had carried away, was as glad as a hungry lion when he finds a stag or a goat, and leaped in armour from his chariot, but Paris turned and slunk away, like a man when he meets a great serpent on a narrow path in the hills. Then Hector rebuked Paris for his cowardice, and Paris was ashamed and offered to end the war by fighting Menelaus. If he himself fell, the Trojans must give up Helen and all her jewels; if Menelaus fell, the Greeks were to return without fair Helen. The Greeks accepted this plan, and both sides disarmed themselves to look on at the fight in comfort, and they meant to take the most solemn oaths to keep peace till the combat was lost and won, and the quarrel settled. Hector sent into Troy for two lambs, which were to be sacrificed when the oaths were taken.

In the meantime Helen of the fair hands was at home working at a great purple tapestry on which she embroidered the battles of the Greeks and Trojans. It was just like the tapestry at Bayeux on which Norman ladies embroidered the battles in the Norman Conquest of England. Helen was very fond of embroidering, like poor Mary, Queen of Scots, when a prisoner in Loch Leven Castle. Probably the work kept both Helen and Mary from thinking of their past lives and their sorrows.

When Helen heard that her husband was to fight Paris, she wept, and threw a shining veil over her head, and with her two bower maidens went to the roof of the gate tower, where King Priam was sitting with the old Trojan chiefs. They saw her and said that it was small blame to fight for so beautiful a lady, and Priam called her "dear child," and said, "I do not blame you, I blame the Gods who brought about this war." But Helen said that she wished she had died before she left her little daughter and her husband, and her home: "Alas! Shameless me!" Then she told Priam the names of the chief Greek warriors, and of Odysseus, who was shorter by a head than Agamemnon but broader in chest and shoulders. She wondered that she could not see her own two brothers, Castor and Polydeuces, and thought that they kept aloof in shame for her sin; but the green grass covered their graves, for they had both died in battle, far away in Lacedaemon, their own country.

Then the lambs were sacrificed, and the oaths were taken, and Paris put on his brother's armour: helmet, breastplate, shield, and leg-armour. Lots were drawn to decide whether Paris or Menelaus should throw his spear first, and, as Paris won, he threw his spear, but the point was blunted against the shield of Menelaus. But when Menelaus threw his spear it went clean through the shield of Paris, and through the side of his breastplate, but only grazed his robe. Menelaus drew his sword, and rushed in, and smote the crest of the helmet of Paris, but his bronze blade broke into four pieces. Menelaus caught Paris by the horsehair crest of his helmet, and dragged him towards the Greeks, but the chin-strap broke, and Menelaus turning round threw the helmet into the ranks of the Greeks. But when Menelaus looked again for Paris, with a spear in his hand, he could see him nowhere! The Greeks believed that the beautiful goddess Aphrodite, whom the Romans called Venus, hid him in a thick cloud of darkness and carried him to his own house, where Helen of the fair hands found him and said to him, "Would that thou hadst perished, conquered by that great warrior who was my lord! Go forth again and challenge him to fight thee face to face." But Paris had no more desire to fight, and the Goddess threatened Helen, and compelled her to remain with him in Troy, coward as he had proved himself. Yet on other days Paris fought well; it seems that he was afraid of Menelaus because, in his heart, he was ashamed of himself.

Meanwhile Menelaus was seeking for Paris everywhere, and the Trojans, who hated him, would have shown his hiding place. But they knew not where he was, and the Greeks claimed the victory, and thought that, as Paris had the worst of the fight, Helen would be restored to them, and they would all sail home.

The Young Thief

ONCE UPON A TIME there was a man and he wished to marry. So he went to the Seers and asked them to foretell his future. The Seers looked at their books and said to him, "If you marry you will certainly have a child, a very beautiful boy, but with one blemish; he will be a thief, the biggest thief that ever was."

So that man said, "Never mind, even if he be a thief; I should like to have a son." So he married, and in due time a child was born, a beautiful boy.

The child was carefully brought up till he was old enough to have a teacher. Then the father engaged a professor to come and teach him every day. He built a house a little distance from the town and put him in it, and that professor came every morning and taught him during the day, and in the evening returned home. Now the father ordered the professor never to let his son see any other soul but himself, and he thought by that means that his son would escape the fate that had been decreed by the Seers; for if he never saw any other person he could have no one to teach him to steal.

One day the professor came, and he told the lad about a horse of the Sultan's, which used to go out to exercise by itself and return by itself, and was of great strength and speed.

Then that youth asked where was the Sultan's palace, and his professor took him up on to the flat roof and pointed out to him the palace and its neighbourhood.

That night, after the professor left, the youth slipped out and came to the Sultan's stables, stole the horse, and returned home with it.

Next day the professor was a little late in coming, so the lad asked him, "Sheikh, why have you delayed today?" The professor said, "I stayed to hear the news. Behold, someone has stolen the Sultan's horse which I told you about yesterday."

Then that lad asked, "What does the Sultan propose to do?"

The old man replied, "He thought of sending out his soldiers, but then he heard of a seer who is able to detect a thief by looking at his books, so he is going to ask him first."

So the youth asked, "Where does that seer live?"

The professor then pointed out the seer's house and its neighbourhood.

That night the youth slipped out and came to the seer's house and found that the seer was out. He saw his wife and said to her – "My mistress, the seer has sent me to fetch his box of books."

So the wife brought out the box containing all his books of magic and gave them to him, and he took them and returned with them to his house.

Next day his professor was late, and when he came he said to him, "Father, why have you delayed?"

The old man said, "I stopped to hear the news. Do you remember the seer of whom I told you yesterday, who was to find out the thief for the Sultan? Well, he has now been robbed of his books of magic."

The youth asked, "What does the Sultan intend to do?"

The old man replied, "He was about to send out his soldiers, and then he heard that there was a magician who is able to detect a thief by casting charms, so he is going to consult him."

Then the youth asked, "Where does the magician live?"

So the old man took him on the roof and pointed out the magician's house and its neighbourhood.

That night, after the professor had gone, the youth went out and came to the house of the magician. He found him out, but saw his wife and said to her, "Mother, I fear to ask you, for was not the seer robbed in like manner yesterday? But the magician has sent me to fetch his bag of charms."

That woman said, "Have no fear; the thief's not you, my child;" and she gave him the bag of charms, and he took them and went to his house.

Next day, when the professor came, he asked for the news, and he said, "Did I not tell you yesterday that the Sultan was going to get a magician to tell him the thief by casting his charms? Well, last night the magician had his bag of charms stolen."

Then the youth asked, "What is the Sultan going to do?"

The old man answered, "He was going to send out his soldiers to catch the thief, but he heard that a certain woman said she knew who the thief was, and so he is going to pay her to tell him."

The youth asked where the woman lived, and the old man pointed out her house to him.

That evening the youth went out, and came to the house of that woman and found her outside, and he said to her, "Mother, I am thirsty; give me a drink of water."

So she went to the well to draw some water, and the youth came behind her and pushed her in. Then he went into the house and took her clothes and jewellery and brought them back to his house.

Next day, when the professor came, he asked the news, and he said, "My son, I told you yesterday that there was a woman who said that she could tell the Sultan the name of the thief. Well, last night the thief came and pushed her into the well and stole her things."

Then that youth asked, "What does the Sultan propose to do?"

The old man replied, "He is sending his soldiers out to look for the thief."

That night, after the professor had gone, the youth dressed up as a soldier, and went out and met the soldiers of the Sultan looking for the thief.

He said to them, "That is not the way to look for a thief. The way to look for a thief is to sit down very quietly in a place, and then perhaps you will see or hear him."

So he brought them all to one place and made them sit down, and one by one they all fell asleep. When they were all asleep he took their weapons and all their clothes he could carry and came with them to his house.

Next day, when the professor came, he asked him the news, and he said, "Last night the Sultan sent his soldiers out to look for the thief and behold, the thief stole their arms and their clothes, so that they returned naked."

Then the youth asked, "And now, what does the Sultan propose to do?"

The old man said, "Tonight the Sultan goes himself to look for the thief."

The youth said, "That is good, for the wisdom of Sultans is great."

That night the youth dressed up as a woman and scented himself and went out. He saw in the distance a lamp, and knew that it was the Sultan looking for the thief, so he passed near. When the Sultan smelt those goodly scents, he turned round to see whence they came, and he saw a very beautiful woman.

He asked, "Who are you?"

The lad replied, "I was just returning home when I saw your light, so I stepped aside to let you pass."

The Sultan said, "You must come and talk with me a little."

That lad said, "No, I must go home."

They were just outside the prison, so at last the youth consented to go in and talk for a little while with the Sultan.

When they got inside the courtyard, the youth took a pair of leg-irons and asked the Sultan, "What are these?"

The Sultan replied, "Those are the leg-irons with which we fasten our prisoners."

Then that youth said, "Oh, fasten them on me, that I may see how they work."

The Sultan said, "No, you are a woman, but I will put them on to show you," and he put them on.

The youth looked up and saw a gang-chain and asked, "What is that?"

The Sultan said, "That is what we put round their necks, and the end is fastened to the wall."

So the youth said, "Oh, put it on my neck, that I may see what it is like."

The Sultan replied, "No, you are a woman, but I will put it on my neck to show you;" so he put it on.

Then the youth took the key of the leg-irons and of the gang-chain, and looked up and saw a whip and said, "What is that?"

"That," said the Sultan, "is a whip with which we whip our prisoners if they are bad."

So the youth picked up the whip and began beating the Sultan. After the first few strokes the Sultan said, "Stop, that is enough fun-making."

But the youth went on and beat him soundly, and then went out, leaving the Sultan in chains and chained to the wall, and he also locked the door of the prison and took the key and went home. Next day the Sultan was found to be in the prison, and they could not get in to let him out or free him.

So a crier was sent round the town to cry, "Anyone who can deliver the Sultan from prison will be given a free pardon for any offence he has committed."

So, when the cries came to that youth's house, he said, "Oho, I want that as a certificate in writing before I will say what I know."

When these words were brought to the Wazir, he had a document drawn up, giving a free pardon to anyone who would deliver the Sultan. Then he brought it round to the prison for the Sultan's signature, and as they could not get it in they pushed it through the window on the end of a long pole. Then the Sultan signed it, and it was given to that youth, who handed over the key of the prison and of the chains and fetters. After the Sultan had been released he called that youth to his palace, and the youth took the horse, and the sage's books of magic, and the magician's bag of charms, and the woman's clothes and jewellery, and the soldiers' arms and clothes, and came to the palace.

When the Sultan heard his story he said that he was indeed a very clever youth, so he made him his Wazir.

This is the story of the man who would have a child, even though he should be a thief.

The Physician's Son and the King of the Snakes

ONCE THERE WAS a very learned physician, who died leaving his wife with a little baby boy, whom, when he was old enough, she named, according to his father's wish, Hasseeboo Kareem Ed Deen.

When the boy had been to school, and had learned to read, his mother sent him to a tailor, to learn his trade, but he could not learn it. Then he was sent to a silversmith, but he could not learn his trade either. After that he tried many trades, but could learn none of them. At last his mother said, "Well, stay at home for a while;" and that seemed to suit him.

One day he asked his mother what his father's business had been, and she told him he was a very great physician.

"Where are his books?" he asked.

"Well, it's a long time since I saw them," replied his mother, "but I think they are behind there. Look and see."

So he hunted around a little and at last found them, but they were almost ruined by insects, and he gained little from them.

At last, four of the neighbours came to his mother and said, "Let your boy go along with us and cut wood in the forest." It was their business to cut wood, load it on donkeys, and sell it in the town for making fires.

"All right," said she; "tomorrow I'll buy him a donkey, and he can start fair with you."

So the next day Hasseeboo, with his donkey, went off with those four persons, and they worked very hard and made a lot of money that day. This continued for six days, but on the seventh day it rained heavily, and they had to get under the rocks to keep dry. Now, Hasseeboo sat in a place by himself, and, having nothing else to do, he picked up a stone and began knocking on the ground with it. To his surprise the ground gave forth a hollow sound, and he called to his companions, saying, "There seems to be a hole under here."

Upon hearing him knock again, they decided to dig and see what was the cause of the hollow sound; and they had not gone very deep before they broke into a large pit, like a well, which was filled to the top with honey.

They didn't do any firewood chopping after that, but devoted their entire attention to the collection and sale of the honey.

With a view to getting it all out as quickly as possible, they told Hasseeboo to go down into the pit and dip out the honey, while they put it in vessels and took it to town for sale. They worked for three days, making a great deal of money.

At last there was only a little honey left at the very bottom of the pit, and they told the boy to scrape that together while they went to get a rope to haul him out.

But instead of getting the rope, they decided to let him remain in the pit, and divide the money among themselves. So, when he had gathered the remainder of the honey together, and called for the rope, he received no answer; and after he had been alone in the pit for three days he became convinced that his companions had deserted him.

Then those four persons went to his mother and told her that they had become separated in the forest, that they had heard a lion roaring, and that they could find no trace of either her son or his donkey.

His mother, of course, cried very much, and the four neighbours pocketed her son's share of the money.

To return to Hasseeboo.

He passed the time walking about the pit, wondering what the end would be, eating scraps of honey, sleeping a little, and sitting down to think.

While engaged in the last occupation, on the fourth day, he saw a scorpion fall to the ground – a large one, too – and he killed it.

Then suddenly he thought to himself, "Where did that scorpion come from? There must be a hole somewhere. I'll search, anyhow."

So he searched around until he saw light through a tiny crack; and he took his knife and scooped and scooped, until he had made a hole big enough to pass through; then he went out, and came upon a place he had never seen before.

Seeing a path, he followed it until he came to a very large house, the door of which was not fastened. So he went inside, and saw golden doors, with golden locks, and keys of pearl, and beautiful chairs inlaid with jewels and precious stones, and in a reception room he saw a couch covered with a splendid spread, upon which he lay down.

Presently he found himself being lifted off the couch and put in a chair, and heard someone saying: "Do not hurt him; wake him gently," and on opening his eyes he found himself surrounded by numbers of snakes, one of them wearing beautiful royal colours.

"Hullo!" he cried; "who are you?"

"I am Sultanee Waa Neeoka, king of the snakes, and this is my house. Who are you?"

"I am Hasseeboo Kareem Ed Deen."

"Where do you come from?"

"I don't know where I come from, or where I'm going."

"Well, don't bother yourself just now. Let's eat; I guess you are hungry, and I know I am."

Then the king gave orders, and some of the other snakes brought the finest fruits, and they ate and drank and conversed.

When the repast was ended, the king desired to hear Hasseeboo's story; so he told him all that had happened, and then asked to hear the story of his host.

"Well," said the king of the snakes, "mine is rather a long story, but you shall hear it. A long time ago I left this place, to go and live in the mountains of Al Kaaf, for the change of air. One day I saw a stranger coming along, and I said to him, 'Where are you from?' and he said, 'I am wandering in the wilderness.' 'Whose son are you?' I asked. 'My name is Bolookeea. My father was a sultan; and when he died I opened a small chest, inside of which I found a bag, which contained a small brass box; when I had opened this I found some writing tied up in a woollen cloth, and it was all in praise of a prophet. He was described as such a good and wonderful man, that I longed to see him; but when I made inquiries concerning him I was told he was not yet born. Then I vowed I would wander until I should see him. So I left our town, and all my property, and I am wandering, but I have not yet seen that prophet.'

"Then I said to him, 'Where do you expect to find him, if he's not yet born? Perhaps if you had some serpent's water you might keep on living until you find him. But it's of no use talking about that; the serpent's water is too far away.'

"'Well,' he said, 'goodbye. I must wander on.' So I bade him farewell, and he went his way.

"Now, when that man had wandered until he reached Egypt, he met another man, who asked him, 'Who are you?'

"'I am Bolookeea. Who are you?'

"'My name is Al Faan. Where are you going?'

"'I have left my home, and my property, and I am seeking the prophet.

"'H'm!' said Al Faan; 'I can tell you of a better occupation than looking for a man that is not born yet. Let us go and find the king of the snakes and get him to give us a charm medicine; then we will go to King Solomon and get his rings, and we shall be able to make slaves of the genii and order them to do whatever we wish.'

"And Bolookeea said, 'I have seen the king of the snakes in the mountain of Al Kaaf.'

"'All right,' said Al Faan; 'let's go.'

"Now, Al Faan wanted the ring of Solomon that he might be a great magician and control the genii and the birds, while all Bolookeea wanted was to see the great prophet.

"As they went along, Al Faan said to Bolookeea, 'Let us make a cage and entice the king of the snakes into it; then we will shut the door and carry him off.'

"'All right,' said Bolookeea.

"So they made a cage, and put therein a cup of milk and a cup of wine, and brought it to Al Kaaf; and I, like a fool, went in, drank up all the wine and became drunk. Then they fastened the door and took me away with them.

"When I came to my senses I found myself in the cage, and Bolookeea carrying me, and I said, 'The sons of Adam are no good. What do you want from me?' And they answered, 'We want some medicine to put on our feet, so that we may walk upon the water whenever it is necessary in the course of our journey.' 'Well,' said I, 'go along.'

"We went on until we came to a place where there were a great number and variety of trees; and when those trees saw me, they said, 'I am medicine for this;' 'I am medicine for that;' 'I am medicine for the head;' 'I am medicine for the feet;' and presently one tree said, 'If anyone puts my medicine upon his feet he can walk on water.'

"When I told that to those men they said, 'That is what we want;' and they took a great deal of it.

"Then they took me back to the mountain and set me free; and we said goodbye and parted.

"When they left me, they went on their way until they reached the sea, when they put the medicine on their feet and walked over. Thus they went many days, until they came near to the place of King Solomon, where they waited while Al Faan prepared his medicines.

"When they arrived at King Solomon's place, he was sleeping, and was being watched by genii, and his hand lay on his chest, with the ring on his finger.

"As Bolookeea drew near, one of the genii said to him 'Where are you going?' And he answered, 'I'm here with Al Faan; he's going to take that ring.' 'Go back,' said the genie; 'keep out of the way. That man is going to die.'

"When Al Faan had finished his preparations, he said to Bolookeea, 'Wait here for me.' Then he went forward to take the ring, when a great cry arose, and he was thrown by some unseen force a considerable distance.

"Picking himself up, and still believing in the power of his medicines, he approached the ring again, when a strong breath blew upon him and he was burnt to ashes in a moment.

"While Bolookeea was looking at all this, a voice said, 'Go your way; this wretched being is dead.' So he returned; and when he got to the sea again he put the medicine upon his feet and passed over, and continued to wander for many years.

"One morning he saw a man sitting down, and said 'Good morning,' to which the man replied. Then Bolookeea asked him, 'Who are you?' and he answered: 'My name is Jan Shah. Who are you?' So Bolookeea told him who he was, and asked him to tell him his history. The man, who was weeping and smiling by turns, insisted upon hearing Bolookeea's story first. After he had heard it he said:

"'Well, sit down, and I'll tell you my story from beginning to end. My name is Jan Shah, and my father is Tooeegha'mus, a great sultan. He used to go every day into the forest to shoot game; so one day I said to him, "Father, let me go with you into the forest today;" but he said, "Stay at home. You are better there." Then I cried bitterly, and as I was his only child, whom he loved dearly, he couldn't stand my tears, so he said: "Very well; you shall go. Don't cry."

"'Thus we went to the forest, and took many attendants with us; and when we reached the place we ate and drank, and then everyone set out to hunt.

"'I and my seven slaves went on until we saw a beautiful gazelle, which we chased as far as the sea without capturing it. When the gazelle took to the water I and four of my slaves took a boat, the other three returning to my father, and we chased that gazelle until we lost sight of the shore, but we caught it and killed it. Just then a great wind began to blow, and we lost our way.

"'When the other three slaves came to my father, he asked them, "Where is your master?" and they told him about the gazelle and the boat. Then he cried, "My son is lost! My son is lost!" and returned to the town and mourned for me as one dead.

"'After a time we came to an island, where there were a great many birds. We found fruit and water, we ate and drank, and at night we climbed into a tree and slept till morning.

"'Then we rowed to a second island, and, seeing no one around, we gathered fruit, ate and drank, and climbed a tree as before. During the night we heard many savage beasts howling and roaring near us.

"'In the morning we got away as soon as possible, and came to a third island. Looking around for food, we saw a tree full of fruit like red-streaked apples; but, as we were about to pick some, we heard a voice say, "Don't touch this tree; it belongs to the king." Toward night a number of monkeys came, who seemed much pleased to see us, and they brought us all the fruit we could eat.

"'Presently I heard one of them say, "Let us make this man our sultan." Then another one said: "What's the use? They'll all run away in the morning." But a third one said, "Not if we smash their boat." Sure enough, when we started to leave in the morning, our boat was broken in pieces. So there was nothing for it but to stay there and be entertained by the monkeys, who seemed to like us very much.

"'One day, while strolling about, I came upon a great stone house, having an inscription on the door, which said, "When any man comes to this island, he will find it difficult to leave, because the monkeys desire to have a man for their king. If he looks for a way to escape, he will think there is none; but there is one outlet, which lies to the north. If you go in that direction you will come to a great plain, which is infested with lions, leopards, and snakes. You must fight all of them; and if you overcome them you can go forward. You will then come to another great plain, inhabited by ants as big as dogs; their teeth are like those of dogs, and they are very fierce. You must fight these also, and if you overcome them, the rest of the way is clear."

"'I consulted with my attendants over this information, and we came to the conclusion that, as we could only die, anyhow, we might as well risk death to gain our freedom.

"'As we all had weapons, we set forth; and when we came to the first plain we fought, and two of my slaves were killed. Then we went on to the second plain, fought again; my other two slaves were killed, and I alone escaped.

"'After that I wandered on for many days, living on whatever I could find, until at last I came to a town, where I stayed for some time, looking for employment but finding none.

"'One day a man came up to me and said, "Are you looking for work?" "I am," said I. "Come with me, then," said he; and we went to his house.

"'When we got there he produced a camel's skin, and said, "I shall put you in this skin, and a great bird will carry you to the top of yonder mountain. When he gets you there, he will tear this skin off you. You must then drive him away and push down the precious stones you will find there. When they are all down, I will get you down."

"'So he put me in the skin; the bird carried me to the top of the mountain and was about to eat me, when I jumped up, scared him away, and then pushed down many precious stones. Then I called out to the man to take me down, but he never answered me, and went away.

"'I gave myself up for a dead man, but went wandering about, until at last, after passing many days in a great forest, I came to a house, all by itself; the old man who lived in it gave me food and drink, and I was revived.

"'I remained there a long time, and that old man loved me as if I were his own son.

"'One day he went away, and giving me the keys, told me I could open the door of every room except one which he pointed out to me.

"'Of course, when he was gone, this was the first door I opened. I saw a large garden, through which a stream flowed. Just then three birds came and alighted by the side of the stream. Immediately they changed to three most beautiful women. When they had finished bathing, they put on their clothes, and, as I stood watching them, they changed into birds again and flew away.

PROPHECIES & ORACLES: MYTHS & TALES

"'I locked the door, and went away; but my appetite was gone, and I wandered about aimlessly. When the old man came back, he saw there was something wrong with me, and asked me what was the matter. Then I told him I had seen those beautiful maidens, that I loved one of them very much, and that if I could not marry her I should die.

"'The old man told me I could not possibly have my wish. He said the three lovely beings were the daughters of the sultan of the genii, and that their home was a journey of three years from where we then were.

"'I told him I couldn't help that. He must get her for my wife, or I should die. At last he said, "Well, wait till they come again, then hide yourself and steal the clothes of the one you love so dearly."

"'So I waited, and when they came again I stole the clothes of the youngest, whose name was Sayadaatee Shems.

"'When they came out of the water, this one could not find her clothes. Then I stepped forward and said, "I have them." "Ah," she begged, "give them to me, their owner; I want to go away." But I said to her, "I love you very much. I want to marry you." "I want to go to my father," she replied. "You cannot go," said I.

"'Then her sisters flew away, and I took her into the house, where the old man married us. He told me not to give her those clothes I had taken, but to hide them; because if she ever got them she would fly away to her old home. So I dug a hole in the ground and buried them.

"'But one day, when I was away from home, she dug them up and put them on; then, saying to the slave I had given her for an attendant, "When your master returns tell him I have gone home; if he really loves me he will follow me," she flew away.

"'When I came home they told me this, and I wandered, searching for her, many years. At last I came to a town where one asked me, "Who are you?" and I answered, "I am Jan Shah." "What was your father's name?" "Taaeeghamus." "Are you the man who married our mistress?" "Who is your mistress?" "Sayadaatee Shems." "I am he!" I cried with delight.

"'They took me to their mistress, and she brought me to her father and told him I was her husband; and everybody was happy.

"'Then we thought we should like to visit our old home, and her father's genii carried us there in three days. We stayed there a year and then returned, but in a short time my wife died. Her father tried to comfort me, and wanted me to marry another of his daughters, but I refused to be comforted, and have mourned to this day. That is my story.'

"Then Bolookeea went on his way, and wandered till he died."

Next Sultaanee Waa Neeoka said to Hasseeboo, "Now, when you go home you will do me injury."

Hasseeboo was very indignant at the idea, and said, "I could not be induced to do you an injury. Pray, send me home."

"I will send you home," said the king; "but I am sure that you will come back and kill me."

"Why, I dare not be so ungrateful," exclaimed Hasseeboo. "I swear I could not hurt you."

"Well," said the king of the snakes, "bear this in mind: when you go home, do not go to bathe where there are many people."

And he said, "I will remember." So the king sent him home, and he went to his mother's house, and she was overjoyed to find that he was not dead.

Now, the sultan of the town was very sick; and it was decided that the only thing that could cure him would be to kill the king of the snakes, boil him, and give the soup to the sultan.

For a reason known only to himself, the vizir had placed men at the public baths with this instruction: "If anyone who comes to bathe here has a mark on his stomach, seize him and bring him to me."

When Hasseeboo had been home three days he forgot the warning of Sultaanee Waa Neeoka, and went to bathe with the other people. All of a sudden he was seized by some soldiers, and brought before the vizir, who said, "Take us to the home of the king of the snakes."

"I don't know where it is," said Hasseeboo.

"Tie him up," commanded the vizir.

So they tied him up and beat him until his back was all raw, and being unable to stand the pain he cried, "Let up! I will show you the place."

So he led them to the house of the king of the snakes, who, when he saw him, said, "Didn't I tell you you would come back to kill me?"

"How could I help it?" cried Hasseeboo. "Look at my back!"

"Who has beaten you so dreadfully?" asked the king.

"The vizir."

"Then there's no hope for me. But you must carry me yourself."

As they went along, the king said to Hasseeboo, "When we get to your town I shall be killed and cooked. The first skimming the vizir will offer to you, but don't you drink it; put it in a bottle and keep it. The second skimming you must drink, and you will become a great physician. The third skimming is the medicine that will cure your sultan. When the vizir asks you if you drank that first skimming say, 'I did.' Then produce the bottle containing the first, and say, 'This is the second, and it is for you.' The vizir will take it, and as soon as he drinks it he will die, and both of us will have our revenge."

Everything happened as the king had said. The vizir died, the sultan recovered, and Hasseeboo was loved by all as a great physician.

Sudika-Mbambi the Invincible

SUDIKA-MBAMBI was the son of Nzua dia Kimanaweze, who married the daughter of the Sun and Moon. The young couple were living with Nzua's parents, when one day Kimanaweze sent his son away to Loanda to trade. The son demurred, but the father insisted, so he went. While he was gone certain cannibal monsters, called *makishi*, descended on the village and sacked it – all the people who were not killed fled. Nzua, when he returned, found no houses and no people; searching over the cultivated ground, he at last came across his wife, but she was so changed that he did not recognize her at first. "The *makishi* have destroyed us," was her explanation of what had happened.

They seem to have camped and cultivated as best they could; and in due course Sudika-Mbambi ('the Thunderbolt') was born. He was a wonder-child, who spoke before his entrance into the world, and came forth equipped with knife, stick, and his *kilembe* (a 'mythic plant', explained as 'life-tree'), which he requested his mother to plant at the back of the house. Scarcely had he made his appearance when another voice was heard, and his twin brother Kabundungulu was born. The first thing they did was to cut down poles and build a house for their parents. Soon after this, Sudika-Mbambi announced that he was going to fight the *makishi*. He told Kabundungulu to stay at home and to keep an eye on the *kilembe*: if it withered he would know that his brother was dead; he then set out. On his way he was joined by four beings who called themselves *kipalendes* and boasted various accomplishments – building a house on the bare rock (a sheer impossibility under local conditions), carving ten clubs a day, and other more recondite operations, none of which, however, as the event proved, they could accomplish successfully. When they had gone a certain distance through the bush Sudika-Mbambi directed them to halt and build a house, in order to fight the *makishi*. As soon as he had cut one pole all the others needed cut themselves. He ordered the *kipalende* who had said he could erect a house on a rock to begin building, but as fast as a pole was set up it fell down again. The leader then took the work in hand, and it was speedily finished.

Next day he set out to fight the *makishi*, with three *kipalendes*, leaving the fourth in the house. To him soon after appeared an old woman, who told him that he might marry her granddaughter if he would fight her (the grandmother) and overcome her. They wrestled, but the old woman soon threw the *kipalende*, placed a large stone on top of him as he lay on the ground, and left him there, unable to move.

Sudika-Mbambi, who had the gift of second-sight, at once knew what had happened, returned with the other three, and released the *kipalende*. He told his story, and the others derided him for being beaten by a woman. Next day he accompanied the rest, the second *kipalende* remaining in the house. No details are given of the fighting with the *makishi*, beyond the statement that "they are firing." The second *kipalende* met with the same fate as his brother, and again Sudika-Mbambi was immediately aware of it. The incident was repeated on the third and on the fourth day. On the fifth Sudika-Mbambi sent the *kipalendes* to the war, and stayed behind himself. The old woman challenged him; he fought her and killed her – she seems to have been a peculiarly malignant kind of witch, who had kept her granddaughter shut up in a stone house, presumably as a lure for unwary strangers. It is not stated what she intended to do with the captives whom she secured under heavy stones, but, judging from what takes place in other stories of this kind, one may conclude that they were kept to be eaten in due course.

Sudika-Mbambi married the old witch's granddaughter, and they settled down in the stone house. The *kipalendes* returned with the news that the *makishi* were completely defeated, and all went well for a time.

Treachery of the Kipalendes

The *kipalendes*, however, became envious of their leader's good fortune, and plotted to kill him. They dug a hole in the place where he usually rested and covered it with mats; when he came in tired they pressed him to sit down, which he did, and immediately fell into the hole. They covered it up, and thought they had made an end of him. His younger brother, at

THE CHOSEN ONES

home, went to look at the 'life-tree', and found that it had withered. Thinking that, perhaps, there was still some hope, he poured water on it, and it grew green again.

Sudika-Mbambi was not killed by the fall; when he reached the bottom of the pit he looked round and saw an opening. Entering this, he found himself in a road – the road, in fact, which leads to the country of the dead. When he had gone some distance he came upon an old woman, or, rather, the upper half of one (half-beings are very common in African folklore, but they are usually split lengthways, having one eye, one arm, one leg, and so on), hoeing her garden by the wayside. He greeted her, and she returned his greeting. He then asked her to show him the way, and she said she would do so if he would hoe a little for her, which he did. She set him on the road, and told him to take the narrow path, not the broad one, and before arriving at Kalunga-ngombe's house he must carry a jug of red pepper and a jug of wisdom. It is not explained how he was to procure these, though it is evident from the sequel that he did so, nor how they were to be used, except that Kalunga-ngombe makes it a condition that anyone who wants to marry his daughter must bring them with him. We have not previously been told that this was Sudika-Mbambi's intention. On arriving at the house a fierce dog barked at him; he scolded it, and it let him pass. He entered, and was courteously welcomed by people who showed him into the guest house and spread a mat for him. He then announced that he had come to marry the daughter of Kalunga-ngombe. Kalunga answered that he consented if Sudika-Mbambi had fulfilled the conditions. He then retired for the night, and a meal was sent in to him a live cock and a bowl of the local porridge (*Junji*). He ate the porridge, with some meat which he had brought with him; instead of killing the cock he kept him under his bed. Evidently it was thought he would assume that the fowl was meant for him to eat (perhaps we have here a remnant of the belief, not known to or not understood by the narrator of the story, that the living must not eat of the food of the dead), and a trick was intended, to prevent his return to the Upper World. In the middle of the night he heard people inquiring who had killed Kalunga's cock; but the cock crowed from under the bed, and Sudika-Mbambi was not trapped. Next morning, when he reminded Kalunga of his promise, he was told that the daughter had been carried off by the huge serpent called Kinyoka kya Tumba, and that if he wanted to marry her he must rescue her.

Sudika-Mbambi started for Kinyoka's abode, and asked for him. Kinyoka's wife said, "He has gone shooting." Sudika-Mbambi waited a while, and presently saw driver ants approaching – the dreaded ants which would consume any living thing left helpless in their path. He stood his ground and beat them off; they were followed by red ants, these by a swarm of bees, and these by wasps, but none of them harmed him. Then Kinyoka's five heads appeared, one after the other. Sudika-Mbambi cut off each as it came, and when the fifth fell the snake was dead. He went into the house, found Kalunga's daughter there, and took her home to her father.

But Kalunga was not yet satisfied. There was a giant fish, Kimbiji, which kept catching his goats and pigs. Sudika-Mbambi baited a large hook with a sucking pig and caught Kimbiji, but even he was not strong enough to pull the monster to land. He fell into the water, and Kimbiji swallowed him.

Kabundungulu, far away at their home, saw that his brother's life-tree had withered once more, and set out to find him. He reached the house where the *kipalendes* were keeping Sudika-Mbambi's wife captive, and asked where he was. They denied all knowledge of him, but he felt certain there had been foul play. "You have killed him.

Uncover the grave." They opened up the pit, and Kabundungulu descended into it. He met with the old woman, and was directed to Kalunga-ngombe's dwelling. On inquiring for his brother he was told, "Kimbiji has swallowed him." Kabundungulu asked for a pig, baited his hook, and called the people to his help. Between them they landed the fish, and Kabundungulu cut it open. He found his brother's bones inside it, and took them out. Then he said, "My elder, arise!" and the bones came to life. Sudika-Mbambi married Kalunga-ngombe's daughter, and set out for home with her and his brother. They reached the pit, which had been filled in, and the ground cracked and they got out. They drove away the four *kipalendes* and, having got rid of them, settled down to a happy life.

Kabundungulu felt that he was being unfairly treated, since his brother had two wives, while he had none, and asked for one of them to be handed over to him. Sudika-Mbambi pointed out that this was impossible, as he was already married to both of them, and no more was said for the time being. But some time later, when Sudika-Mbambi returned from hunting, his wife complained to him that Kabundungulu was persecuting them both with his attentions. This led to a desperate quarrel between the brothers, and they fought with swords, but could not kill each other. Both were endowed with some magical power, so that the swords would not cut, and neither could be wounded. At last they got tired of fighting and separated, the elder going east and the younger west.

Morena-y-a-Letsatsi, or the Sun Chief

IN THE TIME OF THE GREAT FAMINE, when our fathers' fathers were young, there lived across the mountains, many days' journey, a great chief, who bore upon his breast the signs of the sun, the moon, and eleven stars. Greatly was he beloved, and marvellous was his power. When all around were starving, his people had plenty, and many journeyed to his village to implore his protection. Amongst others came two young girls, the daughters of one mother. Tall and lovely as a deep still river was the elder, gentle and timid as the wild deer, and her they called Siloane (the tear-drop.)

Of a different mould was her sister Mokete. Plump and round were her limbs, bright as the stars her eyes, like running water was the music of her voice, and she feared not man nor spirit. When the chief asked what they could do to repay him for helping them in their need, Mokete replied, "Lord, I can cook, I can grind corn, I can make 'leting', I can do all a woman's work."

Gravely the chief turned to Siloane – "And you," he asked, "what can you do?"

"Alas, lord!" Siloane replied, "what can I say, seeing that my sister has taken all words out of my mouth."

"It is enough," said the chief, "you shall be my wife. As for Mokete, since she is so clever, let her be your servant."

Now the heart of Mokete burned with black hate against her sister, and she vowed to humble her to the dust; but no one must see into her heart, so with a smiling face she embraced Siloane.

The next day the marriage feast took place, amidst great rejoicing, and continued for many days, as befitted the great Sun Chief. Many braves came from far to dance at the feast, and to delight the people with tales of the great deeds they had done in battle. Beautiful maidens were there, but none so beautiful as Siloane. How happy she was, how beloved! In the gladness of her heart she sang a song of praise to her lord – "Great is the sun in the heavens, and great are the moon and stars, but greater and more beautiful in the eyes of his handmaiden is my lord. Upon his breast are the signs of his greatness, and by their power I swear to love him with a love so strong, so true, that his son shall be in his image, and shall bear upon his breast the same tokens of the favour of the heavens."

Many moons came and went, and all was peace and joy in the hearts of the Sun Chief and his bride; but Mokete smiled darkly in her heart, for the time of her revenge approached. At length came the day, when Siloane should fulfil her vow, when the son should be born. The chief ordered that the child should be brought to him at once, that he might rejoice in the fulfilment of Siloane's vow. In the dark hut the young mother lay with great content, for had not Mokete assured her the child was his father's image, and upon his breast were the signs of the sun, the moon, and eleven stars?

Why then this angry frown on the chief's face, this look of triumph in the eyes of Mokete? What is this which she is holding covered with a skin? She turns back the covering, and, with a wicked laugh of triumph, shows the chief, not the beautiful son he had looked for, but an ugly, deformed child with the face of a baboon. "Here, my lord," she said, "is the long-desired son. See how well Siloane loves you, see how well she has kept her vow! Shall I tell her of your heart's content?"

"Woman," roared the disappointed chief, "speak not thus to me. Take from my sight both mother and child, and tell my headman it is my will that they be destroyed ere the sun hide his head in yonder mountains."

Sore at heart, angry and unhappy, the chief strode away into the lands, while Mokete hastened to the headman to bid him carry out his master's orders; but ere they could be obeyed, a messenger came from the chief to say the child alone was to be destroyed, but Siloane should become a servant, and on the morrow should witness his marriage to Mokete.

Bitter tears rolled down Siloane's cheeks. What evil thing had befallen her, that the babe she had borne, and whom she had felt in her arms, strong and straight, should have been so changed ere the eyes of his father had rested upon him? Not once did she doubt Mokete. Was she not her own sister? What reason would she have for casting the "Evil Eye" upon the child? It was hard to lose her child, hard indeed to lose the love of her lord; but he had not banished her altogether from his sight, and perhaps some day the spirits might be willing that she should once again find favour in his sight, and should bear him a child in his own image.

Meanwhile Mokete had taken the real baby to the pigs, hoping they would devour him, for each time she tried to kill him some unseen power held her hand; but the pigs took the babe and nourished him, and many weeks went by – weeks of triumph for Mokete, but of bitter sorrow for Siloane.

At length Mokete bethought her of the child, and wondered if the pigs had left any trace of him. When she reached the kraal, she started back in terror, for there, fat, healthy, and happy, lay the babe, while the young pigs played around him. What should she do? Had Siloane seen him? No, she hardly thought so, for the child was in every way the image of the chief. Siloane would at once have known who he was.

Hurriedly returning to her husband, Mokete begged him to get rid of all the pigs, and have their kraal burnt, as they were all ill of a terrible disease. So the chief gave orders to do as Mokete desired; but the spirits took the child to the elephant which lived in the great bush, and told it to guard him.

After this Mokete was at peace for many months, but no child came to gladden the heart of her lord, and to take away her reproach. In her anger and bitterness she longed to kill Siloane, but she was afraid.

One day she wandered far into the bush, and there she beheld the child, grown more beautiful than ever, playing with the elephant. Mad with rage, she returned home, and gave her lord no rest until he consented to burn the bush, which she told him was full of terrible wild beasts, which would one day devour the whole village if they were not destroyed. But the spirits took the child and gave him to the fishes in the great river, bidding them guard him safely.

Many moons passed, many crops were reaped and Mokete had almost forgotten about the child, when one day, as she walked by the river bank, she saw him, a beautiful youth, playing with the fishes. This was terrible. Would nothing kill him? In her rage she tore great rocks from their beds and rolled them into the water; but the spirits carried the youth to a mountain, where they gave him a wand. "This wand," said they, "will keep you safe. If danger threatens you from above, strike once with the wand upon the ground, and a path will be opened to you to the country beneath. If you wish to return to this Upper World, strike twice with the wand, and the path will reopen."

So again they left him, and the youth, fearing the vengeance of his stepmother, struck once upon the ground with his wand. The earth opened, showing a long narrow passage. Down this the youth went, and, upon reaching the other end, found himself at the entrance to a large and very beautiful village. As he walked along, the people stood to gaze at him, and all, when they saw the signs upon his breast, fell down and worshipped him, saying, "Greetings, lord!" At length, he was informed that for many years these people had had no chief, but the spirits had told them that at the proper time a chief would appear who should bear strange signs upon his breast; him the people were to receive and to obey, for he would be the chosen one, and his name should be Tsepitso, or the promise.

From that day the youth bore the name of Tsepitso, and ruled over that land; but he never forgot his mother, and often wandered to the world above, to find how she fared and to watch over her. On these journeys he always clothed himself in old skins, and covered up his breast that none might behold the signs. One day, as he wandered, he found himself in a strange village, and as he passed the well, a maiden greeted him, saying, "Stranger, you look weary. Will you not rest and drink of this fountain?"

Tsepitso gazed into her eyes, and knew what love meant. Here, he felt, was the wife the spirits intended him to wed. He must not let her depart, so he sat down by the well and drank of the cool, delicious water, while he questioned the maid. She told him her name was Ma Thabo (mother of joy), and that her father was chief of that part of the country. Tsepitso told her he was a poor youth looking for work, whereupon she took him to her father, who consented to employ him.

One stipulation Tsepitso made, which was that for one hour every day before sunset he should be free from his duties. This was agreed to, and for several moons he worked for the old chief, and grew more and more in favour, both with him and with his daughter. The hour before sunset each day he spent amongst his own people, attending to their wants and giving judgement. At length he told Ma Thabo of his love, and read her answering love in her beautiful eyes. Together they sought the old chief, to whom Tsepitso told his story, and revealed his true self. The marriage was soon after celebrated, with much rejoicing, and Tsepitso bore his bride in triumph to his beautiful home in the world beneath, where she was received with every joy.

But amidst all his happiness Tsepitso did not forget his mother, and after the feasting and rejoicing were ended, he took Ma Thabo with him, for the time had at length come when he might free his mother forever from the power of Mokete.

When they approached his father's house, Mokete saw them, and, recognizing Tsepitso, knew that her time had come. With a scream she fled to the hut, but Tsepitso followed her, and sternly demanded his mother. Mokete only moaned as she knelt at her lord's feet. The old chief arose, and said, "Young man, I know not who you are, nor who your mother is; but this woman is my wife, and I pray you speak to her not thus rudely."

Tsepitso replied, "Lord, I am thy son."

"Nay now, thou art a liar," said the old man sadly, "I have no son."

"Indeed, my father, I am thy son, and Siloane is my mother. Dost need proof of the truth of my words? Then look," and turning to the light, Tsepitso revealed to his father the signs upon his breast, and the old chief, with a great cry, threw himself upon his son's neck and wept. Siloane was soon called, and knew that indeed she had fulfilled her vow, that here before her stood in very truth the son she had borne, and a great content filled her heart. Tsepitso and Ma Thabo soon persuaded her to return with them, knowing full well that her life would no longer be safe were she to remain near Mokete; so, when the old chief was absent, in the dusk of the evening they departed to their own home.

When the Sun Chief discovered their flight, he determined to follow, and restore his beloved Siloane to her rightful place; but Mokete followed him, though many times he ordered her to return to the village, for that never again would she be wife of his, and that if she continued to follow him, he would kill her. At length he thought, "If I cut off her feet she will not be able to walk," so, turning round suddenly, he seized Mokete, and cut off her feet. "Now, wilt thou leave me in peace, woman? Take care nothing worse befall thee." So saying, he left her, and continued his journey.

But Mokete continued to follow him, till the sun was high in the heavens. Each time he saw her close behind him, he stopped and cut off more of her legs, till only her body was left; even then she was not conquered, but continued to roll after him. Thoroughly enraged, the Sun Chief seized her, and called down fire from the heavens to consume her, and a wind from the edge of the world to scatter her ashes.

When this was done, he went on his way rejoicing, for surely now she would trouble him no more. Then as he journeyed, a voice rose in the evening air, "I follow, I follow, to the edge of the world, yea, even beyond, shall I follow thee."

Placing his hands over his ears to shut out the voice, the Sun Chief ran with the fleetness of a young brave, until, at the hour when the spirits visit the abodes of men, he overtook Tsepitso and the two women, and with them entered the kingdom of his son.

How he won pardon from Siloane, and gained his son's love, and how it was arranged that he and Siloane should again be married, are old tales now in the country of Tsepitso. When the marriage feast was begun, a cloud of ashes dashed against the Sun Chief, and an angry voice was heard from the midst of the cloud, saying, "Nay, thou shalt not wed

Siloane, for I have found thee, and I shall claim thee forever." Hastily the witch doctor was called to free the Sun Chief from the power of Mokete. As the old man approached the cloud, chanting a hymn to the gods, everyone gazed in silence. Raising his wand, the wizard made some mystic signs, the cloud vanished, and only a handful of ashes lay upon the ground.

Thus was the Evil Eye of Mokete stilled for evermore, and peace reigned in the hearts of the Sun Chief and his wife Siloane.

Tau-wau-chee-hezkaw, or The White Feather

THERE WAS AN OLD MAN LIVING in the centre of a forest, with his grandson, whom he had taken when quite an infant. The child had no parents, brothers, or sisters; they had all been destroyed by six large giants, and he had been informed that he had no other relative living besides his grandfather. The band to whom he belonged had put up their children on a wager in a race against those of the giants, and had thus lost them. There was an old tradition in the band, that it would produce a great man, who would wear a white feather, and who would astonish every one with his skill and feats of bravery.

The grandfather, as soon as the child could play about, gave him a bow and arrows to amuse himself. He went into the edge of the woods one day, and saw a rabbit; but not knowing what it was, he ran home and described it to his grandfather. He told him what it was, that its flesh was good to eat, and that if he would shoot one of his arrows into its body, he would kill it. He did so, and brought the little animal home, which he asked his grandfather to boil, that they might feast on it. He humoured the boy in this, and encouraged him to go on in acquiring the knowledge of hunting, until he could kill deer and larger animals; and he became, as he grew up, an expert hunter. As they lived alone, and away from other Indians, his curiosity was excited to know what was passing in the world. One day he came to the edge of a prairie, where he saw ashes like those at his grandfather's lodge, and lodge-poles left standing. He returned and inquired whether his grandfather put up the poles and made the fire. He was answered no, nor did he believe that he had seen anything of the kind. It was all imagination.

Another day he went out to see what there was curious; and, on entering the woods, he heard a voice calling out to him, "Come here, you destined wearer of the White Feather. You do not yet wear it, but you are worthy of it. Return home and take a short nap. You will dream of hearing a voice, which will tell you to rise and smoke. You will see in your dream a pipe, smoking sack, and a large white feather. When you awake you will find these articles. Put the feather on your head, and you will become a great hunter, a great warrior, and a great man, capable of doing anything. As a proof that you will become a great hunter, when you smoke, the smoke will turn into pigeons." The voice then informed him who he was, and disclosed the true character of his grandfather, who had imposed upon him. The voice-spirit then gave him a vine, and told him he was of an age to revenge the injuries of his relations. "When you meet your enemy," continued the spirit, "you will run a race with him. He will not see the vine, because it is enchanted. While you are running, you will throw it over his head and entangle him, so that you will win the race."

Long ere this speech was ended, he had turned to the quarter from which the voice proceeded, and was astonished to behold a man, for as yet he had never seen any man besides his grandfather, whose object it was to keep him in ignorance. But the circumstance that gave him the most surprise was, that this man, who had the looks of great age, was composed of wood from his breast downward, and appeared to be fixed in the earth.

He returned home, slept, heard the voice, awoke, and found the promised articles. His grandfather was greatly surprised to find him with a white feather on his forehead, and to see flocks of pigeons flying out of his lodge. He then recollected what had been predicted, and began to weep at the prospect of losing his charge.

Invested with these honours, the young man departed the next morning to seek his enemies and gratify his revenge. The giants lived in a very high lodge in the middle of a wood. He travelled on till he came to this lodge, where he found that his coming had been made known by the little spirits who carry the news. The giants came out, and gave a cry of joy as they saw him coming. When he approached nearer, they began to make sport of him, saying, "Here comes the little man with the white feather, who is to achieve such wonders." They, however, spoke very fair to him when he came up, saying he was a brave man, and would do brave things. This they said to encourage, and the more surely to deceive him. He, however, understood the object.

He went fearlessly up to the lodge. They told him to commence the race with the smallest of their number. The point to which they were to run was a peeled tree towards the rising sun, and then back to the starting-place, which was marked by a Chaunkahpee, or war-club, made of iron. This club was the stake, and whoever won it was to use it in beating the other's brains out. If he beat the first giant, he was to try the second, and so on until they had all measured speed with him. He won the first race by a dexterous use of the vine, and immediately despatched his competitor, and cut off his head. Next morning he ran with the second giant, whom he also outran, killed, and decapitated. He proceeded in this way for five successive mornings, always conquering by the use of his vine, cutting off the heads of the vanquished. The survivor acknowledged his power, but prepared secretly to deceive him. He wished him to leave the heads he had cut off, as he believed he could again reunite them with the bodies, by means of one of their medicines. White Feather insisted, however, in carrying all the heads to his grandfather. One more contest was to be tried, which would decide the victory; but, before going to the giant's lodge on the sixth morning, he met his old counsellor in the woods, who was stationary. He told him that he was about to be deceived. That he had never known any other sex but his own; but that, as he went on his way to the lodge, he would meet the most beautiful woman in the world. He must pay no attention to her, but, on meeting her, he must wish himself changed into a male elk. The transformation would take place immediately, when he must go to feeding and not regard her.

He proceeded towards the lodge, met the female, and became an elk. She reproached him for having turned himself into an elk on seeing her; said she had travelled a great distance for the purpose of seeing him, and becoming his wife. Now this woman was the sixth giant, who had assumed this disguise; but Tau-Wau-Chee-Hezkaw remained in ignorance of it. Her reproaches and her beauty affected him so much, that he wished himself a man again, and he at once resumed his natural shape. They sat down together, and he began to caress her, and make love to her. He finally ventured to lay his head on her lap, and went to sleep. She pushed his head aside at first, for the purpose of trying if he was really asleep; and when she was satisfied he was, she took her axe and broke his back. She then assumed her natural shape, which was in the form of the sixth giant, and afterwards changed him into a dog, in which degraded form he followed his enemy to the lodge. He took the white feather from his brow, and wore it as a trophy on his own head.

There was an Indian village at some distance, in which there lived two girls, who were rival sisters, the daughters of a chief. They were fasting to acquire power for the purpose of enticing the wearer of the white feather to visit their village. They each secretly hoped to engage his affections. Each one built herself a lodge at a short distance from the village. The giant knowing this, and having now obtained the valued plume, went immediately to visit them. As he approached, the girls saw and recognized the feather. The eldest sister prepared her lodge with great care and parade, so as to attract the eye. The younger, supposing that he was a man of sense, and would not be enticed by mere parade, touched nothing in her lodge, but left it as it ordinarily was. The eldest went out to meet him, and invited him in. He accepted her invitation, and made her his wife. The younger invited the enchanted dog into her lodge, and made him a good bed, and treated him with as much attention as if he were her husband.

The giant, supposing that whoever possessed the white feather possessed also all its virtues, went out upon the prairie to hunt, but returned unsuccessful. The dog went out the same day a hunting upon the banks of a river. He drew a stone out of the water, which immediately became a beaver. The next day the giant followed the dog, and hiding behind a tree, saw the manner in which the dog went into the river and drew out a stone, which at once turned into a beaver. As soon as the dog left the place, the giant went to the river, and observing the same manner, drew out a stone, and had the satisfaction of seeing it transformed into a beaver. Tying it to his belt, he carried it home, and, as is customary, threw it down at the door of the lodge before he entered. After being seated a short time, he told his wife to bring in his belt or hunting girdle. She did so, and returned with it, with nothing tied to it but a stone.

The next day, the dog, finding his method of catching beavers had been discovered, went to a wood at some distance, and broke off a charred limb from a burned tree, which instantly became a bear. The giant, who had again watched him, did the same, and carried a bear home; but his wife, when she came to go out for it, found nothing but a black stick tied to his belt.

The giant's wife determined she would go to her father, and tell him what a valuable husband she had, who furnished her lodge with abundance. She set out while her husband went to hunt. As soon as they had departed, the dog made signs to his mistress to sweat him after the manner of the Indians. She accordingly made a lodge just large enough for him to creep in. She then put in heated stones, and poured on water. After this had been continued the usual time, he came out a very handsome young man, but had not the power of speech.

Meantime, the elder daughter had reached her father's, and told him of the manner in which her sister supported a dog, treating him as her husband, and of the singular skill this animal had in hunting. The old man, suspecting there was some magic in it, sent a deputation of young men and women to ask her to come to him, and bring her dog along. When this deputation arrived, they were surprised to find, in the place of the dog, so fine a young man. They both accompanied the messengers to the father, who was no less astonished. He assembled all the old and wise men of the nation to see the exploits which, it was reported, the young man could perform. The giant was among the number. He took his pipe and filled it, and passed it to the Indians, to see if anything would happen when they smoked. It was passed around to the dog, who made a sign to hand it to the giant first, which was done, but nothing affected. He then took it himself. He made a sign to them to put the white feather upon his head. This was done, and immediately he regained his speech. He then commenced smoking, and behold! immense flocks of white and blue pigeons rushed from the smoke.

The chief demanded of him his history, which he faithfully recounted. When it was finished, the chief ordered that the giant should be transformed into a dog, and turned into the middle of the village, where the boys should pelt him to death with clubs. This sentence was executed.

The chief then ordered, on the request of the White Feather, that all the young men should employ themselves four days in making arrows. He also asked for a buffalo robe. This robe he cut into thin shreds, and sowed in the prairie. At the end of the four days he invited them to gather together all their arrows, and accompany him to a buffalo hunt. They found that these shreds of skin had grown into a very large herd of buffalo. They killed as many as they pleased, and enjoyed a grand festival, in honour of his triumph over the giants.

Having accomplished their labour, the White Feather got his wife to ask her father's permission to go with him on a visit to his grandfather. He replied to this solicitation, that a woman must follow her husband into whatever quarter of the world he may choose to go.

The young men then placed the white feather in his frontlet, and, taking his war-club in his hand, led the way into the forest, followed by his faithful wife.

Tulla, the Hiding Nook of the Snake

NO DOUBT YOU REMEMBER that the wise men built a Dark House in Nachan to hold the National Book, and such other treasures as the Golden Hearted did not wish to carry with him. And you also remember that he left a number of wise men in charge, and that he promised to return. The great pyramid at Cholula was not all finished, but it was far enough along so he could leave the son of Guatamo to go on with the work while he paid a visit to his old friends in Nachan.

When he arrived there, he found a splendid city having whole houses of silver, others of turquoise, some of white and red shells and some of rich feathers. Cotton grew there in all colours, so it was not necessary to dye it, and the people were rich and prosperous. A great and mighty king ruled them, but he finally grew jealous because the people seemed to think that all their good fortune came from obeying the commands given them by the Golden Hearted when he visited them as a mere youth.

They did everything in their power to honour the good prince. When he promulgated a new law, they ran to the mountain-tops and proclaimed it in a loud voice, and then the swift-footed couriers dashed through the country with lighted torches and repeated it to everyone they met. One day a young man came to him and said:

"Good prince, be on your guard. The king no longer loves you."

"Why do you say this to me?" asked the Golden Hearted.

"Because I know he plots to injure you. He is angry because you are helping the wise men build Tulla. He calls it the Hiding Nook of the Snake to show contempt for you."

"Again I ask why do you say such things to me?" There was so much reproach in the tones of the voice of the Golden Hearted that the young man hung his head and stammered:

"Forgive me, but I wanted you to know there is danger for you here, and I am ready to serve you faithfully."

The Golden Hearted made no reply, but taking a thoroughly dried cactus needle from a shelf, stuck it through his ears and was beginning to pierce his tongue when the young man sprang forward and caught his hand.

"Why, good prince," he cried in a startled voice, "do you maltreat your poor ears and tongue? It is I who have spoken evil, not you."

"But I listened, and that is an offense against the Good Law. Do you think I will not punish myself for disobedience?"

"Oh," said the young man, with tears streaming down his face, "the sight of blood makes my heart ache, and I, too, will be punished." And with that he stuck cactus needles through his ears and tongue.

"My friend," said the Golden Hearted, "I thank you for your kind thought of me, but I must beautify Tulla even if it does displease the king, and he is right in calling it the Hiding Nook of the Snake, because it will be a treasure-house of the wisdom inherited from the philosophers and wise men of your race. You should always bear in mind that a serpent is a symbol of wisdom, and not a thing to despise. The king compliments me, even though he knows it not."

The young man went out of the room with the thorns still sticking in his ears, and when he spat blood, his companions said:

"Why does your mouth bleed?" and he answered:

"Because I have been speaking evil of someone."

"Open your mouth and let us see," they said.

"It is only needful to examine the tongue. I have pierced it with the sharp needle of the cactus."

"Who gave you leave to do such a thing?"

"No one," he answered, "but when the Good Prince inflicted that penalty on himself for merely hearing what I said, I could do no less than follow his example."

"And we will do likewise," they said, and in after years, every devotee of the teachings of the Golden Hearted punished himself in this manner for evil speaking or listening to others saying unkind things of a fellow creature.

Of course we know that the king really was jealous of the Golden Hearted, and was determined that he should not stay long in Tulla, which bade fair to rival his own city with which it was connected by the secret passageway containing the Dark House. During the years of his absence, the wise men left in Nachan had been at work on this wonderful city, and it was very beautiful indeed, even before the Golden Hearted saw it at all. When he came the inhabitants received him with great rejoicing, and then the king of Nachan began to be afraid that he would have too great a following.

The king had no excuse to fight the Golden Hearted, because he always put his fingers in his ears when they talked of war in his presence, and under no circumstances would he have been made king himself. He only wanted to teach and help the people in a peaceable and kind way.

The king knew all this, but he was uneasy and wanted the Golden Hearted to go away. So he hired a native wizard to play a cunning trick upon the Golden Hearted. Disguising himself as one of the wise men, the wizard went to his house and said to his servant:

"I wish to see and speak to your master."

"Go away, old man, you cannot see the prince for he is sick. You will annoy him and cause him heaviness."

"But I must see him," persisted the pretended old man.

"Wait a moment and I will ask him," said the servant, and he went and told the Golden Hearted that a strange old man was determined to see him.

"Let him come in," said the sick man.

Tottering up to the bedside as if he were very feeble, the intruder said with well-feigned sympathy:

"How are you, my lord? Here is a medicine I have brought for you."

"You are welcome; I have been expecting you for many days," and the Golden Hearted held out his hand in a friendly manner.

"How is your body, and how is your health?" again asked the visitor, seating himself by the bedside.

"I am exceedingly sick. All my body is in pain, and I cannot move my hands nor my feet."

"The medicine I have is good and wholesome. If you will drink it you will be healed and eased at heart." As he said this, the wizard held up a small silver cup and put a white powder in it. "Drink this and you will then have in mind the toils and fatigues of death, and of your departure."

"Where have I to go?" cried his listener in surprise.

"To Tlapalla (which was their name for the Happy Island), where The Old Man of the Sea is waiting for you. He has much to tell you, and when you return you will be young and handsome. Indeed you will be a mere boy again." Seeing that the Golden Hearted merely stared at him, he said: "Sir, drink this medicine."

But the sick man did not wish to do so.

"Drink, my lord, or you will be sorry for it hereafter," urged the wizard.

"No, no; I will not drink it."

"At least rub some on your brow and taste a sip." So the Golden Hearted drank a little to try it, saying:

"What is this? It seems to be a thing very good and savoury. Already I feel myself healed. I am well."

"Drink some more, my lord, since it is good. The more you drink, the better you will feel."

The sick man swallowed considerably more and then he was drunk. It was not medicine at all that the wizard gave him, but a white wine made from the maguey plant and the powder he put in it was to make the Golden Hearted believe that he must go away.

For days after he was very sad and wept continuously, but he began to get ready to leave Tulla. No matter what was said to dissuade him, he could never get rid of the idea that he must take all of his followers and go as quickly as possible.

The wise men, seeing that he was determined, gathered up all the picture writings they had made as a record of their journeys, and putting them into an ark, carried it swung on a pole with them. Before leaving, they called the people together and said:

"Know that the Golden Hearted commands you to remain here in these lands of which he makes you master and gives you possession. He goes to the place whence he and we came, but he will return to visit you when it shall be time for the world to come to an end. You must await him in these lands, possessing them and all contained in them since for this purpose came we hither. Remain, therefore, for we go with the Golden Hearted."

The Stolen Child

A STRANGE and unlooked for event cast a shadow, though only for a brief period, over the Inca Rocca's life. He had married a very beautiful girl named Micay, the daughter of a neighbouring chief who ruled over a small tribe called Pata Huayllacan. She was the mother of four princes: Cusi Hualpa, the heir, Paucar, Huaman, and Vicaquirau, the future general.

We are told that Micay, the Inca's wife, had previously been promised by her father to Tocay Ccapac, the powerful chief of the Ayamarcas, a much more numerous tribe than the Huayllacans. Her marriage with the Inca caused a deadly feud between those two tribes. Hostilities were continued for a long time, and at last the Huayllacans prayed for peace. It was granted, but with a secret clause that the chief of the Huayllacans would entice away the Inca's eldest son and heir, and deliver him into the hands of his father's enemy, the chief of the Ayamarcas. If this condition was not complied with, Tocay Ccapac declared that he would continue the war until the Huayllacans were blotted out of existence.

These Ayamarcas were at one time a very powerful tribe, in a mountainous region about twenty miles S.S.W. of Cuzco; while the Huayllacans were in a fertile valley between the Ayamarcas and that city.

In accordance with the agreement, a treacherous plot was laid. An earnest request was sent to the Inca that his heir, the young Cusi Hualpa, might be allowed to visit his mother's relations, so as to become acquainted with them. Quite unsuspicious, the Inca consented and sent the child, who was then about eight years of age, to Micucancha, or Paulu, the chief place of the Huayllacans, with about twenty attendants. The young prince was received with great festivities, which lasted for several days. It was summer time. The sun was scorching, and the child passed his time in a verandah or trelhs work, called *arapa*, covered with bright flowers.

One day it was announced that the whole tribe must march to some distance to harvest the crops. As it was still very hot, the Huayllacan chief insisted that the young prince should remain in the shade, and not accompany the harvesters, who had to go a considerable distance under the blazing sun. The prince's attendants consented, and all the tribe, old and young, boys and girls, marched up the hills to the harvesting, singing songs with choruses. All was bright sunshine, and their *haylli*, or harvest song, was in praise of the shade:

Seek the shadow, seek the shade,
Hide us in the blessed shade.

Yahahaha,
Yahaha.

Where is it? where, where, O where?
Here it is, here, here, O here.

Yahahaha,
Yahaha.

Where the pretty cantut blooms,
Where the chihua's flower smiles,
Where the sweet amancay droops.
Yahahaha,
Yahaha.

There it is! there, there, O there!
Yes, we answer, there, O there.
Yahahaha,
Yahaha.

The child listened to the sounds of singing as the harvesters passed away out of sight, and then played among the flowers, surrounded by his personal attendants. The place was entirely deserted. When the sound of the singers had died away in the distance there was profound silence. Suddenly, without the slightest warning, the war cry "Atau! Atau!" was heard in all directions, and the little party was surrounded by armed men. The Orejones struggled valorously in defence of their precious charge until they were all killed, when the young prince was carried off.

Tocay Ccapac waited to hear the result of his treacherous raid in his chief abode, called Ahuayracancha, or 'the place of woof and warp.' When the raiders returned they entered their chief's presence, with the young prince, shouting "Behold the prisoner we have brought you." The chief said, "Is this the child of Mama Micay, who should have been my wife?" The Prince answered, "I am the son of the great Inca Rocca and of Mama Micay." Unsoftened by his tender years, or by his likeness to his beautiful mother, the savage chief ordered the child to be taken out and killed.

Then a strange thing happened. Surrounded by cruel enemies with no pitying eye to look on him, young Cusi Hualpa, a child of eight years, stood up to defy them. He must show himself a child of the sun, and maintain the honour of his race. With a look of indignation beyond his years he uttered a curse upon his captors. His shrill young voice was heard amidst the portentous silence of his enemies. "I tell you," he cried, "that as sure as you murder me there will fall such a curse upon you and your children that you will all come to an end, without any memory being left of your nation." He ceased, and, to the astonishment of his captors, tears of blood flowed from his eyes.

"*Yahuar huaccac!*, *Yahuar huaccac!*, He weeps blood," they shouted in horror. His curse and this unheard-of phenomenon filled the Ayamarcas with superstitious fear. They recoiled from the murder. Tocay Ccapac and his people thought that the curse from so young a child and the tears of blood betokened some great mystery. They dared not kill him. He stood up in their midst unhurt.

Tocay Ccapac saw that his people would not kill the young prince then, or with their own hands at any time, yet he did not give up his intention of gratifying his thirst for vengeance. He resolved to take the child's life by a course of starvation and exposure. He gave him into the charge of shepherds who tended flocks of llamas on the lofty height overlooking the great plain of Suriti, where the climate is exceedingly rigorous. The shepherds had orders to reduce his food, day by day, until he died.

Young Cusi Hualpa had the gift of making friends. The shepherds did not starve him, though for a year he was exposed to great hardships. No doubt, however, the life he led on those frozen heights improved his health and invigorated his frame.

The Inca was told that his son had mysteriously disappeared, and that his attendants were also missing. The Huayllacan chief expressed sorrow, and pretended that diligent searches had been made. Inca Rocca suspected the Ayamarcas, but did not then attack them, lest, if the child was alive, they might kill him. As time went on the bereaved father began to despair of ever seeing his beloved son again.

Meanwhile the prince was well watched by the shepherds and by a strong guard, which had been sent to ensure his remaining in unknown captivity. But help was at hand. One of the concubines of Tocay Ccapac, named Chimpu Urma, or 'the fallen halo,' had probably been a witness of the impressive scene when the child wept blood. At all events, she was filled with pity and the desire to befriend the forlorn prince. She was a native of Anta, a small town at no great distance from Cuzco. As a friend of Tocay Ccapac she was free to go where she liked, within his dominions and those of the chief of Anta, who was her father.

Chimpu Urma persuaded her relations and friends at Anta to join with her in an attempt to rescue the young prince. It had been arranged by the shepherds and guards that, on a certain day, some boys, including Cusi Hualpa, should have a race up to the top of a hill in front of the shepherds' huts. Hearing this, Chimpu Urma stationed her friends from Anta, well armed, on the other side of the same hill. The race was started, and the prince reached the summit first, where he was taken up in the arms of his Anta friends, who made a rapid retreat. The other boys gave the alarm, and the jailers (shepherds and guards) followed in chase. On the banks of a small lake called Huaylla-punu, the men of Anta, finding that they were being overtaken, made a stand. There was a fierce battle, which resulted in the total defeat of the Ayamarcas. The men of Anta continued their journey, and brought the prince safely to their town, where he was received with great rejoicings.

Cusi Hualpa quite won the hearts of the people of Anta. They could not bear to part with him, and they kept him with great secrecy, delaying to send the joyful news to the Inca. Anta is a small town built up the side of a hill which bounds the vast plain of Suriti to the south. There is a glorious view from it, but the climate is severe. At last, after nearly a year, the Anta people sent messengers to inform the Inca. The child had been given up for lost. All hope had been abandoned. Rocca examined the messengers himself, but still he felt doubt. He feared the news was too good to be true. He secretly sent a man he could trust, as one seeking charity, to Anta, to find out the truth. The Inca's emissary returned with assurances that the young prince was certainly liberated, and was at Anta.

The Inca at last gave way to rejoicing, all doubt being removed. Principal lords were sent with rich presents of gold and silver to the chief of Anta, requesting him to send back the heir to the throne. The chief replied that all his people wished that Cusi Hualpa could remain, for they felt much love for the boy, yet they were bound to restore him to his father. He declined to receive the presents, but he made one condition. It was that he and his people should be accepted as relations of the Inca. So the young prince came back to his parents, and was joyfully received. Inca Rocca then visited Anta in person, and declared that the chief and his people were, from henceforward, raised to the rank of Orejones. The Huayllacans made abject submission, and, as Cusi Hualpa generously interceded for them, they were forgiven. Huaman Poma furnishes a curious corroboration of the story of the stolen child. Of all his portraits of the Incas, Rocca is the only one who is portrayed with a little boy. Huaman Poma did not know the story of the kidnapping and the recovered boy – at least, he never mentions it. All he knew was that only Inca Rocca was to be portrayed with a little boy.

Inca Rocca died after a long and glorious reign, during which he firmly laid the foundations of a great empire. His son Cusi Hualpa succeeded at the age of nineteen. He was commonly known by his surname of Yahuar Huaccac, or 'weeping blood.' His reign was memorable for the changes that took place in the system and objects of Inca warfare. The campaigns were no longer mere raids on hostile or rebellious tribes. The Inca's brother, Vicaquirau, and his cousin, Apu Mayta, were administrators quite as much as generals. Every attack on a hostile tribe ended in complete annexation. As the fame of the generals spread, the greater number of tribes submitted without resistance. Those who resisted were made terrible examples of, and if necessary a garrison was left in their principal place. The Ayamarcas were entirely crushed. Thus the Inca realm was every year extended, and at the same time consolidated.

Cusi Hualpa had five sons: Pahuac Hualpa Mayta, so named from his agility as a runner; Hatun Tupac, Vicchu Tupac, Marca Yutu, and Rocca. The Huayllacans, unimpressed by the pardon for their former treachery, conspired to make Marca Yutu the successor of his father, because he was more nearly related to their chief. With this object they enticed Pahuac Hualpa into their power and murdered him. For this there could be no forgiveness, and the tribe was entirely wiped out of existence by the Inca's generals. The second son, Hatun Tupac, then became the heir.

The new heir to the throne had, rather blasphemously, added to his real name of Hatun Tupac the surname of Uira-cocha, which was that of the Deity. One reason that is given was that, being at Urcos, a town about twenty-five miles south of Cuzco, a vision of the Deity appeared to him in a dream. When he related his experience to his attendants next morning, his tutor, named Hualpa Rimachi, offered congratulations and hailed the young prince as Inca Uira-cocha. Others say that he took the name because he adopted the Deity as his godfather, when he was armed and went through other ceremonies at the festival of Huarachicu. Be this how it may, he always called himself Uira-cocha. His father, mindful of the debt of gratitude he owed to the people of Anta, married his heir to a daughter of their chief, and niece of his deliverer, Chimpu Urma. The lady's name was Runtu-caya.

In the fullness of time Cusi Hualpa (Yahuar Huaccac) was succeeded by his son Hatun Tupac, calling himself Uira-cocha. The policy of the two great generals was continued, and the whole region between the rivers Apurimac and Vilcamayu, the Inca region, was annexed and consolidated into one realm under the Inca. The names of Uira-cocha's sons by Runtu-caya were Rocca, Tupac and Cusi. By a beautiful concubine named Ccuri-chulpa the Inca had two other sons named Urco and Sucso. For the sake of Ccuri-chulpa he favoured her children, and even declared the bastard Urco to be his heir. His eldest son was a valiant young warrior, trained in the school of Vicaquirau and Apu Mayta, and, when his age was sufficient, this Prince Rocca became their colleague. Cusi was the most promising youth of the rising generation, endowed with rare gifts, beautiful in form and feature, of dauntless courage and universally beloved.

The Divine Messengers

NOW AT THAT TIME the Gods assembled in the High Plain of Heaven were aware of continual disturbances in the Central Land of Reed-Plains (Idzumo). We are told that "Plains, the rocks, tree-stems, and herbage have still the power of speech. At night they make a clamour like that of flames of fire; in the day-time they swarm up like flies in the fifth month." In addition certain deities made themselves objectionable. The Gods determined to put an end to these disturbances, and after a consultation Takamimusubi decided to send his grandchild Ninigi to govern the Central Land of Reed-Plains, to wipe out insurrection, and to bring peace and prosperity to the country. It was deemed necessary to send messengers to prepare the way in advance. The first envoy was Ama-no-ho; but as he spent three years in the country without reporting to the Gods, his son was sent in his place. He adopted the same course as his father, and defied the orders of the Heavenly Ones. The third messenger was Ame-waka ('Heaven-young-Prince'). He, too, was disloyal, in spite of his noble weapons, and instead of going about his duties he fell in love and took to wife Shita-teru-hime ('Lower-shine-Princess').

Now the assembled Gods grew angry at the long delay, and sent a pheasant down to ascertain what was going on in Idzumo. The pheasant perched on the top of a cassia-tree before Ame-waka's gate. When Ame-waka saw the bird he immediately shot it. The arrow went through the bird, rose into the Place of Gods, and was hurled back again, so that it killed the disloyal and idle Ame-waka.

The weeping of Lower-shine-Princess reached Heaven, for she loved her lord and failed to recognize in his sudden death the just vengeance of the Gods. She wept so loud and so pitifully that the Heavenly Ones heard her. A swift wind descended, and the body of Ame-waka floated up into the High Plain of Heaven. A mortuary house was made, in which the deceased was laid. Mr Frank Rinder writes: "For eight days and eight nights there was wailing and lamentation. The wild goose of the river, the heron, the kingfisher, the sparrow, and the pheasant mourned with a great mourning."

Now it happened that a friend of Ame-waka, Aji-shi-ki by name, heard the sad dirges proceeding from Heaven. He therefore offered his condolence. He so resembled the deceased that when Ame-waka's parents, relations, wife, and children saw him, they exclaimed: "Our lord is still alive!" This greatly angered Aji-shi-ki, and he drew his sword and cut down the mortuary house, so that it fell to the Earth and became the mountain of Moyama.

We are told that the glory of Aji-shi-ki was so effulgent that it illuminated the space of two hills and two valleys. Those assembled for the mourning celebrations uttered the following song:

"Like the string of jewels
Worn on the neck
Of the Weaving-maiden,
That dwells in Heaven:
Oh! the lustre of the jewels
Flung across two valleys
From Aji-suki-taka-hiko-ne!

"To the side-pool:
The side-pool
Of the rocky stream
Whose narrows are crossed
By the country wenches
Afar from Heaven,
Come hither, come hither!
(The women are fair)
And spread across thy net
In the side-pool
Of the rocky stream."

Two more Gods were sent to the Central Land of Reed-Plains, and these Gods were successful in their mission. They returned to Heaven with a favourable report, saying that all was now ready for the coming of the August Grandchild.

The Coming of the August Grandchild

Amaterasu presented her grandson Ninigi, or Prince Rice-Ear-Ruddy-Plenty, with many gifts. She gave him precious stones from the mountain steps of Heaven, white crystal balls, and, most valuable gift of all, the divine sword that Susanoo had discovered in the serpent. She also gave him the star mirror into which she had gazed when peeping out of her cave. Several deities accompanied Ninigi, including that lively maiden of mirth and dance Uzume, whose dancing, it will be remembered, so amused the Gods.

Ninigi and his companions had hardly broken through the clouds and arrived at the eight-forked road of Heaven, when they discovered, much to their alarm, a gigantic creature with large and brightly shining eyes. So formidable was his aspect that Ninigi and all his companions, except the merry and bewitching Uzume, started to turn back with intent to abandon their mission. But Uzume went up to the giant and demanded who it was that dared to impede their progress. The giant replied: "I am the Deity of the Field-paths. I come to pay my homage to Ninigi, and beg to have the honour to be his guide. Return to your master, O fair Uzume, and give him this message."

So Uzume returned and gave her message to the Gods, who had so ignominiously retreated. When they heard the good news they greatly rejoiced, burst once more through the clouds, rested on the Floating Bridge of Heaven, and finally reached the summit of Takachihi.

The August Grandchild, with the Deity of the Field-paths for guide, travelled from end to end of the kingdom over which he was to rule. When he had reached a particularly charming spot, he built a palace.

Ninigi was so pleased with the service the Deity of the Field-paths had rendered him that he gave that giant the merry Uzume to wife.

Ninigi, after having romantically rewarded his faithful guide, began to feel the stirring of love himself, when one day, while walking along the shore, he saw an extremely lovely maiden. "Who are you, most beautiful lady?" inquired Ninigi. She replied: "I am the daughter of the Great-Mountain-Possessor. My name is Ko-no-Hana, the princess who makes the Flowers of the Trees Blossom."

Ninigi fell in love with Ko-no-Hana. He went with all haste to her father, Oho-yama, and begged that he would favour him with his daughter's hand.

Oho-yama had an elder daughter, Iha-naga, Princess Long-as-the-Rocks. As her name implies, she was not at all beautiful; but her father desired that Ninigi's children should have life as eternal as the life of rocks. He therefore presented both his daughters to Ninigi, expressing the hope that the suitor's choice would fall upon Iha-naga. Just as Cinderella, and not her ugly sisters, is dear to children of our own country, so did Ninigi remain true to his choice, and would not even look upon Iha-naga. This neglect made Princess Long-as-the-Rocks extremely angry. She cried out, with more vehemence than modesty: "Had you chosen me, you and your children would have lived long in the land. Now that you have chosen my sister, you and yours will perish as quickly as the blossom of trees, as quickly as the bloom on my sister's cheek."

However, Ninigi and Ko-no-Hana lived happily together for some time; but one day jealousy came to Ninigi and robbed him of his peace of mind. He had no cause to be jealous, and Ko-no-Hana much resented his treatment. She retired to a little wooden hut, and set it on fire. From the flames came three baby boys. We need only concern ourselves with two of them – Hoderi ('Fire-shine') and Hoori ('Fire-fade'). Hoori, as we shall see later on, was the grandfather of the first Mikado of Japan.

The Temple to the God of War

YI HANG-BOK. – When he was a child a blind fortune-teller came and cast his future, saying, "This boy will be very great indeed."

At seven years of age his father gave him for subject to write a verse on "The Harp and the Sword," and he wrote –

> *"The Sword pertains to the Hand of the Warrior*
> *And the Harp to the Music of the Ancients."*

At eight he took the subject of the "Willow before the Door," and wrote –

> *"The east wind brushes the brow of the cliff*
> *And the willow on the edge nods fresh and green."*

On seeing a picture of a great banquet among the fierce Turks of Central Asia, he wrote thus –

> *"The hunt is off in the wild dark hills,*
> *And the moon is cold and gray,*
> *While the tramping feet of a thousand horse*
> *Ring on the frosty way.*
> *In the tents of the Turk the music thrills*
> *And the wine-cups chink for joy,*
> *'Mid the noise of the dancer's savage tread*
> *And the lilt of the wild hautboy."*

At twelve years of age he was proud, we are told, and haughty. He dressed well, and was envied by the poorer lads of the place, and once he took off his coat and gave it to a boy who looked with envy on him. He gave his shoes as well, and came back barefoot. His mother, wishing to know his mind in the matter, pretended to reprimand him, but he replied, saying, "Mother, when others wanted it so, how could I refuse giving?" His mother pondered these things in her heart.

When he was fifteen he was strong and well-built, and liked vigorous exercise, so that he was a noted wrestler and skilful at shuttlecock. His mother, however, frowned upon these things, saying that they were not dignified, so that he gave them up and confined his attention to literary studies, graduating at twenty-five years of age.

In 1592, during the Japanese War, when the king escaped to Eui-ju, Yi Hang-bok went with him in his flight, and there he met the Chinese (Ming) representative, who said in surprise to his Majesty, "Do you mean to tell me that you have men in Cho-sen like Yi Hang-bok?" Yang Ho, the general of the rescuing forces, also continually referred to him for advice and counsel. He lived to see the troubles in the reign of the wicked Kwang-hai, and at last went into exile to Puk-chong. When he crossed the Iron Pass near Wonsan, he wrote –

> *"From the giddy height of the Iron Peak,*
> *I call on the passing cloud,*
> *To take up a lonely exile's tears*
> *In the folds of its feathery shroud,*

*And drop them as rain on the Palace Gates,
On the King, and his shameless crowd."*

During the Japanese War in the reign of Son-jo, the Mings sent a great army that came east, drove out the enemy and restored peace. At that time the general of the Mings informed his Korean Majesty that the victory was due to the help of Kwan, the God of War. "This being the case," said he, "you ought not to continue without temples in which to express your gratitude to him." So they built him houses of worship and offered him sacrifice. The Temples built were one to the south and one to the east of the city. In examining sites for these they could not agree on the one to the south. Some wanted it nearer the wall and some farther away. At that time an official, called Yi Hang-bok, was in charge of the conference. On a certain day when Yi was at home a military officer called and wished to see him. Ordering him in he found him a great strapping fellow, splendidly built. His request was that Yi should send out all his retainers till he talked to him privately. They were sent out, and then the stranger gave his message. After he had finished, he said goodbye and left.

Yi had at that time an old friend stopping with him. The friend went out with the servants when they were asked to leave, and now he came back again. When he came in he noticed that the face of the master had a very peculiar expression, and he asked him the reason of it. Yi made no reply at first, but later told his friend that a very extraordinary thing had happened. The military man who had come and called was none other than a messenger of the God of War. His coming, too, was on account of their not yet having decided in regard to the site for the Temple. "He came," said Yi, "to show me where it ought to be. He urged that it was not a matter for time only, but for the eternities to come. If we do not get it right the God of War will find no peace. I told him in reply that I would do my best. Was this not strange?"

The friend who heard this was greatly exercised, but Yi warned him not to repeat it to anyone. Yi used all his efforts, and at last the building was placed on the approved site, where it now stands.

The Story of Saiáwush

EARLY ONE MORNING as the cock crew, Tús arose, and accompanied by Gíw and Gúdarz and a company of horsemen, proceeded on a hunting excursion, not far from the banks of the Jihún, where, after ranging about the forest for some time, they happened to fall in with a damsel of extreme beauty, with smiling lips, blooming cheeks, and fascinating mien. They said to her:

*"Never was seen so sweet a flower,
In garden, vale, or fairy bower;
The moon is on thy lovely face,
Thy cypress-form is full of grace;*

> *But why, with charms so soft and meek,*
> *Dost thou the lonely forest seek?"*

She replied that her father was a violent man, and that she had left her home to escape his anger. She had crossed the river Jihún, and had travelled several leagues on foot, in consequence of her horse being too much fatigued to bear her farther. She had at that time been three days in the forest. On being questioned respecting her parentage, she said her father's name was Shíwer, of the race of Feridún. Many sovereigns had been suitors for her hand, but she did not approve of one of them. At last he wanted to marry her to Poshang, the ruler of Túrán, but she refused him on account of his ugliness and bad temper! This she said was the cause of her father's violence, and of her flight from home.

> *"But when his angry mood is o'er,*
> *He'll love his daughter as before;*
> *And send his horsemen far and near,*
> *To take me to my mother dear;*
> *Therefore, I would not further stray,*
> *But here, without a murmur, stay."*

The hearts of both Tús and Gíw were equally inflamed with love for the damsel, and each was equally determined to support his own pretensions, in consequence of which a quarrel arose between them. At length it was agreed to refer the matter to the king, and to abide by his decision. When, however, the king beheld the lovely object of contention, he was not disposed to give her to either claimant, but without hesitation took her to himself, after having first ascertained that she was of distinguished family and connection. In due time a son was born to him, who was, according to the calculations of the astrologers, of wonderful promise, and named Saiáwush. The prophecies about his surprising virtues, and his future renown, made Káus anxious that justice should be done to his opening talents, and he was highly gratified when Rustem agreed to take him to Zábulistán, and there instruct him in all the accomplishments which were suitable to his illustrious rank. He was accordingly taught horsemanship and archery, how to conduct himself at banquets, how to hunt with the falcon and the leopard, and made familiar with the manners and duty of kings, and the hardy chivalry of the age. His progress in the attainment of every species of knowledge and science was surprising, and in hunting he never stooped to the pursuit of animals inferior to the lion or the tiger. It was not long before the youth felt anxious to pay a visit to his father, and Rustem willingly complying with his wishes, accompanied his accomplished pupil to the royal court, where they were both received with becoming distinction, Saiáwush having fulfilled Káus's expectations in the highest degree, and the king's gratitude to the champion being in proportion to the eminent merit of his services on the interesting occasion. After this, however, preceptors were continued to enlighten his mind seven years longer, and then he was emancipated from further application and study.

One day Súdáveh, the daughter of the Sháh of Hámáverán, happened to see Saiáwush sitting with his father, the beauty of his person made an instantaneous impression on her heart.

The fire of love consumed her breast,
The thoughts of him denied her rest.
For him alone she pined in grief,
From him alone she sought relief,
And called him to her secret bower,
To while away the passing hour:
But Saiáwush refused the call,
He would not shame his father's hall.

The enamoured Súdáveh, however, was not to be disappointed without further effort, and on a subsequent day she boldly went to the king, and praising the character and attainments of his son, proposed that he should be united in marriage to one of the damsels of royal lineage under her care. For the pretended purpose therefore of making his choice, she requested he might be sent to the harem, to see all the ladies and fix on one the most suited to his taste. The king approved of the proposal, and intimated it to Saiáwush; but Saiáwush was modest, timid, and bashful, and mentally suspected in this overture some artifice of Súdáveh. He accordingly hesitated, but the king overcame his scruples, and the youth at length repaired to the shubistán, as the retired apartments of the women are called, with fear and trembling. When he entered within the precincts of the sacred place, he was surprised by the richness and magnificence of everything that struck his sight. He was delighted with the company of beautiful women, and he observed Súdáveh sitting on a splendid throne in an interior chamber, like Heaven in beauty and loveliness, with a coronet on her head, and her hair floating round her in musky ringlets. Seeing him she descended gracefully, and clasping him in her arms, kissed his eyes and face with such ardour and enthusiasm that he thought proper to retire from her endearments and mix among the other damsels, who placed him on a golden chair and kept him in agreeable conversation for some time. After this pleasing interview he returned to the king, and gave him a very favourable account of his reception, and the heavenly splendour of the retirement, worthy of Jemshíd, Feridún, or Húsheng, which gladdened his father's heart. Káús repeated to him his wish that he would at once choose one of the lights of the harem for his wife, as the astrologers had prophesied on his marriage the birth of a prince. But Saiáwush endeavoured to excuse himself from going again to Súdáveh's apartments. The king smiled at his weakness, and assured him that Súdáveh was alone anxious for his happiness, upon which the youth found himself again in her power. She was surrounded by the damsels as before, but, whilst his eyes were cast down, they shortly disappeared, leaving him and the enamoured Súdáveh together. She soon approached him, and lovingly said:

"O why the secret keep from one,
Whose heart is fixed on thee alone!
Say who thou art, from whom descended,
Some Peri with a mortal blended.
For every maid who sees that face,
That cypress-form replete with grace,
Becomes a victim to the wiles
Which nestle in those dimpled smiles;
Becomes thy own adoring slave,
Whom nothing but thy love can save."

To this Saiáwush made no reply. The history of the adventure of Káús at Hámáverán, and what the king and his warriors endured in consequence of the treachery of the father of Súdáveh, flashed upon his mind. He therefore was full of apprehension, and breathed not a word in answer to her fondness. Súdáveh observing his silence and reluctance, threw away from herself the veil of modesty,

And said: "O be my own, for I am thine,
And clasp me in thy arms!" And then she sprang
To the astonished boy, and eagerly
Kissed his deep crimsoned cheek, which filled his soul
With strange confusion. "When the king is dead,
O take me to thyself; see how I stand,
Body and soul devoted unto thee."
In his heart he said: "This never can be:
This is a demon's work – shall I be treacherous?
What! to my own dear father? Never, never;
I will not thus be tempted by the devil;
Yet must I not be cold to this wild woman,
For fear of further folly."

Saiáwush then expressed his readiness to be united in marriage to her daughter, and to no other; and when this intelligence was conveyed to Káús by Súdáveh herself, his Majesty was extremely pleased, and munificently opened his treasury on the happy occasion. But Súdáveh still kept in view her own design, and still labouring for its success, sedulously read her own incantations to prevent disappointment, at any rate to punish the uncomplying youth if she failed. On another day she sent for him, and exclaimed:

"I cannot now dissemble; since I saw thee
I seem to be as dead – my heart all withered.
Seven years have passed in unrequited love—
Seven long, long years. O! be not still obdurate,
But with the generous impulse of affection,
Oh, bless my anxious spirit, or, refusing,
Thy life will be in peril; thou shalt die!"
"Never," replied the youth; "O, never, never;
Oh, ask me not, for this can never be."

Saiáwush then rose to depart precipitately, but Súdáveh observing him, endeavoured to cling round him and arrest his flight. The endeavour, however, was fruitless; and finding at length her situation desperate, she determined to turn the adventure into her own favour, by accusing Saiáwush of an atrocious outrage on her own person and virtue. She accordingly tore her dress, screamed aloud, and rushed out of her apartment to inform Káús of the indignity she had suffered. Among her women the most clamorous lamentations arose, and echoed on every side. The king, on hearing that Saiáwush had preferred Súdáveh to her daughter, and that he had meditated so abominable an offence, thought that death alone could expiate his crime. He therefore summoned him to his presence; but satisfied that it would be difficult, if not impossible, to ascertain the truth of the case from either party concerned, he had recourse to a test which he thought would be infallible and conclusive. He first smelt the hands of Saiáwush, and then his garments, which had the scent of rose-water; and then he took the garments of Súdáveh, which, on the contrary, had a strong flavour of wine and musk. Upon this discovery, the king resolved on the death of Súdáveh, being convinced of the falsehood of the accusation she had made against his son. But when his indignation subsided, he was induced on various accounts to forego that resolution. Yet he said to her, "I am sure that Saiáwush is innocent, but let that remain concealed." Súdáveh, however, persisted in asserting his guilt, and continually urged him to punish the reputed offender, but without being attended to.

At length he resolved to ascertain the innocence of Saiáwush by the ordeal of fire; and the fearless youth prepared to undergo the terrible trial to which he was sentenced, telling his father to be under no alarm.

> *"The truth (and its reward I claim),*
> *Will bear me safe through fiercest flame."*

A tremendous fire was accordingly lighted on the adjacent plain, which blazed to an immense distance. The youth was attired in his golden helmet and a white robe, and mounted on a black horse. He put up a prayer to the Almighty for protection, and then rushed amidst the conflagration, as collectedly as if the act had been entirely free from peril. When Súdáveh heard the confused exclamations that were uttered at that moment, she hurried upon the terrace of the palace and witnessed the appalling sight, and in the fondness of her heart, wished even that she could share his fate, the fate of him of whom she was so deeply enamoured. The king himself fell from his throne in horror on seeing him surrounded and enveloped in the flames, from which there seemed no chance of extrication; but the gallant youth soon rose up, like the moon from the bursting element, and went through the ordeal unharmed and untouched by the fire. Káús, on coming to his senses, rejoiced exceedingly on the happy occasion, and his severest anger was directed against Súdáveh, whom he now determined to put to death, not only for her own guilt, but for exposing his son to such imminent danger. The noble youth, however, interceded for her. Súdáveh, notwithstanding, still continued to practise her charms and incantations in secret, to the end that Saiáwush might be put out of the way; and in this pursuit she was indeed indefatigable.

Suddenly intelligence was received that Afrásiyáb had assembled another army, for the purpose of making an irruption into Irán; and Káús, seeing that a Tartar could neither be bound by promise nor oath, resolved that he would on this occasion take the field himself, penetrate as far as Balkh, and seizing the country, make an example of the inhabitants. But Saiáwush perceiving in this prospect of affairs an opportunity of becoming free from the machinations and witchery of Súdáveh, earnestly requested to be employed, adding that, with the advice and bravery of Rustem, he would be sure of success. The king referred the matter to Rustem, who candidly declared that there was no necessity whatever for his Majesty proceeding personally to the war; and upon this assurance he threw open his treasury, and supplied all the resources of the empire to equip the troops appointed to accompany them. After one month the army marched toward Balkh, the point of attack.

On the other side Gersíwaz, the ruler of Balghar, joined the Tartar legions at Balkh, commanded by Bármán, who both sallied forth to oppose the Persian host, and after a conflict of three days were defeated, and obliged to abandon the fort. When the accounts of this calamity reached Afrásiyáb, he was seized with the utmost terror, which was increased by a dreadful dream. He thought he was in a forest abounding with serpents, and that the air was darkened by the appearance of countless eagles. The ground was parched with heat, and a whirlwind hurled down his tent and overthrew his banners. On every side flowed a river of blood, and the whole of his army had been defeated and butchered in his sight. He was afterwards taken prisoner, and ignominiously conducted to Káús, in whose company he beheld a gallant youth, not more than fourteen years of age, who, the moment he saw him, plunged a dagger in his loins, and with the scream of agony produced by the wound, he awoke. Gersíwaz had in the meantime returned with the remnant of his force; and being informed of these particulars, endeavoured to console Afrásiyáb, by assuring him that the true interpretation of dreams was the reverse of appearances. But Afrásiyáb was not to be consoled in this manner. He referred to his astrologers, who, however, hesitated, and were unwilling to afford an explanation of the mysterious vision. At length one of them, upon the solicited promise that the king would not punish him for divulging the truth, described the nature of the warning implied in what had been witnessed.

> *"And now I throw aside the veil,*
> *Which hides the darkly shadowed tale.*
> *Led by a prince of prosperous star,*
> *The Persian legions speed to war,*
> *And in his horoscope we scan*
> *The lordly victor of Túrán.*
> *If thou shouldst to the conflict rush,*
> *Opposed to conquering Saiáwush,*
> *Thy Turkish cohorts will be slain,*
> *And all thy saving efforts vain.*
> *For if he, in the threatened strife,*
> *Should haply chance to lose his life;*
> *Thy country's fate will be the same,*
> *Stripped of its throne and diadem."*

Afrásiyáb was satisfied with this interpretation, and felt the prudence of avoiding a war so pregnant with evil consequences to himself and his kingdom. He therefore deputed Gersíwaz to the headquarters of Saiáwush, with splendid presents, consisting of horses richly caparisoned, armour, swords, and other costly articles, and a written dispatch, proposing a termination to hostilities.

In the meantime Saiáwush was anxious to pursue the enemy across the Jihún, but was dissuaded by his friends. When Gersíwaz arrived on his embassy he was received with distinction, and the object of his mission being understood, a secret council was held upon what answer should be given. It was then deemed proper to demand: first, one hundred distinguished heroes as hostages; and secondly, the restoration of all the provinces which the Túránians had taken from Irán. Gersíwaz sent immediately to Afrásiyáb to inform him of the conditions required, and without the least delay they were approved. A hundred warriors were soon on their way; and Bokhára, and Samerkánd, and Haj, and the Punjáb, were faithfully delivered over to Saiáwush. Afrásiyáb himself retired towards Gungduz, saying, "I have had a terrible dream, and I will surrender whatever may be required from me, rather than go to war."

The negotiations being concluded, Saiáwush sent a letter to his father by the hands of Rustem. Rumour, however, had already told Káús of Afrásiyáb's dream, and the terror he had been thrown into in consequence. The astrologers in his service having prognosticated from it the certain ruin of the Túránian king, the object of Rustem's mission was directly contrary to the wishes of Káús; but Rustem contended that the policy was good, and the terms were good, and he thereby incurred his Majesty's displeasure. On this account Káús appointed Tús the leader of the Persian army, and commanded him to march against Afrásiyáb, ordering Saiáwush at the same time to return, and bring with him his hundred hostages. At this command Saiáwush was grievously offended, and consulted with his chieftains, Báhrám, and Zinga, and Sháwerán, on the fittest course to be pursued, saying, "I have pledged my word to the fulfilment of the terms, and what will the world say if I do not keep my faith?" The chiefs tried to quiet his mind, and recommended him to write again to Káús, expressing his readiness to renew the war, and return the hundred hostages. But Saiáwush was in a different humor, and thought as Tús had been actually appointed to the command of the Persian army, it would be most advisable for him to abandon his country and join Afrásiyáb. The chiefs, upon hearing this singular resolution, unanimously attempted to dissuade him from pursuing so wild a course as throwing himself into the power of his enemy; but he was deaf to their entreaties, and in the stubbornness of his spirit, wrote to Afrásiyáb, informing him that Káús had refused to ratify the treaty of peace, that he was compelled to return the hostages, and even himself to seek protection in Túrán from the resentment of his father, the warrior Tús having been already entrusted with the charge of the army. This unexpected intelligence excited considerable surprise in the mind of Afrásiyáb, but he had no hesitation in selecting the course to be followed. The ambassadors, Zinga and Sháwerán, were soon furnished with a reply, which was to this effect: – "I settled the terms of peace with thee, not with thy father. With him I have nothing to do. If thy choice be retirement and tranquillity, thou shalt have a peaceful and independent province allotted to thee; but if war be thy object, I will furnish thee with a large army: thy father is old and infirm, and with the aid of Rustem, Persia will be an easy conquest." Having thus obtained the promised favour and support of Afrásiyáb, Saiáwush gave in charge to Báhrám the city of Balkh, the army and treasure, in order that they might be delivered over to Tús on his arrival; and taking with him three hundred chosen horsemen, passed the Jihún, in progress to the court of Afrásiyáb. On taking this decisive step, he again wrote to Káús, saying:

"From my youth upward I have suffered wrong.
At first Súdáveh, false and treacherous,
Sought to destroy my happiness and fame;
And thou hadst nearly sacrificed my life
To glut her vengeance. The astrologers
Were all unheeded, who pronounced me innocent,
And I was doomed to brave devouring fire,
To testify that I was free from guilt;
But God was my deliverer! Victory now
Has marked my progress. Balkh, and all its spoils,
Are mine, and so reduced the enemy,

That I have gained a hundred hostages,
To guarantee the peace which I have made;
And what my recompense! a father's anger,
Which takes me from my glory. Thus deprived
Of thy affection, whither can I fly?
Be it to friend or foe, the will of fate
Must be my only guide – condemned by thee."

The reception of Saiáwush by Afrásiyáb was warm and flattering. From the gates of the city to the palace, gold and incense were scattered over his head in the customary manner, and exclamations of welcome uttered on every side.

"Thy presence gives joy to the land,
Which awaits thy command;
It is thine! it is thine!
All the chiefs of the state have assembled to meet thee,
All the flowers of the land are in blossom to greet thee!"

The youth was placed on a golden throne next to Afrásiyáb, and a magnificent banquet prepared in honour of the stranger, and music and the songs of beautiful women enlivened the festive scene. They chanted the praises of Saiáwush, distinguished, as they said, among men for three things: first, for being of the line of Kai-kobád; secondly, for his faith and honour; and, thirdly, for the wonderful beauty of his person, which had gained universal love and admiration. The favourable sentiments which characterized the first introduction of Saiáwush to Afrásiyáb continued to prevail, and indeed the king of Túrán seemed to regard him with increased attachment and friendship, as the time passed away, and showed him all the respect and honour to which his royal birth would have entitled him in his own country. After the lapse of a year, Pírán-wísah, one of Afrásiyáb's generals, said to him: "Young prince, thou art now high in the favour of the king, and at a great distance from Persia, and thy father is old; would it not therefore be better for thee to marry and take up thy residence among us for life?" The suggestion was a rational one, and Saiáwush readily expressed his acquiescence; accordingly, the lovely Gúlshaher, who was also named Jaríra, having been introduced to him, he was delighted with her person, and both consenting to a union, the marriage ceremony was immediately performed.

And many a warm delicious kiss,
Told how he loved the wedded bliss.

Some time after this union, Pírán suggested another alliance, for the purpose of strengthening his political interest and power, and this was with Ferangís, the daughter of Afrásiyáb. But Saiáwush was so devoted to Gúlshaher that he first consulted with her on the subject, although the hospitality and affection of the king constituted such strong claims on his gratitude that refusal was impossible. Gúlshaher, however, was a heroine, and willingly sacrificed her own feelings for the good of Saiáwush, saying she would rather condescend to be the very handmaid of Ferangís than that the happiness and prosperity of her lord should be compromised. The second marriage accordingly took place, and Afrásiyáb was so pleased with the match that he bestowed on the bride and her husband the sovereignty of Khoten, together with countless treasure in gold, and a great number of horses, camels, and elephants. In a short time they proceeded to the seat of the new government.

Meanwhile Káús suffered the keenest distress and sorrow when he heard of the flight of Saiáwush into Túrán, and Rustem felt such strong indignation at the conduct of the king that he abruptly quit the court, without permission, and retired to Sístán. Káús thus found himself in an embarrassed condition, and deemed it prudent to recall both Tús and the army from Balkh, and relinquish further hostile measures against Afrásiyáb.

The first thing that Saiáwush undertook after his arrival at Khoten was to order the selection of a beautiful site for his residence, and Pírán devoted his services to fulfil that object, exploring all the provinces, hills, and dales, on every side. At last he discovered a beautiful spot, at the distance of about a month's journey, which combined all the qualities and advantages required by the anxious prince. It was situated on a mountain, and surrounded by scenery of exquisite richness and variety. The trees were fresh and green, birds warbled on every spray, transparent rivulets murmured through the meadows, the air was neither oppressively hot in summer, nor cold in winter, so that the temperature, and the attractive objects which presented themselves at every glance, seemed to realize the imagined charms and fascinations of Paradise. The inhabitants enjoyed perpetual health, and every breeze was laden with music and perfume. So lovely a place could not fail to yield pleasure to Saiáwush, who immediately set about building a palace there, and garden-temples, in which he had pictures painted of the most remarkable persons of his time, and also the portraits of ancient kings. The walls were decorated with the likenesses of Kai-kobád, of Kai-káús, Poshang, Afrásiyáb, and Sám, and Zál, and Rustem, and other champions of Persia and Túrán. When completed, it was a gorgeous retreat, and the sight of it sufficient to give youthful vigour to the withered faculties of age. And yet Saiáwush was not happy! Tears started into his eyes and sorrow weighed upon his heart, whenever he thought upon his own estrangement from home!

It happened that the lovely Gúlshaher, who had been left in the house of her father, was delivered of a son in due time, and he was named Ferúd.

Afrásiyáb, on being informed of the proceedings of Saiáwush, and of the heart-expanding residence he had chosen, was highly gratified; and to show his affectionate regard, despatched to him with the intelligence of the birth of a son, presents of great value and variety. Gersíwaz, the brother of Afrásiyáb, and who had from the first looked upon Saiáwush with a jealous and malignant eye, being afraid of his interfering with his own prospects in Túrán, was the person sent on this occasion. But he hid his secret thoughts under the veil of outward praise and approbation. Saiáwush was pleased with the intelligence and the presents, but failed to pay the customary respect to Gersíwaz on his arrival, and, in consequence, the lurking indignation and hatred formerly felt by the latter were considerably augmented. The attention of Saiáwush respecting his army and the concerns of the state, was unremitting, and noted by the visitor with a jealous and scrutinizing eye, so that Gersíwaz, on his return to the court of Afrásiyáb, artfully talked much of the pomp and splendour of the prince, and added: "Saiáwush is far from being the amiable character thou hast supposed; he is artful and ambitious, and he has collected an immense army; he is in fact dissatisfied. As a proof of his haughtiness, he paid me but little attention, and doubtless very heavy calamity will soon befall Túrán, should he break out, as I apprehend he will, into open rebellion:

"For he is proud, and thou has yet to learn
The temper of thy daughter Ferangís,

Now bound to him in duty and affection;
Their purpose is the same, to overthrow
The kingdom of Túrán, and thy dominion;
To merge the glory of this happy realm
Into the Persian empire!"

But plausible and persuasive as were the observations and positive declarations of Gersíwaz, Afrásiyáb would not believe the imputed ingratitude and hostility of Saiáwush. "He has sought my protection," said he; "he has thrown himself upon my generosity, and I cannot think him treacherous. But if he has meditated anything unmerited by me, and unworthy of himself, it will be better to send him back to Kai-káús, his father." The artful Gersíwaz, however, was not to be diverted from his object: he said that Saiáwush had become personally acquainted with Túrán, its position, its weakness, its strength, and resources, and aided by Rustem, would soon be able to overrun the country if he was suffered to return, and therefore he recommended Afrásiyáb to bring him from Khoten by some artifice, and secure him. In conformity with this suggestion, Gersíwaz was again deputed to the young prince, and a letter of a friendly nature written for the purpose of blinding him to the real intentions of his father-in-law. The letter was no sooner read than Saiáwush expressed his desire to comply with the request contained in it, saying that Afrásiyáb had been a father to him, and that he would lose no time in fulfilling in all respects the wishes he had received.

This compliance and promptitude, however, was not in harmony with the sinister views of Gersíwaz, for he foresaw that the very fact of answering the call immediately would show that some misrepresentation had been practised, and consequently it was his business now to promote procrastination, and an appearance of evasive delay. He therefore said to him privately that it would be advisable for him to wait a little, and not manifest such implicit obedience to the will of Afrásiyáb; but Saiáwush replied that both his duty and affection urged him to a ready compliance. Then Gersíwaz pressed him more warmly, and represented how inconsistent, how unworthy of his illustrious lineage it would be to betray so meek a spirit, especially as he had a considerable army at his command, and could vindicate his dignity and his rights. And he addressed to him these specious arguments so incessantly and with such earnestness, that the deluded prince was at last induced to put off his departure, on account of his wife Ferangís pretending that she was ill, and saying that the moment she was better he would return to Túrán. This was quite enough for treachery to work upon; and as soon as the dispatch was sealed, Gersíwaz conveyed it with the utmost expedition to Afrásiyáb. Appearances, at least, were thus made strong against Saiáwush, and the tyrant of Túrán, now easily convinced of his falsehood, and feeling in consequence his former enmity renewed, forthwith assembled an army to punish his refractory son-in-law. Gersíwaz was appointed the leader of that army, which was put in motion without delay against the unoffending youth. The news of Afrásiyáb's warlike preparations satisfied the mind of Saiáwush that Gersíwaz had given him good advice, and that he had been a faithful monitor, for immediate compliance, he now concluded, would have been his utter ruin. When he communicated this unwelcome intelligence to Ferangís, she was thrown into the greatest alarm and agitation; but ever fruitful in expedients, suggested the course that it seemed necessary he should instantly adopt, which was to fly by a circuitous route back to Irán. To this he expressed no dissent, provided she would accompany him; but she said it was impossible to do so on account of the condition she was in. "Leave me," she added, "and save thy own life!" He therefore called together his three hundred Iránians, and requesting Ferangís, if she happened to be delivered of a son, to call him Kai-khosráu, set off on his journey.

"I go, surrounded by my enemies;
The hand of merciless Afrásiyáb
Lifted against me."

It was not the fortune of Saiáwush, however, to escape so easily as had been anticipated by Ferangís. Gersíwaz was soon at his heels, and in the battle that ensued, all the Iránians were killed, and also the horse upon which the unfortunate prince rode, so that on foot he could make but little progress. In the meantime Afrásiyáb came up, and surrounding him, wanted to shoot him with an arrow, but he was restrained from the violent act by the intercession of his people, who recommended his being taken alive, and only kept in prison. Accordingly he was again attacked and secured, and still Afrásiyáb wished to put him to death; but Pílsam, one of his warriors, and the brother of Pírán, induced him to relinquish that diabolical intention, and to convey him back to his own palace. Saiáwush was then ignominiously fettered and conducted to the royal residence, which he had himself erected and ornamented with such richness and magnificence. The sight of the city and its splendid buildings filled everyone with wonder and admiration. Upon the arrival of Afrásiyáb, Ferangís hastened to him in a state of the deepest distress, and implored his clemency and compassion in favour of Saiáwush.

"O father, he is not to blame,
Still pure and spotless is his name;
Faithful and generous still to me,
And never – never false to thee.
This hate to Gersíwaz he owes,
The worst, the bitterest of his foes;
Did he not thy protection seek,
And wilt thou overpower the weak?
Spill royal blood thou shouldest bless,
In cruel sport and wantonness?
And earn the curses of mankind,
Living, in this precarious state,
And dead, the torments of the mind,
Which hell inflicts upon the great
Who revel in a murderous course,
And rule by cruelty and force.

"It scarce becomes me now to tell,
What the accursed Zohák befel,
Or what the punishment which hurled
Sílim and Túr from out the world.
And is not Káús living now,
With rightful vengeance on his brow?
And Rustem, who alone can make
Thy kingdom to its centre quake?
Gúdarz, Zúára, and Fríburz,

And Tús, and Girgín, and Frámurz;
And others too of fearless might,
To challenge thee to mortal fight?
O, from this peril turn away,
Close not in gloom so bright a day;
Some heed to thy poor daughter give,
And let thy guiltless captive live."

The effect of this appeal, solemnly and urgently delivered, was only transitory. Afrasiyáb felt a little compunction at the moment, but soon resumed his ferocious spirit, and to ensure, without interruption, the accomplishment of his purpose, confined Ferangís in one of the remotest parts of the palace:

And thus to Gersíwaz unfeeling spoke:
"Off with his head, down with the enemy;
But take especial notice that his blood
Stains not the earth, lest it should cry aloud
For vengeance on us. Take good care of that!"

Gersíwaz, who was but too ready an instrument, immediately directed Karú-zíra, a kinsman of Afrásiyáb, who had been also one of the most zealous in promoting the ruin of the Persian prince, to inflict the deadly blow; and Saiáwush, whilst under the grasp of the executioner, had but time to put up a prayer to Heaven, in which he hoped that a son might be born to him to vindicate his good name, and be revenged on his murderer. The executioner then seized him by the hair, and throwing him on the ground, severed the head from the body. A golden vessel was ready to receive the blood, as commanded by Afrásiyáb; but a few drops happened to be spilt on the soil, and upon that spot a tree grew up, which was afterwards called Saiáwush, and believed to possess many wonderful virtues! The blood was carefully conveyed to Afrásiyáb, the head fixed on the point of a javelin, and the body was buried with respect and affection by his friend Pílsam, who had witnessed the melancholy catastrophe. It is also related that a tremendous tempest occurred at the time this amiable prince was murdered, and that a total darkness covered the face of the earth, so that the people could not distinguish each other's faces. Then was the name of Afrásiyáb truly execrated and abhorred for the cruel act he had committed, and all the inhabitants of Khoten long cherished the memory of Saiáwush.

Ferangís was frantic with grief when she was told of the sad fate of her husband, and all her household uttered the loudest lamentations. Pílsam gave the intelligence to Pírán and the proverb was then remembered: "It is better to be in hell, than under the rule of Afrásiyáb!" When the deep sorrow of Ferangís reached the ears of her father, he determined on a summary procedure, and ordered Gersíwaz to have her privately made away with, so that there might be no issue of her marriage with Saiáwush.

Pírán with horror heard this stern command,
And hasten'd to the king, and thus addressed him:
"What! wouldst thou hurl thy vengeance on a woman,
That woman, too, thy daughter? Is it wise,
Or natural, thus to sport with human life?

Already hast thou taken from her arms
Her unoffending husband – that was cruel;
But thus to shed an innocent woman's blood,
And kill her unborn infant – that would be
Too dreadful to imagine! Is she not
Thy own fair daughter, given in happier time
To him who won thy favour and affection?
Think but of that, and from thy heart root out
This demon wish, which leads thee to a crime,
Mocking concealment; vain were the endeavour
To keep the murder secret, and when known,
The world's opprobrium would pursue thy name.
And after death, what would thy portion be!
No more of this – honour me with the charge,
And I will keep her with a father's care,
In my own mansion." Then Afrásiyáb
Readily answered: "Take her to thy home,
But when the child is born, let it be brought
Promptly to me – my will must be obeyed."

Pírán rejoiced at his success; and assenting to the command of Afrásiyáb, took Ferangís with him to Khoten, where in due time a child was born, and being a son, was called Kai-khosráu. As soon as he was born, Pírán took measures to prevent his being carried off to Afrásiyáb, and committed him to the care of some peasants on the mountain Kalún. On the same night Afrásiyáb had a dream, in which he received intimation of the birth of Kai-khosráu; and upon this intimation he sent for Pírán to know why his commands had not been complied with. Pírán replied, that he had cast away the child in the wilderness. "And why was he not sent to me?" inquired the despot. "Because," said Pírán, "I considered thy own future happiness; thou hast unjustly killed the father, and God forbid that thou shouldst also kill the son!" Afrásiyáb was abashed, and it is said that ever after the atrocious murder of Saiáwush, he had been tormented with the most terrible and harrowing dreams. Gersíwaz now became hateful to his sight, and he began at last deeply to repent of his violence and inhumanity.

Kai-khosráu grew up under the fostering protection of the peasants, and showed early marks of surprising talent and activity. He excelled in manly exercises; and hunting ferocious animals was his peculiar delight. Instructors had been provided to initiate him in all the arts and pursuits cultivated by the warriors of those days, and even in his twelfth year accounts were forwarded to Pírán of several wonderful feats which he had performed.

Then smiled the good old man, and joyful said:
"'Tis ever thus – the youth of royal blood
Will not disgrace his lineage, but betray
By his superior mien and gallant deeds
From whence he sprung. 'Tis by the luscious fruit
We know the tree, and glory in its ripeness!"

Pírán could not resist paying a visit to the youth in his mountainous retreat, and, happy to find him, beyond all expectation, distinguished for the elegance of his external appearance, and the superior qualities of his mind, related to him the circumstances under which he had been exposed, and the rank and misfortunes of his father. An artifice then occurred to him which promised to be of ultimate advantage. He afterwards told Afrásiyáb that the offspring of Ferangís, thrown by him into the wilderness to perish, had been found by a peasant and brought up, but that he understood the boy was little better than an idiot. Afrásiyáb, upon this information, desired that he might be sent for, and in the meantime Pírán took especial care to instruct Kai-khosráu how he should act; which was to seem in all respects insane, and he accordingly appeared before the king in the dress of a prince with a golden crown on his head, and the royal girdle round his loins. Kai-khosráu proceeded on horseback to the court of Afrásiyáb, and having performed the usual salutations, was suitably received, though with strong feelings of shame and remorse on the part of the tyrant. Afrásiyáb put several questions to him, which were answered in a wild and incoherent manner, entirely at variance with the subject proposed. The king could not help smiling, and supposing him to be totally deranged, allowed him to be sent with presents to his mother, for no harm, he thought, could possibly be apprehended from one so forlorn in mind. Pírán triumphed in the success of his scheme, and lost no time in taking Kai-khosráu to his mother. All the people of Khoten poured blessings on the head of the youth, and imprecations on the merciless spirit of Afrásiyáb. The city built by Saiáwush had been razed to the ground by the exterminating fury of his enemies, and wild animals and reptiles occupied the place on which it stood. The mother and son visited the spot where Saiáwush was barbarously killed, and the tree, which grew up from the soil enriched by his blood, was found verdant and flourishing, and continued to possess in perfection its marvellous virtues.

The tale of Saiáwush is told;
And now the pages bright unfold,
Rustem's revenge – Súdáveh's fate—
Afrásiyáb's degraded state,
And that terrific curse and ban
Which fell at last upon Túrán!

When Kai-káús heard of the fate of his son, and all its horrible details were pictured to his mind, he was thrown into the deepest affliction. His warriors, Tús, and Gúdarz, and Báhrám, and Fríburz, and Ferhád, felt with equal keenness the loss of the amiable prince, and Rustem, as soon as the dreadful intelligence reached Sístán, set off with his troops to the court of the king, still full of indignation at the conduct of Káús, and oppressed with sorrow respecting the calamity which had occurred. On his arrival he thus addressed the weeping and disconsolate father of Saiáwush, himself at the same time drowned in tears:

"How has thy temper turned to nought, the seed
Which might have grown, and cast a glorious shadow;
How is it scattered to the barren winds!
Thy love for false Súdáveh was the cause
Of all this misery; she, the Sorceress,
O'er whom thou hast so oft in rapture hung,
Enchanted by her charms; she was the cause
Of this destruction. Thou art woman's slave!
Woman, the bane of man's felicity!
Who ever trusted woman? Death were better

> *Than being under woman's influence;*
> *She places man upon the foamy ridge*
> *Of the tempestuous wave, which rolls to ruin,*
> *Who ever trusted woman? – Woman! woman!"*
> *Káús looked down with melancholy mien,*
> *And, half consenting, thus to Rustem said:—*
> *"Súdáveh's blandishments absorbed my soul,*
> *And she has brought this wretchedness upon me."*
> *Rustem rejoined – "The world must be revenged*
> *Upon this false Súdáveh; – she must die."*
> *Káús was silent; but his tears flowed fast,*
> *And shame withheld resistance. Rustem rushed*
> *Without a pause towards the shubistán;*
> *Impatient, nothing could obstruct his speed*
> *To slay Súdáveh; – her he quickly found,*
> *And rapidly his sanguinary sword*
> *Performed its office. Thus the Sorceress died.*
> *Such was the punishment her crimes received.*

Having thus accomplished the first part of his vengeance, he proceeded with the Iránian army against Afrásiyáb, and all the Iránian warriors followed his example. When he had penetrated as far as Túrán, the enemy sent forward thirty thousand men to oppose his progress; and in the conflict which ensued, Ferámurz took Sarkhá, the son of Afrásiyáb, prisoner. Rustem delivered him over to Tús to be put to death precisely in the same manner as Saiáwush; but the captive represented himself as the particular friend of Saiáwush, and begged to be pardoned on that account. Rustem, however, had sworn that he would take his revenge, without pity or remorse, and accordingly death was inflicted upon the unhappy prisoner, whose blood was received in a dish, and sent to Káús, and the severed head suspended over the gates of the king's palace. Afrásiyáb hearing of this catastrophe, which sealed the fate of his favourite son, immediately collected together the whole of the Túránian army, and hastened himself to resist the conquering career of the enemy.

> *As on they moved; with loud and dissonant clang;*
> *His numerous troops shut out the prospect round;*
> *No sun was visible by day; no moon,*
> *Nor stars by night. The tramp of men and steeds,*
> *And rattling drums, and shouts, were only heard,*
> *And the bright gleams of armour only seen.*

Ere long the two armies met, when Pílsam, the brother of Pírán, was ambitious of opposing his single arm against Rustem, upon which Afrásiyáb said: – "Subdue Rustem, and thy reward shall be my daughter, and half my kingdom." Pírán, however, observed that he was too young to be a fit match for the experience and valour of the Persian champion, and would have dissuaded him from the unequal contest, but the choice was his own, and he was consequently permitted by Afrásiyáb to put his bravery to the test. Pílsam accordingly went forth and summoned Rustem to the fight; but Gíw, hearing the call, accepted the challenge himself, and had nearly been thrown from his horse by the superior activity of his opponent.

Ferámurz luckily saw him at the perilous moment, and darting forward, with one stroke of his sword shattered Pílsam's javelin to pieces, and then a new strife began. Pílsam and Ferámurz fought together with desperation, till both were almost exhausted, and Rustem himself was surprised to see the display of so much valour. Perceiving the wearied state of the two warriors he pushed forward Rakush, and called aloud to Pílsam: "Am I not the person challenged?" and immediately the Túránian chief proceeded to encounter him, striking with all his might at the head of the champion; but though the sword was broken by the blow, not a hair of his head was disordered.

> *Then Rustem urging on his gallant steed,*
> *Fixed his long javelin in the girdle band*
> *Of his ambitious foe, and quick unhorsed him;*
> *Then dragged him on towards Afrásiyáb,*
> *And, scoffing, cast him at the despot's feet.*
> *"Here comes the glorious conqueror," he said;*
> *"Now give to him thy daughter and thy treasure,*
> *Thy kingdom and thy soldiers; has he not*
> *Done honour to thy country? – Is he not*
> *A jewel in thy crown of sovereignty?*
> *What arrogance inspired the fruitless hope!*
> *Think of thy treachery to Saiáwush;*
> *Thy savage cruelty, and never look*
> *For aught but deadly hatred from mankind;*
> *And in the field of fight defeat and ruin."*
> *Thus scornfully he spoke, and not a man,*
> *Though in the presence of Afrásiyáb,*
> *Had soul to meet him; fear o'ercame them all*
> *Monarch and warriors, for a time. At length*
> *Shame was awakened, and the king appeared*
> *In arms against the champion. Fiercely they*
> *Hurled their sharp javelins – Rustem's struck the head*
> *Of his opponent's horse, which floundering fell,*
> *And overturned his rider. Anxious then*
> *The champion sprang to seize the royal prize;*
> *But Húmán rushed between, and saved his master,*
> *Who vaulted on another horse and fled.*

Having thus rescued Afrásiyáb, the wary chief exercised all his cunning and adroitness to escape himself, and at last succeeded. Rustem pursued him, and the Túránian troops, who had followed the example of the king; but though thousands were slain in the chase which continued for many farsangs, no further advantage was obtained on that day. Next morning, however, Rustem resumed his pursuit; and the enemy hearing of his approach, retreated into Chinese Tartary, to secure, among other advantages, the person of Kaikhosráu; leaving the kingdom of Túrán at the mercy of the invader, who mounted the throne, and ruled there, it is said, about seven years, with memorable severity, proscribing and putting to death every person who mentioned the name of Afrásiyáb. In the meantime he made splendid presents to Tús and Gúdarz, suitable to their rank and services; and Zúára, in revenge for the monstrous outrage committed upon Saiáwush, burnt and destroyed everything that came in his way; his wrath being exasperated by the sight of the places in which the young prince had resided, and recreated himself with hunting and other sports of the field. The whole realm, in fact, was delivered over to plunder and devastation; and every individual of the army was enriched by the appropriation of public and private wealth. The companions of Rustem, however, grew weary of residing in Túrán, and they strongly represented to him the neglect which Kai-káús had suffered for so many years, recommending his return to Persia, as being more honourable than the exile they endured in an ungenial climate. Rustem's abandonment of the kingdom was at length carried into effect; and he and his warriors did not fail to take away with them all the immense property that remained in jewels and gold; part of which was conveyed by the champion to Zábul and Sístán, and a goodly proportion to the king of kings in Persia.

> *When to Afrásiyáb was known*
> *The plunder of his realm and throne,*
> *That the destroyer's reckless hand*
> *With fire and sword had scathed the land,*
> *Sorrow and anguish filled his soul,*
> *And passion raged beyond control;*
> *And thus he to his warriors said:—*
> *"At such a time, is valour dead?*
> *The man who hears the mournful tale,*
> *And is not by his country's bale*
> *Urged on to vengeance, cannot be*
> *Of woman born; accursed is he!*
> *The time will come when I shall reap*
> *The harvest of resentment deep;*
> *And till arrives that fated hour,*
> *Farewell to joy in hall or bower."*

Rustem, in taking revenge for the murder of Saiáwush, had not been unmindful of Kai-khosráu, and had actually sent to the remote parts of Tartary in quest of him.

It is said that Gúdarz beheld in a dream the young prince, who pointed out to him his actual residence, and intimated that of all the warriors of Káús, Gíw was the only one destined to restore him to the world and his birth-right. The old man immediately requested his son Gíw to go to the place where the stranger would be found. Gíw readily complied, and in his progress provided himself at every stage successively with a guide, whom he afterwards slew to prevent discovery, and in this manner he proceeded till he reached the boundary of Chín, enjoying no comfort by day, or sleep by night. His only food was the flesh of the wild ass, and his only covering the skin of the same animal. He went on traversing mountain and forest, enduring every privation, and often did he hesitate, often did he think of returning, but honour urged him forward in spite of the trouble and impediments with which he was continually assailed. Arriving in a desert one day, he happened to meet with several persons, who upon being interrogated, said that they were sent by Pírán-wísah in search of Kai-káús. Gíw kept his own secret, saying that he was amusing himself with hunting the wild ass, but took care to ascertain from them the direction in which they were going. During the night the parties separated, and in the morning Gíw proceeded rapidly on his route, and after some time discovered a youth sitting by the side of a fountain, with a cup in his hand, whom he supposed to be Kai-khosráu. The youth also spontaneously thought, "This must be Gíw"; and when the traveller approached him, and said, "I am sure thou art the son of Saiáwush"; the youth observed, "I am equally sure that thou art Gíw the son of Gúdarz." At this Gíw was amazed, and falling to his feet, asked how, and from what circumstance, he recognized him. The youth replied that he knew all the warriors of Káús; Rustem, and Kishwád, and Tús, and Gúdarz, and the rest, from their portraits in his father's gallery, they being deeply impressed on his mind. He then asked in what way Gíw had discovered him to be Kai-khosráu, and Gíw answered, "Because I perceived something kingly in thy countenance. But let me again examine thee!" The youth, at this request, removed his garments, and Gíw beheld that mark on his body which was the heritage of the race of Kai-kobád. Upon this discovery he rejoiced, and congratulating himself and the young prince on the success of his mission, related to him the purpose for which he had come. Kai-khosráu was soon mounted on horseback, and Gíw accompanied him respectfully on foot. They, in the first instance, pursued their way towards the abode of Ferangís, his mother. The persons sent by Pírán-wísah did not arrive at the place where Kai-khosráu had been kept till long after Gíw and the prince departed; and then they were told that a Persian horseman had come and carried off the youth, upon which they immediately returned, and communicated to Pírán what had occurred. Ferangís, in recovering her son, mentioned to Gíw, with the fondness of a mother, the absolute necessity of going on without delay, and pointed out to him the meadow in which some of Afrásiyáb's horses were to be met with, particularly one called Behzád, which once belonged to Saiáwush, and which her father had kept in good condition for his own riding. Gíw, therefore, went to the meadow, and throwing his kamund, secured Behzád and another horse; and all three being thus accommodated, hastily proceeded on their journey towards Irán.

Tidings of the escape of Kai-khosráu having reached Afrásiyáb, he despatched Kulbád with three hundred horsemen after him; and so rapid were his movements that he overtook the fugitives in the vicinity of Bulgharia. Khosráu and his mother were asleep, but Gíw being awake, and seeing an armed force evidently in pursuit of his party, boldly put on his armour, mounted Behzád, and before the enemy came up, advanced to the charge. He attacked the horsemen furiously with sword, and mace, for he had heard the prophecy, which declared that Kai-khosráu was destined to be the king of kings, and therefore he braved the direst peril with confidence, and the certainty of success. It was this feeling which enabled him to perform such a prodigy of valour, in putting Kulbád and his three hundred horsemen to the rout. They all fled defeated, and dispersed precipitately before him. After this surprising victory, he returned to the halting place, and told Kai-khosráu what he had done. The prince was disappointed at not having been awakened to participate in the exploit, but Gíw said, "I did not wish to disturb thy sweet slumbers unnecessarily. It was thy good fortune and prosperous star, however, which made me triumph over the enemy." The three travellers then resuming their journey:

> *Through dreary track, and pathless waste,*
> *And wood and wild, their way they traced.*

The return of the defeated Kulbád excited the greatest indignation in the breast of Pírán. "What! three hundred soldiers to fly from the valour of one man! Had Gíw possessed even the activity and might of Rustem and Sám, such a shameful discomfiture could scarcely have happened." Saying this, he ordered the whole force under his command to be got ready, and set off himself to overtake and intercept the fugitives, who, fatigued with the toilsome march, were only able to proceed one stage in the day. Píran, therefore, who travelled at the rate of one hundred leagues a day, overtook them before they had passed through Bulgharia. Ferangís, who saw the enemy's banner floating in the air, knew that it belonged to Píran, and instantly awoke the two young men from sleep. Upon this occasion, Khosráu insisted on acting his part, instead of being left ignominiously idle; but Gíw was still resolute and determined to preserve him from all risk, at the peril of his own life. "Thou art destined to be the king of the world; thou art yet young, and a novice, and hast never known the toils of war; Heaven forbid that any misfortune should befall thee: indeed, whilst I live, I will never suffer thee to go into battle!" Khosráu then proposed to give him assistance; but Gíw said he wanted no assistance, not even from Rustem; "for," he added, "in art and strength we are equal, having frequently tried our skill together." Rustem had given his daughter in marriage to Gíw, he himself being married to Gíw's sister. "Be of good cheer," resumed he, "get upon some high place, and witness the battle between us.

"Fortune will still from Heaven descend,
The god of victory is my friend."

As soon as he took the field, Píran thus addressed him: "Thou hast once, singly, defeated three hundred of my soldiers; thou shalt now see what punishment awaits thee at my hands.

"For should a warrior be a rock of steel,
A thousand ants, gathered on every side,
In time will make him but a heap of dust."

In reply, Gíw said to Píran, "I am the man who bound thy two women, and sent them from China to Persia – Rustem and I are the same in battle. Thou knowest, when he encountered a thousand horsemen, what was the result, and what he accomplished! Thou wilt find me the same: is not a lion enough to overthrow a thousand kids?

"If but a man survive of thy proud host,
Brand me with coward – say I'm not a warrior.
Already have I triumphed o'er Kulbád,
And now I'll take thee prisoner, yea, alive!
And send thee to Káús – there thou wilt be
Slain to avenge the death of Saiáwush;
Túrán shall perish, and Afrásiyáb,
And every earthly hope extinguished quite."
Hearing this awful threat, Píran turned pale
And shook with terror – trembling like a reed;
And saying: "Go, I will not fight with thee!"
But Gíw asked fiercely: "Why?" And on he rushed
Against the foe, who fled – but 'twas in vain.
The kamund round the old man's neck was thrown,
And he was taken captive. Then his troops
Showered their sharp arrows on triumphant Gíw,

To free their master, who was quickly brought
Before Kai-khosráu, and the kamund placed
Within his royal hands. This service done,
Gív sped against the Tartars, and full soon
Defeated and dispersed them.

On his return, Gív expressed his astonishment that Pírán was still alive; when Ferangís interposed, and weeping, said how much she had been indebted to his interposition and the most active humanity on various occasions, and particularly in saving herself and Kai-khosráu from the wrath of Afrásiyáb after the death of Saiáwush. "If," said she, "after so much generosity he has committed one fault, let it be forgiven.

"Let not the man of many virtues die,
For being guilty of one trifling error.
Let not the friend who nobly saved my life,
And more, the dearer life of Kai-khosráu,
Suffer from us. O, he must never, never,
Feel the sharp pang of foul ingratitude,
From a true prince of the Kaiánian race."

But Gív paused, and said, "I have sworn to crimson the earth with his blood, and I must not pass from my oath." Khosráu then suggested to him to pierce the lobes of Pírán's ears, and drop the blood on the ground to stain it, in order that he might not depart from his word; and this humane fraud was accordingly committed. Khosráu further interceded; and instead of being sent a captive to Káús, the good old man was set at liberty.

When the particulars of this event were described to Afrásiyáb by Pírán-wísah, he was exceedingly sorrowful, and lamented deeply that Kai-khosráu had so successfully effected his escape. But he had recourse to a further expedient, and sent instructions to all the ferrymen of the Jihún, with a minute description of the three travellers, to prevent their passing that river, announcing at the same time that he himself was in pursuit of them. Not a moment was lost in preparing his army for the march, and he moved forward with the utmost expedition, night and day. At the period when Gív arrived on the banks of the Jihún, the stream was very rapid and formidable, and he requested the ferrymen to produce their certificates to show themselves equal to their duty. They pretended that their certificates were lost, but demanded for their fare the black horse upon which Gív rode. Gív replied, that he could not part with his favourite horse; and they rejoined, "Then give us the damsel who accompanies you." Gív answered, and said, "This is not a damsel, but the mother of that youth!" – "Then," observed they, "give us the youth's crown." But Gív told them that he could not comply with their demand; yet he was ready to reward them with money to any extent. The pertinacious ferrymen, who were not anxious for money, then demanded his armour, and this was also refused; and such was their independence or their effrontery, that they replied, "If not one of these four things you are disposed to grant, cross the river as best you may." Gív whispered to Kai-khosráu, and told him that there was no time for delay. "When Kavah, the blacksmith," said he, "rescued thy great ancestor, Feridún, he passed the stream in his armour without impediment; and why should we, in a cause of equal glory, hesitate for a moment?" Under the inspiring influence of an auspicious omen, and confiding in the protection of the Almighty, Kai-khosráu at once impelled his foaming horse into the river; his mother, Ferangís, followed with equal intrepidity, and then Gíw; and notwithstanding the perilous passage, they all successfully overcame the boiling surge, and landed in safety, to the utter amazement of the ferrymen, who of course had expected they would be drowned,

It so happened that at the moment they touched the shore, Afrásiyáb with his army arrived, and had the mortification to see the fugitives on the other bank, beyond his reach. His wonder was equal to his disappointment.

"What spirits must they have to brave
The terrors of that boiling wave—
With steed and harness, riding o'er
The billows to the further shore."

It was a cheering sight, they say,
To see how well they kept their way,
How Ferangís impelled her horse
Across that awful torrent's course,
Guiding him with heroic hand,
To reach unhurt the friendly strand."

Afrásiyáb continued for some time mute with astonishment and vexation, and when he recovered, ordered the ferrymen to get ready their boats to pass him over the river; but Húmán dissuaded him from that measure, saying that they could only convey a few troops, and they would doubtless be received by a large force of the enemy on the other side. At these words, Afrásiyáb seemed to devour his own blood with grief and indignation, and immediately retracing his steps, returned to Túrán.

As soon as Gíw entered within the boundary of the Persian empire, he poured out thanksgivings to God for his protection, and sent intelligence to Káús of the safe arrival of the party in his dominions. The king rejoiced exceedingly, and appointed an honorary deputation under the direction of Gúdarz, to meet the young prince on the road. On first seeing him, the king moved forward to receive him; and weeping affectionately, kissed his eyes and face, and had a throne prepared for him exactly like his own, upon which he seated him; and calling the nobles and warriors of the land together, commanded them to obey him. All readily promised their allegiance, excepting Tús, who left the court in disgust, and repairing forthwith to the house of Fríburz, one of the sons of Káús, told him that he would only pay homage and obedience to him, and not to the infant whom Gíw had just brought out of a desert. Next day the great men and leaders were again assembled to declare publicly by an official act their fealty to Kai-khosráu, and Tús was also invited to the banquet, which was held on the occasion, but he refused to go. Gíw was deputed to repeat the invitation; and he then said, "I shall pay homage to Fríburz, as the heir to the throne, and to no other.

"For is he not the son of Kai-káús,
And worthy of the regal crown and throne?
I want not any of the race of Poshang—
None of the proud Túránian dynasty—

> *Fruitless has been thy peril, Gíw, to bring*
> *A silly child among us, to defraud*
> *The rightful prince of his inheritance!"*

Gíw, in reply, vindicated the character and attainments of Khosráu, but Tús was not to be appeased. He therefore returned to his father and communicated to him what had occurred. Gúdarz was roused to great wrath by this resistance to the will of the king, and at once took twelve thousand men and his seventy-eight kinsmen, together with Gíw, and proceeded to support his cause by force of arms. Tús, apprised of his intentions, prepared to meet him, but was reluctant to commit himself by engaging in a civil war, and said, internally:—

> *"If I unsheath the sword of strife,*
> *Numbers on either side will fall,*
> *I would not sacrifice the life*
> *Of one who owns my sovereign's thrall.*
>
> *"My country would abhor the deed,*
> *And may I never see the hour*
> *When Persia's sons are doomed to bleed,*
> *But when opposed to foreign power.*
>
> *"The cause must be both good and true,*
> *And if their blood in war must flow,*
> *Will it not seem of brighter hue,*
> *When shed to crush the Tartar foe?"*

Possessing these sentiments, Tús sent an envoy to Gúdarz, suggesting the suspension of any hostile proceedings until information on the subject had been first communicated to the king. Káús was extremely displeased with Gúdarz for his precipitancy and folly, and directed both him and Tús to repair immediately to court. Tús there said frankly, "I now owe honour and allegiance to king Káús; but should he happen to lay aside the throne and the diadem, my obedience and loyalty will be due to Fríburz his heir, and not to a stranger." To this, Gúdarz replied, "Saiáwush was the eldest son of the king, and unjustly murdered, and therefore it becomes his majesty to appease and rejoice the soul of the deceased, by putting Kai-khosráu in his place. Kai-khosráu, like Feridún, is worthy of empire; all the nobles of the land are of this opinion, excepting thyself, which must arise from ignorance and vanity.

> *"From Nauder certainly thou are descended,*
> *Not from a stranger, not from foreign loins;*
> *But though thy ancestor was wise and mighty*
> *Art thou of equal merit? No, not thou!*
> *Regarding Khosráu, thou hast neither shown*
> *Reason nor sense – but most surprising folly!"*
> *To this contemptuous speech, Tús thus replied:*
> *"Ungenerous warrior! wherefore thus employ*
> *Such scornful words to me? Who art thou, pray!*

Who, but the low descendant of a blacksmith?
No Khosráu claims thee for his son, no chief
Of noble blood; whilst I can truly boast
Kindred to princes of the highest worth,
And merit not to be obscured by thee!"
To him then Gúdarz: "Hear me for this once,
Then shut thy ears for ever. Need I blush
To be the kinsman of the glorious Kavah?
It is my humour to be proud of him.
Although he was a blacksmith – that same man,
Who, when the world could still boast of valour,
Tore up the name-roll of the fiend Zohák,
And gave the Persians freedom from the fangs
Of the devouring serpents. He it was,
Who raised the banner, and proclaimed aloud,
Freedom for Persia! Need I blush for him?
To him the empire owes its greatest blessing,
The prosperous rule of virtuous Feridún."
Tús wrathfully rejoined: "Old man! thy arrow
May pierce an anvil – mine can pierce the heart
Of the Káf mountain! If thy mace can break
A rock asunder – mine can strike the sun!"

The anger of the two heroes beginning to exceed all proper bounds, Káús commanded silence; when Gúdarz came forward, and asked permission to say one word more: "Call Khosráu and Fríburz before thee, and decide impartially between them which is the most worthy of sovereignty – let the wisest and the bravest only be thy successor to the throne of Persia." Káús replied:

"The father has no choice among his children,
He loves them all alike – his only care
Is to prevent disunion; to preserve
Brotherly kindness and respect among them."

After a pause, he requested the attendance of Fríburz and Khosráu, and told them that there was a demon-fortress in the vicinity of his dominions called Bahmen, from which fire was continually issuing. "Go, each of you," said he, "against this fortress, supported by an army with which you shall each be equally provided, and the conqueror shall be the sovereign of Persia." Fríburz was not sorry to hear of this probationary scheme, and only solicited to be sent first on the expedition. He and Tús looked upon the task as perfectly easy, and promised to be back triumphant in a short time.

But when the army reached that awful fort,
The ground seemed all in flames on every side;
One universal fire raged round and round,
And the hot wind was like the scorching breath
Which issues from red furnaces, where spirits

Infernal dwell. Full many a warrior brave,
And many a soldier perished in that heat,
Consumed to ashes. Nearer to the fort
Advancing, they beheld it in mid-air,
But not a living thing – nor gate, nor door;
Yet they remained one week, hoping to find
Some hidden inlet, suffering cruel loss
Hour after hour – but none could they descry.
At length, despairing, they returned, worn out,
Scorched, and half-dead with watching, care, and toil.
And thus Fríburz and Tús, discomfited
And sad, appeared before the Persian king.

Then was it Khosráu's turn, and him Káús
Despatched with Gíw, and Gúdarz, and the troops
Appointed for that enterprise, and blessed them.
When the young prince approached the destined scene
Of his exploit, he saw the blazing fort
Reddening the sky and earth, and well he knew
This was the work of sorcery, the spell
Of demon-spirits. In a heavenly dream,
He had been taught how to destroy the charms
Of fell magicians, and defy their power,
Though by the devil, the devil himself, sustained,
He wrote the name of God, and piously
Bound it upon his javelin's point, and pressed
Fearlessly forward, showing it on high;
And Gíw displayed it on the magic walls
Of that proud fortress – breathing forth a prayer
Craving the aid of the Almighty arm;
When suddenly the red fires died away,
And all the world was darkness, Khosráu's troops
Following the orders of their prince, then shot
Thick clouds of arrows from ten thousand bows,
In the direction of the enchanted tower.
The arrows fell like rain, and quickly slew
A host of demons – presently bright light
Dispelled the gloom, and as the mist rolled off
In sulphury circles, the surviving fiends
Were seen in rapid flight; the fortress, too,
Distinctly shone, and its prodigious gate,
Through which the conquerors passed. Great wealth they found,
And having sacked the place, Khosráu erected
A lofty temple, to commemorate
His name and victory there, then back returned
Triumphantly to gladden King Káús,
Whose heart expanded at the joyous news.

The result of Kai-khosráu's expedition against the enchanted castle, compared with that of Fríburz, was sufficient of itself to establish the former in the king's estimation, and accordingly it was announced to the princes and nobles and warriors of the land, that he should succeed to the throne, and be crowned on a fortunate day. A short time afterwards the coronation took place with great pomp and splendour; and Khosráu conducted himself towards men of every rank and station with such perfect kindness and benevolence, that he gained the affections of all and never failed daily to pay a visit to his grandfather Káús, and to familiarize himself with the affairs of the kingdom which he was destined to govern.

> *Justice he spread with equal hand,*
> *Rooting oppression from the land;*
> *And every desert, wood, and wild,*
> *With early cultivation smiled;*
> *And every plain, with verdure clad,*
> *And every Persian heart was glad.*

The Ram with the Golden Fleece

ONCE UPON A TIME when a certain hunter went to the mountains to hunt, there came toward him a ram with golden fleece. The hunter took his rifle to shoot it, but the ram rushed at him and, before he could fire, pierced him with its horns, and he fell dead. A few days later some of his friends found his body; they knew not who had killed him, and they took the body home and interred it. The hunter's wife hung up the rifle on the wall in her cottage, and when her son grew up he begged his mother to let him take it and go hunting. She, however, would not consent, saying, "You must never ask me again to give you that rifle! It did not save your father's life, and do you wish that it should be the cause of your death?"

One day, however, the youth took the rifle secretly and went out into the forest to hunt. Very soon the same ram rushed out of a thicket and said, "I killed your father; now it is your turn!" This frightened the youth, and he exclaimed, "God help me!" He pressed the trigger of his rifle and, lo! the ram fell dead.

The youth was exceedingly glad to have killed the golden-fleeced ram, for there was not another like it throughout the land. He took off its skin and carried the fleece home, feeling very proud of his prowess. By and by the news spread over the country till it reached the Court, and the king ordered the young hunter to bring him the ram's skin, so that he might see what kind of beasts were to be found in his forests. When the youth brought the skin to the king, the latter said to him, "Ask whatever you like for this skin, and I will give you what you ask!" But the youth answered, "I would not sell it for anything."

It happened that the prime minister was an uncle of the young hunter, but he was not his friend; on the contrary, he was his greatest enemy. So he said to the king, "As he does not wish to sell you the skin, set him something to do which is surely impossible!" The king called the youth back and ordered him to plant a vineyard and to bring him, in seven days' time, some new wine from it. The youth began to weep, and implored that he might be excused from such an impossible task. But the king insisted, saying, "If you do not obey me within seven days, your head shall be cut off!"

The Youth Finds a Friend

Still weeping, the youth went home and told his mother all about his audience with the king, and she answered, "Did I not tell you, my son, that that rifle would cost you your life?" In deep sorrow and bewilderment, the youth went out of the village and walked a long way into the wood. Suddenly a girl appeared before him and asked, "Why do you weep, my brother?" And he answered, somewhat angrily, "Go your way! You cannot help me!" He then went on, but the maiden followed him, and again begged him to tell her the reason of his tears. "For perhaps," she added, "I may, after all, be able to help you." Then he stopped and said, "I will tell you, but I know that God alone can help me." And then he told her all that had happened to him, and about the task he had been set to do.

When she heard the story, she said, "Do not fear, my brother, but go and ask the king to say exactly where he would like the vineyard planted, and then have it dug in perfectly straight lines. Next you must go and take a bag with a sprig of basil in it, and lie down to sleep in the place where the vineyard is to be, and in seven days you will see that there are ripe grapes."

He returned home and told his mother how he had met a maiden who had told him to do a ridiculous thing. His mother, however, said earnestly, "Go, go, my son, do as the maiden bade; you cannot be in a worse case anyhow." So he went to the king as the girl had directed him, and the king gratified his wish. However, he was still very sad when he went to lie down in the indicated place with his sprig of basil.

When he awoke next morning, he saw that the vines were already planted, on the second morning they were clothed with leaves, and by the seventh day they bore ripe grapes. Notwithstanding the girl's promise, the youth was surprised to find ripe grapes at a time of year when they were nowhere to be found. But he gathered them, made wine, and, taking a basketful of the ripe fruit with him, went to the king.

The Second Task

When he reached the palace, the king and the whole court were amazed. The prime minister said, "We must order him to do something absolutely impossible!" And he advised the king to command the youth to build a castle of elephants' tusks.

Upon hearing this cruel order, the youth went home weeping and told his mother what had transpired, adding, "This, my mother, is utterly impossible!" But the mother again advised him, and said, "Go, my son, beyond the village. Maybe you will again meet that maiden!"

The youth obeyed, and, indeed, as soon as he came to the place where he had found the girl before, she appeared before him and said, "You are again sad and tearful, my brother!" And he began to complain of the second impossible task which the king had set him to perform. Hearing this, the girl said, "This will also be easy. But first go to the king and ask him to give you a ship with three hundred barrels of wine and as many kegs of brandy, and also twenty carpenters. Then, when you arrive at such and such a place, which you will find between two mountains, dam the water there, and pour into it all the wine and brandy. Elephants will come down to that spot to drink the water, and will get drunk and fall on the ground. Then your carpenters must at once cut off their tusks and carry them to the place where the king wishes his castle to be built. There you may all lie down to sleep, and within seven days the castle will be ready."

When the youth heard this, he hurried home, and told his mother all about the plan of the maiden. The mother was quite confident, and counselled her son to do everything as directed by the maiden. So he went to the king and asked him for the ship, the three hundred barrels of wine and brandy, as well as the twenty carpenters; and the king gave him all he wanted. Next he went where the girl had told him, and did everything she had advised. Indeed, the elephants came as was expected, drank, and then duly fell down intoxicated. The carpenters cut off the innumerable tusks, took them to the chosen place, and began building, and in seven days the castle was ready. When the king saw this, he was again amazed, and said to his prime minister, "Now what shall I do with him? He is not an ordinary youth! God alone knows who he is!" Thereupon the officer answered, "Give him one more order, and if he executes it successfully, he will prove that he is a supernatural being."

The Third Task

Thus he again advised the king, who called the youth and said to him, "I command you to go and bring me the princess of a certain kingdom, who is living in such and such a castle. If you do not bring her to me, you will surely lose your life!" When the youth heard this, he went straight to his mother and told her of this new task, whereupon the mother advised him to seek his friend once more. He hurried to where beyond the village he had met the girl before, and as he came to the spot, she reappeared.

She listened intently to the youth's account of his last visit to the court, and then said, "Go and ask the king to give you a galley; in the galley there must be made twenty shops with different merchandise in each; in each shop there must, also, be a handsome youth to sell the wares. On your voyage you will meet a man who carries an eagle; you must buy his eagle and pay for it whatever price he may ask. Then you will meet a second man, in a boat carrying in his net a carp with golden scales; you must buy the carp at any cost. The third man whom you will meet will be carrying a dove, which you must also buy. Then you must take a feather from the eagle's tail, a scale from the carp, and a feather from the left wing of the dove, and give the creatures their freedom.

"When you reach that distant kingdom and are near the castle in which the princess resides, you must open all shops and order each youth to stand at his door. And the girls who come down to the shore to fetch water are sure to say that no one ever saw a ship loaded with such wonderful and beautiful things in their town before; and then they will go and spread the news all over the place. The news will reach the ears of the princess, who will at once ask her father's permission to go and visit the galley. When she comes on board with her ladies-in-waiting, you must lead the party from one shop to another, and bring out and exhibit before her all the finest merchandise you have; thus divert her and keep her on board your galley until evening, then you must suddenly set sail; for by that time it will be so dark that your departure will be unnoticed.

THE CHOSEN ONES

"The princess will have a favourite bird on her shoulder, and, when she perceives that the galley is sailing off, she will turn the bird loose, and it will fly to the palace with a message to her father of what has befallen her. When you see that the bird has flown, you must burn the eagle's feather; the eagle will appear, and, when you command it to catch the bird, it will instantly do so. Next, the princess will throw a pebble into the sea, and the galley will immediately be still. Upon this you must burn the scale of the carp at once; the carp will come to you and you must instruct it to find the pebble and swallow it. As soon as this is done, the galley will sail on again.

"Then you will proceed in peace for a while; but, when you reach a certain spot between two mountains, your galley will be suddenly petrified, and you will be greatly alarmed. The princess will then order you to bring her some water of life, whereupon you must burn the feather of the dove, and when the bird appears, you must give it a small flask in which it will bring you the elixir, after which your galley will sail on again and you will arrive home with the princess without further adventure."

The youth returned to his mother, and she advised him to do as the girl counselled him. So he went to the king and asked for all that was necessary for his undertaking, and the king again gave him all he asked for.

On his voyage everything was accomplished as the girl had foretold, and he succeeded in bringing home the princess in triumph. The king and his prime minister from the balcony of the palace saw the galley returning, and the prime minister said, "Now you really must have him killed as soon as he lands, otherwise you will never be able to get rid of him!"

When the galley reached the port, the princess first came ashore with her ladies-in-waiting, then the handsome young men who had sold the wares, and finally the youth himself. The king had ordered an executioner to be in readiness, and as soon as the youth stepped on shore, he was seized by the king's servants and his head was chopped off.

It was the king's intention to espouse the beautiful princess, and, as soon as he saw her, he approached her with compliments and flattery. But the princess would not listen to his honeyed words; she turned away and asked, "Where is my captor who did so much for me?" And, when she saw that his head had been cut off, she immediately took the small flask and poured some of its contents over the body and, lo! the youth arose in perfect health. When the king and his minister saw this marvellous thing, the latter said, "This young man must now be wiser than ever, for was he not dead, and has he not returned to life?" Whereupon the king, desirous of knowing if it were true that one who has been dead knows all things when he returns to life, ordered the executioner to chop off his head, that the princess might bring him to life again by the power of her wonderful water of life.

But, when the king's head was off, the princess would not hear of restoring him to life, but immediately wrote to her father, telling him of her love for the youth and declaring her wish to marry him, and she described to her father all that had happened. Her father replied, saying that he approved of his daughter's choice, and he issued a proclamation which stated that, unless the people would elect the youth to be their ruler, he would declare war against them. The men of that country immediately recognized that this would be only just, and so the youth became king, wedded the fair princess, and gave large estates and titles to all the handsome youths who had helped him on his expedition.

He Whom God Helps No One Can Harm

ONCE UPON A TIME there lived a man and his wife, and they were blessed with three sons. The youngest son was the most handsome, and he possessed a better heart than his brothers, who thought him a fool. When the three brothers had arrived at the man's estate, they came together to their father, each of them asking permission to marry. The father was embarrassed with this sudden wish of his sons, and said he would first take counsel with his wife as to his answer.

The First Quest

A few days later the man called his sons together and told them to go to the neighbouring town and seek for employment. "He who brings me the finest rug will obtain my permission to marry first," he said.

The brothers started off to the neighbouring town together. On the way, the two elder brothers began to make fun of the youngest, mocking his simplicity, and finally they forced him to take a different road.

Abandoned by his malicious brothers, the young man prayed for God to grant him good fortune. At length he came to a lake, on the further shore of which was a magnificent castle. The castle belonged to the daughter of a tyrannous and cruel prince who had died long ago. The young princess was uncommonly beautiful, and many a suitor had come there to ask for her hand. The suitors were always made very welcome, but when they went to their rooms at night, the late master of the castle would invariably come as a vampire and suffocate them.

As the youngest brother stood upon the shore wondering how to cross the lake, the princess noticed him from her window and at once gave an order to the servants to take a boat and bring the young man before her. When he appeared, he was a little confused, but the noble maiden reassured him with some kind words – for he had, indeed, made a good impression upon her, and she liked him at first sight. She asked him whence he came and where he intended to go, and the young man told her all about his father's command.

When the princess heard that, she said to the young man, "You will remain here for the night, and tomorrow morning we will see what we can do about your rug."

After they had supped, the princess conducted her guest to a green room, and, bidding him goodnight, said, "This is your room. Do not be alarmed if during the night anything unusual should appear to disturb you."

Being a simple youth, he could not even close his eyes, so deep was the impression made by the beautiful things which surrounded him, when suddenly, toward midnight, there was a great noise. In the midst of the commotion, he heard distinctly a mysterious voice whisper, "This youth will inherit the princely crown; no one can do him harm!" The young man took refuge in earnest prayer, and, when day dawned, he arose safe and sound.

When the princess awoke, she sent a servant to summon the young man to her presence, and he was greatly astonished to find the young man alive; so also was the princess and everyone in the castle.

After breakfast the princess gave her guest a rich rug, saying, "Take this rug to your father, and if he desires aught else, you have only to come back." The young man thanked his fair hostess and with a deep bow took his leave of her.

When he arrived home, he found his two brothers already there; they were showing their father the rugs they had brought. When the youngest exhibited his, they were astounded, and exclaimed, "How did you get hold of such a costly rug? You must have stolen it!"

The Second Quest

At length the father, in order to quieten them, said, "Go once more into the world, and he who brings back a chain long enough to encircle our house nine times shall have my permission to marry first!" Thus the father succeeded in pacifying his sons. The two elder brothers went their way, and the youngest hurried back to the princess. When he appeared, she asked him, "What has your father ordered you to do now?" And he answered, "That each of us should bring a chain long enough to encircle our house nine times." The princess again made him welcome and, after supper, she showed him into a yellow room, saying, "Somebody will come again to frighten you during the night, but you must not pay any attention to him, and tomorrow we will see what we can do about your chain."

And sure enough, about midnight there came many ghosts dancing round his bed and making fearful noises, but he followed the advice of the princess and remained calm and quiet. Next morning a servant came once more to conduct him to the princess, and, after breakfast, she gave him a fine box, saying, "Take this to your father, and if he should desire anything more, you have but to come to me." The young man thanked her and took his leave.

Again he found that his brothers had reached home first with their chains, but these were not long enough to encircle the house even once, and they were greatly astonished when their youngest brother produced from the box the princess had given an enormous gold chain of the required length. Filled with envy, they exclaimed, "You will ruin the reputation of our house, for you must have stolen this chain!"

The Third Quest

At length the father, tired of their jangling, sent them away, saying, "Go, bring each of you his sweetheart, and I will give you permission to marry." Thereupon the two elder brothers went joyfully to fetch the girls they loved, and the youngest hurried away to the princess to tell her what was now his father's desire. When she heard, the princess said, "You must pass a third night here, and then we shall see what we can do."

So, after supping together, she took him into a red room. During the night he heard again a blood-curdling noise, and from the darkness a mysterious voice said, "This young man is about to take possession of my estates and crown!" He was assaulted by ghosts and vampires, and was dragged from his bed. But through all the young man strove earnestly in prayer, and God saved him.

Next morning when he appeared before the princess, she congratulated him on his bravery, and declared that he had won her love. The young man was overwhelmed with happiness, for although he would never have dared to reveal the secret of his heart, he also loved the princess. A barber was now summoned to attend upon the young man, and a tailor to dress him like a prince. This done, the couple went together to the castle chapel and were wedded.

A few days later they drove to the young man's village, and as they stopped outside his home, they heard great rejoicing and music, whereat they understood that his two elder brothers were celebrating their marriage feasts. The youngest brother knocked on the gate, and when his father came, he did not recognize his son in the richly attired prince who stood before him. He was surprised that such distinguished guests should pay him a visit, and still more so when the prince said, "Good man, will you give us your hospitality for tonight?" The father answered, "Most gladly, but we are having festivities in our house, and I fear that these common people will disturb you with their singing and music." To this the young prince said, "Oh, no, it would please me to see the peasants feasting, and my wife would like it even more than I."

They now entered the house, and as the hostess curtsied deeply before them, the prince congratulated her, saying, "How happy you must be to see your two sons wedded on the same day!" The woman sighed. "Ah," said she, "on one hand I have joy and on the other mourning; I had a third son, who went out in the world, and who knows what ill fate may have befallen him?"

After a time the young prince found an opportunity to step into his old room, and put on one of his old suits over his costly attire. He then returned to the room where the feast was spread and stood behind the door. Soon his two brothers saw him, and they called out, "Come here, father, and see your much-praised son, who went and stole like a thief!" The father turned, and seeing the young man, he exclaimed, "Where have you been for so long, and where is your sweetheart?"

Then the youngest son said, "Do not reproach me. All is well with me and with you!" As he spake, he took off his old garments and stood revealed in his princely dress. Then he told his story and introduced his wife to his parents.

The brothers now expressed contrition for their conduct, and received the prince's pardon, after which they all embraced; the feasting was renewed, and the festivities went on for several days. Finally, the young prince distributed amongst his father and brothers large portions of his new lands, and they all lived long and happily together.

The Cattle-Raid of Cualnge

A great hosting was brought together by the Connaughtmen, that is, by Ailill and Medb; and they sent to the three other provinces. And messengers were sent by Ailill to the seven sons of Magach: Ailill, Anluan, Mocorb, Cet, En, Bascall, and Doche; a cantred with each of them. And to Cormac Condlongas Mac Conchobair with his three hundred, who was billeted in Connaught. Then they all come to Cruachan Ai.

Now Cormac had three troops which came to Cruachan. The first troop had many-coloured cloaks folded round them; hair like a mantle; the tunic falling to the knee, and long shields; and a broad grey spearhead on a slender shaft in the hand of each man.

The second troop wore dark grey cloaks, and tunics with red ornamentation down to their calves, and long hair hanging behind from their heads, and white shields, and five-pronged spears were in their hands.

"This is not Cormac yet," said Medb.

Then comes the third troop; and they wore purple cloaks and hooded tunics with red ornamentation down to their feet, hair smooth to their shoulders, and round shields with engraved edges, and spears as large as the pillars of a palace in the hand of each man.

"This is Cormac now," said Medb.

Then the four provinces of Ireland were assembled, till they were in Cruachan Ai. And their poets and their druids did not let them go thence till the end of a fortnight, for waiting for a good omen. Medb said then to her charioteer the day that they set out:

"Everyone who parts here today from his love or his friend will curse me," said she, "for it is I who have gathered this hosting."

"Wait then," said the charioteer, "till I turn the chariot with the sun, and till there come the power of a good omen that we may come back again."

Then the charioteer turned the chariot, and they set forth. Then they saw a full-grown maiden before them. She had yellow hair, and a cloak of many colours, and a golden pin in it; and a hooded tunic with red embroidery. She wore two shoes with buckles of gold. Her face was narrow below and broad above. Very black were her two eyebrows; her black delicate eyelashes cast a shadow into the middle of her two cheeks. You would think it was with *partaing* her lips were adorned. You would think it was a shower of pearls that was in her mouth, that is, her teeth. She had three tresses: two tresses round her head above, and a tress behind, so that it struck her two thighs behind her. A shuttle (a beam used for making fringe) of white metal, with an inlaying of gold, was in her hand. Each of her two eyes had three pupils. The maiden was armed, and there were two black horses to her chariot.

"What is your name?" said Medb to the maiden.

"Fedelm, the prophetess of Connaught, is my name," said the maiden.

"Whence do you come?" said Medb.

"From Scotland, after learning the art of prophecy," said the maiden.

"Have you the inspiration which illumines?" said Medb.

"Yes, indeed," said the maiden.

"Look for me how it will be with my hosting," said Medb.

Then the maiden looked for it; and Medb said: "O Fedelm the prophetess, how seest thou the host?"

Fedelm answered and said: "I see very red, I see red."

"That is not true," said Medb; 'for Conchobar is in his sickness at Emain and the Ulstermen with him, with all the best of their warriors; and my messengers have come and brought me tidings thence.

"Fedelm the prophetess, how seest thou our host?" said Medb.

"I see red," said the maiden.

"That is not true," said Medb; "for Celtchar Mac Uithichair is in Dun Lethglaise, and a third of the Ulstermen with him; and Fergus, son of Roich, son of Eochaid, is here with us, in exile, and a cantred with him. Fedelm the prophetess, how seest thou our host?"

"I see very red, I see red," said the maiden.

"That matters not," said Medb; "for there are mutual angers, and quarrels, and wounds very red in every host and in every assembly of a great army. Look again for us then, and tell us the truth. Fedelm the prophetess, how seest thou our host?"

"I see very red, I see red," said Fedelm.

> *"I see a fair man who will make play*
> *With a number of wounds on his girdle;*
> *A hero's flame over his head,*
> *His forehead a meeting-place of victory.*
>
> *"There are seven gems of a hero of valour*
> *In the middle of his two irises;*
> *There is – on his cloak,*
> *He wears a red clasped tunic.*
>
> *"He has a face that is noble,*
> *Which causes amazement to women.*
> *A young man who is fair of hue*
> *Comes –*
>
> *"Like is the nature of his valour*
> *To Cuchulainn of Murthemne.*
> *I do not know whose is the Hound*
> *Of Culann, whose fame is the fairest.*
> *But I know that it is thus*
> *That the host is very red from him.*
>
> *"I see a great man on the plain*
> *He gives battle to the hosts;*
> *Four little swords of feats*
> *There are in each of his two hands.*
>
> *"Two* Gae-bolga, *he carries them,*
> *Besides an ivory-hilted sword and spear;*
> *– he wields to the host;*
> *Different is the deed for which each arm goes from him.*
>
> *"A man in a battle-girdle, of a red cloak,*
> *He puts – every plain.*
> *He smites them, over left chariot wheel;*
> *The* Riastartha *wounds them.*
> *The form that appeared to me on him hitherto,*
> *I see that his form has been changed.*

"He has moved forward to the battle,
If heed is not taken of him it will be treachery.
I think it likely it is he who seeks you:
Cuchulainn Mac Sualtaim.

"He will strike on whole hosts,
He will make dense slaughters of you,
Ye will leave with him many thousands of heads.
The prophetess Fedelm conceals not.

"Blood will rain from warriors' wounds
At the hand of a warrior – 'twill be full harm.
He will slay warriors, men will wander
Of the descendants of Deda Mac Sin.
Corpses will be cut off, women will lament
Through the Hound of the Smith that I see."

How Fin Went to the Kingdom of the Big Men

FIN AND HIS MEN were in the Harbour of the Hill of Howth on a hillock, behind the wind and in front of the sun, where they could see every person, and nobody could see them, when they saw a speck coming from the west. They thought at first it was the blackness of a shower; but when it came nearer, they saw it was a boat. It did not lower sail till it entered the harbour. There were three men in it; one for guide in the bow, one for steering in the stern, and one for the tackle in the centre. They came ashore, and drew it up seven times its own length in dry grey grass, where the scholars of the city could not make it stock for derision or ridicule.

They then went up to a lovely green spot, and the first lifted a handful of round pebbles or shingle, and commanded them to become a beautiful house, that no better could be found in Ireland; and this was done. The second one lifted a slab of slate, and commanded it to be slate on the top of the house, that there was not better in Ireland; and this was done. The third one caught a bunch of shavings and commanded them to be pine wood and timber in the house, that there was not in Ireland better; and this was done.

This caused much wonder to Fin, who went down where the men were, and made inquiries of them, and they answered him. He asked whence they were, or whither they were going. They said, "We are three Heroes whom the King of the Big Men has sent to ask combat of the Fians." He then asked, "What was the reason for doing this?" They said they did not know, but they heard that they were strong men, and they came to ask combat of Heroes from them. "Is Fin at Home?"

"He is not." (Great is a man's leaning towards his own life.) Fin then put them under crosses and under enchantments, that they were not to move from the place where they were till they saw him again.

He went away and made ready his coracle, gave its stern to land and prow to sea, hoisted the spotted towering sails against the long, tough, lance-shaped mast, cleaving the billows in the embrace of the wind in whirls, with a soft gentle breeze from the height of the sea-coast, and from the rapid tide of the red rocks, that would take willom from the hill, foliage from the tree, and heather from its stock and roots. Fin was guide in her prow, helm in her stern, and tackle in her middle; and stopping of head or foot he did not make till he reached the Kingdom of the Big Men. He went ashore and drew up his coracle in grey grass. He went up, and a Big Wayfarer met him. Fin asked who he was.

"I am," he said, "the Red-haired Coward of the King of the Big Men; and," said he to Fin, "you are the one I am in quest of. Great is my esteem and respect towards you; you are the best maiden I have ever seen; you will yourself make a dwarf for the King, and your dog (this was Bran) a lapdog. It is long since the King has been in want of a dwarf and a lapdog." He took with him Fin; but another Big Man came, and was going to take Fin from him. The two fought; but when they had torn each other's clothes, they left it to Fin to judge. He chose the first one. He took Fin with him to the palace of the King, whose worthies and high nobles assembled to see the little man. The king lifted him upon the palm of his hand, and went three times round the town with Fin upon one palm and Bran upon the other. He made a sleeping-place for him at the end of his own bed. Fin was waiting, watching, and observing everything that was going on about the house. He observed that the King, as soon as night came, rose and went out, and returned no more till morning. This caused him much wonder, and at last he asked the King why he went away every night and left the Queen by herself. "Why," said the King, "do you ask?"

"For satisfaction to myself," said Fin; "for it is causing me much wonder." Now the King had a great liking for Fin; he never saw anything that gave him more pleasure than he did; and at last he told him. "There is," he said, "a great Monster who wants my daughter in marriage, and to have half my kingdom to himself; and there is not another man in the kingdom who can meet him but myself; and I must go every night to hold combat with him."

"Is there," said Fin, "no man to combat with him but yourself?"

"There is not," said the King, "one who will war with him for a single night."

"It is a pity," said Fin, "that this should be called the Kingdom of the Big Men. Is he bigger than yourself?"

"Never you mind," said the King.

"I will mind," said Fin; "take your rest and sleep tonight, and I shall go to meet him."

"Is it you?" said the King; "you would not keep half a stroke against him."

When night came, and all men went to rest, the King was for going away as usual; but Fin at last prevailed upon him to allow himself to go. "I shall combat him," said he, "or else he knows a trick."

"I think much," said the King, "of allowing you to go, seeing he gives myself enough to do."

"Sleep you soundly tonight," said Fin, "and let me go; if he comes too violently upon me, I shall hasten home."

Fin went and reached the place where the combat was to be. He saw no one before him, and he began to pace backwards and forwards. At last he saw the sea coming in kilns of fire and as a darting serpent, till it came down below where he was. A Huge Monster came up and looked towards him, and from him. "What little speck do I see there?" he said.

THE CHOSEN ONES

"It is I," said Fin. "What are you doing here?"

"I am a messenger from the King of the Big Men; he is under much sorrow and distress; the Queen has just died, and I have come to ask if you will be so good as to go home tonight without giving trouble to the kingdom."

"I shall do that," said he; and he went away with the rough humming of a song in his mouth.

Fin went home when the time came, and lay down in his own bed, at the foot of the King's bed. When the King awoke, he cried out in great anxiety, "My kingdom is lost, and my dwarf and my lapdog are killed!"

"They are not," said Fin; "I am here yet; and you have got your sleep, a thing you were saying it was rare for you to get."

"How," said the King, "did you escape, when you are so little, while he is enough for myself, though I am so big."

"Though you," said Fin, "are so big and strong, I am quick and active."

Next night the King was for going; but Fin told him to take his sleep tonight again. "I shall stand myself in your place, or else a better hero than yonder one must come."

"He will kill you," said the King. "I shall take my chance," said Fin.

He went, and as happened the night before, he saw no one; and he began to pace backwards and forwards. He saw the sea coming in fiery kilns and as a darting serpent; and that Huge Man came up. "Are you here tonight again?" said he. "I am, and this is my errand: when the Queen was being put in the coffin, and the King heard the coffin being nailed, and the joiner's stroke, he broke his heart with pain and grief; and the Parliament has sent me to ask you to go home tonight till they get the King buried." The Monster went this night also, roughly humming a song; and Fin went home when the time came.

In the morning the King awoke in great anxiety, and called out, "My kingdom is lost, and my dwarf and my lapdog are killed!" and he greatly rejoiced that Fin and Bran were alive, and that he himself got rest, after being so long without sleep.

Fin went the third night, and things happened as before. There was no one before him, and he took to pacing to and fro. He saw the sea coming till it came down below him: the Big Monster came up; he saw the little black speck, and asked who was there, and what he wanted. "I have come to combat you," said Fin.

Fin and Bran began the combat. Fin was going backwards, and the Huge Man was following. Fin called to Bran, "Are you going to let him kill me?" Bran had a venomous shoe; and he leaped and struck the Huge Man with the venomous shoe on the breast-bone, and took the heart and lungs out of him. Fin drew his sword, Mac-a-Luin, cut off his head, put it on a hempen rope, and went with it to the Palace of the King. He took it into the Kitchen, and put it behind the door. In the morning the servant could not turn it, nor open the door. The King went down; he saw the Huge Mass, caught it by the top of the head, and lifted it, and knew it was the head of the Man who was for so long a time asking combat from him, and keeping him from sleep. "How at all," said he, "has this head come here? Surely it is not my dwarf that has done it."

"Why," said Fin, "should he not?"

Next night the King wanted to go himself to the place of combat; "because," said he, "a bigger one than the former will come tonight, and the kingdom will be destroyed, and you yourself killed; and I shall lose the pleasure I take in having you with me." But Fin went, and that Big Man came, asking vengeance for his son, and to have the kingdom for himself, or equal combat. He and Fin fought; and Fin was going backwards. He spoke to Bran, "Are you going to allow him to kill me?" Bran whined, and went and sat down on the beach. Fin was ever being driven back, and he called out again to Bran. Then Bran jumped and struck the Big Man with the venomous shoe, and took the heart and the lungs out of him. Fin cut the head off, and took it with him, and left it in front of the house. The King awoke in great terror, and cried out, "My kingdom is lost, and my dwarf and my lapdog are killed!" Fin raised himself up and said, "They are not"; and the King's joy was not small when he went out and saw the head that was in front of the house.

The next night a Big Hag came ashore, and the tooth in the door of her mouth would make a distaff. She sounded a challenge on her shield: "You killed," she said, "my husband and my son."

"I did kill them," said Fin. They fought; and it was worse for Fin to guard himself from the tooth than from the hand of the Big Hag. When she had nearly done for him Bran struck her with the venomous shoe, and killed her as he had done to the rest. Fin took with him the head, and left it in front of the house. The King awoke in great anxiety, and called out, "My kingdom is lost, and my dwarf and my lapdog are killed!"

"They are not," said Fin, answering him; and when they went out and saw the head, the King said, "I and my kingdom will have peace ever after this. The mother herself of the brood is killed; but tell me who you are. It was foretold for me that it would be Fin-mac-Coul that would give me relief, and he is only now eighteen years of age. Who are you, then, or what is your name?"

"There never stood," said Fin, "on hide of cow or horse, one to whom I would deny my name. I am Fin, the Son of Coul, son of Looach, son of Trein, son of Fin, son of Art, son of the young High King of Erin; and it is time for me now to go home. It has been with much wandering out of my way that I have come to your kingdom; and this is the reason why I have come, that I might find out what injury I have done to you, or the reason why you sent the three Heroes to ask combat from me, and bring destruction on my Men."

"You never did any injury to me," said the King; "and I ask a thousand pardons. I did not send the heroes to you. It is not the truth they told. They were three men who were courting three fairy women, and these gave them their shirts; and when they have on their shirts, the combat of a hundred men is upon the hand of every one of them. But they must put off the shirts every night, and put them on the backs of chairs; and if the shirts were taken from them they would be next day as weak as other people."

Fin got every honour, and all that the King could give him, and when he went away, the King and the Queen and the people went down to the shore to give him their blessing.

Fin now went away in his coracle, and was sailing close by the side of the shore, when he saw a young man running and calling out to him. Fin came in close to land with his coracle, and asked what he wanted.

"I am," said the young man, "a good servant wanting a master."

"What work can you do?" said Fin.

"I am," said he, "the best soothsayer that there is."

"Jump into the boat then." The soothsayer jumped in, and they went forward.

They did not go far when another youth came running. "I am," he said, "a good servant wanting a master."

"What work can you do?" said Fin.

"I am as good a thief as there is."

"Jump into the boat, then"; and Fin took with him this one also. They saw then a third young man running and calling out. They came close to land. "What man are you?" said Fin.

"I am," said he, "the best climber that there is. I will take up a hundred pounds on my back in a place where a fly could not stand on a calm summer day."

"Jump in"; and this one came in also. "I have my pick of servants now," said Fin; "it cannot be but these will suffice."

They went; and stop of head or foot they did not make till they reached the Harbour of the Hill of Howth. He asked the soothsayer what the three Big Men were doing. "They are," he said, "after their supper, and making ready for going to bed."

He asked a second time. "They are," he said, "after going to bed; and their shirts are spread on the back of chairs."

After a while, Fin asked him again, "What are the Big Men doing now?"

"They are," said the soothsayer, "sound asleep."

"It would be a good thing if there was now a thief to go and steal the shirts."

"I would do that," said the thief, "but the doors are locked, and I cannot get in."

"Come," said the climber, "on my back, and I shall put you in." He took him up upon his back to the top of the chimney, and let him down, and he stole the shirts.

Fin went where the Fian band was; and in the morning they came to the house where the three Big Men were. They sounded a challenge upon their shields, and asked them to come out to combat.

They came out. "Many a day," said they, "have we been better for combat than we are today," and they confessed to Fin everything as it was. "You were," said Fin, "impertinent, but I will forgive you"; and he made them swear that they would be faithful to himself ever after, and ready in every enterprise he would place before them.

The Prophecies of Merlin, and the Birth of Arthur

King Vortigern the usurper sat upon his throne in London, when, suddenly, upon a certain day, ran in a breathless messenger, and cried aloud—

"Arise, Lord King, for the enemy is come; even Ambrosius and Uther, upon whose throne thou sittest – and full twenty thousand with them – and they have sworn by a great oath, Lord, to slay thee, ere this year be done; and even now they march towards thee as the north wind of winter for bitterness and haste."

At those words Vortigern's face grew white as ashes, and, rising in confusion and disorder, he sent for all the best artificers and craftsmen and mechanics, and commanded them vehemently to go and build him straightway in the furthest west of his lands a great and strong castle, where he might fly for refuge and escape the vengeance of his master's sons – "and, moreover," cried he, "let the work be done within a hundred days from now, or I will surely spare no life amongst you all."

Then all the host of craftsmen, fearing for their lives, found out a proper site whereon to build the tower, and eagerly began to lay in the foundations. But no sooner were the walls raised up above the ground than all their work was overwhelmed and broken down by night invisibly, no man perceiving how, or by whom, or what. And the same thing happening again, and yet again, all the workmen, full of terror, sought out the king, and threw themselves upon their faces before him, beseeching him to interfere and help them or to deliver them from their dreadful work.

Filled with mixed rage and fear, the king called for the astrologers and wizards, and took counsel with them what these things might be, and how to overcome them. The wizards worked their spells and incantations, and in the end declared that nothing but the blood of a youth born without mortal father, smeared on the foundations of the castle, could avail to make it stand. Messengers were therefore sent forthwith through all the land to find, if it were possible, such a child. And, as some of them went down a certain village street, they saw a band of lads fighting and quarrelling, and heard them shout at one – "Avaunt, thou imp! – avaunt! Son of no mortal man! go, find thy father, and leave us in peace."

At that the messengers looked steadfastly on the lad, and asked who he was. One said his name was Merlin; another, that his birth and parentage were known by no man; a third, that the foul fiend alone was his father. Hearing the things, the officers seized Merlin, and carried him before the king by force.

But no sooner was he brought to him than he asked in a loud voice, for what cause he was thus dragged there?

"My magicians," answered Vortigern, "told me to seek out a man that had no human father, and to sprinkle my castle with his blood, that it may stand."

"Order those magicians," said Merlin, "to come before me, and I will convict them of a lie."

The king was astonished at his words, but commanded the magicians to come and sit down before Merlin, who cried to them—

"Because ye know not what it is that hinders the foundation of the castle, ye have advised my blood for a cement to it, as if that would avail; but tell me now rather what there is below that ground, for something there is surely underneath that will not suffer the tower to stand?"

The wizards at these words began to fear, and made no answer. Then said Merlin to the king—

"I pray, Lord, that workmen may be ordered to dig deep down into the ground till they shall come to a great pool of water."

This then was done, and the pool discovered far beneath the surface of the ground.

Then, turning again to the magicians, Merlin said, "Tell me now, false sycophants, what there is underneath that pool?" – but they were silent. Then said he to the king, "Command this pool to be drained, and at the bottom shall be found two dragons, great and huge, which now are sleeping, but which at night awake and fight and tear each other. At their great struggle all the ground shakes and trembles, and so casts down thy towers, which, therefore, never yet could find secure foundations."

The king was amazed at these words, but commanded the pool to be forthwith drained; and surely at the bottom of it did they presently discover the two dragons, fast asleep, as Merlin had declared.

But Vortigern sat upon the brink of the pool till night to see what else would happen.

Then those two dragons, one of which was white, the other red, rose up and came near one another, and began a sore fight, and cast forth fire with their breath. But the white dragon had the advantage, and chased the other to the end of the lake. And he, for grief at his flight, turned back upon his foe, and renewed the combat, and forced him to retire in turn. But in the end the red dragon was worsted, and the white dragon disappeared no man knew where.

When their battle was done, the king desired Merlin to tell him what it meant. Whereat he, bursting into tears, cried out this prophecy, which first foretold the coming of King Arthur.

"Woe to the red dragon, which figureth the British nation, for his banishment cometh quickly; his lurkingholes shall be seized by the white dragon – the Saxon whom thou, O king, hast called to the land. The mountains shall be levelled as the valleys, and the rivers of the valleys shall run blood; cities shall be burned, and churches laid in ruins; till at length the oppressed shall turn for a season and prevail against the strangers. For a Boar of Cornwall shall arise and rend them, and trample their necks beneath his feet. The island shall be subject to his power, and he shall take the forests of Gaul. The house of Romulus shall dread him – all the world shall fear him – and his end shall no man know; he shall be immortal in the mouths of the people, and his works shall be food to those that tell them.

"But as for thee, O Vortigern, flee thou the sons of Constantine, for they shall burn thee in thy tower. For thine own ruin wast thou traitor to their father, and didst bring the Saxon heathens to the land. Aurelius and Uther are even now upon thee to revenge their father's murder; and the brood of the white dragon shall waste thy country, and shall lick thy blood. Find out some refuge, if thou wilt! but who may escape the doom of God?"

The king heard all this, trembling greatly; and, convicted of his sins, said nothing in reply. Only he hasted the builders of his tower by day and night, and rested not till he had fled thereto.

In the meantime, Aurelius, the rightful king, was hailed with joy by the Britons, who flocked to his standard, and prayed to be led against the Saxons. But he, till he had first killed Vortigern, would begin no other war. He marched therefore to Cambria, and came before the tower which the usurper had built. Then, crying out to all his knights, "Avenge ye on him who hath ruined Britain and slain my father and your king!" he rushed with many thousands at the castle walls. But, being driven back again and yet again, at length he thought of fire, and ordered blazing brands to be cast into the building from all sides. These finding soon a proper fuel, ceased not to rage, till spreading to a mighty conflagration, they burned down the tower and Vortigern within it.

Then did Aurelius turn his strength against Hengist and the Saxons, and, defeating them in many places, weakened their power for a long season, so that the land had peace.

Anon the king, making many journeys to and fro, restoring ruined churches and, creating order, came to the monastery near Salisbury, where all those British knights lay buried who had been slain there by the treachery of Hengist. For when in former times Hengist had made a solemn truce with Vortigern, to meet in peace and settle terms, whereby himself and all his Saxons should depart from Britain, the Saxon soldiers carried every one of them beneath his garment a long dagger, and, at a given signal, fell upon the Britons, and slew them, to the number of nearly five hundred.

The sight of the place where the dead lay moved Aurelius to great sorrow, and he cast about in his mind how to make a worthy tomb over so many noble martyrs, who had died there for their country.

When he had in vain consulted many craftsmen and builders, he sent, by the advice of the archbishop, for Merlin, and asked him what to do. "If you would honour the burying-place of these men," said Merlin, "with an everlasting monument, send for the Giants' Dance which is in Killaraus, a mountain in Ireland; for there is a structure of stone there which none of this age could raise without a perfect knowledge of the arts. They are stones of a vast size and wondrous nature, and if they can be placed here as they are there, round this spot of ground, they will stand for ever."

At these words of Merlin, Aurelius burst into laughter, and said, "How is it possible to remove such vast stones from so great a distance, as if Britain, also, had no stones fit for the work?"

"I pray the king," said Merlin, "to forbear vain laughter; what I have said is true, for those stones are mystical and have healing virtues. The giants of old brought them from the furthest coast of Africa, and placed them in Ireland while they lived in that country: and their design was to make baths in them, for use in time of grievous illness. For if they washed the stones and put the sick into the water, it certainly healed them, as also it did them that were wounded in battle; and there is no stone among them but hath the same virtue still."

When the Britons heard this, they resolved to send for the stones, and to make war upon the people of Ireland if they offered to withhold them. So, when they had chosen Uther the king's brother for their chief, they set sail, to the number of 15,000 men, and came to Ireland. There Gillomanius, the king, withstood them fiercely, and not till after a great battle could they approach the Giants' Dance, the sight of which filled them with joy and admiration. But when they sought to move the stones, the strength of all the army was in vain, until Merlin, laughing at their failures, contrived machines of wondrous cunning, which took them down with ease, and placed them in the ships.

When they had brought the whole to Salisbury, Aurelius, with the crown upon his head, kept for four days the feast of Pentecost with royal pomp; and in the midst of all the clergy and the people, Merlin raised up the stones, and set them round the sepulchre of the knights and barons, as they stood in the mountains of Ireland.

Then was the monument called "Stonehenge," which stands, as all men know, upon the plain of Salisbury to this very day.

Soon thereafter it befell that Aurelius was slain by poison at Winchester, and was himself buried within the Giants' Dance.

At the same time came forth a comet of amazing size and brightness, darting out a beam, at the end whereof was a cloud of fire shaped like a dragon, from whose mouth went out two rays, one stretching over Gaul, the other ending in seven lesser rays over the Irish sea.

At the appearance of this star a great dread fell upon the people, and Uther, marching into Cambria against the son of Vortigern, himself was very troubled to learn what it might mean. Then Merlin, being called before him, cried with a loud voice: "O mighty loss! O stricken Britain! Alas! the great prince is gone from us. Aurelius Ambrosius is dead, whose death will be ours also, unless God help us. Haste, therefore, noble Uther, to destroy the enemy; the victory shall be thine, and thou shalt be king of all Britain. For the star with the fiery dragon signifies thyself; and the ray over Gaul portends that thou shalt have a son, most mighty, whom all those kingdoms shall obey which the ray covers."

Thus, for the second time, did Merlin foretell the coming of King Arthur. And Uther, when he was made king, remembered Merlin's words, and caused two dragons to be made in gold, in likeness of the dragon he had seen in the star. One of these he gave to Winchester Cathedral, and had the other carried into all his wars before him, whence he was ever after called Uther Pendragon, or the dragon's head.

Now, when Uther Pendragon had passed through all the land, and settled it – and even voyaged into all the countries of the Scots, and tamed the fierceness of that rebel people – he came to London, and ministered justice there. And it befell at a certain great banquet and high feast which the king made at Easter-tide, there came, with many other earls and barons, Gorlois, Duke of Cornwall, and his wife Igerna, who was the most famous beauty in all Britain. And soon thereafter, Gorlois being slain in battle, Uther determined to make Igerna his own wife. But in order to do this, and enable him to come to her – for she was shut up in the high castle of Tintagil, on the furthest coast of Cornwall – the king sent for Merlin, to take counsel with him and to pray his help. This, therefore, Merlin promised him on one condition – namely, that the king should give him up the first son born of the marriage. For Merlin by his arts foreknew that this firstborn should be the long-wished prince, King Arthur.

When Uther, therefore, was at length happily wedded, Merlin came to the castle on a certain day, and said, "Sir, thou must now provide thee for the nourishing of thy child."

And the king, nothing doubting, said, "Be it as thou wilt."

"I know a lord of thine in this land," said Merlin, "who is a man both true and faithful; let him have the nourishing of the child. His name is Sir Ector, and he hath fair possessions both in England and in Wales. When, therefore, the child is born, let him be delivered unto me, unchristened, at yonder postern-gate, and I will bestow him in the care of this good knight."

So when the child was born, the king bade two knights and two ladies to take it, bound in rich cloth of gold, and deliver it to a poor man whom they should discover at the postern-gate. And the child being delivered thus to Merlin, who himself took the guise of a poor man, was carried by him to a holy priest and christened by the name of Arthur, and then was taken to Sir Ector's house, and nourished at Sir Ector's wife's own breasts. And in the same house he remained privily for many years, no man soever knowing where he was, save Merlin and the king.

Anon it befell that the king was seized by a lingering distemper, and the Saxon heathens, taking their occasion, came back from over sea, and swarmed upon the land, wasting it with fire and sword. When Uther heard thereof, he fell into a greater rage than his weakness could bear, and commanded all his nobles to come before him, that he might upbraid them for their cowardice. And when he had sharply and hotly rebuked them, he swore that he himself, nigh unto death although he lay, would lead them forth against the enemy. Then causing a horse-litter to be made, in which he might be carried – for he was too faint and weak to ride – he went up with all his army swiftly against the Saxons.

But they, when they heard that Uther was coming in a litter, disdained to fight with him, saying it would be shame for brave men to fight with one half dead. So they retired into their city; and, as it were in scorn of danger, left the gates wide open. But Uther straightway commanding his men to assault the town, they did so without loss of time, and had already reached the gates, when the Saxons, repenting too late of their haughty pride, rushed forth to the defence. The battle raged till night, and was begun again next day; but at last, their leaders, Octa and Eosa, being slain, the Saxons turned their backs and fled, leaving the Britons a full triumph.

The king at this felt so great joy, that, whereas before he could scarce raise himself without help, he now sat upright in his litter by himself, and said, with a laughing and merry face, "They called me the half-dead king, and so indeed I was; but victory to me half dead is better than defeat and the best health. For to die with honour is far better than to live disgraced."

But the Saxons, although thus defeated, were ready still for war. Uther would have pursued them; but his illness had by now so grown that his knights and barons kept him from the adventure. Whereat the enemy took courage, and left nothing undone to destroy the land; until, descending to the vilest treachery, they resolved to kill the king by poison.

To this end, as he lay sick at Verulam, they sent and poisoned stealthily a spring of clear water, whence he was wont to drink daily; and so, on the very next day, he was taken with the pains of death, as were also a hundred others after him, before the villainy was discovered, and heaps of earth thrown over the well.

The knights and barons, full of sorrow, now took counsel together, and came to Merlin for his help to learn the king's will before he died, for he was by this time speechless. "Sirs, there is no remedy," said Merlin, "and God's will must be done; but be ye all tomorrow before him, for God will make him speak before he die."

So on the morrow all the barons, with Merlin, stood round the bedside of the king; and Merlin said aloud to Uther, "Lord, shall thy son Arthur be the king of all this realm after thy days?"

Then Uther Pendragon turned him about, and said, in the hearing of them all, "God's blessing and mine be upon him. I bid him pray for my soul, and also that he claim my crown, or forfeit all my blessing;" and with those words he died.

Then came together all the bishops and the clergy, and great multitudes of people, and bewailed the king; and carrying his body to the convent of Ambrius, they buried it close by his brother's grave, within the "Giants' Dance."

The Fourth Branch of the Mabinogi

MATH THE SON OF Mathonwy was lord over Gwynedd, and Pryderi the son of Pwyll was lord over the one-and-twenty Cantrevs of the South; and these were the seven Cantrevs of Dyved, and the seven Cantrevs of Morganwc, the four Cantrevs of Ceredigiawn, and the three of Ystrad Tywi.

At that time, Math the son of Mathonwy could not exist unless his feet were in the lap of a maiden, except only when he was prevented by the tumult of war. Now the maiden who was with him was Goewin, the daughter of Pebin of Dôl Pebin, in Arvon, and she was the fairest maiden of her time who was known there.

And Math dwelt always at Caer Dathyl, in Arvon, and was not able to go the circuit of the land, but Gilvaethwy the son of Don, and Eneyd the son of Don, his nephews, the sons of his sisters, with his household, went the circuit of the land in his stead.

Now the maiden was with Math continually, and Gilvaethwy the son of Don set his affections upon her, and loved her so that he knew not what he should do because of her, and therefrom behold his hue, and his aspect, and his spirits changed for love of her, so that it was not easy to know him.

One day his brother Gwydion gazed steadfastly upon him. "Youth," said he, "what aileth thee?" "Why," replied he, "what seest thou in me?" "I see," said he, "that thou hast lost thy aspect and thy hue; what, therefore, aileth thee?" "My lord brother," he answered, "that which aileth me, it will not profit me that I should own to any." "What may it be, my soul?" said he.

"Thou knowest," he said, "that Math the son of Mathonwy has this property, that if men whisper together, in a tone how low soever, if the wind meet it, it becomes known unto him." "Yes," said Gwydion, "hold now thy peace, I know thy intent, thou lovest Goewin."

When he found that his brother knew his intent, he gave the heaviest sigh in the world. "Be silent, my soul, and sigh not," he said. "It is not thereby that thou wilt succeed. I will cause," said he, "if it cannot be otherwise, the rising of Gwynedd, and Powys, and Deheubarth, to seek the maiden. Be thou of glad cheer therefore, and I will compass it."

So they went unto Math the son of Mathonwy. "Lord," said Gwydion, "I have heard that there have come to the South some beasts, such as were never known in this island before." "What are they called?" he asked. "Pigs, lord." "And what kind of animals are they?" "They are small animals, and their flesh is better than the flesh of oxen." "They are small, then?" "And they change their names. Swine are they now called." "Who owneth them?" "Pryderi the son of Pwyll; they were sent him from Annwvyn, by Arawn the king of Annwvyn, and still they keep that name, half hog, half pig." "Verily," asked he, "and by what means may they be obtained from him?" "I will go, lord, as one of twelve, in the guise of bards, to seek the swine." "But it may be that he will refuse you," said he. "My journey will not be evil, lord," said he; "I will not come back without the swine." "Gladly," said he, "go thou forward."

So he and Gilvaethwy went, and ten other men with them. And they came into Ceredigiawn, to the place that is now called Rhuddlan Teivi, where the palace of Pryderi was. In the guise of bards they came in, and they were received joyfully, and Gwydion was placed beside Pryderi that night.

"Of a truth," said Pryderi, "gladly would I have a tale from some of your men yonder." "Lord," said Gwydion, "we have a custom that the first night that we come to the Court of a great man, the chief of song recites. Gladly will I relate a tale." Now Gwydion was the best teller of tales in the world, and he diverted all the Court that night with pleasant discourse and with tales, so that he charmed everyone in the Court, and it pleased Pryderi to talk with him.

And after this, "Lord," said he unto Pryderi, "were it more pleasing to thee, that another should discharge my errand unto thee, than that I should tell thee myself what it is?" "No," he answered, "ample speech hast thou." "Behold then, lord," said he, "my errand. It is to crave from thee the animals that were sent thee from Annwvyn." "Verily," he replied, "that were the easiest thing in the world to grant, were there not a covenant between me and my land concerning them. And the covenant is that they shall not go from me, until they have produced double their number in the land." "Lord," said he, "I can set thee free from those words, and this is the way I can do so; give me not the swine tonight, neither refuse them unto me, and tomorrow I will show thee an exchange for them."

And that night he and his fellows went unto their lodging, and they took counsel. "Ah, my men," said he, "we shall not have the swine for the asking." "Well," said they, "how may they be obtained?" "I will cause them to be obtained," said Gwydion.

Then he betook himself to his arts, and began to work a charm. And he caused twelve chargers to appear, and twelve black greyhounds, each of them white-breasted, and having upon them twelve collars and twelve leashes, such as no one that saw them could know to be other than gold. And upon the horses twelve saddles, and every part which should have been of iron was entirely of gold, and the bridles were of the same workmanship. And with the horses and the dogs he came to Pryderi.

"Good day unto thee, lord," said he. "Heaven prosper thee," said the other, "and greetings be unto thee." "Lord," said he, "behold here is a release for thee from the word which thou spakest last evening concerning the swine; that thou wouldst neither give nor sell them. Thou mayest exchange them for that which is better. And I will give these twelve horses, all caparisoned as they are, with their saddles and their bridles, and these twelve greyhounds, with their collars and their leashes as thou seest, and the twelve gilded shields that thou beholdest yonder." Now these he had formed of fungus. "Well," said he, "we will take counsel." And they consulted together, and determined to give the swine to Gwydion, and to take his horses and his dogs and his shields.

Then Gwydion and his men took their leave, and began to journey forth with the pigs. "Ah, my comrades," said Gwydion, "it is needful that we journey with speed. The illusion will not last but from the one hour to the same tomorrow."

And that night they journeyed as far as the upper part of Ceredigiawn, to the place which, from that cause, is called Mochdrev still. And the next day they took their course through Melenydd, and came that night to the town which is likewise for that reason called Mochdrev between Keri and Arwystli. And thence they journeyed forward; and that night they came as far as that Commot in Powys, which also upon account thereof is called Mochnant, and there tarried they that night. And they journeyed thence to the Cantrev of Rhos, and the place where they were that night is still called Mochdrev.

"My men," said Gwydion, "we must push forward to the fastnesses of Gwynedd with these animals, for there is a gathering of hosts in pursuit of us." So they journeyed on to the highest town of Arllechwedd, and there they made a sty for the swine, and therefore was the name of Creuwyryon given to that town. And after they had made the sty for the swine, they proceeded to Math the son of Mathonwy, at Caer Dathyl. And when they came there, the country was rising. "What news is there here?" asked Gwydion. "Pryderi is assembling one-and-twenty Cantrevs to pursue after you," answered they. "It is marvellous that you should have journeyed so slowly." "Where are the animals whereof you went in quest?" said Math. "They have had a sty made for them in the other Cantrev below," said Gwydion.

Thereupon, lo, they heard the trumpets and the host in the land, and they arrayed themselves and set forward and came to Penardd in Arvon.

And at night Gwydion the son of Don, and Gilvaethwy his brother, returned to Caer Dathyl; and Gilvaethwy took Math the son of Mathonwy's couch. And while he turned out the other damsels from the room discourteously, he made Goewin unwillingly remain.

And when they saw the day on the morrow, they went back unto the place where Math the son of Mathonwy was with his host; and when they came there, the warriors were taking counsel in what district they should await the coming of Pryderi, and the men of the South. So they went in to the council. And it was resolved to wait in the strongholds of Gwynedd, in Arvon. So within the two Maenors they took their stand, Maenor Penardd and Maenor Coed Alun. And there Pryderi attacked them, and there the combat took place. And great was the slaughter on both sides; but the men of the South were forced to flee. And they fled unto the place which is still called Nantcall. And thither did they follow them, and they made a vast slaughter of them there, so that they fled again as far as the place called Dol Pen Maen, and there they halted and sought to make peace.

And that he might have peace, Pryderi gave hostages, Gwrgi Gwastra gave he and three-and-twenty others, sons of nobles. And after this they journeyed in peace even unto Traeth Mawr; but as they went on together towards Melenryd, the men on foot could not be restrained from shooting. Pryderi dispatched unto Math an embassy to pray him to forbid his people, and to leave it between him and Gwydion the son of Don, for that he had caused all this. And the messengers came to Math. "Of a truth," said Math, "I call Heaven to witness, if it be pleasing unto Gwydion the son of Don, I will so leave it gladly. Never will I compel any to go to fight, but that we ourselves should do our utmost."

"Verily," said the messengers, "Pryderi saith that it were more fair that the man who did him this wrong should oppose his own body to his, and let his people remain unscathed." "I declare to Heaven, I will not ask the men of Gwynedd to fight because of me. If I am allowed to fight Pryderi myself, gladly will I oppose my body to his." And this answer they took back to Pryderi. "Truly," said Pryderi, "I shall require no one to demand my rights but myself."

Then these two came forth and armed themselves, and they fought. And by force of strength, and fierceness, and by the magic and charms of Gwydion, Pryderi was slain. And at Maen Tyriawc, above Melenryd, was he buried, and there is his grave.

And the men of the South set forth in sorrow towards their own land; nor is it a marvel that they should grieve, seeing that they had lost their lord, and many of their best warriors, and for the most part their horses and their arms.

The men of Gwynedd went back joyful and in triumph. "Lord," said Gwydion unto Math, "would it not be right for us to release the hostages of the men of the South, which they pledged unto us for peace? for we ought not to put them in prison." "Let them then be set free," saith Math. So that youth, and the other hostages that were with him, were set free to follow the men of the South.

Math himself went forward to Caer Dathyl. Gilvaethwy the son of Don, and they of the household that were with him, went to make the circuit of Gwynedd as they were wont, without coming to the Court. Math went into his chamber, and caused a place to be prepared for him whereon to recline, so that he might put his feet in the maiden's lap. "Lord," said Goewin, "seek now another to hold thy feet, for I am now a wife." "What meaneth this?" said he. "An attack, lord, was made unawares upon me; but I held not my peace, and there was no one in the Court who knew not of it. Now the attack was made by thy nephews, lord, the sons of thy sister, Gwydion the son of Don, and Gilvaethwy the son of Don; unto me they did wrong, and unto thee dishonour." "Verily," he exclaimed, "I will do to the utmost of my power concerning this matter. But first I will cause thee to have compensation, and then will I have amends made unto myself. As for thee, I will take thee to be my wife, and the possession of my dominions will I give unto thy hands."

And Gwydion and Gilvaethwy came not near the Court, but stayed in the confines of the land until it was forbidden to give them meat and drink. At first they came not near unto Math, but at the last they came. "Lord," said they, "good day to thee." "Well," said he, "is it to make me compensation that ye are come?" "Lord," they said, "we are at thy will." "By my will I would not have lost my warriors, and so many arms as I have done. You cannot compensate me my shame, setting aside the death of Pryderi. But since ye come hither to be at my will, I shall begin your punishment forthwith."

Then he took his magic wand, and struck Gilvaethwy, so that he became a deer, and he seized upon the other hastily lest he should escape from him. And he struck him with the same magic wand, and he became a deer also. "Since now ye are in bonds, I will that ye go forth together and be companions, and possess the nature of the animals whose form ye bear. And this day twelvemonth come hither unto me."

At the end of a year from that day, lo there was a loud noise under the chamber wall, and the barking of the dogs of the palace together with the noise. "Look," said he, "what is without." "Lord," said one, "I have looked; there are there two deer, and a fawn with them." Then he arose and went out. And when he came he beheld the three animals. And he lifted up his wand. "As ye were deer last year, be ye wild hogs each and either of you, for the year that is to come." And thereupon he struck them with the magic wand. "The young one will I take and cause to be baptized." Now the name that he gave him was Hydwn. "Go ye and be wild swine, each and either of you, and be ye of the nature of wild swine. And this day twelvemonth be ye here under the wall."

At the end of the year the barking of dogs was heard under the wall of the chamber. And the Court assembled, and thereupon he arose and went forth, and when he came forth he beheld three beasts. Now these were the beasts that he saw; two wild hogs of the woods, and a well-grown young one with them. And he was very large for his age. "Truly," said Math, "this one will I take and cause to be baptized." And he struck him with his magic wand, and he become a fine fair auburn-haired youth, and the name that he gave him was Hychdwn. "Now as for you, as ye were wild hogs last year, be ye wolves each and either of you for the year that is to come." Thereupon he struck them with his magic wand, and they became wolves. "And be ye of like nature with the animals whose semblance ye bear, and return here this day twelvemonth beneath this wall."

And at the same day at the end of the year, he heard a clamour and a barking of dogs under the wall of the chamber. And he rose and went forth. And when he came, behold, he saw two wolves, and a strong cub with them. "This one will I take," said Math, "and I will cause him to be baptized; there is a name prepared for him, and that is Bleiddwn. Now these three, such are they:

The three sons of Gilvaethwy the false,
The three faithful combatants,
Bleiddwn, Hydwn, and Hychdwn the Tall."

Then he struck the two with his magic wand, and they resumed their own nature. "Oh men," said he, "for the wrong that ye did unto me sufficient has been your punishment and your dishonour. Prepare now precious ointment for these men, and wash their heads, and equip them." And this was done.

And after they were equipped, they came unto him. "Oh men," said he, "you have obtained peace, and you shall likewise have friendship. Give your counsel unto me, what maiden I shall seek." "Lord," said Gwydion the son of Don, "it is easy to give thee counsel; seek Arianrod, the daughter of Don, thy niece, thy sister's daughter."

And they brought her unto him, and the maiden came in. "Ha, damsel," said he, "art thou the maiden?" "I know not, lord, other than that I am." Then he took up his magic wand, and bent it. "Step over this," said he, "and I shall know if thou art the maiden." Then stepped she over the magic wand, and there appeared forthwith a fine chubby yellow-haired boy. And at the crying out of the boy, she went towards the door. And thereupon some small form was seen; but before anyone could get a second glimpse of it, Gwydion had taken it, and had flung a scarf of velvet around it and hidden it. Now the place where he hid it was the bottom of a chest at the foot of his bed.

"Verily," said Math the son of Mathonwy, concerning the fine yellow-haired boy, "I will cause this one to be baptized, and Dylan is the name I will give him."

So they had the boy baptized, and as they baptized him he plunged into the sea. And immediately when he was in the sea, he took its nature, and swam as well as the best fish that was therein. And for that reason was he called Dylan, the son of the Wave. Beneath him no wave ever broke. And the blow whereby he came to his death was struck by his uncle Govannon. The third fatal blow was it called.

As Gwydion lay one morning on his bed awake, he heard a cry in the chest at his feet; and though it was not loud, it was such that he could hear it. Then he arose in haste, and opened the chest: and when he opened it, he beheld an infant boy stretching out his arms from the folds of the scarf, and casting it aside. And he took up the boy in his arms, and carried him to a place where he knew there was a woman that could nurse him. And he agreed with the woman that she should take charge of the boy. And that year he was nursed.

And at the end of the year he seemed by his size as though he were two years old. And the second year he was a big child, and able to go to the Court by himself. And when he came to the Court, Gwydion noticed him, and the boy became familiar with him, and loved him better than anyone else. Then was the boy reared at the Court until he was four years old, when he was as big as though he had been eight.

And one day Gwydion walked forth, and the boy followed him, and he went to the Castle of Arianrod, having the boy with him; and when he came into the Court, Arianrod arose to meet him, and greeted him and bade him welcome. "Heaven prosper thee," said he. "Who is the boy that followeth thee?" she asked. "This youth, he is thy son," he answered. "Alas," said she, "what has come unto thee that thou shouldst shame me thus? wherefore dost thou seek my dishonour, and retain it so long as this?" "Unless thou suffer dishonour greater than that of my bringing up such a boy as this, small will be thy disgrace." "What is the name of the boy?" said she. "Verily," he replied, "he has not yet a name." "Well," she said, "I lay this destiny upon him, that he shall never have a name until he receives one from me." "Heaven bears me witness," answered he, "that thou art a wicked woman. But the boy shall have a name how displeasing soever it may be unto thee. As for thee, that which afflicts thee is that thou art no longer called a damsel." And thereupon he went forth in wrath, and returned to Caer Dathyl and there he tarried that night.

And the next day he arose and took the boy with him, and went to walk on the seashore between that place and Aber Menei. And there he saw some sedges and seaweed, and he turned them into a boat. And out of dry sticks and sedges he made some Cordovan leather, and a great deal thereof, and he coloured it in such a manner that no one ever saw leather more beautiful than it. Then he made a sail to the boat, and he and the boy went in it to the port of the castle of Arianrod. And he began forming shoes and stitching them, until he was observed from the castle. And when he knew that they of the castle were observing him, he disguised his aspect, and put another semblance upon himself, and upon the boy, so that they might not be known. "What men are those in yonder boat?" said Arianrod. "They are cordwainers," answered they. "Go and see what kind of leather they have, and what kind of work they can do."

So they came unto them. And when they came he was colouring some Cordovan leather, and gilding it. And the messengers came and told her this. "Well," said she, "take the measure of my foot, and desire the cordwainer to make shoes for me." So he made the shoes for her, yet not according to the measure, but larger. The shoes then were brought unto her, and behold they were too large. "These are too large," said she, "but he shall receive their value. Let him also make some that are smaller than they." Then he made her others that were much smaller than her foot, and sent them unto her. "Tell him that these will not go on my feet," said she. And they told him this. "Verily," said he, "I will not make her any shoes, unless I see her foot." And this was told unto her. "Truly," she answered, "I will go unto him."

So she went down to the boat, and when she came there, he was shaping shoes and the boy stitching them. "Ah, lady," said he, "good day to thee." "Heaven prosper thee," said she. "I marvel that thou canst not manage to make shoes according to a measure." "I could not," he replied, "but now I shall be able."

Thereupon behold a wren stood upon the deck of the boat, and the boy shot at it, and hit it in the leg between the sinew and the bone. Then she smiled. "Verily," said she, "with a steady hand did the lion aim at it." "Heaven reward thee not, but now has he got a name. And a good enough name it is. Llew Llaw Gyffes be he called henceforth."

Then the work disappeared in seaweed and sedges, and he went on with it no further. And for that reason was he called the third Gold-shoemaker. "Of a truth," said she, "thou wilt not thrive the better for doing evil unto me." "I have done thee no evil yet," said he. Then he restored the boy to his own form. "Well," said she, "I will lay a destiny upon this boy, that he shall never have arms and armour until I invest him with them." "By Heaven," said he, "let thy malice be what it may, he shall have arms."

Then they went towards Dinas Dinllev, and there he brought up Llew Llaw Gyffes, until he could manage any horse, and he was perfect in features, and strength, and stature. And then Gwydion saw that he languished through the want of horses and arms. And he called him unto him. "Ah, youth," said he, "we will go tomorrow on an errand together. Be therefore more cheerful than thou art." "That I will," said the youth.

Next morning, at the dawn of day, they arose. And they took way along the sea coast, up towards Bryn Aryen. And at the top of Cevn Clydno they equipped themselves with horses, and went towards the Castle of Arianrod. And they changed their form, and pricked towards the gate in the semblance of two youths, but the aspect of Gwydion was more staid than that of the other. "Porter," said he, "go thou in and say that there are here bards from Glamorgan." And the porter went in. "The welcome of Heaven be unto them, let them in," said Arianrod.

With great joy were they greeted. And the hall was arranged, and they went to meat. When meat was ended, Arianrod discoursed with Gwydion of tales and stories. Now Gwydion was an excellent teller of tales. And when it was time to leave off feasting, a chamber was prepared for them, and they went to rest.

In the early twilight Gwydion arose, and he called unto him his magic and his power. And by the time that the day dawned, there resounded through the land uproar, and trumpets and shouts. When it was now day, they heard a knocking at the door of the chamber, and therewith Arianrod asking that it might be opened. Up rose the youth and opened unto her, and she entered and a maiden with her. "Ah, good men," she said, "in evil plight are we." "Yes, truly," said Gwydion, "we have heard trumpets and shouts; what thinkest thou that they may mean?" "Verily," said she, "we cannot see the colour of the ocean by reason of all the ships, side by side. And they are making for the land with all the speed they can. And what can we do?" said she. "Lady," said Gwydion, "there is none other counsel than to close the castle upon us, and to defend it as best we may." "Truly," said she, "may Heaven reward you. And do you defend it. And here may you have plenty of arms."

And thereupon went she forth for the arms, and behold she returned, and two maidens, and suits of armour for two men, with her. "Lady," said he, "do you accoutre this stripling, and I will arm myself with the help of thy maidens. Lo, I hear the tumult of the men approaching." "I will do so, gladly." So she armed him fully, and that right cheerfully. "Hast thou finished arming the youth?" said he. "I have finished," she answered. "I likewise have finished," said Gwydion. "Let us now take off our arms, we have no need of them." "Wherefore?" said she. "Here is the army around the house." "Oh, lady, there is here no army." "Oh," cried she, "whence then was this tumult?" "The tumult was but to break thy prophecy and to obtain arms for thy son. And now has he got arms without any thanks unto thee." "By Heaven," said Arianrod, "thou art a wicked man. Many a youth might have lost his life through the uproar thou hast caused in this Cantrev today. Now will I lay a destiny upon this youth," she said, "that he shall never have a wife of the race that now inhabits this earth." "Verily," said he, "thou wast ever a malicious woman, and no one ought to support thee. A wife shall he have notwithstanding."

They went thereupon unto Math the son of Mathonwy, and complained unto him most bitterly of Arianrod. Gwydion showed him also how he had procured arms for the youth. "Well," said Math, "we will seek, I and thou, by charms and illusion, to form a wife for him out of flowers. He has now come to man's stature, and he is the comeliest youth that was ever beheld." So they took the blossoms of the oak, and the blossoms of the broom, and the blossoms of the meadow-sweet, and produced from them a maiden, the fairest and most graceful that man ever saw. And they baptized her, and gave her the name of Blodeuwedd.

After she had become his bride, and they had feasted, said Gwydion, "It is not easy for a man to maintain himself without possessions." "Of a truth," said Math, "I will give the young man the best Cantrev to hold." "Lord," said he, "what Cantrev is that?" "The Cantrev of Dinodig," he answered. Now it is called at this day Eivionydd and Ardudwy. And the place in the Cantrev where he dwelt, was a palace of his in a spot called Mur y Castell, on the confines of Ardudwy. There dwelt he and reigned, and both he and his sway were beloved by all.

One day he went forth to Caer Dathyl, to visit Math the son of Mathonwy. And on the day that he set out for Caer Dathyl, Blodeuwedd walked in the Court. And she heard the sound of a horn. And after the sound of the horn, behold a tired stag went by, with dogs and huntsmen following it. And after the dogs and the huntsmen there came a crowd of men on foot. "Send a youth," said she, "to ask who yonder host may be." So a youth went, and inquired who they were. "Gronw Pebyr is this, the lord of Penllyn," said they. And thus the youth told her.

Gronw Pebyr pursued the stag, and by the river Cynvael he overtook the stag and killed it. And what with flaying the stag and baiting his dogs, he was there until the night began to close in upon him. And as the day departed and the night drew near, he came to the gate of the Court. "Verily," said Blodeuwedd, "the Chieftain will speak ill of us if we let him at this hour depart to another land without inviting him in." "Yes, truly, lady," said they, "it will be most fitting to invite him."

Then went messengers to meet him and bid him in. And he accepted her bidding gladly, and came to the Court, and Blodeuwedd went to meet him, and greeted him, and bade him welcome. "Lady," said he, "Heaven repay thee thy kindness."

When they had disaccoutred themselves, they went to sit down. And Blodeuwedd looked upon him, and from the moment that she looked on him she became filled with his love. And he gazed on her, and the same thought came unto him as unto her, so that he could not conceal from her that he loved her, but he declared unto her that he did so. Thereupon she was very joyful. And all their discourse that night was concerning the affection and love which they felt one for the other, and which in no longer space than one evening had arisen. And that evening passed they in each other's company.

The next day he sought to depart. But she said, "I pray thee go not from me today." And that night he tarried also. And that night they consulted by what means they might always be together. "There is none other counsel," said he, "but that thou strive to learn from Llew Llaw Gyffes in what manner he will meet his death. And this must thou do under the semblance of solicitude concerning him."

The next day Gronw sought to depart. "Verily," said she, "I will counsel thee not to go from me today." "At thy instance will I not go," said he, "albeit, I must say, there is danger that the chief who owns the palace may return home." "Tomorrow," answered she, "will I indeed permit thee to go forth."

The next day he sought to go, and she hindered him not. "Be mindful," said Gronw, "of what I have said unto thee, and converse with him fully, and that under the guise of the dalliance of love, and find out by what means he may come to his death."

That night Llew Llaw Gyffes returned to his home. And the day they spent in discourse, and minstrelsy, and feasting. And at night they went to rest, and he spoke to Blodeuwedd once, and he spoke to her a second time. But, for all this, he could not get from her one word. "What aileth thee?" said he, "art thou well?" "I was thinking," said she, "of that which thou didst never think of concerning me; for I was sorrowful as to thy death, lest thou shouldst go sooner than I." "Heaven reward thy care for me," said he, "but until Heaven take me I shall not easily be slain." "For the sake of Heaven, and for mine, show me how thou mightest be slain. My memory in guarding is better than thine." "I will tell thee gladly," said he. "Not easily can I be slain, except by a wound. And the spear wherewith I am struck must be a year in the forming. And nothing must be done towards it except during the sacrifice on Sundays." "Is this certain?" asked she. "It is in truth," he answered. "And I cannot be slain within a house, nor without. I cannot be slain on horseback nor on foot." "Verily," said she, "in what manner then canst thou be slain?" "I will tell thee," said he. "By making a bath for me by the side of a river, and by putting a roof over the cauldron, and thatching it well and tightly, and bringing a buck, and putting it beside the cauldron. Then if I place one foot on the buck's back, and the other on the edge of the cauldron, whosoever strikes me thus will cause my death." "Well," said she, "I thank Heaven that it will be easy to avoid this."

No sooner had she held this discourse than she sent to Gronw Pebyr. Gronw toiled at making the spear, and that day twelvemonth it was ready. And that very day he caused her to be informed thereof.

"Lord," said Blodeuwedd unto Llew, "I have been thinking how it is possible that what thou didst tell me formerly can be true; wilt thou show me in what manner thou couldst stand at once upon the edge of a cauldron and upon a buck, if I prepare the bath for thee?" "I will show thee," said he.

Then she sent unto Gronw, and bade him be in ambush on the hill which is now called Bryn Kyvergyr, on the bank of the river Cynvael. She caused also to be collected all the goats that were in the Cantrev, and had them brought to the other side of the river, opposite Bryn Kyvergyr.

And the next day she spoke thus. "Lord," said she, "I have caused the roof and the bath to be prepared, and lo! they are ready." "Well," said Llew, "we will go gladly to look at them."

The day after they came and looked at the bath. "Wilt thou go into the bath, lord?" said she. "Willingly will I go in," he answered. So into the bath he went, and he anointed himself. "Lord," said she, "behold the animals which thou didst speak of as being called bucks." "Well," said he, "cause one of them to be caught and brought here." And the buck was brought. Then Llew rose out of the bath, and put on his trousers, and he placed one foot on the edge of the bath and the other on the buck's back.

Thereupon Gronw rose up from the bill which is called Bryn Kyvergyr, and he rested on one knee, and flung the poisoned dart and struck him on the side, so that the shaft started out, but the head of the dart remained in. Then he flew up in the form of an eagle and gave a fearful scream. And thenceforth was he no more seen.

As soon as he departed Gronw and Blodeuwedd went together unto the palace that night. And the next day Gronw arose and took possession of Ardudwy. And after he had overcome the land, he ruled over it, so that Ardudwy and Penllyn were both under his sway.

Then these tidings reached Math the son of Mathonwy. And heaviness and grief came upon Math, and much more upon Gwydion than upon him. "Lord," said Gwydion, "I shall never rest until I have tidings of my nephew." "Verily," said Math, "may Heaven be thy strength." Then Gwydion set forth and began to go forward. And he went through Gwynedd and Powys to the confines. And when he had done so, he went into Arvon, and came to the house of a vassal, in Maenawr Penardd. And he alighted at the house, and stayed there that night. The man of the house and his house-hold came in, and last of all came there the swineherd. Said the man of the house to the swineherd, "Well, youth, hath thy sow come in tonight?" "She hath," said he, "and is this instant returned to the pigs." "Where doth this sow go to?" said Gwydion. "Every day, when the sty is opened, she goeth forth and none can catch sight of her, neither is it known whither she goeth more than if she sank into the earth." "Wilt thou grant unto me," said Gwydion, "not to open the sty until I am beside the sty with thee?" "This will I do, right gladly," he answered.

That night they went to rest; and as soon as the swineherd saw the light of day, he awoke Gwydion. And Gwydion arose and dressed himself, and went with the swineherd, and stood beside the sty. Then the swineherd opened the sty. And as soon as he opened it, behold she leaped forth, and set off with great speed. And Gwydion followed her, and she went against the course of a river, and made for a brook, which is now called Nant y Llew. And there she halted and began feeding. And Gwydion came under the tree, and looked what it might be that the sow was feeding on. And he saw that she was eating putrid flesh and vermin. Then looked he up to the top of the tree, and as he looked he beheld on the top of the tree an eagle, and when the eagle shook itself, there fell vermin and putrid flesh from off it, and these the sow devoured. And it seemed to him that the eagle was Llew. And he sang an Englyn:

> *"Oak that grows between the two banks;*
> *Darkened is the sky and hill!*
> *Shall I not tell him by his wounds,*
> *That this is Llew?"*

Upon this the eagle came down until he reached the centre of the tree. And Gwydion sang another Englyn:

> *"Oak that grows in upland ground,*
> *Is it not wetted by the rain? Has it not been drenched*

By nine score tempests?
It bears in its branches Llew Llaw Gyffes!"

Then the eagle came down until he was on the lowest branch of the tree, and thereupon this Englyn did Gwydion sing:

"Oak that grows beneath the steep;
Stately and majestic is its aspect!
Shall I not speak it?
That Llew will come to my lap?"

And the eagle came down upon Gwydion's knee. And Gwydion struck him with his magic wand, so that he returned to his own form. No one ever saw a more piteous sight, for he was nothing but skin and bone.

Then he went unto Caer Dathyl, and there were brought unto him good physicians that were in Gwynedd, and before the end of the year he was quite healed.

"Lord," said he unto Math the son of Mathonwy, "it is full time now that I have retribution of him by whom I have suffered all this woe." "Truly," said Math, "he will never be able to maintain himself in the possession of that which is thy right." "Well," said Llew, "the sooner I have my right, the better shall I be pleased."

Then they called together the whole of Gwynedd, and set forth to Ardudwy. And Gwydion went on before and proceeded to Mur y Castell. And when Blodeuwedd heard that he was coming, she took her maidens with her, and fled to the mountain. And they passed through the river Cynvael, and went towards a court that there was upon the mountain, and through fear they could not proceed except with their faces looking backwards, so that unawares they fell into the lake. And they were all drowned except Blodeuwedd herself, and her Gwydion overtook. And he said unto her, "I will not slay thee, but I will do unto thee worse than that. For I will turn thee into a bird; and because of the shame thou hast done unto Llew Llaw Gyffes, thou shalt never show thy face in the light of day henceforth; and that through fear of all the other birds. For it shall be their nature to attack thee, and to chase thee from wheresoever they may find thee. And thou shalt not lose thy name, but shalt be always called Blodeuwedd." Now Blodeuwedd is an owl in the language of this present time, and for this reason is the owl hateful unto all birds. And even now the owl is called Blodeuwedd.

Then Gronw Pebyr withdrew unto Penllyn, and he dispatched thence an embassy. And the messengers he sent asked Llew Llaw Gyffes if he would take land, or domain, or gold, or silver, for the injury he had received. "I will not, by my confession to Heaven," said he. "Behold this is the least that I will accept from him; that he come to the spot where I was when he wounded me with the dart, and that I stand where he did, and that with a dart I take my aim at him. And this is the very least that I will accept."

And this was told unto Gronw Pebyr. "Verily," said he, "is it needful for me to do thus? My faithful warriors, and my household, and my foster-brothers, is there not one among you who will stand the blow in my stead?" "There is not, verily," answered they. And because of their refusal to suffer one stroke for their lord, they are called the third disloyal tribe even unto this day. "Well," said he, "I will meet it."

Then they two went forth to the banks of the river Cynvael, and Gronw stood in the place where Llew Llaw Gyffes was when he struck him, and Llew in the place where Gronw was. Then said Gronw Pebyr unto Llew, "Since it was through the wiles of a woman that I did unto thee as I have done, I adjure thee by Heaven to let me place between me and the blow, the slab thou seest yonder on the river's bank." "Verily," said Llew, "I will not refuse thee this." "Ah," said he, "may Heaven reward thee." So Gronw took the slab and placed it between him and the blow.

Then Llew flung the dart at him, and it pierced the slab and went through Gronw likewise, so that it pierced through his back. And thus was Gronw Pebyr slain. And there is still the slab on the bank of the river Cynvael, in Ardudwy, having the hole through it. And therefore is it even now called Llech Gronw.

A second time did Llew Llaw Gyffes take possession of the land, and prosperously did he govern it. And, as the story relates, he was lord after this over Gwynedd.

And thus ends this fourth part of the Mabinogi.

The Birth of Cúchulainn

KING CONCHOBAR MAC NESSA was ruler of Ulster at the time when Cúchulainn, the mightiest hero of the Red Guard, came to be born. It happened that one day, the King's sister Dechtire, whom he cherished above all others, disappeared from the palace without warning, taking fifty of her maidens and her most valuable possessions with her. Although Conchobar summoned every known person in the court before him for questioning, no explanation could be discovered for his sister's departure. For three long years, the King's messengers scoured the country in search of Dechtire, but not one among them ever brought him news of her whereabouts.

At last, one summer's morning, a strange flock of birds descended on the palace gardens of Emain Macha and began to gorge themselves on every fruit tree and vegetable patch in sight. Greatly disturbed by the greed and destruction he witnessed, the King immediately gathered together a party of his hunters, and they set off in pursuit of the birds, armed with powerful slings and the sharpest of arrows. Fergus mac Roig, Conchobar's chief huntsman and guide, was among the group, as were his trusted warriors Amergin and Bricriu. As the day wore on, they found themselves being lured a great distance southward by the birds, across Sliab Fuait, towards the Plain of Gossa, and with every step taken they grew more angry and frustrated that not one arrow had yet managed to ruffle a single feather.

Nightfall had overtaken them before they had even noticed the light begin to fade, and the King, realizing that they would never make it safely back to the palace, gave the order for Fergus and some of the others to go out in search of a place of lodging for the party. Before long, Fergus came upon a small hut whose firelight was extremely inviting, and he approached and knocked politely on the door. He received a warm and hearty welcome from the old married couple within, and they at once offered him food and a comfortable bed for the evening. But Fergus would not accept their kind hospitality, knowing that his companions were still abroad without shelter.

"Then they are all invited to join us," said the old woman, and as she bustled about, preparing food and wine for her visitors, Fergus went off to deliver his good news to Conchobar and the rest of the group.

Bricriu had also set off in search of accommodation, and as he had walked to the opposite side of the woodlands, he was certain that he heard the gentle sound of harp music. Instinctively drawn towards the sweet melody, he followed the winding path through the trees until he came upon a regal mansion standing proudly on the banks of the river Boyne. He timidly approached the noble structure, but there was no need for him to knock, since the door was already ajar and a young maiden, dressed in a flowing gown of shimmering gold, stood in the entrance hall ready to greet him. She was accompanied by a young man of great stature and splendid appearance who smiled warmly at Bricriu and extended his hand in friendship:

"You are indeed welcome," said the handsome warrior, "we have been waiting patiently for your visit to our home this day."

"Come inside, Bricriu," said the beautiful maiden, "why is it that you linger out of doors?"

"Can it be that you do not recognize the woman who appears before you?" asked the warrior.

"Her great beauty stirs a memory from the past," replied Bricriu, "but I cannot recall anything more at present."

"You see before you Dechtire, sister of Conchobar mac Nessa," said the warrior, "and the fifty maidens you have been seeking these three years are also in this house. They have today visited Emain Macha in the form of birds in order to lure you here."

"Then I must go at once to the King and inform him of what I have discovered," answered Bricriu, "for he will be overjoyed to know that Dechtire has been found and will be eager for her to accompany him back to the palace where there will be great feasting and celebration."

He hurried back through the woods to rejoin the King and his companions. And when Conchobar heard the news of Bricriu's discovery, he could scarcely contain his delight and was immediately anxious to be reunited with his sister. A messenger was sent forth to invite Dechtire and the warrior to share in their evening meal, and a place was hurriedly prepared for the couple at the table inside the welcoming little hut. But Dechtire was already suffering the first pangs of childbirth by the time Conchobar's messenger arrived with his invitation. She excused herself by saying that she was tired and agreed instead to meet up with her brother at dawn on the following morning.

When the first rays of sunshine had brightened the heavens, Conchobar arose from his bed and began to prepare himself for Dechtire's arrival. He had passed a very peaceful night and went in search of Fergus and the others in the happiest of moods. Approaching the place where his men were sleeping, he became convinced that he had heard the stifled cries of an infant. Again, as he drew nearer, the sound was repeated. He stooped down and began to examine a small, strange bundle lying on the ground next to Bricriu. As he unwrapped it, the bundle began to wriggle in his arms and a tiny pink hand revealed itself from beneath the cloth covering.

Dechtire did not appear before her brother that morning, or on any morning to follow. But she had left the King a great gift – a newborn male child fathered by the noble warrior, Lugh of the Long Arm, a child destined to achieve great things for Ulster. Conchobar took the infant back to the palace with him and gave him to his sister Finnchoem to look after. Finnchoem reared the child alongside her own son Conall and grew to love him as if he had been born of her own womb. He was given the name of Setanta, a name he kept until the age of six, and the druid Morann made the following prophecy over him:

> *"His praise will be sung by the most valorous knights,*
> *And he will win the love of all*
> *His deeds will be known throughout the land*
> *For he will answer Ulster's call."*

Briar-Rose

A LONG TIME AGO there were a king and queen who said every day, "Ah, if only we had a child!" but they never had one. But it happened that once when the queen was bathing, a frog crept out of the water on to the land, and said to her, "Your wish shall be fulfilled; before a year has gone by, you shall have a daughter."

What the frog had said came true, and the queen had a little girl who was so pretty that the king could not contain himself for joy, and ordered a great feast. He invited not only his kindred, friends and acquaintance, but also the wise women, in order that they might be kind and well-disposed towards the child. There were thirteen of them in his kingdom, but, as he had only twelve golden plates for them to eat out of, one of them had to be left at home.

The feast was held with all manner of splendour and when it came to an end the wise women bestowed their magic gifts upon the baby: one gave virtue, another beauty, a third riches, and so on with everything in the world that one can wish for.

When eleven of them had made their promises, suddenly the thirteenth came in. She wished to avenge herself for not having been invited, and without greeting, or even looking at anyone, she cried with a loud voice, "The king's daughter shall in her fifteenth year prick herself with a spindle, and fall down dead."

And, without saying a word more, she turned round and left the room.

They were all shocked; but the twelfth, whose good wish still remained unspoken, came forward, and as she could not undo the evil sentence, but only soften it, she said, "It shall not be death, but a deep sleep of a hundred years, into which the princess shall fall."

The king, who would fain keep his dear child from the misfortune, gave orders that every spindle in the whole kingdom should be burnt. Meanwhile the gifts of the wise women were plenteously fulfilled on the young girl, for she was so beautiful, modest, good-natured, and wise, that everyone who saw her was bound to love her.

It happened that on the very day when she was fifteen years old, the king and queen were not at home, and the maiden was left in the palace quite alone. So she went round into all sorts of places, looked into rooms and bedchambers just as she liked, and at last came to an old tower. She climbed up the narrow winding staircase, and reached a little door. A rusty key was in the lock, and when she turned it the door sprang open, and there in a little room sat an old woman with a spindle, busily spinning her flax.

"Good day, old dame," said the king's daughter; "what are you doing there?"

"I am spinning," said the old woman, and nodded her head.

"What sort of thing is that, that rattles round so merrily?" said the girl, and she took the spindle and wanted to spin too. But scarcely had she touched the spindle when the magic decree was fulfilled, and she pricked her finger with it.

And, in the very moment when she felt the prick, she fell down upon the bed that stood there, and lay in a deep sleep. And this sleep extended over the whole palace; the king and queen who had just come home, and had entered the great hall, began to go to sleep, and the whole of the court with them. The horses, too, went to sleep in the stable, the dogs in the yard, the pigeons upon the roof, the flies on the wall; even the fire that was flaming on the hearth became quiet and slept, the roast meat left off frizzling, and the cook, who was just going to pull the hair of the scullery boy, because he had forgotten something, let him go, and went to sleep. And the wind fell, and on the trees before the castle not a leaf moved again.

But round about the castle there began to grow a hedge of thorns, which every year became higher, and at last grew close up round the castle and all over it, so that there was nothing of it to be seen, not even the flag upon the roof.

But the story of the beautiful sleeping 'Briar-rose', for so the princess was named, went about the country, so that from time to time kings' sons came and tried to get through the thorny hedge into the castle.

But they found it impossible, for the thorns held fast together, as if they had hands, and the youths were caught in them, could not get loose again, and died a miserable death.

After long, long years a king's son came again to that country, and heard an old man talking about the thorn-hedge, and that a castle was said to stand behind it in which a wonderfully beautiful princess, named Briar-rose, had been asleep for a hundred years; and that the king and queen and the whole court were asleep likewise. He had heard, too, from his grandfather, that many kings' sons had already come, and had tried to get through the thorny hedge, but they had remained sticking fast in it, and had died a pitiful death. Then the youth said, "I am not afraid, I will go and see the beautiful Briar-rose."

The good old man might dissuade him as he would, he did not listen to his words.

But by this time the hundred years had just passed, and the day had come when Briar-rose was to awake again. When the king's son came near to the thorn-hedge, it was nothing but large and beautiful flowers, which parted from each other of their own accord, and let him pass unhurt, then they closed again behind him like a hedge. In the courtyard he saw the horses and the spotted hounds lying asleep; on the roof sat the pigeons with their heads under their wings. And when he entered the house, the flies were asleep upon the wall, the cook in the kitchen was still holding out his hand to seize the boy, and the maid was sitting by the black hen which she was going to pluck.

He went on farther, and in the great hall he saw the whole of the court lying asleep, and up by the throne lay the king and queen.

Then he went on still farther, and all was so quiet that a breath could be heard, and at last he came to the tower, and opened the door into the little room where Briar-rose was sleeping. There she lay, so beautiful that he could not turn his eyes away; and he stooped down and gave her a kiss. But as soon as he kissed her, Briar-rose opened her eyes and awoke, and looked at him quite sweetly.

Then they went down together, and the king awoke, and the queen, and the whole court, and looked at each other in great astonishment. And the horses in the courtyard stood up and shook themselves; the hounds jumped up and wagged their tails; the pigeons upon the roof pulled out their heads from under their wings, looked round, and flew into the open country; the flies on the wall crept again; the fire in the kitchen burned up and flickered and cooked the meat; the joint began to turn and frizzle again, and the cook gave the boy such a box on the ear that he screamed, and the maid plucked the fowl ready for the spit.

And then the marriage of the king's son with Briar-rose was celebrated with all splendour, and they lived contented to the end of their days.

The Devil with the Three Golden Hairs

THERE WAS ONCE a poor woman who gave birth to a little son; and as he came into the world with a caul on, it was predicted that in his fourteenth year he would have the king's daughter for his wife. It happened that soon afterwards the king came into the village, and no one knew that he was the king, and when he asked the people what news there was, they answered, "A child has just been born with a caul on; whatever anyone so born undertakes turns out well. It is prophesied, too, that in his fourteenth year he will have the king's daughter for his wife."

The king, who had a bad heart, and was angry about the prophecy, went to the parents, and, seeming quite friendly, said, "You poor people, let me have your child, and I will take care of it."

At first they refused, but when the stranger offered them a large amount of gold for it, and they thought, "It is a luck-child, and everything must turn out well for it," they at last consented, and gave him the child.

The king put it in a box and rode away with it until he came to a deep piece of water; then he threw the box into it and thought, "I have freed my daughter from her unlooked-for suitor."

The box, however, did not sink, but floated like a boat, and not a drop of water made its way into it. And it floated to within two miles of the king's chief city, where there was a mill, and it came to a stand-still at the mill-dam. A miller's boy, who by good luck was standing there, noticed it and pulled it out with a hook, thinking that he had found a great treasure, but when he opened it there lay a pretty boy inside, quite fresh and lively.

He took him to the miller and his wife, and as they had no children they were glad, and said, "God has given him to us."

They took great care of the foundling, and he grew up in all goodness.

It happened that once in a storm, the king went into the mill, and he asked the mill-folk if the tall youth was their son.

"No," answered they, "he's a foundling. Fourteen years ago he floated down to the mill-dam in a box, and the mill-boy pulled him out of the water."

Then the king knew that it was none other than the luck-child which he had thrown into the water, and he said, "My good people, could not the youth take a letter to the queen; I will give him two gold pieces as a reward?"

"Just as the king commands," answered they, and they told the boy to hold himself in readiness. Then the king wrote a letter to the queen, wherein he said, "As soon as the boy arrives with this letter, let him be killed and buried, and all must be done before I come home."

The boy set out with this letter; but he lost his way, and in the evening came to a large forest. In the darkness he saw a small light; he went towards it and reached a cottage. When he went in, an old woman was sitting by the fire quite alone. She started when she saw the boy, and said, "Whence do you come, and whither are you going?"

"I come from the mill," he answered, "and wish to go to the queen, to whom I am taking a letter; but as I have lost my way in the forest I should like to stay here overnight."

"You poor boy," said the woman, "you have come into a den of thieves, and when they come home they will kill you."

"Let them come," said the boy, "I am not afraid; but I am so tired that I cannot go any farther": and he stretched himself upon a bench and fell asleep.

Soon afterwards the robbers came, and angrily asked what strange boy was lying there?

"Ah," said the old woman, "it is an innocent child who has lost himself in the forest, and out of pity I have let him come in; he has to take a letter to the queen."

The robbers opened the letter and read it, and in it was written that the boy as soon as he arrived should be put to death. Then the hard-hearted robbers felt pity, and their leader tore up the letter and wrote another, saying that as soon as the boy came, he should be married at once to the king's daughter. Then they let him lie quietly on the bench until the next morning, and when he awoke they gave him the letter, and showed him the right way.

And the queen, when she had received the letter and read it, did as was written in it, and had a splendid wedding feast prepared, and the king's daughter was married to the luck-child, and as the youth was handsome and agreeable she lived with him in joy and contentment.

After some time the king returned to his palace and saw that the prophecy was fulfilled, and the luck-child married to his daughter.

"How has that come to pass?" said he; "I gave quite another order in my letter."

So the queen gave him the letter, and said that he might see for himself what was written in it. The king read the letter and saw quite well that it had been exchanged for the other. He asked the youth what had become of the letter entrusted to him, and why he had brought another instead of it.

"I know nothing about it," answered he; "it must have been changed in the night, when I slept in the forest."

The king said in a passion, "You shall not have everything quite so much your own way; whosoever marries my daughter must fetch me from hell three golden hairs from the head of the devil; bring me what I want, and you shall keep my daughter."

In this way the king hoped to be rid of him forever.

But the luck-child answered, "I will fetch the golden hairs, I am not afraid of the devil"; thereupon he took leave of them and began his journey.

The road led him to a large town, where the watchman by the gates asked him what his trade was, and what he knew.

"I know everything," answered the luck-child.

"Then you can do us a favour," said the watchman, "if you will tell us why our market fountain, which once flowed with wine, has become dry and no longer gives even water?"

"That you shall know," answered he; "only wait until I come back."

Then he went farther and came to another town, and there also the gatekeeper asked him what was his trade, and what he knew.

"I know everything," answered he.

"Then you can do us a favour and tell us why a tree in our town which once bore golden apples now does not even put forth leaves?"

"You shall know that," answered he; "only wait until I come back."

Then he went on and came to a wide river over which he must go. The ferryman asked him what his trade was, and what he knew.

"I know everything," answered he.

"Then you can do me a favour," said the ferryman, "and tell me why I must always be rowing backwards and forwards, and am never set free?"

"You shall know that," answered he; "only wait until I come back."

When he had crossed the water he found the entrance to Hell. It was black and sooty within, and the devil was not at home, but his grandmother was sitting in a large armchair.

"What do you want?" said she to him, but she did not look so very wicked.

"I should like to have three golden hairs from the devil's head," answered he, "else I cannot keep my wife."

"That is a good deal to ask for," said she; "if the devil comes home and finds you, it will cost you your life; but as I pity you, I will see if I cannot help you."

She changed him into an ant and said, "Creep into the folds of my dress, you will be safe there."

"Yes," answered he, "so far, so good; but there are three things besides that I want to know: why a fountain which once flowed with wine has become dry, and no longer gives even water; why a tree which once bore golden apples does not even put forth leaves; and why a ferryman must always be going backwards and forwards, and is never set free?"

"Those are difficult questions," answered she, "but only be silent and quiet and pay attention to what the devil says when I pull out the three golden hairs."

As the evening came on, the devil returned home. No sooner had he entered than he noticed that the air was not pure.

"I smell man's flesh," said he; "all is not right here."

Then he pried into every corner, and searched, but could not find anything.

His grandmother scolded him. "It has just been swept," said she, "and everything put in order, and now you are upsetting it again; you have always got man's flesh in your nose. Sit down and eat your supper."

When he had eaten and drunk he was tired, and laid his head in his grandmother's lap, and before long he was fast asleep, snoring and breathing heavily. Then the old woman took hold of a golden hair, pulled it out, and laid it down near her.

"Oh!" cried the devil, "What are you doing?"

"I have had a bad dream," answered the grandmother, "so I seized hold of your hair."

"What did you dream then?" said the devil.

"I dreamed that a fountain in a marketplace from which wine once flowed was dried up, and not even water would flow out of it; what is the cause of it?"

"Oh, ho! If they did but know it," answered the devil; "there is a toad sitting under a stone in the well; if they killed it, the wine would flow again."

He went to sleep again and snored until the windows shook. Then she pulled the second hair out.

"Ha! What are you doing?" cried the devil angrily.

"Do not take it ill," said she, "I did it in a dream."

"What have you dreamt this time?" asked he.

"I dreamt that in a certain kingdom there stood an apple-tree which had once borne golden apples, but now would not even bear leaves. What, think you, was the reason?"

"Oh! if they did but know," answered the devil. "A mouse is gnawing at the root; if they killed this they would have golden apples again, but if it gnaws much longer the tree will wither altogether. But leave me alone with your dreams: if you disturb me in my sleep again you will get a box on the ear."

The grandmother spoke gently to him until he fell asleep again and snored. Then she took hold of the third golden hair and pulled it out. The devil jumped up, roared out, and would have treated her ill if she had not quieted him once more and said, "Who can help bad dreams?"

"What was the dream, then?" asked he, and was quite curious.

"I dreamt of a ferryman who complained that he must always ferry from one side to the other, and was never released. What is the cause of it?"

"Ah! The fool," answered the devil; "when anyone comes and wants to go across he must put the oar in his hand, and the other man will have to ferry and he will be free."

As the grandmother had plucked out the three golden hairs, and the three questions were answered, she let the old serpent alone, and he slept until daybreak.

When the devil had gone out again the old woman took the ant out of the folds of her dress, and gave the luck-child his human shape again.

"There are the three golden hairs for you," said she.

"What the devil said to your three questions, I suppose you heard?"

"Yes," answered he, "I heard, and will take care to remember."

"You have what you want," said she, "and now you can go your way."

He thanked the old woman for helping him in his need, and left Hell well content that everything had turned out so fortunately.

When he came to the ferryman he was expected to give the promised answer.

"Ferry me across first," said the luck-child, "and then I will tell you how you can be set free," and when he reached the opposite shore he gave him the devil's advice: "Next time anyone comes, who wants to be ferried over, just put the oar in his hand."

He went on and came to the town wherein stood the unfruitful tree, and there too the watchman wanted an answer. So he told him what he had heard from the devil: "Kill the mouse which is gnawing at its root, and it will again bear golden apples."

Then the watchman thanked him, and gave him as a reward two asses laden with gold, which followed him.

At last he came to the town whose well was dry. He told the watchman what the devil had said: "A toad is in the well beneath a stone; you must find it and kill it, and the well will again give wine in plenty."

The watchman thanked him, and also gave him two asses laden with gold.

At last the luck-child got home to his wife, who was heartily glad to see him again, and to hear how well he had prospered in everything.

To the king he took what he had asked for, the devil's three golden hairs, and when the king saw the four asses laden with gold he was quite content, and said, "Now all the conditions are fulfilled, and you can keep my daughter. But tell me, dear son-in-law, where did all that gold come from? This is tremendous wealth!"

"I was rowed across a river," answered he, "and got it there; it lies on the shore instead of sand."

"Can I too fetch some of it?" said the king; and he was quite eager about it.

"As much as you like," answered he. "There is a ferryman on the river; let him ferry you over, and you can fill your sacks on the other side."

The greedy king set out in all haste, and when he came to the river he beckoned to the ferryman to put him across. The ferryman came and bade him get in, and when they got to the other shore he put the oar in his hand and sprang out. But from this time forth the king had to ferry, as a punishment for his sins.

Perhaps he is ferrying still?

If he is, it is because no one has taken the oar from him.

Oracles, Seers & Sages

Introduction

"I HAVE SEEN THEE, and I have not lain down in death; I have stood over thee, and I have risen like a god. I have cackled like a goose, and I have alighted like a hawk by the divine clouds and by the great dew. I have journeyed from the earth to heaven." So says the scribe of the ancient Egyptian Papyrus of Nu – a deity associated with the primordial ocean that preceded the creation of the world. Dark depths, and yet this is a message more of triumph than of fear or gloom, the seer exultant in his ability to travel into far-off spiritual realms. By comparison, the bard Taliesin seems something of a stay-at-home, though he's no more than a boy when, in fluent verse, he tells the wondering Welsh king:

> *I was with my Lord in the highest sphere,*
> *On the fall of Lucifer into the depth of hell*
> *I have borne a banner before Alexander;*
> *I know the names of the stars from north to south;*

The stories in this section are of mystic, spiritual or imaginative travel; of minds transcending the narrow bounds of ordinary earthly life.

Oedipus

LAIUS AND JOCASTA, King and Queen of Thebes, in Boeotia, were greatly delighted at the birth of a little son. In their joy they sent for the priests of Apollo, and bade them foretell the glorious deeds their heir would perform; but all their joy was turned to grief when told that the child was destined to kill his father, marry his mother, and bring great misfortunes upon his native city.

To prevent the fulfillment of this dreadful prophecy, Laius bade a servant carry the new-born child out of the city, and end its feeble little life. The king's mandate was obeyed only in part; for the servant, instead of killing the child, hung it up by its ankles to a tree in a remote place, and left it there to perish from hunger and exposure if it were spared by the wild beasts.

When he returned, none questioned how he had performed the appointed task, but all sighed with relief to think that the prophecy could never be accomplished. The child, however, was not dead, as all supposed. A shepherd in quest of a stray lamb had heard his cries, delivered him from his painful position, and carried him to Polybus, King of Corinth, who, lacking an heir of his own, gladly adopted the little stranger. The Queen of Corinth and her handmaidens hastened with tender concern to bathe the swollen ankles, and called the babe Oedipus (swollen-footed).

Years passed by. The young prince grew up in total ignorance of the unfortunate circumstances under which he had made his first appearance at court, until one day at a banquet one of his companions, heated by drink, began to quarrel with him, and taunted him about his origin, declaring that those whom he had been accustomed to call parents were in no way related to him.

These words, coupled with a few meaning glances hastily exchanged by the guests, excited Oedipus's suspicions, and made him question the queen, who, afraid lest he might do himself an injury in the first moment of his despair if the truth were revealed to him, had recourse to prevarication, and quieted him by the assurance that he was her beloved son.

Something in her manner, however, left a lingering doubt in Oedipus's mind, and made him resolve to consult the oracle of Delphi, whose words he knew would reveal the exact truth. He therefore went to this shrine; but, as usual, the oracle answered somewhat ambiguously, and merely warned him that fate had decreed he should kill his father, marry his mother, and cause great woes to his native city.

What! Kill Polybus, who had ever been such an indulgent father, and marry the queen, whom he revered as his mother! Never! Rather than perpetrate these awful crimes, and bring destruction upon the people of Corinth, whom he loved, he would wander away over the face of the earth, and never see city or parents again.

But his heart was filled with intense bitterness, and as he journeyed he did not cease to curse the fate which drove him away from home. After some time, he came to three crossroads; and while he stood there, deliberating which direction to take, a chariot, wherein an aged man was seated, came rapidly towards him.

The herald who preceded it haughtily called to the youth to stand aside and make way for his master; but Oedipus, who, as Polybus's heir, was accustomed to be treated with deference, resented the commanding tone, and refused to obey. Incensed at what seemed unparalleled impudence, the herald struck the youth, who, retaliating, stretched his assailant lifeless at his feet.

This affray attracted the attention of the master and other servants. They immediately attacked the murderer, who slew them all, thus unconsciously accomplishing the first part of the prophecy; for the aged man was Laius, his father, journeying incognito from Thebes to Delphi, where he wished to consult the oracle.

Oedipus then leisurely pursued his way until he came to the gates of Thebes, where he found the whole city in an uproar, "because the king had been found lifeless by the roadside, with all his attendants slain beside him, presumably the work of a band of highway robbers or assassins."

Of course, Oedipus did not connect the murder of such a great personage as the King of Thebes by an unknown band of robbers with the death he had dealt to an arrogant old man, and he therefore composedly inquired what the second calamity alluded to might be.

With lowered voices, as if afraid of being overheard, the Thebans described the woman's head, bird's wings and claws, and lion's body, which were the outward presentment of a terrible monster called the Sphinx, which had taken up its station without the city gates beside the highway, and would allow none to pass in or out without propounding a difficult riddle. Then, if any hesitated to give the required answer, or failed to give it correctly, they were mercilessly devoured by the terrible Sphinx, which no one dared attack or could drive away.

While listening to these tidings, Oedipus saw a herald pass along the street, proclaiming that the throne and the queen's hand would be the reward of any man who dared encounter the Sphinx, and was fortunate enough to free the country of its terrible presence.

As Oedipus attached no special value to the life made desolate by the oracle's predictions, he resolved to slay the dreaded monster, and, with that purpose in view, advanced slowly, sword in hand, along the road where lurked the Sphinx. He soon found the monster, which from afar propounded the following enigma, warning him, at the same time, that he forfeited his life if he failed to give the right answer.

Oedipus was not devoid of intelligence, by any manner of means, and soon concluded that the animal could only be man, who in infancy, when too weak to stand, creeps along on hands and knees, in manhood walks erect, and in old age supports his tottering steps with a staff.

This reply, evidently as correct as unexpected, was received by the Sphinx with a hoarse cry of disappointment and rage as it turned to fly; but ere it could effect its purpose, it was stayed by Oedipus, who drove it at his sword's point over the edge of a neighbouring precipice, where it was killed. On his return to the city, Oedipus was received with cries of joy, placed on a chariot, crowned King of Thebes, and married to his own mother, Jocasta, unwittingly fulfilling the second fearful clause of the prophecy.

A number of happy and moderately uneventful years now passed by, and Oedipus became the father of two manly sons, Eteocles and Polynices, and two beautiful daughters, Ismene and Antigone; but prosperity was not doomed to favour him long.

Just when he fancied himself most happy, and looked forward to a peaceful old age, a terrible scourge visited Thebes, causing the death of many faithful subjects, and filling the hearts of all with great terror. The people now turned to him, beseeching him to aid them, as he had done once before when threatened by the Sphinx; and Oedipus sent messengers to consult the Delphic oracle, who declared the plague would cease only when the former king's murderers had been found and punished.

Messengers were sent in every direction to collect all possible information about the murder committed so long ago, and after a short time they brought unmistakable proofs which convicted Oedipus of the crime. At the same time the guilty servant confessed that he had not killed the child, but had exposed it on a mountain, whence it was carried to Corinth's king.

The chain of evidence was complete, and now Oedipus discovered that he had involuntarily been guilty of the three crimes to avoid which he had fled from Corinth. The rumour of these dreadful discoveries soon reached Jocasta, who, in her despair at finding herself an accomplice, committed suicide.

Oedipus, apprised of her intention, rushed into her apartment too late to prevent its being carried out, and found her lifeless. This sight was more than the poor monarch could bear, and in his despair he blinded himself with one of her ornaments.

Penniless, blind, and on foot, he then left the scene of his awful crimes, accompanied by his daughter Antigone, the only one who loved him still, and who was ready to guide his uncertain footsteps wherever he wished to go. After many days of weary wandering, father and daughter reached Colonus, where grew a mighty forest sacred to the avenging deities, the Furies, or Eumenides.

Here Oedipus expressed his desire to remain, and, after bidding his faithful daughter an affectionate farewell, he groped his way into the dark forest alone. The wind rose, the lightning flashed, the thunder pealed; but although, as soon as the storm was over, a search was made for Oedipus, no trace of him was ever found, and the ancients fancied that the Furies had dragged him down to Hades to receive the punishment for all his crimes.

Antigone, no longer needed by her unhappy father, slowly wended her way back to Thebes, where she found that the plague had ceased, but that her brothers had quarrelled about the succession to the throne. A compromise was finally decided upon, whereby it was decreed that Eteocles, the elder son, should reign one year, and at the end of that period resign the throne to Polynices for an equal space of time, both brothers thus exercising the royal authority in turn. This arrangement seemed satisfactory to Eteocles; but when, at the end of the first year, Polynices returned from his travels in foreign lands to claim the sceptre, Eteocles refused to relinquish it, and, making use of his power, drove the claimant away.

Themis

THEMIS, WHO HAS already been alluded to as the wife of Zeus, was the daughter of Cronus and Rhea, and personified those divine laws of justice and order by means of which the well-being and morality of communities are regulated. She presided over the assemblies of the people and the laws of hospitality. To her was entrusted the office of convoking the assembly of the gods, and she was also mistress of ritual and ceremony. On account of her great wisdom Zeus himself frequently sought her counsel and acted upon her advice. Themis was a prophetic divinity, and had an oracle near the river Cephissus in Boeotia.

She is usually represented as being in the full maturity of womanhood, of fair aspect, and wearing a flowing garment, which drapes her noble, majestic form; in her right hand she holds the sword of justice, and in her left the scales, which indicate the impartiality with which every cause is carefully weighed by her, her eyes being bandaged so that the personality of the individual should carry no weight with respect to the verdict.

This divinity is sometimes identified with Tyche, sometimes with Ananke.

Themis, like so many other Greek divinities, takes the place of a more ancient deity of the same name who was a daughter of Uranus and Gaea. This elder Themis inherited from her mother the gift of prophecy, and when she became merged into her younger representative she transmitted to her this prophetic power.

The Norns' Web

THE NORTHERN GODDESSES OF FATE, who were called Norns, were in nowise subject to the other gods, who might neither question nor influence their decrees. They were three sisters, probably descendants of the giant Norvi, from whom sprang Nott (night). As soon as the Golden Age was ended, and sin began to steal even into the heavenly homes of Asgard, the Norns made their appearance under the great ash Yggdrasil, and took up their abode near the Urdar fountain. According to some mythologists, their mission was to warn the gods of future evil, to bid them make good use of the present, and to teach them wholesome lessons from the past.

These three sisters, whose names were Urd, Verdandi, and Skuld, were personifications of the past, present, and future. Their principal occupations were to weave the web of fate, to sprinkle daily the sacred tree with water from the Urdar fountain, and to put fresh clay around its roots, that it might remain fresh and ever green.

Some authorities further state that the Norns kept watch over the golden apples which hung on the branches of the tree of life, experience, and knowledge, allowing none but Idunn to pick the fruit, which was that with which the gods renewed their youth.

The Norns also fed and tenderly cared for two swans which swam over the mirror-like surface of the Urdar fountain, and from this pair of birds all the swans on earth are supposed to be descended. At times, it is said, the Norns clothed themselves with swan plumage to visit the earth, or sported like mermaids along the coast and in various lakes and rivers, appearing to mortals, from time to time, to foretell the future or give them sage advice.

The Norns sometimes wove webs so large that while one of the weavers stood on a high mountain in the extreme east, another waded far out into the western sea. The threads of their woof resembled cords, and varied greatly in hue, according to the nature of the events about to occur, and a black thread, tending from north to south, was invariably considered an omen of death. As these sisters flashed the shuttle to and fro, they chanted a solemn song. They did not seem to weave according to their own wishes, but blindly, as if reluctantly executing the wishes of Orlog, the eternal law of the universe, an older and superior power, who apparently had neither beginning nor end.

Two of the Norns, Urd and Verdandi, were considered to be very beneficent indeed, while the third, it is said, relentlessly undid their work, and often, when nearly finished, tore it angrily to shreds, scattering the remnants to the winds of heaven. As personifications of time, the Norns were represented as sisters of different ages and characters, Urd (Wurd, weird) appearing very old and decrepit, continually looking backward, as if absorbed in contemplating past events and people; Verdandi, the second sister, young, active, and fearless, looked straight before her, while Skuld, the type of the future, was generally represented as closely veiled, with head turned in the direction opposite to where Urd was gazing, and holding a book or scroll which had not yet been opened or unrolled.

These Norns were visited daily by the gods, who loved to consult them; and even Odin himself frequently rode down to the Urdar fountain to bespeak their aid, for they generally answered his questions, maintaining silence only about his own fate and that of his fellow gods.

The Story of Nornagesta

ON ONE OCCASION the three sisters visited Denmark, and entered the dwelling of a nobleman as his first child came into the world. Entering the apartment where the mother lay, the first Norn promised that the child should be handsome and brave, and the second that he should be prosperous and a great scald – predictions which filled the parents' hearts with joy. Meantime news of what was taking place had gone abroad, and the neighbours came thronging the apartment to such a degree that the pressure of the curious crowd caused the third Norn to be pushed rudely from her chair.

Angry at this insult, Skuld proudly rose and declared that her sister's gifts should be of no avail, since she would decree that the child should live only as long as the taper then burning near the bedside. These ominous words filled the mother's heart with terror, and she tremblingly clasped her babe closer to her breast, for the taper was nearly burned out and its extinction could not be very long delayed. The eldest Norn, however, had no intention of seeing her prediction thus set at naught; but as she could not force her sister to retract her words, she quickly seized the taper, put out the light, and giving the smoking stump to the child's mother, bade her carefully treasure it, and never light it again until her son was weary of life.

The boy was named Nornagesta, in honour of the Norns, and grew up to be as beautiful, brave, and talented as any mother could wish. When he was old enough to comprehend the gravity of the trust his mother told him the story of the Norns' visit, and placed in his hands the taper end, which he treasured for many a year, placing it for safe-keeping inside the frame of his harp. When his parents were dead, Nornagesta wandered from place to place, taking part and distinguishing himself in every battle, singing his heroic lays wherever he went. As he was of an enthusiastic and poetic temperament, he did not soon weary of life, and while other heroes grew wrinkled and old, he remained young at heart and vigorous in frame. He therefore witnessed the stirring deeds of the heroic ages, was the boon companion of the ancient warriors, and after living three hundred years, saw the belief in the old heathen gods gradually supplanted by the teachings of Christian missionaries. Finally Nornagesta came to the court of King Olaf Tryggvesson, who, according to his usual custom, converted him almost by force, and compelled him to receive baptism. Then, wishing to convince his people that the time for superstition was past, the king forced the aged scald to produce and light the taper which he had so carefully guarded for more than three centuries.

In spite of his recent conversion, Nornagesta anxiously watched the flame as it flickered, and when, finally, it went out, he sank lifeless to the ground, thus proving that in spite of the baptism just received, he still believed in the prediction of the Norns.

In the middle ages, and even later, the Norns figure in many a story or myth, appearing as fairies or witches, as, for instance, in the tale of 'The Sleeping Beauty,' and Shakespeare's tragedy of *Macbeth*.

Sometimes the Norns bore the name of Vala, or prophetesses, for they had the power of divination – a power which was held in great honour by all the Northern races, who believed that it was restricted to the female sex. The predictions of the Vala were never questioned, and it is said that the Roman general Drusus was so terrified by the appearance of Veleda, one of these prophetesses, who warned him not to cross the Elbe, that he actually beat a retreat. She foretold his approaching death, which indeed happened shortly after through a fall from his steed.

These prophetesses, who were also known as Idises, Dises, or Hagedises, officiated at the forest shrines and in the sacred groves, and always accompanied invading armies. Riding ahead, or in the midst of the host, they would vehemently urge the warriors on to victory, and when the battle was over they would often cut the bloody-eagle upon the bodies of the captives. The blood was collected into great tubs, wherein the Dises plunged their naked arms up to the shoulders, previous to joining in the wild dance with which the ceremony ended.

It is not to be wondered at that these women were greatly feared. Sacrifices were offered to propitiate them, and it was only in later times that they were degraded to the rank of witches, and sent to join the demon host on the Brocken, or Blocksberg, on Valpurgisnacht.

Besides the Norns or Dises, who were also regarded as protective deities, the Northmen ascribed to each human being a guardian spirit named Fylgie, which attended him through life, either in human or brute shape, and was invisible except at the moment of death by all except the initiated few.

The allegorical meaning of the Norns and of their web of fate is too patent to need explanation; still some mythologists have made them demons of the air, and state that their web was the woof of clouds, and that the bands of mists which they strung from rock to tree, and from mountain to mountain, were ruthlessly torn apart by the suddenly rising wind. Some authorities, moreover, declare that Skuld, the third Norn, was at times a Valkyr, and at others personated the goddess of death, the terrible Hel.

Hermod

ANOTHER OF ODIN'S SONS was Hermod, his special attendant, a bright and beautiful young god, who was gifted with great rapidity of motion and was therefore designated as the swift or nimble god.

On account of this important attribute Hermod was usually employed by the gods as messenger, and at a mere sign from Odin he was always ready to speed to any part of creation. As a special mark of favour, Allfather gave him a magnificent corselet and helmet, which he often donned when he prepared to take part in war, and sometimes Odin entrusted to his care the precious spear Gungnir, bidding him cast it over the heads of combatants about to engage in battle, that their ardour might be kindled into murderous fury.

Hermod delighted in battle, and was often called 'the valiant in battle', and confounded with the god of the universe, Irmin. It is said that he sometimes accompanied the Valkyrs on their ride to earth, and frequently escorted the warriors to Valhalla, wherefore he was considered the leader of the heroic dead.

Hermod's distinctive attribute, besides his corselet and helm, was a wand or staff called Gambantein, the emblem of his office, which he carried with him wherever he went.

Once, oppressed by shadowy fears for the future, and unable to obtain from the Norns satisfactory answers to his questions, Odin bade Hermod don his armour and saddle Sleipnir, which he alone, besides Odin, was allowed to ride, and hasten off to the land of the Finns. This people, who lived in the frozen regions of the pole, besides being able to call up the cold storms which swept down from the North, bringing much ice and snow in their train, were supposed to have great occult powers.

The most noted of these Finnish magicians was Rossthiof (the horse thief) who was wont to entice travellers into his realm by magic arts, that he might rob and slay them; and he had power to predict the future, although he was always very reluctant to do so.

Hermod, 'the swift,' rode rapidly northward, with directions to seek this Finn, and instead of his own wand, he carried Odin's runic staff, which Allfather had given him for the purpose of dispelling any obstacles that Rossthiof might conjure up to hinder his advance. In spite, therefore, of phantom-like monsters and of invisible snares and pitfalls, Hermod was enabled safely to reach the magician's abode, and upon the giant attacking him, he was able to master him with ease, and he bound him hand and foot, declaring that he would not set him free until he promised to reveal all that he wished to know.

Rossthiof, seeing that there was no hope of escape, pledged himself to do as his captor wished, and upon being set at liberty, he began forthwith to mutter incantations, at the mere sound of which the sun hid behind the clouds, the earth trembled and quivered, and the storm winds howled like a pack of hungry wolves.

Pointing to the horizon, the magician bade Hermod look, and the swift god saw in the distance a great stream of blood reddening the ground. While he gazed wonderingly at this stream, a beautiful woman suddenly appeared, and a moment later a little boy stood beside her. To the god's amazement, this child grew with such marvellous rapidity that he soon attained his full growth, and Hermod further noticed that he fiercely brandished a bow and arrows.

Rossthiof now began to explain the omens which his art had conjured up, and he declared that the stream of blood portended the murder of one of Odin's sons, but that if the father of the gods should woo and win Rinda, in the land of the Ruthenes (Russia), she would bear him a son who would attain his full growth in a few hours and would avenge his brother's death.

Hermod listened attentively to the words of Rossthiof and upon his return to Asgard he reported all he had seen and heard to Odin, whose fears were confirmed and who thus definitely ascertained that he was doomed to lose a son by violent death. He consoled himself, however, with the thought that another of his descendants would avenge the crime and thereby obtain the satisfaction which a true Northman ever required.

King Kitamba kia Shiba (and the Kingdom of Death)

KITAMBA WAS A CHIEF who lived at Kasanji. He lost his head-wife, Queen Muhongo, and mourned for her many days. Not only did he mourn himself, but he insisted on his people sharing his grief. "My village, too, no man shall do anything therein. The young people shall not shout; the women shall not pound; no one shall speak in the village."

His headmen remonstrated with him, but Kitamba was obdurate, and declared that he would neither speak nor eat nor allow anyone else to do so till his queen was restored to him. The headmen consulted together, and called in a 'doctor' (*kimbanda*). Having received his fee (first a gun, and then a cow) and heard their statement of the case, he said, "All right," and set off to gather herbs. These he pounded in a 'medicine-mortar', and, having prepared some sort of decoction, ordered the king and all the people to wash themselves with it. He next directed some men to "dig a grave in my guest-hut at the fireplace," which they did, and he entered it with his little boy, giving two last instructions to his wife: to leave off her girdle (i.e., to dress negligently, as if in mourning) and to pour water every day on the fireplace. Then the men filled in the grave. The doctor saw a road open before him; he walked along it with his boy till he came to a village, where he found Queen Muhongo sitting, sewing a basket. She saw him approaching, and asked, "Whence comest thou?" He answered, in the usual form demanded by native politeness, "Thou thyself, I have sought thee. Since thou art dead King Kitamba will not eat, will not drink, will not speak. In the village they pound not; they speak not; he says, 'If I shall talk, if I eat, go ye and fetch my head-wife.' That is what brought me here. I have spoken."

The queen then pointed out a man seated a little way off, and asked the doctor who he was. As he could not say, she told him, "He is Lord Kalunga-ngombe; he is always consuming us, us all." Directing his attention to another man, who was chained, she asked if he knew him, and he answered, "He looks like King Kitamba, whom I left where I came from." It was indeed Kitamba, and the queen further informed the messenger that her husband had not many years to live, and also that "Here in Kalunga never comes one here to return again." She gave him the armlet which had been buried with her, to show to Kitamba as a proof that he had really visited the abode of the dead, but enjoined on him not to tell the king that he had seen him there. And he must not eat anything in Kalunga; otherwise he would never be permitted to return to earth.

Meanwhile the doctor's wife had kept pouring water on the grave. One day she saw the earth beginning to crack; the cracks opened wider, and, finally, her husband's head appeared. He gradually made his way out, and pulled his small son up after him. The child fainted when he came out into the sunlight, but his father washed him with some 'herb-medicine', and soon brought him to.

Next day the doctor went to the headmen, presented his report, was repaid with two slaves, and returned to his home. The headmen told Kitamba what he had said, and produced the token. The only comment he is recorded to have made, on looking at the armlet, is "Truth, it is the same." We do not hear whether he countermanded the official mourning, but it is to be presumed he did so, for he made no further difficulty about eating or drinking. Then, after a few years, he died, and the story concludes, "They wailed the funeral; they scattered."

Piqua

A GREAT WHILE AGO THE SHAWANOS nation took up the war-talk against the Walkullas, who lived on their own lands on the borders of the Great Salt Lake, and near the Burning Water. Part of the nation were not well pleased with the war. The head chief and the counsellors said the Walkullas were very brave and cunning, and the priests said their god was mightier than ours. The old and experienced warriors said the counsellors were wise, and had spoken well; but the Head Buffalo, the young warriors, and all who wished for war, would not listen to their words. They said that our fathers had beaten their fathers in many battles, that the Shawanos were as brave and strong as they ever were, and the Walkullas much weaker and more cowardly. They said the old and timid, the faint heart and the failing knee, might stay at home to take care of the women and children, and sleep and dream of those who had never dared bend a bow or look upon a painted cheek or listen to a war-whoop, while the young warriors went to war and drank much blood. When two moons were gone they said they would come back with many prisoners and scalps, and have a great feast. The arguments of the fiery young men prevailed with all the youthful warriors, but the elder and wiser listened to the priests and counsellors, and remained in their villages to see the leaf fall and the grass grow, and to gather in the nut and follow the trail of the deer.

Two moons passed, then a third, then came the night enlivened by many stars, but the warriors returned not. As the land of the Walkullas lay but a woman's journey of six suns from the villages of our nation, our people began to fear that our young men had been overcome in battle and were all slain. The head chief, the counsellors, and all the warriors who had remained behind, came together in the great wigwam, and called the priests to tell them where their sons were. Chenos, who was the wisest of them all (as well he might be, for he was older than the oak-tree whose top dies by the hand of Time), answered that they were killed by their enemies, the Walkullas, assisted by men of a strange speech and colour, who lived beyond the Great Salt Lake, fought with thunder and lightning, and came to our enemies on the back of a great bird with many white wings. When he had thus made known to our people the fate of the warriors there was a dreadful shout of horror throughout the village. The women wept aloud, and the men sprang up and seized their bows and arrows to go to war with the Walkullas and the strange warriors who had helped to slay their sons, but Chenos bade them sit down again.

"There is one yet living," said he. "He will soon be here. The sound of his footsteps is in my ear as he crosses the hollow hills. He has killed many of his enemies; he has glutted his vengeance fully; he has drunk blood in plenteous draughts. Long he fought with the men of his own race, and many fell before him, but he fled from the men who came to the battle armed with the real lightning, and hurling unseen death. Even now I see him coming; the shallow streams he has forded; the deep rivers he has swum. He is tired and hungry, and his quiver has no arrows, but he brings a prisoner in his arms. Lay the deer's flesh on the fire, and bring hither the pounded corn. Taunt him not, for he is valiant, and has fought like a hungry bear."

As the wise Chenos spoke these words to the grey-bearded counsellors and warriors the Head Buffalo walked calm and cool into the midst of them. There he stood, tall and straight as a young pine, but he spoke no word, looking on the head chief and the counsellors. There was blood upon his body, dried on by the sun, and the arm next his heart was bound up with the skin of the deer. His eye was hollow and his body gaunt, as though he had fasted long. His quiver held no arrows.

"Where are our sons?" inquired the head chief of the warrior.

"Ask the wolf and the panther," he answered.

"Brother! tell us where are our sons!" exclaimed the chief. "Our women ask us for their sons. They want them. Where are they?"

"Where are the snows of last year?" replied the warrior. "Have they not gone down the swelling river into the Great Lake? They have, and even so have your sons descended the stream of Time into the great Lake of Death. The great star sees them as they lie by the water of the Walkulla, but they see him not. The panther and the wolf howl unheeded at their feet, and the eagle screams, but they hear them not. The vulture whets his beak on their bones, the wild-cat rends their flesh, both are unfelt, for your sons are dead."

When the warrior told these things to our people, they set up their loud death-howl. The women wept; but the men sprang up and seized their weapons, to go to meet the Walkullas, the slayers of their sons. The chief warrior rose again –

"Fathers and warriors," said he, "hear me and believe my words, for I will tell you the truth. Who ever heard the Head Buffalo lie, and who ever saw him afraid of his enemies? Never, since the time that he chewed the bitter root and put on the new moccasins, has he lied or fled from his foes. He has neither a forked tongue nor a faint heart. Fathers, the Walkullas are weaker than us. Their arms are not so strong, their hearts are not so big, as ours. As well might the timid deer make war upon the hungry wolf, as the Walkullas upon the Shawanos. We could slay them as easily as a hawk pounces into a dove's nest and steals away

ORACLES, SEERS & SAGES

her unfeathered little ones. The Head Buffalo alone could have taken the scalps of half the nation. But a strange tribe has come among them – men whose skin is white as the folds of the cloud, and whose hair shines like the great star of day. They do not fight as we fight, with bows and arrows and with war-axes, but with spears which thunder and lighten, and send unseen death. The Shawanos fall before it as the berries and acorns fall when the forest is shaken by the wind in the sturgeon moon. Look at the arm nearest my heart. It was stricken by a bolt from the strangers' thunder; but he fell by the hands of the Head Buffalo, who fears nothing but shame, and his scalp lies at the feet of the head chief.

"Fathers, this was our battle. We came upon the Walkullas, I and my brothers, when they were unprepared. They were just going to hold the dance of the green corn. The whole nation had come to the dance; there were none left behind save the sick and the very old. None were painted; they were all for peace, and were as women. We crept close to them, and hid in the thick bushes which grew upon the edge of their camp, for the Shawanos are the cunning adder and not the foolish rattlesnake. We saw them preparing to offer a sacrifice to the Great Spirit. We saw them clean the deer, and hang his head, horns, and entrails upon the great white pole with a forked top, which stood over the roof of the council wigwam. They did not know that the Master of Life had sent the Shawanos to mix blood with the sacrifices. We saw them take the new corn and rub it upon their hands, breasts, and faces. Then the head chief, having first thanked the Master of Life for his goodness to the Walkullas, got up and gave his brethren a talk. He told them that the Great Spirit loved them, and had made them victorious over all their enemies; that he had sent a great many fat bears, deer, and moose to their hunting-ground, and had given them fish, whose heads were very small and bodies very big; that he had made their corn grow tall and sweet, and had ordered his suns to ripen it in the beginning of the harvest moon, that they might make a great feast for the strangers who had come from a far country on the wings of a great bird to warm themselves at the Walkullas' fire. He told them they must love the Great Spirit, take care of the old men, tell no lies, and never break the faith of the pipe of peace; that they must not harm the strangers, for they were their brothers, but must live in peace with them, and give them lands, and wives from among their women. If they did these things the Great Spirit, he said, would make their corn grow taller than ever, and direct them to hunting-grounds where the moose should be as thick as the stars.

"Fathers and warriors, we heard these words; but we knew not what to do. We feared not the Walkullas; the God of War, we saw, had given them into our hands. But who were the strange tribe? Were they armed as we were, and was their Great Medicine (Great Spirit) like ours? Warriors, you all knew the Young Eagle, the son of the Old Eagle, who is here with us; but his wings are feeble, he flies no more to the field of blood. The Young Eagle feared nothing but shame, and he said:

"'I see many men sit round a fire, I will go and see who they are!'

"He went. The Old Eagle looks at me as if he would say, 'Why went not the chief warrior himself?' I will tell you. The Head Buffalo is a head taller than the tallest man of his tribe. Can the moose crawl into the fox's hole? Can the swan hide himself under a little leaf? The Young Eagle was little, save in his soul. He was not full-grown, save in his heart. He could go and not be seen or heard. He was the cunning black-snake which creeps silently in the grass, and none thinks him near till he strikes.

"He came back and told us there were many strange men a little way before us whose faces were white, and who wore no skins, whose cabins were white as the snow upon the

Backbone of the Great Spirit (the Alleghany Mountains), flat at the top, and moving with the wind like the reeds on the bank of a river; that they did not talk like the Walkullas, but spoke a strange tongue, the like of which he had never heard before. Many of our warriors would have turned back to our own lands. The Flying Squirrel said it was not cowardice to do so; but the Head Buffalo never turns till he has tasted the blood of his foes. The Young Eagle said he had eaten the bitter root and put on the new moccasins, and had been made a man, and his father and the warriors would cry shame on him if he took no scalp. Both he and the Head Buffalo said they would go and attack the Walkullas and their friends alone. The young warriors then said they would also go to the battle, and with a great heart, as their fathers had done. Then the Shawanos rushed upon their foes.

"The Walkullas fell before us like rain in the summer months. We were as a fire among rushes. We went upon them when they were unprepared, when they were as children; and for a while the Great Spirit gave them into our hands. But a power rose up against us that we could not withstand. The strange men came upon us armed with thunder and lightning. Why delays my tongue to tell its story? Fathers, your sons have fallen like the leaves of a forest-tree in a high wind, like the flowers of spring after a frost, like drops of rain in the sturgeon moon! Warriors, the sprouts which sprang up from the withered oaks have perished, the young braves of our nation lie food for the eagle and the wild-cat by the arm of the Great Lake!

"Fathers, the bolt from the strangers' thunder entered my flesh, yet I did not fly. These six scalps I tore from the Walkullas, but this has yellow hair. Have I done well?"

The head chief and the counsellors answered he had done very well, but Chenos answered:

"No. You went into the Walkullas' camp when the tribe were feasting to the Great Spirit, and you disturbed the sacrifice, and mixed human blood with it. Therefore has this evil come upon us, for the Great Spirit is very angry."

Then the head chief and the counsellors asked Chenos what must be done to appease the Master of Breath.

Chenos answered:

"The Head Buffalo, with the morning, will offer to him that which he holds dearest."

The Head Buffalo looked upon the priests, and said:

"The Head Buffalo fears the Great Spirit. He will kill a deer, and, in the morning, it shall be burned to the Great Spirit."

Chenos said to him:

"You have told the council how the battle was fought and who fell; you have shown the spent quiver and the scalps, but you have not spoken of your prisoner. The Great Spirit keeps nothing hid from his priests, of whom Chenos is one. He has told me you have a prisoner, one with tender feet and a trembling heart."

"Let anyone say the Head Buffalo ever lied," replied the warrior. "He never spoke but truth. He has a prisoner, a woman taken from the strange camp, a daughter of the sun, a maiden from the happy islands which no Shawano has ever seen, and she shall live with me, and become the mother of my children."

"Where is she?" asked the head chief.

"She sits on the bank of the river at the bend where we dug up the bones of the great beast, beneath the tree which the Master of Breath shivered with his lightnings. I placed her there because the spot is sacred, and none dare disturb her. I will go and fetch her to the council fire, but let no one touch her or show anger, for she is fearful as a young deer, and weeps like a child for its mother."

Soon he returned, and brought with him a woman. She shook like a reed in the winter's wind, and many tears ran down her cheeks. The men sat as though their tongues were frozen. Was she beautiful? Go forth to the forest when it is clothed with the flowers of spring, look at the tall maize when it waves in the wind, and ask if they are beautiful. Her skin was white as the snow which falls upon the mountains beyond our lands, save upon her cheeks, where it was red – not such red as the Indian paints when he goes to war, but such as the Master of Life gives to the flower which grows among thorns. Her eyes shone like the star which never moves. Her step was like that of the deer when it is a little scared.

The Head Buffalo said to the council:

"This is my prisoner. I fought hard for her. Three warriors, tall, strong, and painted, three pale men, armed with red lightning, stood at her side. Where are they now? I bore her away in my arms, for fear had overcome her. When night came on I wrapped skins around her, and laid her under the leafy branches of the tree to keep off the cold, and kindled a fire, and watched by her till the sun rose. Who will say she shall not live with the Head Buffalo, and be the mother of his children?"

Then the Old Eagle got up, but he could not walk strong, for he was the oldest warrior of his tribe, and had seen the flowers bloom many times, the infant trees of the forest die of old age, and the friends of his boyhood laid in the dust. He went to the woman, laid his hands on her head, and wept. The other warriors, who had lost their kindred and sons in the war with the Walkullas, shouted and lamented. The woman also wept.

"Where is the Young Eagle?" asked the Old Eagle of the Head Buffalo. The other warriors, in like manner, asked for their kindred who had been killed.

"Fathers, they are dead," answered the warrior. "The Head Buffalo has said they are dead, and he never lies. But let my fathers take comfort. Who can live for ever? The foot of the swift step and the hand of the stout bow become feeble. The eye grows dim, and the heart of many days quails at the fierce glance of warriors. 'Twas better they should die like brave men in their youth than become old men and faint."

"We must have revenge," they all cried. "We will not listen to the young warrior who pines for the daughter of the sun."

Then they began to sing a mournful song. The strange woman wept. Tears rolled down her cheeks, and she often looked up to the house of the Great Spirit and spoke, but none could understand her. All the time the Old Eagle and the other warriors begged that she should be burned to revenge them.

"Brothers and warriors," said Chenos, "our sons did wrong when they broke in upon the sacred dance the Walkullas made to their god, and he lent his thunder to the strange warriors. Let us not draw down his vengeance further by doing we know not what. Let the beautiful woman remain this night in the wigwam of the council, covered with skins, and let none disturb her. Tomorrow we will offer a sacrifice of deer's flesh to the Great Spirit, and if he will not give her to the raging fire and the torments of the avengers, he will tell us so by the words of his mouth. If he does not speak, it shall be done to her as the Old Eagle and his brothers have said."

The head chief said:

"Chenos has spoken well; wisdom is in his words. Make for the strange woman a soft bed of skins, and treat her kindly, for it may be she is a daughter of the Great Spirit."

Then they all returned to their cabins and slept, save the Head Buffalo, who, fearing for the woman's life, laid himself down at the door of the lodge, and watched.

When the morning came the warrior went to the forest and killed a deer which he brought to Chenos, who prepared it for a sacrifice, and sang a song while the flesh lay on the fire.

"Let us listen," said Chenos, stopping the warriors in their dance. "Let us see if the Great Spirit hears us."

They listened, but could hear nothing. Chenos asked him why he did not speak, but he did not answer. Then they sang again.

"Hush!" said Chenos listening. "I hear the crowing of the Great Turkey-cock. I hear him speaking."

They stopped, and Chenos went close to the fire and talked with his master, but nobody saw with whom he talked.

"What does the Great Spirit tell his prophet?" asked the head chief.

"He says," answered Chenos, "the young woman must not be offered to him. He wills her to live and become the mother of many children."

Many were pleased that she was to live, but those who had lost brothers or sons were not appeased, and they said:

"We will have blood. We will go to the priest of the Evil Spirit, and ask him if his master will not give us revenge."

Not far from where our nation had their council fire was a great hill, covered with stunted trees and moss, and rugged rocks. There was a great cave in it, in which dwelt Sketupah, the priest of the Evil One, who there did worship to his master. Sketupah would have been tall had he been straight, but he was more crooked than a bent bow. His hair was like a bunch of grapes, and his eyes like two coals of fire. Many were the gifts our nation made to him to gain his favour, and the favour of his master.

Who but he feasted on the fattest buffalo hump? Who but he fed on the earliest ear of milky corn, on the best things that grew on the land or in the water?

The Old Eagle went to the mouth of the cave and cried with a loud voice:

"Sketupah!"

"Sketupah!" answered the hoarse voice of the Evil One from the hollow cave. He soon came and asked the Old Eagle what he wanted.

"Revenge for our sons who have been killed by the Walkullas and their friends. Will your master hear us?"

"My master must have a sacrifice; he must smell blood," answered Sketupah. "Then we shall know if he will give revenge. Bring hither a sacrifice in the morning."

So in the morning they brought a sacrifice, and the priest laid it on the fire while he danced around. He ceased singing and listened, but the Evil Spirit answered not. Just as he was going to commence another song the warriors saw a large ball rolling very fast up the hill to the spot where they stood. It was the height of a man. When it came up to them it began to unwind itself slowly, until at last a little strange-looking man crept out of the ball, which was made of his own hair. He was no higher than one's shoulders. One of his feet made a strange track, such as no warrior had ever seen before. His face was as black as the shell of the butter-nut or the feathers of the raven, and his eyes as green as grass. His hair was of the colour of moss, and so long that, as the wind blew it out, it seemed the tail of a fiery star.

"What do you want of me?" he asked.

The priest answered:

"The Shawanos want revenge. They want to sacrifice the beautiful daughter of the sun, whom the Head Buffalo has brought from the camp of the Walkullas."

ORACLES, SEERS & SAGES

"They shall have their wish," said the Evil Spirit. "Go and fetch her."

Then Old Eagle and the warriors fetched her. Head Buffalo would have fought for her, but Chenos commanded him to be still.

"My master," he said, "will see she does not suffer." Then they fastened her to the stake. The head warrior had stood still, for he hoped that the priest of the Great Spirit should snatch her away from the Evil One. Now he shouted his war cry and rushed upon Sketupah. It was in vain. Sketupah's master did but breathe upon the face of the warrior when he fell as though he had struck him a blow, and never breathed more. Then the Evil One commanded them to seize Chenos.

"Come, my master," cried Chenos, "for the hands of the Evil One are upon me."

As soon as he had said this, very far over the tall hills, which Indians call the Backbone of the Great Spirit, the people saw two great lights, brighter and larger than stars, moving very fast towards the land of the Shawanos. One was just as high as another, and they were both as high as the goat-sucker flies before a thunderstorm. At first they were close together, but as they came nearer they grew wider apart. Soon our people saw that they were two eyes, and in a little while the body of a great man, whose head nearly reached the sky, came after them. Brothers, the eyes of the Great Spirit always go before him, and nothing is hid from his sight. Brothers, I cannot describe the Master of Life as he stood before the warriors of our nation. Can you look steadily on the star of the morning?

When the Evil Spirit saw the Spirit of Good coming, he began to grow in stature, and continued swelling until he was as tall and big as he. When the Spirit of Good came near and saw how the Evil Spirit had grown, he stopped, and, looking angry, said, with a voice that shook the hills:

"You lied; you promised to stay among the white people and the nations towards the rising sun, and not trouble my people more."

"This woman," replied the Evil Spirit, "comes from my country; she is mine."

"She is mine," said the Great Spirit. "I had given her for a wife to the warrior whom you have killed. Tell me no more lies, bad manito, lest I punish you. Away, and see you trouble my people no more."

The cowardly spirit made no answer, but shrank down to the size he was when he first came. Then he began as before to roll himself up in his hair, which he soon did, and then disappeared as he came. When he was gone, the Great Spirit shrank till he was no larger than a Shawano, and began talking to our people in a soft sweet voice:

"Men of the Shawanos nation, I love you and have always loved you. I bade you conquer your enemies; I gave your foes into your hands. I sent herds of deer and many bears and moose to your hunting-ground, and made my suns shine upon your corn. Who lived so well, who fought so bravely as the Shawanos? Whose women bore so many sons as yours?

"Why did you disturb the sacrifice which the Walkullas were offering to me at the feast of green corn? I was angry, and gave your warriors into the hands of their enemies.

"Shawanos, hear my words, and forget them not; do as I bid you, and you shall see my power and my goodness. Offer no further violence to the white maiden, but treat her kindly. Go now and rake up the ashes of the sacrifice fire into a heap, gathering up the brands. When the great star of evening rises, open the ashes, put in the body of the Head Buffalo, lay on much wood, and kindle a fire on it. Let all the nation be called together, for all must assist in laying wood on the fire, but they must put on no pine, nor the tree which bears white flowers, nor the grape-vine which yields no fruit, nor the shrub whose dew blisters the flesh. The fire must be kept burning two whole moons. It must not go out; it must burn night and day. On the first day of the third moon put no wood on the fire, but let it die. On the morning of the second day the Shawanos must all come to the heap of ashes – every man, woman, and child must come, and the aged who cannot walk must be helped to it. Then Chenos and the head chief must bring out the beautiful woman, and place her near the ashes. This is the will of the Great Spirit."

When he had finished these words he began to swell until he had reached his former bulk and stature. Then at each of his shoulders came out a wing of the colour of the gold-headed pigeon. Gently shaking these, he took flight from the land of the Shawanos, and was never seen in those beautiful regions again.

The Shawanos did as he bade them. They raked the ashes together, laid the body of Head Buffalo in them, lighted the fire, and kept it burning the appointed time. On the first day of the third moon they let the fire out, assembled the nation around, and placed the beautiful woman near the ashes. They waited, and looked to see what would happen. At last the priests and warriors who were nearest began to shout, crying out:

"Piqua!" which in the Shawanos tongue means a man coming out of the ashes, or a man made of ashes.

They told no lie. There he stood, a man tall and straight as a young pine, looking like a Shawano, but handsomer than any man of our nation. The first thing he did was to cry the war-whoop, and demand paint, a club, a bow and arrows, and a hatchet – all of which were given him. Looking around he saw the white woman, and he walked up to her, and gazed in her eyes. Then he came to the head chief and said:

"I must have that woman for my wife."

"What are you?" asked the chief.

"A man of ashes," he replied.

"Who made you?"

"The Great Spirit; and now let me go, that I may take my bow and arrows, kill my deer, and come back and take the beautiful maiden for my wife."

The chief asked Chenos:

"Shall he have her? Does the Great Spirit give her to him?"

"Yes," replied the priest. "The Great Spirit has willed that he shall have her, and from them shall arise a tribe to be called Piqua."

Brothers, I am a Piqua, descended from the man made of ashes. If I have told you a lie, blame not me, for I have but told the story as I heard it. Brothers, I have done.

The Spirits of the Yellow River

THE SPIRITS OF the Yellow River are called Dai Wang – Great King. For many hundreds of years past the river inspectors had continued to report that all sorts of monsters show themselves in the waves of the stream, at times in the shape of dragons, at others in that of cattle and horses, and whenever such a creature makes an appearance a great flood follows. Hence temples are built along the river banks. The higher spirits of the river are honoured as kings, the lower ones as captains, and hardly a day goes by without their being honoured with sacrifices or theatrical performances. Whenever, after a dam has been broken, the leak is closed again, the emperor sends officials with sacrifices and ten great bars of Tibetan incense. This incense is burned in a great sacrificial censer in the temple court, and the river inspectors and their subordinates all go to the temple to thank the gods for their aid. These river gods, it is said, are good and faithful servants of former rulers, who died in consequence of their toil in keeping the dams unbroken. After they died their spirits became river-kings; in their physical bodies, however, they appear as lizards, snakes and frogs.

The mightiest of all the river-kings is the Golden Dragon-King. He frequently appears in the shape of a small golden snake with a square head, low forehead and four red dots over his eyes. He can make himself large or small at will, and cause the waters to rise and fall. He appears and vanishes unexpectedly, and lives in the mouths of the Yellow River and the Imperial Canal. But in addition to the Golden Dragon-King there are dozens of river-kings and captains, each of whom has his own place. The sailors of the Yellow River all have exact lists in which the lives and deeds of the river-spirits are described in detail.

The river-spirits love to see theatrical performances. Opposite every temple is a stage. In the hall stands the little spirit-tablet of the river-king, and on the altar in front of it a small bowl of golden lacquer filled with clean sand. When a little snake appears in it, the river-king has arrived. Then the priests strike the gong and beat the drum and read from the holy books. The official is at once informed and he sends for a company of actors. Before they begin to perform the actors go up to the temple, kneel, and beg the king to let them know which play they are to give. And the river-god picks one out and points to it with his head; or else he writes signs in the sand with his tail. The actors then at once begin to perform the desired play.

The river-god cares naught for the fortunes or misfortunes of human beings. He appears suddenly and disappears in the same way, as best suits him.

Between the outer and the inner dam of the Yellow River are a number of settlements. Now it often happens that the yellow water moves to the very edge of the inner walls. Rising perpendicularly, like a wall, it gradually advances. When people see it coming they hastily burn incense, bow in prayer before the waters, and promise the river-god a theatrical performance. Then the water retires and the word goes round: "The river-god has asked for a play again!"

In a village in that section there once dwelt a wealthy man. He built a stone wall, twenty feet high, around the village, to keep away the water. He did not believe in the spirits of the river, but trusted in his strong wall and was quite unconcerned.

One evening the yellow water suddenly rose and towered in a straight line before the village. The rich man had them shoot cannon at it. Then the water grew stormy, and surrounded the wall to such a height that it reached the openings in the battlements. The water foamed and hissed, and seemed about to pour over the wall. Then everyone in the village was very much frightened. They dragged up the rich man and he had to kneel and beg for pardon. They promised the river-god a theatrical performance, but in vain; but when they promised to build him a temple in the middle of the village and give regular performances, the water sank more and more and gradually returned to its bed. And the village fields suffered no damage, for the earth, fertilized by the yellow slime, yielded a double crop.

Once a scholar was crossing the fields with a friend in order to visit a relative. On their way they passed a temple of the river-god where a new play was just being performed. The friend asked the scholar to go in with him and look on. When they entered the temple court they saw two great snakes upon the front pillars, who had wound themselves about the columns, and were thrusting out their heads as though watching the performance. In the hall of the temple stood the altar with the bowl of sand. In it lay a small snake with a golden body, a green head and red dots above his eyes. His neck was thrust up and his glittering little eyes never left the stage. The friend bowed and the scholar followed his example.

Softly he said to his friend: "What are the three river-gods called?"

"The one in the temple," was the reply, "is the Golden Dragon-King. The two on the columns are two captains. They do not dare to sit in the temple together with the king."

This surprised the scholar, and in his heart he thought: "Such a tiny snake! How can it possess a god's power? It would have to show me its might before I would worship it."

He had not yet expressed these secret thoughts before the little snake suddenly stretched forth his head from the bowl, above the altar. Before the altar burned two enormous candles. They weighed more than ten pounds and were as thick as small trees. Their flame burned like the flare of a torch. The snake now thrust his head into the middle of the candle-flame. The flame must have been at least an inch broad, and was burning red. Suddenly its radiance turned blue, and was split into two tongues. The candle was so enormous and its fire so hot that even copper and iron would have melted in it; but it did not harm the snake.

Then the snake crawled into the censer. The censer was made of iron, and was so large one could not clasp it with both arms. Its cover showed a dragon design in open-work. The snake crawled in and out of the holes in this cover, and wound his way through all of them, so that he looked like an embroidery in threads of gold. Finally all the openings of the cover, large and small, were filled by the snake. In order to do so, he must have made himself several dozen feet long. Then he stretched out his head at the top of the censer and once more watched the play.

Thereupon the scholar was frightened, he bowed twice, and prayed: "Great King, you have taken this trouble on my account! I honour you from my heart!"

No sooner had he spoken these words than, in a moment, the little snake was back in his bowl, and just as small as he had been before.

In Dsiningdschou they were celebrating the river god's birthday in his temple. They were giving him a theatrical performance for a birthday present. The spectators crowded around as thick as a wall, when who should pass but a simple peasant from the country, who said in a loud voice: "Why, that is nothing but a tiny worm! It is a great piece of folly to honour it like a king!"

Before ever he had finished speaking the snake flew out of the temple. He grew and grew, and wound himself three times around the stage. He became as thick around as a small pail, and his head seemed like that of a dragon. His eyes sparkled like golden lamps, and he spat out red flame with his tongue. When he coiled and uncoiled the whole stage trembled and it seemed as though it would break down. The actors stopped their music and fell down on the stage in prayer. The whole multitude was seized with terror and bowed to the ground. Then some of the old men came along, cast the peasant on the ground, and gave him a good thrashing. So he had to cast himself on his knees before the snake and worship him. Then all heard a noise as though a great many firecrackers were being shot off. This lasted for some time, and then the snake disappeared.

East of Shantung lies the city of Dongschou. There rises an observation-tower with a great temple. At its feet lies the water-city, with a sea-gate at the North, through which the flood-tide rises up to the city. A camp of the boundary guard is established at this gate.

Once upon a time there was an officer who had been transferred to this camp as captain. He had formerly belonged to the land forces, and had not yet been long at his new post. He gave some friends of his a banquet, and before the pavilion in which they feasted lay a great stone shaped somewhat like a table. Suddenly a little snake was seen crawling on this stone. It was spotted with green, and had red dots on its square head. The soldiers were about to kill the little creature, when the captain went out to look into the matter. When he had looked he laughed and said: "You must not harm him! He is the river-king of Dsiningdschou. When I was stationed in Dsiningdschou he sometimes visited me, and then I always gave sacrifices and performances in his honour. Now he has come here expressly in order to wish his old friend luck, and to see him once more."

There was a band in camp; the bandsmen could dance and play like a real theatrical troupe. The captain quickly had them begin a performance, had another banquet with wine and delicate foods prepared, and invited the river-god to sit down to the table.

Gradually evening came and yet the river-god made no move to go.

So the captain stepped up to him with a bow and said: "Here we are far removed from the Yellow River, and these people have never yet heard your name spoken. Your visit has been a great honour for me. But the women and fools who have crowded together chattering outside, are afraid of hearing about you. Now you have visited your old friend, and I am sure you wish to get back home again."

With these words he had a litter brought up; cymbals were beaten and fire-works set off, and finally a salute of nine guns was fired to escort him on his way. Then the little snake crawled into the litter, and the captain followed after. In this order they reached the port, and just when it was about time to say farewell, the snake was already swimming in the water. He had grown much larger, nodded to the captain with his head, and disappeared.

Then there were doubts and questionings: "But the river-god lives a thousand miles away from here, how does he get to this place?"

Said the captain: "He is so powerful that he can get to any place, and besides, from where he dwells a waterway leads to the sea. To come down that way and swim to sea is something he can do in a moment's time!"

The Vengeance of the Goddess

IN A CERTAIN TEMPLE in the northern part of the Empire, there once lived a famous priest named Hien-Chung, whose reputation had spread far and wide, not merely for the sanctity of his life, but also for the supernatural powers which he was known to possess, and which he had exhibited on several remarkable occasions. Men would have marvelled less about him had they known that the man dressed in the long slate-coloured robe, with shaven head, and saintly looking face, over which no one had ever seen a smile flicker, was in reality a pilgrim on his way to the Western Heaven, which he hoped to reach in time, and to become a fairy there.

One night Hien-Chung lay asleep in a room opening out of the main hall in which the great image of the Goddess of Mercy, with her benevolent, gracious face, sat enshrined amidst the darkness that lay thickly over the temple. All at once, there stood before him a most striking and stately looking figure. The man had a royal look about him, as though he had been accustomed to rule. On his head there was a crown, and his dress was such as no mere subject would ever be allowed to wear.

Hien-Chung gazed at him in wonder, and was at first inclined to believe that he was some evil spirit who had assumed this clever disguise in order to deceive him. As this thought flashed through his mind, the man began to weep. It was pitiable indeed to see this kingly person affected with such oppressive grief that the tears streamed down his cheeks, and with the tenderness that was distinctive of him Hien-Chung expressed his deep sympathy for a sorrow so profound.

"Three years ago," said his visitor, "I was the ruler of this 'Kingdom of the Black Flower'. I was indeed the founder of my dynasty, for I carved my own fortune with my sword, and made this little state into a kingdom. For a long time I was very happy, and my people were most devoted in their allegiance to me. I little dreamed of the sorrows that were coming on me, and the disasters which awaited me in the near future.

"Five years ago my kingdom was visited with a very severe drought. The rains ceased to fall; the streams which used to fall down the mountain-sides and irrigate the plains dried up; and the wells lost the fountains which used to fill them with water. Everywhere the crops failed, and the green herbage on which the cattle browsed was slowly blasted by the burning rays of the sun.

"The common people suffered in their homes from want of food, and many of the very poorest actually died of starvation. This was a source of great sorrow to me, and every day my prayers went up to Heaven, that it would send down rain upon the dried-up land and so deliver my people from death. I knew that this calamity had fallen on my kingdom because of some wrong that I had done, and so my heart was torn with remorse.

"One day while my mind was full of anxiety, a man suddenly appeared at my palace and begged my ministers to be allowed to have an audience with me. He said that it was of the utmost importance that he should see me, for he had come to propose a plan for the deliverance of my country.

"I gave orders that he should instantly be brought into my presence, when I asked him if he had the power to cause the rain to descend upon the parched land.

"'Yes,' he replied, 'I have, and if you will step with me now to the front of your palace I will prove to you that I have the ability to do this, and even more.'

"Striding out to a balcony which overlooked the capital, and from which one could catch a view of the hills in the distance, the stranger lifted up his right hand towards the heavens and uttered certain words which I was unable to understand.

"Instantly, and as if by magic, a subtle change crept through the atmosphere. The sky became darkened, and dense masses of clouds rolled up and blotted out the sun. The thunder began to mutter, and vivid flashes of lightning darted from one end of the heavens to the other, and before an hour had elapsed the rain was descending in torrents all over the land, and the great drought was at an end.

"My gratitude to this mysterious stranger for the great deliverance he had wrought for my kingdom was so great that there was no favour which I was not willing to bestow upon him. I gave him rooms in the palace, and treated him as though he were my equal. I had the truest and the tenderest affection for him, and he seemed to be equally devoted to me.

ORACLES, SEERS & SAGES

"One morning we were walking hand in hand in the royal gardens. The peach blossoms were just out, and we were enjoying their perfume and wandering up and down amongst the trees which sent forth such exquisite fragrance.

"As we sauntered on, we came by-and-by upon a well which was hidden from sight by a cluster of oleander trees. We stayed for a moment to peer down its depths and to catch a sight of the dark waters lying deep within it. Whilst I was gazing down, my friend gave me a sudden push and I was precipitated head first into the water at the bottom. The moment I disappeared, he took a broad slab of stone and completely covered the mouth of the well. Over it he spread a thick layer of earth, and in this he planted a banana root, which, under the influence of the magic powers he possessed, in the course of a few hours had developed into a full-grown tree. I have lain dead in the well now for three years, and during all that time no one has arisen to avenge my wrong or to bring me deliverance."

"But have your ministers of State made no efforts during all these three years to discover their lost king?" asked Hien-Chung. "And what about your wife and family? Have they tamely submitted to have you disappear without raising an outcry that would resound throughout the whole kingdom? It seems to me inexplicable that a king should vanish from his palace and that no hue and cry should be raised throughout the length and breadth of the land until the mystery should be solved and his cruel murder fully avenged."

"It is here," replied the spirit of the dead king, "that my enemy has shown his greatest cunning. The reason why men never suspect that any treason has been committed is because by his enchantments he has transformed his own appearance so as to become the exact counterpart of myself. The man who called down the rain and saved my country from drought and famine has simply disappeared, so men think, and I the King still rule as of old in my kingdom. Not the slightest suspicion as to the true state of things has ever entered the brain of anyone in the nation, and so the usurper is absolutely safe in the position he occupies today."

"But have you never appealed to Yam-lo, the ruler of the Land of Shadows?" asked Hien-Chung. "He is the great redresser of the wrongs and crimes of earth, and now that you are a spirit and immediately within his jurisdiction, you should lay your complaint before him and pray him to avenge the sufferings you have been called upon to endure."

"You do not understand," the spirit hastily replied. "The one who has wrought such ruin in my life is an evil spirit. He has nothing in common with men, but has been let loose from the region where evil spirits are confined to punish me for some wrong that I have committed in the past. He therefore knows the ways of the infernal regions, and is hand in glove with the rulers there, and even with Yam-lo himself. He is, moreover, on the most friendly terms with the tutelary God of my capital, and so no complaint of mine would ever be listened to for a moment by any of the powers who rule in the land of the dead.

"There is another very strong reason, too, why any appeal that I might make for justice would be disregarded. My soul has not yet been loosed from my body, but is still confined within it in the well. The courts of the Underworld would never recognize me, because I still belong to this life, over which they have no control.

"Only today," he continued, "a friendly spirit whispered in my ear that my confinement in the well was drawing to a close, and that the three years I had been adjudged to stay there would soon be up. He strongly advised me to apply to you, for you are endowed, he said, with powers superior to those possessed by my enemy, and if you are only pleased to exercise them I shall speedily be delivered from his evil influence."

Now the Goddess of Mercy had sent Hien-Chung a number of familiar spirits to be a protection to him in time of need. Next morning, accordingly, he summoned the cleverest of these, whose name was Hing, in order to consult with him as to how the king might be delivered from the bondage in which he had been held for the three years.

"The first thing we have to do," said Hing, "is to get the heir to the Throne on our side. He has often been suspicious at certain things in the conduct of his supposed father, one of which is that for three years he has never been allowed to see his mother. All that is needed now is to get some tangible evidence to convince him that there is some mystery in the palace, and we shall gain him as our ally.

"I have been fortunate," he continued, "in obtaining one thing which we shall find very useful in inducing the Prince to listen to what we have to say to him about his father. You may not know it, but about the time when the King was thrown into the well, the seal of the kingdom mysteriously disappeared and a new one had to be cut.

"Knowing that you were going to summon me to discuss this case, I went down into the well at dawn this morning, and found the missing seal on the body of the King. Here it is, and now we must lay our plans to work on the mind of the son for the deliverance of the father. Tomorrow I hear that the Prince is going out hunting on the neighbouring hills. In one of the valleys there is a temple to the Goddess of Mercy, and if you will take this seal and await his coming there, I promise you that I will find means to entice him to the shrine."

Next morning the heir to the Throne of the "Kingdom of the Black Flower" set out with a noisy retinue to have a day's hunting on the well-wooded hills overlooking the capital. They had scarcely reached the hunting grounds when great excitement was caused by the sudden appearance of a remarkable-looking hare. It was decidedly larger than an ordinary hare, but the curious feature about it was its colour, which was as white as the driven snow.

No sooner had the hounds caught sight of it, than with loud barkings and bayings they dashed madly in pursuit. The hare, however, did not seem to show any terror, but with graceful bounds that carried it rapidly over the ground, it easily out-distanced the fleetest of its pursuers. It appeared, indeed, as though it were thoroughly enjoying the facility with which it could outrun the dogs, while the latter grew more and more excited as they always saw the quarry before them and yet could never get near enough to lay hold upon it.

Another extraordinary thing was that this hare did not seem anxious to escape. It took no advantage of undergrowth or of clumps of trees to hide the direction in which it was going. It managed also to keep constantly in view of the whole field; and when it had to make sudden turns in the natural windings of the road which led to a valley in the distance, where there stood a famous temple, it hesitated for a moment and allowed the baying hounds to come perilously near, before it darted off with the speed of lightning and left the dogs far behind it.

Little did the hunters dream that the beautiful animal which was giving them such an exciting chase was none other than the fairy Hing, who had assumed this disguise in order to bring the Prince to the lonely temple in the secluded valley, where, beyond the possibility of being spied upon by his father's murderer, the story of treachery could be told, and means be devised for his restoration to the throne.

ORACLES, SEERS & SAGES

Having arrived close to the temple, the mysterious hare vanished as suddenly as it had appeared, and not a trace was left to enable the dogs, which careered wildly round and round, to pick up the scent.

The Prince, who was a devoted disciple of the Goddess of Mercy, now dismounted and entered the temple, where he proceeded to burn incense before her shrine and in muttered tones to beseech her to send down blessings upon him.

After a time, he became considerably surprised to find that the presiding priest of the temple, instead of coming forward to attend upon him and to show him the courtesies due to his high position, remained standing in a corner where the shadows were darkest, his eyes cast upon the ground and with a most serious look overspreading his countenance.

Accordingly, when he had finished his devotions to the Goddess, the Prince approached the priest, and asked him in a kindly manner if anything was distressing him.

"Yes," replied Hien-Chung, "there is, and it is a subject which materially affects your Royal Highness. If you will step for a moment into my private room, I shall endeavour to explain to you the matter which has filled my mind with the greatest possible anxiety."

When they entered the abbot's room, Hien-Chung handed the Prince a small box and asked him to open it and examine the article it contained.

Great was the Prince's amazement when he took it out and cast a hurried glance over it. A look of excitement passed over his face and he cried out, "Why, this is the great seal of the kingdom which was lost three years ago, and of which no trace could ever be found! May I ask how it came into your possession and what reason you can give for not having restored it to the King, who has long wished to discover it?"

"The answer to that is a long one, your Highness, and to satisfy you, I must go somewhat into detail."

Hien-Chung then told the Prince of the midnight visit his father had made him, and the tragic story of his murder by the man who was now posing as the King, and of his appeal to deliver him from the sorrows of the well in which he had been confined for three years.

"With regard to the finding of the seal," he continued, "my servant Hing, who is present, will describe how by the supernatural powers with which he is endowed, he descended the well only this very morning and discovered it on the body of your father."

"We have this absolute proof," he said, "that the vision I saw only two nights ago was not some imagination of the brain, but that it was really the King who appealed to me to deliver him from the power of an enemy who seems bent upon his destruction.

"We must act, and act promptly," he went on, "for the man who is pretending to be the ruler of your kingdom is a person of unlimited ability, and as soon as he gets to know that his secret has been divulged, he will put into operation every art he possesses to frustrate our purpose.

"What I propose is that your Highness should send back the greater part of your retinue to the palace, with an intimation to the effect that you are going to spend the night here in a special service to the Goddess, whose birthday it fortunately happens to be today. After night has fallen upon the city, Hing shall descend into the well and bring the body of your father here. You will then have all the proof you need of the truth of the matter, and we can devise plans as to our future action."

A little after midnight, Hing having faithfully carried out the commission entrusted to him by Hien-Chung, arrived with the body of the King, which was laid with due ceremony and respect in one of the inner rooms of the temple. With his marvellous wonder-working powers and with the aid of invisible forces which he had been able to summon to his assistance, he had succeeded in transporting it from the wretched place where it had lain so long to the friendly temple of the Goddess of Mercy.

The Prince was deeply moved by the sight of his father's body. Fortunately it had suffered no change since the day when it was thrown to the bottom of the well. Not a sign of decay could be seen upon the King's noble features. It seemed as though he had but fallen asleep, and presently would wake up and talk to them as he used to do. The fact that in some mysterious way the soul had not been separated from the body accounted for its remarkable preservation. Nevertheless to all appearance the King was dead, and the great question now was how he could be brought back to life, so that he might be restored to his family and his kingdom.

"The time has come," said Hien-Chung, "when heroic measures will have to be used if the King is ever to live again. Two nights ago he made a passionate and urgent request to me to save him, for one of the gods informed him that I was the only man who could do so. So far, we have got him out of the grip of the demon that compassed his death, and now it lies with me to provide some antidote which shall bring back the vital forces and make him a living man once more.

"I have never had to do with such a serious case as this before, but I have obtained from the Patriarch of the Taoist Church a small vial of the Elixir of Life, which has the marvellous property of prolonging the existence of whoever drinks it. We shall try it on the King and, as there is no sign of vital decay, let us hope that it will be effective in restoring him to life."

Turning to a desk that was kept locked, he brought out a small black earthenware bottle, from which he dropped a single drop of liquid on to the lips of the prostrate figure. In a few seconds a kind of rosy flush spread over the King's features. Another drop, and a look of life flashed over the pallid face. Still another, and after a short interval the eyes opened and looked with intelligence upon the group surrounding his couch. Still one more, and the King arose and asked how long he had been asleep, and how it came about that he was in this small room instead of being in his own palace.

He was soon restored to his family and to his position in the State, for the usurper after one or two feeble attempts to retain his power ignominiously fled from the country.

A short time after, Hien-Chung had a private interview with the King. "I am anxious," he said, "that your Majesty should understand the reason why such a calamity came into your life.

"Some years ago without any just reason you put to death a Buddhist priest. You never showed any repentance for the great wrong you had done, and so the Goddess sent a severe drought upon your Kingdom. You still remained unrepentant, and then she sent one of her Ministers to afflict you, depriving you of your home and your royal power. The man who pushed you down the well was but carrying out the instructions he had received from the Goddess. Your stay down the well for three years was part of the punishment she had decreed for your offence, and when the time was up, I was given the authority to release you.

"Kings as well as their subjects are under the great law of righteousness, and if they violate it they must suffer like other men. I would warn your Majesty that unless you show some evidence that you have repented for taking away a man's life unjustly, other sorrows will most certainly fall upon you in the future."

The Mysterious Buddhist Robe

THE SHORT VISIT which the Emperor Li Shih-Ming paid to the Land of Shadows had produced a profound impression on his mind. The pain and misery that men had to endure there, because of the evils they had committed in this life by their own voluntary action, had been brought before him in a most vivid manner. He had seen with his own eyes what he had always been unwilling to believe – namely, that wrong-doing is in every case followed by penalties, which have to be paid either in this world or the next.

He was now convinced that the doctrine of the sages on this point was true, for he had witnessed the horrors that criminals who had practically escaped punishment in this life had to suffer when they came under the jurisdiction of Yam-lo.

What distressed him most of all, however, was the grim thought which clung to him and refused to be silenced, that a large number of those in the Land of Shadows who were suffering from hunger and nakedness, were there as the result of his own cruelty and injustice, and that the cries of these men and women would reach to Heaven, and in due time bring down vengeance on himself.

With this fear of coming judgement there was at the same time mingled in his mind an element of compassion, for he was really sorry for the poor wretches whom he had seen in the 'City of the Wronged Ones', and whose reproaches and threats of divine vengeance had entered into his very soul.

He therefore determined to institute a magnificent service for those spirits of the dead, who through the injustice of rulers, or the impotence of law, or private revenge, had lost their lives and were suffering untold hardships in the other world. He would have prayers said for their souls, that would flood their lives with plenty, and in course of time would open up the way for their being reborn into the world of men.

In this way he would propitiate those whom he had injured, and at the same time accumulate such an amount of merit for his benevolence that the gods would make it easy for him when his time of reckoning came, and the accounts of his life were made up and balanced.

As this ceremony was to be one such as had never before been held at any period of Chinese history, he was anxious that the man who should be the leader and conductor of it should not be one of the men of indifferent lives who are usually found in the Buddhist temples and monasteries. He must be a man of sterling character, and of a life so pure and holy that no stain could be found upon it to detract from the saintly reputation he had acquired.

His Majesty accordingly sent out edicts to all the Viceroys in the Empire, commanding them to issue proclamations throughout the length and breadth of the country, telling the people of the great religious service which he was going to hold in the capital for the unhappy spirits in the Land of Shadows. In these edicts he ordered that search should be made for a priest of unblemished character – one who had proved his love for his fellow-men by great acts of sympathy for them. This man was to be invited to present himself before the Emperor, to take charge of the high and splendid service which had been designed by the Sovereign himself.

The tidings of this noble conception of Li Shih-Ming spread with wonderful rapidity throughout his dominions, and even reached the far-off Western Heaven, where the mysterious beings who inhabit that happy land are ever on the alert to welcome any movement for the relief of human suffering. The Goddess of Mercy considered the occasion of such importance that she determined to take her share of responsibility for this distinguished service, by providing suitable vestments in which the leader of the great ceremony should be attired.

So it came to pass that while men's minds were excited about the proposed celebration for the dead, two priests suddenly appeared in the streets of the capital. No one had ever seen such old-fashioned and weird-looking specimens of manhood before. They were mean and insignificant in appearance, and the distinctive robes in which they were dressed were so travel-stained and unclean that it was evident they had not been washed for many a long day.

Men looked at them with astonishment as they passed along the road, for there was something so strange about them that they seemed to have come down from a far-off distant age, and to have suddenly burst into a civilization which had long out-grown the type from which they were descended. But by-and-by their curious old-world appearance was forgotten in amazement at the articles they carried with them. These were carefully wrapped in several folds of cloth to keep them from being soiled, though the two priests were perfectly willing to unfold the wrappers, and exhibit them to anyone who wished to examine them.

The precious things which were preserved with such jealous care were a hat and robe such as an abbot might wear on some great occasion when the Buddhist church was using its most elabourate ceremonial to perform some function of unusual dignity and importance. There was also a crosier, beautifully wrought with precious stones, which was well worthy of being held in the hand of the highest functionary of the Church in any of its most sacred and solemn services. The remarkable thing about the hat and robe was their exquisite beauty. The richness of the embroidered work, the quaint designs, the harmonious blending of colours, and the subtle exhibition of the genius of the mind which had fashioned and perfected them, arrested the attention of even the lowest class in the crowds of people who gathered round the two priests to gaze upon the hat and robe, with awe and admiration in their faces.

Some instinct that flashed through the minds of the wondering spectators told them that these rare and fairy-like vestments were no ordinary products manufactured in any of the looms throughout the wide domains of the Empire. No human mind or hand had ever designed or worked out the various hues and shades of such marvellous colours as those which flashed before their eyes, and which possessed a delicacy and beauty such as none of the great artists of the past had ever been able to produce.

The priests from the various temples and monasteries of the capital soon heard the reports that spread through the city about the marvellous hat and robe, and flocked in large numbers to see these wonderful things, which the two curious-looking men were displaying to all who cared to gaze upon them.

"Do you wish to dispose of these things?" asked one of the city priests.

"If anyone can pay the price at which alone we are prepared to sell, we shall be willing to part with them to him," was the reply.

"And what may the price be?" anxiously enquired the priest.

"The hat and robe will cost four thousand taels, and the crosier, which is of the rarest materials and manufacture, will be sold for the same amount."

At this a great laugh resounded through the crowd. In those days eight thousand taels was a huge fortune which only one or two of the wealthiest men of the State could have afforded to give. The boisterous mirth, however, which convulsed the crowd when they heard the fabulous sums asked by these strangers for their articles, soon became hushed when the latter proceeded to explain that the sums demanded were purposely prohibitive, in order that the sacred vestments should not fall into the hands of anyone who was unworthy to possess them.

"You are all aware," said one of the strangers, "that his Majesty the Emperor, recognizing that the service for the dead which he is about to hold is one of momentous importance, not only to the spirits suffering in the Land of Shadows, but also to the prosperity and welfare of the Chinese Empire, has already issued edicts to secure the presence of some saintly and godly priest, who shall be worthy to superintend the prayers that will be said for the men and women who are leading dreary lives in the land over which Yam-lo rules."

The story of these two men spread with great rapidity throughout the homes of all classes in the metropolis, and when it was understood that they had no desire to make money by the rare and beautiful articles which they readily displayed to the crowds that followed them whenever they appeared on the streets, they began to be surrounded with a kind of halo of romance. Men whispered to each other that these were no common denizens of the earth, but fairies in disguise, who had come as messengers from the Goddess of Mercy. The garments which they had with them were such as no mortal eyes had ever beheld, and were clearly intended for use only at some special ceremony of exceptional importance such as that which the Emperor was planning to have carried out.

At length rumours reached the palace of the strange scenes which were daily taking place in the streets of the capital, and Li Shih-Ming sent officers to command the two strange priests to appear in his presence.

When they were brought before him, and he saw the wonderful robe embroidered in delicate hues and colours such as no workman had ever been known to design before, and grasped the crosier which sparkled and flashed with the brilliancy of the precious stones adorning it, the Emperor felt that the invisible gods had approved of his design for the solemn service for the dead and had prepared vestments for the High Priest which would be worthy of the exalted position he would occupy in the great ceremony.

"I hear that you want eight thousand taels for these articles," said the Emperor to the two men, who stood respectfully before him.

"We are not anxious, your Majesty," replied one of the strangers, "about the price. That is to us of very little importance. We have mentioned this large sum simply to prevent any man of unworthy mind from becoming their possessor.

"There is a peculiarity about that robe," he continued. "Any person of pure and upright heart who wears it will be preserved from every kind of disaster that can possibly assail him in this world. No sorrow can touch him, and the schemes of the most malignant of evil spirits will have no influence upon him. On the other hand, any man who is under the dominion of any base passion, if he dares to put on that mystic robe, will find himself involved in all kinds of calamities and sorrows, which will never leave him until he has put it off and laid it aside for ever.

"What we are really here for," he concluded, "is to endeavour to assist your Majesty in the discovery of a priest of noble and blameless life who will be worthy of presiding at the service you are about to hold for the unhappy spirits in the Land of Shadows. When we have found him we shall consider that our mission has been fulfilled, and we can then return and report the success we have achieved."

At this moment despatches from high officials throughout the country were presented to the Emperor, all recommending Sam-Chaong as the only man in the dominions who was fit to act as High Priest in the proposed great service. As Sam-Chaong happened to be then in the capital, he was sent for and, being approved of by his Majesty, was at once appointed to the sacred office, which he alone of the myriads of priests in China seemed to be worthy of occupying.

The two strangers, who had been noting the proceedings with anxious and watchful eyes, expressed their delight at the decision that had been arrived at. Stepping up to Sam-Chaong with the most reverential attitude, they presented him with the costly vestments which had excited the wonder and admiration of everyone who had seen them. Refusing to receive any remuneration for them, they bowed gracefully to the Emperor and retired. As the door of the audience-chamber closed upon them they vanished from human sight, and no trace of them could anywhere be found.

On the great day appointed by the Emperor, such a gathering was assembled as China in all the long history of the past had never before witnessed. Abbots from far-off distant monasteries were there, dressed in their finest vestments. Aged priests, with faces wrinkled by the passage of years, and young bonzes in their slate-coloured gowns, had travelled over the hills and mountains of the North to be present, and took up their positions in the great building. Men of note, too, who had made themselves famous by their devoted zeal for the ceremonies of the Buddhist Church and by their munificent gifts to the temples and shrines, had come with great retinues of their clansmen to add to the splendour and dignity of the occasion.

But the chief glory and attraction of the day to the assembled crowds was the Emperor, Li Shih-Ming. Never had he been seen in such pomp and circumstance as on this occasion. Close round him stood the princes of the royal family, the great officers of state and the members of the Cabinet in their rich and picturesque dresses. Immediately beyond were earls and dukes, viceroys of provinces and great captains and commanders, whose fame for mighty deeds of valour in the border warfare had spread through every city and town and hamlet in the Empire.

There were also present some of the most famous scholars of China, who, though not members of the Buddhist Church, yet felt that they could not refuse the invitation which the Emperor had extended to them.

In short, the very flower of the Empire was gathered together to carry out the benevolent purpose of rescuing the spirits of the dead from an intolerable state of misery which only the living had the power of alleviating.

The supreme moment, however, was when Sam-Chaong and more than a hundred of the priests most distinguished for learning and piety in the whole of the church, marched in solemn procession, chanting a litany, and took their places on the raised platform from which they were to conduct the service for the dead.

During the ceremony, much to his amazement, Li Shih-Ming saw the two men who had bestowed the fairy vestments on Sam-Chaong, standing one on each side of him; but though they joined heartily in the proceedings, he could not help noticing that a look of dissatisfaction and occasionally of something which seemed like contempt, rested like a shadow on their faces.

At the close of the service he commanded them to appear before him, and expressed his surprise at their conduct, when they explained that the discontent they had shown was entirely due to a feeling that the ritual which had been used that day was one entirely inadequate to the occasion. It was so wanting in dignity and loftiness of conception, they said, that though some ease might be brought to the spirits suffering in the Land of Shadows from the service which had been performed, it would utterly fail in the most important particular of all – namely, their deliverance from Hades, and their rebirth into the land of the living.

That this was also a matter which had given the Goddess of Mercy a vast amount of concern was soon made evident to the Emperor, for in the midst of this conversation there suddenly sounded, throughout the great hall in which the vast congregation still lingered, a voice saying: "Send Sam-Chaong to the Western Heaven to obtain the ritual which shall there be given him and which shall be worthy of being chanted by a nation."

This command from the invisible Goddess produced such an impression upon the Emperor that he made immediate preparations for the departure of Sam-Chaong on his momentous journey; and in a few days, supplied with everything necessary for so toilsome an undertaking, the famous priest started on what seemed a wild and visionary enterprise in pursuit of an object which anyone with less faith than himself would have deemed beyond the power of any human being to accomplish.

In order to afford him protection by the way and to act as his body-servants, the Emperor appointed two men to accompany Sam-Chaong on the long journey which he had undertaken at the command of the Goddess of Mercy. His Majesty would indeed have given him a whole regiment of soldiers, if he had been willing to accept them; but he absolutely refused to take more than just two men. He relied chiefly on the fairy robe which he had received, for that secured him from all danger from any foes whom he might meet on the road. Moreover, his mission, as he assured the Emperor, was one of peace and good-will, and it would not harmonize either with his own wishes or with those of the Goddess for him to be in a position to avenge his wrongs by the destruction of human life.

Before many days had elapsed Sam-Chaong began to realize the perilous nature of the service he had been called upon to perform. One afternoon, the travellers were jogging leisurely along in a wild and unsettled district, when suddenly two fierce-looking hobgoblins swooped down upon them, and almost before a word could be said had swallowed up both his poor followers. They were proceeding to do the same with Sam-Chaong when a fairy appeared upon the scene, and sent them flying with screams of terror to the caverns in the neighbouring hills where their homes seemed to be.

For a moment or two, Sam-Chaong was in extreme distress. He had just escaped an imminent peril; he was absolutely alone in an apparently uninhabited region; and the shadows of night were already darkening everything around. He was wondering where he would spend the night, when a man appeared upon the scene and invited him to come home with him to a mountain village on the spur of the hills which rose abruptly some distance away in front of them.

Although an entire stranger, who had never even heard Sam-Chaong's name, this man treated his guest right royally and gave him the very best that his house contained. Deeply impressed with the generous treatment he had received, Sam-Chaong determined that he would repay his host's generosity by performing an act which would be highly gratifying both to him and to all the members of his household.

Arranging a temporary altar in front of the image of the household god, who happened to be the Goddess of Mercy, he chanted the service for the dead before it with such acceptance that the spirit of the father of his host, who had been confined in the Land of Shadows, was released from that sunless land and was allowed to be reborn and take his place amongst the living. Moreover, that very night, the father appeared before his son in a vision, and told him that in consequence of the intercession of Sam-Chaong, whose reputation for piety was widely known in the dominions of Yam-lo, he had been allowed to leave that dismal country and had just been born into a family in the province of Shensi.

The son was rejoiced beyond measure at this wonderful news, and in order to show his gratitude for this generous action, he volunteered to accompany Sam-Chaong right to the very frontiers of China and to share with him any dangers and hardships he might have to endure by the way.

After many weary days of travelling this part of the journey was at last accomplished, and they were about to separate at the foot of a considerable hill which lay on the border line between China and the country of the barbarians beyond, when a loud and striking voice was heard exclaiming, "The priest has come! The priest has come!"

Sam-Chaong asked his companion the meaning of these words and to what priest they referred.

"There is a tradition in this region," replied the man, "that five hundred years ago, a certain fairy, inflamed with pride, dared to raise himself in rebellion against the Goddess of Mercy in the Western Heaven. To punish him she turned him into a monkey, and confined him in a cave near the top of this hill. There she condemned him to remain until Sam-Chaong should pass this way, when he could earn forgiveness by leading the priest into the presence of the Goddess who had commanded him to appear before her."

Ascending the hill in the direction of the spot from whence the cry, "The priest has come!" kept ringing through the air, they came upon a natural cavern, the mouth of which was covered by a huge boulder, nicely poised in such a position that all exit from it was rendered an impossibility. Peering through the crevices at the side, they could distinctly see the figure of a monkey raising its face with an eager look of expectation in the direction of Sam-Chaong and his companion.

"Let me out," it cried, "and I will faithfully lead you to the Western Heaven, and never leave you until you find yourself standing in the presence of the Goddess of Mercy."

"But how am I to get you out?" asked Sam-Chaong. "The boulder that shuts you in is too large for human hands to move, and so, though I pity you in your misfortune and greatly desire your help to guide me along the unknown paths that lie before me, I fear that the task of setting you free must fall to other hands than mine."

"Deliverance is more easy than you imagine," replied the monkey. "Cast your eye along the edge of this vast rock, which the Goddess with but a simple touch of one of her fingers moved into its place five hundred years ago, as though it had been the airiest down that ever floated in a summer's breeze, and you will see something yellow standing out in marked contrast to the black lichen-covered stone. That is the sign-manual of the Goddess. She printed it on the rock when she condemned me centuries ago to be enclosed within this narrow cell until you should come and release me. Your hand alone can remove that mystic symbol and save me from the penalty of a living death."

Following the directions of the monkey, Sam-Chaong carefully scraped away the yellow-coloured tracings which he tried in vain to decipher; and when the last faint scrap had been finally removed, the huge, gigantic boulder silently moved aside with a gentle, easy motion and tilted itself to one side until the prisoner had emerged, when once more it slid gracefully back into its old position.

Under the guidance of the monkey, who had assumed the appearance of a strong and vigorous young athlete, Sam-Chaong proceeded on his journey – over mountains so high that they seemed to touch the very heavens, and through valleys which lay at their foot in perpetual shadow, except only at noon-tide when the sun stood directly overhead. Then again they travelled across deserts whose restless, storm-tossed, sandy billows left no traces of human footsteps, and where death seemed, like some cunning foe, to be lying in wait to destroy their lives.

It was here that Sam-Chaong realized the protecting care of the Goddess in providing such a valuable companion as the monkey proved himself to be. He might have been born in these sandy wastes, so familiar was he with their moods. There was something in the air, and in the colours of the sky at dawn and at sunset, that told him what was going to happen, and he could say almost to a certainty whether any storm was coming to turn these silent deserts into storm-tossed oceans of sand, which more ruthless even than the sea, would engulf all living things within their pitiless depths. He knew, moreover, where the hidden springs of water lay concealed beneath the glare and glitter that pained the eyes simply to look upon them; and without a solitary landmark in the boundless expanse, by unerring instinct, he would travel straight to the very spot where the spring bubbled up from the great fountains below.

Having crossed these howling wildernesses, where Sam-Chaong must have perished had he travelled alone, they came to a region inhabited by a pastoral people, but abounding in bands of robbers. Monkey was a daring fellow and was never afraid to meet any foe in fair fight; yet for the sake of Sam-Chaong, whose loving disposition had been insensibly taming his wild and fiery nature, he tried as far as possible to avoid a collision with any evil characters, whether men or spirits, who might be inclined to have a passage of arms with them.

One day they had passed over a great plain, where herds of sheep could be seen in all directions browsing under the watchful care of their shepherds, and they had come to the base of the foot-hills leading to a mountainous country beyond, when the profound meditation in which Sam-Chaong was usually absorbed was suddenly interrupted by a startled cry from Monkey.

Drawing close up to him, he said in a low voice, "Do you see those six men who are descending the hill and coming in our direction? They look like simple-minded farmers, and yet they are all devils who have put on the guise of men in order to be able to take us unawares. Their real object is to kill you, and thus frustrate the gracious purpose of the Goddess, who wishes to deliver the souls in the Land of Shadows from the torments they are enduring there.

"I know them well," he went on; "they are fierce and malignant spirits and very bold, for rarely have they ever been put to flight in any conflict in which they have been engaged. They little dream, however, who it is you have by your side. If they did they would come on more warily, for though I am single-handed they would be chary of coming to issues with me.

"But I am glad," he continued, "that they have not yet discovered who I am, for my soul has long desired just such a day as this, when in a battle that shall be worthy of the gods, my fame shall spread throughout the Western Heaven and even into the wide domains of the Land of Shadows."

With a cry of gladness, as though some wondrous good-fortune had befallen him, he bounded along the road to meet the coming foe, and in contemptuous tones challenged them to mortal combat.

No sooner did they discover who it was that dared to champion Sam-Chaong with such bold and haughty front, than with hideous yells and screams they rushed tumultuously upon him, hoping by a combined attack to confuse him and to make him fly in terror before them.

In this however they had reckoned without their host. With a daring quite as great as theirs, but with a skill far superior to that of the six infuriated demons, Monkey seized a javelin which came gleaming through the air just at the precise moment that he needed it, and hurled it at one of his opponents with such fatal effect that he lay sprawling on the ground, and with a cry that might have come from a lost spirit breathed his last.

And now the battle became a mighty one indeed. Arrows shot from invisible bows flew quicker than flashes of light against this single mighty fighter, but they glanced off a magic shield which fairy arts had interposed in front of him. Weapons such as mortal hands had never wielded in any of the great battles of the world were now brought into play; but never for a moment did Monkey lose his head. With marvellous intrepidity he warded them off, and striking back with one tremendous lunge, he laid another of the demons dead at his feet.

Dismay began to raise the coward in the minds of those who were left, and losing heart they turned to those subtle and cunning devices that had never before failed in their attacks on mankind. Their great endeavour now was to inveigle Monkey into a position where certain destruction would be sure to follow. Three-pronged spears were hurled against him with deadly precision, and had he not at that precise moment leaped high into the air no power on earth could have saved him.

It was at this tremendous crisis in the fight that Monkey won his greatest success. Leaping lightly to the ground whilst the backs of his foes were still turned towards him, he was able with the double-edged sword which he held in each of his hands to despatch three more of his enemies. The last remaining foe was so utterly cowed when he beheld his comrades lying dead upon the road that he took to flight, and soon all that was to be seen of him was a black speck slowly vanishing on the distant horizon.

Thus ended the great battle in which Monkey secured such a signal victory over the wild demons of the frozen North, and Sam-Chaong drew near to gaze upon the mangled bodies of the fierce spirits who but a moment ago were fighting so desperately for their very lives.

Now, Sam-Chaong was a man who naturally had the tenderest heart for every living thing; and so, as he looked, a cloud of sadness spread over his countenance and he sighed as he thought of the destruction of life which he had just witnessed. It was true that the demons had come with the one settled purpose of killing him, and there was no reason therefore why he should regret their death. But life to him was always precious, no matter in what form it might be enshrined. Life was the special gift of Heaven, and could not be wilfully destroyed without committing a crime against the gods.

So absorbed did Sam-Chaong become in this thought, and so sombre were the feelings filling his heart, that he entirely forgot to thank the hero by his side who had risked his life for him, and but for whose prowess he would have fallen a victim to the deadly hatred of these enemies of mankind. Feelings of resentment began to spring up in the mind of Monkey as he saw that Sam-Chaong seemed to feel more pity for the dead demons than gratitude for the heroic efforts which had saved him from a cruel death.

"Are you dissatisfied with the services I have rendered to you today?" he asked him abruptly.

"My heart is deeply moved by what you have done for me," replied Sam-Chaong. "My only regret is that you could not have delivered me without causing the death of these poor wretched demons, and thus depriving them of the gift of life, a thing as dear to them as it is to you or me."

Now Monkey, who was of a fierce and hasty temper, could not brook such meagre praise as this, and so in passionate and indignant language he declared that no longer would he be content to serve so craven a master, who, though beloved of the Goddess, was not a man for whom he would care to risk his life again.

With these words he vaulted into the air, and soared away into the distance, on and on through countless leagues of never-ending sky, until he came to the verge of a wide-spreading ocean. Plunging into this as though it had been the home in which he had always lived, he made his way by paths with which he seemed familiar, until he reached the palace of the Dragon Prince of the Sea, who received him with the utmost cordiality and gave him an invitation to remain with him as his guest as long as he pleased.

For some time he entertained himself with the many marvellous sights which are hidden away beneath the waters of the great ocean and which have a life and imagery of their own, stranger and more mysterious perhaps than those on which men are accustomed to look. But in time he became restless and dissatisfied with himself. The unpleasant thought crept slowly into his heart that in a moment of passion he had basely deserted Sam-Chaong and had left him helpless in a strange and unknown region; and worse still that he had been unfaithful to the trust which the Goddess had committed to him. He became uncomfortably conscious, too, that though he had fled to the depths of the ocean he could never get beyond the reach of her power, and that whenever she wished to imprison him in the mountain cavern where he had eaten out his heart for five hundred years, she could do so with one imperious word of command.

In this mood of repentance for his past errors, he happened to cast his eye upon a scroll which hung in one of the rooms of the palace. As he read the story on it his heart smote him, and from that moment he determined to hasten back to the post from which he had fled.

The words on the scroll were written in letters of gold and told how on a certain occasion in the history of the past the fairies determined to assist the fortunes of a young man named Chang-lung, who had gained their admiration because of the nobility of character which he had exhibited in his ordinary conduct in life. He belonged to an extremely poor family, and so without some such aid as they could give him, he could never attain to that eminence in the State which would enable him to be of service to his country. But he must first be tested to see whether he had the force of character necessary to bear the strain which greatness would put upon him. Accordingly one of the most experienced amongst their number was despatched to make the trial.

Assuming the guise of an old countryman in poor and worn-out clothing, the fairy sat down on a bridge over a stream close to the village where the favourite of the gods lived. By-and-by Chang-lung came walking briskly along. Just as he came up to the disguised fairy, the latter let one of his shoes drop into the water below. With an air of apparent distress, he begged the young man to wade into the stream and pick it up for him.

Cheerfully smiling, Chang-lung at once jumped into the water. In a moment he had returned with the shoe and was handing it to the old man, when the latter requested him to put it on his foot for him. This was asking him to do a most menial act, which most men would have scornfully resented; but Chang-lung, pitying the decrepit-looking old stranger, immediately knelt on the ground and carefully fastened the dripping shoe on to his foot.

Whilst he was in the act of doing this, the fairy, as if by accident, skilfully managed to let the other shoe slip from his foot over the edge of the bridge into the running stream. Apologizing for his stupidity, and excusing himself on the ground that he was an old man and that his fingers were not as nimble as they used to be, he begged Chang-lung to repeat his kindness and do him the favour of picking up the second shoe and restoring it to him.

With the same cheery manner, as though he were not being asked to perform a servile task, Chang-lung once more stepped into the shallow brook and bringing back the shoe, proceeded without any hesitation to repeat the process of putting it on the old man's foot.

The fairy was now perfectly satisfied. Thanking Chang-lung for his kindness, he presented him with a book, which he took out of one of the sleeves of his jacket, and urging him to study it with all diligence, vanished out of his sight. The meeting that day on the country bridge had an important influence on the destiny of Chang-lung, who in time rose to great eminence and finally became Prime Minister of China.

As Monkey studied the golden words before him, he contrasted his own conduct with that of Chang-lung, and, pricked to the heart by a consciousness of his wrong, he started at once, without even bidding farewell to the Dragon Prince of the Sea, to return to the service of Sam-Chaong.

He was just emerging from the ocean, when who should be standing waiting for him on the yellow sands of the shore but the Goddess of Mercy herself, who had come all the way from her distant home to warn him of the consequences that would happen to him were he ever again to fail in the duty she had assigned him of leading Sam-Chaong to the Western Heaven.

Terrified beyond measure at the awful doom which threatened him, and at the same time truly repentant for the wrong he had committed, Monkey bounded up far above the highest mountains which rear their peaks to the sky, and fled with incredible speed until he stood once more by the side of Sam-Chaong.

No reproof fell from the latter's lips as the truant returned to his post. A tender gracious smile was the only sign of displeasure that he evinced.

"I am truly glad to have you come back to me," he said, "for I was lost without your guidance in this unknown world in which I am travelling. I may tell you, however, that since you left me the Goddess appeared to me and comforted me with the assurance that you would ere long resume your duties and be my friend, as you have so nobly been in the past. She was very distressed at my forlorn condition and was so determined that nothing of the kind should happen again in the future, that she graciously presented me with a mystic cap wrought and embroidered by the fairy hands of the maidens in her own palace.

"'Guard this well,' she said, 'and treasure it as your very life, for it will secure you the services of one who for five hundred years was kept in confinement in order that he might be ready to escort you on the way to the Western Heaven. He is the one man who has the daring and the courage to meet the foes who will endeavour to destroy you on your journey, but he is as full of passion as the storm when it is blowing in its fury. Should he ever desert you again, you have but to place this cap on his head, and he will be wrung with such awful and intolerable agonies that though he were a thousand miles away he would hurry back with all the speed he could command to have you take it off again, so that he might be relieved from the fearful pains racking his body.'"

After numerous adventures too long to relate, Sam-Chaong reached the borders of an immense lake, many miles in extent, spanned by a bridge of only a single foot in width. With fear and trembling, as men tremble on the brink of eternity, and often with terror in his eyes and a quivering in his heart as he looked at the narrow foothold on which he was treading, he finally crossed in safety, when he found to his astonishment that the pulsations of a new life had already begun to beat strongly within him. Beyond a narrow strip of land, which bounded the great expanse of water over which he had just passed, was a wide flowing river, and on its bank was a boat with a ferryman in it ready to row him over.

When they had reached the middle of the stream, Sam-Chaong saw a man struggling in the water as if for dear life. Moved with pity he urged upon the boatman to go to his rescue and deliver him from drowning. He was sternly told, however, to keep silence. "The figure you see there," said the boatman, "is yourself – or rather, it is but the shell of your old self, in which you worked out your redemption in the world beyond, and which you could never use in the new life upon which you have entered."

On the opposite bank of the river stood the Goddess of Mercy, who with smiling face welcomed him into the ranks of the fairies.

Since then, it is believed by those whose vision reaches further than the grey and common scenes of earthly life, Sam-Chaong has frequently appeared on earth, in various disguises, when in some great emergency more than human power was required to deliver men from destruction. There is one thing certain at least – these gifted people declare – and that is that in the guise of a priest Sam-Chaong did once more revisit this world and delivered to the Buddhist Church the new ritual which the Goddess of Mercy had prepared for it, and which is used today in its services throughout the East.

In the Palace of the Sea God

HODERI WAS A GREAT FISHERMAN, while his younger brother, Hoori, was an accomplished hunter. One day they exclaimed: "Let us for a trial exchange gifts." This they did, but the elder brother, who could catch fish to some purpose, came home without any spoil when he went a-hunting. He therefore returned the bow and arrows, and asked his younger brother for the fish-hook. Now it so happened that Hoori had lost his brother's fish-hook. The generous offer of a new hook to take the place of the old one was scornfully refused. He also refused to accept a heaped-up tray of fish-hooks. To this offer the elder brother replied: "These are not my old fish-hook: though they are many, I will not take them."

Now Hoori was sore troubled by his brother's harshness, so he went down to the seashore and there gave way to his grief. A kind old man by the name of Shiko-tsutsu no Oji ('Salt-sea-elder') said: "Why dost thou grieve here?" When the sad tale was told, the old man replied: "Grieve no more. I will arrange this matter for thee."

True to his word, the old man made a basket, set Hoori in it, and then sank it in the sea. After descending deep down in the water Hoori came to a pleasant strand rich with all manner of fantastic seaweed. Here he abandoned the basket and eventually arrived at the Palace of the Sea God.

Now this palace was extremely imposing. It had battlements and turrets and stately towers. A well stood at the gate, and over the well there was a cassia-tree. Here Hoori loitered in the pleasant shade. He had not stood there long before a beautiful woman appeared. As she was about to draw water, she raised her eyes, saw the stranger, and immediately returned, with much alarm, to tell her mother and father what she had seen.

The God of the Sea, when he had heard the news, "prepared an eightfold cushion" and led the stranger in, asking his visitor why he had been honoured by his presence. When Hoori explained the sad loss of his brother's fish-hook the Sea God assembled all the fishes of his kingdom, "broad of fin and narrow of fin." And when the thousands upon thousands of fishes were assembled, the Sea God asked them if they knew anything about the missing fish-hook. "We know not," answered the fishes. "Only the Red-woman (the *tai*) has had a sore mouth for some time past, and has not come." She was accordingly summoned, and on her mouth being opened the lost fish-hook was discovered.

Hoori then took to wife the Sea God's daughter, Toyotama ('Rich-jewel'), and they dwelt together in the palace under the sea. For three years all went well, but after a time Hoori hungered for a sight of his own country, and possibly he may have remembered that he had yet to restore the fish-hook to his elder brother. These not unnatural feelings troubled the heart of the loving Toyotama, and she went to her father and told him of her sorrow. But the Sea God, who was always urbane and courteous, in no way resented his son-in-law's behaviour. On the contrary he gave him the fish-hook, saying: "When thou givest this fish-hook to thy elder brother, before giving it to him, call to it secretly, and say, 'A poor hook!'" He also presented Hoori with the Jewel of the Flowing Tide and the Jewel of the Ebbing Tide, saying: "If thou dost dip the Tide-flowing Jewel, the tide will suddenly flow, and therewithal thou shalt drown thine elder brother. But in case thy elder brother should repent and beg forgiveness, if, on the contrary, thou dip the Tide-ebbing Jewel, the tide will spontaneously ebb, and therewithal thou shalt save him. If thou harass him in this way thy elder brother will of his own accord render submission."

Just before Hoori was about to depart his wife came to him and told him that she was soon to give him a child. Said she: "On a day when the winds and waves are raging I will surely come forth to the seashore. Build for me a house, and await me there."

Hoderi and Hoori Reconciled

When Hoori reached his own home he found his elder brother, who admitted his offence and begged for forgiveness, which was readily granted.

Toyotama and her younger sister bravely confronted the winds and waves, and came to the seashore. There Hoori had built a hut roofed with cormorant feathers, and there in due season she gave birth to a son. When Toyotama had blessed her lord with offspring, she turned into a dragon and slipped back into the sea. Hoori's son married his aunt, and was the father of four children, one of whom was Kamu-Yamato-Iware-Biko, who is said to have been the first human Emperor of Japan, and is now known as Jimmu Tenno.

Fate

ONCE UPON A TIME there were two brothers who lived together in a house. The one did all the work, whereas the other went about idling and never did anything but eat and drink. And they had abundance of everything, and were blessed with cattle, horses, sheep, pigs, and bees.

Then the brother who did all the work one day said to himself, "Why should I work for that lazy bones as well? It is much better we separate; I shall work for myself and he may do what he likes." And so he told his brother, "It is not fair that I have to manage everything whilst you never lend me a hand. You think of nothing but eating and drinking. I have, therefore, made up my mind. We are going to part." The brother, however, tried to dissuade him and said, "You have the management of everything, both of your property and of mine. And you know I am quite content and agree with everything you do." But the industrious brother insisted, so that the other one had to give in, and he said, "Very well, I shall not be cross with you about it. Go and give me my share according to what you think is mine." Then everything was divided up. The lazy brother took his share, and at once he appointed a cow-keeper for his cattle, a stableboy for his horses, a goatherd, a swineherd, and a beekeeper, and he said to them, "All my property I leave in your hands and God's." And after that he stayed at home, unconcerned, and without troubling himself about anything. The other brother went on working hard as before, looked after his herds, and was most careful. Yet in spite of that, he did not thrive, but suffered many losses, and his affairs became daily worse and worse. At last he was so poor that he had not even a pair of latchet shoes, and had to walk about barefooted. Then he said to himself, "I will go to my brother to see how he is getting on."

His way led him past the meadow, in which there was a flock of sheep, and when he came nearer he saw there was no shepherd, but an exceedingly beautiful maiden who was spinning a golden thread. After he had greeted the girl with a friendly "God be with you", he asked her whose were those sheep. She replied, "To whom I belong, his are also the sheep." Then he asked her, "Who are you?" whereupon she answered, "I am your brother's Good Luck." Then, overcome with violent anger, he asked, "Where is my Good Luck?" The maiden said, "Oh, that is very far from you." "And could I find it?" he asked. "You may," she said. "Go and search for it." And when he had heard this and seen that his brother's sheep were so fine that one cannot possibly imagine any sheep more valuable, then he was no longer inclined to view the other herds, but he went straightaway to his brother. When the latter beheld him, he pitied him, and with tears in his eyes he said, "Where have you been all this time?" And noticing the poor garments and bare feet, he gave him a pair of latchet shoes and some money. After he had been entertained for a few days, the poor brother started again for home. Arrived there, he took a knapsack over his shoulders, put some bread in it, took a staff in his hands, and went into the wide world to find his Good Luck.

When he had been walking for some time, he came into a big forest, and there he found an ugly trollop sleeping underneath a shrub. Then he lifted his stick and struck her on the back to awaken her. She got up with difficulty, could hardly open her bleared eyes, and said, "You may thank God that I had fallen asleep here, for had I been awake, you would not have received those lovely shoes." Then he asked her, "Who are you that on your account I should not have been given these shoes?" The slut said, "I am your Good Luck." When he heard this, he grew very angry, saying, "So you are my Good Luck? I wish God would kill you. Who is it that has given you unto me?" The slut, however, interrupted him. "Fate has given me unto you." Then he asked, "Where is this Fate?" And she said, "Go and search for it!" With which words she disappeared.

Thereupon the man started again on his way in order to find Fate. And whilst he was thus going along, he came to a village, and there stood a fine house in which a large fire was burning. Then he thought to himself, "Here must be a wedding, or they are celebrating some other feast day!" He entered, and saw hanging over the fire a big kettle in which the supper was cooking, and the master of the house sat by the fire. He wished him a good evening, to which the master of the house replied, "May God bestow on you all good things!" He invited him to take a seat near him, and asked him who he was and whither he was going. Then he told everything, how he, too, had been a householder, how he had become poor, and that he was now on his way to ask Fate herself why just he himself should remain so poor. Hereupon he asked the master of the house why and for whom he was cooking such a big meal. Then the latter said, "Alas, my brother! I am the master of a house and have abundance of everything, but nevertheless I am unable to appease the hunger of my people; it is as though dragons were hidden in their stomachs. Just observe my people when we are going to supper, then you will see it." And when they sat down for supper, the men snatched and grabbed one another's food, and in a few minutes the large cauldron was empty. After supper, the host's young wife collected all the bones and threw them on a heap behind the stove. And when the stranger was wondering at this, suddenly two very old persons thin as skeletons crawled forth in order to suck the bones. Then the stranger asked the master of the house, "Who are those behind the stove?" And he answered, "They are my father and my mother, and they will not die, just as though they were chained to this world."

The next morning when they parted, the stranger was requested kindly to ask Fate why the people in his house could not be sufficiently fed, and why his father and mother were so long in dying. The visitor promised to do so, and took his leave in order to find Fate.

After he had been on the road for ever such a long time, one evening he came into another village, entered one of the houses, and asked for a night's shelter. Readily he was received, and when asked what was his destination, he told them everything. Then the people in the house said, "For God's sake, brother, when you have reached your goal, do ask why our cattle do not thrive but are getting thinner and thinner." He promised to ask Fate about it, and the next morning he set out again.

And he came to a river and called out, "Oh, water, water, carry me over to the other bank." The water asked him, "Where are you going?" And he told the water. Then the water carried him across and said, "Please, brother, ask Fate why nothing can live within me." And he promised to do the water this favour and went on.

After ever such a long time, at last he came into a forest, and here he met a hermit, whom he asked whether he could give him any information about Fate. And the hermit said to him, "Go from here straight across the mountains, then you will arrive exactly in front of Fate's castle. But there you must not say a word, only do all the time precisely the same thing Fate is doing until she puts questions to you." The man thanked the hermit, and set out on his journey across the mountains. When he arrived at the castle of Fate, what things he did behold! Everywhere imperial splendour, and a great number of servants, men and women, were running about. But Fate sat quite alone at a table eating her supper. When the man saw her for whom he had been searching such a long time, he sat down by her side and shared the supper. After supper, Fate lay down to rest. So did he. Toward midnight, there was the most awful noise and turmoil in the castle, but above all the turmoil a voice was audible that said, "O Fate! O Fate! One hundred thousand souls have been born today. Give them something according to your pleasure!" Then Fate rose, opened a treasure box full of gold, took out of it glittering sovereigns, and scattered them all over the floor of the room. At the same time she said, "As I am faring today, they shall fare all their lives."

At daybreak the magnificent castle was gone, and in its place stood quite a small house of modest appearance. Yet there was in it enough and to spare of everything. When evening fell, Fate again sat down to supper; so did our friend, and neither spoke a word. And after supper both lay down to rest. Toward midnight there was again the most awful noise and turmoil, and above all the turmoil a voice was again audible that said, "O Fate! O Fate! One hundred thousand souls have been born today. Give them something according to your pleasure!" Then Fate rose, and opened a money box, but there were no sovereigns, only silver coins with an occasional sovereign hidden away amongst them, and Fate scattered silver coins all over the floor of the room. At the same time she said, "As I am faring today they shall fare all their lives."

And at daybreak that small but comfortable house was gone too, and in its place stood one ever so much smaller. So it happened every night and every morning the house was smaller, until at last there remained but a wretched hut, and Fate took a spade and began digging. Then the man, our friend, likewise took a spade and began digging, and both kept on digging throughout the day. When evening fell, Fate took a piece of bread, halved it, and gave one half to the man. That was their supper, and when they had eaten it they lay down to rest. Toward midnight, there was again the most awful noise and turmoil, and above all the turmoil a voice was yet again audible that said, "O Fate! O Fate! One hundred thousand souls have been born today. Give them something according to your pleasure!" Then Fate rose, opened a box, and began scattering about small potsherds like those with which children play, and amongst them a very few coins. At the same time she said, "As I am faring today they shall fare all their lives."

But when day broke again, the hut had once more been changed into a large palace, just as grand as the one which the man found when he arrived. And now at last Fate spoke to him and asked him, "Why did you come here?" And then he related all the particulars of his distress and his troubles, and that he had come to ask Fate personally why she had given unto him such a Bad Luck. Then Fate said to him, "You have seen how during the first night I was scattering sovereigns, and you have noticed, I hope, everything that happened during that night. Exactly as I am faring during the night in the course of which a man is born, thus he will fare throughout his life. You have been born in a night of poverty, and therefore you will remain poor as long as you live. Your brother, on the other hand, has seen the light of the world during a fortunate night, and he will be a fortunate man until the end of his days. But since you have taken so much trouble and come in quest of me, I will tell you how you can help yourself. Your brother has a daughter; her name is Milica, and she is just as fortunate as her father. When you get home again, take her to you into your house, and of everything that you may gain say, "It is Milica's!"

Then he thanked Fate and said, "I know of a rich farmer who has more than enough of everything, yet he never succeeds in feeding his household well; at every meal they empty a brewer's copper full of food, and even that is not enough for them. And the father and the mother of this farmer, as though they were chained to this earth, have grown quite black with age and they are shrivelled up like ghosts, yet they cannot die. Therefore he begged me when I was his guest for a night to ask you what is the reason of all that." Then Fate replied, "All that happens because he does not honour his father and mother, and just throws some food at them behind the stove. If he would put them in the place of honour at his table and hand to them the first glass of wine and the first glass of whisky, they would soon breathe their last, and the people of the farmer's household would no longer eat so much."

Then he asked Fate, "In another village where I was staying a night, a man complained to me that his cattle would not thrive, and he urged me to find out from you whose fault it is." And Fate said, "It is because on the day of the patron saint of his house, he slaughters the most wretched cow he has. If, on the other hand, he would kill the very best, all his cattle would thrive." Finally, he also inquired on behalf of the water. "And how is it that nothing can live in that water?" And Fate answered, "Because no human being has yet been drowned in it. But take heed not to tell the water about this secret before you have been carried across, lest the water should at once drown you!"

Once again he thanked Fate, and started on his journey home. When he came to the water, it asked, "Well, what did Fate say?" And he answered, "First carry me across, and then I will tell you." Hardly had the water carried him across than he began running, and when he was a good distance away, he turned round and called out, "O, Water, it is because you have never drowned a human being that nothing will live in you." On hearing this, the water rushed after him over the fields and meadows, and only with great difficulty he escaped.

When he came into the village to the man whose cattle were not thriving, he was already impatiently awaited. "What news do you bring me, brother? Have you questioned Fate?" Whereupon he replied, "Yes, I have done so, and Fate said it is because you always offer up the worst cow on the feast day of your household saint. But if you would sacrifice your best, all your cattle would thrive." Having heard this, the farmer said, "Brother, stay with us! There are but three days to the feast of our patron saint, and if that is true which you tell me, I'll show you my gratitude." When now the feast day came, the father of the family killed the finest bullock which he had, and from that moment onwards his cattle began to thrive. Then he gave the man five oxen as a present. And the man set out again.

And when he arrived in the village where the ever-hungry household was, he was greeted with the words, "For God's sake, tell me, brother, how are you and what did Fate say?" And he replied, "Fate says you are not honouring your father and your mother, and you always throw the food at them behind the stove. If you would put them at the table, and, moreover, in the place of honour at the top of the table, and hand them the first glass of wine and the first glass of whisky, the inmates of your house would not eat half as much, and your father and mother would depart this life." When the master of the house had heard this, he told his wife at once to wash and to comb her father- and mother-in-law and to dress them nicely. When the evening came, the two were placed at the top of the table, and the first glass of wine and the first glass of whisky were handed to them. From that moment onwards the inmates of that household could no longer eat so much, and the father and mother in a few days died peaceably. Then the grateful master of the house gave our friend two bullocks, and the latter, after thanking his host, went home.

When he came into his native place, his acquaintances met him and asked him, "Whose are these beautiful cattle?" And he said each time, "My friend, they belong to Milica, my brother's daughter." When he arrived home, he went at once to his brother and begged him, "Do give me Milica, brother, as you know I have no one to care for me." And his brother replied, "I do not mind at all. Go and take Milica with you." Then he led his brother's daughter to his house. From that moment onwards, he prospered much, but of everything gained, he said, "It is Milica's."

One day he went out over his fields to see how the corn was going on. It was most lovely to look at. Then a wanderer came along, who asked him, "Whose is this corn field?" And, forgetting himself for a moment, he said, "It's mine." In the moment he said that, flames burst out of the corn and the fire spread rapidly. Quickly he ran after the wanderer and exclaimed, "Stop, my friend, the corn does not belong to me at all; it is Milica's." At once the fire ceased. Henceforth he lived happily with Milica, and to the end of his days all he did prospered.

The Flaming Horse

THERE WAS ONCE a land that was dreary and dark as the grave, for the sun of heaven never shone upon it. The king of the country had a wonderful horse that had, growing right on his forehead, a flaming sun. In order that his subjects might have the light that is necessary for life, the king had this horse led back and forth from one end of his dark kingdom to the other. Wherever he went his flaming head shone out and it seemed like beautiful day.

Suddenly this wonderful horse disappeared. Heavy darkness that nothing could dispel settled down on the country. Fear spread among the people and soon they were suffering terrible poverty, for they were unable to cultivate the fields or do anything else that would earn them a livelihood. Confusion increased until the king saw that the whole country was likely to perish. In order then, if possible, to save his people, he gathered his army together and set out in search of the missing horse.

Through heavy darkness they groped their way slowly and with difficulty to the far boundaries of the kingdom. At last they reached the ancient forests that bordered the neighbouring state and they saw gleaming through the trees faint rays of the sunshine with which that kingdom was blessed.

Here they came upon a small lonely cottage which the king entered in order to find out where he was and to ask directions for moving forward.

A man was sitting at the table reading diligently from a large open book. When the king bowed to him, he raised his eyes, returned the greeting, and stood up. His whole appearance showed that he was no ordinary man but a seer.

"I was just reading about you," he said to the king, "that you were gone in search of the flaming horse. Exert yourself no further, for you will never find him. But trust the enterprise to me and I will get him for you."

"If you do that, my man," the king said, "I will pay you royally."

"I seek no reward. Return home at once with your army, for your people need you. Only leave here with me one of your serving men."

The king did exactly as the seer advised and went home at once.

The next day the seer and his man set forth. They journeyed far and long until they had crossed six different countries. Then they went on into the seventh country which was ruled over by three brothers who had married three sisters, the daughters of a witch.

They made their way to the front of the royal palace, where the seer said to his man: "Do you stay here while I go in and find out whether the kings are at home. It is they who stole the flaming horse and the youngest brother rides him."

Then the seer transformed himself into a green bird and flew up to the window of the eldest queen and flitted about and pecked until she opened the window and let him into her chamber. When she let him in, he alighted on her white hand and the queen was as happy as a child.

"You pretty thing!" she said, playing with him. "If my husband were home how pleased he would be! But he's off visiting a third of his kingdom and he won't be home until evening."

Suddenly the old witch came into the room and as soon as she saw the bird she shrieked to her daughter: "Wring the neck of that cursed bird, or it will stain you with blood!"

"Why should it stain me with blood, the dear innocent thing?"

"Dear innocent mischief!" shrieked the witch. "Here, give it to me and I'll wring its neck!"

She tried to catch the bird, but the bird changed itself into a man and was already out of the door before they knew what had become of him.

After that he changed himself again into a green bird and flew up to the window of the second sister. He pecked at it until she opened it and let him in. Then he flitted about her, settling first on one of her white hands, then on the other.

"What a dear bird you are!" cried the queen. "How you would please my husband if he were at home. But he's off visiting two-thirds of his kingdom and he won't be back until tomorrow evening."

At that moment the witch ran into the room and as soon as she saw the bird she shrieked out: "Wring the neck of that wretched bird, or it will stain you with blood!"

"Why should it stain me with blood?" the daughter answered. "The dear innocent thing!"

"Dear innocent mischief!" shrieked the witch. "Here, give it to me and I'll wring its neck!"

She reached out to catch the bird, but in less time than it takes to clap a hand, the bird had changed itself into a man who ran through the door and was gone before they knew where he was.

A moment later he again changed himself into a green bird and flew up to the window of the youngest queen. He flitted about and pecked until she opened the window and let him in. Then he alighted at once on her white hand and this pleased her so much that she laughed like a child and played with him.

"Oh, what a dear bird you are!" she cried. "How you would delight my husband if he were home. But he's off visiting all three parts of his kingdom and he won't be back until the day after tomorrow in the evening."

At that moment the old witch rushed into the room. "Wring the neck of that cursed bird!" she shrieked, "or it will stain you with blood."

"My dear mother," the queen answered, "why should it stain me with blood – beautiful innocent creature that it is?"

"Beautiful innocent mischief!" shrieked the witch. "Here, give it to me and I'll wring its neck!"

But at that moment the bird changed itself into a man, disappeared through the door, and they never saw him again.

The seer knew now where the kings were and when they would come home. So he made his plans accordingly. He ordered his servant to follow him and they set out from the city at a quick pace. They went on until they came to a bridge which the three kings as they came back would have to cross.

The seer and his man hid themselves under the bridge and lay there in wait until evening. As the sun sank behind the mountains, they heard the clatter of hoofs approaching the bridge. It was the eldest king returning home. At the bridge his horse stumbled on a log which the seer had rolled there.

"What scoundrel has thrown a log here?" cried the king angrily.

Instantly the seer leaped out from under the bridge and demanded of the king how he dared to call him a scoundrel. Clamouring for satisfaction he drew his sword and attacked the king. The king, too, drew sword and defended himself, but after a short struggle he fell from his horse dead. The seer bound the dead king to his horse and then with a cut of the whip started the horse homewards.

The seer hid himself again and he and his man lay in wait until the next evening.

On that evening near sunset the second king came riding up to the bridge. When he saw the ground sprinkled with blood, he cried out: "Surely there has been a murder here! Who has dared to commit such a crime in my kingdom!"

At these words the seer leaped out from under the bridge, drew his sword, and shouted: "How dare you insult me? Defend yourself as best you can!"

The king drew, but after a short struggle he, too, yielded up his life to the sword of the seer.

The seer bound the dead king to his horse and with a cut of the whip started the horse homewards.

Then the seer hid himself again under the bridge and he and his man lay there in wait until the third evening.

On the third evening just at sunset the youngest king came galloping home on the flaming steed. He was hurrying fast because he had been delayed. But when he saw red blood at the bridge he stopped short and looked around.

"What audacious villain," he cried, "has dared to kill a man in my kingdom!"

Hardly had he spoken when the seer stood before him with drawn sword demanding satisfaction for the insult of his words.

"I don't know how I've insulted you," the king said, "unless you're the murderer."

When the seer refused to parley, the king, too, drew his sword and defended himself.

To overcome the first two kings had been mere play for the seer, but it was no play this time. They both fought until their swords were broken and still victory was doubtful.

"We shall accomplish nothing with swords," the seer said. "That is plain. I tell you what: let us turn ourselves into wheels and start rolling down the hill and the wheel that gets broken let him yield."

"Good!" said the king. "I'll be a cartwheel and you be a lighter wheel."

"No, no," the seer answered quickly. "You be the light wheel and I'll be the cartwheel."

To this the king agreed. So they went up the hill, turned themselves into wheels and started rolling down. The cartwheel went whizzing into the lighter wheel and broke its spokes.

"There!" cried the seer, rising up from the cartwheel. "I am victor!"

"Not so, brother, not so!" said the king, standing before the seer. "You only broke my fingers! Now I tell you what: let us change ourselves into two flames and let the flame that burns up the other be victor. I'll be a red flame and do you be a white one."

"Oh, no," the seer interrupted. "You be the white flame and I'll be the red one."

The king agreed to this. So they went back to the road that led to the bridge, turned themselves into flames, and began burning each other mercilessly. But neither was able to burn up the other.

Suddenly a beggar came down the road, an old man with a long grey beard and a bald head, with a scrip at his side and a heavy staff in his hand.

"Father," the white flame said, "get some water and pour it on the red flame and I'll give you a penny."

But the red flame called out quickly: "Not so, father! Get some water and pour it on the white flame and I'll give you a shilling!"

Now of course the shilling appealed to the beggar more than the penny. So he got some water, poured it on the white flame and that was the end of the king.

The red flame turned into a man who seized the flaming horse by the bridle, mounted him and, after he had rewarded the beggar, called his servant and rode off.

Meanwhile at the royal palace there was deep sorrow for the murdered kings. The halls were draped in black and people came from miles around to gaze at the mutilated bodies of the two elder brothers which the horses had carried home.

The old witch was beside herself with rage. As soon as she had devised a plan whereby she could avenge the murder of her sons-in-law, she took her three daughters under her arm, mounted an iron rake, and sailed off through the air.

The seer and his man had already covered a good part of their journey and were hurrying on over rough mountains and across desert plains, when the servant was taken with a terrible hunger. There wasn't anything in sight that he could eat, not even a wild berry. Then suddenly they came upon an apple tree that was bending beneath a load of ripe fruit. The apples were red and pleasant to the sight and sent out a fragrance that was most inviting.

The servant was delighted. "Glory to God!" he cried. "Now I can feast to my heart's content on these apples!"

He was already running to the tree when the seer called him back.

"Wait! Don't touch them! I will pick them for you myself!"

But instead of picking an apple, the seer drew his sword and struck a mighty blow into the apple tree. Red blood gushed forth.

"Just see, my man! You would have perished if you had eaten one apple. This apple tree is the eldest queen, whom her mother, the witch, placed here for our destruction."

Presently they came to a spring. Its water bubbled up clear as crystal and most tempting to the tired traveller.

"Ah," said the servant, "since we can get nothing better, at least we can take a drink of this good water."

"Wait!" cried the seer. "I will draw some for you."

But instead of drawing water he plunged his naked sword into the middle of the spring. Instantly it was covered with blood and blood began to spurt from the spring in thick streams.

"This is the second queen, whom her mother, the witch, placed here to work our doom."

Presently they came to a rosebush covered with beautiful red roses that scented all the air with their fragrance.

"What beautiful roses!" said the servant. "I have never seen any such in all my life. I'll go pluck a few. As I can't eat or drink, I'll comfort myself with roses."

"Don't dare to pluck them!" cried the seer. "I'll pluck them for you."

With that he cut into the bush with his sword and red blood spurted out as though he had cut a human vein.

"This is the youngest queen," said the seer, "whom her mother, the witch, placed here in the hope of revenging herself on us for the death of her sons-in-law."

After that they proceeded without further adventures.

When they crossed the boundaries of the dark kingdom, the sun in the horse's forehead sent out its blessed rays in all directions. Everything came to life. The earth rejoiced and covered itself with flowers.

The king felt he could never thank the seer enough and he offered him the half of his kingdom.

But the seer replied: "You are the king. Keep on ruling over the whole of your kingdom and let me return to my cottage in peace."

He bade the king farewell and departed.

The Three Fates

THERE WAS A VERY POOR MAN who had no house in which to live. Driven by this, he hiked out to a nearby mountain, found a good spot near the main road, and built himself a humble cottage in which he settled with his wife and children.

A very rich man was travelling on horseback along that road and was overtaken by night just near the cottage. As he rode along, he became more and more fearful as his saddlebags were full of money. He happened to peer towards the little house, where a fire was glowing invitingly, and he decided to see if he would be able to spend the night there. He backtracked, deciding to first find out what sort of people lived there; if they seemed decent, he'd stay, if not, he'd continue on his way. Scared or not, what else could he do on that lonely mountain?

When he looked through the window of the cottage, he saw that a man and his wife with several children were warming themselves around the fire.

"Thank goodness," said the rich man to himself. "This is a family home, just what I was hoping for." He called out, "Good evening, friends."

"Good evening to you," replied the poor man.

"If it's possible, would you be able to put me up for the night, as it's too dark to keep travelling?" he asked.

"Of course, friend. There are no problems about that, but I'm sorry I can't offer you any dinner. There's no food in the house – we've eaten all we had. But as far as sleeping goes, you're welcome," offered the poor man.

"I don't expect you to provide me with food. I have plenty with me. I only want somewhere to lie down," said the rich traveller. "Thank you for your offer."

With that, he tethered his horses, took his things into the house and sat close to the fire to thaw out from the bitter cold outside. From his saddlebags, he shared out the food he was carrying and, together with the family, ate his dinner.

"It's as if you've been sent from heaven, noble sir," said his host. "You've arrived with all sorts of fine things to eat on this, the third night after the birth of our son. Hopefully it's a good-luck omen. We don't want him to suffer as much as we have."

"Congratulations. I hope it is for the best and that God grants him a good life," said the traveller.

They sat for a while, then, when the time came, they lay down to sleep. All of them dozed off, except for the rich man who just couldn't sleep. He suspected the poor man might be planning to rob and kill him during the night. So he was wide awake at midnight when the three Fates appeared to determine the new baby's destiny.

"What do you think, sister?" said the first Fate to the second. "What future should we write out for this baby, this son of a poor man?"

"What should we write? Why, we should that he should live for only forty days. Otherwise he'll be another burden on his poor father," she replied. "Yes, that's what we should do."

"But wouldn't it be better if we decided that he should live, and when he grows up, he should marry the daughter of this rich traveller who's staying here overnight?" suggested the third.

"Most fitting! What a good idea!" chorused the two others. "Yes, let's do that." They opened their Book of Destiny and wrote, "This boy will become the rich man's son-in-law and inherit all his property".

The rich man heard what the three Fates said, and he became so agitated that even by morning, he hadn't closed his eyes to sleep. He just lay there thinking up ways to get rid of the baby.

"Ha! The chances of this yokel's son becoming my son-in-law and getting his hands on my property are zilch!" he thought.

Morning arrived, and the rich man started preparing for his departure. As he did, he said to his poverty-stricken hosts, "Listen, friends. Why don't you give me the baby boy to adopt, seeing I have no children. I've got more assets than I know what to do with! Why, you already have four other children, long may they live."

"Oh no!" they exclaimed. "What mother and father can give up their baby, no matter how poor they are? You can't expect us to do that!"

The rich man then tried to convince them with money. "It's true that no parents would willingly give up their child, but somehow I think I can change your minds. Look, here's one hundred gold coins. They will enable you to buy a house in town where you can live comfortably. And your boy will live in even more comfort at my place."

When they heard that proposal and saw the gold, they reconsidered. They found some rags in which they wrapped the baby, gave him a fig that he could suck on like a dummy, and handed him over to the rich man to adopt. The rich man mounted his horse, cradling the baby in his arms, and started down the road, thinking all the while about how to do away with the poor child. He considered maybe murdering it by hurling it against some rocks, but that was too cruel. He wondered about just leaving it abandoned on the road, but he was worried lest someone find it. On he rode, thinking these thoughts, when he espied a cave not far off the road. He carried the baby into it and abandoned it there, believing that it would die alone without anyone knowing a thing.

That cave happened to be a bears' den, and in it there were two small cubs that had been recently born. When the rich man dumped the baby, it tumbled and rolled right across to where the cubs were. Because it was crying, the little cubs were curious and started to play with it, one passing it to the other and back again. Just then, the mother bear returned from grazing to find the baby crying. She felt sorry for it, so she fed it and nursed it to sleep. Thankfully, when God wills it, He can even inspire a bear to suckle a human baby rather than eat it. What with today and tomorrow, the bear nurtured the infant and raised it to a toddler. The little boy too started to wander out with the bear family in search of food, such as wild apples, berries and other things that grew on the mountain.

One day, as the boy was climbing a tree to gather fruit, he was spotted by some goat herders and coal merchants. They were amazed and wondered where that naked boy who roamed around with the mountain bears could be from. They started to track him to discover where he hid and lived. After many days, they saw him as he entered his cave and resolved to capture him. Many villagers equipped themselves with whatever they could find and concealed themselves around the bears' den.

When the mother bear headed out, the boy followed, and the villagers started to chase him. He ran – they pursued, till finally they grabbed him and took him to the village. But who should look after him? Who? They came to the decision to give him to a childless widow, who gratefully accepted him and raised him as her own till he grew into a fine young man. Then she found him an apprenticeship with an important businessman in town.

"But what's the boy's name, Granny?" asked the businessman.

"His name is Bearboy, sir, because he was found living with the mountain bears," she explained.

Bearboy had just settled in to his new job when, in order for the destiny pronounced by the three Fates to be fulfilled, the rich man who had "adopted" him came in to the office. He was in town for a few months on business and sat down to discuss some deal with Bearboy's employer.

"Bearboy, go and order some coffee for our visitor," instructed his boss. Bearboy ran off on his errand, and some dim memory prompted the rich visitor to ask, "Why do you call your apprentice Bearboy?"

"His story is quite incredible," replied the businessman.

"Why? What's so incredible about it? Tell me!" insisted his visitor.

"Alright. This lad was found by some villagers living in the mountains with the bears. Apparently, there was a bear cave near the main road and that's where he was trapped. They gave him to a widow who looked after him, and because she didn't know his name, she christened him Bearboy. So that's why I call him Bearboy too."

After hearing that story, the rich man was quite certain that Bearboy was the one and same child that he had thrown into the cave. He immediately figured out a plan to destroy him.

"Would you mind sending your apprentice to deliver a very important and urgent letter for me? It has to go as far as my house in the village and be given to my wife," he said.

"Of course! He can take it at once," replied Bearboy's employer.

The rich man sat far over on the other side and composed the letter for Bearboy to deliver to his house. Bearboy rushed the letter there and, luckily for him, the rich man's wife was not home, so he gave it to their daughter instead.

She opened it to read and, oh, you should have seen what he'd written! The rich man had instructed his wife to kill Bearboy, to either slaughter or poison him, because he claimed that Bearboy had caused him so much damage that they were nearly ruined.

When she read those awful words, the daughter was overcome with hatred for her father and filled with love for Bearboy. She decided to outsmart her father and win Bearboy for herself. It seemed that fate would run its course. She grabbed another sheet of paper and wrote a very different message:

> *"Dear wife. The bearer of this letter is the finest and most intelligent man I've ever met. Accordingly, I want you to build a grand new house on our property and arrange that our daughter marries him. And the sooner the better, because it seems that we have been destined to be united with a young man so remarkable, it would be impossible to find his match anywhere."*

She sealed the letter, not a moment too soon, for her mother arrived home, and Bearboy handed the new letter to her. On reading it, the woman was delighted. She was taken with the handsome young Bearboy, so straight away she summoned the builders and lost no time in organizing the marriage between Bearboy and her daughter.

Some three or four months later, the rich man finally was able to return to his village. He couldn't wait to find out how Bearboy had been done away with. As he neared his estate, he saw a brand-new house had been built.

"What the devil!" he exclaimed. "What's been going on here? What's this new house doing here?" He stormed up to his wife and demanded an explanation.

"But it's all in accordance with what you told me to do in the letter you sent with Bearboy. I did exactly as you said. I built the house and arranged for our daughter to marry him," she said.

When he heard that, the rich man was flabbergasted. "Ah, the devil take him. I'll fix that cur, that Bearboy, just wait! That bastard will soon find out what I have in store for him." He uttered these threats under his breath, but at the same time he pretended to his wife that indeed she had followed his instructions to the letter and praised her for carrying them out so well.

"Yes, that's right! You've done everything perfectly," he lied.

"I know what I'm doing," she answered happily. "It's all been so wonderful."

The rich man entered his house and was greeted by his daughter and her husband Bearboy, as well as his own son. They each shook his hand and welcomed him warmly. The rich man kept up his pretense, making out he was ever so fond of Bearboy, and congratulated him heartily for everything.

The next day, even before dawn had broken, the rich man headed out towards his sheep pens. He did this without anyone knowing. When he arrived there, he bullied the shepherd into digging a grave and gave him the following order:

"Listen here, shepherd. There's a job I want you to do, and once it's done, you can depend on me to look after you for the rest of your days. This is what it is. Tomorrow morning a young man will come here asking you for a ram to roast. You are to kill him and bury him in this grave. Do not ask any questions and do not say a word to a soul about it. If anyone asks, you don't know anything, right? Is that all clear?"

"You can count on me, sir, I won't let you down," replied the shepherd.

The rich man hurried home and persuaded his wife to throw a big celebratory dinner party. The rich man's plan was that Bearboy would go to the shepherd the next morning to pick up the ram for roasting.

Even before the sun had risen, the rich man's wife tiptoed into Bearboy's bedroom to wake him for his errand, but he was fast asleep in her daughter's loving arms. She waited a little while, but decided she couldn't disturb him, so instead she went and woke up her own son and sent him in place of Bearboy.

The lad went off, and as soon as he asked the shepherd for a ram, he was grabbed and given a lot more than he asked for. The shepherd rammed his staff against his throat, and he dragged the lad's body over to the grave and pushed it in.

Later, the rich man rose from his bed and asked his wife whether she'd sent Bearboy to pick up the ram.

"No, I didn't send Bearboy in the end, because I felt sorry to wake him so early," she replied. "I sent our own son instead, because really, he's so much better at that sort of thing."

That reply had the same effect as a snake bite would. The rich man rushed to the sheep pens to see what the shepherd had done.

"What happened, shepherd? Did my boy come?"

"He came, alright, and I finished him off good and proper, sir!"

"Bravo. You did well," said the rich man through his tears, and he sobbed all the way home. "Ah, you cursed Fates. Will what you decreed really come true? Will all my efforts come to nothing? I refuse to let that yokel's son end up with all my hard-earned money. Just wait and see what I'm going to do to him now!"

With that, he hired a trained assassin for I don't know how high a price. The rich man arranged for the assassin to kill Bearboy. His instructions were that a man and his wife would be walking past a particular spot on the road to a certain village, and he was to shoot the man.

To set his plan in action, the rich man said to his wife, "Listen, let's all go out tonight and dine at such and such a restaurant, but I think it would be nice if Bearboy and his wife went early so they can have some time to themselves. We'll follow later to arrive just before dinner."

"Yes dear, what a good idea," she agreed.

The rich lady told Bearboy and her daughter of the plan, so the young couple got dressed and off they went. However, they got hot walking in the afternoon sun and decided to turn off into a field to rest under the cool shade of the trees. Both Bearboy and his wife stretched out, and before long they fell fast asleep.

Several hours later, as dusk was failing, they awoke to the sound of a gunshot nearby on the road. It was the sort of bang that a gun makes when it's fired into a piece of wood.

"I don't like the sound of that shot," said Bearboy. "It sounds to me as though someone's been hit."

They hurried along the road, when suddenly they came face to face with the rich man's wife, who was crying and running for all she was worth.

"What's happened? Why are you running, mother?" asked her daughter.

"Oh, it's too dreadful," she cried, "Your father has been shot! He's dead!"

"He dug a grave for Bearboy but fell into it himself," replied her daughter, unmoved. Only then, did she tell her mother about the original letter that Bearboy had delivered. After that, the rich man's strange behaviour became as clear as day to his widow.

So there, everything happens according to what the Fates decree.

How Cobbler Ahmet Became the Chief Astrologer

EVERY DAY COBBLER AHMET, year in and year out, measured the breadth of his tiny cabin with his arms as he stitched old shoes. To do this was his Kismet, his decreed fate, and he was content – and why not? His business brought him quite sufficient to provide the necessaries of life for both himself and his wife. And had it not been for a coincidence that occurred, in all probability he would have mended old boots and shoes to the end of his days.

One day cobbler Ahmet's wife went to the Hamam (bath), and while there she was much annoyed at being obliged to give up her compartment, owing to the arrival of the Harem and retinue of the chief astrologer to the sultan. Much hurt, she returned home and vented her pique upon her innocent husband.

"Why are you not the chief astrologer to the sultan?" she said. "I will never call or think of you as my husband until you have been appointed chief astrologer to his majesty."

Ahmet thought that this was another phase in the eccentricity of woman which in all probability would disappear before morning, so he took small notice of what his wife said. But Ahmet was wrong. His wife persisted so much in his giving up his present means of earning a livelihood and becoming an astrologer, that finally, for the sake of peace, he complied with her desire. He sold his tools and collection of sundry old boots and shoes, and, with the proceeds purchased an inkwell and reeds. But this, alas! did not constitute him an astrologer, and he explained to his wife that this mad idea of hers would bring him to an unhappy end. She, however, could not be moved, and insisted on his going to the highway, there to wisely practise the art, and thus ultimately become the chief astrologer.

In obedience to his wife's instructions, Ahmet sat down on the highroad, and his oppressed spirit sought comfort in looking at the heavens and sighing deeply. While in this condition a Hanoum in great excitement came and asked him if he communicated with the stars. Poor Ahmet sighed, saying that he was compelled to converse with them.

"Then please tell me where my diamond ring is, and I will both bless and handsomely reward you."

The Hanoum, with this, immediately squatted on the ground, and began to tell Ahmet that she had gone to the bath that morning and that she was positive that she then had the ring, but every corner of the Hamam had been searched, and the ring was not to be found.

"Oh! Astrologer, for the love of Allah, exert your eye to see the unseen."

"Hanoum Effendi," replied Ahmet, the instant her excited flow of language had ceased, "I perceive a rent," referring to a tear he had noticed in her shalvars, or baggy trousers.

Up jumped the Hanoum, exclaiming: "A thousand holy thanks! You are right! Now I remember! I put the ring in a crevice of the cold water fountain." And in her gratitude she handed Ahmet several gold pieces.

In the evening he returned to his home, and, giving the gold to his wife, said: "Take this money, wife; may it satisfy you, and in return all I ask is that you allow me to go back to the trade of my father, and not expose me to the danger and suffering of trudging the road shoeless."

But her purpose was unmoved. Until he became the chief astrologer she would neither call him nor think of him as her husband.

In the meantime, owing to the discovery of the ring, the fame of Ahmet the cobbler spread far and wide. The tongue of the Hanoum never ceased to sound his praise.

It happened that the wife of a certain Pasha had appropriated a valuable diamond necklace, and as a last resort, the Pasha determined, seeing that all the astrologers, Hodjas, and diviners had failed to discover the article, to consult Ahmet the cobbler, whose praises were in every mouth.

The Pasha went to Ahmet, and, in fear and trembling, the wife who had appropriated the necklace sent her confidential slave to overhear what the astrologer would say. The Pasha told Ahmet all he knew about the necklace, but this gave no clue, and in despair he asked how many diamonds the necklace contained. On being told that there were twenty-four, Ahmet, to put off the evil hour, said it would take an hour to discover each diamond; consequently would the Pasha come on the morrow at the same hour when, Inshallah, he would perhaps be able to give him some news.

The Pasha departed, and no sooner was he out of earshot, than the troubled Ahmet exclaimed in a loud voice: "Oh woman! Oh woman! What evil influence impelled you to go the wrong path, and drag others with you? When the twenty-four hours are up, you will perhaps repent! Alas! Too late. Your husband gone from you forever! Without a hope even of being united in paradise."

Ahmet was referring to himself and his wife, for he fully expected to be cast into prison on the following day as an impostor. But the slave who had been listening gave another interpretation to his words, and hurrying off, told her mistress that the astrologer knew all about the theft. The good man had even bewailed the separation that would inevitably take place. The Pasha's wife was distracted, and hurried off to plead her cause in person with the astrologer. On approaching Ahmet, the first words she said, in her excitement, were:

"Oh learned Hodja, you are a great and good man. Have compassion on my weakness and do not expose me to the wrath of my husband! I will do such penance as you may order, and bless you five times daily as long as I live."

"How can I save you?" innocently asked Ahmet. "What is decreed is decreed!"

And then, though silent, looked volumes, for he instinctively knew that words unuttered were arrows still in the quiver.

"If you won't pity me," continued the Hanoum, in despair, "I will go and confess to my Pasha, and perhaps he will forgive me."

To this appeal Ahmet said he must ask the stars for their views on the subject. The Hanoum inquired if the answer would come before the twenty-four hours were up. Ahmet's reply to this was a long and concentrated gaze at the heavens.

"Oh Hodja Effendi, I must go now, or the Pasha will miss me. Shall I give you the necklace to restore to the Pasha without explanation, when he comes tomorrow for the answer?"

Ahmet now realized what all the trouble was about, and in consideration of a fee, he promised not to reveal her theft on the condition that she would at once return home and place the necklace between the mattresses of her Pasha's bed. This the grateful woman agreed to do, and departed invoking blessings on Ahmet, who in return promised to exercise his influence on her behalf for astral intervention.

When the Pasha came to the astrologer at the appointed time, he explained to him that if he wanted both the necklace and the thief or thieves, it would take a long time, as it was impossible to hurry the stars; but if he would be content with the necklace alone, the horoscope indicated that the stars would oblige him at once. The Pasha said that he would be quite satisfied if he could get his diamonds again, and Ahmet at once told him where to find them. The Pasha returned to his home not a little sceptical, and immediately searched for the necklace where Ahmet had told him it was to be found. His joy and astonishment on discovering the article knew no bounds, and the fame of Ahmet the cobbler was the theme of every tongue.

Having received handsome payment from both the Pasha and the Hanoum, Ahmet earnestly begged of his wife to desist and not bring down sorrow and calamity upon his head. But his pleadings were in vain. Satan had closed his wife's ear to reason with envy. Resigned to his fate, all he could do was to consult the stars, and after mature thought give their communication, or assert that the stars had, for some reason best known to the applicant, refused to commune on the subject.

It happened that forty cases of gold were stolen from the Imperial Treasury, and every astrologer having failed to get even a clue as to where the money was or how it had disappeared, Ahmet was approached. Poor man, his case now looked hopeless! Even the chief astrologer was in disgrace. What might be his punishment he did not know – most probably death. Ahmet had no idea of the numerical importance of forty; but concluding that it must be large, he asked for a delay of forty days to discover the forty cases of gold. Ahmet gathered up the implements of his occult art, and before returning to his home, went to a shop and asked for forty beans – neither one more nor one less. When he got home and laid them down before him, he appreciated the number of cases of gold that had been stolen, and also the number of days he had to live. He knew it would be useless to explain to his wife the seriousness of the case, so that evening he took from his pocket the forty beans and mournfully said: "Forty cases of gold, forty thieves, forty days; and here is one of them," handing a bean to his wife. "The rest remain in their place until the time comes to give them up."

While Ahmet was saying this to his wife, one of the thieves was listening at the window. The thief was sure he had been discovered when he heard Ahmet say, "And here is one of them," and hurried off to tell his companions.

The thieves were greatly distressed, but decided to wait till the next evening and see what would happen then, and another of the number was sent to listen and see if the report would be verified. The listener had not long been stationed at his post when he heard Ahmet say to his wife: "And here is another of them," meaning another of the forty days of his life. But the thief understood the words otherwise, and hurried off to tell his chief that the astrologer knew all about it and knew that he had been there. The thieves consequently decided to send a delegation to Ahmet, confessing their guilt and offering to return the forty cases of gold intact. Ahmet received them, and on hearing their confession, accompanied with their condition to return the gold, boldly told them that he did not require their aid; that it was in his power to take possession of the forty cases of gold whenever he wished, but that he had no special desire to see them all executed, and he would plead their cause if they would go and put the gold in a place he indicated. This was agreed to, and Ahmet continued to give his wife a bean daily – but now with another purpose; he no longer feared the loss of his head, but discounted by degrees the great reward he hoped to receive. At last the final bean was given to his wife, and Ahmet was summoned to the palace. He went, and explained to his Majesty that the stars refused both to reveal the thieves and the gold, but whichever of the two his Majesty wished would be immediately granted. The Treasury being low, it was decided that, provided the cases were returned with the gold intact, his majesty would be satisfied. Ahmet conducted them to the place where the gold was buried, and amidst great rejoicing it was taken back to the palace. The sultan was so pleased with Ahmet, that he appointed him to the office of chief astrologer, and his wife attained her desire.

The sultan was one day walking in his palace grounds accompanied by his Chief Astrologer; wishing to test his powers, he caught a grasshopper, and, holding his closed hand out to the astrologer, asked him what it contained. Ahmet, in a pained and reproachful tone, answered the Sultan by a much-quoted proverb: "Alas! Your Majesty! the grasshopper never knows where its third leap will land it," figuratively alluding to himself and the dangerous hazard of guessing what was in the clenched hand of his Majesty. The Sultan was so struck by the reply that Ahmet was never again troubled to demonstrate his powers.

The Beresford Ghost

"THERE IS at Curraghmore, the seat of Lord Waterford, in Ireland, a manuscript account of the tale, such as it was originally received and implicitly believed in by the children and

ORACLES, SEERS & SAGES

grandchildren of the lady to whom Lord Tyrone is supposed to have made the supernatural appearance after death. The account was written by Lady Betty Cobbe, the youngest daughter of Marcus, Earl of Tyrone, and granddaughter of Nicola S., Lady Beresford. She lived to a good old age, in full use of all her faculties, both of body and mind. I can myself remember her, for when a boy I passed through Bath on a journey with my mother, and we went to her house there, and had luncheon. She appeared to my juvenile imagination a very appropriate person to revise and transmit such a tale, and fully adapted to do ample justice to her subject-matter. It never has been doubted in the family that she received the full particulars in early life, and that she heard the circumstances, such as they were believed to have occurred, from the nearest relatives of the two persons, the supposed actors in this mysterious interview, viz., from her own father, Lord Tyrone, who died in 1763, and from her aunt, Lady Riverston, who died in 1763 also.

"These two were both with their mother, Lady Beresford, on the day of her decease, and they, without assistance or witness, took off from their parent's wrist the black bandage which she had always worn on all occasions and times, even at Court, as some very old persons who lived well into the eighteenth century testified, having received their information from eyewitnesses of the fact. There was an oil painting of this lady in Tyrone House, Dublin, representing her with a black ribbon bound round her wrist. This portrait disappeared in an unaccountable manner. It used to hang in one of the drawing-rooms in that mansion, with other family pictures. When Henry, Marquis of Waterford, sold the old town residence of the family and its grounds to the Government as the site of the Education Board, he directed Mr. Watkins, a dealer in pictures, and a man of considerable knowledge in works of art and vertu, to collect the pictures, etc., etc., which were best adapted for removal to Curraghmore. Mr. Watkins especially picked out this portrait, not only as a good work of art, but as one which, from its associations, deserved particular care and notice. When, however, the lot arrived at Curraghmore and was unpacked, no such picture was found; and though Mr. Watkins took great pains and exerted himself to the utmost to trace what had become of it, to this day (nearly forty years), not a hint of its existence has been received or heard of.

"John le Poer, Lord Decies, was the eldest son of Richard, Earl of Tyrone, and of Lady Dorothy Annesley, daughter of Arthur, Earl of Anglesey. He was born 1665, succeeded his father 1690, and died 14th October, 1693. He became Lord Tyrone at his father's death, and is the 'ghost' of the story.

"Nicola Sophie Hamilton was the second and youngest daughter and co-heiress of Hugh, Lord Glenawley, who was also Baron Lunge in Sweden. Being a zealous Royalist, he had, together with his father, migrated to that country in 1643, and returned from it at the Restoration. He was of a good old family, and held considerable landed property in the county Tyrone, near Ballygawley. He died there in 1679. His eldest daughter and co-heiress, Arabella Susanna, married, in 1683, Sir John Macgill, of Gill Hall, in the county Down.

"Nicola S. (the second daughter) was born in 1666, and married Sir Tristram Beresford in 1687. Between that and 1693 two daughters were born, but no son to inherit the ample landed estates of his father, who most anxiously wished and hoped for an heir. It was under these circumstances, and at this period, that the manuscripts state that Lord Tyrone made his appearance after death; and all the versions of the story, without variation, attribute the same cause and reason, viz., a solemn promise mutually interchanged in early life between John le Poer, then Lord Decies, afterwards Lord Tyrone, and Nicola S. Hamilton, that whichever of the two died the first, should, if permitted, appear to the survivor for the object of declaring the approval or rejection by the Deity of the revealed religion as generally acknowledged: of which the departed one must be fully cognisant, but of which they both had in their youth entertained unfortunate doubts.

"In the month of October, 1693, Sir Tristram and Lady Beresford went on a visit to her sister, Lady Macgill, at Gill Hall, now the seat of Lord Clanwilliam, whose grandmother was eventually the heiress of Sir J. Macgill's property. One morning Sir Tristram rose early, leaving Lady Beresford asleep, and went out for a walk before breakfast. When his wife joined the table very late, her appearance and the embarrassment of her manner attracted general attention, especially that of her husband. He made anxious inquiries as to her health, and asked her apart what had occurred to her wrist, which was tied up with black ribbon tightly bound round it. She earnestly entreated him not to inquire more then, or thereafter, as to the cause of her wearing or continuing afterwards to wear that ribbon; 'for,' she added, 'you will never see me without it'. He replied, 'Since you urge it so vehemently, I promise you not to inquire more about it'.

"After completing her hurried breakfast she made anxious inquiries as to whether the post had yet arrived. It had not yet come in; and Sir Tristram asked: 'Why are you so particularly eager about letters today?' 'Because I expect to hear of Lord Tyrone's death, which took place on Tuesday.' 'Well,' remarked Sir Tristram, 'I never should have put you down for a superstitious person; but I suppose that some idle dream has disturbed you.' Shortly after, the servant brought in the letters; one was sealed with black wax. 'It is as I expected,' she cries; 'he is dead.' The letter was from Lord Tyrone's steward to inform them that his master had died in Dublin, on Tuesday, 14th October, at 4 p.m. Sir Tristram endeavoured to console her, and begged her to restrain her grief, when she assured him that she felt relieved and easier now that she knew the actual fact. She added, 'I can now give you a most satisfactory piece of intelligence, viz., that I am with child, and that it will be a boy.' A son was born in the following July. Sir Tristram survived its birth little more than six years. After his death Lady Beresford continued to reside with her young family at his place in the county of Derry, and seldom went from home. She hardly mingled with any neighbours or friends, excepting with Mr. and Mrs. Jackson, of Coleraine. He was the principal personage in that town, and was, by his mother, a near relative of Sir Tristram. His wife was the daughter of Robert Gorges, LL.D. (a gentleman of good old English family, and possessed of a considerable estate in the county Meath), by Jane Loftus, daughter of Sir Adam Loftus, of Rathfarnham, and sister of Lord Lisburn. They had an only son, Richard Gorges, who was in the army, and became a general officer very early in life. With the Jacksons Lady Beresford maintained a constant communication and lived on the most intimate terms, while she seemed determined to eschew all other society and to remain in her chosen retirement.

"At the conclusion of three years thus passed, one luckless day 'Young Gorges' most vehemently professed his passion for her, and solicited her hand, urging his suit in a most passionate appeal, which was evidently not displeasing to the fair widow, and which, unfortunately for her, was successful. They were married in 1704. One son and two daughters were born to them, when his abandoned and dissolute conduct forced her to seek and to obtain a separation. After this had continued for four years, General Gorges pretended extreme penitence for his past misdeeds, and with the most solemn promises of amendment induced his wife to live with him again, and she became the mother of a second son. The day a month after her confinement happened to be her birthday, and having recovered and feeling herself equal to some exertion, she sent for her son, Sir Marcus Beresford, then twenty years old, and her married daughter, Lady Riverston. She also invited Dr. King, the Archbishop of

Dublin (who was an intimate friend), and an old clergyman who had christened her, and who had always kept up a most kindly intercourse with her during her whole life, to make up a small party to celebrate the day.

"In the early part of it Lady Beresford was engaged in a kindly conversation with her old friend the clergyman, and in the course of it said: 'You know that I am forty-eight this day'. 'No, indeed,' he replied; 'you are only forty-seven, for your mother had a dispute with me once on the very subject of your age, and I in consequence sent and consulted the registry, and can most confidently assert that you are only forty-seven this day.' 'You have signed my death-warrant, then,' she cried; 'leave me, I pray, for I have not much longer to live, but have many things of grave importance to settle before I die. Send my son and my daughter to me immediately.' The clergyman did as he was bidden. He directed Sir Marcus and his sister to go instantly to their mother; and he sent to the archbishop and a few other friends to put them off from joining the birthday party.

"When her two children repaired to Lady Beresford, she thus addressed them: 'I have something of deep importance to communicate to you, my dear children, before I die. You are no strangers to the intimacy and the affection which subsisted in early life between Lord Tyrone and myself. We were educated together when young, under the same roof, in the pernicious principles of Deism. Our real friends afterwards took every opportunity to convince us of our error, but their arguments were insufficient to overpower and uproot our infidelity, though they had the effect of shaking our confidence in it, and thus leaving us wavering between the two opinions. In this perplexing state of doubt we made a solemn promise one to the other, that whichever died first should, if permitted, appear to the other for the purpose of declaring what religion was the one acceptable to the Almighty. One night, years after this interchange of promises, I was sleeping with your father at Gill Hall, when I suddenly awoke and discovered Lord Tyrone sitting visibly by the side of the bed. I screamed out, and vainly endeavoured to rouse Sir Tristram. "Tell me," I said, "Lord Tyrone, why and wherefore are you here at this time of the night?" "Have you then forgotten our promise to each other, pledged in early life? I died on Tuesday, at four o'clock. I have been permitted thus to appear in order to assure you that the revealed religion is the true and only one by which we can be saved. I am also suffered to inform you that you are with child, and will produce a son, who will marry my heiress; that Sir Tristram will not live long, when you will marry again, and you will die from the effects of childbirth in your forty-seventh year." I begged from him some convincing sign or proof so that when the morning came I might rely upon it, and feel satisfied that his appearance had been real, and that it was not the phantom of my imagination. He caused the hangings of the bed to be drawn in an unusual way and impossible manner through an iron hook. I still was not satisfied, when he wrote his signature in my pocket-book. I wanted, however, more substantial proof of his visit, when he laid his hand, which was cold as marble, on my wrist; the sinews shrunk up, the nerves withered at the touch. "Now," he said, "let no mortal eye, while you live, ever see that wrist," and vanished. While I was conversing with him my thoughts were calm, but as soon as he disappeared I felt chilled with horror and dismay, a cold sweat came over me, and I again endeavoured but vainly to awaken Sir Tristram; a flood of tears came to my relief, and I fell asleep.

"'In the morning your father got up without disturbing me; he had not noticed anything extraordinary about me or the bed-hangings. When I did arise I found a long broom in the gallery outside the bedroom door, and with great difficulty I unhooded the curtain, fearing that the position of it might excite surprise and cause inquiry. I bound up my wrist with black ribbon before I went down to breakfast, where the agitation of my mind was too visible not to attract attention. Sir Tristram made many anxious inquiries as to my health, especially as to my sprained wrist, as he conceived mine to be. I begged him to drop all questions as to the bandage, even if I continued to adopt it for any length of time. He kindly promised me not to speak of it any more, and he kept his promise faithfully. You, my son, came into the world as predicted, and your father died six years after. I then determined to abandon society and its pleasures and not mingle again with the world, hoping to avoid the dreadful predictions as to my second marriage; but, alas! In the one family with which I held constant and friendly intercourse I met the man, whom I did not regard with perfect indifference. Though I struggled to conquer by every means the passion, I at length yielded to his solicitations, and in a fatal moment for my own peace I became his wife. In a few years his conduct fully justified my demand for a separation, and I fondly hoped to escape the fatal prophecy. Under the delusion that I had passed my forty-seventh birthday, I was prevailed upon to believe in his amendment, and to pardon him. I have, however, heard from undoubted authority that I am only forty-seven this day, and I know that I am about to die. I die, however, without the dread of death, fortified as I am by the sacred precepts of Christianity and upheld by its promises. When I am gone, I wish that you, my children, should unbind this black ribbon and alone behold my wrist before I am consigned to the grave.'

"She then requested to be left that she might lie down and compose herself, and her children quitted the apartment, having desired her attendant to watch her, and if any change came on to summon them to her bedside. In an hour the bell rang, and they hastened to the call, but all was over. The two children having ordered everyone to retire, knelt down by the side of the bed, when Lady Riverston unbound the black ribbon and found the wrist exactly as Lady Beresford had described it – every nerve withered, every sinew shrunk.

"Her friend, the Archbishop, had had her buried in the Cathedral of St. Patrick, in Dublin, in the Earl of Cork's tomb, where she now lies."

* * *

The writer now professes his disbelief in any spiritual presence, and explains his theory that Lady Beresford's anxiety about Lord Tyrone deluded her by a vivid dream, during which she hurt her wrist.

Of all ghost stories the Tyrone, or Beresford Ghost, has most variants. Following Monsieur Haureau, in the *Journal des Savants*, I have tracked the tale, the death compact, and the wound inflicted by the ghost on the hand, or wrist, or brow, of the seer, through Henry More, and Melanchthon, and a medieval sermon by Eudes de Shirton, to William of Malmesbury, a range of 700 years. Mrs. Grant of Laggan has a rather recent case, and I have heard of another in the last ten years! Calmet has a case in 1625, the spectre leaves

> *The sable score of fingers four on a board of wood.*
> *Now for a modern instance of a gang of ghosts with a purpose!*

When I narrated the story which follows to an eminent moral philosopher, he remarked, at a given point, "Oh, the ghost spoke, did she?" and displayed scepticism. The evidence, however, left him, as it leaves me, at a standstill, not convinced, but agreeably perplexed. The ghosts here are truly old-fashioned.

My story is, and must probably remain, entirely devoid of proof, as far as any kind of ghostly influence is concerned. We find ghosts appearing, and imposing a certain course of action on a living witness, for definite purposes of their own. The course of action prescribed was undeniably pursued, and apparently the purpose of the ghosts was fulfilled, but what that purpose was their agent declines to state, and conjecture is hopelessly baffled.

The documents in the affair have been published by the Society for Psychical Research (Proceedings, vol. xi., p. 547), and are here used for reference. But I think the matter will be more intelligible if I narrate it exactly as it came under my own observation. The names of persons and places are all fictitious, and are the same as those used in the documents published by the S.P.R.

The Terrible Head

ONCE UPON A TIME there was a king whose only child was a girl. Now the king had been very anxious to have a son, or at least a grandson, to come after him, but he was told by a prophet whom he consulted that his own daughter's son should kill him. This news terrified him so much that he determined never to let his daughter be married, for he thought it was better to have no grandson at all than to be killed by his grandson. He therefore called his workmen together, and bade them dig a deep round hole in the earth, and then he had a prison of brass built in the hole, and then, when it was finished, he locked up his daughter. No man ever saw her, and she never saw even the fields and the sea, but only the sky and the sun, for there was a wide open window in the roof of the house of brass.

So the princess would sit looking up at the sky, watching the clouds float across, and wonder whether she should ever get out of her prison. Now one day it seemed to her that the sky opened above her, and a great shower of shining gold fell through the window in the roof, and lay glittering in her room. Not very long after, the princess had a baby, a little boy, but when the king, her father, heard of it he was very angry and afraid, for now the child was born that should be his death. Yet, cowardly as he was, he had not quite the heart to kill the princess and her baby outright, but he had them put in a huge brass-bound chest and thrust out to sea, that they might either be drowned or starved, or perhaps come to a country where they would be out of his way.

So the princess and the baby floated and drifted in the chest on the sea all day and night, but the baby was not afraid of the waves nor of the wind, for he did not know that they could hurt him, and he slept quite soundly. And the princess sang a song over him, and this was her song:

> *"Child, my child, how sound you sleep!*
> *Though your mother's care is deep,*
> *You can lie with heart at rest*

In the narrow brass-bound chest;
In the starless night and drear
You can sleep, and never hear
Billows breaking, and the cry
Of the night-wind wandering by;
In soft purple mantle sleeping
With your little face on mine,
Hearing not your mother weeping
And the breaking of the brine."

Well, the daylight came at last, and the great chest was driven by the waves against the shore of an island. There the brass-bound chest lay, with the princess and her baby in it, till a man of that country came past, and saw it, and dragged it on to the beach, and when he had broken it open, behold! There was a beautiful lady and a little boy. So he took them home, and was very kind to them, and brought up the boy till he was a young man. Now when the boy had come to his full strength, the king of that country fell in love with his mother, and wanted to marry her, but he knew that she would never part from her boy. So he thought of a plan to get rid of the boy, and this was his plan: A great queen of a country not far off was going to be married, and this king said that all his subjects must bring him wedding presents to give her. And he made a feast to which he invited them all, and they all brought their presents; some brought gold cups, and some brought necklaces of gold and amber, and some brought beautiful horses; but the boy had nothing, though he was the son of a princess, for his mother had nothing to give him. Then the rest of the company began to laugh at him, and the king said: "If you have nothing else to give, at least you might go and fetch the Terrible Head."

The boy was proud, and spoke without thinking:

"Then I swear that I *will* bring the Terrible Head, if it may be brought by a living man. But of what head you speak I know not."

Then they told him that somewhere, a long way off, there dwelt three dreadful sisters, monstrous ogrish women, with golden wings and claws of brass, and with serpents growing on their heads instead of hair. Now these women were so awful to look on that whoever saw them was turned at once into stone. And two of them could not be put to death, but the youngest, whose face was very beautiful, could be killed, and it was *her* head that the boy had promised to bring. You may imagine it was no easy adventure.

When he heard all this he was perhaps sorry that he had sworn to bring the Terrible Head, but he was determined to keep his oath. So he went out from the feast, where they all sat drinking and making merry, and he walked alone beside the sea in the dusk of the evening, at the place where the great chest, with himself and his mother in it, had been cast ashore.

There he went and sat down on a rock, looking toward the sea, and wondering how he should begin to fulfill his vow. Then he felt some one touch him on the shoulder; and he turned, and saw a young man like a king's son, having with him a tall and beautiful lady, whose blue eyes shone like stars. They were taller than mortal men, and the young man had a staff in his hand with golden wings on it, and two golden serpents twisted round it, and he had wings on his cap and on his shoes. He spoke to the boy, and asked him why he was so unhappy; and the boy told him how he had sworn to bring the Terrible Head, and knew not how to begin to set about the adventure.

Then the beautiful lady also spoke, and said that "it was a foolish oath and a hasty, but it might be kept if a brave man had sworn it." Then the boy answered that he was not afraid, if only he knew the way.

Then the lady said that to kill the dreadful woman with the golden wings and the brass claws, and to cut off her head, he needed three things: first, a Cap of Darkness, which would make him invisible when he wore it; next, a Sword of Sharpness, which would cleave iron at one blow; and last, the Shoes of Swiftness, with which he might fly in the air.

The boy answered that he knew not where such things were to be procured, and that, wanting them, he could only try and fail. Then the young man, taking off his own shoes, said: "First, you shall use these shoes till you have taken the Terrible Head, and then you must give them back to me. And with these shoes you will fly as fleet as a bird, or a thought, over the land or over the waves of the sea, wherever the shoes know the way. But there are ways which they do not know, roads beyond the borders of the world. And these roads have you to travel. Now first you must go to the three grey sisters, who live far off in the north, and are so very cold that they have only one eye and one tooth among the three. You must creep up close to them, and as one of them passes the eye to the other you must seize it, and refuse to give it up till they have told you the way to the three fairies of the garden, and *they* will give you the Cap of Darkness and the Sword of Sharpness, and show you how to wing beyond this world to the land of the Terrible Head."

Then the beautiful lady said: "Go forth at once, and do not return to say goodbye to your mother, for these things must be done quickly, and the Shoes of Swiftness themselves will carry you to the land of the three grey sisters – for they know the measure of that way."

So the boy thanked her, and he fastened on the Shoes of Swiftness, and turned to say goodbye to the young man and the lady. But, behold! they had vanished, he knew not how or where! Then he leaped in the air to try the Shoes of Swiftness, and they carried him more swiftly than the wind, over the warm blue sea, over the happy lands of the south, over the northern peoples who drank mare's milk and lived in great wagons, wandering after their flocks. Across the wide rivers, where the wild fowl rose and fled before him, and over the plains and the cold North Sea he went, over the fields of snow and the hills of ice, to a place where the world ends, and all water is frozen, and there are no men, nor beasts, nor any green grass. There in a blue cave of the ice he found the three grey sisters, the oldest of living things. Their hair was as white as the snow, and their flesh of an icy blue, and they mumbled and nodded in a kind of dream, and their frozen breath hung round them like a cloud. Now the opening of the cave in the ice was narrow, and it was not easy to pass in without touching one of the grey sisters. But, floating on the Shoes of Swiftness, the boy just managed to steal in, and waited till one of the sisters said to another, who had their one eye:

"Sister, what do you see? Do you see old times coming back?"

"No, Sister."

"Then give *me* the eye, for perhaps I can see farther than you."

Then the first sister passed the eye to the second, but as the second groped for it the boy caught it cleverly out of her hand.

"Where is the eye, Sister?" said the second grey woman.

"You have taken it yourself, Sister," said the first grey woman.

"Have you lost the eye, Sister? Have you lost the eye?" said the third grey woman; "Shall we *never* find it again, and see old times coming back?"

Then the boy slipped from behind them out of the cold cave into the air, and he laughed aloud.

When the grey women heard that laugh they began to weep, for now they knew that a stranger had robbed them, and that they could not help themselves, and their tears froze as they fell from the hollows where no eyes were, and rattled on the icy ground of the cave. Then they began to implore the boy to give them their eye back again, and he could not help being sorry for them, they were so pitiful. But he said he would never give them the eye till they told him the way to the fairies of the garden.

Then they wrung their hands miserably, for they guessed why he had come, and how he was going to try to win the Terrible Head. Now the dreadful women were akin to the three grey sisters, and it was hard for them to tell the boy the way. But at last they told him to keep always south, and with the land on his left and the sea on his right, till he reached the Island of the Fairies of the Garden. Then he gave them back the eye, and they began to look out once more for the old times coming back again. But the boy flew south between sea and land, keeping the land always on his left hand, till he saw a beautiful island crowned with flowering trees. There he alighted, and there he found the three fairies of the garden. They were like three very beautiful young women, dressed one in green, one in white, and one in red, and they were dancing and singing round an apple tree with apples of gold, and this was their song:

The Song of the Western Fairies

Round and round the apples of gold,
Round and round dance we;
Thus do we dance from the days of old
About the enchanted tree;
Round, and round and round we go,
While the spring is green, or the stream shall flow,
Or the wind shall stir the sea!

There is none may taste of the golden fruit
Till the golden new time come
Many a tree shall spring from shoot,
Many a blossom be withered at root,
Many a song be dumb;
Broken and still shall be many a lute
Or ever the new times come!

Round and round the tree of gold,
Round and round dance we,
So doth the great world spin from of old,
Summer and winter, and fire and cold,
Song that is sung, and tale that is told,
Even as we dance, that fold and unfold
Round the stem of the fairy tree!

These grave dancing fairies were very unlike the grey women, and they were glad to see the boy, and treated him kindly. Then they asked him why he had come; and he told them how he was sent to find the Sword of Sharpness and the Cap of Darkness. And the fairies gave him these, and a wallet, a shield, and belted the sword which had a diamond blade, round his waist, and the cap they set on his head, and told him that now even they could not see him though they were fairies. Then he took it off, and they each kissed him and wished him good fortune, and then they began again their eternal dance round the golden tree, for it is their business to guard it till the new times come, or till the world's ending. So the boy put the cap on his head, and hung the wallet round his waist, and the shining shield on his shoulders, and flew beyond the great river that lies coiled like a serpent round the whole world. And by the banks of that river, there he found the three terrible women all asleep beneath a poplar tree, and the dead poplar leaves lay all about them. Their golden wings were folded and their brass claws were crossed, and two of them slept with their hideous heads beneath their wings like birds, and the serpents in their hair writhed out from under the feathers of gold. But the youngest slept between her two sisters, and she lay on her back, with her beautiful sad face turned to the sky; and though she slept her eyes were wide open. If the boy had seen her he would have been changed into stone by the terror and the pity of it, she was so awful; but he had thought of a plan for killing her without looking on her face. As soon as he caught sight of the three from far off he took his shining shield from his shoulders, and held it up like a mirror, so that he saw the dreadful women reflected in it, and did not see the Terrible Head itself. Then he came nearer and nearer, till he reckoned that he was within a sword's stroke of the youngest, and he guessed where he should strike a back blow behind him. Then he drew the Sword of Sharpness and struck once, and the Terrible Head was cut from the shoulders of the creature, and the blood leaped out and struck him like a blow. But he thrust the Terrible Head into his wallet, and flew away without looking behind. Then the two dreadful sisters who were left wakened, and rose in the air like great birds; and though they could not see him because of his Cap of Darkness, they flew after him up the wind, following by the scent through the clouds, like hounds hunting in a wood. They came so close that he could hear the clatter of their golden wings, and their shrieks to each other: *"Here, here, No, there; this way he went,"* as they chased him. But the Shoes of Swiftness flew too fast for them, and at last their cries and the rattle of their wings died away as he crossed the great river that runs round the world.

Now when the horrible creatures were far in the distance, and the boy found himself on the right side of the river, he flew straight eastward, trying to seek his own country. But as he looked down from the air he saw a very strange sight – a beautiful girl chained to a stake at the high-water mark of the sea. The girl was so frightened or so tired that she was only prevented from falling by the iron chain about her waist, and there she hung, as if she were dead. The boy was very sorry for her and flew down and stood beside her. When he spoke she raised her head and looked round, but his voice only seemed to frighten her. Then he remembered that he was wearing the Cap of Darkness, and that she could only hear him, not see him. So he took it off, and there he stood before her, the handsomest young man she had ever seen in all her life, with short curly yellow hair, and blue eyes, and a laughing face. And he thought her the most beautiful girl in the world. So first with one blow of the Sword of Sharpness he cut the iron chain that bound her, and then he asked her what she did there, and why men treated her so cruelly. And she told him that she was the daughter of the King of that country, and that she was tied there to be eaten by a monstrous beast out of the sea; for the beast came and devoured a girl every day. Now the lot had fallen on her; and as she was just saying this a long fierce head of a cruel sea creature rose out of the waves and snapped at the girl. But the beast had been too greedy and too hurried, so he missed his aim the first time. Before he could rise and bite again the boy had whipped the Terrible Head out of his wallet and held it up. And when the sea beast leaped out once more its eyes fell on the head, and instantly it was turned into a stone. And the stone beast is there on the sea-coast to this day.

Then the boy and the girl went to the palace of the king, her father, where everyone was weeping for her death, and they could hardly believe their eyes when they saw her come back well. And the king and queen made much of the boy, and could not contain themselves for delight when they found he wanted to marry their daughter. So the two were married with the most splendid rejoicings, and when they had passed some time at court they went home in a ship to the boy's own country. For he could not carry his bride through the air, so he took the Shoes of Swiftness, and the Cap of Darkness, and the Sword of Sharpness up to a lonely place in the hills. There he left them, and there they were found by the man and woman who had met him at home beside the sea, and had helped him to start on his journey.

When this had been done the boy and his bride set forth for home, and landed at the harbour of his native land. But whom should he meet in the very street of the town but his own mother, flying for her life from the wicked King, who now wished to kill her because he found that she would never marry him! For if she had liked the king ill before, she liked him far worse now that he had caused her son to disappear so suddenly. She did not know, of course, where the boy had gone, but thought the king had slain him secretly. So now she was running for her very life, and the wicked king was following her with a sword in his hand. Then, behold! she ran into her son's very arms, but he had only time to kiss her and step in front of her, when the king struck at him with his sword. The boy caught the blow on his shield, and cried to the king:

"I swore to bring you the Terrible Head, and see how I keep my oath!"

Then he drew forth the head from his wallet, and when the king's eyes fell on it, instantly he was turned into stone, just as he stood there with his sword lifted!

Now all the people rejoiced, because the wicked king should rule them no longer. And they asked the boy to be their king, but he said no, he must take his mother home to her father's house. So the people chose for king the man who had been kind to his mother when first she was cast on to the island in the great chest.

Presently the boy and his mother and his wife set sail for his mother's own country, from which she had been driven so unkindly. But on the way they stayed at the court of a king, and it happened that he was holding games, and giving prizes to the best runners, boxers and quoit-throwers. Then the boy would try his strength with the rest, but he threw the quoit so far that it went beyond what had ever been thrown before, and fell in the crowd, striking a man so that he died. Now this man was no other than the father of the boy's mother, who had fled away from his own kingdom for fear his grandson should find him and kill him after all. Thus he was destroyed by his own cowardice and by chance, and thus the prophecy was fulfilled. But the boy and his wife and his mother went back to the kingdom that was theirs, and lived long and happily after all their troubles.

The Seer's Death

MACINTYRE SUPPLIES the following account of the Seaforth prophecy and the Seer's death, as related at this day, in the Black Isle:

Coinneach's supernatural power was at length the cause which led to his untimely and cruel death. At a time when there was a convivial gathering in Brahan Castle, a large concourse of local aristocratic guests was present. As the youthful portion were amusing themselves in the beautiful grounds or park surrounding the castle, and displaying their noble forms and features as they thought to full advantage, a party remarked in Coinneach Odhar's hearing, that such a gathering of gentlemen's children could rarely be seen. The seer answered with a sneer, "that he saw more in the company of the children of footmen and grooms than of the children of gentlemen," (Is mo th'ann do chlann ghillean-buird agus do chlann ghillean-stabuil na th'ann do chlann dhaoin' uaisle), a remark which soon came to the ears of Lady Seaforth and the other ladies present, who were so much offended and provoked at this base insinuation as to the paternity of the Brahan guests that they determined at once to have condign punishment on the once-respected seer. He was forthwith ordered to be seized; and, after eluding the search of his infuriated pursuers for some time, was at last apprehended. Seeing he had no way of escape, he once more applied the magic stone to his eye, and uttered the well-known prophetic curse [already given] against the Brahan family, and then threw the stone into a cow's footmark, which was full of water, declaring that a child would be born with two navels, or as some say, with four thumbs and six toes, who would in course of time discover it inside a pike, and who then would be gifted with Coinneach's prophetic power. As it was the purpose of his pursuers to obtain possession of this wonderful stone, as well as of the prophet's person, search was eagerly made for it in the muddy waters in the footprint, when, lo! it was found that more water was copiously oozing from the boggy ground around, and rapidly forming a considerable lake, that effectually concealed the much-coveted stone. The waters steadily increased, and the result, as the story goes, was the formation of Loch Ussie (Oozie). The poor prophet was then taken to Chanonry Point, where the stern arm of ecclesiastical authority, with unrelenting severity, burnt him to death in a tar barrel for witchcraft.

It is currently reported that a person answering to the foregoing description was actually born in the neighbourhood of Conon, near Loch Ussie, and is still living. Of this I have been credibly informed by a person who saw him several times at the Muir of Ord markets.

We see from the public prints, our correspondent humorously continues, that the Magistrates and Police Commissioners of Dingwall contemplate to bring a supply of water for 'Baile-'Chail' from Loch Ussie. Might we humbly suggest with such a view in prospect, as some comfort to the burdened ratepayers, that there may be, to say the least, a probability in the course of such an undertaking of recovering the mystic stone, so long compelled to hide its prophetic light in the depths of Loch Ussie, and so present the world with the novel sight of having not only an individual gifted with second-sight, but also a Corporation; and, further, what would be a greater terror to evil-doers, a magistracy capable, in the widest sense of the word, of discerning between right and wrong, good and evil, and thus compelling the lieges in the surrounding towns and villages to exclaim involuntarily – *O si sic omnes!* They might go the length even of lending it out, and giving you the use of it occasionally in Inverness.

When Coinneach Odhar was being led to the stake, fast bound with cords, Lady Seaforth exultingly declared that, having had so much unhallowed intercourse with the unseen world, he would never go to Heaven. But the seer, looking round upon her with an eye from which his impending fate had not banished the ray of a joyful hope of rest in a future state, gravely answered – "*I* will go to Heaven, but *you* never shall; and this will be a sign whereby you can determine whether my condition after death is one of everlasting happiness or of eternal misery; a raven and a dove, swiftly flying in opposite directions will meet, and for a second hover over my ashes, on which they will instantly alight. If the raven be foremost, you have spoken truly; but if the dove, then my hope is well-founded." And, accordingly, tradition relates, that after the cruel sentence of his hard-hearted enemies had been executed upon the Brahan Seer, and his ashes lay scattered among the smouldering embers of the fagot, his last prophecy was most literally fulfilled; for those messengers, emblematically denoting – the one sorrow, the other joy – came speeding to the fatal spot, when the dove, with characteristic flight, closely followed by the raven, darted downwards and was first to alight on the dust of the departed Coinneach Odhar; thus completely disproving the positive and uncharitable assertion of the proud and vindictive Lady of Brahan, to the wonder and consternation of all the beholders.

Mr. Maclennan describes the cause of Coinneach's doom in almost identical terms; the only difference being, that while the former has the young ladies amusing themselves on the green outside, the latter describes them having a grand dance in the great hall of the castle. The following is his account of the prophet's end:

In terms of her expressed resolution, Lady Seaforth, some days after this magnificent entertainment, caused the seer to be seized, bound hand and foot, and carried forthwith to the Ness of Chanonry, where, despite his pitiful looks and lamentable cries, he was inhumanly thrown, head foremost, into a barrel of burning tar, the inside of which was thickly studded with sharp and long spikes driven in from the outside. On the very day upon which Coinneach was sent away from the castle to meet his cruel fate, Lord Seaforth arrived, and was immediately informed of his lady's resolution, and that Coinneach was already well on his way to the Chanonry, where he was to be burned that very day, under clerical supervision and approval. My lord, knowing well the vindictive and cruel nature of his Countess, believed the story to be only too true. He waited neither for food nor refreshment; called neither for groom nor for servant, but hastened immediately to the stable, saddled his favourite steed with his own hands, for lairds were not so proud in those days, and set off at full speed, hoping to reach Chanonry Point before the diabolical intention of her ladyship and her religious advisers should be carried into effect. Never before nor since did Seaforth ride so furiously as he did on that day. He was soon at Fortrose, when he observed a dense smoke rising higher and higher from the promontory below. He felt his whole frame giving way, and a cold sweat came over his body, for he felt that the foul deed was, or was about to be, perpetrated. He pulled himself together, however, and with fresh energy and redoubled vigour, spurred his steed, which had already been driven almost beyond its powers of endurance, to reach the fatal spot to save the seer's life. Within a few paces of where the smoke was rising the poor brute could endure the strain no longer; it fell down under him and died on the spot. Still determined, if possible, to arrive in time, he rushed forward on foot, crying out at the height of his voice to those congregated at the spot to save their victim. It was, however, too late, for whether Seaforth's cries were heard or not, the victim of his lady's rage and vindictive nature had been thrown into the burning barrel a few moments before his intended deliverer had reached the fatal spot.

The time when this happened is not so very remote as to lead us to suppose that tradition could so grossly blunder as to record such a horrible and barbarous murder by a lady so widely and well-known as Lady Seaforth was, had it not taken place.

It is too much to suppose that if the seer had been allowed to die a peaceful and natural death, that such a story as this would have ever originated, be carried down and believed in from generation to generation, and be so well authenticated in many quarters as it now is. It may be stated that a large stone slab, now covered under the sand, lies a few yards east from the road leading from Fortrose to Fort-George Ferry, and about 250 yards northwest from the lighthouse, which is still pointed out as marking the spot where this inhuman tragedy was consummated, under the eyes and with the full approval of the highest dignitaries of the church.

The Tale of Taliesin

IN TIMES PAST there lived in Penllyn a man of gentle lineage, named Tegid Voel, and his dwelling was in the midst of the lake Tegid, and his wife was called Caridwen. And there was born to him of his wife a son named Morvran ab Tegid, and also a daughter named Creirwy, the fairest maiden in the world was she; and they had a brother, the most ill-favoured man in the world, Avagddu. Now Caridwen his mother thought that he was not likely to be admitted among men of noble birth, by reason of his ugliness, unless he had some exalted merits or knowledge. For it was in the beginning of Arthur's time and of the Round Table.

So she resolved, according to the arts of the books of the Fferyllt, to boil a cauldron of Inspiration and Science for her son, that his reception might be honourable because of his knowledge of the mysteries of the future state of the world.

Then she began to boil the cauldron, which from the beginning of its boiling might not cease to boil for a year and a day, until three blessed drops were obtained of the grace of Inspiration.

And she put Gwion Bach the son of Gwreang of Llanfair in Caereinion, in Powys, to stir the cauldron, and a blind man named Morda to kindle the fire beneath it, and she charged them that they should not suffer it to cease boiling for the space of a year and a day. And she herself, according to the books of the astronomers, and in planetary hours, gathered every day of all charm-bearing herbs. And one day, towards the end of the year, as Caridwen was culling plants and making incantations, it chanced that three drops of the charmed liquor flew out of the cauldron and fell upon the finger of Gwion Bach. And by reason of their great heat he put his finger to his mouth, and the instant he put those marvel-working drops into his mouth, he foresaw everything that was to come, and perceived that his chief care must be to guard against the wiles of Caridwen, for vast was her skill. And in very great fear he fled towards his own land. And the cauldron burst in two, because all the liquor within it except the three charm-bearing drops was poisonous, so that the horses of Gwyddno Garanhir were poisoned by the water of the stream into which the liquor of the cauldron ran, and the confluence of that stream was called the Poison of the Horses of Gwyddno from that time forth.

Thereupon came in Caridwen and saw all the toil of the whole year lost. And she seized a billet of wood and struck the blind Morda on the head until one of his eyes fell out upon his cheek. And he said, "Wrongfully hast thou disfigured me, for I am innocent. Thy loss was not because of me." "Thou speakest truth," said Caridwen, "it was Gwion Bach who robbed me."

And she went forth after him, running. And he saw her, and changed himself into a hare and fled. But she changed herself into a greyhound and turned him. And he ran towards a river, and became a fish. And she in the form of an otter-bitch chased him under the water, until he was fain to turn himself into a bird of the air. She, as a hawk, followed him and gave him no rest in the sky. And just as she was about to stoop upon him, and he was in fear of death, he espied a heap of winnowed wheat on the floor of a barn, and he dropped among the wheat, and turned himself into one of the grains.

Then she transformed herself into a high-crested black hen, and went to the wheat and scratched it with her feet, and found him out and swallowed him. And, as the story says, she bore him nine months, and when she was delivered of him, she could not find it in her heart to kill him, by reason of his beauty. So she wrapped him in a leathern bag, and cast him into the sea to the mercy of God, on the twenty-ninth day of April.

And at that time the weir of Gwyddno was on the strand between Dyvi and Aberystwyth, near to his own castle, and the value of an hundred pounds was taken in that weir every May eve. And in those days Gwyddno had an only son named Elphin, the most hapless of youths, and the most needy. And it grieved his father sore, for he thought that he was born in an evil hour. And by the advice of his council, his father had granted him the drawing of the weir that year, to see if good luck would ever befall him, and to give him something wherewith to begin the world.

And the next day when Elphin went to look, there was nothing in the weir. But as he turned back he perceived the leathern bag upon a pole of the weir. Then said one of the weir-ward unto Elphin, "Thou wast never unlucky until tonight, and now thou hast destroyed the virtues of the weir, which always yielded the value of an hundred pounds every May eve, and tonight there is nothing but this leathern skin within it." "How now," said Elphin, "there may be therein the value of an hundred pounds." Well, they took up the leathern bag, and he who opened it saw the forehead of the boy, and said to Elphin, "Behold a radiant brow!" [1] "Taliesin be he called," said Elphin. And he lifted the boy in his arms, and lamenting his mischance, he placed him sorrowfully behind him. And he made his horse amble gently, that before had been trotting, and he carried him as softly as if he had been sitting in the easiest chair in the world. And presently the boy made a Consolation and praise to Elphin, and foretold honour to Elphin; and the Consolation was as you may see:

"Fair Elphin, cease to lament!
Let no one be dissatisfied with his own,
To despair will bring no advantage.
No man sees what supports him;
The prayer of Cynllo will not be in vain;
God will not violate his promise.
Never in Gwyddno's weir
Was there such good luck as this night.
Fair Elphin, dry thy cheeks!
Being too sad will not avail.
Although thou thinkest thou hast no gain,
Too much grief will bring thee no good;
Nor doubt the miracles of the Almighty:
Although I am but little, I am highly gifted.
From seas, and from mountains,
And from the depths of rivers,
God brings wealth to the fortunate man.
Elphin of lively qualities,
Thy resolution is unmanly;
Thou must not be over sorrowful:
Better to trust in God than to forbode ill.
Weak and small as I am,
On the foaming beach of the ocean,
In the day of trouble I shall be
Of more service to thee than three hundred salmon.
Elphin of notable qualities,
Be not displeased at thy misfortune;
Although reclined thus weak in my bag,
There lies a virtue in my tongue.
While I continue thy protector
Thou hast not much to fear;
Remembering the names of the Trinity,
None shall be able to harm thee."

And this was the first poem that Taliesin ever sang, being to console Elphin in his grief for that the produce of the weir was lost, and, what was worse, that all the world would consider that it was through his fault and ill-luck. And then Gwyddno Garanhir [2] asked him what he was, whether man or spirit. Whereupon he sang this tale, and said:

"First, I have been formed a comely person,
In the court of Caridwen I have done penance;
Though little I was seen, placidly received,
I was great on the floor of the place to where I was led;
I have been a prized defence, the sweet muse the cause,

And by law without speech I have been liberated
By a smiling black old hag, when irritated
Dreadful her claim when pursued:
I have fled with vigour, I have fled as a frog,
I have fled in the semblance of a crow, scarcely finding rest;
I have fled vehemently, I have fled as a chain,
I have fled as a roe into an entangled thicket;
I have fled as a wolf cub, I have fled as a wolf in a wilderness,
I have fled as a thrush of portending language;
I have fled as a fox, used to concurrent bounds of quirks;
I have fled as a martin, which did not avail;
I have fled as a squirrel, that vainly hides,
I have fled as a stag's antler, of ruddy course,
I have fled as iron in a glowing fire,
I have fled as a spear-head, of woe to such as has a wish for it;
I have fled as a fierce bull bitterly fighting,
I have fled as a bristly boar seen in a ravine,
I have fled as a white grain of pure wheat,
On the skirt of a hempen sheet entangled,
That seemed of the size of a mare's foal,
That is filling like a ship on the waters;
Into a dark leathern bag I was thrown,
And on a boundless sea I was sent adrift;
Which was to me an omen of being tenderly nursed,
And the Lord God then set me at liberty."

Then came Elphin to the house or court of Gwyddno his father, and Taliesin with him. And Gwyddno asked him if he had had a good haul at the weir, and he told him that he had got that which was better than fish. "What was that?" said Gwyddno. "A bard," answered Elphin. Then said Gwyddno, "Alas, what will he profit thee?" And Taliesin himself replied and said, "He will profit him more than the weir ever profited thee." Asked Gwyddno, "Art thou able to speak, and thou so little?" And Taliesin answered him, "I am better able to speak than thou to question me." "Let me hear what thou canst say," quoth Gwyddno. Then Taliesin sang:

"In water there is a quality endowed with a blessing;
On God it is most just to meditate aright;
To God it is proper to supplicate with seriousness,
Since no obstacle can there be to obtain a reward from him.
Three times have I been born, I know by meditation;
It were miserable for a person not to come and obtain
All the sciences of the world, collected together in my breast,
For I know what has been, what in future will occur.
I will supplicate my Lord that I get refuge in him,
A regard I may obtain in his grace;
The Son of Mary is my trust, great in him is my delight,
For in him is the world continually upholden.

God has been to instruct me and to raise my expectation,
The true Creator of heaven, who affords me protection;
It is rightly intended that the saints should daily pray,
For God, the renovator, will bring them to him."

And forthwith Elphin gave his haul to his wife, and she nursed him tenderly and lovingly. Thenceforward Elphin increased in riches more and more day after day, and in love and favour with the king, and there abode Taliesin until he was thirteen years old, when Elphin son of Gwyddno went by a Christmas invitation to his uncle, Maelgwn Gwynedd, who some time after this held open court at Christmastide in the castle of Dyganwy, for all the number of his lords of both degrees, both spiritual and temporal, with a vast and thronged host of knights and squires. And amongst them there arose a discourse and discussion. And thus was it said.

"Is there in the whole world a king so great as Maelgwn, or one on whom Heaven has bestowed so many spiritual gifts as upon him? First, form, and beauty, and meekness, and strength, besides all the powers of the soul!" And together with these they said that Heaven had given one gift that exceeded all the others, which was the beauty, and comeliness, and grace, and wisdom, and modesty of his queen; whose virtues surpassed those of all the ladies and noble maidens throughout the whole kingdom. And with this they put questions one to another amongst themselves: Who had braver men? Who had fairer or swifter horses or greyhounds? Who had more skilful or wiser bards – than Maelgwn?

Now at that time the bards were in great favour with the exalted of the kingdom; and then none performed the office of those who are now called heralds, unless they were learned men, not only expert in the service of kings and princes, but studious and well versed in the lineage, and arms, and exploits of princes and kings, and in discussions concerning foreign kingdoms, and the ancient things of this kingdom, and chiefly in the annals of the first nobles; and also were prepared always with their answers in various languages, Latin, French, Welsh, and English. And together with this they were great chroniclers, and recorders, and skilful in framing verses, and ready in making englyns in every one of those languages. Now of these there were at that feast within the palace of Maelgwn as many as four-and-twenty, and chief of them all was one named Heinin Vardd.

When they had all made an end of thus praising the king and his gifts, it befell that Elphin spoke in this wise. "Of a truth none but a king may vie with a king; but were he not a king, I would say that my wife was as virtuous as any lady in the kingdom, and also that I have a bard who is more skilful than all the king's bards." In a short space some of his fellows showed the king all the boastings of Elphin; and the king ordered him to be thrown into a strong prison, until he might know the truth as to the virtues of his wife, and the wisdom of his bard.

Now when Elphin had been put in a tower of the castle, with a thick chain about his feet (it is said that it was a silver chain, because he was of royal blood), the king, as the story relates, sent his son Rhun to inquire into the demeanour of Elphin's wife. Now Rhun was the most graceless man in the world, and there was neither wife nor maiden with whom he had held converse, but was evil spoken of. While Rhun went in haste towards Elphin's dwelling, being fully minded to bring disgrace upon his wife, Taliesin told his mistress how that the king had placed his master in durance in prison, and how that Rhun was coming in haste to strive to bring disgrace upon her. Wherefore he caused his mistress to array one of the maids of her kitchen in her apparel; which the noble lady gladly did; and she loaded her hands with the best rings that she and her husband possessed.

In this guise Taliesin caused his mistress to put the maiden to sit at the board in her room at supper, and he made her to seem as her mistress, and the mistress to seem as the maid. And when they were in due time seated at their supper in the manner that has been said, Rhun suddenly arrived at Elphin's dwelling, and was received with joy, for all the servants knew him plainly; and they brought him in haste to the room of their mistress, in the semblance of whom the maid rose up from supper and welcomed him gladly. And afterwards she sat down to supper again the second time, and Rhun with her. Then Rhun began jesting with the maid, who still kept the semblance of her mistress. And verily this story shows that the maiden became so intoxicated, that she fell asleep; and the story relates that it was a powder that Rhun put into the drink, that made her sleep so soundly that she never felt it when he cut from off her hand her little finger, whereupon was the signet ring of Elphin, which he had sent to his wife as a token, a short time before. And Rhun returned to the king with the finger and the ring as a proof, to show that he had cut it from off her hand, without her awaking from her sleep of intemperance.

The king rejoiced greatly at these tidings, and he sent for his councillors, to whom he told the whole story from the beginning. And he caused Elphin to be brought out of his prison, and he chided him because of his boast. And he spake unto Elphin on this wise. "Elphin, be it known to thee beyond a doubt that it is but folly for a man to trust in the virtues of his wife further than he can see her; and that thou mayest be certain of thy wife's vileness, behold her finger, with thy signet ring upon it, which was cut from her hand last night, while she slept the sleep of intoxication." Then thus spake Elphin. "With thy leave, mighty king, I cannot deny my ring, for it is known of many; but verily I assert strongly that the finger around which it is, was never attached to the hand of my wife, for in truth and certainty there are three notable things pertaining to it, none of which ever belonged to any of my wife's fingers. The first of the three is, that it is certain, by your grace's leave, that wheresoever my wife is at this present hour, whether sitting, or standing, or lying down, this ring would never remain upon her thumb, whereas you can plainly see that it was hard to draw it over the joint of the little finger of the hand whence this was cut; the second thing is, that my wife has never let pass one Saturday since I have known her without paring her nails before going to bed, and you can see fully that the nail of this little finger has not been pared for a month. The third is, truly, that the hand whence this finger came was kneading rye dough within three days before the finger was cut therefrom, and I can assure your goodness that my wife has never kneaded rye dough since my wife she has been."

Then the king was mightily wroth with Elphin for so stoutly withstanding him, respecting the goodness of his wife, wherefore he ordered him to his prison a second time, saying that he should not be loosed thence until he had proved the truth of his boast, as well concerning the wisdom of his bard as the virtues of his wife.

In the meantime his wife and Taliesin remained joyful at Elphin's dwelling. And Taliesin showed his mistress how that Elphin was in prison because of them, but he bade her be glad, for that he would go to Maelgwn's court to free his master. Then she asked him in what manner he would set him free. And he answered her:

> "A journey will I perform,
> And to the gate I will come;

The hall I will enter,
And my song I will sing;
My speech I will pronounce
To silence royal bards,
In presence of their chief,
I will greet to deride,
Upon them I will break
And Elphin I will free.
Should contention arise,
In presence of the prince,
With summons to the bards,
For the sweet flowing song,
And wizards' posing lore
And wisdom of Druids,
In the court of the sons of the Distributor
Some are who did appear
Intent on wily schemes,
By craft and tricking means,
In pangs of affliction
To wrong the innocent,
Let the fools be silent,
As erst in Badon's fight, –
With Arthur of liberal ones
The head, with long red blades;
Through feats of testy men,
And a chief with his foes.
Woe be to them, the fools,
When revenge comes on them.
I Taliesin, chief of bards,
With a sapient Druid's words,
Will set kind Elphin free
From haughty tyrant's bonds.
To their fell and chilling cry,
By the act of a surprising steed,
From the far distant North,
There soon shall be an end.
Let neither grace nor health
Be to Maelgwn Gwynedd,
For this force and this wrong;
And be extremes of ills
And an avenged end
To Rhun and all his race:
Short be his course of life,
Be all his lands laid waste;
And long exile be assigned
To Maelgwn Gwynedd!"

After this he took leave of his mistress, and came at last to the Court of Maelgwn, who was going to sit in his hall and dine in his royal state, as it was the custom in those days for kings and princes to do at every chief feast. And as soon as Taliesin entered the hall, he placed himself in a quiet corner, near the place where the bards and the minstrels were wont to come in doing their service and duty to the king, as is the custom at the high festivals when the bounty is proclaimed. And so, when the bards and the heralds came to cry largesse, and to proclaim the power of the king and his strength, at the moment that they passed by the corner wherein he was crouching, Taliesin pouted out his lips after them, and played "Blerwm, blerwm," with his finger upon his lips. Neither took they much notice of him as they went by, but proceeded forward till they came before the king, unto whom they made their obeisance with their bodies, as they were wont, without speaking a single word, but pouting out their lips, and making mouths at the king, playing "Blerwm, blerwm," upon their lips with their fingers, as they had seen the boy do elsewhere. This sight caused the king to wonder and to deem within himself that they were drunk with many liquors. Wherefore he commanded one of his lords, who served at the board, to go to them and desire them to collect their wits, and to consider where they stood, and what it was fitting for them to do. And this lord did so gladly. But they ceased not from their folly any more than before. Whereupon he sent to them a second time, and a third, desiring them to go forth from the hall. At the last the king ordered one of his squires to give a blow to the chief of them named Heinin Vardd; and the squire took a broom and struck him on the head, so that he fell back in his seat. Then he arose and went on his knees, and besought leave of the king's grace to show that this their fault was not through want of knowledge, neither through drunkenness, but by the influence of some spirit that was in the hall. And after this Heinin spoke on this wise. "Oh, honourable King, be it known to your Grace, that not from the strength of drink, or of too much liquor, are we dumb, without power of speech like drunken men, but through the influence of a spirit that sits in the corner yonder in the form of a child." Forthwith the king commanded the squire to fetch him; and he went to the nook where Taliesin sat, and brought him before the king, who asked him what he was, and whence he came. And he answered the king in verse.

"Primary chief bard am I to Elphin,
And my original country is the region of the summer stars;
Idno and Heinin called me Merddin,
At length every king will call me Taliesin.

I was with my Lord in the highest sphere,
On the fall of Lucifer into the depth of hell
I have borne a banner before Alexander;
I know the names of the stars from north to south;
I have been on the galaxy at the throne of the Distributor;
I was in Canaan when Absalom was slain;
I conveyed the Divine Spirit to the level of the vale of Hebron;
I was in the court of Don before the birth of Gwdion.
I was instructor to Eli and Enoc;
I have been winged by the genius of the splendid crosier;
I have been loquacious prior to being gifted with speech;
I was at the place of the crucifixion of the merciful Son of God;

I have been three periods in the prison of Arianrod;
I have been the chief director of the work of the tower of Nimrod;
I am a wonder whose origin is not known.
I have been in Asia with Noah in the ark,
I have seen the destruction of Sodom and Gomorra;
I have been in India when Roma was built,
I am now come here to the remnant of Troia.

I have been with my Lord in the manger of the ass:
I strengthened Moses through the water of Jordan;
I have been in the firmament with Mary Magdalene;
I have obtained the muse from the cauldron of Caridwen;
I have been bard of the harp to Lleon of Lochlin.
I have been on the White Hill, in the court of Cynvelyn,
For a day and a year in stocks and fetters,
I have suffered hunger for the Son of the Virgin,
I have been fostered in the land of the Deity,
I have been teacher to all intelligences,
I am able to instruct the whole universe.
I shall be until the day of doom on the face of the earth;
And it is not known whether my body is flesh or fish.

Then I was for nine months
In the womb of the hag Caridwen;
I was originally little Gwion,
And at length I am Taliesin."

And when the king and his nobles had heard the song, they wondered much, for they had never heard the like from a boy so young as he. And when the king knew that he was the bard of Elphin, he bade Heinin, his first and wisest bard, to answer Taliesin and to strive with him. But when he came, he could do no other but play 'blerwm' on his lips; and when he sent for the others of the four-and-twenty bards they all did likewise, and could do no other. And Maelgwn asked the boy Taliesin what was his errand, and he answered him in song.

"Puny bards, I am trying
To secure the prize, if I can;
By a gentle prophetic strain
I am endeavouring to retrieve
The loss I may have suffered;
Complete the attempt I hope,
Since Elphin endures trouble
In the fortress of Teganwy,
On him may there not be laid
Too many chains and fetters;
The Chair of the fortress of Teganwy
Will I again seek;
Strengthened by my muse I am powerful;

Mighty on my part is what I seek,
For three hundred songs and more
Are combined in the spell I sing.
There ought not to stand where I am
Neither stone, neither ring;
And there ought not to be about me
Any bard who may not know
That Elphin the son of Gwyddno
Is in the land of Artro,
Secured by thirteen locks,
For praising his instructor;
And then I Taliesin,
Chief of the bards of the west,
Shall loosen Elphin
Out of a golden fetter."

* * *

"If you be primary bards
To the master of sciences,
Declare ye mysteries
That relate to the inhabitants of the world;
There is a noxious creature,
From the rampart of Satanas,
Which has overcome all
Between the deep and the shallow;
Equally wide are his jaws
As the mountains of the Alps;
Him death will not subdue,
Nor hand or blades;
There is the load of nine hundred wagons
In the hair of his two paws;
There is in his head an eye
Green as the limpid sheet of icicle;
Three springs arise
In the nape of his neck;
Sea-roughs thereon
Swim through it;
There was the dissolution of the oxen
Of Deivrdonwy the water-gifted.
The names of the three springs
From the midst of the ocean;
One generated brine
Which is from the Corina,
To replenish the flood
Over seas disappearing;
The second, without injury

ORACLES, SEERS & SAGES

It will fall on us,
When there is rain abroad,
Through the whelming sky;
The third will appear
Through the mountain veins,
Like a flinty banquet,
The work of the King of kings,
You are blundering bards,
In too much solicitude;
You cannot celebrate
The kingdom of the Britons;
And I am Taliesin,
Chief of the bards of the west,
Who will loosen Elphin
Out of the golden fetter."

* * *

"Be silent, then, ye unlucky rhyming bards,
For you cannot judge between truth and falsehood.
If you be primary bards formed by heaven,
Tell your king what his fate will be.
It is I who am a diviner and a leading bard,
And know every passage in the country of your king;
I shall liberate Elphin from the belly of the stony tower;
And will tell your king what will befall him.
A most strange creature will come from the sea marsh of Rhianedd
As a punishment of iniquity on Maelgwn Gwynedd;
His hair, his teeth, and his eyes being as gold,
And this will bring destruction upon Maelgwn Gwynedd."

* * *

"Discover thou what is
The strong creature from before the flood,
Without flesh, without bone,
Without vein, without blood,
Without head, without feet,
It will neither be older nor younger
Than at the beginning;
For fear of a denial,
There are no rude wants
With creatures.
Great God! how the sea whitens
When first it comes!
Great are its gusts
When it comes from the south;

Great are its evaporations
When it strikes on coasts.
It is in the field, it is in the wood,
Without hand, and without foot,
Without signs of old age,
Though it be co-æval
With the five ages or periods
And older still,
Though they be numberless years.
It is also so wide
As the surface of the earth;
And it was not born,
Nor was it seen.
It will cause consternation
Wherever God willeth.
On sea, and on land,
It neither sees, nor is seen.
Its course is devious,
And will not come when desired;
On land and on sea,
It is indispensable.
It is without an equal,
It is four-sided;
It is not confined,
It is incomparable;
It comes from four quarters;
It will not be advised,
It will not be without advice.
It commences its journey
Above the marble rock,
It is sonorous, it is dumb,
It is mild,
It is strong, it is bold,
When it glances over the land,
It is silent, it is vocal,
It is clamorous,
It is the most noisy
On the face of the earth.
It is good, it is bad,
It is extremely injurious.
It is concealed,
Because sight cannot perceive it.
It is noxious, it is beneficial;
It is yonder, it is here;
It will discompose,
But will not repair the injury;
It will not suffer for its doings,

Seeing it is blameless.
It is wet, it is dry,
It frequently comes,
Proceeding from the heat of the sun,
And the coldness of the moon.
The moon is less beneficial,
Inasmuch as her heat is less.
One Being has prepared it,
Out of all creatures,
By a tremendous blast,
To wreak vengeance
On Maelgwn Gwynedd."

And while he was thus singing his verse near the door, there arose a mighty storm of wind, so that the king and all his nobles thought that the castle would fall on their heads. And the king caused them to fetch Elphin in haste from his dungeon, and placed him before Taliesin. And it is said, that immediately he sang a verse, so that the chains opened from about his feet.

"I adore the Supreme, Lord of all animation, –
Him that supports the heavens, Ruler of every extreme,
Him that made the water good for all,
Him who has bestowed each gift, and blesses it; –
May abundance of mead be given Maelgwn of Anglesey, who supplies us,
From his foaming meadhorns, with the choicest pure liquor.
Since bees collect, and do not enjoy,
We have sparkling distilled mead, which is universally praised.
The multitude of creatures which the earth nourishes
God made for man, with a view to enrich him; –
Some are violent, some are mute, he enjoys them,
Some are wild, some are tame; the Lord makes them; –
Part of their produce becomes clothing;
For food and beverage till doom will they continue.
I entreat the Supreme, Sovereign of the region of peace,
To liberate Elphin from banishment,
The man who gave me wine, and ale, and mead,
With large princely steeds, of beautiful appearance;
May he yet give me; and at the end,
May God of his good will grant me, in honour,
A succession of numberless ages, in the retreat of tranquillity.
Elphin, knight of mead, late be thy dissolution!"

And afterwards he sang the ode which is called 'The Excellence of the Bards'.

"What was the first man
Made by the God of heaven;
What the fairest flattering speech

That was prepared by Ieuav;
What meat, what drink,
What roof his shelter;
What the first impression
Of his primary thinking;
What became his clothing;
Who carried on a disguise,
Owing to the wilds of the country,
In the beginning?
Wherefore should a stone be hard;
Why should a thorn be sharp-pointed?
Who is hard like a flint;
Who is salt like brine;
Who is sweet like honey;
Who rides on the gale;
Why ridged should be the nose;
Why should a wheel be round;
Why should the tongue be gifted with speech
Rather than another member?
If thy bards, Heinin, be competent,
Let them reply to me, Taliesin."

And after that he sang the address which is called 'The Reproof of the Bards.'

"If thou art a bard completely imbued
With genius not to be controlled,
Be thou not untractable
Within the court of thy king;
Until thy rigmarole shall be known,
Be thou silent, Heinin,
As to the name of thy verse,
And the name of thy vaunting;
And as to the name of thy grandsire
Prior to his being baptized.
And the name of the sphere,
And the name of the element,
And the name of thy language,
And the name of thy region.
Avaunt, ye bards above,
Avaunt, ye bards below!
My beloved is below,
In the fetter of Ariansod
It is certain you know not
How to understand the song I utter,
Nor clearly how to discriminate
Between the truth and what is false;
Puny bards, crows of the district,

Why do you not take to flight?
A bard that will not silence me,
Silence may he not obtain,
Till he goes to be covered
Under gravel and pebbles;
Such as shall listen to me,
May God listen to him."

Then sang he the piece called 'The Spite of the Bards.'

"Minstrels persevere in their false custom,
Immoral ditties are their delight;
Vain and tasteless praise they recite;
Falsehood at all times do they utter;
The innocent persons they ridicule;
Married women they destroy,
Innocent virgins of Mary they corrupt;
As they pass their lives away in vanity,
Poor innocent persons they ridicule;
At night they get drunk, they sleep the day;
In idleness without work they feed themselves;
The Church they hate, and the tavern they frequent;
With thieves and perjured fellows they associate;
At courts they inquire after feasts;
Every senseless word they bring forward;
Every deadly sin they praise;
Every vile course of life they lead;
Through every village, town, and country they stroll;
Concerning the gripe of death they think not;
Neither lodging nor charity do they give;
Indulging in victuals to excess.
Psalms or prayers they do not use,
Tithes or offerings to God they do not pay,
On holidays or Sundays they do not worship;
Vigils or festivals they do not heed.
The birds do fly, the fish do swim,
The bees collect honey, worms do crawl,
Every thing travails to obtain its food,
Except minstrels and lazy useless thieves.

I deride neither song nor minstrelsy,
For they are given by God to lighten thought;
But him who abuses them,
For blaspheming Jesus and his service."

Taliesin having set his master free from prison, and having protected the innocence
of his wife, and silenced the bards, so that not one of them dared to say a word, now

brought Elphin's wife before them, and showed that she had not one finger wanting. Right glad was Elphin, right glad was Taliesin.

Then he bade Elphin wager the king that he had a horse both better and swifter than the king's horses. And this Elphin did, and the day, and the time, and the place were fixed, and the place was that which at this day is called Morva Rhiannedd: and thither the king went with all his people, and four-and-twenty of the swiftest horses he possessed. And after a long process the course was marked, and the horses were placed for running. Then came Taliesin with four-and-twenty twigs of holly, which he had burnt black, and he caused the youth who was to ride his master's horse to place them in his belt, and he gave him orders to let all the king's horses get before him, and as he should overtake one horse after the other, to take one of the twigs and strike the horse with it over the crupper, and then let that twig fall; and after that to take another twig, and do in like manner to every one of the horses, as he should overtake them, enjoining the horseman strictly to watch when his own horse should stumble, and to throw down his cap on the spot. All these things did the youth fulfil, giving a blow to every one of the king's horses, and throwing down his cap on the spot where his horse stumbled. And to this spot Taliesin brought his master after his horse had won the race. And he caused Elphin to put workmen to dig a hole there; and when they had dug the ground deep enough, they found a large cauldron full of gold. And then said Taliesin, "Elphin, behold a payment and reward unto thee, for having taken me out of the weir, and for having reared me from that time until now." And on this spot stands a pool of water, which is to this time called Pwllbair.

After all this, the king caused Taliesin to be brought before him, and he asked him to recite concerning the creation of man from the beginning; and thereupon he made the poem which is now called 'One of the Four Pillars of Song'.

"The Almighty made,
Down the Hebron vale,
With his plastic hands,
Adam's fair form:

And five hundred years,
Void of any help,
There he remained and lay
Without a soul.

He again did form,
In calm paradise,
From a left-side rib,
Bliss-throbbing Eve.

Seven hours they were
The orchard keeping,
Till Satan brought strife,
With wiles from hell.

Thence were they driven,
Cold and shivering,

To gain their living,
Into this world.

To bring forth with pain
Their sons and daughters,
To have possession
Of Asia's land.

Twice five, ten and eight,
She was self-bearing,
The mixed burden
Of man-woman.

And once, not hidden,
She brought forth Abel,
And Cain the forlorn,
The homicide.

To him and his mate
Was given a spade,
To break up the soil,
Thus to get bread.

The wheat pure and white,
Summer tilth to sow,
Every man to feed,
Till great yule feast.

An angelic hand
From the high Father,
Brought seed for growing
That Eve might sow;

But she then did hide
Of the gift a tenth,
And all did not sow
Of what was dug.

Black rye then was found,
And not pure wheat grain,
To show the mischief
Thus of thieving.

For this thievish act,
It is requisite,
That all men should pay
Tithe unto God.

Of the ruddy wine,
Planted on sunny days,
And on new-moon nights;
And the white wine.

The wheat rich in grain
And red flowing wine
Christ's pure body make,
Son of Alpha.

The wafer is flesh,
The wine is spilt blood,
The Trinity's words
Sanctify them.

The concealed books
From Emmanuel's hand
Were brought by Raphael
As Adam's gift,

When in his old age,
To his chin immersed
In Jordan's water,
Keeping a fast,

Moses did obtain
In Jordan's water,
The aid of the three
Most special rods.

Solomon did obtain
In Babel's tower,
All the sciences
In Asia land.

So did I obtain,
In my bardic books,
All the sciences
Of Europe and Africa.

Their course, their bearing,
Their permitted way,
And their fate I know,
Unto the end.

Oh! what misery,
Through extreme of woe,

Prophecy will show
On Troia's race!

A coiling serpent
Proud and merciless,
On her golden wings,
From Germany.

She will overrun
England and Scotland,
From Lychlyn sea-shore
To the Severn.

Then will the Brython
Be as prisoners,
By strangers swayed,
From Saxony.

Their Lord they will praise,
Their speech they will keep,
Their land they will lose,
Except wild Walia.

Till some change shall come,
After long penance,
When equally rife
The two crimes come.

Britons then shall have
Their land and their crown,
And the stranger swarm
Shall disappear.

All the angels' words,
As to peace and war,
Will be fulfilled
To Britain's race."

He further told the king various prophecies of things that should be in the world, in songs...

The original manuscript breaks off at this point.

Footnotes for *The Tale of Taliesin*

1. 'Taliesin' means 'radiant brow'.
2. The mention of Gwyddno Garanhir instead of Elphin ab Gwyddno in this place is evidently an error of some transcriber of the MS.

The Curse of the Fires and of the Shadows

ONE SUMMER NIGHT, when there was peace, a score of Puritan troopers under the pious Sir Frederick Hamilton broke through the door of the Abbey of the White Friars which stood over the Gara Lough at Sligo. As the door fell with a crash they saw a little knot of friars, gathered about the altar, their white habits glimmering in the steady light of the holy candles. All the monks were kneeling except the abbot, who stood upon the altar steps with a great brazen crucifix in his hand. "Shoot them!" cried Sir Frederick Hamilton, but none stirred, for all were new converts, and feared the crucifix and the holy candles. The white lights from the altar threw the shadows of the troopers up on to roof and wall. As the troopers moved about, the shadows began a fantastic dance among the corbels and the memorial tablets. For a little while all was silent, and then five troopers who were the body-guard of Sir Frederick Hamilton lifted their muskets, and shot down five of the friars. The noise and the smoke drove away the mystery of the pale altar lights, and the other troopers took courage and began to strike. In a moment the friars lay about the altar steps, their white habits stained with blood. "Set fire to the house!" cried Sir Frederick Hamilton, and at his word one went out, and came in again carrying a heap of dry straw, and piled it against the western wall, and, having done this, fell back, for the fear of the crucifix and of the holy candles was still in his heart. Seeing this, the five troopers who were Sir Frederick Hamilton's body-guard darted forward, and taking each a holy candle set the straw in a blaze. The red tongues of fire rushed up and flickered from corbel to corbel and from tablet to tablet, and crept along the floor, setting in a blaze the seats and benches. The dance of the shadows passed away, and the dance of the fires began. The troopers fell back towards the door in the southern wall, and watched those yellow dancers springing hither and thither.

For a time the altar stood safe and apart in the midst of its white light; the eyes of the troopers turned upon it. The abbot whom they had thought dead had risen to his feet and now stood before it with the crucifix lifted in both hands high above his head. Suddenly he cried with a loud voice, "Woe unto all who smite those who dwell within the Light of the Lord, for they shall wander among the ungovernable shadows, and follow the ungovernable fires!" And having so cried he fell on his face dead, and the brazen crucifix rolled down the steps of the altar. The smoke had now grown very thick, so that it drove the troopers out into the open air. Before them were burning houses. Behind them shone the painted windows of the Abbey filled with saints and martyrs, awakened, as from a sacred trance, into an angry and animated life. The eyes of the troopers were dazzled, and for a while could see nothing but the flaming faces of saints and martyrs. Presently, however, they saw a man covered with dust who came running towards them. "Two messengers," he cried, "have been sent by the defeated Irish to raise against you the whole country about Manor Hamilton, and if you do not

ORACLES, SEERS & SAGES

stop them you will be overpowered in the woods before you reach home again! They ride northeast between Ben Bulben and Cashel-na-Gael."

Sir Frederick Hamilton called to him the five troopers who had first fired upon the monks and said, "Mount quickly, and ride through the woods towards the mountain, and get before these men, and kill them."

In a moment the troopers were gone, and before many moments they had splashed across the river at what is now called Buckley's Ford, and plunged into the woods. They followed a beaten track that wound along the northern bank of the river. The boughs of the birch and quicken trees mingled above, and hid the cloudy moonlight, leaving the pathway in almost complete darkness. They rode at a rapid trot, now chatting together, now watching some stray weasel or rabbit scuttling away in the darkness. Gradually, as the gloom and silence of the woods oppressed them, they drew closer together, and began to talk rapidly; they were old comrades and knew each other's lives. One was married, and told how glad his wife would be to see him return safe from this harebrained expedition against the White Friars, and to hear how fortune had made amends for rashness. The oldest of the five, whose wife was dead, spoke of a flagon of wine which awaited him upon an upper shelf; while a third, who was the youngest, had a sweetheart watching for his return, and he rode a little way before the others, not talking at all. Suddenly the young man stopped, and they saw that his horse was trembling. "I saw something," he said, "and yet I do not know but it may have been one of the shadows. It looked like a great worm with a silver crown upon his head." One of the five put his hand up to his forehead as if about to cross himself, but remembering that he had changed his religion he put it down, and said: "I am certain it was but a shadow, for there are a great many about us, and of very strange kinds." Then they rode on in silence. It had been raining in the earlier part of the day, and the drops fell from the branches, wetting their hair and their shoulders. In a little they began to talk again. They had been in many battles against many a rebel together, and now told each other over again the story of their wounds, and so awakened in their hearts the strongest of all fellowships, the fellowship of the sword, and half forgot the terrible solitude of the woods.

Suddenly the first two horses neighed, and then stood still, and would go no further. Before them was a glint of water, and they knew by the rushing sound that it was a river. They dismounted, and after much tugging and coaxing brought the horses to the river-side. In the midst of the water stood a tall old woman with grey hair flowing over a grey dress. She stood up to her knees in the water, and stooped from time to time as though washing. Presently they could see that she was washing something that half floated. The moon cast a flickering light upon it, and they saw that it was the dead body of a man, and, while they were looking at it, an eddy of the river turned the face towards them, and each of the five troopers recognized at the same moment his own face. While they stood dumb and motionless with horror, the woman began to speak, saying slowly and loudly: "Did you see my son? He has a crown of silver on his head, and there are rubies in the crown." Then the oldest of the troopers, he who had been most often wounded, drew his sword and cried: "I have fought for the truth of my God, and need not fear the shadows of Satan," and with that rushed into the water. In a moment he returned. The woman had vanished, and though he had thrust his sword into air and water he had found nothing.

The five troopers remounted, and set their horses at the ford, but all to no purpose. They tried again and again, and went plunging hither and thither, the horses foaming and rearing. "Let us," said the old trooper, "ride back a little into the wood, and strike the river higher up." They rode in under the boughs, the ground-ivy crackling under the hoofs, and the branches striking against their steel caps. After about twenty minutes' riding they came out again upon the river, and after another ten minutes found a place where it was possible to cross without sinking below the stirrups. The wood upon the other side was very thin, and broke the moonlight into long streams. The wind had arisen, and had begun to drive the clouds rapidly across the face of the moon, so that thin streams of light seemed to be dancing a grotesque dance among the scattered bushes and small fir-trees. The tops of the trees began also to moan, and the sound of it was like the voice of the dead in the wind; and the troopers remembered the belief that tells how the dead in purgatory are spitted upon the points of the trees and upon the points of the rocks. They turned a little to the south, in the hope that they might strike the beaten path again, but they could find no trace of it.

Meanwhile, the moaning grew louder and louder, and the dance of the white moon-fires more and more rapid. Gradually they began to be aware of a sound of distant music. It was the sound of a bagpipe, and they rode towards it with great joy. It came from the bottom of a deep, cup-like hollow. In the midst of the hollow was an old man with a red cap and withered face. He sat beside a fire of sticks, and had a burning torch thrust into the earth at his feet, and played an old bagpipe furiously. His red hair dripped over his face like the iron rust upon a rock. "Did you see my wife?" he cried, looking up a moment; "she was washing! she was washing!" "I am afraid of him," said the young trooper, "I fear he is one of the Sidhe." "No," said the old trooper, "he is a man, for I can see the sun-freckles upon his face. We will compel him to be our guide"; and at that he drew his sword, and the others did the same. They stood in a ring round the piper, and pointed their swords at him, and the old trooper then told him that they must kill two rebels, who had taken the road between Ben Bulben and the great mountain spur that is called Cashel-na-Gael, and that he must get up before one of them and be their guide, for they had lost their way. The piper turned, and pointed to a neighbouring tree, and they saw an old white horse ready bitted, bridled, and saddled. He slung the pipe across his back, and, taking the torch in his hand, got upon the horse, and started off before them, as hard as he could go.

The wood grew thinner and thinner, and the ground began to slope up toward the mountain. The moon had already set, and the little white flames of the stars had come out everywhere. The ground sloped more and more until at last they rode far above the woods upon the wide top of the mountain. The woods lay spread out mile after mile below, and away to the south shot up the red glare of the burning town. But before and above them were the little white flames. The guide drew rein suddenly, and pointing upwards with the hand that did not hold the torch, shrieked out, "Look; look at the holy candles!" and then plunged forward at a gallop, waving the torch hither and thither. "Do you hear the hoofs of the messengers?" cried the guide. "Quick, quick! or they will be gone out of your hands!" and he laughed as with delight of the chase. The troopers thought they could hear far off, and as if below them, rattle of hoofs; but now the ground began to slope more and more, and the speed grew more headlong moment by moment. They tried to pull up, but in vain, for the horses seemed to have gone mad. The guide had thrown the reins on to the neck of the old white horse, and was waving his arms and singing a wild Gaelic song. Suddenly they saw the thin gleam of a river, at an immense distance below, and knew that they were upon the brink of the abyss that is now called Lug-na-Gael, or in English the Stranger's Leap. The six horses sprang forward, and five screams went up into the air, a moment later five men and horses fell with a dull crash upon the green slopes at the foot of the rocks.

Clairvoyant Visions & Dreams

Introduction

BENTEN IS JAPAN'S Shinto goddess of everything that flows, so water – obviously – but also poetry and music. It's appropriate, then, that it's at her temple, beside a spring marked Tanjo-Sui ('Birth-Water') that a young poet falls in love with the woman whose fair hand he knows must have written the lines exquisitely written on the scrap of paper the wind blows across his path. In the dreamlike world of myth it's an inevitability that he meets her and marries and lives with her for happy years which themselves have the character of a dream. One day, while walking through an unfamiliar part of town, he's summoned to a house whose patriarch tells him he fits the description of the man who – it's been revealed to him by Benten in yet another vision – will be husband to his young daughter. The young man is about to make his excuses when he realizes that his appointed bride is the wife he's long since been living with – this one is flesh-and-blood, though: he must have been living with his own wife's ghost. In myth, the dimensions of dream and waking life can coexist, interpenetrate and inform each other; an imaginative realm in which we may immerse ourselves.

Balder and the Mistletoe

LOKI HAD GIVEN UP trying to revenge himself upon Thor. The Thunder Lord seemed proof against his tricks. And indeed nowadays Loki hated him no more than he did the other gods. He hated some because they always frowned at him; he hated others because they only laughed and jeered. Some he hated for their distrust and some for their fear. But he hated them all because they were happy and good and mighty, while he was wretched, bad, and of little might. Yet it was all his own fault that this was so. He might have been an equal with the best of them, if he had not chosen to set himself against everything that was good. He had made them all his enemies, and the more he did to injure them, the more he hated them, – which is always the way with evil-doers. Loki longed to see them all unhappy. He slunk about in Asgard with a glum face and wrinkled forehead. He dared not meet the eyes of anyone, lest they should read his heart. For he was plotting evil, the greatest of evils, which should bring sorrow to all his enemies at once and turn Asgard into a land of mourning. The Aesir did not guess the whole truth, yet they felt the bitterness of the thoughts which Loki bore; and whenever in the dark he passed unseen, the gods shuddered as if a breath of evil had blown upon them, and even the flowers drooped before his steps.

Now at this time Balder the beautiful had a strange dream. He dreamed that a cloud came before the sun, and all Asgard was dark. He waited for the cloud to drift away, and for the sun to smile again. But no; the sun was gone forever, he thought; and Balder awoke feeling very sad. The next night Balder had another dream. This time he dreamed that it was still dark as before; the flowers were withered and the gods were growing old; even Idun's magic apples could not make them young again. And all were weeping and wringing their hands as though some dreadful thing had happened. Balder awoke feeling strangely frightened, yet he said no word to Nanna his wife, for he did not want to trouble her.

When it came night again Balder slept and dreamed a third dream, a still more terrible one than the other two had been. He thought that in the dark, lonely world there was nothing but a sad voice, which cried, "The sun is gone! The spring is gone! Joy is gone! For Balder the beautiful is dead, dead, dead!"

This time Balder awoke with a cry, and Nanna asked him what was the matter. So he had to tell her of his dream, and he was sadly frightened; for in those days dreams were often sent to folk as messages, and what the gods dreamed usually came true. Nanna ran sobbing to Queen Frigga, who was Balder's mother, and told her all the dreadful dream, asking what could be done to prevent it from coming true.

Now Balder was Queen Frigga's dearest son. Thor was older and stronger, and more famous for his great deeds; but Frigga loved far better gold-haired Balder. And indeed he was the best-beloved of all the Aesir; for he was gentle, fair, and wise, and wherever he went folk grew happy and light-hearted at the very sight of him, just as we do when we first catch a glimpse of spring peeping over the hilltop into Winterland. So when Frigga heard of Balder's woeful dream, she was frightened almost out of her wits.

"He must not die! He shall not die!" she cried. "He is so dear to all the world, how could there be anything which would hurt him?"

And then a wonderful thought came to Frigga. "I will travel over the world and make all things promise not to injure my boy," she said. "Nothing shall pass my notice. I will get the word of everything."

So first she went to the gods themselves, gathered on Ida Plain for their morning exercise; and telling them of Balder's dream, she begged them to give the promise. Oh, what a shout arose when they heard her words!

"Hurt Balder! – Our Balder! Not for the world, we promise! The dream is wrong, – there is nothing so cruel as to wish harm to Balder the beautiful!" they cried. But deep in their hearts they felt a secret fear which would linger until they should hear that all things had given their promise. What if harm were indeed to come to Balder. The thought was too dreadful.

Then Frigga went to see all the beasts who live in field or forest or rocky den. Willingly they gave their promise never to harm hair of gentle Balder. "For he is ever kind to us," they said, "and we love him as if he were one of ourselves. Not with claws or teeth or hoofs or horns will any beast hurt Balder."

Next Frigga spoke to the birds and fishes, reptiles and insects. And all – even the venomous serpents – cried that Balder was their friend, and that they would never do aught to hurt his dear body. "Not with beak or talon, bite or sting or poison fang, will one of us hurt Balder," they promised.

After doing this, the anxious mother travelled over the whole round world, step by step; and from all the things that are she got the same ready promise never to harm Balder the beautiful. All the trees and plants promised; all the stones and metals; earth, air, fire, and water; sun, snow, wind, and rain, and all diseases that men know, – each gave to Frigga the word of promise which she wanted. So at last, footsore and weary, she came back to Asgard with the joyful news that Balder must be safe, for that there was nothing in the world but had promised to be his harmless friend.

Then there was rejoicing in Asgard, as if the gods had won one of their great victories over the giants. The noble Aesir and the heroes who had died in battle upon the earth, and who had come to Valhalla to live happily ever after, gathered on Ida Plain to celebrate the love of all nature for Balder.

There they invented a famous game, which was to prove how safe he was from the bite of death. They stationed Balder in the midst of them, his face glowing like the sun with the bright light which ever shone from him. And as he stood there all unarmed and smiling, by turns they tried all sorts of weapons against him; they made as if to beat him with sticks, they stoned him with stones, they shot at him with arrows and hurled mighty spears straight at his heart.

It was a merry game, and a shout of laughter went up as each stone fell harmless at Balder's feet, each stick broke before it touched his shoulders, each arrow overshot his head, and each spear turned aside. For neither stone nor wood nor flinty arrow-point nor barb of iron would break the promise which each had given. Balder was safe with them, just as if he were bewitched. He remained unhurt among the missiles which whizzed about his head, and which piled up in a great heap around the charmed spot whereon he stood.

Now among the crowd that watched these games with such enthusiasm, there was one face that did not smile, one voice that did not rasp itself hoarse with cheering. Loki saw how everyone and everything loved Balder, and he was jealous. He was the only creature in all the world that hated Balder and wished for his death. Yet Balder had never done harm to him. But the wicked plan that Loki had been cherishing was almost ripe, and in this poison fruit was the seed of the greatest sorrow that Asgard had ever known.

CLAIRVOYANT VISIONS & DREAMS

While the others were enjoying their game of love, Loki stole away unperceived from Ida Plain, and with a wig of grey hair, a long gown, and a staff, disguised himself as an old woman. Then he hobbled down Asgard streets till he came to the palace of Queen Frigga, the mother of Balder.

"Good day, my lady," quoth the old woman, in a cracked voice. "What is that noisy crowd doing yonder in the green meadow? I am so deafened by their shouts that I can hardly hear myself think."

"Who are you, good mother, that you have not heard?" said Queen Frigga in surprise. "They are shooting at my son Balder. They are proving the word which all things have given me, – the promise not to injure my dear son. And that promise will be kept."

The old crone pretended to be full of wonder. "So, now!" she cried. "Do you mean to say that *every single thing* in the whole world has promised not to hurt your son? I can scarce believe it; though, to be sure, he is as fine a fellow as I ever saw." Of course this flattery pleased Frigga.

"You say true, mother," she answered proudly, "he is a noble son. Yes, everything has promised, – that is, everything except one tiny little plant that is not worth mentioning."

The old woman's eyes twinkled wickedly. "And what is that foolish little plant, my dear?" she asked coaxingly.

"It is the mistletoe that grows in the meadow west of Valhalla. It was too young to promise, and too harmless to bother with," answered Frigga carelessly.

After this her questioner hobbled painfully away. But as soon as she was out of sight from the Queen's palace, she picked up the skirts of her gown and ran as fast as she could to the meadow west of Valhalla. And there sure enough, as Frigga had said, was a tiny sprig of mistletoe growing on a gnarled oak-tree. The false Loki took out a knife which she carried in some hidden pocket and cut off the mistletoe very carefully. Then she trimmed and shaped it so that it was like a little green arrow, pointed at one end, but very slender.

"Ho, ho!" chuckled the old woman. "So you are the only thing in all the world that is too young to make a promise, my little mistletoe. Well, young as you are, you must go on an errand for me today. And maybe you shall bear a message of my love to Balder the beautiful."

Then she hobbled back to Ida Plain, where the merry game was still going on around Balder. Loki quietly passed unnoticed through the crowd, and came close to the elbow of a big dark fellow who was standing lonely outside the circle of weapon-throwers. He seemed sad and forgotten, and he hung his head in a pitiful way. It was Hodur, the blind brother of Balder.

The old woman touched his arm. "Why do you not join the game with the others?" she asked, in her cracked voice. "Are you the only one to do your brother no honour? Surely, you are big and strong enough to toss a spear with the best of them yonder."

Hodur touched his sightless eyes madly. "I am blind," he said. "Strength I have, greater than belongs to most of the Aesir. But I cannot see to aim a weapon. Besides, I have no spear to test upon him. Yet how gladly would I do honour to dear Balder!" and he sighed deeply.

"It were a pity if I could not find you at least a little stick to throw," said Loki sympathetically. "I am only a poor old woman, and of course I have no weapon. But ah, – here is a green twig which you can use as an arrow, and I will guide your arm, poor fellow."

Hodur's dark face lighted up, for he was eager to take his turn in the game. So he thanked her, and grasped eagerly the little arrow which she put into his hand. Loki held him by the arm, and together they stepped into the circle which surrounded Balder. And when it was Hodur's turn to throw his weapon, the old woman stood at his elbow and guided his big arm as it hurled the twig of mistletoe towards where Balder stood.

325

Oh, the sad thing that befell! Straight through the air flew the little arrow, straight as magic and Loki's arm could direct it. Straight to Balder's heart it sped, piercing through jerkin and shirt and all, to give its bitter message of "Loki's love," as he had said. With a cry Balder fell forward on the grass. And that was the end of sunshine and spring and joy in Asgard, for the dream had come true, and Balder the beautiful was dead.

When the Aesir saw what had happened, there was a great shout of fear and horror, and they rushed upon Hodur, who had thrown the fatal arrow.

"What is it? What have I done?" asked the poor blind brother, trembling at the tumult which had followed his shot.

"You have slain Balder!" cried the Aesir. "Wretched Hodur, how could you do it?"

"It was the old woman – the evil old woman, who stood at my elbow and gave me a little twig to throw," gasped Hodur. "She must be a witch."

Then the Aesir scattered over Ida Plain to look for the old woman who had done the evil deed; but she had mysteriously disappeared.

"It must be Loki," said wise Heimdall. "It is Loki's last and vilest trick."

"Oh, my Balder, my beautiful Balder!" wailed Queen Frigga, throwing herself on the body of her son. "If I had only made the mistletoe give me the promise, you would have been saved. It was I who told Loki of the mistletoe, – so it is I who have killed you. Oh, my son, my son!"

But Father Odin was speechless with grief. His sorrow was greater than that of all the others, for he best understood the dreadful misfortune which had befallen Asgard. Already a cloud had come before the sun, so that it would never be bright day again. Already the flowers had begun to fade and the birds had ceased to sing. And already the Aesir had begun to grow old and joyless, – all because the little mistletoe had been too young to give a promise to Queen Frigga.

"Balder the beautiful is dead!" the cry went echoing through all the world, and everything that was sorrowed at the sound of the Aesir's weeping.

Balder's brothers lifted up his beautiful body upon their great war shields and bore him on their shoulders down to the seashore. For, as was the custom in those days, they were going to send him to Hel, the Queen of Death, with all the things he best had loved in Asgard. And these were, – after Nanna his wife, – his beautiful horse, and his ship Hringhorni. So that they would place Balder's body upon the ship with his horse beside him, and set fire to this wonderful funeral pyre. For by fire was the quickest passage to Hel's kingdom.

But when they reached the shore, they found that all the strength of all the Aesir was unable to move Hringhorni, Balder's ship, into the water. For it was the largest ship in the world, and it was stranded far up the beach.

"Even the giants bore no ill-will to Balder," said Father Odin. "I heard the thunder of their grief but now shaking the hills. Let us for this once bury our hatred of that race and send to Jotunheim for help to move the ship."

So they sent a messenger to the giantess Hyrrockin, the hugest of all the frost people. She was weeping for Balder when the message came.

"I will go, for Balder's sake," she said. Soon she came riding fast upon a giant wolf, with a serpent for the bridle; and mighty she was, with the strength of forty Aesir. She dismounted from her wolf-steed, and tossed the wriggling reins to one of the men-heroes who had followed Balder and the Aesir from Valhalla. But he could not hold the beast, and it took four heroes to keep him quiet, which they could only do by throwing him upon the ground and sitting upon him in a row. And this mortified them greatly.

Then Hyrrockin the giantess strode up to the great ship and seized it by the prow. Easily she gave a little pull and presto! it leaped forward on its rollers with such force that sparks flew from the flint stones underneath and the whole earth trembled. The boat shot into the waves and out toward open sea so swiftly that the Aesir were likely to have lost it entirely, had not Hyrrockin waded out up to her waist and caught it by the stern just in time.

Thor was angry at her clumsiness, and raised his hammer to punish her. But the other Aesir held his arm.

"She cannot help being so strong," they whispered. "She meant to do well. She did not realize how hard she was pulling. This is no time for anger, brother Thor." So Thor spared her life, as indeed he ought, for her kindness.

Then Balder's body was borne out to the ship and laid upon a pile of beautiful silks, and furs, and cloth-of-gold, and woven sunbeams which the dwarfs had wrought. So that his funeral pyre was more grand than anything which had ever been seen. But when Nanna, Balder's gentle wife, saw them ready to kindle the flames under this gorgeous bed, she could bear her grief no longer. Her loving heart broke, and they laid her beside him, that they might comfort each other on their journey to Hel. Thor touched the pile gently with his hammer that makes the lightning, and the flames burst forth, lighting up the faces of Balder and Nanna with a glory. Then they cast upon the fire Balder's war-horse, to serve his master in the dark country to which he was about to go. The horse was decked with a harness all of gold, with jewels studding the bridle and headstall. Last of all Odin laid upon the pyre his gift to Balder, Draupnir, the precious ring of gold which the dwarf had made, from which every ninth night there dropped eight other rings as large and brightly golden.

"Take this with you, dear son, to Hel's palace," said Odin. "And do not forget the friends you leave behind in the now lonely halls of Asgard."

Then Hyrrockin pushed the great boat out to sea, with its bonfire of precious things. And on the beach stood all the Aesir watching it out of sight, all the Aesir and many besides. For there came to Balder's funeral great crowds of little dwarfs and multitudes of huge frost giants, all mourning for Balder the beautiful. For this one time they were all friends together, forgetting their quarrels of so many centuries. All of them loved Balder, and were united to do him honour.

The great ship moved slowly out to sea, sending up a red fire to colour all the heavens. At last it slid below the horizon softly, as you have often seen the sun set upon the water, leaving a brightness behind to lighten the dark world for a little while.

This indeed was the sunset for Asgard. The darkness of sorrow came in earnest after the passing of Balder the beautiful.

But the punishment of Loki was a terrible thing. And that came soon and sore.

Ryangombe and Binego

RYANGOMBE'S FATHER WAS BABINGA, described as the 'king of the ghosts (*imandwa*)'; his mother, originally called Kalimulore, was an uncomfortable sort of person, who had the power of turning herself into a lioness, and took to killing her father's cattle, till he forbade her to herd them, and sent someone else in her place. She so frightened her first husband that he took her home to her parents and would have no more to do with her. After her second marriage, to Babinga, there seems to have been no further trouble.

When Babinga died, his son, Ryangombe, announced that he was going to take his father's place. This was disputed by one of Babinga's followers named Mpumutimuchuni, and the two agreed to decide the question by a game of *kisoro*, which Ryangombe lost.

Ryangombe passed some time in exile. He went out hunting, and heard a prophecy from some herd-lads which led to his marriage. After some difficulties with his parents in-law he settled down with his wife, and had a son, Binego, but soon left them and returned to his own home.

As soon as Binego was old enough, his mother's brother set him to herd the cattle; he speared a heifer the first day, a cow and her calf the next, and when his uncle objected he speared him too. He then called his mother, and they set out for Ryangombe's place, which they reached in due course, Binego having, on the way, killed two men who refused to leave their work and guide him, and a baby, for no particular reason.

When he arrived, he found his father playing the final game with Mpumutimuchuni. The decision had been allowed to stand over during the interval, and Ryangombe, if he lost this game, was not only to hand over the kingdom, but to let his opponent shave his head – that is, deprive him of the crest of hair which marked his royal rank. Binego went and stood behind his father to watch the game, suggested a move which enabled him to win, and when Mpumutimuchuni protested, stabbed him. Thus he secured his father in the kingship, which, apparently, was so far counted to him for righteousness as to outweigh all the murders he had committed. Ryangombe named him, first as his second-in-command and afterwards as his successor, and Binego, as will be seen, avenged his death. Like all the *imandwa*, with the exception of Ryangombe himself, who is uniformly kind and beneficent, Binego is mischievous and cruel.

Ryangombe's Death

The story of his death is as follows.

Ryangombe one day went hunting, accompanied by his sons, Kagoro and Ruhanga, two of his sisters, and several other *imandwa*. His mother tried to dissuade him from going, as during the previous night she had had four strange dreams, which seemed to her prophetic of evil. She had seen, first, a small beast without a tail; then an animal all of one colour; thirdly, a stream running two ways at once; and, fourthly, an immature girl carrying a baby without a *ngobe* (the skin in which an African woman carries a baby on her back; the Zulus call it *imbeleko*). She was very uneasy about these dreams, and begged her son to stay at home, but, unlike most Africans, who attach great importance to such things, he paid no attention to her words, and set out. Before he had gone very far he killed a hare, which, when examined, was found to have no tail. His personal attendant at once exclaimed that this was the fulfilment of Nyiraryangombe's dream, but Ryangombe only said, "Don't repeat a woman's words while we are after game."

Soon after this they encountered the second and third portents (the "animal all of one colour" was a black hyena), but Ryangombe still refused to be impressed. Then they met a young girl carrying a baby, without the usual skin in which it is supported. She stopped Ryangombe and asked him to give her a *ngobe*. He offered her the skin of one animal after another; but she refused them all, till he produced a buffalo hide. Then she said she must have it properly dressed, which he did, and also gave her the thongs to tie it with.

Thereupon she said, "Take up the child." He objected, but gave in when she repeated her demand, and even, at her request, gave the infant a name. Finally, weary of her importunity, he said, "Leave me alone!" and the girl rushed away, was lost to sight among the bushes, and became a buffalo. Ryangombe's dogs, scenting the beast, gave chase, one after the other, and when they did not return he sent his man, Nyarwambali, to see what had become of them. Nyarwambali came back and reported: "There is a beast here which has killed the dogs." Ryangombe followed him, found the buffalo, speared it, and thought he had killed it, but just as he was shouting his song of triumph it sprang up, charged, and gored him. He staggered back and leaned against a tree; the buffalo changed into a woman, picked up the child, and went away.

At the very moment when he fell, a bloodstained leaf dropped out of the air on his mother's breast. She knew then that her dream had in fact been a warning of disaster; but it was not till a night and a day had passed that she heard what had happened. Ryangombe, as soon as he knew he had got his death-wound, called all the *imandwa* together, and told first one and, on his refusal, another to go and call his mother and Binego. One after another all refused, except the maidservant, Nkonzo, who set off at once, travelling night and day, till she came to Nyiraryangombe's house and gave her the news. She came at once with Binego, and found her son still living. Binego, when he had heard the whole story, asked his father in which direction the buffalo had gone; having had it pointed out, he rushed off, overtook the woman, brought her back, and killed her, with the child, cutting both in pieces. So he avenged his father.

Ryangombe then gave directions for the honours to be paid him after his death; these are, so to speak, the charter of the Kubandwa society which practises the cult of the *imandwa*. He specially insisted that Nkonzo, as a reward for her services, should have a place in these rites. Then at the moment when his throat tightened, he named Binego as his successor, and so died.

Berossus's Account of the Deluge

MORE IMPORTANT is his account of the deluge. There is more than one Babylonian version of the deluge: that which is to be found in the *Gilgamesh Epic*, and Berossus's account. As the latter is quite as important, we shall give it in his own words:

"After the death of Ardates, his son (Sisuthrus) succeeded and reigned eighteen sari. In his time happened the great deluge; the history of which is given in this manner. The Deity, Cronus, appeared to him in a vision; and gave him notice, that upon the fifteenth day of the month Daesius there would be a flood, by which mankind would be destroyed. He therefore enjoined him to commit to writing a history of the beginning, procedure and final conclusion of all things, down to the present term; and to bury these accounts securely in the City of the Sun at Sippara. He then ordered Sisuthrus to build a vessel, and to take with him into it his friends and relations; and trust himself to the deep. The latter implicitly obeyed: and having conveyed on board everything necessary to sustain life, he took in also all species of animals, that either fly, or rove upon the surface of the earth. Having asked the Deity where he was to go, he was answered, To the gods: upon which he offered up a prayer for the good of mankind. Thus he obeyed the divine admonition: and the vessel, which he built, was five stadia in length, and in breadth two. Into this he put everything which he had got ready; and last of all conveyed into it his wife, children and friends.

"After the flood had been upon the earth, and was in time abated, Sisuthrus sent out some birds from the vessel; which not finding any food, nor any place to rest their feet, returned to him again. After an interval of some days; he sent them forth a second time: and they now returned with their feet tinged with mud. He made trial a third time with these birds: but they returned to him no more: from whence he formed a judgement, that the surface of the earth was now above the waters. Having therefore made an opening in the vessel, and finding upon looking out, that the vessel was driven to the side of a mountain, he immediately quitted it, being attended with his wife, children and the pilot. Sisuthrus immediately paid his adoration to the earth: and having constructed an altar, offered sacrifices to the gods. These things being duly performed, both Sisuthrus, and those who came out of the vessel with him, disappeared. They, who remained in the vessel, finding that the others did not return, came out with many lamentations and called continually on the name of Sisuthrus. Him they saw no more; but they could distinguish his voice in the air, and could hear him admonish them to pay due regard to the gods; and likewise inform them, that it was upon account of his piety that he was translated to live with the gods; that his wife and children, with the pilot, had obtained the same honour. To this he added, that he would have them make the best of their way to Babylonia, and search for the writings at Sippara, which were to be made known to all mankind. The place where these things happened was in Armenia. The remainder having heard these words, offered sacrifices to the gods; and, taking a circuit, journeyed towards Babylonia."

Berossus adds that the remains of the vessel were to be seen in his time upon one of the Corcyrean mountains in Armenia; and that people used to scrape off the bitumen, with which it had been outwardly coated, and made use of it by way of an antidote for poison or amulet. In this manner they returned to Babylon; and having found the writings at Sippara, they set about building cities and erecting temples; and Babylon was thus inhabited again.

Nebuchadnezzar

BUT STRANGELY ENOUGH the older seat of power, Babylon, still flourished to some extent. By superhuman exertions, Nebuchadnezzar II (or Nebuchadrezzar), who reigned for forty-three years, sent the standard of Babylonia far and wide through the known world. In 567 BCE he invaded Egypt. In one of his campaigns he marched against Jerusalem and put its king, Jehoiakim, to death, but the king whom the Babylonian monarch set up in his place was deposed and the royal power vested in Zedekiah. Zedekiah revolted in 558 BCE and once more Jerusalem was taken and destroyed, the principal inhabitants were carried captive to Babylon, and the city was reduced to a condition of insignificance.

CLAIRVOYANT VISIONS & DREAMS

This, the first exile of the Jews, lasted for seventy years. The story of this captivity and of Nebuchadnezzar's treatment of the Jewish exiles is graphically told in the Book of Daniel, whom the Babylonians called Belteshazzar. Daniel refused to eat the meat of the Babylonians, probably because it was not prepared according to Jewish rite. He and his companions ate pulses and drank water, and fared upon it better than the Babylonians on strong meats and wines. The King, hearing of this circumstance, sent for them and found them much better informed than all his magicians and astrologers. Nebuchadnezzar dreamed dreams, and informed the Babylonian astrologers that if they were unable to interpret them they would be cut to pieces and their houses destroyed, whereas did they interpret the visions they would be held in high esteem. They answered that if the King would tell them his dream they would show the interpretation thereof; but the King said that if they were wise men in truth they would know the dream without requiring to be told it, and upon some of the astrologers of the court replying that the request was unreasonable, he was greatly incensed and ordered all of them to be slain. But in a vision of the night the secret was revealed to Daniel, who begged that the wise men of Babylon be not destroyed, and going to a court official he offered to interpret the dream. He told the King that in his dream he had beheld a great image, whose brightness and form were terrible. The head of this image was of fine gold, the breast and arms of silver, and the other parts of brass, excepting the legs which were of iron, and the feet which were partly of that metal and partly of clay. But a stone was cast at it which smote the image upon its feet and it brake into pieces and the wind swept away the remnants. The stone that had smitten it became a great mountain and filled the whole earth.

Then Daniel proceeded to the interpretation. The King, he said, represented the golden head of the image; the silver an inferior kingdom which would rise after Nebuchadnezzar's death; and a third of brass which should bear rule over all the earth. The fourth dynasty from Nebuchadnezzar would be as strong as iron, but since the toes of the image's feet were partly of iron and partly of clay, so should that kingdom be partly strong and partly broken. Nebuchadnezzar was so awed with the interpretation that he fell upon his face and worshipped Daniel, telling him how greatly he honoured the God who could have revealed such secrets to him; and he set him as ruler over the whole province of Babylon, and made him chief of the governors over all the wise men of that kingdom.

But Daniel's three companions – Shadrach, Meshach and Abednego – refused to worship a golden image which the King had set up, and he commanded that they should be cast into a fiery furnace, through which they passed unharmed.

This circumstance still more turned the heart of Nebuchadnezzar in the direction of the God of Israel. A second dream which he had, he begged Daniel to interpret. He said he had seen a tree in the midst of the earth of more than natural height, which flourished and was exceedingly strong, so that it reached to heaven. So abundant was the fruit of this tree that it provided meat for the whole earth, and so ample its foliage that the beasts of the field had shadow under it, and the fowl of the air dwelt in its midst. A spirit descended from heaven and called aloud, demanding that the tree should be cut down and its leaves and fruit scattered, but that its roots should be left in the earth surrounded by a band of iron and brass. Then, ordering that the tree should be treated as if it were a man, the voice of the spirit continued to ask that it should be wet with the dew of heaven, and that its portion should be with the beasts in the grass of the earth. "Let his heart be changed from a man's," said the voice, "and let a beast's heart be given him; and let seven times pass over him."

Then was Daniel greatly troubled. He kept silence for a space until the King begged him to take heart and speak. The tree, he announced, represented Nebuchadnezzar himself, and what had happened to it in the vision would come to pass regarding the great King of Babylon. He would be driven from among men and his dwelling would be with the beasts of the field. He would be made to eat grass as oxen and be wet with the dew of heaven, and seven times would pass over him, till he knew and recognized that the Most High ruled in the kingdom of man and gave it to whomsoever he desired.

Twelve months after this Nebuchadnezzar was in the midst of his palace at Babylon, boasting of what he had accomplished during his reign, when a voice from heaven spoke, saying: "O King Nebuchadnezzar, to thee it is spoken, the kingdom is departed from thee", and straightway was Nebuchadnezzar driven from man and he did eat grass as an ox and his body was wet with the dew of heaven, till his hair was grown like eagle's feathers and his nails like bird's claws.

At the termination of his time of trial Nebuchadnezzar lifted his eyes to heaven, and praising the Most High admitted his domination over the whole earth. Thus was the punishment of the boaster completed.

It has been stated with some show of probability that the judgement upon Nebuchadnezzar was connected with that weird disease known as lycanthropy, from the Greek words *lukos*, a wolf, and *anthropos*, a man. It develops as a kind of hysteria and is characterized by a belief on the part of the victim that he has become an animal. There are, too, cravings for strange food, and the afflicted person runs about on all fours. Among primitive peoples such a seizure is ascribed to supernatural agency, and garlic or onion – the common scourge of vampires – is held to the nostrils.

Iosco, or The Prairie Boys' Visit to the Sun and the Moon

ONE PLEASANT MORNING, five young men and a boy about ten years of age, called Ioscoda, went out a shooting with their bows and arrows. They left their lodges with the first appearance of daylight, and having passed through a long reach of woods, had ascended a lofty eminence before the sun arose. While standing there in a group, the sun suddenly burst forth in all its effulgence. The air was so clear that it appeared to be at no great distance. "How very near it is," they all said. "It cannot be far," said the eldest, "and if you will accompany me, we will see if we cannot reach it." A loud assent burst from every lip. Even the boy, Ioscoda, said he would go. They told him he was too young; but he replied, "If you do not permit me to go with you, I will mention your design to each of your parents." They then said to him, "You shall also go with us, so be quiet."

They then fell upon the following arrangement. It was resolved that each one should obtain from his parents as many pairs of moccasins as he could, and also new clothing of leather. They fixed on a spot where they would conceal all their articles, until they were ready

CLAIRVOYANT VISIONS & DREAMS

to start on their journey, and which would serve, in the mean time, as a place of rendezvous, where they might secretly meet and consult. This being arranged, they returned home.

A long time passed before they could put their plan into execution. But they kept it a profound secret, even to the boy. They frequently met at the appointed place, and discussed the subject. At length everything was in readiness, and they decided on a day to set out. That morning the boy shed tears for a pair of new leather leggings. "Don't you see," said he to his parents, "how my companions are dressed?" This appeal to their pride and envy prevailed. He obtained the leggings. Artifices were also resorted to by the others, under the plea of going out on a special hunt. They said to one another, but in a tone that they might be overheard, "We will see who will bring in the most game." They went out in different directions, but soon met at the appointed place, where they had hid the articles for their journey, with as many arrows as they had time to make. Each one took something on his back, and they began their march. They travelled day after day, through a thick forest, but the sun was always at the same distance. "We must," said they, "travel toward Waubunong, and we shall get to the object, some time or other." No one was discouraged, although winter overtook them. They built a lodge and hunted, till they obtained as much dried meat as they could carry, and then continued on. This they did several times; season followed season. More than one winter overtook them. Yet none of them became discouraged, or expressed dissatisfaction.

One day the travellers came to the banks of a river, whose waters ran toward Waubunong. They followed it down many days. As they were walking, one day, they came to rising grounds, from which they saw something white or clear through the trees. They encamped on this elevation. Next morning they came, suddenly, in view of an immense body of water. No land could be seen as far as the eye could reach. One or two of them lay down on the beach to drink. As soon as they got the water in their mouths, they spat it out, and exclaimed, with surprise, "Shewetagon awbo!" [salt water.] It was the sea. While looking on the water, the sun arose as if from the deep, and went on its steady course through the heavens, enlivening the scene with his cheering and animating beams. They stood in fixed admiration, but the object appeared to be as distant from them as ever. They thought it best to encamp, and consult whether it were advisable to go on, or return. "We see," said the leader, "that the sun is still on the opposite side of this great water, but let us not be disheartened. We can walk around the shore." To this they all assented.

Next morning they took the northerly shore, to walk around it, but had only gone a short distance when they came to a large river. They again encamped, and while sitting before the fire, the question was put, whether any one of them had ever dreamed of water, or of walking on it. After a long silence, the eldest said he had. Soon after they lay down to sleep. When they arose the following morning, the eldest addressed them: "We have done wrong in coming north. Last night my spirit appeared to me, and told me to go south, and that but a short distance beyond the spot we left yesterday, we should come to a river with high banks. That by looking off its mouth, we should see an island, which would approach to us. He directed that we should all get on it. He then told me to cast my eyes toward the water. I did so, and I saw all he had declared. He then informed me that we must return south, and wait at the river until the day after tomorrow. I believe all that was revealed to me in this dream, and that we shall do well to follow it."

The party immediately retraced their footsteps in exact obedience to these intimations. Toward the evening they came to the borders of the indicated river. It had high banks, behind which they encamped, and here they patiently awaited the fulfilment of the dream. The appointed day arrived. They said, "We will see if that which has been said will be seen."

Midday is the promised time. Early in the morning two had gone to the shore to keep a look-out. They waited anxiously for the middle of the day, straining their eyes to see if they could discover anything. Suddenly they raised a shout. "Ewaddee suh neen! There it is! There it is!" On rushing to the spot they beheld something like an island steadily advancing toward the shore. As it approached, they could discover that something was moving on it in various directions. They said, "It is a Manito, let us be off into the woods." "No, no," cried the eldest, "let us stay and watch." It now became stationary, and lost much of its imagined height. They could only see three trees, as they thought, resembling trees in a pinery that had been burnt. The wind, which had been off the sea, now died away into a perfect calm. They saw something leaving the fancied island and approaching the shore, throwing and flapping its wings, like a loon when he attempts to fly in calm weather. It entered the mouth of the river. They were on the point of running away, but the eldest dissuaded them. "Let us hide in this hollow," he said, "and we will see what it can be." They did so. They soon heard the sounds of chopping, and quickly after they heard the falling of trees. Suddenly a man came up to the place of their concealment. He stood still and gazed at them. They did the same in utter amazement. After looking at them for some time, the person advanced and extended his hand towards them. The eldest took it, and they shook hands. He then spoke, but they could not understand each other. He then cried out for his comrades. They came, and examined very minutely their dresses. They again tried to converse. Finding it impossible, the strangers then motioned to the Naubequon, and to the Naubequonais, wishing them to embark. They consulted with each other for a short time. The eldest then motioned that they should go on board. They embarked on board the boat, which they found to be loaded with wood. When they reached the side of the supposed island, they were surprised to see a great number of people, who all came to the side and looked at them with open mouths. One spoke out, above the others, and appeared to be the leader. He motioned them to get on board. He looked at and examined them, and took them down into the cabin, and set things before them to eat. He treated them very kindly.

When they came on deck again, all the sails were spread, and they were fast losing sight of land. In the course of the night and the following day they were sick at the stomach, but soon recovered. When they had been out at sea ten days, they became sorrowful, as they could not converse with those who had hats on.

The following night Ioscoda dreamed that his spirit appeared to him. He told him not to be discouraged, that he would open his ears, so as to be able to understand the people with hats. I will not permit you to understand much, said he, only sufficient to reveal your wants, and to know what is said to you. He repeated this dream to his friends, and they were satisfied and encouraged by it. When they had been out about thirty days, the master of the ship told them, and motioned them to change their dresses of leather, for such as his people wore; for if they did not, his master would be displeased. It was on this occasion that the elder first understood a few words of the language. The first phrase he comprehended was *La que notte*, and from one word to another he was soon able to speak it.

One day the men cried out, "Land!" and soon after they heard a noise resembling thunder, in repeated peals. When they had got over their fears, they were shown the large guns which made this noise. Soon after they saw a vessel smaller than their own, sailing out of a bay, in the direction towards them. She had flags on her masts, and when she came near she fired a gun. The large vessel also hoisted her flags, and the boat came alongside. The master told the person who came in it, to tell his master or king, that he had six strangers on board, such as had never been seen before, and that they were coming to visit him. It was some time after the departure of this messenger before the vessel got up to the town. It was then dark, but they could see people, and horses and odawbons ashore. They were landed and placed in a covered vehicle, and driven off. When they stopped, they were taken into a large and splendid room. They were here told that the great chief wished to see them. They were shown into another large room, filled with men and women. All the room was Shoneancauda. The chief asked them their business, and the object of their journey. They told him where they were from, and where they were going, and the nature of the enterprise which they had undertaken. He tried to dissuade them from its execution, telling them of the many trials and difficulties they would have to undergo; that so many days' march from his country dwelt a bad spirit, or Manito, who foreknew and foretold the existence and arrival of all who entered into his country. It is impossible, he said, my children, for you ever to arrive at the object you are in search of.

Ioscoda replied: "Nosa," and they could see the chief blush in being called father, "we have come so far on our way, and we will continue it; we have resolved firmly that we will do so. We think our lives are of no value, for we have given them up for this object. Nosa," he repeated, "do not then prevent us from going on our journey." The chief then dismissed them with valuable presents, after having appointed the next day to speak to them again, and provided everything that they needed or wished for.

Next day they were again summoned to appear before the king. He again tried to dissuade them. He said he would send them back to their country in one of his vessels: but all he said had no effect. "Well," said he, "if you will go, I will furnish you all that is needed for your journey." He had everything provided accordingly. He told them, that three days before they reached the Bad Spirit he had warned them of, they would hear his Shéshegwun. He cautioned them to be wise, for he felt that he should never see them all again.

They resumed their journey, and travelled sometimes through villages, but they soon left them behind and passed over a region of forests and plains, without inhabitants. They found all the productions of a new country: trees, animals, birds, were entirely different from those they were accustomed to, on the other side of the great waters. They travelled, and travelled, till they wore out all of the clothing that had been given to them, and had to take to their leather clothing again.

The three days the chief spoke of meant three years, for it was only at the end of the third year that they came within the sight of the spirit's shéshegwun. The sound appeared to be near, but they continued walking on, day after day, without apparently getting any nearer to it. Suddenly they came to a very extensive plain; they could see the blue ridges of distant mountains rising on the horizon beyond it; they pushed on, thinking to get over the plain before night, but they were overtaken by darkness; they were now on a stony part of the plain, covered by about a foot's depth of water; they were weary and fatigued; some of them said, let us lie down; no, no, said the others, let us push on. Soon they stood on firm ground, but it was as much as they could do to stand, for they were very weary. They, however, made an effort to encamp, lighted up a fire, and refreshed themselves by eating. They then commenced conversing about the sound of the spirit's shéshegwun, which they had heard for several days. Suddenly the instrument commenced; it sounded as if it was subterraneous, and it shook the ground: they tied up their bundles and went towards the spot.

They soon came to a large building, which was illuminated. As soon as they came to the door, they were met by a rather elderly man. "How do ye do," said he, "my grandsons? Walk in, walk in; I am glad to see you: I knew when you started: I saw you encamp this evening: sit down, and tell me the news of the country you left, for I feel interested in it." They complied with his wishes, and when they had concluded, each one presented him with a piece of tobacco. He then revealed to them things that would happen in their journey, and predicted its successful accomplishment. "I do not say that all of you," said he, "will successfully go through it. You have passed over three-fourths of your way, and I will tell you how to proceed after you get to the edge of the earth. Soon after you leave this place, you will hear a deafening sound: it is the sky descending on the edge, but it keeps moving up and down; you will watch, and when it moves up, you will see a vacant space between it and the earth. You must not be afraid. A chasm of awful depth is there, which separates the unknown from this earth, and a veil of darkness conceals it. Fear not. You must leap through; and if you succeed, you will find yourselves on a beautiful plain, and in a soft and mild light emitted by the moon." They thanked him for his advice. A pause ensued.

"I have told you the way," he said; "now tell me again of the country you have left; for I committed dreadful ravages while I was there: does not the country show marks of it? and do not the inhabitants tell of me to their children? I came to this place to mourn over my bad actions, and am trying, by my present course of life, to relieve my mind of the load that is on it." They told him that their fathers spoke often of a celebrated personage called Manabozho, who performed great exploits. "I am he," said the spirit. They gazed with astonishment and fear. "Do you see this pointed house?" said he, pointing to one that resembled a sugar-loaf; "you can now each speak your wishes, and will be answered from that house. Speak out, and ask what each wants, and it shall be granted." One of them, who was vain, asked with presumption that he might live forever, and never be in want. He was answered, "Your wish shall be granted." The second made the same request, and received the same answer. The third asked to live longer than common people, and to be always successful in his war excursions, never losing any of his young men. He was told, "Your wishes are granted." The fourth joined in the same request, and received the same reply. The fifth made an humble request, asking to live as long as men generally do, and that he might be crowned with such success in hunting as to be able to provide for his parents and relatives. The sixth made the same request, and it was granted to both, in pleasing tones, from the pointed house.

After hearing these responses they prepared to depart. They were told by Manabozho that they had been with him but one day, but they afterwards found that they had remained there upward of a year. When they were on the point of setting out, Manabozho exclaimed, "Stop! You two, who asked me for eternal life, will receive the boon you wish immediately." He spake, and one was turned into a stone called Shin-gauba-wossin, and the other into a cedar tree. "Now," said he to the others, "you can go." They left him in fear, saying, "We were fortunate to escape so, for the king told us he was wicked, and that we should not probably escape from him." They had not proceeded far, when they began to hear the sound of the beating sky. It appeared to be near at hand, but they had a long interval to travel before they came near, and the sound was then stunning to their senses; for when the sky came down, its pressure would force gusts of wind from the opening, so strong that it was with difficulty they could keep their feet, and the sun passed but a short distance above their heads. They however approached boldly, but had to wait sometime before they could muster courage enough to leap through the dark veil that covered the passage. The sky would come down with violence, but it would rise slowly and gradually. The two who had made the humble request, stood near the edge, and with no little exertion succeeded, one after the other, in leaping through, and gaining a firm foothold. The remaining two were fearful and undecided: the others spoke to them through the darkness, saying, "Leap! leap! The sky is on its way down." These two looked up and saw it descending, but fear paralyzed their efforts; they made but a feeble attempt, so as to reach the opposite side with their hands; but the sky at the same time struck on the earth with great violence and a terrible sound, and forced them into the dreadful black chasm.

The two successful adventurers, of whom Iosco now was chief, found themselves in a beautiful country, lighted by the moon, which shed around a mild and pleasant light. They could see the moon approaching as if it were from behind a hill. They advanced, and an aged woman spoke to them; she had a white face and pleasing air, and looked rather old, though she spoke to them very kindly: they knew from her first appearance that she was the moon: she asked them several questions: she told them that she knew of their coming, and was happy to see them: she informed them that they were half way to her brother's, and that from the earth to her abode was half the distance. "I will, by and by, have leisure," said she, "and will go and conduct you to my brother, for he is now absent on his daily course: you will succeed in your object, and return in safety to your country and friends, with the good wishes, I am sure, of my brother." While the travellers were with her, they received every attention. When the proper time arrived, she said to them, "My brother is now rising from below, and we shall see his light as he comes over the distant edge: come," said she, "I will lead you up." They went forward, but in some mysterious way, they hardly knew how: they rose almost directly up, as if they had ascended steps. They then came upon an immense plain, declining in the direction of the sun's approach. When he came near, the moon spake – "I have brought you these persons, whom we knew were coming;" and with this she disappeared. The sun motioned with his hand for them to follow him. They did so, but found it rather difficult, as the way was steep: they found it particularly so from the edge of the earth till they got halfway between that point and midday: when they reached this spot, the sun stopped, and sat down to rest. "What, my children," said he, "has brought you here? I could not speak to you before: I could not stop at any place but this, for this is my first resting-place – then at the centre, which is at midday, and then halfway from that to the western edge. Tell me," he continued, "the object of your undertaking this journey and all the circumstances which have happened to you on the way." They complied, Iosco told him their main object was to see him. They had lost four of their friends on the way, and they wished to know whether they could return in safety to the earth, that they might inform their friends and relatives of all that had befallen them. They concluded by requesting him to grant their wishes. He replied, "Yes, you shall certainly return in safety; but your companions were vain and presumptuous in their demands. They were Gug-ge-baw-diz-ze-wug. They aspired to what Manitoes only could enjoy. But you two, as I said, shall get back to your country, and become as happy as the hunter's life can make you. You shall never be in want of the necessaries of life, as long as you are permitted to live; and you will have the satisfaction of relating your journey to your friends, and also of telling them of me. Follow me, follow me," he said, commencing his course again. The ascent was now gradual, and they soon came to a level plain. After travelling some time he again sat down to rest, for they had arrived at Nau-we-qua. "You see," said he, "it is level at this place, but a short distance onwards, my way descends gradually to my last resting-place, from which there is an abrupt descent." He repeated his assurance that they should be shielded from danger, if they relied firmly on his power. "Come here quickly," he said, placing something before them on which they could descend; "keep firm," said he, as they resumed the descent. They went downward as if they had been let down by ropes.

In the mean time the parents of these two young men dreamed that their sons were returning, and that they should soon see them. They placed the fullest confidence in their dreams. Early in the morning they left their lodges for a remote point in the forest, where they expected to meet them. They were not long at the place before they saw the adventurers returning, for they had descended not far from that place. The young men knew they were their fathers. They met, and were happy. They related all that had befallen them. They did not conceal anything; and they expressed their gratitude to the different Manitoes who had preserved them, by feasting and gifts, and particularly to the sun and moon, who had received them as their children.

The Undying Head

IN A REMOTE PART OF THE NORTH lived a man and his only sister who had never seen another human being. Seldom, if ever, had the man any cause to go from home, for if he wanted food he had only to go a little distance from the lodge, and there place his arrows with their barbs in the ground. He would then return to the lodge and tell his sister where the arrows had been placed, when she would go in search of them, and never fail to find each struck through the heart of a deer. These she dragged to the lodge and dressed for food. Thus she lived until she attained womanhood. One day her brother, who was named Iamo, said to her:

"Sister, the time is near when you will be ill. Listen to my advice, for if you do not it will probably be the cause of my death. Take the implements with which we kindle our fires, go some distance from our lodge and build a separate fire. When you are in want of food I will tell you where to find it. You must cook for yourself and I for myself. When you are ill do not attempt to come near the lodge or bring to it any of the utensils you use. Be sure to always have fastened to your belt whatever you will need in your sickness, for you do not know when the time of your indisposition will come. As for myself, I must do the best I can." His sister promised to obey him in all he said.

Shortly after her brother had cause to go from home. His sister was alone in the lodge combing her hair, and she had just untied and laid aside the belt to which the implements were fastened when suddenly she felt unwell. She ran out of the lodge, but in her haste forgot the belt. Afraid to return she stood some time thinking, and finally she determined to return to the lodge and get it, for she said to herself:

"My brother is not at home, and I will stay but a moment to catch hold of it."

She went back, and, running in, suddenly seized the belt, and was coming out, when her brother met her. He knew what had happened.

"Did I not tell you," said he, "to take care? Now you have killed me."

His sister would have gone away, but he spoke to her again.

CLAIRVOYANT VISIONS & DREAMS

"What can you do now? What I feared has happened. Go in, and stay where you have always lived. You have killed me."

He then laid aside his hunting dress and accoutrements, and soon after both his feet began to inflame and turn black, so that he could not move. He directed his sister where to place his arrows, so that she might always have food. The inflammation continued to increase, and had now reached his first rib.

"Sister," said he, "my end is near. You must do as I tell you. You see my medicine-sack and my war-club tied to it. It contains all my medicines, my war-plumes, and my paints of all colours. As soon as the inflammation reaches my chest, you will take my war-club, and with the sharp point of it cut off my head. When it is free from my body, take it, place its neck in the sack, which you must open at one end. Then hang it up in its former place. Do not forget my bow and arrows. One of the last you will take to procure food. Tie the others to my sack, and then hang it up so that I can look towards the door. Now and then I will speak to you, but not often."

His sister again promised to obey.

In a little time his chest became affected.

"Now," cried he, "take the club and strike off my head."

His sister was afraid, but he told her to muster up courage.

"Strike," said he, with a smile upon his face.

Calling up all her courage, his sister struck and cut off the head.

"Now," said the head, "place me where I told you."

Fearful, she obeyed it in all its commands.

Retaining its animation, it looked round the lodge as usual, and it would command its sister to go to such places where it thought she could best procure the flesh of the different animals she needed. One day the head said:

"The time is not distant when I shall be freed from this situation, but I shall have to undergo many sore evils. So the Superior Manito decrees, and I must bear all patiently."

In a certain part of the country was a village inhabited by a numerous and warlike band of Indians. In this village was a family of ten young men, brothers. In the spring of the year the youngest of these blackened his face and fasted. His dreams were propitious, and having ended his fast, he sent secretly for his brothers at night, so that the people in the village should not be aware of their meeting. He told them how favourable his dreams had been, and that he had called them together to ask them if they would accompany him in a war excursion. They all answered they would. The third son, noted for his oddities, swinging his war-club when his brother had ceased speaking, jumped up: "Yes," said he, "I will go, and this will be the way I will treat those we go to fight with." With those words he struck the post in the centre of the lodge, and gave a yell. The other brothers spoke to him, saying:

"Gently, gently, Mudjikewis, when you are in other people's lodges." So he sat down. Then, in turn, they took the drum, sang their songs, and closed the meeting with a feast. The youngest told them not to whisper their intention to their wives, but to prepare secretly for their journey. They all promised obedience, and Mudjikewis was the first to do so.

The time for departure drew near. The youngest gave the word for them to assemble on a certain night, when they would commence their journey. Mudjikewis was loud in his demands for his moccasins, and his wife several times demanded the reason of his impatience.

"Besides," said she, "you have a good pair on."

"Quick, quick," replied Mudjikewis; "since you must know, we are going on a war excursion."

Thus he revealed the secret.

That night they met and started. The snow was on the ground, and they travelled all night lest others should follow them. When it was daylight, the leader took snow, made a ball of it, and tossing it up in the air, said:

"It was in this way I saw snow fall in my dream, so that we could not be tracked."

Immediately snow began to fall in large flakes, so that the leader commanded the brothers to keep close together for fear of losing one another. Close as they walked together it was with difficulty they could see one another. The snow continued falling all that day and the next night, so that it was impossible for anyone to follow their track.

They walked for several days, and Mudjikewis was always in the rear. One day, running suddenly forward, he gave the saw-saw-quan (war cry), and struck a tree with his war-club, breaking the tree in pieces as if it had been struck by lightning.

"Brothers," said he, "this is the way I will serve those we are going to fight."

The leader answered:

"Slowly, slowly, Mudjikewis. The one I lead you to is not to be thought of so lightly."

Again Mudjikewis fell back and thought to himself, "What, what! Who can this be he is leading us to?"

He felt fearful, and was silent. Day after day they travelled on till they came to an extensive plain, on the borders of which human bones were bleaching in the sun. The leader said:

"These are the bones of those who have gone before us. None has ever yet returned to tell the sad tale of their fate."

Again Mudjikewis became restless, and, running forward, gave the accustomed yell. Advancing to a large rock which stood above the ground he struck it, and it fell to pieces.

"See, brothers," said he, "thus will I treat those we are going to fight."

"Be quiet," said the leader. "He to whom I am leading you is not to be compared to that rock."

Mudjikewis fell back quite thoughtful, saying to himself, "I wonder who this can be that he is going to attack;" and he was afraid.

They continued to see the remains of former warriors who had been to the place to which they were now going, and had retreated thus far back again. At last they came to a piece of rising ground, from which they plainly saw on a distant mountain an enormous bear. The distance between them was very great, but the size of the animal caused it to be seen very clearly.

"There," said the leader; "it is to him I am leading you. Here our troubles will only commence, for he is a mishemokwa" (a she-bear, or a male-bear as ferocious as a she-bear) "and a manito. It is he who has what we prize so dearly, to obtain which the warriors whose bones we saw sacrificed their lives. You must not be fearful. Be manly; we shall find him asleep."

The warriors advanced boldly till they came near to the bear, when they stopped to look at it more closely. It was asleep, and there was a belt around its neck.

"This," said the leader, touching the belt, "is what we must get. It contains what we want."

The eldest brother then tried to slip the belt over the bear's head, the animal appearing to be fast asleep, and not at all disturbed by his efforts. He could not, however, remove the belt, nor was any of the brothers more successful till the one next to the youngest tried in his turn. He slipped the belt nearly over the beast's head, but could not get it quite off. Then the youngest laid his hands on it, and with a pull succeeded. Placing the belt on the eldest brother's back, he said:

"Now we must run," and they started off at their best pace. When one became tired with the weight of the belt another carried it. Thus they ran till they had passed the bones of all the warriors, and when they were some distance beyond, looking back, they saw the monster slowly rising. For some time it stood still, not missing the belt. Then they heard a tremendous howl, like distant thunder, slowly filling the sky. At last they heard the bear cry:

"Who can it be that has dared to steal my belt? Earth is not so large but I can find them," and it descended the hill in pursuit. With every jump of the bear the earth shook as if it were convulsed. Very soon it approached the party. They, however, kept the belt, exchanging it from one to another, and encouraging each other. The bear, however, gained on them fast.

"Brothers," said the leader, "have none of you, when fasting, ever dreamed of some friendly spirit who would aid you as a guardian?"

A dead silence followed.

"Well," continued he, "once when I was fasting I dreamed of being in danger of instant death, when I saw a small lodge, with smoke curling up from its top. An old man lived in it, and I dreamed that he helped me, and may my dream be verified soon."

Having said this, he ran forward and gave a yell and howl. They came upon a piece of rising ground, and, behold! a lodge with smoke curling from its top appeared before them. This gave them all new strength, and they ran forward and entered the lodge. In it they found an old man, to whom the leader said:

"Nemesho (my grandfather), help us. We ask your protection, for the great bear would kill us."

"Sit down and eat, my grandchildren," said the old man. "Who is a great manito? There is none but me; but let me look;" and he opened the door of the lodge, and saw at a little distance the enraged bear coming on with slow but great leaps. The old man closed the door.

"Yes," said he; "he is indeed a great manito. My grandchildren, you will be the cause of my losing my life. You asked my protection, and I granted it; so now, come what may, I will protect you. When the bear arrives at the door you must run out at the other end of the lodge."

Putting his hand to the side of the lodge where he sat, he took down a bag, and, opening it, took out of it two small black dogs, which he placed before him.

"These are the ones I use when I fight," said he, and he commenced patting with both hands the sides of one of the dogs, which at once commenced to swell out until it filled the lodge, and it had great strong teeth. When the dog had attained its full size it growled, and, springing out at the door, met the bear, which, in another leap, would have reached the lodge. A terrible combat ensued. The sky rang with the howls of the monsters. In a little while the second dog took the field. At the commencement of the battle the brothers, acting on the advice of the old man, escaped through the opposite side of the lodge. They had not proceeded far in their flight before they heard the death-cry of one of the dogs, and soon after that of the other.

"Well," said the leader, "the old man will soon share their fate, so run, run! The bear will soon be after us."

The brothers started with fresh vigour, for the old man had refreshed them with food; but the bear very soon came in sight again, and was evidently fast gaining upon them. Again the leader asked the warriors if they knew of any way in which to save themselves. All were silent. Running forward with a yell and a howl, the leader said:

"I dreamed once that, being in great trouble, an old man, who was a manito, helped me. We shall soon see his lodge."

Taking courage, the brothers still went on, and, after going a short distance, they saw a lodge. Entering it, they found an old man, whose protection they claimed, saying that a manito was pursuing them.

"Eat," said the old man, putting meat before them. "Who is a manito? There is no manito but me. There is none whom I fear."

Then he felt the earth tremble as the bear approached, and, opening the door of the lodge, he saw it coming. The old man shut the door slowly, and said:

"Yes, my grandchildren, you have brought trouble upon me."

Taking his medicine sack, he took out some small war-clubs of black stone, and told the young men to run through the other side of the lodge. As he handled the clubs they became an enormous size, and the old man stepped out as the bear reached the door. He struck the beast with one of his clubs, which broke in pieces, and the bear stumbled. The old man struck it again with the other club, and that also broke, but the bear fell insensible. Each blow the old man struck sounded like a clap of thunder, and the howls of the bear ran along the skies.

The brothers had gone some distance before they looked back. They then saw that the bear was recovering from the blows. First it moved its paws, and then they saw it rise to its feet. The old man shared the fate of the first, for the warriors heard his cries as he was torn in pieces. Again the monster was in pursuit, and fast overtaking them. Not yet discouraged, the young men kept on their way, but the bear was so close to them that the leader once more applied to his brothers, but they could do nothing.

"Well," said he, "my dreams will soon be exhausted. After this I have but one more."

He advanced, invoking his guardian spirit to aid him.

"Once," said he, "I dreamed that, being sorely pressed, I came to a large lake, on the shore of which was a canoe, partly out of water, and having ten paddles all in readiness. Do not fear," he cried, "we shall soon get to it."

It happened as he had said. Coming to the lake, the warriors found the canoe with the ten paddles, and immediately took their places in it. Putting off, they paddled to the centre of the lake, when they saw the bear on the shore. Lifting itself on its hind-legs, it looked all around. Then it waded into the water until, losing its footing, it turned back, and commenced making the circuit of the lake. Meanwhile the warriors remained stationary in the centre watching the animal's movements. It travelled round till it came to the place whence it started. Then it commenced drinking up the water, and the young men saw a strong current fast setting in towards the bear's mouth. The leader encouraged them to paddle hard for the opposite shore. This they had nearly reached, when the current became too strong for them, and they were drawn back by it, and the stream carried them onwards to the bear.

Then the leader again spoke, telling his comrades to meet their fate bravely.

"Now is the time, Mudjikewis," said he, "to show your prowess. Take courage, and sit in the bow of the canoe, and, when it approaches the bear's mouth, try what effect your club will have on the beast's head."

Mudjikewis obeyed, and, taking his place, stood ready to give the blow, while the leader, who steered, directed the canoe to the open mouth of the monster.

Rapidly advancing, the canoe was just about to enter the bear's mouth, when Mudjikewis struck the beast a tremendous blow on the head, and gave the saw-saw-quan. The bear's limbs doubled under it, and it fell stunned by the blow, but before Mudjikewis could strike again the monster sent from its mouth all the water it had swallowed with such force that the canoe was immediately carried by the stream to the other side of the lake. Leaving the canoe, the brothers fled, and on they went till they were completely exhausted. Again they felt the earth shake, and, looking back, saw the monster hard after them. The young men's spirits drooped, and they felt faint-hearted. With words and actions the leader exerted himself to cheer them, and once more he asked them if they could do nothing, or think of nothing, that might save them. All were silent as before.

"Then," said he, "this is the last time I can apply to my guardian spirit. If we do not now succeed, our fate is decided."

He ran forward, invoking his spirit with great earnestness, and gave the yell.

"We shall soon arrive," said he to his brothers, "at the place where my last guardian spirit dwells. In him I place great confidence. Do not be afraid, or your limbs will be fear-bound. We shall soon reach his lodge. Run, run!"

What had in the meantime passed in the lodge of Iamo? He had remained in the same condition, his head in the sack, directing his sister where to place the arrows to procure food, and speaking at long intervals.

One day the girl saw the eyes of the head brighten as if with pleasure. At last it spoke.

"O sister!" it said, "in what a pitiful situation you have been the cause of placing me! Soon, very soon, a band of young men will arrive and apply to me for aid; but alas! how can I give what I would with so much pleasure have afforded them? Nevertheless, take two arrows, and place them where you have been in the habit of placing the others, and have meat cooked and prepared before they arrive. When you hear them coming, and calling on my name, go out and say, 'Alas! it is long ago since an accident befell him. I was the cause of it.' If they still come near, ask them in, and set meat before them. Follow my directions strictly. A bear will come. Go out and meet him, taking my medicine sack, bow and arrows, and my head. You must then untie the sack, and spread out before you my paints of all colours, my war eagle-feathers, my tufts of dried hair, and whatsoever else the sack contains. As the bear approaches take these articles, one by one, and say to him, 'This is my dead brother's paint,' and so on with all the articles, throwing each of them as far from you as you can. The virtue contained in the things will cause him to totter. Then, to complete his destruction, you must take my head and cast it as far off as you can, crying aloud, 'See, this is my dead brother's head!' He will then fall senseless. While this is taking place the young men will have eaten, and you must call them to your aid. You will, with their assistance, cut the carcass of the bear into pieces – into small pieces – and scatter them to the winds, for unless you do this he will again come to life."

The sister promised that all should be done as he commanded, and she had only time to prepare the meal when the voice of the leader of the band of warriors was heard calling on Iamo for aid. The girl went out and did as she had been directed. She invited the brothers in and placed meat before them, and while they were eating the bear was heard approaching. Untying the medicine sack and taking the head the girl made all ready for its approach. When it came up she did as her brother directed, and before she had cast down all the paints the bear began to totter, but, still advancing, came close to her. Then she took the head and cast it from her as far as she could, and as it rolled upon the ground the bear, tottering, fell with a tremendous noise. The girl cried for help, and the young men rushed out.

Mudjikewis, stepping up, gave a yell, and struck the bear a blow on the head. This he repeated till he had dashed out its brains. Then the others, as quickly as possible, cut the monster up into very small pieces and scattered them in all directions. As they were engaged in this they were surprised to find that wherever the flesh was thrown small black bears appeared, such as are seen at the present day, which, starting up, ran away. Thus from this monster the present race of bears derives its origin.

Having overcome their pursuer the brothers returned to the lodge, and the girl gathered together the articles she had used, and placed the head in the sack again. The head remained silent, probably from its being fatigued with its exertion in overcoming the bear.

Having spent so much time, and having traversed so vast a country in their flight, the young men gave up the idea of ever returning to their own country, and game being plentiful about the lodge, they determined to remain where they were. One day they moved off some distance from the lodge for the purpose of hunting, and left the belt with the girl. They were very successful, and amused themselves with talking and jesting. One of them said:

"We have all this sport to ourselves. Let us go and ask our sister if she will not let us bring the head to this place, for it is still alive."

So they went and asked for the head. The girl told them to take it, and they carried it to their hunting-grounds and tried to amuse it, but only at times did they see its eyes beam with pleasure. One day, while they were busy in their encampment, they were unexpectedly attacked by unknown enemies. The fight was long and fierce. Many of the foes were slain, but there were thirty of them to each warrior. The young men fought desperately till they were all killed, and then the attacking party retreated to a high place to muster their men and count the missing and the slain. One of the men had strayed away, and happened to come to where the head was hung up. Seeing that it was alive he eyed it for some time with fear and surprise. Then he took it down, and having opened the sack he was much pleased to see the beautiful feathers, one of which he placed on his head.

It waved gracefully over him as he walked to his companions' camp, and when he came there he threw down the head and sack and told his friends how he had found them, and how the sack was full of paints and feathers. The men all took the head and made sport of it. Many of the young men took the paint and painted themselves with it; and one of the band, taking the head by the hair, said:

"Look, you ugly thing, and see your paints on the faces of warriors."

The feathers were so beautiful that many of the young men placed them on their heads, and they again subjected the head to all kinds of indignity. They were, however, soon punished for their insulting conduct, for all who had worn the feathers became sick and died. Then the chief commanded the men to throw all the paints and feathers away.

"As for the head," he said, "we will keep that and take it home with us; we will there see what we can do with it. We will try to make it shut its eyes."

Meanwhile for several days the sister had been waiting for the brothers to bring back the head; till at last, getting impatient, she went in search of them. She found them lying within short distances of one another, dead, and covered with wounds. Other bodies lay scattered around. She searched for the head and sack, but they were nowhere to be found, so she raised her voice and wept, and blackened her face. Then she walked in different directions till she came to the place whence the head had been taken, and there she found the bow and arrows, which had been left behind. She searched further, hoping to find her brother's head, and, when she came to a piece of rising ground she found some of his paints and feathers. These she carefully put by, hanging them to the branch of a tree.

At dusk she came to the first lodge of a large village. Here she used a charm employed by Indians when they wish to meet with a kind reception, and on applying to the old man and the woman who occupied the lodge she was made welcome by them. She told them her errand, and the old man, promising to help her, told her that the head was hung up before the council fire, and that the chiefs and young men of the village kept watch over it continually. The girl said she only desired to see the head, and would be satisfied if she could only get to the door of the lodge in which it was hung, for she knew she could not take it by force.

"Come with me," said the old man, "I will take you there."

So they went and took their seats in the lodge near to the door. The council lodge was filled with warriors amusing themselves with games, and constantly keeping up the fire to smoke the head to dry it. As the girl entered the lodge the men saw the features of the head move, and, not knowing what to make of it, one spoke and said:

"Ha! ha! it is beginning to feel the effects of the smoke."

The sister looked up from the seat by the door; her eyes met those of her brother, and tears began to roll down the cheeks of the head.

"Well," said the chief, "I thought we would make you do something at last. Look! look at it shedding tears," said he to those around him, and they all laughed and made jokes upon it. The chief, looking around, observed the strange girl, and after some time said to the old man who brought her in:

"Who have you got there? I have never seen that woman before in our village."

"Yes," replied the old man, "you have seen her. She is a relation of mine, and seldom goes out. She stays in my lodge, and she asked me to bring her here."

In the centre of the lodge sat one of those young men who are always forward, and fond of boasting and displaying themselves before others.

"Why," said he, "I have seen her often, and it is to his lodge I go almost every night to court her."

All the others laughed and continued their games. The young man did not know he was telling a lie to the girl's advantage, who by means of it escaped.

She returned to the old man's lodge, and immediately set out for her own country. Coming to the spot where the bodies of her adopted brothers lay, she placed them together with their feet towards the east. Then taking an axe she had she cast it up into the air, crying out:

"Brothers, get up from under it or it will fall on you!"

This she repeated three times, and the third time all the brothers rose and stood on their feet. Mudjikewis commenced rubbing his eyes and stretching himself.

"Why," said he, "I have overslept myself."

"No, indeed," said one of the others. "Do you not know we were all killed, and that it is our sister who has brought us to life?"

The brothers then took the bodies of their enemies and burned them. Soon after the girl went to a far country, they knew not where, to procure wives for them, and she returned with the women, whom she gave to the young men, beginning with the eldest. Mudjikewis stepped to and fro, uneasy lest he should not get the one he liked, but he was not disappointed, for she fell to his lot; and the two were well matched, for she was a female magician.

345

The young men and their wives all moved into a very large lodge, and their sister told them that one of the women must go in turns every night to try and recover the head of her brother, untying the knots by which it was hung up in the council lodge. The women all said they would go with pleasure. The eldest made the first attempt. With a rushing noise she disappeared through the air.

Towards daylight she returned. She had failed, having only succeeded in untying one of the knots. All the women save the youngest went in turn, and each one succeeded in untying only one knot each time. At length the youngest went. As soon as she arrived at the lodge she went to work. The smoke from the fire in the lodge had not ascended for ten nights. It now filled the place and drove all the men out. The girl was alone, and she carried off the head.

The brothers and Iamo's sister heard the young woman coming high through the air, and they heard her say:

"Prepare the body of our brother."

As soon as they heard that they went to where Iamo's body lay, and, having got it ready, as soon as the young woman arrived with the head they placed it to the body, and Iamo was restored in all his former manliness and beauty. All rejoiced in the happy termination of their troubles, and when they had spent some time joyfully together, Iamo said:

"Now I will divide the treasure," and taking the bear's belt he commenced dividing what it contained amongst the brothers, beginning with the eldest. The youngest brother, however, got the most splendid part of the spoil, for the bottom of the belt held what was richest and rarest.

Then Iamo told them that, since they had all died and been restored to life again, they were no longer mortals but spirits, and he assigned to each of them a station in the invisible world. Only Mudjikewis' place was, however, named. He was to direct the west wind. The brothers were commanded, as they had it in their power, to do good to the inhabitants of the earth, and to give all things with a liberal hand.

The spirits then, amid songs and shouts, took their flight to their respective places, while Iamo and his sister, Iamoqua, descended into the depths below.

The Shepherd and the Daughter of the Sun

IN THE SNOW-CLAD CORDILLERA above the valley of Yucay, called Pitu-siray, a shepherd watched the flock of white llamas intended for the Inca to sacrifice to the Sun. He was a native of Laris, named Acoya-napa, a very well disposed and gentle youth. He strolled behind his flock, and presently began to play upon his flute very softly and sweetly, neither feeling anything of the amorous desires of youth, nor knowing anything of them.

He was carelessly playing his flute one day when two daughters of the Sun came to him. They could wander in all directions over the green meadows, and never failed to find one of their houses at night, where the guards and porters looked out that nothing came that could do them harm. Well! the two girls came to the place where the shepherd rested quite at his ease, and they asked him about his llamas.

The shepherd, who had not seen them until they spoke, was surprised, and fell on his knees, thinking that they were the embodiments of two out of the four crystalline fountains which were very famous in those parts. So he did not dare to answer them. They repeated their question about the flock, and told him not to be afraid, for they were children of the Sun, who was lord of all the land, and to give him confidence they took him by the arm. Then the shepherd stood up and kissed their hands. After talking together for some time the shepherd said that it was time for him to collect his flock, and asked their permission. The elder princess, named Chuqui-llantu, had been struck by the grace and good disposition of the shepherd. She asked him his name and of what place he was a native. He replied that his home was at Laris and that his name was Acoya-napa. While he was speaking Chuqui-llantu cast her eyes upon a plate of silver which the shepherd wore over his forehead, and which shone and glittered very prettily. Looking closer she saw on it two figures, very subtilely contrived, who were eating a heart. Chuqui-llantu asked the shepherd the name of that silver ornament, and he said it was called *utusi*. The princess returned it to the shepherd, and took leave of him, carrying well in her memory the name of the ornament and the figures, thinking with what delicacy they were drawn, almost seeming to her to be alive. She talked about it with her sister until they came to their palace. On entering, the doorkeepers looked to see if they brought with them anything that would do harm, because it was often found that women had brought with them, hidden in their clothes, such things as fillets and necklaces. After having looked well, the porters let them pass, and they found the women of the Sun cooking and preparing food. Chuqui-llantu said that she was very tired with her walk, and that she did not want any supper. All the rest supped with her sister, who thought that Acoya-napa was not one who could cause inquietude. But Chuqui-llantu was unable to rest owing to the great love she felt for the shepherd Acoya-napa, and she regretted that she had not shown him what was in her breast. But at last she went to sleep.

In the palace there were many richly furnished apartments in which the women of the Sun dwelt. These virgins were brought from all the four provinces which were subject to the Inca, namely Chincha-suyu, Cunti-suyu, Anti-suyu and Colla-suyu. Within, there were four fountains which flowed towards the four provinces, and in which the women bathed, each in the fountain of the province where she was born. They named the fountains in this way. That of Chincha-suyu was called Chuclla-puquio, that of Cunti-suyu was known as Ocoruro-puquio, Siclla-puquio was the fountain of Anti-suyu, and Llulucha-puquio of Colla-suyu. The most beautiful child of the Sun, Chuqui-llantu, was wrapped in profound sleep. She had a dream. She thought she saw a bird flying from one tree to another, and singing very softly and sweetly. After having sung for some time, the bird came down and regarded the princess, saying that she should feel no sorrow, for all would be well. The princess said that she mourned for something for which there could be no remedy. The singing bird replied that it would find a remedy, and asked the princess to tell her the cause of her sorrow. At last Chuqui-llantu told the bird of the great love she felt for the shepherd boy named Acoya-napa, who guarded the white flock. Her death seemed inevitable. She could have no cure but to go to him whom she so dearly loved, and if she did her father the Sun would order her to be killed. The answer of the singing bird, by name Checollo, was that she should arise and sit between the four fountains. There she was to sing what she had most in her memory. If the fountains repeated her words, she might then safely do what she wanted. Saying this the bird flew away, and the princess awoke. She was terrified. But she dressed very quickly and put herself between the four fountains. She began to repeat what she remembered to have seen of the two figures on the silver plate, singing:

Micuc isutu cuyuc utusi cucim.

Presently all the fountains began to sing the same verse.

Seeing that all the fountains were very favourable, the princess went to repose for a little while, for all night she had been conversing with the *checollo* in her dream.

When the shepherd boy went to his home he called to mind the great beauty of Chuqui-llantu. She had aroused his love, but he was saddened by the thought that it must be love without hope. He took up his flute and played such heart-breaking music that it made him shed many tears, and he lamented, saying: "Ay! ay! ay! for the unlucky and sorrowful shepherd, abandoned and without hope, now approaching the day of your death, for there can be no remedy and no hope." Saying this, he also went to sleep.

The shepherd's mother lived in Laris, and she knew, by her power of divination, the cause of the extreme grief into which her son was plunged, and that he must die unless she took order for providing a remedy. So she set out for the mountains, and arrived at the shepherd's hut at sunrise. She looked in and saw her son almost moribund, with his face covered with tears. She went in and awoke him. When he saw who it was he began to tell her the cause of his grief, and she did what she could to console him. She told him not to be downhearted, because she would find a remedy within a few days. Saying this she departed and, going among the rocks, she gathered certain herbs which are believed to be cures for grief. Having collected a great quantity she began to cook them, and the cooking was not finished before the two princesses appeared at the entrance of the hut. For Chuqui-llantu, when she was rested, had set out with her sister for a walk on the green slopes of the mountains, taking the direction of the hut. Her tender heart prevented her from going in any other direction. When they arrived they were tired, and sat down by the entrance. Seeing an old dame inside they saluted her, and asked her if she could give them anything to eat. The mother went down on her knees and said she had nothing but a dish of herbs. She brought it to them, and they began to eat with excellent appetites. Chuqui-llantu then walked round the hut without finding what she sought, for the shepherd's mother had made Acoya-napa lie down inside the hut, under a cloak. So the princess thought that he had gone after his flock. Then she saw the cloak and told the mother that it was a very pretty cloak, asking where it came from. The old woman told her that it was a cloak which, in ancient times, belonged to a woman beloved by Pachacamac, a deity very celebrated in the valleys on the coast. She said it had come to her by inheritance; but the princess, with many endearments, begged for it until at last the mother consented. When Chuqui-llantu took it into her hands she liked it better than before and, after staying a short time longer in the hut, she took leave of the old woman, and walked along the meadows looking about in hopes of seeing him whom she longed for.

We do not treat further of the sister, as she now drops out of the story, but only of Chuqui-llantu. She was very sad and pensive when she could see no signs of her beloved shepherd on her way back to the palace. She was in great sorrow at not having seen him, and when, as was usual, the guards looked at what she brought, they saw nothing but the cloak. A splendid supper was provided, and when everyone went to bed the princess took the cloak and placed it at her bedside. As soon as she was alone she began to weep, thinking of the shepherd. She fell asleep at last, but it was not long before the cloak was changed into the being it had been before. It began to call Chuqui-llantu by her own name. She was terribly frightened, got out of bed, and beheld the shepherd on his knees before her, shedding many tears. She was satisfied on seeing him, and inquired how he had got inside the palace. He replied that the cloak which she carried had arranged that. Then Chuqui-llantu embraced him, and put her finely worked *lipi* mantles on him, and they slept together. When they wanted to get up in the morning, the shepherd again became the cloak. As soon as the sun rose, the princess left the palace of her father with the cloak, and when she reached a ravine in the mountains, she found herself again with her beloved shepherd, who had been changed into himself. But one of the guards had followed them, and when he saw what had happened he gave the alarm with loud shouts. The lovers fled into the mountains which are near the town of Calca. Being tired after a long journey, they climbed to the top of a rock and went to sleep. They heard a great noise in their sleep, so they arose. The princess took one shoe in her hand and kept the other on her foot. Then looking towards the town of Calca both were turned into stone. To this day the two statues may be seen between Calca and Huayllapampa.

The Vision of Yupanqui

THE INCA YUPANQUI before he succeeded to the sovereignty is said to have gone to visit his father, Viracocha Inca. On his way he arrived at a fountain called Susur-pugaio. There he saw a piece of crystal fall into the fountain, and in this crystal he saw the figure of an Indian, with three bright rays as of the sun coming from the back of his head. He wore a *bautu*, or royal fringe, across the forehead like the Inca. Serpents wound round his arms and over his shoulders. He had ear-pieces in his ears like the Incas, and was also dressed like them. There was the head of a lion between his legs, and another lion was about his shoulders.

Inca Yupanqui took fright at this strange figure, and was running away when a voice called to him by name telling him not to be afraid, because it was his father, the sun, whom he beheld, and that he would conquer many nations, but he must remember his father in his sacrifices and raise revenues for him, and pay him great reverence. Then the figure vanished, but the crystal remained, and the Inca afterwards saw all he wished in it. When he became king he had a statue of the sun made, resembling the figure as closely as possible, and ordered all the tribes he had conquered to build splendid temples and worship the new deity instead of the creator.

Benten-of-the-Birth-Water

HANAGAKI BAISHU, a young poet and scholar, attended a great festival to celebrate the rebuilding of the Amadera temple. He wandered about the beautiful grounds, and eventually reached the place of a spring from which he had often quenched his thirst. He found that what had originally been a spring was now a pond, and, moreover, that at one corner of the pond there was a tablet bearing the words *Tanjō-Sui* ('Birth-Water'), and also a small but attractive temple dedicated to Benten. While Baishu was noting the changes in the temple grounds the wind blew to his feet a charmingly written love-poem. He picked it up, and discovered that it had been inscribed by a female hand, that the characters were exquisitely formed, and that the ink was fresh.

Baishu went home and read and re-read the poem. It was not long before he fell in love with the writer, and finally he resolved to make her his wife. At length he went to the temple of Benten-of-the-Birth-Water, and cried: "Oh, Goddess, come to my aid, and help me to find the woman who wrote these wind-blown verses!" Having thus prayed, he promised to perform a seven days' religious service, and to devote the seventh night in ceaseless worship before the sacred shrine of Benten, in the grounds of the Amadera.

On the seventh night of the vigil Baishu heard a voice calling for admittance at the main gateway of the temple grounds. The gate was opened, and an old man, clad in ceremonial robes and with a black cap upon his head, advanced and silently knelt before the temple of Benten. Then the outer door of the temple mysteriously opened, and a bamboo curtain was partially raised, revealing a handsome boy, who thus addressed the old man: "We have taken pity on a young man who desires a certain love-union, and have called you to inquire into the matter, and to see if you can bring the young people together."

The old man bowed, and then drew from his sleeve a cord which he wound round Baishu's body, igniting one end in a temple-lantern, and waving his hand the while, as if beckoning some spirit to appear out of the dark night. In a moment a young girl entered the temple grounds, and, with her fan half concealing her pretty face, she knelt beside Baishu.

Then the beautiful boy thus addressed Baishu: "We have heard your prayer, and we have known that recently you have suffered much. The woman you love is now beside you." And having uttered these words the divine youth departed, and the old man left the temple grounds.

When Baishu had given thanks to Benten-of-the-Birth-Water he proceeded homeward. On reaching the street outside the temple grounds he saw a young girl, and at once recognized her as the woman he loved. Baishu spoke to her, and when she replied the gentleness and sweetness of her voice filled the youth with joy. Together they walked through the silent streets until at last they came to the house where Baishu lived. There was a moment's pause, and then the maiden said: "Benten has made me your wife," and the lovers entered the house together.

The marriage was an extremely fortunate one, and the happy Baishu discovered that his wife, apart from her excellent domestic qualities, was accomplished in the art of arranging flowers and in the art of embroidery, and that her delicate writing was not less pleasing than her charming pictures. Baishu knew nothing about her family, but as she had been presented to him by the Goddess Benten he considered that it was unnecessary to question her in the matter. There was only one thing that puzzled the loving Baishu, and that was that the neighbours seemed to be totally unaware of his wife's presence.

One day, while Baishu was walking in a remote quarter of Kyoto, he saw a servant beckoning to him from the gateway of a private house. The man came forward, bowed respectfully, and said: "Will you deign to enter this house? My master is anxious to have the honour of speaking to you." Baishu, who knew nothing of the servant or his master, was not a little surprised by this strange greeting, but he allowed himself to be conducted to the guest-room, and thus his host addressed him:

"I most humbly apologize for the very informal manner of my invitation, but I believe that I have acted in compliance with a message I received from the Goddess Benten. I have a daughter, and, as I am anxious to find a good husband for her, I sent her written poems to all the temples of Benten in Kyoto. In a dream the Goddess came to me, and told me that she had secured an excellent husband for my daughter, and that he would visit me during the coming winter. I was not inclined to attach very much importance to this dream; but last night Benten again revealed herself to me in a vision, and said that tomorrow the husband she had chosen for my daughter would call upon me, and that I could then arrange the marriage. The Goddess described the appearance of the young man so minutely that I am assured that you are my daughter's future husband."

These strange words filled Baishu with sorrow, and when his courteous host proposed to present him to the lady he was unable to summon up sufficient courage to tell his would-be father-in-law that he already had a wife. Baishu followed his host into another apartment, and to his amazement and joy he discovered that the daughter of the house was none other than his own wife! And yet there was a subtle difference, for the woman who now smiled upon him was the body of his wife, and she who had appeared before the temple of Benten-of-the-Birth-Water was her soul. We are told that Benten performed this miracle for the sake of her worshippers, and thus it came to pass that Baishu had a strange dual marriage with the woman he loved.

Dutiful Daughter

THERE ONCE LIVED in Korea a rich merchant and his wife who had no children, though they greatly desired them and prayed every day that a child might be granted them.

They had been married sixteen years and were no longer young, when the wife had a wonderful dream.

In her dream she walked in a garden full of beauteous fruits and flowers and singing birds, and as she walked, suddenly a star fell from heaven into her bosom.

As soon as the wife awoke, she told this dream to her husband. "I feel assured," said she, "that this dream can mean only one thing, and that is that heaven is about to send us a child, and that this child will be as a star for beauty and wonder and grace."

The merchant could hardly believe that this good fortune was really to be theirs; but it was indeed as the wife had said, and in due time a daughter was born to the couple, and this child was so beautiful that she was the wonder of all who saw her.

The husband and wife, who had hoped for a son, were greatly disappointed that the long-wished-for child was only a daughter, but their disappointment was soon forgotten in the joy and pride they felt in her beauty and wit and goodness.

Unhappily, while Sim Ching (for so the girl was named) was still a child, her mother died, and her father's grief over the loss of his wife was so great that he became completely blind.

He was now obliged to leave the most of his business affairs in the hands of his servants, and these servants were so dishonest and so idle that they either wasted or stole all his money. At last he became so poor that he could scarcely provide enough food to keep himself and his daughter alive.

One day the merchant in his unhappiness wandered away from home, and being blind and so unable to tell where he was going, he fell into a deep pit out of which he was unable to climb.

He feared he would die there, but presently, hearing footsteps on the road above, he called out loudly for help.

The footsteps he heard were those of a greedy and dishonest priest who lived near by. Every day he passed by this way on his walks to and from the temple.

Hearing the voice from the pit, the priest went to the edge of it and looking down into it, saw the blind man there below.

"Who are you?" asked the priest, "and how have you fallen into this pit?"

"I am a poor blind man, who was once a rich merchant," replied the man in the pit. "I lost at once both my sight and my wealth, and because I cannot see I fell into this pit from which I am not able to climb. For the sake of mercy reach down your hand and draw me out."

"Not so," replied the priest. "That would be a foolish thing for me to do. Instead of drawing you out, I might myself be pulled in. But if you will promise to give me a hundred and fifty bags of rice that I may offer them up in the temple, I will go and get a rope, and throw the end of it down to you, and by that means I may be able to pull you out without danger to either of us."

The priest asked for the rice for the temple not because he really wished to make an offering of it, for indeed he meant to keep it for himself, but he thought, "If this man was once rich, no doubt he must still know some wealthy people, and if he goes to them and asks for rice to offer up in the temple they will be more likely to give it to him than if he told them it was for me."

When the poor man heard that the priest demanded his promise of a hundred and fifty bags of rice before he would help him, he cried aloud with grief and wonder.

"How is it possible I should promise you such a thing as that?" he cried. "None but a very rich man could make such a gift to the temple, and I am so poor that I cannot even provide food enough for myself and my daughter."

"Your daughter!" cried the priest. "You have then a daughter?"

"Yes; and she is so beautiful that no one in the whole land can compare with her for fairness, and she is as good as she is beautiful, and as witty as she is good."

"Now listen!" said the priest. "If you will swear to give me the bags of rice, not only will I pull you out of the pit, but I foresee that because of this gift your daughter will be raised to the highest place in the land, and you yourself will receive great wealth and honour, and your sight will return to you."

This the priest said, not because he really foresaw anything of the kind, but because he wished to tempt the blind man into making him the promise of the rice.

The poor man still declared that he had no means of making such an offering, but the priest urged and begged and threatened, until at last the blind man gave his promise.

The priest then ran and got a rope, and soon pulled the blind merchant out of the pit.

"Now remember!" said he. "Exactly a month from now I will send my servants for the rice, and you must in some way have it ready, whether you beg or borrow or steal it, and

CLAIRVOYANT VISIONS & DREAMS

if you do not, you shall receive a good beating for breaking your bargain with me, and be thrown into a prison that is worse than any pit."

The priest then went on to the temple, while the blind man returned home, very sad and sorrowful.

As soon as he entered the door, his daughter saw by his look that something unfortunate had happened and begged him to tell her what it was.

At first he would not say because he feared to frighten her, but she asked him so many questions that at last he was obliged to tell her the whole story.

Sim Ching was indeed terrified when she heard what her father had promised the priest.

"Alas! Alas!" she cried. "How can we possibly get the rice ready for him? You know it is only by the kindness of the neighbours that we have the handful that I have cooked for our dinner today."

The poor man began to weep. "What you say is true," he cried. "Better that I should have died in the pit than be thrown into prison as will surely happen to me if I cannot give the priest the hundred and fifty bags that I promised him."

The blind man now set out to beg, telling everyone his sad story and asking them to help him to collect the rice, but the people of the village were themselves poor and had no more than enough food for their own families.

Time slipped by, until at last the day arrived when the priest's servants were to come to demand the rice, and the blind man had not yet been able to get together even one bagful of rice, let alone a hundred and fifty.

He and his daughter sat together very sorrowful, and now and then the blind man bemoaned himself as he thought of how he was to be beaten and thrown into prison, for he had now learned enough about the priest to know that he could expect no mercy from one as cruel and greedy as he.

Now there lived in another city, not far away, a very rich merchant who owned many ships that traded in foreign lands. This merchant had become so proud of his wealth and his power that he called himself the Prince of the Sea, and so it was that he obliged others to address him. This greatly offended a powerful Water Spirit who lived under the sea over which the ships of the merchant sailed. And now, in order to punish the merchant, the Water Spirit sent storms down upon the ships. Many were destroyed, and others were driven on to reefs, or back to the ports they sailed from. So many misfortunes overtook the vessels that sailors became afraid to sail on them, and the merchant began to fear he would be ruined.

In his trouble he sent for a number of wise men and magicians and asked them why he was now so unlucky, and what he could do to bring back good fortune.

The wise men and magicians studied their books and consulted together for a long time, and then they came to the merchant and said, "We have found why you are so unlucky. Your pride has offended a powerful Water Spirit, and it is he who is wrecking your ships or driving them back into port. There is only one way in which to turn aside his anger. If a young and beautiful maiden can be found who will willingly offer herself as a sacrifice to him, then he will be satisfied and will punish you no further. Otherwise he will certainly destroy every vessel you send out, and so in the end you will be ruined."

When the merchant heard this, he was in despair. "Now indeed there is no hope for me," he cried, "for I am very sure there is not, in the whole of Korea, a maiden who would be willing to be sacrificed to this Water Spirit, however great the reward I might offer. For indeed of what use would any reward be to her, if in order to gain it she must be drowned in the sea."

353

PROPHECIES & ORACLES: MYTHS & TALES

However, his head steward, who had charge of his affairs, begged him at least to send out a proclamation and to offer a reward to the family of any maiden who would consent to the sacrifice. "It may be that such a one will be found," said he; – "someone who values the fortunes of her parents even above her own life."

The merchant finally agreed to the wishes of his steward, and messengers were sent forth to read the proclamation aloud in every city, town and village in the country. They went this way and that, East, West, North and South, and finally one of them came to the place where the blind man and his daughter lived. The day the messenger came to the village was the very day when the servants of the wicked priest were to come and demand the hundred and fifty bags of rice from the blind man.

The merchant's messenger took his stand not far from the blind man's house, and from there he read aloud the proclamation as to the sacrifice and the reward that would be paid to the parents of any maiden who would be willing to be thrown to the Water Spirit.

The people of the village gathered about him in a great crowd to listen, but after they had heard what he said, they began to make a great noise, with cries and laughter.

"Some parents there may be," they cried, "who would be wicked enough to sacrifice their daughters for the sake of the reward, but what girl would ever go willingly to such a fate; and the messenger himself tells us that unless the maiden went willingly, the sacrifice would be useless."

Sim Ching heard the noise outside, the voice of the messenger, and the laughter of the crowd, and as she was of a very curious nature, she went to the door to hear what was going on.

The man was already turning away, and Sim Ching asked a woman who was standing near what the man had been saying. The woman told her, laughing as she spoke. "How could anyone suppose that any maiden would consent to be thrown to this monster in order that her family might have the reward!" cried the woman.

But Sim Ching ran after the man and caught him by the sleeve.

"Wait!" cried she. "Do not go until you have told me something. You say your master will richly reward the family of any maiden who will willingly give herself to this Water Spirit. Would he give as much as a hundred and fifty bags of rice to such a family?"

"That and more," replied the messenger. "My master is very rich, and the reward will be generous."

"Then I will go with you and be the sacrifice," said Sim Ching. "Permit me only to go and bid farewell to my father, and then I will be ready."

The messenger was rejoiced that he had been able to secure the maiden for his master and gladly consented to wait until she had spoken with her father.

But when Sim Ching went back into the house and told her father what she intended to do he was in despair. He wept aloud and rent his clothes. "Never, never will I consent to such a sacrifice," cried he.

But his daughter comforted him. "Do you forget," said she, "what the priest promised you? Did he not tell you that if you offered up this rice to the temple, all would be well with us, and that I would be raised to the highest place in the kingdom? Let us have faith and believe that the gods of the temple can save me at the last even though I be thrown into the sea."

As her father listened to her, he grew quieter, and at last gave his consent for her to go.

The neighbors who had heard what she meant to do gathered about to bid her farewell and could not but weep for pity, even while they praised her for her dutifulness toward her father.

Sim Ching at once set out with the messenger, who was in haste to bring her before his master. Indeed he feared that if she thought too long of what she had consented to do, she might repent of her bargain.

When he reached the merchant's house and told him he had found a maiden for the sacrifice, his master could scarcely believe him. "Does she understand what is required of her, and is she willing?" he asked.

The messenger assured him that she understood perfectly and was rejoiced at the thought of securing the reward for her father.

Sim Ching was now brought before the merchant, and when he saw her beauty and youth, and her modest, gentle air, he was filled with pity for her. He would even have commanded that she should be taken back again to her father, but to this Sim Ching would not consent.

"No," said she. "I have come here to do a certain thing. I have promised, and I do not wish to break my word. All I ask is to be assured that the bags of rice will certainly be sent to my father, and that at once."

"Let it then be as you desire," said the merchant. "And be assured that my part of the bargain shall be kept as faithfully as yours." He then ordered that one hundred and fifty bags of rice should be loaded on as many mules and sent to the blind man at once, that Sim Ching might herself have the comfort of seeing them set forth.

This was done, and after the train of mules had departed, Sim Ching was taken to a chamber where magnificent robes and veils and jewels had been laid ready for her. Her attendants dressed her and hung the jewels on her neck and arms, and when all was done, she was so beautiful that even the attendants wept to think she must be sacrificed.

A barge had been made ready and hung about with garlands, and in it sat musicians to make sweet music while the rowers rowed to where the sacrifice was to be made.

And now Sim Ching would have been afraid, but she fixed her thoughts upon her father and on how he would now be saved from the cruelty of the priest, and then she became quite happy and was no longer frightened.

When the barge came to the place under which the Water Spirit lived, Sim Ching leaned over the side of the boat and looked down into the water. It was very deep and green, and it seemed to her that beneath she could see shining walls and towers, as though of some great castle, and that the spirits of the water were beckoning to her to come. Lower and lower she leaned, until, as though drawn by some power beneath, she sank over the side of the vessel and down and down through the water until she was lost to the sight of those above her.

Then the rowers took the barge back to the shore and told the merchant the sacrifice had been accepted.

The merchant was glad that now again his ships might sail in safety; but at the same time he felt pity for Sim Ching, believing she had been drowned.

But such was not the case. After she had sunk down and down through the waters for what seemed to her a long distance, she came to the land where the Water Spirit is king. All about her were things strange and beautiful. There were water weeds so tall they were like trees waving high above her, and through them, like birds, darted the shining fishes. There were water flowers of colours she had never seen before, and shining shells, and before her rose a castle made of mother of pearl and studded with precious stones that shone and glittered like stars in the light that came down through the water.

While she was looking at it, the doors of the castle swung open, and a train of attendants came out to meet her. These attendants were all dressed in green, and many of them would have been very handsome except that they themselves were green. Their faces, their hands, their hair, and eyes, – everything about them was green.

They spoke to Sim Ching in a strange language, but soon she understood them and knew they had come to bring her before their King who was waiting for her.

Sim Ching felt no doubt but that this King was the Water Spirit himself, and she was very much frightened, but still she did not hesitate, but went with them willingly, for it was for this purpose she had come hither.

The attendants led her through one room after another, until they came to the place where the Water Spirit sat upon a crystal throne, and he, too, was green, but his crown was of gold, and his garments were set all over with pearls and precious stones.

The King looked at Sim Ching kindly and bade her have no fear. "I intend you no harm," said he, "and indeed I wished for no sacrifice. My only wish was to punish the rich merchant for his pride, and so it was that I set him a task that I thought impossible for him to perform. But because of your dutifulness and your love for your father, he has been able to make the sacrifice. Now you must stay here patiently for a year and teach the sea-maidens the ways of the world above, and at the end of that time you shall return to the earth, and receive the happiness you deserve."

Sim Ching listened to him wondering, and when he had made an end of speaking, she gladly agreed to serve for a time in the palace and to teach the sea-people all she knew. So for a twelvemonth Sim Ching stayed there and was very happy, for though the ways and manners of the sea-people were strange to her, they themselves were kind and gentle, so that she soon lost all fear of them.

At the end of the twelve months, the King sent for Sim Ching, and when she had come before him, he said, "Sim Ching, for a year you have served us both faithfully and well, and now the time has come for you to return to the Upper World. But in that world there are many dangers, and you have no one to protect you. I have, therefore, caused a great flower to be prepared for you. When you enter into this flower, the leaves will fold about you and hide you, so that none may suspect you are within it. The leaves will afford you food and drink as well as shelter. In this way you can live protected and in safety until fate sends you a husband to love and guard you."

After speaking thus, the Water Spirit led Sim Ching into another room and there showed her the flower that he had caused to be prepared for her. This flower was very large and of a beautiful rose colour, and the leaves were of some rich, thick substance that had a most delicious smell and was good to eat. The juice of the leaves also afforded a delicious drink. Sim Ching, as she examined it, knew not how to express her wonder and admiration.

The King bade her step into the flower. She did so, and at once the leaves closed about her, so that she was completely hidden, and at the same time the most delightful music breathed softly from the flower. It now floated softly up and up, through the roof of the palace, and through the waters above, until it reached the surface of the sea. There it rested, rocking gently with the motion of the waves.

Now it so happened that the place where the flower floated on the sea was not far from the palace of the young King of that country. The morning it arose through the waters, the King was looking from a window across the sea toward a pleasure island where he sometimes went. Suddenly, between himself and the island, he saw something glittering in the sunlight out upon the waters.

356

He could not make out what the object was, and he ordered that some of the castle servants should row out to it, see what it was, and if possible bring it back with them. This was done and when the rowers returned, they brought the flower with them and carried it in to where the young King was awaiting them.

When the King saw the flower, he was filled with wonder and admiration. Never before had he seen such a blossom. He examined it on all sides and exclaimed over its size and beauty.

"It must be some magic," said he, "that has created such a flower. A room shall be built for it, and there I will keep it, and if indeed, it has been made by magic, as I suspect, it may be that in time some fruit will come from it that will be even more beautiful than the flower itself."

The room that was now prepared for the flower was so magnificent that no other apartment in the palace could compare with it. The walls were of gold, overlaid with paintings and hung with silken embroidered hangings. The floors were set with precious stones. There were fountains, and couches heaped with soft cushions, and from the ceiling hung seven alabaster lamps that were kept burning both night and day.

When the room was finished, the King caused the flower to be carefully carried into it and placed in the centre upon a raised dais covered with embroidered velvet. After this no one was allowed to enter the room except himself, and he carried the key of it hung on a jewelled chain about his neck. Every day he spent long hours with the flower admiring its beauty, enjoying its delicious perfume, and listening to the delicate music that sometimes breathed out from among its leaves.

All the while Sim Ching lay hidden in the centre of the flower without the King's once suspecting it. All day the leaves were closed about her, and only at night did they open to allow her to come forth.

The first time they unfolded, she was very much surprised to find herself in a room of a palace, instead of out upon the sea as she had supposed. Wondering, she looked about her, and then she stepped from the flower and began, timidly, to examine the apartment to which she had been brought. The beauty of it delighted her. She rested among the soft cushions, and bathed in the fountains, and dressed her hair. But toward morning she re-entered the flower, and the leaves closed about her so that she was again hidden from view.

For some time life went on in this manner. All day Sim Ching slept in the flower, and only at night did she come forth, and as the King only visited the room in the daytime he never saw her, nor even guessed that a living maiden was inclosed by the leaves of the flower he admired so greatly.

But it so happened that one night the King could not sleep, and he took a fancy to visit the flower and see it by the light of the lamps. He therefore made his way along the corridors, and fitting the key into the lock, he turned it without having made a sound.

What was his surprise, when he opened the door, to see a maiden of surpassing beauty sitting beside a fountain and amusing herself by catching the water in her hands.

When Sim Ching saw the King, she gave a cry, and would have run back into the flower to hide, but the King called to her gently, bidding her stay.

"I will not harm you," said he. "Do but tell me who you are and how you have come here. It must be you are some spirit or fairy, for no human being could be as beautiful as you."

"I am no spirit, nor am I a fairy," answered Sim Ching, "but only the daughter of a poor blind beggar, and as to how I came here I know not. I was placed inside that flower by a Water Spirit, but who has brought the flower here, or why, I cannot tell."

The King then told her of how he had seen the flower floating on the sea, and how he had had it brought to the palace, and had ordered this room to be built for it, and after he had made an end of speaking, Sim Ching told him her history from the time her father had become blind and fallen into the pit, to the hour when the Water Spirit had bade her enter the flower and the leaves had closed about her.

The young King listened and wondered. "Yours is indeed a strange story," said he, "and this mischievous priest shall be sought out and punished as he deserves. And yet it may be his promises shall all come true, and you shall indeed be exalted to the highest place in the kingdom."

He then told Sim Ching he loved her and desired nothing in the world so much as to make her his wife.

To this Sim Ching joyfully consented for the young King was so handsome and gracious, and spoke so well and wisely, that she could not but love him with all her heart, even as he loved her.

All night they sat and talked together, and in the morning he opened the door of the chamber and led her forth, and called the courtiers and nobles together, and told them she was to be his bride.

Then there was great rejoicing, and everyone who saw Sim Ching wondered at her beauty and loved her for her gentle and gracious manner.

Soon after she and the King were married, and they loved each other so dearly that Sim Ching would have been perfectly happy except for the thought of her old father and his griefs and sorrows.

Immediately after she was married, she sent messengers to the village where she had lived, bidding them find her father and bring him to her, but the old man had disappeared, and no one knew what had become of him.

Then the Queen had a great feast prepared and sent word throughout the length and breadth of the Kingdom that all who were both poor and blind were bidden to the palace to eat of it. All would be welcome, and none should be turned away.

Then from far and near the blind and poor came flocking to the palace, scores and hundreds of them. The tables for the feast were laid in a great hall, and the young King and Queen sat on raised thrones at one end of it. All who came to the feast were obliged to pass before this throne before they might take their places at the table, and as each one passed, the Queen looked at him eagerly, hoping to recognize her father, but none of all the multitude was the one she sought. At last every one was seated; the attendants were about to close the doors, when another beggar, the last of all, came stumbling into the hall. He was so feeble and so old that he could scarcely make his way to the throne, but no sooner did the Queen see him than she knew him as her father.

Then she gave a great cry, and came down from the throne, and threw her arms about him, and wept over him.

"It is I, oh, my father! It is thy daughter, Sim Ching," she wept.

Then her father knew her voice and cried aloud with joy. "Oh, my daughter, I had thought thee dead," he cried, "and now thou art alive and I can feel thy arms about me."

As he spoke the tears of joy ran down his cheeks, and these tears washed away the mists of sorrow that had clouded his eyes and he found he could see again.

Then there was great rejoicing, and the King called the old man father and made him welcome, and in due time he who had been blind and now could see was raised to great wealth and honour, and so the words of the priest, that he had spoken without believing, came true.

But as for the priest himself, the King had him sought for, and when he was found, he was thrown into prison and punished as he deserved for his greed and cruelty.

The Dream of the King's Son

THERE WAS ONCE a king who had three sons. One evening, when the young princes were going to sleep, the king ordered them to take good note of their dreams and come and tell them to him next morning.

So the next day the princes went to their father as soon as they awoke, and the moment the king saw them he asked of the eldest, "Well, what have you dreamt?"

The prince answered, "I dreamt that I should be the heir to your throne."

And the second said, "And I dreamt that I should be the first subject in the kingdom."

Then the youngest said, "*I* dreamt that I was going to wash my hands, and that the princes, my brothers, held the basin, whilst the queen, my mother, held fine towels for me to dry my hands with, and Your Majesty's self poured water over them from a golden ewer."

The king, hearing this last dream, became very angry, and exclaimed, "What! I – the king – pour water over the hands of my own son! Go away this instant out of my palace, and out of my kingdom! You are no longer my son."

The poor young prince tried hard to make his peace with his father, saying that he was really not to be blamed for what he had only dreamed, but the king grew more and more furious, and at last actually thrust the prince out of the palace.

So the young prince was obliged to wander up and down in different countries, until one day, being in a large forest, he saw a cave, and entered it to rest. There, to his great surprise and joy, he found a large kettle full of Indian corn boiling over a fire and, being exceedingly hungry, began to help himself to the corn. In this way he went on until he was shocked to see he had eaten up nearly all the maize, and then, being afraid some mischief would come of it, he looked about for a place in which to hide himself. At this moment, however, a great noise was heard at the cave mouth, and he had only time to hide himself in a dark corner before a blind old man entered, riding on a great goat and driving a number of goats before him.

The old man rode straight up to the kettle, but as soon as he found that the corn was nearly all gone, he began to suspect someone was there, and groped about the cave until he caught hold of the prince.

"Who are you?" asked he sharply. And the prince answered, "I am a poor, homeless wanderer about the world, and have come now to beg you to be good enough to receive me."

"Well," said the old man, "why not? I shall at least have someone to mind my corn whilst I am out with my goats in the forest."

So they lived together for some time; the prince remained in the cave to boil the maize, whilst the old man drove out his goats every morning into the forest.

One day, however, the old man said to the prince, "I think you shall take out the goats today, and I will stay at home to mind the corn."

This the prince consented to very gladly, as he was tired of living so long quietly in the cave. But the old man added, "Mind only one thing! There are nine different mountains, and you can let the goats go freely over eight of them, but you must on no account go on the ninth. The Vilas (fairies) live there, and they will certainly put out your eyes as they have put out mine, if you venture on their mountain."

The prince thanked the old man for his warning, and then, mounting the great goat, drove the rest of the goats before him out of the cave.

Following the goats, he had passed over all the mountains to the eighth, and from this he could see the ninth mountain, and could not resist the temptation he felt to go upon it. So he said to himself, "I will venture up, whatever happens!"

Hardly had he stepped on the ninth mountain before the fairies surrounded him, and prepared to put out his eyes. But happily a thought came into his head, and he exclaimed quickly, "Dear Vilas, why take this sin on your heads? Better let us make a bargain, that if you spring over a tree that I will place ready to jump over, you shall put out my eyes, and I will not blame you!"

So the Vilas consented to this, and the prince went and brought a large tree, which he cleft down the middle almost to the root. This done, he placed a wedge to keep the two halves of the trunk open a little.

When it was fixed upright, he himself first jumped over it, and then he said to the Vilas, "Now it is your turn. Let us see if you can spring over the tree!"

One Vila attempted to spring over, but at the same moment the prince knocked the wedge out, and the trunk closing, at once held the Vila fast. Then all the other fairies were alarmed, and begged him to open the trunk and let their sister free, promising, in return, to give him anything he might ask. The prince said, "I want nothing except to keep my own eyes, and to restore eyesight to that poor old man." So the fairies gave him a certain herb, and told him to lay it over the old man's eyes, and then he would recover his sight. The prince took the herb, opened the tree a little so as to let the fairy free, and then rode back on the goat to the cave, driving the other goats before him. When he arrived there, he placed at once the herb on the old man's eyes, and in a moment his eyesight came back, to his exceeding surprise and joy.

Next morning the old man, before he drove out his goats, gave the prince the keys of eight closets in the cave, but warned him on no account to open the ninth closet, although the key hung directly over the door. Then he went out, telling the prince to take good care that the corn was ready for their suppers.

Left alone in the cave, the young man began to wonder what might be in the ninth closet, and at last he could not resist the temptation to take down the key and open the door to look in.

What was his surprise to see there a golden horse, with a golden greyhound beside him, and near them a golden hen and golden chicks were busy picking up golden millet seeds.

The young prince gazed at them for some time, admiring their beauty, and then he spoke to the golden horse: "Friend, I think we had better leave this place before the old man comes back again."

CLAIRVOYANT VISIONS & DREAMS

"Very well," answered the golden horse, "I am quite willing to go away, only you must take heed to what I am going to tell. Go and find linen cloth enough to spread over the stones at the mouth of the cave, for if the old man hears the ring of my hoofs he will be certain to kill you. Then you must take with you a little stone, a drop of water, and a pair of scissors, and the moment I tell you to throw them down you must obey me quickly, or you are lost."

The prince did everything that the golden horse had ordered him, and then, taking up the golden hen with her chicks in a bag, he placed it under his arm, and mounted the horse and rode quickly out of the cave, leading with him, in a leash, the golden greyhound. But the moment they were in the open air, the old man, although he was very far off tending his goats on a distant mountain, heard the clang of the golden hoofs, and cried to his great goat, "They have run away. Let us follow them at once."

In a wonderfully short time, the old man on his great goat came so near the prince on his golden horse that the latter shouted, "Throw now the little stone!"

The moment the prince had thrown it down, a high rocky mountain rose up between him and the old man, and before the goat had climbed over it, the golden horse had gained much ground. Very soon, however, the old man was so nearly catching them that the horse shouted, "Throw now the drop of water!" The prince obeyed instantly, and immediately saw a broad river flowing between him and his pursuer.

It took the old man on his goat so long to cross the river that the prince on his golden horse was far away before them. But for all that, it was not very long before the horse heard the goat so near behind him that he shouted, "Throw the scissors!" The prince threw them, and the goat, running over them, injured one of his forelegs very badly. When the old man saw this, he exclaimed, "Now I see I cannot catch you, so you may keep what you have taken. But you will do wisely to listen to my counsel. People will be sure to kill you for the sake of your golden horse, so you had better buy at once a donkey, and take the hide to cover your horse. And do the same with your golden greyhound."

Having said this, the old man turned and rode back to his cave. And the prince lost no time in attending to his advice, and covered with donkey hide his golden horse and his golden hound.

After travelling a long time, the prince came unawares to the kingdom of his father. There he heard that the king had had a ditch dug – three hundred yards wide and four hundred yards deep – and had proclaimed that whosoever should leap his horse over it should have the princess, his daughter, for wife.

Almost a whole year had elapsed since the proclamation was issued, but as yet no one had dared to risk the leap. When the prince heard this, he said, "I will leap over it with my donkey and my dog!" And he leapt over it.

But the king was very angry when he heard that a poorly dressed man on a donkey had dared to leap over the great ditch which had frightened back his bravest knights. So he had the disguised prince thrown into one of his deepest dungeons, together with his donkey and his dog.

Next morning the king sent some of his servants to see if the man was still living, and these soon ran back to him, full of wonder, and told him that they had found in the dungeon, instead of a poor man and his donkey, a young man, beautifully dressed, a golden horse, a golden greyhound, and a golden hen, surrounded by golden chicks, which were picking up golden millet seeds from the ground.

Then the king said, "That must be some powerful prince." So he ordered the queen, and the princes, his sons, to prepare all things for the stranger to wash his hands. Then he went down himself into the dungeon, and led the prince up with much courtesy, desiring thus to make amends for the past ill-treatment.

The king himself took a golden ewer full of water, and poured some over the prince's hands, whilst the two princes held the basin under them, and the queen held out fine towels to dry them on.

This done, the young prince exclaimed, "Now, my dream is fulfilled." And they all at once recognized him, and were very glad to see him once again amongst them.

Water of Youth, Water of Life, and Water of Death

IN A CERTAIN KINGDOM IN A CERTAIN LAND there lived a Tsar; that Tsar had three sons – two crafty, and the third simple. Somehow the Tsar had a dream that beyond the thrice ninth land, in the thirtieth kingdom, there was a beautiful maiden, from whose hands and feet water was flowing, and that whoever would drink that water would become thirty years younger. The Tsar was very old. He summoned his sons and counsellors, and asked, "Can anyone explain my dream?"

The counsellors answered the Tsar: "We have not seen with sight nor heard with hearing of such a beautiful maiden, and how to go to her is unknown to us."

Now the eldest son, Dmitri Tsarevich, spoke up: "Father, give me thy blessing to go in all four directions, look at people, show myself, and make search for the beautiful maiden."

The Tsar gave his parental blessing. "Take," said he, "treasure as much as thou wishest, and all kinds of troops as many as are necessary."

Dmitri Tsarevich took one hundred thousand men and set out on the road, on the journey. He rode a day, he rode a week, he rode a month, and two and three months. No matter whom he asked, no one knew of the beautiful maiden, and he came to such desert places that there were only heaven and earth. He urged his horse on, and behold before him was a lofty mountain; he could not see the top with his eyes. Somehow he climbed the mountain and found there an ancient, a grey old man.

"Hail, grandfather!"

"Hail, brave youth! Art fleeing from labour, or seekest thou labour?"

"I am seeking labour."

"What dost thou need?"

"I have heard that beyond the thrice ninth land, in the thirtieth kingdom, is a beautiful maiden, from whose hands and feet healing water flows, and that whoever gets and drinks this water will grow thirty years younger."

"Well, brother, thou canst not go there."

"Why not?"

"Because there are three broad rivers on the road, and on these rivers three ferries: at the first ferry they will cut off thy right hand, at the second thy left foot, at the third they will take thy head."

Dmitri Tsarevich was grieved; he hung his stormy head below his shoulders, and thought, "Must I spare my father's head? Must I spare my own? I'll turn back."

He came down from the mountain, went back to his father, and said, "No, father, I have not been able to find her; there is nothing to be heard of that maiden."

The second son, Vassili Tsarevich, began to beg, "Father, give me thy blessing; perhaps I can find her."

"Go, my son."

Vassili Tsarevich took one hundred thousand men, and set out on his road, on his journey. He rode a day, he rode a week, he rode a month, and two, and three, and entered such places that there was nothing but forests and swamps. He found there Baba-Yaga, boneleg. "Hail, Baba-Yaga, boneleg!"

"Hail, brave youth! Art thou fleeing from labour, or seekest labour?"

"I am seeking labour. I have heard that beyond the thrice ninth land, in the thirtieth kingdom, is a beautiful maiden, from whose feet and hands healing water flows."

"There is, father; only thou canst not go there."

"Why not?"

"Because on the road there are three ferries: at the first ferry they will cut off thy right hand, at the second thy left foot, at the third off with thy head."

"It is not a question of saving my father's head, but sparing my own."

He returned, and said to his father, "No, father, I could not find her; there is nothing to be heard of that maiden."

The youngest son, Ivan Tsarevich, began to beg, "Give me thy blessing, father; maybe I shall find her."

The father gave him his blessing. "Go, my dear son; take troops and treasure all that are needed."

"I need nothing, only give me a good steed and the sword Kládyenets."

Ivan Tsarevich mounted his steed, took the sword Kládyenets, and set out on his way, on his journey. He rode a day, he rode a week, he rode a month, and two and three; and rode into such places that his horse was to the knees in water, to the breast in grass, and he, good youth, had nothing to eat. He saw a cabin on hen's feet, and entered. Inside sat Baba-Yaga, boneleg.

"Hail, grandmother!"

"Hail, Ivan Tsarevich! Art flying from labour, or seekest labour?"

"What labour? I am going to the thirtieth kingdom; there, it is said, lives a beautiful maiden, from whose hands and feet healing water flows."

"There is, Father; though with sight I have not seen her, with hearing I have heard of her. But to her it is not for thee to go."

"Why so?"

"Because there are three ferries on the way: at the first ferry they will cut off thy right hand, at the second thy left foot, at the third off with thy head."

"Well, grandmother, one head is not much; I will go, whatever God gives."

"Ah! Ivan Tsarevich, better turn back; thou art still a green youth, hast never been in places of danger, hast not seen great terror."

"No," said Ivan, "if thou seizest the rope, don't say thou art not strong." He took farewell of Baba-Yaga and went farther.

He rode a day, a second, and a third, and came to the first ferry. The ferrymen were sleeping on the opposite bank. "What is to be done?" thought Ivan. "If I shout, they'll be deaf for the rest of their lives; if I whistle, I shall sink the ferry-boat." He whistled a half whistle. The ferrymen sprang up that minute and ferried him across the river.

"What is the price of your work, brothers?"

"Give us thy right hand."

"Oh, I want that for myself!" Then Ivan Tsarevich struck with his sword on the right, and on the left. He cut down all the ferrymen, mounted his horse, and galloped ahead. At the two other ferries he got away in the same fashion. He was drawing near the thirtieth kingdom. On the boundary stood a wild man, in stature tall as a forest, in thickness the equal of a great stack of hay; he held in his hands an enormous oak tree.

"Oh, worm!" said the giant to Ivan Tsarevich, "whither art thou riding?"

"I am going to the thirtieth kingdom; I want to see the beautiful maiden from whose hands and feet healing water flows."

"How couldst thou, little pigmy, go there? I am a hundred years guarding her kingdom, great, mighty heroes came here – not the like of thee – and they fell from my strong hand. What art thou? Just a little worm!"

Ivan Tsarevich saw that he could not manage the giant, and he turned aside. He travelled and travelled till he came to a sleeping forest; in the forest was a cabin, and in the cabin an old, ancient woman was sitting. She saw the good youth, and said, "Hail, Ivan Tsarevich! Why has God brought thee hither?"

He told her all without concealment. The old woman gave him magic herbs and a ball.

"Go out," said she, "into the open field, make a fire, and throw these herbs on it; but take care to stand on the windward. From these magic herbs the giant will sleep a deep sleep; cut his head off, then let the ball roll, and follow. The ball will take thee to those regions where the beautiful maiden reigns. She lives in a great golden castle, and often rides out with her army to the green meadows to amuse herself. Nine days does she stay there; then sleeps a hero's sleep nine days and nine nights."

Ivan Tsarevich thanked the old woman and went to the open field, where he made a fire and threw into it the magic herbs. The stormy wind bore the smoke to where the wild man was standing on guard. It grew dim in his eyes; he lay on the damp earth and fell soundly asleep. Ivan Tsarevich cut off his head, let the ball roll, and rode on. He travelled and travelled till the golden palace was visible; then he turned from the road, let his horse out to feed, and crept into a thicket himself. He had just hidden, when dust was rising in a column from the front of the palace. The beautiful maiden rode out with her army to amuse herself in the green meadows. The Tsarevich saw that the whole army was formed of maidens alone. One was beautiful, the next surpassed that one; fairer than all, and beyond admiration was the Tsarevna herself.

Nine days was she sporting in the green meadows, and the Tsarevich did not take his eyes from her, still he could not gaze his fill. On the tenth day he went to the golden palace. The beautiful maiden was lying on a couch of down, sleeping a hero's sleep; from her hands and feet healing water was flowing. At the same time her trusty army was sleeping as well.

Ivan Tsarevich took a flask of the healing water. His heroic heart could not withstand her maiden beauty. He tarried awhile, then left the palace, mounted his good steed, and rushed towards home.

Nine days slept the beautiful maiden, and when she woke her rage was dreadful. She stamped, and she screamed with a piercing voice, "What wretch has been here?" She sprang on to her fleet-flying mare, and struck into a chase after Ivan Tsarevich. The mare raced, the ground trembled; she caught up with the good hero, struck him with her sword, and straight in the breast did she strike. The Tsarevich fell on the damp earth; his bright eyes closed, his red blood stiffened. The fair maiden looked at him, and great pity seized her; through the whole world might she search, and not find such a beauty. She placed her white hand on his wound, and moistened it with healing water. All at once the wound closed, and Ivan Tsarevich rose up unharmed.

"Wilt thou take me as wife?" asked she.

"I will, beautiful maiden."

"Well, go home, and wait three years."

Ivan Tsarevich took farewell of his betrothed bride and continued his journey. He was drawing near his own kingdom; but his elder brothers had put guards everywhere, so as not to let him come near his father. The guards gave notice at once that Ivan Tsarevich was coming. The elder brothers met him on the road, drugged him, took the flask of healing water, and threw him into a deep pit. Ivan Tsarevich came out in the underground kingdom.

He travelled and travelled in the underground kingdom. When he came to a certain place, a great storm rose up, lightning flashed, thunder roared, rain fell. He went to a tree to find shelter, looked up, and saw young birds in that tree all wet. He took off his coat, covered them, and sat himself under the tree.

When the old bird flew to the tree, she was so large that she hid the light, and it grew dark as if night were near. When she saw her young covered, she asked, "Who has protected my little birds?" Then, seeing the Tsarevich, she said, "It is thou who didst this. God save thee! Whatever thou wishest, ask of me; I will do everything for thee."

He said, "Bear me out into the Upper World."

"Make ready," said the bird, "a double box. Fill one half of it with every kind of game, and in the other half put water, so as to have something with which to nourish me."

The Tsarevich did all that was asked. The bird took the box on her back, and the Tsarevich sat in the middle. She flew up; and whether it was long or short, she bore him to this Upper World, took farewell of him, and flew home.

Ivan Tsarevich went to his father; but the old Tsar did not like him by reason of the lies which his brothers had told, and sent him into exile. For three whole years Ivan wandered from place to place. When three years had passed, the beautiful maiden sailed in a ship to the capital town of Ivan Tsarevich's father. She sent a letter to the Tsar, demanding the man who had stolen the water, and if he refused she would burn and destroy his kingdom utterly.

The Tsar sent his eldest son; he went to the ship. Two little boys, grandsons of the Tsar, saw him, and asked their mother, "Is that our father?"

"No, that is your uncle."

"How shall we meet him?"

"Take each one a whip and flog him back home."

The eldest Tsarevich returned, looking as if he had eaten something unsalted.

The maiden continued her threats, demanded the guilty man. The Tsar sent his second son, and the same thing happened to him as to the eldest. Now the Tsar gave command to find the youngest Tsarevich.

When the Tsarevich was found, his father wished him to go on the ship to the maiden. But he said, "I will go when a crystal bridge is built to the ship, and on the bridge there shall be many kinds of food and wine set out."

There was no help for it; they built the bridge, prepared the food, brought wines and meat.

The Tsarevich collected his comrades. "Come with me, attend me," said he. "Eat ye and drink, spare nothing."

While he was walking on the bridge the little boys cried out, "Mother, who is that?"

"That is your father."

"How shall we meet him?"

"Take him by the hands and lead him to me."

They did so; there was kissing and embracing. After that they went to the Tsar, told him all just as it had been. The Tsar drove his eldest sons from the castle and lived with Ivan – lived on and gained wealth.

The Three Dreams

THERE WAS ONCE, I don't know where, even beyond the Operencziás Sea, a poor man, who had three sons. Having got up one morning, the father asked the eldest one, "What have you dreamt, my son?" "Well, my dear father," said he, "I sat at a table covered with many dishes, and I ate so much that when I patted my belly all the sparrows in the whole village were startled by the sound." "Well, my son," said the father, "if you had so much to eat, you ought to be satisfied; and, as we are rather short of bread, you shall not have anything to eat today." Then he asked the second one, "What have you dreamt, my son?" "Well, my dear father, I bought such splendid boots with spurs, that when I put them on and knocked my heels together I could be heard over seven countries." "Well, my good son," answered the father, "you have got good boots at last, and you won't want any for the winter." At last he asked the youngest as to what he had dreamt, but this one was reticent, and did not care to tell; his father ordered him to tell what it was he had dreamt, but he was silent.

As fair words were of no avail the old man tried threats, but without success. Then he began to beat the lad. "To flee is shameful, but very useful," they say. The lad followed this good advice, and ran away, his father after him with a stick. As they reached the street the king was just passing down the high road, in a carriage drawn by six horses with golden hair and diamond shoes. The king stopped, and asked the father why he was ill-treating the lad. "Your Majesty, because he won't tell me his dream." "Don't hurt him, my good man," said the monarch; "I'll tell you what, let the lad go with me, and take this purse; I am anxious to know his dream, and will take him with me." The father consented, and the king continued his journey, taking the lad with him. Arriving at home, he commanded the lad to appear before him, and questioned him about his dream, but the lad would not tell him. No imploring, nor threatening, would induce him to disclose his dream. The king grew angry with the lad's obstinacy, and said, in a great

CLAIRVOYANT VISIONS & DREAMS

rage, "You good-for-nothing fellow, to disobey your king, you must know, is punishable by death! You shall die such a lingering death that you will have time to think over what disobedience to the king means." He ordered the warders to come, and gave them orders to take the lad into the tower of the fortress, and to immure him alive in the wall. The lad listened to the command in silence, and only the king's pretty daughter seemed pale, who was quite taken by the young fellow's appearance, and gazed upon him in silent joy. The lad was tall, with snow-white complexion, and had dark eyes and rich raven locks. He was carried away, but the princess was determined to save the handsome lad's life, with whom she had fallen in love at first sight; and she bribed one of the workmen to leave a stone loose, without its being noticed, so that it could be easily taken out and replaced; and so it was done!

And the pretty girl fed her sweetheart in his cell in secret. One day after this, it happened that the powerful ruler of the dog-headed Tartars gave orders that seven white horses should be led into the other king's courtyard; the animals were so much alike that there was not a hair to choose between them, and each of the horses was one year older than another; at the same time the despot commanded that he should choose the youngest from among them, and the others in the order of their ages, including the oldest; if he could not do this, his country should be filled with as many Tartars as there were blades of grass in the land; that he should be impaled; and his daughter become the Tartar chief's wife. The king on hearing this news was very much alarmed, held a council of all the wise men in his realm, but all in vain: and the whole court was in sorrow and mourning. The princess, too, was sad, and when she took the food to her sweetheart she did not smile as usual, but her eyes were filled with tears: he seeing this inquired the cause; the princess told him the reason of her grief, but he consoled her, and asked her to tell her father that he was to get seven different kinds of oats put into seven different dishes, the oats to be the growths of seven different years; the horses were to be let in and they would go and eat the oats according to their different ages, and while they were feeding they must put a mark on each of the horses. And so it was done, The horses were sent back and the ages of them given, and the Tartar monarch found the solution to be right.

But then it happened again that a rod was sent by him both ends of which were of equal thickness; the same threat was again repeated in case the king should not find out which end had grown nearest the trunk of the tree. The king was downcast and the princess told her grief to the lad, but he said, "Don't worry yourself, princess, but tell your father to measure carefully the middle of the rod and to hang it up by the middle on a piece of twine, the heavier end of it will swing downwards, that end will be the one required." The king did so and sent the rod back with the end marked as ordered. The Tartar monarch shook his head but was obliged to admit that it was right. "I will give them another trial," said he in a great rage; "and, as I see that there must be someone at the king's court who wishes to defy me, we will see who is the stronger." Not long after this, an arrow struck the wall of the royal palace, which shook it to its very foundation, like an earthquake; and great was the terror of the people, which was still more increased when they found that the Tartar monarch's previous threats were written on the feathers of the arrow, which threats were to be carried out if the king had nobody who could draw out the arrow and shoot it back. The king was more downcast than ever, and never slept a wink: he called together all the heroes of his realm, and every child born under a lucky star, who was born either with a caul or with a tooth, or with a grey lock; he promised to the successful one, half of his realm and his daughter, if he fulfilled the Tartar king's wish. The princess told the lad, in sad distress, the cause of her latest grief, and he asked her to have the secret opening closed, so that their love might not be found out, and that no trace be left; and then she was to say, that she dreamt that the lad was still alive, and that he would be able to do what was needed, and that they were to have the wall opened. The princess did as she was told; the king was very much astonished, but at the same time treated the matter as an idle dream in the beginning. He had almost entirely forgotten the lad, and thought that he had gone to dust behind the walls long ago. But in times of perplexity, when there is no help to be found in reality, one is apt to believe dreams, and in his fear about his daughter's safety, the king at last came to the conclusion that the dream was not altogether impossible. He had the wall opened; and a gallant knight stepped from the hole. "You have nothing more to fear, my king," said the lad, who was filled with hope, and, dragging out the arrow with his right hand, he shot it towards Tartary with such force that all the finials of the royal palace dropped down with the force of the shock.

Seeing this, the Tartar monarch was not only anxious to see, but also to make the acquaintance of him who did all these things. The lad at once offered to go, and started on the journey with twelve other knights, disguising himself so that he could not be distinguished from his followers; his weapons, his armour, and everything on him was exactly like those around him. This was done in order to test the magic power of the Tartar chief. The lad and his knights were received with great pomp by the monarch, who, seeing that all were attired alike, at once discovered the ruse; but, in order that he might not betray his ignorance, did not dare to inquire who the wise and powerful knight was, but trusted to his mother, who had magic power, to find him out. For this reason the magic mother put them all in the same bedroom for the night, she concealing herself in the room. The guests lay down, when one of them remarked, with great satisfaction, "By Jove! What a good cellar the monarch has!" "His wine is good, indeed," said another, "because there is human blood mixed with it." The magic mother noted from which bed the sound had come; and, when all were asleep, she cut off a lock from the knight in question, and crept out of the room unnoticed, and informed her son how he could recognize the true hero. The guests got up next morning, but our man soon noticed that he was marked, and in order to thwart the design, every one of the knights cut off a lock. They sat down to dinner, and the monarch was not able to recognize the hero.

The next night the monarch's mother again stole into the bedroom, and this time a knight exclaimed, "By Jove! what good bread the Tartar monarch has!" "It's very good, indeed," said another, "because there is woman's milk in it." When they went to sleep, she cut off the end of the moustache from the knight who slept in the bed where the voice came from, and made this sign known to her son; but the knights were more on their guard than before, and having discovered what the sign was, each of them cut off as much from their moustache as the knight's who was marked; and so once more the monarch could not distinguish between them.

The third night the old woman again secreted herself, when one of the knights remarked, "By Jove! what a handsome man the monarch is!" "He is handsome, indeed, because he is a love child," said another. When they went to sleep, she made a scratch on the visor of the knight who spoke last, and told her son. Next morn the monarch saw that all visors were marked alike. At last the monarch took courage and spoke thus: "I can see there is a cleverer man amongst you than I; and this is why I am so much more anxious to know him. I pray, therefore, that he make himself known, so that I may see him, and make the acquaintance of the only living man who wishes to be wiser and more powerful than myself." The lad stepped forward and said, "I do not wish to be wiser or more powerful than you; but I have only carried out what you bade me do; and I am the one who has been marked for the last three nights." "Very well, my lad, now I wish you to prove your words. Tell me, then, how is it possible there can be human blood in my wine?" "Call your cupbearer, Your Majesty, and he will explain it to you," said the lad. The official appeared hastily, and told the king how, when filling the tankards with the wine in question, he cut his finger with his knife, and thus the blood got into the wine. "Then how is it that there is woman's milk in my bread?" asked the monarch. "Call the woman who baked the bread, and she will tell," said the lad. The woman was questioned, and narrated that she was nursing a baby, and that milk had collected in her breasts; and as she was kneading the dough, the breast began to run, and some milk dropped into it. The magic mother had previously informed her son, when telling him what happened the three nights, and now confirmed her previous confession that it was true that the monarch was a love-child. The monarch was not able to keep his temper any longer, and spoke in a great rage and very haughtily, "I cannot tolerate the presence of a man who is my equal: either he or I will die. Defend yourself, lad!" and with these words he flashed his sword, and dashed at the lad. But in doing so, he accidentally slipped and fell, and the lad's life was saved. Before the former had time to get on his feet, the lad pierced him through, cut off his head, and presented it on the point of his sword to the king at home. "These things that have happened to me are what I dreamt," said the victorious lad; "but I could not divulge my secret beforehand, or else it would not have been fulfilled." The king embraced the lad, and presented to him his daughter and half his realm; and they perhaps still live in happiness today, if they have not died since.

The Dream of Maxen Wledig

MAXEN WLEDIG was Emperor of Rome, and he was a comelier man, and a better and a wiser than any emperor that had been before him. And one day he held a council of kings, and he said to his friends, "I desire to go tomorrow to hunt." And the next day in the morning he set forth with his retinue, and came to the valley of the river that flowed towards Rome. And he hunted through the valley until midday. And with him also were two-and-thirty crowned kings, that were his vassals; not for the delight of hunting went the emperor with them, but to put himself on equal terms with those kings.

And the sun was high in the sky over their heads and the heat was great. And sleep came upon Maxen Wledig. And his attendants stood and set up their shields around him upon the shafts of their spears to protect him from the sun, and they placed a gold enamelled shield under his head; and so Maxen slept.

And he saw a dream. And this is the dream that he saw. He was journeying along the valley of the river towards its source; and he came to the highest mountain in the world. And he thought that the mountain was as high as the sky; and when he came over the mountain, it seemed to him that he went through the fairest and most level regions that man ever yet beheld, on the other side of the mountain. And he saw large and mighty rivers descending from the mountain to the sea, and towards the mouths of the rivers he proceeded. And as he journeyed thus, he came to the mouth of the largest river ever seen. And he beheld a great city at the entrance of the river, and a vast castle in the city, and he saw many high towers of various colours in the castle. And he saw a fleet at the mouth of the river, the largest ever seen. And he saw one ship among the fleet; larger was it by far, and fairer than all the others. Of such part of the ship as he could see above the water, one plank was gilded and the other silvered over. He saw a bridge of the bone of a whale from the ship to the land, and he thought that he went along the bridge, and came into the ship. And a sail was hoisted on the ship, and along the sea and the ocean was it borne. Then it seemed that he came to the fairest island in the whole world, and he traversed the island from sea to sea, even to the furthest shore of the island. Valleys he saw, and steeps, and rocks of wondrous height, and rugged precipices. Never yet saw he the like. And thence he beheld an island in the sea, facing this rugged land. And between him and this island was a country of which the plain was as large as the sea, the mountain as vast as the wood. And from the mountain he saw a river that flowed through the land and fell into the sea. And at the mouth of the river he beheld a castle, the fairest that man ever saw, and the gate of the castle was open, and he went into the castle. And in the castle he saw a fair hall, of which the roof seemed to be all gold, the walls of the hall seemed to be entirely of glittering precious gems, the doors all seemed to be of gold. Golden seats he saw in the hall, and silver tables. And on a seat opposite to him he beheld two auburn-haired youths playing at chess. He saw a silver board for the chess, and golden pieces thereon. The garments of the youths were of jet-black satin, and chaplets of ruddy gold bound their hair, whereon were sparkling jewels of great price, rubies, and gems, alternately with imperial stones. Buskins of new Cordovan leather on their feet, fastened by slides of red gold.

And beside a pillar in the hall he saw a hoary-headed man, in a chair of ivory, with the figures of two eagles of ruddy gold thereon. Bracelets of gold were upon his arms, and many rings were on his hands, and a golden torque about his neck; and his hair was bound with a golden diadem. He was of powerful aspect. A chessboard of gold was before him, and a rod of gold, and a steel file in his hand. And he was carving out chessmen.

And he saw a maiden sitting before him in a chair of ruddy gold. Not more easy than to gaze upon the sun when brightest, was it to look upon her by reason of her beauty. A vest of white silk was upon the maiden, with clasps of red gold at the breast; and a surcoat of gold tissue upon her, and a frontlet of red gold upon her head, and rubies and gems were in the frontlet, alternating with pearls and imperial stones. And a girdle of ruddy gold was around her. She was the fairest sight that man ever beheld.

The maiden arose from her chair before him, and he threw his arms about the neck of the maiden, and they two sat down together in the chair of gold: and the chair was not less roomy for them both than for the maiden alone. And as he had his arms about the maiden's neck, and his cheek by her cheek, behold, through the chafing of the dogs at their leashing, and the clashing of the shields as they struck against each other, and the beating together of the shafts of the spears, and the neighing of the horses and their prancing, the emperor awoke.

370

And when he awoke, nor spirit nor existence was left him, because of the maiden whom he had seen in his sleep, for the love of the maiden pervaded his whole frame. Then his household spake unto him. "Lord," said they, "is it not past the time for thee to take thy food?" Thereupon the emperor mounted his palfrey, the saddest man that mortal ever saw, and went forth towards Rome.

And thus he was during the space of a week. When they of the household went to drink wine and mead out of golden vessels, he went not with any of them. When they went to listen to songs and tales, he went not with them there; neither could he be persuaded to do anything but sleep. And as often as he slept, he beheld in his dreams the maiden he loved best; but except when he slept he saw nothing of her, for he knew not where in the world she was.

One day the page of the chamber spake unto him; now, although he was page of the chamber, he was king of the Romans. "Lord," said he, "all the people revile thee." "Wherefore do they revile me?" asked the emperor. "Because they can get neither message nor answer from thee as men should have from their lord. This is the cause why thou art spoken evil of." "Youth," said the emperor, "do thou bring unto me the wise men of Rome, and I will tell them wherefore I am sorrowful."

Then the wise men of Rome were brought to the emperor, and he spake to them. "Sages of Rome," said he, "I have seen a dream. And in the dream I beheld a maiden, and because of the maiden is there neither life, nor spirit, nor existence within me." "Lord," they answered, "since thou judgest us worthy to counsel thee, we will give thee counsel. And this is our counsel; that thou send messengers for three years to the three parts of the world to seek for thy dream. And as thou knowest not what day or what night good news may come to thee, the hope thereof will support thee."

So the messengers journeyed for the space of a year, wandering about the world, and seeking tidings concerning his dream. But when they came back at the end of the year, they knew not one word more than they did the day they set forth. And then was the emperor exceeding sorrowful, for he thought that he should never have tidings of her whom best he loved.

Then spoke the king of the Romans unto the emperor. "Lord," said he, "go forth to hunt by the way thou didst seem to go, whether it were to the east, or to the west." So the emperor went forth to the hunt, and he came to the bank of the river. "Behold," said he, "this is where I was when I saw the dream, and I went towards the source of the river westward."

And thereupon thirteen messengers of the emperor's set forth, and before them they saw a high mountain, which seemed to them to touch the sky. Now this was the guise in which the messengers journeyed; one sleeve was on the cap of each of them in front, as a sign that they were messengers, in order that through what hostile land soever they might pass no harm might be done them. And when they were come over this mountain, they beheld vast plains, and large rivers flowing there through.

"Behold," said they, "the land which our master saw."

And they went along the mouths of the rivers, until they came to the mighty river which they saw flowing to the sea, and the vast city, and the many coloured high towers in the castle. They saw the largest fleet in the world, in the harbour of the river, and one ship that was larger than any of the others. "Behold again," said they, "the dream that our master saw." And in the great ship they crossed the sea, and came to the Island of Britain. And they traversed the island until they came to Snowdon. "Behold," said they,

PROPHECIES & ORACLES: MYTHS & TALES

"the rugged land that our master saw." And they went forward until they saw Anglesey before them, and until they saw Arvon likewise. "Behold," said they, "the land our master saw in his sleep." And they saw Aber Sain, and a castle at the mouth of the river. The portal of the castle saw they open, and into the castle they went, and they saw a hall in the castle. Then said they, "Behold, the hall which he saw in his sleep." They went into the hall, and they beheld two youths playing at chess on the golden bench. And they beheld the hoary-headed man beside the pillar, in the ivory chair, carving chessmen. And they beheld the maiden sitting on a chair of ruddy gold.

The messengers bent down upon their knees. "Empress of Rome, all hail!" "Ha, gentles," said the maiden, "ye bear the seeming of honourable men, and the badge of envoys, what mockery is this ye do to me?" "We mock thee not, lady; but the Emperor of Rome hath seen thee in his sleep, and he has neither life nor spirit left because of thee. Thou shalt have of us therefore the choice, lady, whether thou wilt go with us and be made Empress of Rome, or that the emperor come hither and take thee for his wife?" "Ha, lords," said the maiden, "I will not deny what ye say, neither will I believe it too well. If the emperor love me, let him come here to seek me."

And by day and night the messengers hied them back. And when their horses failed, they bought other fresh ones. And when they came to Rome, they saluted the emperor, and asked their boon, which was given to them according as they named it. "We will be thy guides, lord," said they, "over sea and over land, to the place where is the woman whom best thou lovest, for we know her name, and her kindred, and her race."

And immediately the emperor set forth with his army. And these men were his guides. Towards the Island of Britain they went over the sea and the deep. And he conquered the Island from Beli the son of Manogan, and his sons, and drove them to the sea, and went forward even unto Arvon. And the emperor knew the land when he saw it. And when he beheld the castle of Aber Sain, "Look yonder," said he, "there is the castle wherein I saw the damsel whom I best love." And he went forward into the castle and into the hall, and there he saw Kynan the son of Eudav, and Adeon the son of Eudav, playing at chess. And he saw Eudav the son of Caradawc, sitting on a chair of ivory carving chessmen. And the maiden whom he had beheld in his sleep, he saw sitting on a chair of gold. "Empress of Rome," said he, "all hail!" And the emperor threw his arms about her neck; and that night she became his bride.

And the next day in the morning, the damsel asked her maiden portion. And he told her to name what she would. And she asked to have the Island of Britain for her father, from the Channel to the Irish Sea, together with the three adjacent Islands, to hold under the empress of Rome; and to have three chief castles made for her, an whatever places she might choose in the Island of Britain. And she chose to have the highest castle made at Arvon. And they brought thither earth from Rome that it might be more healthful for the emperor to sleep, and sit, and walk upon. After that the two other castles were made for her, which were Caerlleon and Caermarthen.

And one day the emperor went to hunt at Caermarthen, and he came so far as the top of Brevi Vawr, and there the emperor pitched his tent. And that encamping place is called Cadeir Maxen, even to this day. And because that he built the castle with a myriad of men, he called it Caervyrddin. Then Helen bethought her to make high roads from one castle to another throughout the Island of Britain. And the roads were made. And for this cause are they called the roads of Helen Luyddawc, that she was sprung from a native of this island, and the men of the Island of Britain would not have made these great roads for any save for her.

372

Seven years did the emperor tarry in this island. Now, at that time, the men of Rome had a custom, that whatsoever emperor should remain in other lands more than seven years should remain to his own overthrow, and should never return to Rome again.

So they made a new emperor. And this one wrote a letter of threat to Maxen. There was nought in the letter but only this. 'If thou comest, and if thou ever comest to Rome.' And even unto Caerlleon came this letter to Maxen, and these tidings. Then sent he a letter to the man who styled himself emperor in Rome. There was nought in that letter also but only this. 'If I come to Rome, and if I come.'

And thereupon Maxen set forth towards Rome with his army, and vanquished France and Bugundy, and every land on the way, and sat down before the city of Rome.

A year was the emperor before the city, and he was no nearer taking it than the first day. And after him there came the brothers of Helen Luyddawc from the Island of Britain, and a small host with them, and better warriors were in that small host than twice as many Romans. And the emperor was told that a host was seen, halting close to his army and encamping, and no man ever saw a fairer or better appointed host for its size, nor more handsome standards.

And Helen went to see the hosts, and she knew the standards of her brothers. Then came Kynan the son of Eudav, and Adeon the son of Eudav, to meet the emperor. And the emperor was glad because of them, and embraced them.

Then they looked at the Romans as they attacked the city. Said Kynan to his brother, "We will try to attack the city more expertly than this." So they measured by night the height of the wall, and they sent their carpenters to the wood, and a ladder was made for every four men of their number. Now when these were ready, every day at midday the emperors went to meat, and they ceased to fight on both sides till all had finished eating. And in the morning the men of Britain took their food and they drank until they were invigorated. And while the two emperors were at meat, the Britons came to the city, and placed their ladders against it, and forthwith they came in through the city.

The new emperor had no time to arm himself when they fell upon him, and slew him, and many others with him. And three nights and three days were they subduing the men that were in the city and taking the castle. And others of them kept the city, lest any of the host of Maxen should come therein, until they had subjected all to their will.

Then spake Maxen to Helen Luyddawc. "I marvel, lady," said he, "that thy brothers have not conquered this city for me." "Lord, emperor," she answered, "the wisest youths in the world are my brothers. Go thou thither and ask the city of them, and if it be in their possession thou shalt have it gladly." So the emperor and Helen went and demanded the city. And they told the emperor that none had taken the city, and that none could give it him, but the men of the Island of Britain. Then the gates of the city of Rome were opened, and the emperor sat on the throne, and all the men of Rome submitted them selves unto him.

The emperor then said unto Kynan and Adeon, "Lords," said he, "I have now had possession of the whole of my empire. This host give I unto you to vanquish whatever region ye may desire in the world."

So they set forth and conquered lands, and castles, and cities. And they slew all the men, but the women they kept alive. And thus they continued until the young men that had come with them were grown grey-headed, from the length of time they were upon this conquest.

Then spoke Kynan unto Adeon his brother, "Whether wilt thou rather," said he, "tarry in this land, or go back into the land whence thou didst come forth?" Now he chose to go back to his own land, and many with him. But Kynan tarried there with the other part and dwelt there.

And they took counsel and cut out the tongues of the women, lest they should corrupt their speech. And because of the silence of the women from their own speech, the men of Armorica are called Britons. From that time there came frequently, and still comes, that language from the Island of Britain.

And this dream is called the Dream of Maxen Wledig, emperor of Rome. And here it ends.

Seaforth's Dream

BEFORE PROCEEDING TO RELATE the Seer's remarkable prediction, and the extraordinary minuteness with which it has been fulfilled, we shall give the particulars of a curious dream by Lord Seaforth, which was a peculiar forecast of the loss of his faculties of speech and hearing during the latter part of his eventful life. It has been supplied by a member of the family, who shows an unmistakable interest in everything calculated to throw light on the 'prophecies', and who evidently believes them not to be merely an old wife's tale. We give it *verbatim et literatim*: The last Lord Seaforth was born in full possession of all his faculties. When about twelve years of age scarlet fever broke out in the school at which he was boarding. All the boys who were able to be sent away were returned to their homes at once, and some fifteen or twenty boys who had taken the infection were moved into a large room, and there treated. After a week had passed, some boys naturally became worse than others, and some of them were in great danger. One evening, before dark, the attendant nurse, having left the dormitory for a few minutes, was alarmed by a cry. She instantly returned, and found Lord Seaforth in a state of great excitement. After he became calmer, he told the nurse that he had seen, soon after she had left the room, the door opposite to his bed silently open, and a hideous old woman came in. She had a wallet full of something hanging from her neck in front of her. She paused on entering, then turned to the bed close to the door, and stared steadily at one of the boys lying in it. She then passed to the foot of the next boy's bed, and, after a moment, stealthily moved up to the head, and taking from her wallet a mallet and peg, drove the peg into his forehead. Young Seaforth said he heard the crash of the bones, though the boy never stirred. She then proceeded round the room, looking at some boys longer than at others. When she came to him, his suspense was awful. He felt he could not resist or even cry out, and he never could forget, in years after, that moment's agony, when he saw her hand reaching down for a nail and feeling his ears. At last, after a look, she slunk off, and slowly completing the circuit of the room, disappeared noiselessly through the same door by which she had entered. Then he felt the spell seemed to be taken off, and uttered the cry which had alarmed the nurse. The latter laughed at the lad's story, and told him to go to sleep. When the doctor came, an hour later to make his rounds, he observed that the boy was feverish and excited, and asked the nurse afterwards if she knew the cause, whereupon she reported what had occurred. The doctor, struck with the story, returned to the boy's bedside and made him repeat his dream. He took it down in writing at the moment. The following day nothing eventful happened, but, in course of time, some got worse, a few indeed died, others suffered but slightly, while some, though they recovered, bore some evil trace and consequence of the fever for the rest of their lives. The doctor, to his horror, found that those whom Lord Seaforth had described as having a peg driven into their foreheads were those who died from the fever; those whom the old hag passed by recovered, and were none the worse; whereas those she appeared to look at intently, or handled, all suffered afterwards. Lord Seaforth left his bed of sickness almost stone deaf; and, in later years, grieving over the loss of his four sons, absolutely and entirely ceased to speak.

The Conflagration

OURSON NOW FORBADE VIOLETTE to go alone in the forest. She was no longer allowed to carry him his dinner so he always returned to the house at midday. Violette never left the farm without Ourson.

Three years after the event in the forest, Ourson saw Violette arise in the morning pale and exhausted. She was seeking him.

"Come, come," she said, drawing him along, "I have something to say – something to relate – oh, come!"

Ourson was much alarmed and followed her precipitately.

"What is it, dear Violette? For the love of Heaven, speak to me! What can I do for you?"

"Nothing, nothing, dear Ourson; you can do nothing – only listen to me. You remember the dream I had in my childhood, of the toad! The river! The danger! Well, last night I had this same dream again. It is terrible! Terrible! Ourson, dear Ourson, your life is menaced! If you die, I will die also!"

"How! By whom is my life threatened?"

"Listen! I was sleeping and a toad – still a toad – always a toad – came to me and said:

"'The moment approaches when your dear Ourson is to resume his natural skin. To you he is to be indebted for this change. I hate him! I hate you! You shall not make each other happy! Ourson shall perish and you cannot accomplish the sacrifice which in your folly you meditate. In a few days, yes, perhaps in a few hours I shall take a signal vengeance upon you both. Goodbye – do you hear? – till we meet again!'

"I awoke, suppressed a cry which was about to issue from my lips and saw, as I saw on that day in which you saved me from the water, the hideous toad creeping upon the shutter and gazing at me menacingly. It disappeared, leaving me more dead than alive. I arose dressed myself and came to find you my brother, my friend to warn you against the vengeance of the fairy, Furious, and to entreat you to seek the aid of the good fairy, Drolette."

Ourson listened in great alarm. He was not frightened by the fate which menaced himself – he was agitated by the sacrifice which Furious announced and which he understood but too well. The thought alone of his dear and lovely Violette being muffled up in his hideous bear's skin through devotion to him made him tremble and he preferred death. Ourson's anguish was pictured in his countenance, and Violette, who was watching him closely, threw herself upon his neck and sobbed violently.

"Alas! my brother, my dear brother, you will soon be torn from me. You, who do not know what it is to fear, now tremble. You who comfort me, encourage me and sustain me in all my fears have now no word to utter to restore my failing courage. You who have combated the most terrible dangers now bow your head and are resigned to fate."

"No, Violette, it is not fear which makes me tremble – it is not fear which agitates me. It is a word which the fairy Furious has uttered, of which you do not comprehend the meaning but which I understand perfectly. The threat was addressed to you, my Violette. It is for you I tremble!"

Violette divined from this that the moment of sacrifice had come, that she was about to be called upon to keep the promise she had made to the fairy Drolette. In place of trembling and shrinking, she felt the most lively joy. She could now at last make some return for the devotion, the incessant watchful tenderness of her dear Ourson – could in her turn be useful to him. She made no response to the fears expressed by Ourson but thanked him and spoke to him more tenderly than ever before, thinking that soon perhaps she would be separated from him by death. Ourson had the same thought. They both fervently invoked the protection of the fairy Drolette. Ourson, indeed, called upon her in a loud voice but she did not respond to his appeal.

The day passed away sadly. Neither Ourson nor Violette spoke to Agnella on the subject of their disquiet for fear of aggravating her melancholy which had been constantly increasing as Ourson grew to manhood.

"Already twenty years old!" thought she. "If he persists in living in this solitude and seeing no one and in refusing to change with Violette, who asks nothing better, I am certain, I am convinced, he will wear this bear skin till his death."

Agnella wept, often wept; but her tears brought her no remedy.

The day Violette had her frightful dream, Agnella also had a dream. The fairy Drolette had appeared to her:

"Courage, queen," she said to her, "in a few days Ourson will lose his bear's skin and you can give him his true name of Prince Marvellous."

Agnella had awaked full of hope and happiness. She redoubled her tenderness to Violette, believing that it was to her she would owe the happiness of her son.

Everyone retired at night with different feelings. Violette and Ourson, full of anxiety for the future which appeared so threatening, Agnella's heart bounding with joy at that same future which appeared so near and so replete with happiness, Passerose, astonished at the melancholy of the one and the joy of the other and ignorant of the cause of both.

All slept, however. Violette after weeping profusely. Ourson after having invoked the fairy Drolette; Agnella after smiling and thinking of Ourson handsome and attractive and Passerose after saying to herself a hundred times: "But what is the matter with them all today?"

Scarcely an hour after all at the farm were asleep, Violette was awoken by the smell of fire and smoke. Agnella awoke at the same moment.

"Mother," said Violette, "do you not smell something?"

"The house is on fire," said Agnella. "Look what a light is round about us!"

They sprang from their beds and ran to the parlour. The flames had already taken possession of it and of the neighbouring chambers.

"Ourson! Passerose!" cried Agnella.

"Ourson! Ourson!" exclaimed Violette.

Passerose sprang half clothed into the parlour.

"We are lost, madam! The flames are all through the house. The doors and windows are firmly closed – it is impossible to open them."

"My son! My son!" cried Agnella.

"My brother! My brother!" exclaimed Violette.

They ran to the doors; all their efforts to open them or the windows were ineffectual.

"Oh, my terrible dream!" murmured Violette. "Dear Ourson, adieu forever!"

Ourson had also been awakened by the flames and smoke. He slept out of the farmhouse, and near the stable. His first impulse was to run to the front of the house but notwithstanding his extraordinary strength he could not open it. One would have thought that the door would break to pieces under his efforts. It was evidently held fast by the fairy Furious.

Ourson sprang upon a ladder and passed across the flames into a granary through an open window, then descended into the room where his mother and Violette were embracing, expecting instant death. Before they had time to recognize him, he seized them in his arms and cried to Passerose to follow him. He ran along the granary and descended the ladder with his mother in one arm and Violette in the other and followed by Passerose. The moment after they reached the ground in safety, the ladder and granary became a prey to the flames.

Ourson led Agnella and Violette some distance from the fire. Passerose was self-possessed: she had quite a large package of clothing which she had collected at the commencement of the fire. Agnella and Violette had escaped barefooted and in their night robes, and the clothing brought by Passerose was thus very necessary to protect them from the cold. After having thanked Ourson for saving their lives at the peril of his own they complimented Passerose upon her forethought.

"See," said Passerose, "the advantage of not losing one's senses. Whilst you two were only thinking of your Ourson, I made up this package of necessary things."

"That is true, my good Passerose; but what purpose would your package have served, if my mother and Violette had perished in the flames?"

"Oh, I knew very well that you would not allow them to be burned up alive. Is anyone ever in danger when you are present? Is not this the third time you have saved Violette's life?"

Violette pressed Ourson's hands tenderly and carried them to her lips. Agnella embraced her and said:

"Dear Violette, Ourson is happy in your tenderness which fully rewards him for all he has done for you. I feel assured that on your part you would be happy to sacrifice yourself for him if an occasion offered, that only too willingly would you help him."

Before Violette could speak, Ourson said with animation:

"Mother, do not say anything to Violette of sacrificing herself for me. You know the thought alone makes me wretched."

In place of replying to Ourson, Agnella placed her hand on her forehead and cried out anxiously:

"The casket, Passerose! The casket! Have you saved the casket?"

"I forgot it, madam," said Passerose.

The countenance of Agnella expressed such regret and anxiety that Ourson questioned her as to this precious casket which seemed to trouble her so much.

"The casket was a present of the fairy Drolette. She told me that the happiness of Violette was contained in it. It was in the wardrobe, at the foot of my bed. Alas! By what fatality did I forget it?"

She had scarcely uttered these words when the brave Ourson sprang towards the burning house and notwithstanding the tears and supplications of Agnella, Violette and Passerose, disappeared in the flames exclaiming:

"You shall have the casket, Mother, or I will perish with it!"

A horrible silence followed this act of Ourson. Violette fell on her knees with her arms extended towards the burning house, Agnella with her hands clasped looked with straining eyes at the opening through which Ourson had entered while Passerose was motionless, hiding her face with her hands. Some moments passed thus and they appeared ages to the three women who were expecting a sentence of life or death.

Ourson did not reappear. The crackling of the burning wood, the flashing of the flames, increased in violence. Suddenly, a frightful noise made Violette and Agnella utter a cry of despair.

The roof, covered with flames, had fallen in and Ourson was buried under the ruins – crushed by the ruins, consumed by the fire.

The silence of death succeeded this dreadful catastrophe. The flames diminished, then died away – no sound now interrupted the despair of Agnella and Violette.

Violette had fallen into the arms of Agnella and they sobbed thus a long time in silence. Passerose contemplated the smoking ruins and wept. Poor Ourson was buried there a victim of his courage and his devotion! Agnella and Violette still wept bitterly; they appeared neither to hear nor understand what was passing around them.

"Let us leave this place," said Passerose, at last.

Agnella and Violette made no response.

Passerose tried to lead Violette away.

"Come," said she; "come, Violette, let us seek a shelter for the night – the evening fortunately is mild."

"What shelter do I want?" said Violette. "What is the evening to me or the morning? There are no more beautiful days for me! The sun will shine no more but to illumine my despair!"

"But if we remain here weeping we shall die of hunger, Violette, and in spite of the bitterest grief, we must think of the necessities of life."

"Better to die of hunger than of grief! I will not leave this place where I saw my dear Ourson for the last time – where he perished, a victim of his tenderness for us."

Passerose shrugged her shoulders; she remembered that the stable had not been burned so she ran there with all speed, milked the cow, drank a cupful of milk and tried in vain to make Agnella and Violette do the same.

Agnella rose and said to Violette in a solemn tone:

"Your grief is just, my daughter. Never did a more noble or generous heart beat in a human form than Ourson's and he loved you more than he loved himself – to spare your grief he sacrificed his happiness and his life."

Agnella now recounted to Violette the scene which preceded Ourson's birth, the power Violette had to deliver him from his deformity by accepting it for herself and Ourson's constant prayer that Violette should never be informed of the possibility of such a sacrifice.

It is easy to comprehend the feelings of loving tenderness and regret which filled the heart of Violette after this confidence and she wept more bitterly than ever.

"And now, my daughter," continued Agnella, "there remains one duty to fulfil, that is to give burial to my son. We must clear away these ruins and remove the ashes and when we have found the remains of our well-beloved Ourson—"

Sobs interrupted her speech; she could say no more.

Origin Prophecies

Introduction

THE STORY OF 'The Elephant and the Lion' involves a chain reaction of violence in what was once a peaceful forest. A boastful, swaggering elephant slays a young lion, and his victim's parents come after him. The elephant kills the dead cat's father but is killed in his turn by the lion's brother. Another elephant kills him and is then attacked by a passing man. He mauls the man to death, but is left with a spear in his side. The dead man's wife turns to flee, but the elephant tells her not to fear: 'The happy days in the woods are ended for all the tribes,' he says. 'Animals will be henceforth at constant war one with another. Lions will no more greet elephants, the buffaloes will be shy, the rhinoceroses will live apart, and man when he comes within the shadows will think of nothing else than his terrors, and he will fancy an enemy in every shadow. I am sorely wounded, for thy man stole up to my side and drove his spear into me, and soon I shall die.' Prophecies like this set out the way that the world was to be ordered; the shape that Nature was to take, the directions in which civilizations were to go.

Ion

ION WAS THE SON of Creusa (the beauteous daughter of Erechtheus, King of Athens) and the sun-god Phoebus-Apollo, to whom she was united without the knowledge of her father.

Fearing the anger of Erechtheus, Creusa placed her new-born babe in a little wicker basket, and hanging some golden charms round his neck, invoked for him the protection of the gods, and concealed him in a lonely cave. Apollo, pitying his deserted child, sent Hermes to convey him to Delphi, where he deposited his charge on the steps of the temple. Next morning the Delphic priestess discovered the infant, and was so charmed by his engaging appearance that she adopted him as her own son. The young child was carefully tended and reared by his kind foster-mother, and was brought up in the service of the temple, where he was intrusted with some of the minor duties of the holy edifice.

And now to return to Creusa. During a war with the Euboeans, in which the latter were signally defeated, Xuthus, son of Aeolus, greatly distinguished himself on the side of the Athenians, and as a reward for his valuable services, the hand of Creusa, the king's daughter, was bestowed upon him in marriage. Their union, however, was not blest with children, and as this was a source of great grief to both of them, they repaired to Delphi in order to consult the oracle. The response was, that Xuthus should regard the first person who met him on leaving the sanctuary as his son. Now it happened that Ion, the young guardian of the temple, was the first to greet his view, and when Xuthus beheld the beautiful youth, he gladly welcomed him as his son, declaring that the gods had sent him to be a blessing and comfort to his old age. Creusa, however, who concluded that the youth was the offspring of a secret marriage on the part of her husband, was filled with suspicion and jealousy; when an old servant, observing her grief, begged her to be comforted, assuring her that the cause of her distress should be speedily removed.

When, upon the occasion of the public adoption of his son, Xuthus gave a grand banquet, the old servant of Creusa contrived to mix a strong poison in the wine of the unsuspecting Ion. But the youth – according to the pious custom of the ancients, of offering a libation to the gods before partaking of any repast – poured upon the ground a portion of the wine before putting it to his lips, when suddenly, as if by a miracle, a dove flew into the banquet hall, and sipped of the wine of the libation; whereupon the poor little creature began to quiver in every limb, and in a few moments expired.

Ion's suspicions at once fell upon the obsequious servant of Creusa, who with such officious attention had filled his cup. He violently seized the old man, and accused him of his murderous intentions. Unprepared for this sudden attack he admitted his guilt, but pointed to the wife of Xuthus as the instigator of the crime. Ion was about to avenge himself upon Creusa, when, by means of the divine intervention of Apollo, his foster-mother, the Delphic priestess appeared on the scene, and explained the true relationship which existed between Creusa and Ion. In order to set all doubts at rest, she produced the charms which she had found round the neck of the infant, and also the wicker basket in which he had been conveyed to Delphi.

Mother and son now became reconciled to each other, and Creusa revealed to Ion the secret of his divine origin. The priestess of Delphi foretold that he would become the father of a great nation, called after him the Ionians, and also that Xuthus and Creusa would have a son called Dorus, who would be the progenitor of the Dorian people, both of which predictions were in due time verified.

The Story of the Drummer and the Alligators

THERE WAS ONCE A WOMAN named Affiong Any who lived at Nsidung, a small town to the south of Calabar. She was married to a chief of Hensham Town called Etim Ekeng. They had lived together for several years, but had no children. The chief was very anxious to have a child during his lifetime, and made sacrifices to his Ju Ju, but they had no effect. So he went to a witch man, who told him that the reason he had no children was that he was too rich. The chief then asked the witch man how he should spend his money in order to get a child, and he was told to make friends with everybody, and give big feasts, so that he should get rid of some of his money and become poorer.

The chief then went home and told his wife. The next day his wife called all her company together and gave them a big dinner, which cost a lot of money; much food was consumed, and large quantities of tombo were drunk. Then the chief entertained his company, which cost a lot more money. He also wasted a lot of money in the Egbo house. When half of his property was wasted, his wife told him that she had conceived. The chief, being very glad, called a big play for the next day.

In those days all the rich chiefs of the country belonged to the Alligator Company, and used to meet in the water. The reason they belonged to the company was, first of all, to protect their canoes when they went trading, and secondly, to destroy the canoes and property of the people who did not belong to their company, and to take their money and kill their slaves.

Chief Etim Ekeng was a kind man, and would not join this society, although he was repeatedly urged to do so. After a time a son was born to the chief, and he called him Edet Etim. The chief then called the Egbo society together, and all the doors of the houses in the town were shut, the markets were stopped, and the women were not allowed to go outside their houses while the Egbo was playing. This was kept up for several days, and cost the chief a lot of money. Then he made up his mind that he would divide his property, and give his son half when he became old enough. Unfortunately after three months the chief died, leaving his sorrowing wife to look after their little child.

The wife then went into mourning for seven years for her husband, and after that time she became entitled to all his property, as the late chief had no brothers. She looked after the little boy very carefully until he grew up, when he became a very fine, healthy young man, and was much admired by all the pretty girls of the town; but his mother warned him

ORIGIN PROPHECIES

strongly not to go with them, because they would make him become a bad man. Whenever the girls had a play they used to invite Edet Etim, and at last he went to the play, and they made him beat the drum for them to dance to. After much practice he became the best drummer in the town, and whenever the girls had a play they always called him to drum for them. Plenty of the young girls left their husbands, and went to Edet and asked him to marry them. This made all the young men of the town very jealous, and when they met together at night they considered what would be the best way to kill him. At last they decided that when Edet went to bathe they would induce the alligators to take him. So one night, when he was washing, one alligator seized him by the foot, and others came and seized him round the waist. He fought very hard, but at last they dragged him into the deep water, and took him to their home.

When his mother heard this, she determined to do her best to recover her son, so she kept quite quiet until the morning.

When the young men saw that Edet's mother remained quiet, and did not cry, they thought of the story of the hawk and the owl, and determined to keep Edet alive for a few months.

At cockcrow the mother raised a cry, and went to the grave of her dead husband in order to consult his spirit as to what she had better do to recover her lost son. After a time she went down to the beach with small young green branches in her hands, with which she beat the water, and called upon all the Ju Jus of the Calabar River to help her to recover her son. She then went home and got a load of rods, and took them to a Ju Ju man in the farm. His name was Ininen Okon; he was so called because he was very artful, and had plenty of strong Ju Jus.

When the young boys heard that Edet's mother had gone to Ininen Okon, they all trembled with fear, and wanted to return Edet, but they could not do so, as it was against the rules of their society. The Ju Ju man having discovered that Edet was still alive, and was being detained in the alligators' house, told the mother to be patient. After three days Ininen himself joined another alligators' society, and went to inspect the young alligators' house. He found a young man whom he knew, left on guard when all the alligators had gone to feed at the ebb of the tide, and came back and told the mother to wait, as he would make a Ju Ju which would cause them all to depart in seven days, and leave no one in the house. He made his Ju Ju, and the young alligators said that, as no one had come for Edet, they would all go at the ebb tide to feed, and leave no one in charge of the house. When they returned they found Edet still there, and everything as they had left it, as Ininen had not gone that day.

Three days afterwards they all went away again, and this time went a long way off, and did not return quickly. When Ininen saw that the tide was going down he changed himself into an alligator, and swam to the young alligators' home, where he found Edet chained to a post. He then found an axe and cut the post, releasing the boy. But Edet, having been in the water so long, was deaf and dumb. He then found several loin cloths which had been left behind by the young alligators, so he gathered them together and took them away to show to the king, and Ininen left the place, taking Edet with him.

He then called the mother to see her son, but when she came the boy could only look at her, and could not speak. The mother embraced her boy, but he took no notice, as he did not seem capable of understanding anything, but sat down quietly. Then the Ju Ju man told Edet's mother that he would cure her son in a few days, so he made several Ju Jus, and gave her son medicine, and after a time the boy recovered his speech and became sensible again.

Then Edet's mother put on a mourning cloth, and pretended that her son was dead, and did not tell the people he had come back to her. When the young alligators returned, they found that Edet was gone, and that someone had taken their loin cloths. They were therefore much afraid, and made inquiries if Edet had been seen, but they could hear nothing about him, as he was hidden in a farm, and the mother continued to wear her mourning cloth in order to deceive them.

Nothing happened for six months, and they had quite forgotten all about the matter. Affiong, the mother, then went to the chiefs of the town, and asked them to hold a large meeting of all the people, both young and old, at the palaver house, so that her late husband's property might be divided up in accordance with the native custom, as her son had been killed by the alligators.

The next day the chiefs called all the people together, but the mother in the early morning took her son to a small room at the back of the palaver house, and left him there with the seven loin cloths which the Ju Ju man had taken from the alligators' home. When the chiefs and all the people were seated, Affiong stood up and addressed them, saying –

"Chiefs and young men of my town, eight years ago my husband was a fine young man. He married me, and we lived together for many years without having any children. At last I had a son, but my husband died a few months afterwards. I brought my boy up carefully, but as he was a good drummer and dancer the young men were jealous, and had him caught by the alligators. Is there anyone present who can tell me what my son would have become if he had lived?" She then asked them what they thought of the alligator society, which had killed so many young men.

The chiefs, who had lost a lot of slaves, told her that if she could produce evidence against any members of the society they would destroy it at once. She then called upon Ininen to appear with her son Edet. He came out from the room leading Edet by the hand, and placed the bundle of loin cloths before the chiefs.

The young men were very much surprised when they saw Edet, and wanted to leave the palaver house; but when they stood up to go the chiefs told them to sit down at once, or they would receive three hundred lashes. They then sat down, and the Ju Ju man explained how he had gone to the alligators' home, and had brought Edet back to his mother. He also said that he had found the seven loin cloths in the house, but he did not wish to say anything about them, as the owners of some of the cloths were sons of the chiefs.

The chiefs, who were anxious to stop the bad society, told him, however, to speak at once and tell them everything. Then he undid the bundle and took the cloths out one by one, at the same time calling upon the owners to come and take them. When they came to take their cloths, they were told to remain where they were; and they were then told to name their company. The seven young men then gave the names of all the members of their society, thirty-two in all. These men were all placed in a line, and the chiefs then passed sentence, which was that they should all be killed the next morning on the beach. So they were then all tied together to posts, and seven men were placed as a guard over them. They made fires and beat drums all the night.

Early in the morning, at about 4am, the big wooden drum was placed on the roof of the palaver house, and beaten to celebrate the death of the evildoers, which was the custom in those days.

The boys were then unfastened from the posts, and had their hands tied behind their backs, and were marched down to the beach. When they arrived there, the head chief stood up and addressed the people. "This is a small town of which I am chief, and I am determined to stop this bad custom, as so many men have been killed." He then told a man who had a sharp matchet to cut off one man's head. He then told another man who had a sharp knife to skin another young man alive. A third man who had a heavy stick was ordered to beat another to death, and so the chief went on and killed all the thirty-two young men in the most horrible ways he could think of. Some of them were tied to posts in the river, and left there until the tide came up and drowned them. Others were flogged to death.

After they had all been killed, for many years no one was killed by alligators, but some little time afterwards on the road between the beach and the town the land fell in, making a very large and deep hole, which was said to be the home of the alligators, and the people have ever since tried to fill it up, but have never yet been able to do so.

Why Dead People are Buried

IN THE BEGINNING OF THE WORLD when the Creator had made men and women and the animals, they all lived together in the creation land. The Creator was a big chief, past all men, and being very kind-hearted, was very sorry whenever anyone died. So one day he sent for the dog, who was his head messenger, and told him to go out into the world and give his word to all people that for the future whenever anyone died the body was to be placed in the compound, and wood ashes were to be thrown over it; that the dead body was to be left on the ground, and in twenty-four hours it would become alive again.

When the dog had travelled for half a day he began to get tired; so as he was near an old woman's house he looked in, and seeing a bone with some meat on it he made a meal off it, and then went to sleep, entirely forgetting the message which had been given him to deliver.

After a time, when the dog did not return, the Creator called for a sheep, and sent him out with the same message. But the sheep was a very foolish one, and being hungry, began eating the sweet grasses by the wayside. After a time, however, he remembered that he had a message to deliver, but forgot what it was exactly; so as he went about among the people he told them that the message the Creator had given him to tell the people, was that whenever anyone died they should be buried underneath the ground.

A little time afterwards the dog remembered his message, so he ran into the town and told the people that they were to place wood ashes on the dead bodies and leave them in the compound, and that they would come to life again after twenty-four hours. But the people would not believe him, and said, "We have already received the word from the Creator by the sheep, that all dead bodies should be buried." In consequence of this the dead bodies are now always buried, and the dog is much disliked and not trusted as a messenger, as if he had not found the bone in the old woman's house and forgotten his message, the dead people might still be alive.

How Kimyera Became King of Uganda

MANY AGES AGO Uni reigned as king over Unyoro, a great country which lies to the north and west of Uganda. One day he took to wife Wanyana, a woman of the neighbouring kingdom, who on the first night she had been taken into the inner harem manifested a violent aversion for his person. At that time a man named Kalimera, who was a dealer in cattle, was visiting the court, and had already resided some months there as an honoured guest of the king, on account of his agreeable manners, and his accomplishments on the flute. During his stay he had not failed to note the beauty of the young women who were permitted to crowd around him while he played; but it had long been observed that he had been specially attracted by the charms of Wanyana. It was whispered by a few of the more maliciously disposed among the women that a meeting had taken place, and that an opportunity had been found by them to inform each other of their mutual passion. However that may be, King Uni, surprised at the dislike which she manifested towards him, forbore pressing her for the time, trustfully believing that her sentiments would change for the better after a more intimate acquaintance with him. Meantime he built for her a separate apartment, and palisaded its court closely around with thick cane. His visits were paid to her on alternate days, and each time he brought some gift of bead or bark-cloth, or soft, furry hide, in the hope of winning her favour.

In time she discovered that she was pregnant, and, fearing King Uni's wrath, she made a compact with him that if he would abstain from visiting her for one month she would repay his kindness with all affection. Uni gladly consented to this proposal, and confined his attentions to sending his pages with daily greetings and gifts. Meantime she endeavoured through her own servants to communicate with Kalimera, her lover, but, though no effort on her part was wanting, she could gain no news of him, except a report that soon after she had entered the harem of Uni, Kalimera had disappeared.

In a few days she was delivered of a fine male child, but as she would undoubtedly be slain by the king if the child was discovered, she departed by night with it, and laid it, clad in fur adorned with fine bead-work, at the bottom of a potter's pit. She then hastened to a soothsayer in the neighbourhood, and bribed him to contrive in some way to receive and rear her child until he could be claimed. Satisfied with his assurance that the child would be safe, Wanyana returned to her residence at the court in the same secret manner that she had left it.

Next morning Mugema, the potter, was seen passing the soothsayer's door, and was hailed by the great witch-finder.

"Mugema," said he, "thy pots are now made of rotten clay. They are not at all what they used to be. They now crumble in the hand. Tell me why is this?"

"Ah, doctor, it is just that. I thought to bribe thee to tell me, only I did not wish to disturb thee."

ORIGIN PROPHECIES

"It is well, Mugema; I will tell thee why. Thou hast an enemy who wishes evil to thee, but I will defeat his projects. Haste thou to thy pit, and whatever living thing thou findest there, keep it, and rear it kindly. While it lives thou art safe from all harm."

Wondering at this news, Mugema departed from the soothsayer's house, and proceeded to the pit where he obtained his clay. Peering softly over the edge of the pit, he saw a bundle of bark-cloth and fur. From its external appearance he could not guess what this bundle might contain, but, fearing to disturb it by any precipitate movement, he silently retreated from the pit, and sped away to tell his wife, as he was in duty bound, and obtain her advice and assistance, for the wife in all such matters is safer than the man. His wife on hearing this news cried out at him, saying:

"Why, what a fool thou art! Why didst thou not do as the soothsayer commanded thee? Come, I will go with thee at once, for my mind is troubled with a dream which I had last night, and this thing thou tellest me may have a weighty meaning for us both."

Mugema and his wife hurried together towards the clay-pit, and as her husband insisted on it, she crept silently to its edge to look down. At that moment the child uttered a cry and moved the clothes which covered it.

"Why, it is a babe," cried the woman; "just as I found it in my dream. Hurry, Mugema. Descend quickly, and bring it up to me; and take care not to hurt it."

Mugema wondered so much at his wife's words that he almost lost his wits, but being pushed into the pit he mechanically obeyed, and brought up the bundle and its living occupant, which he handed to his wife without uttering a word.

On opening the bundle there was discovered the form of a beautiful and remarkably lusty child, of such weight, size, and form, that the woman exclaimed:

"Oh! Mugema, was ever anybody's luck like this of ours? My very heart sighed for a child that I could bring up to be our joy, and here the good spirits have given us the pick of all the world. Mugema, thy fortune is made."

"But whose child is it?" asked Mugema, suspiciously.

"How can I tell thee that? Hadst thou not brought the news to me of it being in the pit, I should have been childless all my life. The soothsayer who directed thee hither is a wise man. He knows the secret, I warrant him. But come, Mugema, drop these silly thoughts. What sayest thou? Shall we rear the child, or leave it here to perish?"

"All right, wife. If it prove of joy to thee, I shall live content."

Thus it was that the child of Wanyana found foster-parents, and no woman in Unyoro could be prouder of her child than Mugema's wife came to be of the foundling. The milk of woman, goat, and cow was given to him, and he throve prodigiously; and when Mugema asked the soothsayer what name would be fittest for him, the wise man said:

"Call him Kimyera – the mighty one."

Some months after this, when Kimyera was about a year old, Wanyana came to the potter's house to purchase pots for her household, and while she was seated in the porch selecting the soundest among them, she heard a child crying within.

"Ah, has thy wife had a child lately? I did not observe or hear when I last visited thee that she was likely to become a mother."

"No, princess," replied Mugema; "that is the cry of a child I discovered in the clay-pit about a year ago."

Wanyana's heart gave a great jump, and for a moment she lost all recollection of where she was. Recovering herself with a great effort, she bade Mugema tell her all about the incident: but while he related the story, she was busy thinking how she might assure herself of his secrecy if she declared herself to be the mother of the child.

Mugema, before concluding his story, did not fail to tell Wanyana how for a time he had suspected his wife of having played him falsely, and that though he had no grounds for the suspicion further than that the clay-pit was his own and the child had been found in it, he was not quite clear in his mind yet, and he would be willing to slave a long time for any person who could thoroughly disabuse his mind of the doubt, as, with that exception, his wife was the cleverest and best woman in Unyoro.

Wanyana, perceiving her opportunity, said:

"Well, much as I affected not to know about the child, I know whose child it is, and who placed it in the pit."

"Thou, princess!" he cried.

"Yes, and, if thou wilt take an oath upon the great Muzimu to keep it secret, I will disclose the name of the mother."

"Thou hast my assurance of secrecy upon the condition that the child is not proved to be my wife's. Whosoever else's it may be, matters not to me; the child was found, and is mine by right of the finder. Now name the mother, princess."

"Wanyana!"

"Thine?"

"Even so. It is the offspring of fond love, and Kalimera of Uganda is his father. The young man belongs to one of the four royal clans of Uganda, called the Elephant clan. He is the youngest son of the late king of Uganda. To him, on his father's death, fell his mother's portion, a pastoral district rich in cattle not far from the frontier of Unyoro. It was while he drove fat herds here for sale to Uni that he saw and loved me, and I knew him as my lord. Dreading the king's anger, he fled, and I was left loveless in the power of Uni. One night the child was born, and in the darkness I crept out of the king's court, and bore the babe to thy pit. To the wise man I confided the secret of that birth. Thou knowest the rest."

"Princess, my wife never appeared fairer to me than she does now, and I owe the clear eye to thee. Rest in peace. My wife loves the babe, let her nurse it until happier times, and I will guard it safe as though it were mine own. Ay, the babe, I feel assured, will pay me well when he is grown. The words of the wise man come home to me now, and I see whereby good luck shall come to all. If bone and muscle can make a king, Kimyera's future is sure. But come in to see my wife, and to her discretion and wisdom confide thy tale frankly."

Wanyana soon was hanging over her child, and, amid tears of joy, she made Mugema's wife acquainted with his birth, and obtained from her earnest assurance that he would be tenderly cared for, and her best help in any service she could perform for Kimyera and his mother.

Great friendship sprang up between Princess Wanyana and the potter Mugema and his wife, and she found frequent excuses for visiting the fast-growing child.

Through the influence of the princess, the potter increased in riches, and his herds multiplied; and when Kimyera was grown tall and strong, he was entrusted by his foster-father with the care of the cattle, and he gave him a number of strong youths as assistants. With these Kimyera indulged in manly games, until he became wonderfully dexterous in casting the spear, and drawing the bow, and in wrestling. His swiftness exceeded that of the fleetest antelope; no animal of the plain could escape him when he gave chase. His

ORIGIN PROPHECIES

courage, proved in the defence of his charge, became a proverb among all who knew him. If the cry of the herdsman warned him that a beast sought to prey upon the cattle, Kimyera never lost time to put himself in front, and, with spear and arrow, he often became victor.

With the pride becoming the possessor of so many admirable qualities, he would drive his herds right through the corn-fields of the villagers, and to all remonstrances he simply replied that the herds belonged to Wanyana, favourite wife of Uni. The people belonged to her also, as well as their corn, and who could object to Wanyana's cattle eating Wanyana's corn?

As his reputation for strength and courage was well known, the villagers then submissively permitted him to do as he listed.

As he grew up in might and valour, Uni's regards cooled towards Wanyana, and, as she was not permitted that freedom formerly enjoyed by her, her visits to Kimyera ceased. Mugema sympathized with the mother, and contrived to send Kimyera with pots to sell to the people of the court, with strict charge to discover every piece of news relating to the Princess Wanyana. The mother's heart dilated with pride every time she saw her son, and she contrived in various ways to lengthen the interview. And each time he returned to his home he carried away some gift from Wanyana, such as leopard-skins, strings of beast claws, beads, and crocodile-teeth, girdles of white monkey-skin, parcels of ground ochre, or camwood, or rare shells, to show Mugema and his wife. And often he used to say, "Wanyana bade me ask you to accept this gift from her as a token of her esteem," showing them similar articles.

His mother's presents to him in a short time enabled him to purchase two fine large dogs – one was black as charcoal, which was named by him *Msigissa*, or 'Darkness', the other was white as a cotton tuft, and called *Sema-gimbi*, or 'Wood-burr'. You must know that it is because of the dog Darkness that the Baboon clan of Uganda became so attached to black dogs, by which they perpetuate the memory of Kimyera.

When he had become the owner of Darkness and Wood-burr, he began to absent himself from home for longer periods, leaving the herds in charge of the herdsmen. With these he explored the plains, and hills, and woods to a great distance from his home. Sometimes he would be absent for weeks, causing great anxiety to his kind foster-parents. The further he went the more grew his passion to know what lay beyond the furthest ridge he saw, which, when discovered, he would be again tempted to explore another that loomed in the far distance before him. With every man he met he entered into conversation, and obtained a various knowledge of things of interest relating to the country, the people, and the chiefs. In this manner before many months he had a wide knowledge of every road and river, village and tribe, in the neighbouring lands.

On his return from these daring excursions, he would be strictly questioned by Mugema and his wife as to what he had been doing, but he evaded giving the entire truth by rehearsing the hunting incidents that attended his wanderings, so that they knew not the lands he had seen, nor the distances that he travelled. However, being uneasy in their minds they communicated to Wanyana all that was related to them and all they suspected. Wanyana then sought permission to pay a visit to the potter and his wife, and during the visit she asked Kimyera, "Pray tell me, my son, whither dost thou travel on these long journeys of thine to seek for game?"

"Oh! I travel far through woods, and over grassy hills and plains."

"But is it in the direction of sunrise, or sunset, is it north or is it south of here?"

To which he replied: "I seek game generally in the direction whence the sun rises."

"Ah!" said Wanyana. "In that way lies Ganda, where thy father lives, and whence he came in former days to exchange cattle for salt and hoes."

"My father! What may be my father's name, mother?"

"Kalimera."

"And where did he live?"

"His village is called Willimera, and is near the town of Bakka."

"Bakka! I know the town, for in some of my journeys I entered a long way into Uganda, and have chased the leopard in the woods that border the stream called Myanja, and over the plains beyond the river many an antelope has fallen a victim to my spear."

"It is scarcely credible, my son."

"Nay, but it is true, Mother."

"Then thou must have been near Willimera in that case, and it is a pity that thou shouldst not have seen thy father, and been received by him."

A few days later Kimyera slung his knitted haversack over his shoulder, and with shield, two spears, and his faithful dogs Darkness and Wood-burr, he strode out of the potter's house, and set his face once more towards the Myanja river. At the first village across the stream he questioned the natives if they knew Willimera, and was told that it was but eight hours east. The next day he arrived, and travelled round the village, and rested that night at the house of one of the herdsmen of Kalimera. He made himself very agreeable to his host, and from him he received the fullest information of all matters relating to his father.

The next day he began his return to Unyoro, which he reached in two weeks. He told Mugema and his foster-mother of his success, and they sent a messenger to apprise Wanyana that Kimyera had returned home.

Wanyana, impatient to learn the news, arrived that night at Mugema's house, and implored Kimyera to tell her all that he had heard and seen.

"In brief, it is this," replied Kimyera. "I now know to a certainty where Kalimera lives. I have gone round the village, I know how many natives are in it, how many herds of cattle, and how many herdsmen and slaves he has. Kalimera is well. All these I learned from one of his chief herdsmen with whom I rested a night. I came here straight to let thee and my foster-parents know it."

"It is very well, my son. Now, Mugema, it is time to move," she said to the potter. "Uni daily becomes more intolerable to me. I never have yet mated with him as his wife, and I have been true to the one man who seemed to me to be the comeliest of his kind. Now that I know Kalimera lives, my heart has gone to him, though my body is here. Mugema, speak, my friend."

"Wanyana, my wit is slow and my tongue is heavy. Thou knowest my circumstances. I have one wife, but many cattle. The two cows, Namala and Nakaombeh, thou gavest me first, I possess still. Their milk has always been abundant and sweet. Namala has sufficed to nourish Kimyera into perfect lustiness and strength; Nakaombeh gives more than will feed my wife and I. Let Kimyera take his flute, his dogs, Darkness and Wood-burr, his spears and shield; Sebarija, my cowherd, who taught Kimyera the flute, will also take his flute and staff, and drive Namala and Nakaombeh. My wife will carry a few furs, some of the spoils won by Kimyera's prowess; and, lo! I and my family will follow Wanyana."

"A true friend thou hast been to me and mine, Mugema! We will hence before dawn. In Willimera thou shalt receive tenfold what thou leavest here. The foundling of the clay-pit has grown tall and strong, and at last he has found the way to his father and his father's kindred."

And as Wanyana advised, the journey was undertaken that night, and before the sun arose Wanyana, Mugema and his wife, the slave Sebarija driving the two cows, Namala and Nakaombeh, were far on their way eastward, Kimyera and his two dogs, Darkness and Wood-burr, preceding the emigrants and guiding the way.

The food they took with them sustained them for two days; but on the third day they saw a lonely buffalo, and Kimyera, followed by Mugema and Sebarija, chased him. The buffalo was uncommonly wild, and led them a long chase, far out of sight of the two women. Then Mugema reflected that they had done wrong in thus leaving the two women alone, and called out to Sebarija to hurry back, and to look after the women and two cows. Not long after, Darkness fastened his fangs in the buffalo, until Wood-burr came up and assisted him to bring it to the ground, and there they held him until Kimyera gave him his death-stroke. The two men loaded themselves with the meat, and returned to the place where they had left, but alas! they found no traces of the two women, nor of Sebarija and the two cows.

Day after day Kimyera and Mugema hunted all around the country for news of the missing party, until, finally, to their great sorrow, they were obliged to abandon the search, and came to the conclusion that it was best for them to continue their journey and trust to chance for the knowledge they desired.

Near Ganda another buffalo was sighted by Kimyera, and, bidding Mugema remain at the first house he came to, he went after it with his dogs. The buffalo galloped far, and near noon he stood still under the shelter of a rock. Kimyera bounded to the top, and, exerting all his strength, he shot his spear clean through the back of the animal. That rock is still shown to strangers as the place where Kimyera killed the first game in Uganda, and even the place where he stood may be seen by the marks of his feet which were impressed on it. While resting on the rock he saw a woman pass near by with a gourd of water. He called out to her, and begged for a drop to allay his thirst. She smilingly complied, as the stranger was comely and his manner pleasant. They entered into conversation, during which he learned that she belonged to Ganda, and served as maid to Queen Naku, wife of Sebwana, and that Naku was kind to strangers, and was famed for her hospitality to them.

"Dost thou think she will be kind to me?" asked Kimyera. "I am a native of Unyoro, and I am seeking a house where I may rest."

To which the maid replied: "It is the custom of Naku, and, indeed, of all the princes of Ganda, to entertain the stranger since, in the far olden times, the first prince settled in this land in which he was a stranger. But what may that be which is secured in thy girdle?"

"That is a reed flute on which I imitate when alone the songs of such birds as sound sweetest to me."

"And art thou clever at it?" asked the maid.

"Be thou judge," he said; and forthwith blew on his flute until the maid marvelled greatly.

When he had ended, she clapped her hands gaily and said:

"Thou wilt be more than welcome to Naku and her people. Haste and follow me that I may show thee to her, for thy fortune is made."

"Nay. I have a companion not far from here, and I must not lose him. But thou mayest say thou hast met a stranger who, when he has found his friend, will present himself before Queen Naku and Sebwana before sunset."

The maid withdrew and Kimyera rose, and cutting a large portion of the meat he retraced his steps, and sought and found Mugema, to whom he told all his adventures.

After washing the stains of travel and refreshing themselves, they proceeded into the village to the residence of the queen and her consort Sebwana. Naku was prepared by the favourable reports of the maid to receive Kimyera kindly, but when she saw his noble proportions and handsome figure she became violently in love with him, and turning to Sebwana she said:

"See now, we have guests of worth and breeding. They must have travelled from a far land, for I have heard of no tribe which could boast of such a youth as this. Let us receive him and his old friend nobly. Let a house close by our own be made ready for his lodging, and let it be furnished with abundance of food, with wine (banana wine) and milk, bananas and yams, water and fuel, and let nothing be lacking to show our esteem for them." Sebwana gave orders accordingly and proceeded to select a fit house as a lodging for the guests.

Then Naku said: "I hear that thou art skilled in music. If that is the instrument in thy girdle with which thou hast delighted my maid, I should be pleased to hear thee."

"Yes, Queen Naku, it is my flute; and if my music will delight thee, my best efforts are at thy service."

Then Kimyera, kneeling on the leopard-skins placed for the convenience of himself and Mugema, took out his flute, and after one or two flourishes, poured forth such melodious sounds that Naku, unable to keep her eyes open, closed them and lay down with panting breasts, while her senses were filled as it were with dreams of happier lands, and faces of brighter people than ever she knew in real life. As he varied the notes, so varied the gladsome visions of her mind. When the music gently vibrated on her ears, her body palpitated under the influence of the emotions which swayed her; when they became more enlivened she tossed her arms about, and laughed convulsively; and when the notes took a solemn tone, she sighed and wept as though all her friends had left her only their tender memory. Grieved that Naku should suffer, Kimyera woke the queen from her sorrowful condition with tones that soon started her to her feet, and lo, all at once, those who were present joined in the lively dance, and nothing but gay laughter was heard from them. Oh, it was wonderful what quick changes came over people as they heard the flute of Kimyera. When he ceased people began to look at one another in a foolish and confused way, as though something very strange had happened to them.

But Naku quickly recovered, and went to Kimyera, smiling and saying:

"It is for thee to command, O Kimyera. To resist thy flute would be impossible. Again welcome to Ganda, and we shall see if we cannot keep thee and thy flute amongst us."

She conducted Kimyera and his foster-father Mugema to their house. She examined carefully the arrangements made by the slaves, and when she found anything amiss she corrected it with her own hands. Before she parted from them she called Mugema aside, and questioned him further respecting the youth, by which means she obtained many interesting particulars concerning him.

On arriving at her own house she called all the pages of the court to her, and gave orders that if Sebwana told them to convey such and such things to the strangers next day, that none of them should do so, but carry them to the rear court where only women were admitted.

In consequence of this command Mugema and Kimyera found themselves deserted next day, and not one person went near them. Mugema therefore sought an interview the day after with Queen Naku and said:

ORIGIN PROPHECIES

"The custom of this country seems strange to us, O Queen. On the first day we came thy favours showered abundance on us, but on the next not a single person showed his face to us. Had we been in a wilderness we could not have been more alone. It is possible that we may have offended thee unknown to ourselves. Pray acquaint us with our offence, or permit us to depart at once from Ganda."

"Nay, Mugema, I must ask thee to be patient. Food ye shall have in abundance, through my women, and much more is in store for ye. But come, I will visit the young stranger, and thou shalt lead me to him."

Kimyera had been deep in thought ever since he had parted from Naku, and he had not observed what Mugema had complained of; but on seeing Naku enter his house, he hasted and laid matting on the floor, and, covering it with leopard-skins, begged Naku to be seated on them. He brought fresh banana-leaves in his arms, and spread them near her, on which he arranged meat and salt, and bananas and clotted milk, and kneeled before her like a ready servitor.

Naku observed all his movements, her admiration for his person and graces of body becoming stronger every minute. She peeled a mellow banana and handed it to him, saying, "Let Kimyera taste and eat with me, and I will then know that I am in the house of a friend."

Kimyera accepted the gift with thanks, and ate the banana as though he had never eaten anything so delicious in his life. Then he also peeled a beautiful and ripe banana, and, presenting it to her on a fragment of green leaf with both hands, said to her:

"Queen Naku, it is the custom of my country for the master of the house to wait upon his guests. Wherefore accept, O Queen, this banana as a token of friendship from the hands of Kimyera."

The queen smiled, bent forward with her eyes fixed on his own, and took the yellow fruit, and ate it as though such sweetness was not known in the banana land of Ganda.

When she had eaten she said:

"List, Kimyera, and thou, Mugema, hearken well, for I am about to utter weighty words. In Ganda, since the death of my father, there has been no king. Sebwana is my consort by choice of the elders of the land, but in name only. He is really only my *kate-kiro* (Premier). But I am now old enough to choose a king for myself, and according to custom, I may do so. Wherefore I make known to thee, Mugema, that I have already chosen my lord and husband, and he by due right must occupy the chair of my father, the old king who is dead. I have said to myself since the day before yesterday that my lord and husband shall be Kimyera."

Both Kimyera and Mugema prostrated themselves three times before Naku, and, after the youth had recovered from his confusion and surprise, he replied:

"But, Queen Naku, hast thou thought what the people will say to this? May it not be that they will ask, 'Who is this stranger that he should reign over us?' and they will be wroth with me and try to slay me?"

"Nay. For thou art my father's brother's son, as Mugema told me, and my father having left no male heirs of his body, his daughter may, if she choose, ally herself with a son of his brother. Kalimera is a younger brother of my father. Thou seest, therefore, that thou, Kimyera, hast a right to the king's chair, if I, Naku, will it to be so."

"And how, Naku, dost thou propose to act? In thy cause my arm is ready to strike. Thou hast but to speak."

"In this way. I will now leave thee, for I have some business for Sebwana. When he has gone I will then send for thee, and thou, when thou comest to me, must say, 'Naku, I have come. What can Kimyera do for Queen Naku?' And I will rise and say, 'Kimyera, come and seat thyself in thy father's brother's chair.' And thou wilt step forward, bow three times before me, then six times before the king's chair, and, with thy best spear in hand and shield on arm, thou wilt proceed to the king's chair, and turning to the people who will be present, say in a loud voice thus: 'Lo, people of Ganda, I am Kimyera, son of Kalimera, by Wanyana of Unyoro. I hereby declare that with her own free will I this day do take Naku, my father's brother's daughter, to wife, and seat myself in the king's chair. Let all obey, on pain of death, the king's word.'"

"It is well, Naku; be it according to thy wish," replied Kimyera.

Naku departed and proceeded in search of Sebwana; and, when she found him, she affected great distress and indignation.

"How is this, Sebwana? I gave orders that our guests should be tenderly cared for and supplied with every needful thing. But I find, on inquiring this morning, that all through yesterday they were left alone to wonder at our sudden disregard for their wants. Haste, my friend, and make amends for thy neglect. Go to my fields and plantations, collect all that is choicest for our guests, lest, when they leave us, they will proclaim our unkindness."

Sebwana was amazed at this charge of neglect, and in anger hastened to find out the pages. But the pages, through Naku's good care, absented themselves, and could not be found; so that old Sebwana was obliged to depend upon a few unarmed slaves to drive the cattle and carry the choicest treasures of the queen's fields and plantations for the use of the strangers.

Sebwana having at last left the town, Naku returned to Kimyera, whom she found with a sad and disconsolate aspect.

"Why, what ails thee, Kimyera?" she asked. "The chair is now vacant. Arm thyself and follow me to the audience court."

"Ah, Naku! I but now remembered that as yet I know not whether my mother and good nurse are alive or dead. They may be waiting for me anxiously somewhere near the Myanja, or their bones may be bleaching on one of the great plains we traversed in coming hither."

"Nay, Kimyera, my lord, this is not a time for mourning. Bethink thee of the present needs first. The chair of the king awaits thee. Rise, and occupy it, and tomorrow all Ganda is at thy service to find thy lost mother and nurse. Come, delay not, lest Sebwana return and take vengeance on us all."

"Fear not, Naku, it was but a passing fit of grief which filled my mind. Sebwana must needs be strong and brave to dispossess me when Naku is on my side," saying which Kimyera dressed himself in war-costume, with a crown of cock's tail feathers on his head, a great leopard-skin depending from his neck down his back, a girdle of white monkey-skin round his waist, his body and face brilliantly painted with vermilion and saffron. He then armed himself with two bright shining spears of great length, and bearing a shield of dried elephant hide, which no ordinary spear could penetrate, he strode after Queen Naku towards the audience court in the royal palace. Mugema, somewhat similarly armed, followed his foster-son.

As Kimyera strode proudly on, the great drum of Ganda sounded, and its deep tones were heard far and wide. Immediately the populace, who knew well that the summons of the great drum announced an important event, hastily armed themselves, and filled the great court. Naku, the queen, they found seated in a chair alongside of the king's chair, which was now unfilled, and in front of her was a tall young stranger, who prostrated himself three times before the queen. He was then seen bowing six times before the empty king's chair. Rising to his feet, he stepped towards it, and afterwards faced the multitude, who were looking on wonderingly.

The young stranger, lifting his long spears and raising his shield in an attitude of defence, cried out aloud, so that all heard his voice:

"Lo, people of Ganda! I am Kimyera, son of Kalimera, by Wanyana of Unyoro. I hereby declare that with her own free will I this day do take Naku, my father's brother's daughter, to wife, and seat myself in the king's chair. Let all obey, on pain of death, the king's word."

On concluding this address, he stepped back a pace, and gravely sat in the king's chair. A loud murmur rose from the multitude, and the shafts of spears were seen rising up, when Naku rose to her feet, and said:

"People of Ganda, open your ears. I, Naku, the legitimate queen of Ganda, hereby declare that I have found my father's brother's son, and I, this day, of my own free will and great love for him, do take him for my lord and husband. By full right Kimyera fills the king's chair. I charge you all henceforth to be loyal to him, and him only."

As she ended her speech the people gave a great shout of welcome to the new king, and they waved their spears, and clashed them against their shields, thus signifying their willing allegiance to King Kimyera.

The next day great bodies of strong men were despatched in different directions for the king's mother and his nurse, and for Sebarija and the two cows, Namala and Nakaombeh. If alive they were instructed to convey them with honour and care to Ganda, and if any fatal misadventure had happened to them, their remains were to be borne with all due respect to the king.

Sebwana, meanwhile, had started for the plantations, and hearing the thunder of the great drum, divined that Naku had deposed him in favour of the young stranger. To assure himself of the fact, he sent a confidential slave to discover the truth of the matter, while he sought a place where he could await, unobserved, the return of his messenger. When his slave came back to him he learned what great event had occurred during his short absence, and that his power had been given to another. Knowing the fate attending those thus deposed, he secretly retired to the district that had given him birth, where he lived obscure and safe until he died at a good old age.

After some days Sebarija and Mugema's wife, and the two cows Namala and Nakaombeh, were found by the banks of Myanja, near a rocky hill which contained a cave, whither they had retired to seek a dwelling-place until news could be found of Mugema and Kimyera. But Wanyana, the king's mother, while gathering fuel near the cave during the absence of Sebarija and the potter's wife, had been fatally wounded by a leopard, before her cries brought Sebarija to her rescue. A short time after she had been taken into the cave she had died of her wounds, and her body had been folded in such furs and covering as her friends possessed, that Kimyera, on his return, might be satisfied of the manner of her death.

Kimyera, accompanied by his wife Naku and old Mugema, set out from Ganda with a great escort to receive the long-lost couple and the remains of Wanyana. Mugema rejoiced to see his old wife once more, though he deeply regretted the loss of his friend the princess. As for the king, his grief was excessive, but Naku, with her loving ways, assisted him to bear his great misfortune. A period of mourning, for an entire moon, was enjoined on all the people, after which a great mound was built at Kagoma over the remains of the unfortunate princess, and Sebarija was duly installed as keeper of the monument. Ever since that day it has become the custom to bury the queen-mothers near the grave of Wanyana, and to appoint keepers of the royal cemetery in memory of Sebarija, who first occupied that post.

While he lived Sebarija was honoured with a visit, on the first day of every alternate moon, from Kimyera, who always brought with him a young buffalo as a gift to the faithful cowherd. During these days the king and Sebarija were accustomed to play their flutes together as they did in the old time, and their seats were on mats placed on top of the mound, while the escort and servants of the king and queen sat all round the foot of it, and this was the manner in which Wanyana's memory was honoured during her son's life.

Kimyera finally settled with Queen Naku at Birra, where he built a large town. Mugema and his wife, with their two cows Namala and Nakaombeh, lived near the palace for many years, until they died.

Darkness and Wood-burr accompanied the king on many a hunt in the plains bordering the Myanja, in the woods of Ruwambo, and along the lakelands which look towards Bussi; and they in their turn died and were honourably interred with many folds of bark-cloth. Queen Naku, after giving birth to three sons, died during the birth of her fourth child, and was buried with great honour near Birra, and finally, after living to a great old age, the hunter king, Kimyera, died, mourned by all his people.

The Legend of the Leopardess and Her Two Servants, Dog and Jackal

LONG AGO, IN THE EARLY AGE OF UGANDA, a leopardess, in want of a servant to do chores in her den, was solicited by a jackal to engage him to perform that duty. As Jackal had a very suspicious appearance, with his ears drawn back, and his furtive eyes, and a smile which always seemed to be a leer, Leopardess consulted with Dog, whom she had lately hired as her steward, as to the propriety of trusting such a cunning-looking animal.

Dog trotted out to the entrance of the den to examine the stranger for himself, and, after close inspection of him, asked Jackal what work he could do. Jackal replied humbly and fawningly, and said that he could fetch water from the brook, collect fuel, sweep out the house, and was willing, if necessary, to cook now and then, as he was not a novice in the art of cooking; and, looking at Leopardess, "I am very fond of cubs, and am very clever in nursing them." Mistress Leopardess, on hearing this, seemed to be impressed with the abilities of Jackal, and, without waiting for the advice of Dog, engaged him at once, and said:

"Jackal, you must understand that my custom is to feed my servants well. What is left from my table is so abundant that I have heard no complaints from any who have been with me. Therefore you need fear no starvation, but while you may depend upon

ORIGIN PROPHECIES

being supplied with plenty of meat, the bones must not be touched. Dog shall be your companion, but neither he nor anyone else is permitted to touch the bones."

"I shall be quite content, Mistress Leopardess. Meat is good enough for me, and for good meat you may depend upon it I shall give good work."

The household of Mistress Leopardess was completed; she suffered no anxiety, and enjoyed herself in her own way. The chase was her great delight. The forest and plains were alive with game, and each morning at sunrise it was her custom to set out for the hunt, and scarcely a day passed but she returned with sufficient meat to fatten her household. Dog and Jackal expressed themselves delighted with the luscious repasts which they enjoyed, and a sleek roundness witnessed that they fared nobly. But as it frequently happens with people who have everything they desire, Dog, in a short while, became nicer and fastidious in his tastes. He hankered after the bones which were forbidden him, and was heard to sigh deeply whenever Mistress Leopardess collected the bones and stored them in the interior, and his eyes became filled with tears as he eyed the rich morsels stowed away. His feelings at last becoming intolerable, he resolved to appeal to his mistress one day, as she appeared to be in a more amiable mood than usual, and said:

"Mistress, thanks to you, the house is always well supplied with meat, and none of your servants have any reason to think that they will ever suffer the pangs of hunger; but, speaking for myself, mistress mine, I wish for one thing more, if you will be so good as to grant it."

"And what may that be, greedy one?" asked Leopardess.

"Well, you see, Mistress, I fear you do not understand the nature of dogs very well. You must know dogs delight in marrow, and often prefer it to meat. The latter by itself is good, but however plentiful and good it may be, without an occasional morsel of marrow it is apt to pall. Dogs also love to sharpen their teeth on bones and screw their tongues within the holes for the sake of the rich juice. By itself, marrow would not fatten my ribs; but meat with marrow is most delectable. Now, good mistress, seeing that I have been so faithful in your service, so docile and prompt to do your bidding, will you not be gracious enough to let me gnaw the bones and extract the marrow?"

"No," roared Leopardess decisively, "that is positively forbidden; and let me warn you that the day you venture to do so, a strange event will happen suddenly, which shall have most serious consequences to you and to all in this house.

"And you, Jackal, bear what I say well in mind," she continued, turning to that servile subordinate.

"Yes, mistress; I will, most certainly. Indeed, I do not care very greatly for bones," said Jackal, "and I hope my friend and mate, Dog, will remember, good mistress, what you say."

"I hear, mistress," replied Dog, "and since it is your will, I must needs obey."

The alarming words of Leopardess had the effect of compelling Dog and Jackal for a while to desist from even thinking of marrow, and the entreaty of Dog appeared to be forgotten by Leopardess, though Jackal was well aware, by the sparkles in the covetous eyes of Dog when any large bone was near him, how difficult it was for him to resist the temptation. Day after day Leopardess sallied out from her den, and returned with kids, goats, sheep, antelopes, zebra, and often a young giraffe; and one day she brought a great buffalo to her household, and cubs and servants came running to greet her, and praise her successful hunting.

On this day Dog undertook to prepare the dinner. The buffalo meat was cooked in exquisite fashion, and when it was turned out of the great pot, steaming and trickling over

397

everywhere with juice, Dog caught sight of a thigh-bone and yellow marrow glistening within. The temptation to steal it was too great to resist. He contrived to drop the bone back again into the pot, furnished the tray quickly with the meat, and sent Jackal with it to Leopardess, saying that he would follow with the kabobs and stew. As soon as Jackal had gone out of the kitchen, Dog whipped the bone out of the pot and slyly hid it; then, loading stew and kabobs on a tray, he hurried after Jackal, and began officiously bustling about, fawning upon Leopardess, stroking the cubs as he placed them near their mamma around the smoking trays, scolding Jackal for his laziness, and bidding him hurry up with the steaks. All of which, of course, was due to his delight that he had a rare treat in store for himself snugly hidden away.

Leopardess was pleased to bestow a good many praises upon Dog's cooking, and the cubs even condescended to smile their approval for the excellent way in which their wants were supplied.

Towards evening Mistress Leopardess went out again, but not before reminding Jackal of his duties towards the cubs, and bidding him, if it were late before she returned, on no account to leave them alone in the dark. Dog smilingly followed his mistress to the door, wishing her, in the most fawning manner, every success. When he thought that his mistress was far enough, and Jackal quite occupied with the cubs, Dog hastened to the kitchen, and, taking up his bone, stole out of the house, and carried it to a considerable distance off. When he thought he was safe from observation, he lay down, and, placing the bone between his paws, was about to indulge his craving for marrow, when lo! the bone was seen to fly away back to the den. Wondering at such a curious event, furious at his disappointment, and somewhat alarmed as he remembered Leopardess's warning words, he rushed after it, crying:

"Jackal, Jackal! Shut the door; the bone is coming. Jackal, please shut the door."

Jackal fortunately was at the door, squatting on his haunches, having just arrived there from nursing the cubs, and saw the bone coming straight towards him, and Dog galloping and crying out to shut the door. Quickly perceiving that Dog had at last allowed his appetite to get the better of his duty, and having, truth to say, a fellow feeling for his fellow servant, Jackal closed the door just in time, for in about a second afterwards the bone struck the door with a tremendous force, dinting it deeply.

Then Jackal turned to Dog, on recovering from his astonishment, and angrily asked, "Oh, Dog, do you know what you are doing? Have you no sense? You came near being the death of me this time. I'll tell you what, my friend, if Mistress Leopardess hears of this, your life is not worth a feather."

"Now don't, please, good Jackal – don't say anything of it this time. The fright I have had is quite sufficient to keep me from touching a bone again."

"Well, I am sure I don't wish you any harm, but for your life's sake do not be so dull as to forget the lesson you have learned."

Soon after Leopardess returned with a small antelope for the morrow's breakfast, and cried out to Jackal, as was usual with her on returning from the hunt:

"Now, my Jackal, bring the cubs hither; my dugs are so heavy. How are the little ones?"

"Ah, very well, Ma'am: poor little dears, they have been in a sweet sleep ever since you went out."

A few days later, Leopardess brought a fat young zebra, and Jackal displayed his best skill in preparing it for dinner. Dog also assisted with wise suggestions in the preparation of certain auxiliaries to the feast. When all was ready, Dog laid the table, and as fast as Jackal brought the various dishes, Dog arranged them in the most tempting manner on fresh banana leaves, spread over the ample plateau. Just before sitting down to the meal, Leopardess heard a strange noise without, and bounded to the door, growling angrily at being disturbed. Dog instantly seized the opportunity of her absence to extract a great bone from one of the trays, and stowed it in a recess in the wall of the passage leading from the kitchen. Presently Leopardess came back, and when the cubs were brought the meal was proceeded with in silence. When they had all eaten enough, the good effect of it was followed by commendations upon the cooking, and the juicy flavour of the meat, and how well Jackal had prepared everything. Neither was Dog forgotten by the mistress and her young ones, and he was dismissed with the plenteous remnants of the feast for himself and mate, with the courteous hope that they would find enough and to spare.

In the afternoon Leopardess, having refreshed herself with a nap, sallied out once more, enjoining Jackal, as she was going out of the den, to be attentive to her little ones during her absence.

While his friend Jackal proceeded towards the cubs, Dog surreptitiously abstracted his bone from the cavity in the passage wall, and trotted out unobserved. When he had arrived at a secluded place, he lay down, and, seizing the bone between his paws, was about to give it a preliminary lick, when again, to his dismay and alarm, the bone flew up and away straight for the door. Dog loped after it as fast as his limbs could carry him, crying out:

"Oh, Jackal, Jackal, good Jackal! Shut the door. Hurry up. Shut the door, good Jackal."

Again Jackal heard his friend's cry, and sprang up to close the door, and the instant he had done so the bone struck it with dreadful force.

Turning to the crestfallen and panting Dog, Jackal said sternly: "You are a nice fellow, you are. I well see the end of you. Now listen, this is the last time that I shall help you, my friend. The next time you take a bone you will bear the consequences, so look out."

"Come, Jackal, now don't say any more; I will not look at a bone again, I make you a solemn promise."

"Keep to that, and you will be safe," replied Jackal.

Poor Dog, however, was by no means able to adhere to his promise, for a few days afterwards Leopardess brought a fat young eland, and he found an opportunity to abstract a fine marrowbone before serving his generous mistress. Late in the afternoon, after dinner and siesta, Leopardess, before going out, repeated her usual charge to Jackal, and while the faithful servant retired to his nursing duties, greedy Dog sought his bone, and stole out to the forest with it. This time he went further than usual. Jackal meanwhile finding the cubs indisposed for sleep, led them out to the door of the den, where they frisked and gambolled about with all the liveliness of cubhood. Jackal was sitting at a distance from the door when he heard the cries of Dog. "Oh, Jackal, Jackal, good Jackal! Shut the door quickly. Look out for the bone. It is coming. Shut the door quickly."

"Ha, ha! Friend Dog! At it again, eh?" said the Jackal. "It is too late, too late, Doggie dear, the cubs are in the doorway." He looked up, however, saw the bone coming with terrific speed; he heard it whiz as it flew close over his head, and almost immediately after it struck one of the cubs, killing it instantly.

Jackal appeared to quickly realize the consequences of Dog's act, and his own carelessness, and feeling that henceforth Leopardess's den would be no home for him, he resolved to escape. Just then Dog came up, and when he saw the dead cub he set up a piteous howl.

"Ay," said Jackal. "You fool, you begin to see what your greed has brought upon us all. Howl on, my friend, but you will howl differently when Mistress Leopardess discovers her dead cub. Bethink yourself how all this will end. Our mighty mistress, if she catches you, will make mincemeat of you. Neither may I stay longer here. My home must be a burrow in the wild wood, or in the rocky cave in future. What will you do?"

"I, Jackal? I know not yet. Go, if you will, and starve yourself. I trust to find a better home than a cramped burrow, or the cold shelter of a cave. I love warmth, and kitchen fires, and the smell of roast meats too well to trust myself to the chilly covert you propose to seek, and my coat is too fine for rough outdoor life."

"Hark!" cried Jackal, "do you hear that? That is the mistress's warning note! Fare you well, Doggie. I shall dream of you tonight lying stark under the paw of the Leopardess."

Jackal waited to say no more, but fled from the scene, and from that day to this Jackal has been a vagabond. He loves the darkness, and the twilight. It is at such times you hear his yelp. He is very selfish and cowardly. He has not courage enough to kill anything for himself, but prefers to wait – licking his chops – until the lion or the leopard, who has struck the game, has gorged himself.

As for Dog he was sorely frightened, but after a little deliberation he resolved to face the matter out until he was certain of the danger. He conveyed the cubs, living and dead, quickly within, and then waited with well-dissembled anxiety the coming of his mistress.

Leopardess shortly arrived, and was met at the door by the obsequious Dog with fawning welcome.

"Where is Jackal?" asked Leopardess as she entered.

"I regret to say he has not returned yet from a visit which he said he was bound to pay his friends and family, whom he had not seen for so long," replied Dog.

"Then you go and bring my little ones to me. Poor little dears, they must be hungry by this, and my milk troubles me," commanded the mistress.

Dog departed readily, thinking to himself, "I am in for it now." He soon returned, bearing one of the cubs, and laid it down.

"Bring the other one, quickly," cried Leopardess.

"Yes, ma'am, immediately," he said.

Dog took the same cub up again, but in a brief time returned with it. The cub, already satisfied, would not touch the teat.

"Go and bring the other one, stupid," cried Leopardess, observing that it would not suck.

"This is the other one, mistress," he replied.

"Then why does it not suck?" she asked.

"Perhaps it has not digested its dinner."

"Where is Jackal? Has he not yet returned? Jackal!" she cried. "Where are you, Jackal?"

From the jungle outdoors Jackal shrilly yelped, "Here I am, mistress!"

"Come to me this instant," commanded Leopardess.

"Coming, mistress, coming," responded Jackal's voice faintly, for at the sound of her call he had been alarmed and was trotting off.

"Why, what can be the matter with the brute, trifling with me in this manner? Here, Dog, take this cub to the crib."

Dog hastened to obey, but Leopardess, whose suspicions had been aroused, quietly followed him as he entered the doorway leading into the inner recess of the house where the crib was placed. Having placed the living near the dead cub in the crib,

ORIGIN PROPHECIES

Dog turned to leave, when he saw his dreaded mistress in the doorway, gazing with fierce distended eyes, and it flashed on him that she had discovered the truth, and fear adding speed to his limbs he darted like an arrow between her legs, and rushed out of the den. With a loud roar of fury Leopardess sprang after him, Dog running for dear life. His mistress was gaining upon him, when Dog turned aside, and ran round the trees. Again Leopardess was rapidly drawing near, when Dog shot straight away and increased the distance between them a little. Just as one would think Dog had no hope of escaping from his fierce mistress, he saw a warthog's burrow, into which he instantly dived. Leopardess arrived at the hole in the ground as the tail of Dog disappeared from her sight. Being too large of body to enter, she tore up the entrance to the burrow, now and then extending her paw far within to feel for her victim. But the burrow was of great length, and ran deep downwards, and she was at last obliged to desist from her frantic attempts to reach the runaway.

Reflecting awhile, Leopardess looked around and saw Monkey nearby, sitting gravely on a branch watching her.

"Come down, Monkey," she imperatively commanded, "and sit by this burrow and watch the murdering slave who is within, while I procure materials to smoke him out."

Monkey obeyed, and descending the tree, took his position at the mouth of the burrow. But it struck him that should Dog venture out, his strength would be unable to resist him. He therefore begged Leopardess to stay a moment, while he went to bring a rock with which he could block the hole securely. When this was done Leopardess said, "Now stay here, and do not stir until I return; I will not be long, and when I come I will fix him."

Leopardess, leaving the burrow in charge of Monkey, commenced to collect a large quantity of dry grass, and then proceeded to her house to procure fire wherewith to light it, and suffocate Dog with the smoke.

Dog, soon after entering the burrow had turned himself round and faced the hole, to be ready for all emergencies. He had heard Leopardess give her orders to Monkey, had heard Monkey's plans for blockading him, as well as the threat of Leopardess to smoke him out. There was not much hope for him if he stayed longer.

After a little while he crept close to the rock that blocked his exit, and whispered:

"Monkey, let me out, there's a good fellow."

"It may not be," replied Monkey.

"Ah, Monkey, why are you so cruel? I have not done any harm to you. Why do you stand guard over me to prevent my escape?"

"I am simply obeying orders, Dog. Leopardess said, 'Stay here and watch, and see that Dog does not escape;' and I must do so or harm will come to me, as you know."

Then said Dog, "Monkey, I see that you have a cruel heart, too, though I thought none but the Leopard kind could boast of that. May you feel some day the deep despair I feel in my heart. Let me say one word more to you before I die. Put your head close to me that you may hear it."

Monkey, curious to know what the last word could be about, put his face close between the rock and the earth and looked in, upon which Dog threw so much dust and sand into his cunning eyes as almost to blind him.

Monkey staggered back from the entrance, and while knuckling his eyes to nib the sand out, Dog put his forefeet against the rock and soon rolled it away. Then, after a hasty view around, Dog fled like the wind from the dangerous spot.

401

Monkey, after clearing his eyes from the dirt thrown in them, and reviewing his position, began to be concerned as to his own fate. It was not long before his crafty mind conceived that it would be a good idea to place some soft nuts within the burrow, and roll back the stone into its place.

When Leopardess returned with the fire she was told that Dog was securely imprisoned within, upon which she piled the grass over the burrow and set fire to it.

Presently a crackling sound was heard within.

"What can that be?" demanded Leopardess.

"That must surely be one of Dog's ears that you heard exploding," replied Monkey.

After a short time another crackling sound was heard.

"And what is that?" asked Leopardess.

"Ah, that must be the other ear of course," Monkey answered.

But as the fire grew hotter and the heat increased within there were a great many of these sounds heard, at which Monkey laughed gleefully and cried:

"Ah ha! Do you hear? Dog is splitting to pieces now. Oh, he is burning up finely; every bone in his body is cracking. Ah, but it is a cruel death, though, is it not?"

"Let him die," fiercely cried Leopardess. "He killed one of my young cubs – one of the loveliest little fellows you ever saw."

Both Leopardess and Monkey remained at the burrow until the fire had completely died out, then the first said:

"Now, Monkey, bring me a long stick with a hook at the end of it, that I may rake Dog's bones out and feast my eyes upon them."

Monkey hastened to procure the stick, with which the embers were raked out, when Leopardess exclaimed:

"What a queer smell this is! It is not at all like what one would expect from a burnt dog."

"Ah," replied Monkey, "Dog must be completely burnt by this. Of that there can be no doubt. Did you ever burn a dog before that you know the smell of its burnt body so well?"

"No," said the Leopardess; "but this is not like the smell of roast meat. Rake out all the ashes that I may see the bones and satisfy myself."

Monkey, compelled to do as he was commanded, put in his stick, and drew out several half-baked nuts, the shells of which were cracked and gaping open. These Leopardess no sooner saw than she seized Monkey, and furiously cried:

"You wretch, you have deceived and trifled with me! You have permitted the murderer of my cub to escape, and your life shall now be the forfeit for his."

"Pardon, mighty Leopardess, but let me ask how do you propose to slay me?"

"Why, miserable slave, how else should I kill you but with one scratch of my claws?"

"Nay, then, great Queen, my blood will fall on your head and smother you. It is better for yourself that you should toss me up above that thorny bough, so that when I fall upon it the thorns may penetrate my heart and kill me."

No sooner had Monkey ended than fierce Leopardess tossed Monkey upward as he had directed; but the latter seized the bough and sat up, and from this he sprang upward into another still higher, and thence from branch to branch and from tree to tree until he was safe from all possible pursuit.

Leopardess perceived that another of her intended victims had escaped, and was furious with rage.

"Come down this instant," she cried to Monkey, hoping he would obey her.

"Nay, Leopardess. It has been told me, and the forest is full of the report, that your cruelty has driven from you Jackal and Dog, and that they will never serve you again. Cruel people never can reckon upon friends. I and my tribe, so long servants to you, will henceforth be strangers to you. Fare you well."

A great rustling was heard in the trees overhead as Monkey and his tribe migrated away from the district of the cruel Leopardess who, devoured with rage, was obliged to depart with not one of her vengeful thoughts gratified.

As she was returning to her den, Leopardess bethought herself of the Oracle, who was her friend, who would no doubt, at her solicitations, reveal the hiding places of Jackal and Dog. She directed her steps to the cave of the Oracle, who was a nondescript practising witchcraft in the wildest part of the district.

To this curious being she related the story of the murder of her cub by Jackal and Dog, and requested him to inform her by what means she could discover the criminals and wreak her vengeance on them.

The Oracle replied, "Jackal has gone into the wild wood, and he and his family henceforward will always remain there, to degenerate in time into a suspicious and cowardly race. Dog has fled to take his shelter in the home of man, to be his companion and friend, and to serve man against you and your kind. But lest you accuse me of ill-will to you, I will tell you how you may catch Dog if you are clever and do not allow your temper to exceed your caution. Not far off is a village belonging to one of the human tribes, near which there is a large ant-hill, where moths every morning flit about in the sunshine of the early day. About the same time Dog leaves the village to sport and gambol and chase the moths. If you can find a lurking place not far from it, where you can lie silently in wait, Dog may be caught by you in an unwary moment while at his daily play. I have spoken."

Leopardess thanked the Oracle and retired brooding over its advice. That night the moon was very clear and shining bright, and she stole out of her den, and proceeding due west as she was directed, in a few hours she discovered the village and the ant-hill described by the Oracle. Near the mound she also found a thick dense bush, which was made still more dense by the tall wild grass surrounding it. In the depths of this she crouched, waiting for morning. At dawn the village wherein men and women lived was astir, and at sunrise the gates were opened. A little later Dog signalled himself by his well-known barks as he came out to take his morning's exercise. Unsuspicious of the presence of his late dread mistress he bounded up the hill and began to circle around, chasing the lively moths. Leopardess, urged by her anger, did not wait until Dog, tired with his sport, would of his own accord stray among the bushes, but uttering a loud roar sprang out from her hiding place. Dog, warned by her voice, which he well knew, put his tail between his legs and rushed through the open gates and alarmed his new masters, who came pouring from their houses with dreadful weapons in their hands, who chased her, and would have slain her had she not bounded over the fence. Thus Leopardess lost her last chance of revenging the death of her cub; but as she was creeping homeward her mortification was so great that she vowed to teach her young eternal hostility towards Dog and all his tribe. Dog also, convinced that his late mistress was one who nourished an implacable resentment when offended, became more cautious, and a continued life with his new masters increased his attachment for them. When he finally married, and was blessed with a progeny, he taught his pups various arts by which they might ingratiate themselves more and more with the human race. He lived in comfort and affluence to a good old age, and had the satisfaction to see his family grow more and more in the estimation of their generous masters, until dogs and men became inseparable companions.

Leopardess and her cub removed far away from the house associated with her misfortune, but though time healed the keen sore of her bereavement by blessing her annually with more cubs, her hate for Dog and his kind was lasting and continues to this day. And thus it was that the friendly fellowship which reigned between the forest animals during the golden age of Uganda was broken forever.

The Elephant and the Lion

A HUGE AND SOUR-TEMPERED ELEPHANT went and wandered in the forest. His inside was slack for want of juicy roots and succulent reeds, but his head was as full of dark thoughts as a gadfly is full of blood. As he looked this way and that, he observed a young lion asleep at the foot of a tree. He regarded him for a while, then, as he was in a wicked mood, it came to him that he might as well kill the lion, and he accordingly rushed forward and impaled him with his tusks. He then lifted the body with his trunk, swung it about, and dashed it against the tree, and afterwards kneeled on it until it became as shapeless as a crushed banana pulp. He then laughed and said, "Ha! ha! This is a proof that I am strong. I have killed a lion, and people will say proud things of me, and will wonder at my strength."

Presently a brother elephant came up and greeted him.

"See," said the first elephant, "what I have done. It was I that killed him. I lifted him on high, and lo, he lies like a rotten banana. Do you not think that I am very strong? Come, be frank now, and give me some credit for what I have done."

Elephant Number 2 replied, "It is true that you are strong, but that was only a young lion. There are others of his kind, and I have seen them, who would give you considerable trouble."

"Ho, ho!" laughed the first elephant, "Get out, stupid. You may bring his whole tribe here, and I will show you what I can do. Ay! and to your dam to boot."

"What? My own mother, too?"

"Yes. Go and fetch her if you like."

"Well, well," said Number 2, "you are far gone, there is no doubt. Fare you well."

Number 2 proceeded on his wanderings, resolved in his own mind that if he had an opportunity he would send someone to test the boaster's strength. Number 1 called out to him as he moved off –

"Away you go. Goodbye to you."

In a little while Number 2 Elephant met a lion and lioness, full-grown, and splendid creatures, who turned out to be the parents of the youngster which had been slain. After a sociable chat with them, he said:

"If you go further on along the path I came you will meet a kind of game which requires killing badly. He has just mangled your cub."

Meantime Elephant Number 1, after chuckling to himself very conceitedly, proceeded to the pool nearby to bathe and cool himself. At every step he went you could hear his "Ha, ha, ha! Ioh! I have killed a lion!" While he was in the pool, spurting the water in a shower over his back, he suddenly looked up, and at the water's edge beheld a lion and lioness who were regarding him sternly.

"Well! What do you want?" he asked. "Why are you standing there looking at me in that way?"

"Are you the rogue who killed our child?" they asked.

"Perhaps I am," he answered. "Why do you want to know?"

"Because we are in search of him. If it be you that did it, you will have to do the same to us before you leave this ground."

"Ho! ho!" laughed the elephant loudly. "Well, hark. It was I who killed your cub. Come now, it was I. Do you hear? And if you do not leave here mighty quick, I shall have to serve you both in the same way as I served him."

The lions roared aloud in their fury, and switched their tails violently.

"Ho, ho!" laughed the elephant gaily. "This is grand. There is no doubt I shall run soon, they make me so skeery," and he danced round the pool and jeered at them, then drank a great quantity of water and blew it in a shower over them.

The lions stirred not, but kept steadfastly gazing at him, planning how to make their attack.

Perceiving that they were obstinate, he threw another stream of water over the lions and then backed into the deepest part of the pool, until there was nothing seen of him but the tip of his trunk. When he rose again the lions were still watching him, and had not moved.

"Ho, ho!" he trumpeted, "still there! Wait a little, I am coming to you." He advanced towards the shore, but when he was close enough the lion sire sprang into the air, and alighted on the elephant's back, and furiously tore at the muscles of the neck, and bit deep into the shoulder. The elephant retreated quickly into the deepest part of the pool, and submerged himself and his enemy, until the lion was compelled to abandon his back and begin to swim ashore. No sooner had the elephant felt himself relieved, than he rose to the surface, and hastily followed and seized the lion with his trunk. Despite his struggles he was pressed beneath the surface, dragged under his knees, and trodden into the mud, and in a short time the lion sire was dead.

The elephant laughed triumphantly, and cried, "Ho, ho! am I not strong, Ma Lion? Did you ever see the likes of me before? Two of you! Young Lion and Pa Lion are now killed! Come, Ma Lion, had you not better try now, just to see if you won't have better luck? Come on, old woman, just once."

The lioness fiercely answered, while she retreated from the pool, "Rest where you are. I am going to find my brother, and will be back shortly."

The elephant trumpeted his scorn of her and her kind, and seizing the carcase of her lord, flung it on shore after her, and declared his readiness to abide where he was, that he might make mash of all the lion family.

In a short time the lioness had found her brother, who was a mighty fellow, and full of fight. As they advanced near the pool together, they consulted as to the best means of getting at the elephant. Then the lioness sprang forward to the edge of the pool. The elephant retreated a short distance into deeper water. The lioness upon this crept along the pool, and pretended to lap the water. The elephant moved towards her. The lion waited his chance, and finally, with a great roar, sprang upon his shoulders, and commenced tearing away at the very place which had been torn by lion sire.

The elephant backed quickly into deep water as he had done before, and submerged himself, but the lion maintained his hold and bit deeper. The elephant then sank down until there was nothing to be seen but the tip of his trunk, upon which the lion, to avoid suffocation, relaxed his hold and swam vigorously towards shore. The elephant rose up, and as the lion was stepping on shore, seized him, and drove one of his tusks through his adversary's body; but as he was in the act, the lioness sprang upon the elephant's neck, and bit and tore so furiously that he fell dead, and with his fall crushed the dying lion.

Soon after the close of the terrible combat, Elephant Number 2 came up, and discovered the lioness licking her chops and paws, and said –

"Hello, it seems there has been quite a quarrel here lately. Three lions are dead, and here lies one of my own kind, stiffening."

"Yes," replied lioness, gloomily, "the rogue elephant killed my cub while the little fellow was asleep in the woods. He then killed my husband and brother, and I killed him; but I do not think the elephant has gained much by fighting with us. I did not have much trouble in killing him. Should you meet any friends of his, you may warn them to leave the lioness alone, or she may be tempted to make short work of them."

Elephant Number 2, though a patient person generally, was annoyed at this, and gave her a sudden kick with one of his hind feet, which sent her sprawling a good distance off, and asked –

"How do you like that, Ma Lion?"

"What do you mean by that?" demanded the enraged lioness.

"Oh, because I hate to hear so much bragging."

"Do you also wish to fight?" she asked.

"We should never talk about doing an impossible thing, Ma Lion," he answered. "I have travelled many years through these woods, and I have never fought yet. I find that when a person minds his own business he seldom comes to trouble, and when I meet one who is even stronger than myself I greet him pleasantly, and pass on, and I should advise you to do the same, Ma Lion."

"You are saucy, Elephant. It would be well for you to think upon your stupid brother there, who lies so stark under your nose, before you trouble with your insolence one who slew him."

"Well, words never yet made a plantation; it is the handling of a hoe that makes fields. See here, Ma Lion, if I talked to you all day I could not make you wise. I will just turn my back to you. If you will bite me, you will soon learn how weak you are."

The lioness, angered still more by the elephant's contempt, sprang at his shoulders, and clung to him, upon which he rushed at a stout tree, and pressing his shoulders against it, crushed the breath out of her body, and she ceased her struggles. When he relaxed his pressure, the body fell to the ground, and he knelt upon it, and kneaded it until every bone was broken.

While the elephant was meditatively standing over the body, and thinking what misfortunes happen to boasters, a man came along, carrying a spear, and seeing that the elephant was unaware of his presence, he thought what great luck had happened to him.

Said he, "Ah, what fine tusks he has. I shall be rich with them, and shall buy slaves and cattle, and with these I will get a wife and a farm," saying which he advanced silently, and when he was near enough, darted his spear into a place behind the shoulder.

The elephant turned around quickly, and on beholding his enemy rushed after and overtook him, and mauled him, until in a few moments he was a mangled corpse.

Soon after a woman approached, and seeing four lions, one elephant, and her husband dead, she raised up her hands wonderingly and cried, "How did all this happen?" The elephant, hearing her voice, came from behind a tree, with a spear quivering in his side, and bleeding profusely. At the sight of him the woman turned round to fly, but the elephant cried out to her, "Nay, run not, woman, for I can do you no harm. The happy days in the woods are ended for all the tribes. The memory of this scene will never be forgotten. Animals will be henceforth at constant war one with another. Lions will no more greet elephants, the buffaloes will be shy, the rhinoceroses will live apart, and man when he comes within the shadows will think of nothing else than his terrors, and he will fancy an enemy in every shadow. I am sorely wounded, for thy man stole up to my side and drove his spear into me, and soon I shall die."

When she had heard these words the woman hastened home, and all the villagers, old and young, hurried into the woods, by the pool, where they found four lions, two elephants, and one of their own tribe lying still and lifeless.

The words of the elephant have turned out to be true, for no man goes now-a-days into the silent and deserted woods but he feels as though something were haunting them, and thinks of goblinry, and starts at every sound. Out of the shadows which shift with the sun, forms seem crawling and phantoms appear to glide, and we are in a fever almost from the horrible illusions of fancy. We breathe quickly and fear to speak, for the smallest vibration in the silence would jar on our nerves.

The First of the Rattlesnakes

NOW THERE IS A TAIL TO YOU, *compadre* [friend]," said old Desiderio, nodding at Patricio after we had sat a while in silence around the crackling fire.

Patricio had a broad strip of rawhide across his knee, and was scraping the hair from it with a dull knife. It was high time to be thinking of new soles, for already there was a wee hole in the bottom of each of his moccasins; and as for Benito, his shy little grandson, *his* toes were all abroad.

But shrilly as the cold night-wind outside hinted the wisdom of speedy cobbling, Patricio had no wish to acquire that burro's tail, so, laying the rawhide and knife upon the floor beside him, he deliberately rolled a modest pinch of the aromatic *koo-ah-rée* in a corn-husk, lighted it at the coals, and drew Benito's tousled head to his side.

"You have heard," he said, with a slow puff, "about Nah-chu-rú-chu, the mighty medicine-man who lived here in Isleta in the times of the ancients?"

"*Ah-h!*" (Yes) cried all the boys. "You have promised to tell us how he married the moon!"

"Another time I will do so. But now I shall tell you something that was before that – for Nah-chu-rú-chu had many strange adventures before he married Páh-hlee-oh, the

Moon-Mother. Do you know why the rattlesnake – which is the king of all snakes and alone has the power of death in his mouth – always shakes his *guaje* before he bites?"

"*Een-dah*!" chorused Ramon and Benito, and Fat Juan, and Tomas, very eagerly; for they were particularly fond of hearing about the exploits of the greatest of Tée-wahn medicine-men.

"Listen, then, and you shall hear."

In those days Nah-chu-rú-chu had a friend who lived in a pueblo nearer the foot of the Eagle-Feather Mountain than this, in the Place of the Red Earth, where still are its ruins; and the two young men went often to the mountain together to bring wood and to hunt. Now, Nah-chu-rú-chu had a white heart, and never thought ill; but the friend had the evil road and became jealous, for Nah-chu-rú-chu was a better hunter. But he said nothing, and made as if he still loved Nah-chu-rú-chu truly.

One day the friend came over from his village and said:

"Friend Nah-chu-rú-chu, let us go tomorrow for wood and to have a hunt.

"It is well," replied Nah-chu-rú-chu. Next morning he started very early and came to the village of his friend; and together they went to the mountain. When they had gathered much wood, and lashed it in bundles for carrying, they started off in opposite directions to hunt. In a short time each returned with a fine fat deer.

"But why should we hasten to go home, friend Nah-chu-rú-chu?" said the friend. "It is still early, and we have much time. Come, let us stop here and amuse ourselves with a game."

"It is well, friend," answered Nah-chu-rú-chu; "but what game shall we play? For we have neither *pa-toles*, nor hoops, nor any other game here."

"See! we will roll the *mah-khúr*, for while I was waiting for you I made one that we might play" – and the false friend drew from beneath his blanket a pretty painted hoop; but really he had made it at home, and had brought it hidden, on purpose to do harm to Nah-chu-rú-chu.

"Now go down there and catch it when I roll it," said he; and Nah-chu-rú-chu did so. But as he caught the hoop when it came rolling, he was no longer Nah-chu-rú-chu the brave hunter, but a poor Coyote with great tears rolling down his nose!

"Hu!" said the false friend, tauntingly, "we do this to each other! So now you have all the plains to wander over, to the north, and west, and south; but you can never go to the east. And if you are not lucky, the dogs will tear you; but if you are lucky, they may have pity on you. So now goodbye, for this is the last I shall ever see of you."

Then the false friend went away, laughing, to his village; and the poor Coyote wandered aimlessly, weeping to think that he had been betrayed by the one he had loved and trusted as a brother. For four days he prowled about the outskirts of Isleta, looking wistfully at his home. The fierce dogs ran out to tear him; but when they came near they only sniffed at him, and went away without hurting him. He could find nothing to eat save dry bones, and old thongs or soles of moccasins.

On the fourth day he turned westward, and wandered until he came to Mesita. There was no town of the Lagunas there then, and only a shepherd's hut and corral, in which were an old Queres Indian and his grandson, tending their goats.

Next morning when the grandson went out very early to let the goats from the corral, he saw a Coyote run out from among the goats. It went off a little way, and then sat down and watched him. The boy counted the goats, and none were missing, and he thought it strange. But he said nothing to his grandfather.

ORIGIN PROPHECIES

For three more mornings the very same thing happened; and on the fourth morning the boy told his grandfather. The old man came out, and set the dogs after the Coyote, which was sitting a little way off; but when they came near they would not touch him.

"I suspect there is something wrong here," said the old shepherd; and he called: "Coyote, are you coyote-true, or are you people?"

But the Coyote could not answer; and the old man called again: "Coyote, are you people?"

At that the Coyote nodded his head, "Yes."

"If that is so, come here and be not afraid of us; for we will be the ones to help you out of this trouble."

So the Coyote came to them and licked their hands, and they gave it food – for it was dying of hunger. When it was fed, the old man said:

"Now, son, you are going out with the goats along the creek, and there you will see some willows. With your mind look at two willows, and mark them; and tomorrow morning you must go and bring one of them."

The boy went away tending the goats, and the Coyote stayed with the old man. Next morning, when they awoke very early, they saw all the earth wrapped in a white *manta*.

"Now, son," said the old man, "you must wear only your moccasins and breech-clout, and go like a man to the two willows you marked yesterday. To one of them you must pray; and then cut the other and bring it to me."

The boy did so and came back with the willow stick. The old man prayed, and made a *mah-khúr* hoop; and bidding the Coyote stand a little way off and stick his head through the hoop before it should stop rolling, rolled it towards him. The Coyote waited till the hoop came very close, and gave a great jump and put his head through it before it could stop. And lo! there stood Nah-chu-rú-chu, young and handsome as ever; but his beautiful suit of fringed buckskin was all in rags. For four days he stayed there and was cleansed with the cleansing of the medicine-man; and then the old shepherd said to him:

"Now, friend Nah-chu-rú-chu, there is a road. But take with you this *faja*, for though your power is great, you have submitted to this evil. When you get home, he who did this to you will be first to know, and he will come pretending to be your friend, as if he had done nothing; and he will ask you to go hunting again. So you must go; and when you come to the mountain, with this *faja* you shall repay him."

Nah-chu-rú-chu thanked the kind old shepherd, and started home. But when he came to the Bad Hill and looked down into the valley of the Rio Grande, his heart sank. All the grass and fields and trees were dry and dead – for Nah-chu-rú-chu was the medicine-man who controlled the clouds, so no rain could fall when he was gone; and the eight days he had been a Coyote were in truth eight years. The river was dry, and the springs; and many of the people were dead from thirst, and the rest were dying. But as Nah-chu-rú-chu came down the hill, it began to rain again, and all the people were glad.

When he came into the pueblo, all the famished people came out to welcome him. And soon came the false friend, making as if he had never bewitched him nor had known whither he disappeared.

In a few days the false friend came again to propose a hunt; and next morning they went to the mountain together. Nah-chu-rú-chu had the pretty *faja* wound around his waist; and when the wind blew his blanket aside, the other saw it.

"Ay! What a pretty *faja*!" cried the false friend. "Give it to me, friend Nah-chu-rú-chu."

409

"*Een-dah!*" (No) said "Nah-chu-rú-chu. But the false friend begged so hard that at last he said:

"Then I will roll it to you; and if you can catch it before it unwinds, you may have it."

So he wound it up, and holding by one end gave it a push so that it ran away from him, unrolling as it went. The false friend jumped for it, but it was unrolled before he caught it-

"*Een-dah!*" said Nah-chu-rú-chu, pulling it back. "If you do not care enough for it to be spryer than that, you cannot have it."

The false friend begged for another trial; so Nah-chu-rú-chu rolled it again. This time the false friend caught it before it was unrolled; and lo! instead of a tall young man, there lay a great rattlesnake with tears rolling from his lidless eyes!

"We, too, do this to each other!" said Nah-chu-rú-chu. He took from his medicine-pouch a pinch of the sacred meal and laid it on the snake's flat head for its food; and then a pinch of the corn-pollen to tame it. And the snake ran out its red forked tongue, and licked them.

"Now," said Nah-chu-rú-chu, "this mountain and all rocky places shall be your home. But you can never again do to another harm, without warning, as you did to me. For see, there is a *guaje* in your tail, and whenever you would do any one an injury, you must warn them beforehand with your rattle."

"And is that the reason why Ch'ah-rah-ráh-deh always rattles to give warning before he bites?" asked Fat Juan, who is now quite as often called Juan Biscocho (John Biscuit), since I photographed him one day crawling out of the big adobe bake-oven where he had been hiding.

"That is the very reason. Then Nah-chu-rú-chu left his false friend, from whom all the rattlesnakes are descended, and came back to his village. From that time all went well with Isleta, for Nah-chu-rú-chu was at home again to attend to the clouds. There was plenty of rain, and the river began to run again, and the springs flowed.

The people ploughed and planted again, as they had not been able to do for several years, and all their work prospered. As for the people who lived in the Place of the Red Earth, they all moved down here, because the Apaches were very bad; and here their descendants live to this day."

The Gods of the Azteca

QUETZALCOATL TOLD THE PEOPLE ABOUT THE GODS and about the creation of men and women... At first there was Citlalatonac and Citlalicue, the Sky-father and the Earth-mother. Then Citlalicue gave birth to a knife of flint, and when this knife of flint was flung down it became the sixteen hundred Earth-gods. They had to live as men and women of today have to live – by labouring and searching for their food. But after a while they began to think that it was unfitting that they should have to do this – they, the children of the Sky-father and the Earth-mother. They sent Tlotli the Hawk to their mother, asking that men be made who would serve them, the sixteen hundred Earth-gods.

Now there had been an earth before the earth they lived on, and men and women had been upon it, and the earth and the men and women on it had been destroyed, not once, but many times. Once the earth and all that was on it had been destroyed by floods. Once all had been destroyed by the force of great winds, and once all had been destroyed by fire. Now when the sixteen hundred Earth-gods asked that a race of men and women be created who would serve them, the Earth-mother told them what they should do to bring about this creation.

They were to send one of their number down to Mictlampa, the place where there is no light, and the one who went down was to ask the Lord of that place for a bone, the bone of a man of the last race that had perished. The Earth-gods chose Xolotl for their messenger; they sent him down to Mictlampa, the place where there is no light.

Xolotl went where they sent him; he came before Mictlantecutli, the Lord of Mictlampa, and found him pouring fire into a vessel of blood. And Mictlantecutli, he whose head is a bare skull, thinking that he might beguile one of the Earth-gods and keep him for ever in that place where there is no light, spoke fairly to him. He would give the Earth-gods a bone, he said, a bone of one of the giants who had dwelt upon the earth; this bone should be put into a vessel when it was brought into the Upperworld, and each of the Earth-gods was to put a drop of his blood into the vessel with the bone; out of what would brew in the vessel two who would make the new race of men and women would come.

Xolotl knew that Mictlantecutli intended evil to him. He stole the bone and bore it away through that place of darkness. The bone was a great one, for it was a bone of one who belonged to the giant race. Yet the messenger of the Earth-gods was able to go swiftly with it through the darkness. But when he came near to the Upperworld the great owls that guard Mictlantecutli's realm flew at him and tore at his eyes. Xolotl stumbled and the great bone fell and broke into fragments. He gathered up the fragments and carried them into the Upperworld where the rest of the Earth-gods waited for him.

Then the sixteen hundred Earth-gods put the fragments of the great bone in a vessel, and each of them drew blood from his own body and dropped the blood into the vessel that held the fragments of the bone. For three days they watched over it, stirring what was in the vessel. Their labour, it seemed, was in vain. Then, on the fourth day, what was in the vessel simmered and bubbled. Out of the brew emerged a human child, a boy. The Earth-gods watched over the vessel for another four days. Then out of the brew emerged a human child, a girl. The Earth-gods took the children and nourished them on the juice of the maguey-plant; the children grew to be a man and a woman. They became man and wife, and from them come the men and women of our time.

The bone that Xolotl brought into the Upperworld was in fragments: for that reason the men and women whom it went to form are not great of stature like the giants who had lived on the earth before; the fragments were of different sizes, and for that reason the men and woman of today are not all of one size – some are very tall, and others are small, and there are dwarfs amongst them. The world that the first men and women of our race came into was without sun or moon. Then the great Gods held a council to decide how luminaries might be made for the sky.

At that council the gods declared that it was their will that luminaries should be formed by transformations of a pair of gods; they declared that the two who should enter a fire and allow themselves to be consumed should become the sun and the moon. They built two towers, one for each of the gods who would undertake to make a luminary for the day and for the night, and they strewed the ground with branches and flowers, and they made sacrifices. Two of the gods agreed to cast themselves down into the fires and make themselves into the sun and the moon. These two put on their crowns and their robes of bright feathers and they went up upon the towers. The rest of the gods sat around the fires that had been lighted for four days. Then the two who were upon the towers cast themselves into the fires beneath them; they were consumed.

Then the gods, at that sacred place, waited to witness the resurrection of the pair as the sun and the moon. Four days they waited beside the towers. Then they saw the sky grow red; they knew not what was going to come about; they were terrified. The sun appeared in the sky; it was very red, and none of the gods could look at it because of its blinding rays. Then the moon appeared at the other side of the sky; its light was no less great than the sun's. One of the gods took a rabbit and flung the rabbit in the face of the moon. The rabbit remained there to dim the moon's brightness. And so the moon was made more dim than the sun.

But the two luminaries stayed moveless in the sky. "Die, all of you," they cried down to the gods, "die all of you and create the stars." Then a great wind came. It blew upon them until the gods were destroyed by the force of it. Their remains were carried up to the sky, and in the sky they stay, having become the stars. The wind blew upon the sun; it made it hurry across the sky. It did not blow upon the moon, and so the moon remains moveless in the sky. But the moon comes into the sky at a different time from the sun.

All this Quetzalcoatl told the dwellers in Tollan.

Manco Capac Founds Cuzco

WE ARE TOLD THAT TAMPU-TOCCO was a house on a hill, provided with three windows, named Maras, Sutic, and Capac. Through the first of these came the Maras tribe, through Sutic came the Tampu tribe, and through Capac, the regal window, came four Ayars with their four wives – Ayar Manco and Mama Ocllo; Ayar Auca (the 'joyous', or 'fighting', Ayar) and Mama Huaco (the 'warlike'); Ayar Cachi (the 'Salt' Ayar) and Mama Ipacura (the 'Elder Aunt'); Ayar Uchu (the 'Pepper' Ayar) and Mama Raua.

The four pairs knew no father nor mother, beyond the story they told that they came out of the said window by order of Ticci Viracocha; and they declared that Viracocha created them to be lords; but it was believed that by the counsel of the fierce Mama Huaco they decided to go forth and subjugate peoples and lands. Besides the Maras and Tampu peoples, eight other tribes were associated with the Ayars, as vassals, when they began their quest, taking with them their goods and their families. Manco Capac carrying with him, as a palladium, a falcon, called Indi, or Inti – the name of the Sun-god – bore also a golden rod which was to sink into the land at the site where they were to abide; and Salcamayhua says that, in setting out, the hero was wreathed in rainbows, this being regarded as an omen of success.

The journey was leisurely, and in course of it Sinchi Rocca, who was to be the second Inca, was born to Mama Ocllo and Manco Capac; but then came a series of magic transformations by which the three brothers disappeared, leaving the elder without a rival. Ayar Cachi, who had such great power that, with stones hurled from his sling, he split the hills and hurled them up to the clouds, was the first to excite the envy of his brothers; and on the pretext that certain royal treasures had been forgotten in a cave of Tampu-Tocco, he was sent back to secure them, accompanied by a follower who had secret instructions from the brothers to immure him in the cave, once he was inside. This was done, and though Ayar Cachi made the earth shake in his efforts to break through, he could not do so. Nevertheless, he appeared to his brothers, coming in the air with great wings of coloured feathers; and despite their terror, he commanded them to go on to their destiny, found Cuzco, and establish the empire. "I shall remain in the form and fashion that ye shall see on a hill not distant from here; and it will be for your descendants a place of sanctity and worship, and its name shall be Huanacauri. And in return for the good things that ye will have received from me, I pray that ye will always adore me as god and in that place will set up altars whereat to offer sacrifices. If ye do this, ye shall receive help from me in war; and as a sign that from henceforth ye are to be esteemed, honoured, and feared, your ears shall be bored in the manner that ye now behold mine." (It was from this custom of boring and enlarging the ears that the Spaniards called the ruling caste *Orejones* ('Big-Ears'); and it was at the hill of Huanacauri that the Ayar instructed the Incas in the rites by which they initiated youths into the warrior caste. At this mount, which became one of the great Inca shrines, both the Salt and the Pepper Ayars were reputed to have been transformed into stones, or idols, and it was here that the rainbow sign of promise was given.)

As they approached the hill, they saw near the rainbow what appeared to be a man-shaped idol; and Ayar Uchu offered himself to go to it, for they said that he was very like it. He did so, sat upon the stone, and himself became stone, crying: "O Brothers, an evil work ye have wrought for me. It was for your sakes that I came where I must remain forever, apart from your company. Go! go! happy brethren, I announce to you that ye shall be great lords. I therefore pray that, in recognition of the desire I have always had to please you, ye shall honour and venerate me in all your festivals and ceremonies, and that I shall be the first to whom ye make offerings, since I remain here for your sakes. When ye celebrate the *huarochico* (the arming of the sons as knights), ye shall adore me as their father, for I shall remain here forever."

Finally Manco Capac's staff sank into the ground and from their camp the hero pointed to a heap of stones on the site of Cuzco. Showing this to his brother, Ayar Auca, he said, "Brother! thou rememberest how it was arranged between us that thou shouldst go to take possession of the land where we are to settle. Well! behold that stone." Pointing it out, he continued, "Go thither flying," for they say that Ayar Auca had developed some wings; "and seating thyself there, take possession of the land seen from that heap of rocks. We will presently come and settle and reside." When Ayar Auca heard the words of his brother, opening his wings, he flew to that place which Manco Capac had pointed out; and seating himself there, he was presently turned into stone, being made the stone of possession. In the ancient language of this valley the heap was called cozco, whence the site has had the name of Cuzco to this day.

The Prophecy of Chilam Balam and the Story of Antonio Martinez

LET IT BE KNOWN that the day then arrived when the tenth katun was established, when the katun of the plumeria flower was established. For three moons had been established Yuma-une-tziuit, the quetzal, the green bird. Then there shall be present the forceful one, there would be Nine Mountains, Yuma-une-tziuit, the quetzal, the green bird. No one understands the penance among the rulers in the twelfth tun when he declared his name. Like a jaguar is his head, long is his tooth, withered is his body, like a dog is his body. His heart is pierced with sorrow. Sweet is his food, sweet is his drink. Perchance he does not speak, perchance he will not hear. They say his speech is false and mad. Nowhere do the younger sisters, native to the land, surrender themselves. They shall be taken away from the land here. So it shall always be with the maidens, the daughters whom they shall bear tomorrow and day after tomorrow. Give yourselves up, my younger brothers, my older brothers, submit to the unhappy destiny of the katun which is to come. If you do not submit, you shall be moved from where your feet are rooted. If you do not submit, you shall gnaw the trunks of trees and herbs. If you do not submit, it shall be as when the deer die, so that they go forth from your settlement. Then even when the ruler himself goes forth, he shall return within your settlement bearing nothing. Also there shall come such a pestilence that the vultures enter the houses, a time of great death among the wild animals. There shall be three kinds of bread, the bread-nut shall be their bread in the katun of the plumeria flower. Then comes the time when thirteen layers of mats are laid down for the very mad one, for the adulterer. Then comes the papal bull of six divisions. Three times the bull shall be announced. Then the judge of the bull shall come, when he who bears the gold staff shall judge, when white wax candles shall be exchanged. It is to be white wax, when justice shall descend from Heaven, for Christian men to come up before the eye of justice. Then it shall shake heaven and earth. In sorrow shall end the katun of the plumeria flower. No one shall fulfil his promises. The prop roots of the trees shall be bent over. There shall be an earthquake all over the land. The fulfilment of the prophecy of the katun of the plumeria flower shall be for sale. There is no reason or necessity for you to submit to the Archbishop. When he comes, you shall go and hide yourselves in the forest. If you surrender yourselves, you shall follow Christ, when he shall come. Then his visitation shall end. Then shall come to pass the shaking of the plumeria flower. Then you shall understand. Then it shall thunder from a dry sky. Then shall be spoken that which is written on the wall. Then you shall set up God, that is, you shall admit his divinity to your hearts. I hardly know what wise man among you will understand. He who understands will go into the forest to serve Christianity. Who will understand it?

After only fourteen years of chieftainship, permanently the son shall arrive, Don Antonio Martínez and Saul. These were his names when he departed from heaven. At that time he went to Tzimentan, and when he was at Tzimentan a certain queen said she would marry him. For seven years he was married, when the golden doors of the house of four apartments were opened. Here he was shown how, and he equipped a fleet of thirteen ships. Then he began a war with the land of Havana. The king had a friend at Havana, and the king was advised by his friend. The public prosecutor was there with him. Then he went and heard that the man was to be seized. Whereupon he departed and went to Tzimentan. It was three months after he was seized that the man who took him departed. Then he arrived at Tzimentan. When the man was seized, he cut short the words of him who took him when he arrived at Tzimentan, and he said: "Go, man." These were his words to him. "It is three months since I arrived," he said. "It is three months now since you departed. It was three months ago that you arrived, since you arrived, since you are shut up in the prison; in the meantime I come. I will take you out of prison. You two captains shall follow me," he said.

"Let nine chairs be raised up for us to sit on. The sea shall burn. I shall be raised up." There was fire in his eye. Sand and spray shall be raised aloft. The face of the sun shall be darkened by the great tempest. Whereupon the captain accoutered himself. Everything shall be blown to the ground by the wind. In the meantime I sit on my chair; in the meantime the fleet of thirteen ships comes. Then the king accouters himself also. "Prepare yourself, my Lord! There come the French." These were his words to me. "We shall be killed by these men. For what reason does your strength fail because of your compatriots? Let me go and direct the ship from the middle." My own spirits are raised also. The sea upon which I go burns. The face of the heavens is tilted. But when I came down into his presence, the ship was lost. "What man are you?" he said to me. "I am without compunction. It is I whom you have aided, I am he whom you have caused to live again." Then he said: "I shall put my name to the test, it is Martinez. God the Father, God the Son, God the Holy Spirit is my name." These were his words. Then I brought out the book of seven generations to read. In three months it was finished.

Now the town officials went elsewhere. Whereupon he said he would give his town, half of the men in it, to me. "Where is your town? It is all my town," he said. "You shall pay for my town, I was the first to arrive."

Then, I tell you, justice shall descend to the end that Christianity and salvation may arise. Thus shall end the men of the plumeria flower. Then the rulers of the towns shall be asked for their proofs and titles of ownership, if they know of them. Then they shall come forth from the forests and from among the rocks and live like men; then towns shall be established again. There shall be no fox to bite them. This shall be in Katun Ahau. Five years shall run until the end of my prophecy, and then shall come the time for the tribute to come down. Then there shall be an end to the paying for the wars which our fathers raised against the Spaniards. You shall not call the katun which is to come a hostile one, when Jesus Christ, the guardian of our souls, shall come. Just as we are saved here on earth, so shall he bear our souls to his holy heaven also. You are sons of the true God. Amen.

The Origin of the Deity Fehuluni

IT IS SAID that there were two parents that had nine children. And suddenly one day the eldest died. And after he was buried, then the next eldest died; and after he was buried, then the next eldest died and so on, continued day after day till the sixth was reached. And after the burial of the sixth, the man who was the seventh said: 'You remain here while I go and see what is the matter with us; for we are nearly all dead; perhaps there is someone that is carrying us off.' Thus he told them. 'I am going, and I will leave my dead body in the cave (the name of which was Makatuuua: *maka*, stone; *tuu*, appear as a spirit; *ua*, two); and should I be away a long time don't bury my body, but leave it for me to return to it.'

And he took a fine mat as a loin cloth, then he went down to Pulotu. And when he reached Pulotu he found a house and some fire that was smoking outside. Behold! it was the home of Hikuleo. And he went up to it and found a yam on the fire baking. The name of that yam was *lokolokamangavalu* (*lokoloka*, rough skin; *manga*, forked; *valu*, eight). And he broke off one of the forks (the yam had eight forks), and ate it. And Hikuleo came and turned the baking yam. Lo! one of the forks was gone. And he shouted and said, 'Who is the person that has taken the fork of my yam; just like Tui Haatala but is he not still in the world?' Then he (the intruder) again crawled forth and broke off another fork. Then again came Hikuleo and again he shouted and they repeated this, till six of the forks were taken. Then the lad appeared before Hikuleo, and said, 'It is I, Tui Haatala. I have come from the world.' It is said that Hikuleo was blind. And Hikuleo called softly, 'Come, come, why have you come to this bad place?' And then he (Hikuleo) said, 'Go to that water and bathe; and there is that cloth to wipe with; then come and we will talk.'

And he did according to Hikuleo's instructions; and he took his fine mat from earth that he had used as loin cloth, and washed it in the water. And put it on wet, and then went up and left it outside while he entered the house to talk with Hikuleo. And he told Hikuleo, 'There is something about which I have come, because we have nearly all died. We were nine in number, but there are only three of us left. Why is it, kindly tell me, that we die like that; for we die one after the other in succession and not a day passes (without a death).' And Hikuleo told him, 'All right; I have brought them to dwell with me; here we are all together, and we cannot bear for you to dwell in poverty on earth.' And he again said, 'This day it was arranged to bring you, and you have come quicker.' He had gone down before the sixth had been buried. 'But you shall return; and those that remain shall escape.'

And Tui Haatala went outside and took his fine mat which was still wet, and went up to the earth. And when he went to his body, behold they had buried it as he was so long in returning. And he cried in grief, and he took off his fine mat which was still wet, as he had brought it with him from Pulotu, and hung it on a big pandanus tree. And the fine mat dripped water, which caused a little stream which is called Maaeatanu; that stream is still in existence. And he said, 'I will not stay here; I will go and wander in other lands, and I will not go to Pulotu, because Hikuleo has said we shall dwell on earth we who are left.' And he came from Eua to Eueiki, and from there he came to Tongatabu, and from there he went to Haapai; and from there he went to Vavau; and from there he went to Samoa, and from there he went to Fiji. And he is seen at these islands, but he is never seen at Eua. And he is called by different names in the various islands. He is called by the Tongans Fehuluni (To move about); and he is called by the Samoans Moso; and he is called by another name in Fiji; but he is still Tui Haatala.

His father was Tui Haatala, and he and their mother were the first to die, and then they (his brothers) died one after the other as has been stated.

And they were the grandchildren of Hikuleo, and since then there has been no more Tui Haatala, the man that went to Pulotu was the last one. The way of their death was perplexing, one died and another was appointed, and he died and another was appointed. They were just like that. And the Tui Haatala that went to Pulotu was the last. When he went he was already appointed, and it is said that none were appointed after him; he went without dying and was to return. And it was difficult (for another) to take (his title), because he had returned but was unable to become a man because his body had been buried. And it has been so ever since.

And there are also some things about bygone days, his (hair) lime is a big stone, which if chipped and made into a hair wash is like cooked lime.

The Twelve Brothers

THERE WERE ONCE on a time a king and a queen who lived happily together and had twelve children, but they were all boys. Then said the King to his wife, "If the thirteenth child which thou art about to bring into the world is a girl, the twelve boys shall die, in order that her possessions may be great, and that the kingdom may fall to her alone."

He caused likewise twelve coffins to be made, which were already filled with shavings, and in each lay the little pillow for the dead, and he had them taken into a locked-up room, and then he gave the Queen the key of it, and bade her not to speak of this to anyone.

The mother, however, now sat and lamented all day long, until the youngest son, who was always with her, and whom she had named Benjamin, from the Bible, said to her, "Dear mother, why art thou so sad?"

"Dearest child," she answered, "I may not tell thee."

But he let her have no rest until she went and unlocked the room, and showed him the twelve coffins ready filled with shavings. Then she said, "My dearest Benjamin, thy father has had these coffins made for thee and for thy eleven brothers, for if I bring a little girl into the world, you are all to be killed and buried in them."

And as she wept while she was saying this, the son comforted her and said, "Weep not, dear mother, we will save ourselves, and go hence."

But she said, "Go forth into the forest with thy eleven brothers, and let one sit constantly on the highest tree which can be found, and keep watch, looking towards the tower here in the castle. If I give birth to a little son, I will put up a white flag, and then you may venture to come back, but if I bear a daughter, I will hoist a red flag, and then fly hence as quickly as you are able, and may the good God protect you. And every night I will rise up and pray for you – in winter that you may be able to warm yourself at a fire, and in summer that you may not faint away in the heat."

After she had blessed her sons therefore, they went forth into the forest. They each kept watch in turn, and sat on the highest oak and looked towards the tower. When eleven days had passed and the turn came to Benjamin, he saw that a flag was being raised. It was, however, not the white, but the blood-red flag which announced that they were all to die. When the brothers heard that, they were very angry and said, "Are we all to suffer death for the sake of a girl? We swear that we will avenge ourselves! – Wheresoever we find a girl, her red blood shall flow."

Thereupon they went deeper into the forest, and in the midst of it, where it was the darkest, they found a little bewitched hut, which was standing empty. Then said they, "Here we will dwell, and thou Benjamin, who art the youngest and weakest, thou shalt stay at home and keep house, we others will go out and get food."

Then they went into the forest and shot hares, wild deer, birds and pigeons, and whatsoever there was to eat; this they took to Benjamin, who had to dress it for them in order that they might appease their hunger. They lived together ten years in the little hut, and the time did not appear long to them.

The little daughter which their mother the Queen had given birth to was now grown up; she was good of heart, and fair of face, and had a golden star on her forehead. Once, when it was the great washing, she saw twelve men's shirts among the things, and asked her mother, "To whom do these twelve shirts belong, for they are far too small for father?"

Then the Queen answered with a heavy heart, "Dear child, these belong to thy twelve brothers."

Said the maiden, "Where are my twelve brothers, I have never yet heard of them?"

She replied, "God knows where they are, they are wandering about the world."

Then she took the maiden and opened the chamber for her, and showed her the twelve coffins with the shavings, and pillows for the head. "These coffins," said she, "were destined for thy brothers, but they went away secretly before thou wert born," and she related to her how everything had happened; then said the maiden, "Dear mother, weep not, I will go and seek my brothers."

So she took the twelve shirts and went forth, and straight into the great forest. She walked the whole day, and in the evening she came to the bewitched hut. Then she entered it and found a young boy, who asked, "From whence comest thou, and whither art thou bound?" and was astonished that she was so beautiful, and wore royal garments, and had a star on her forehead. And she answered, "I am a king's daughter, and am seeking my twelve brothers, and I will walk as far as the sky is blue until I find them." She likewise showed him the twelve shirts which belonged to them. Then Benjamin saw that she was his sister, and said, "I am Benjamin, thy youngest brother." And she began to weep for joy, and Benjamin wept also, and they kissed and embraced each other with the greatest love. But after this he said, "Dear sister, there is still one difficulty. We have agreed that every maiden whom we meet shall die, because we have been obliged to leave our kingdom on account of a girl."

Then said she, "I will willingly die, if by so doing I can deliver my twelve brothers."

"No," answered he, "thou shalt not die, seat thyself beneath this tub until our eleven brothers come, and then I will soon come to an agreement with them."

She did so, and when it was night the others came from hunting, and their dinner was ready. And as they were sitting at table, and eating, they asked, "What news is there?"

Said Benjamin, "Don't you know anything?"

"No," they answered.

He continued, "You have been in the forest and I have stayed at home, and yet I know more than you do."

"Tell us then," they cried. He answered, "But promise me that the first maiden who meets us shall not be killed."

"Yes," they all cried, "she shall have mercy, only do tell us."

Then said he, "Our sister is here," and he lifted up the tub, and the King's daughter came forth in her royal garments with the golden star on her forehead, and she was beautiful, delicate and fair. Then they were all rejoiced, and fell on her neck, and kissed and loved her with all their hearts.

Now she stayed at home with Benjamin and helped him with the work. The eleven went into the forest and caught game, and deer, and birds, and wood-pigeons that they might have food, and the little sister and Benjamin took care to make it ready for them. She sought for the wood for cooking and herbs for vegetables, and put the pans on the fire so that the dinner was always ready when the eleven came. She likewise kept order in the little house, and put beautifully white clean coverings on the little beds, and the brothers were always contented and lived in great harmony with her.

Once on a time the two at home had prepared a beautiful entertainment, and when they were all together, they sat down and ate and drank and were full of gladness. There was, however, a little garden belonging to the bewitched house wherein stood twelve lily flowers, which are likewise called students. She wished to give her brothers pleasure, and plucked the twelve flowers, and thought she would present each brother with one while at dinner. But at the self-same moment that she plucked the flowers the twelve brothers were changed into twelve ravens, and flew away over the forest, and the house and garden vanished likewise. And now the poor maiden was alone in the wild forest, and when she looked around, an old woman was standing near her who said, "My child, what hast thou done? Why didst thou not leave the twelve white flowers growing? They were thy brothers, who are now for evermore changed into ravens."

The maiden said, weeping, "Is there no way of delivering them?"

"No," said the woman, "there is but one in the whole world, and that is so hard that thou wilt not deliver them by it, for thou must be dumb for seven years, and mayst not speak or laugh, and if thou speakest one single word, and only an hour of the seven years is wanting, all is in vain, and thy brothers will be killed by the one word."

Then said the maiden in her heart, "I know with certainty that I shall set my brothers free," and went and sought a high tree and seated herself in it and span, and neither spoke nor laughed. Now it so happened that a king was hunting in the forest, who had a great greyhound which ran to the tree on which the maiden was sitting, and sprang about it, whining, and barking at her. Then the King came by and saw the beautiful King's daughter with the golden star on her brow, and was so charmed with her beauty that he called to ask her if she would be his wife.

She made no answer, but nodded a little with her head.

So he climbed up the tree himself, carried her down, placed her on his horse, and bore her home. Then the wedding was solemnized with great magnificence and rejoicing, but the bride neither spoke nor smiled.

When they had lived happily together for a few years, the King's mother, who was a wicked woman, began to slander the young Queen, and said to the King, "This is a common beggar girl whom thou hast brought back with thee. Who knows what impious tricks she practises secretly! Even if she be dumb, and not able to speak, she still might laugh for once; but those who do not laugh have bad consciences."

At first the King would not believe it, but the old woman urged this so long, and accused her of so many evil things, that at last the King let himself be persuaded and sentenced her to death.

And now a great fire was lighted in the courtyard in which she was to be burnt, and the King stood above at the window and looked on with tearful eyes, because he still loved her so much. And when she was bound fast to the stake, and the fire was licking at her clothes with its red tongue, the last instant of the seven years expired.

Then a whirring sound was heard in the air, and twelve ravens came flying towards the place, and sank downwards, and when they touched the earth they were her twelve brothers, whom she had delivered. They tore the fire asunder, extinguished the flames, set their dear sister free, and kissed and embraced her. And now as she dared to open her mouth and speak, she told the King why she had been dumb, and had never laughed. The King rejoiced when he heard that she was innocent, and they all lived in great unity until their death. The wicked step-mother was taken before the judge, and put into a barrel filled with boiling oil and venomous snakes, and died an evil death.

Biographies & Text Sources

The stories in this book derive from a multitude of original sources, often from the nineteenth century and often based on the writer's first-hand accounts of tales narrated to them by natives, while others are their own retellings of traditional tales. Authors, works and contributors to this book include:

Richard Stoneman
Foreword
Richard Stoneman is an honorary visiting professor at the University of Exeter. The core of his research and interest has been the continuity of the Greek world and Greek tradition up to the present day. He is Series Editor for *Understanding Classics*, which aims to introduce major writers of the classical and early Christian worlds, providing a map of the scholarship and critical response for the benefit of students as well as scholars in other fields. He has written anthologies and travel guides reflecting these interests, one notable title being *The Ancient Oracles: Making the Gods Speak* (Yale University Press, 2011). His most recent books are a biography of *Xerxes* (Yale Uuniversity Press, 2015) and *The Greek Experience of India* (Princeton University Press, 2019).

Cyrus Adler
How Cobbler Ahmet Became the Chief Astrologer
Cyrus Adler (1863–1940) was an American Jewish educator, scholar, editor and Jewish leader. He was a professor of Semitic languages and went on to be commissioner for the world's Columbian exposition to the Orient in 1890 securing exhibits for over 16 months.

Jón Árnason
The Story of Grímur, Who Killed Skeljúngur
Jón Árnason (1819–1888) was an Icelandic author, museum director and librarian. He is known for publishing the world's first collection of Icelandic folktales. This collection, entitled *Íslenzk Aefintýri* (Icelandic Folktales), was published in 1852 and co-edited with Árnason's friend Magnús Grímsson. It was later republished in two volumes as *Íslenzkar Þjóðsögur og Aefintýri* (Icelandic Folktales and Legends) between 1862 and 1864. Árnason was the original collector of the Icelandic tale 'The Witch in the Stone Boat'. He also wrote biographies, served as the first National Librarian of Iceland and was the first curator of what would become the National Museum of Iceland.

James Atkinson
The Story of Saiáwush
James Atkinson (1780–1852) was a surgeon, an artist, and a Persian scholar. He was born in County Durham in England, and studied medicine in both Edinburgh and London, although he also showed an affinity for languages and art from a young age. He worked as a Surgeon's Mate and Assistant Surgeon on ships with the East India Trading Company, and it was during his time in India that he began to study and translate Persian. Among his works are a translation of *Firdusi's Shahnameh* (1832) and of *Nizami's Laili and Majnun* (1836).

George W. Bateman
The Physician's Son and the King of Snakes
George W. Bateman (1850–1940) was the British-born author of the famous *Zanzibar Tales: Told by Natives of the East Coast of Africa* (1901), in which he presented stories, "translated from the Original Swahili", told to him in Zanzibar, by locals "whose ancestors told them to them, who had received them from their ancestors, and so back." Reportedly many of these tales were the inspiration for several Disney films such as *Bambi*, *The Lion King* and so on.

E.M. Berens
The Loves of Apollo; Ion
E.M. Berens was a scholar and author of classical mythology and folklore. His most important and best-known work is *Myths and Legends of Ancient Greece and Rome* (1894).

Abbie Farwell Brown
Balder and the Misteltoe
American author Abbie Farwell Brown (1871–1927) was born in Boston and attended the Girls' Latin School. While attending school she set up a school newspaper and also contributed articles to other magazines. Brown's books were most often retellings of old tales for children such as in *The Book of Saints and Friendly Beasts*. She also published a collection of tales from Norse mythology, *In the Days of Giants*, which became the common text held by many libraries for several generations.

Padraic Colum
Gods of the Azteca
Padraic Colum (1881–1972) was born in County Longford, Ireland. He wrote prolifically as a poet, biographer, novelist, playwright, dramatist, children's book author and folklore collector. A prominent figure in the late nineteenth-century Irish Literary Revival, Colum developed connections with numerous well-known Irish writers including James Joyce and W.B. Yeats. His first book, a poetry collection entitled *Wild Earth*, was published in 1907. Later living in the US, Colum ventured into prose fiction and children's books, and taught at Columbia University and CCNY.

Jeremiah Curtin
Water of Youth, Water of Life and Water of Death
Jeremiah Curtin (1835–1906) was a Detroit-born ethnographer and folklorist. While much of his work focused on collecting myths and folktales from around the world, Curtin was also renowned for his translations of works by Polish author Henryk Sienkiewicz. Between 1883 and 1891 Curtin's interests would focus closer to home, when he worked as a field researcher recording the myths and customs of Native American people, which would later result in the publication of the book *Creation Myths of Primitive America* (1898).

Lucy Crane
The Twelve Brothers
Lucy Crane (1842–1882) was a talented musician and artist. She translated the Brothers Grimm's *Household Stories* collection from German to English in 1882.

BIOGRAPHIES & TEXT SOURCES

F. Hadland Davis
Tobikawa Imitates a Tengu; Chrysanthemum-Old-Man; The White Hare of Inaba; The Divine Messengers; In the Palace of the Sea God; Benten-of-the-Birth-Water
Frederick Hadland Davis was a writer and a historian – author of *The Land of the Yellow Spring and Other Japanese Stories* (1910) and *The Persian Mystics* (1908 and 1920). His books describe these cultures to the Western world and tell stories of ghosts, creation, mystical creatures and more. He is best known for his book *Myths and Legends of Japan* (1912).

Elphinstone Dayrell
The Orphan Boy and the Magic Stone; The Story of the Drummer and the Alligators; Why Dead People are Buried
Elphinstone Dayrell (1869–1917) collected his tales after hearing many first-hand from the Efik and Ibibio peoples of South East Nigeria when he was District Commissioner of South Nigeria. His collections of folklore include *Folk Stories From Southern Nigeria* (1910) and *Ikom Folk Stories From Southern Nigeria*, the latter published by the Royal Anthropological Institute of Great Briain and Ireland in 1913.

Alice Dracott
The Man Who Went to Seek His Fortune
Alice Elizabeth Dracott was the author of *Simla Village Tales*: Or, *Folk Tales From the Himalayas* (1906), the source of the story 'The Man Who Went to Seek His Fortune'.

L. Winifred Faraday
The Cattle-Raid of Cualnge
L. Winifred Faraday (1872–1948) was a teacher and folklorist. The above translation was the first English translation based on two incomplete and early versions of the Táin.

Parker Fillmore
Katcha and the Devil; The Flaming Horse
Parker Fillmore (1878–1944) was an American author born in Cincinnati, Ohio. Upon taking a job as a teacher in the Philippines, Fillmore was given no textbooks to teach his students English, and so he crafted his own stories for this purpose, launching his career in writing. Returning to the US and moving to a primarily Czech neighbourhood in New York City, he gained a great passion for the Czechoslovakian folklore that his neighbours shared with him. This led to his publication of several collections of these stories including *Czechoslovak Fairy Tales* (1919) and *The Shoemaker's Apron* (1920).

James S. Gale
The Temple to the God of War
The work of classical Korean storytellers Im Bang and Yi Ryuk was translated from the Korean by James S. Gale (1863–1937) and published as *Korean Folk Tales: Imps, Ghosts and Fairies* in 1913. Gale was a Canadian missionary, educator and Bible translator who was sent to Korea in 1888.

Pedro Sarmiento de Gamboa
Manco Capac Founds Cuzco
Pedro Sarmiento de Gamboa (1532–92) was a Spanish explorer, historian, author, astronomer

and mathematician. He sailed to 'New Spain' (present-day Mexico) in 1555, marking the beginning of his career in exploration. He later joined an expedition which resulted in the discovery of the Solomon Islands. In 1572, the fifth Viceroy of Peru, Francisco de Toledo, commissioned Sarmiento de Gamboa to write a history of the Incan civilization. The resulting work, *History of the Incas*, preserved meticulous details of the Incas' culture and history.

Edward Winslow Gifford
The Origin of the Deity Fehuluni
Edward Winslow Gifford (1887–1959) was a professor of anthropology in California as well as being an archaeologist. His anthropological expedition to the Tonga Islands was a notable achievement and he went on to write *Tongan Society* (1929).

H. A. Guerber
Tyr's Sword, Ragnarok, Oedipus, The Norns' Web; The Story of Nornagesta; Hermod; Vidar
Hélène Adeline Guerber (1859–1929) was a British historian who published a large number of works, largely focused on myths and legends. Guerber's most famous publication is *Myths of the Norsemen: From the Eddas and Sagas*, a history of Germanic mythology. Her works continue to be published today and include *The Myths of Greece and Rome*, *The Story of the Greeks* and *Legends of the Middle Ages*.

Lady Charlotte Guest
The Fourth Branch of the Mabinogi; Tale of Taliesin; The Dream of Maxen Wledig
Lady Charlotte Elizabeth Guest (née Bertie; 1812–95), later Lady Charlotte Schreiber, was an English aristocrat who became a prominent figure in the study of literature, as well as a philanthropist, educator and collector. She is best known as the first publisher, in 1838–45, in modern print format in Welsh and English, of the Middle Welsh prose stories known as *The Mabinogion*.

James A. Honey, M.D
Horse Cursed by Sun (from South Africa)
Dr James Albert Burnside Honeij (1880–1924) was born in Bloemfontein in Free State, South Africa, but worked and died in Cambridge, Massachusetts. Though a doctor, he had an apparent interest in folklore, publishing a collection of *South-African Folk-Tales* (1910) for an American audience, stating that many of them have "appeared among English collections previous to 1880, others have been translated from the Dutch, and a few have been written from childhood remembrance."

Margaret Hunt
Briar-Rose; The Devil with the Three Golden Hairs
Margaret Raine Hunt (1831–1912) was a British translator and author. Hunt was born in Durham, and later lived in London during the late nineteenth century. She is best known for her English translations of German fairy tales by the Brothers Grimm. She published a two-volume English-language collection of their tales in 1884, entitled *Grimm's Household Tales*, featuring an introduction by Andrew Lang. Hunt also published works under the pen-name Averil Beaumont. Her novels include *Under Seal of Confession* (1874), *The Leaden Casket* (1880), and *Thornicroft's Model* (1881).

BIOGRAPHIES & TEXT SOURCES

Joseph Jacobs
How Fin Went to the Kingdom of Big Men
Joseph Jacobs (1854–1916) was born in Australia and settled in New York. He is most famous for his collections of English folklore and fairytales including 'Jack and the Beanstalk' and 'The Three Little Pigs'. He also published Celtic, Jewish and Indian fairytales during his career. Jacobs was an editor of books and journals centred on folklore and a member of The Folklore Society in England.

Charles Kingsley
How the Argonauts Sailed to Colchis
Charles Kingsley (1819–75) was an English priest, professor, social reformer, historian, novelist and poet, whose most famous works are probably the novels *Westward Ho!* (1855) and *The Water- Babies, A Fairy Tale for a Land Baby* (1863). Though he held some questionable views, his knack for storytelling is evident in *The Heroes, or Greek Fairy Tales* (1856).

Sir James Knowles
The Prophecies of Merlin, and the Birth of Arthur
Sir James Knowles (1831–1908) Alongside his career in architecture, he also branched into the literary sphere and published *The Legends of King Arthur and His Knights* in 1860.

Lewis L. Kropp
The Three Dreams, The Three Princes, The Three Dragons, and the Woman with the Iron Nose
Lewis L. Kropp (1852–1939) studied at the Budapest University of Technology and Economics. He translated and edited *The Folk-tales of the Magyars* (1889) with the Rev W. Henry Jones.

Ignácz Kúnos
The Rose Beauty
Ignácz Kúnos (1860–1945) was a Hungarian linguist, author and Turkologist. He was a prominent scholar of Turkish folk literature and dialectology. Having studied linguistics at Budapest University and spending five years studying the Turkish language and culture in Constantinople (now Istanbul), he became professor of Turkish philology at Budapest University in 1890. He later worked as a professor at various other institutions and established the Department of Folkloristics at Istanbul University in 1925. His folktale collections include *Turkish Fairy Tales and Folk Tales* (1896) and *Forty-Four Turkish Fairy Tales* (1914).

Andrew Lang
The Death of Achilles; The Stealing of Helen; The Beresford Ghost; The Terrible Head; Trojan Victories
Poet, novelist and anthropologist Andrew Lang (1844–1912) was born in Selkirk, Scotland. He is now best known for his collections of fairy stories and publications on folklore, mythology and religion. Inspired by the traditional folklore tales of his home on the English-Scottish border, Lang compiled twelve coloured fairy books which collected 798 stories from French, Danish, Russian and Romanian sources, amongst others. This series was hugely popular and had a wide influence on increasing the popularity of fairy tales in children's literature.

Charles Lummis
The First of the Rattlesnakes
Charles Fletcher Lummis (1859–1928) was born in Lynn, Massachusetts. Moving to the Southwest, he developed a passion for the region and its indigenous peoples, and he wrote extensively on these cultures. As a writer, journalist and activist, he advocated for the rights of Native Americans and the preservation of their cultures. Lummis created the Sequoya League, a Native American rights group, and he battled the US Bureau of Indian Affairs. In 1907 he founded the Southwest Museum of the American Indian in Los Angeles.

Rev. J. Macgowan
The Reward of a Benevolent Life; The Vengence of the Goddess; The Mytserious Buddhist Robe
John Macgowan (1835–1922) was born in Belfast and became a missionary to China with the London Missionary Society, where he helped to found the anti-footbinding Natural Foot Society. He was author of many books about Chinese culture and history. As well as *Chinese Folk-Lore Tales* (1910), his works include *English and Chinese Dictionary of the Amoy Dialect* (1883) and *Men and Manners of Modern China* (1912).

Alexander Mackenzie
The Seer's Death; Seaforth's Dream
Alexander Mackenzie (1838–1898) was a Scottish author, historian, politician, and magazine editor. Born in Gairloch, Scotland, Mackenzie worked as a labourer and ploughman before starting a business in the cloth trade. Later he became an editor and publisher of *Celtic Magazine* and *Scottish Highlander*. His best-known work is his collections entitled *Historical Tales and Legends of the Highlands* (1878). He also penned histories of a number of Scottish clans. He became a member of the Society of Antiquaries of Scotland and a founding member of the Gaelic Society of Inverness.

Donald A. Mackenzie
An End to the Exile; Yama and Savitri
Donald Alexander Mackenzie (1873–1936) was a Scottish journalist and folklorist and a prolific writer on religion, mythology and anthropology in the early twentieth century. Born in Cromarty, he became a journalist in Glasgow, later moving to be editor and/or owner of publications in Dingwall, Dundee and Edinburgh. He wrote nearly fifty books, mostly on ancient history and mythology, as well as articles and poems. He often gave lectures, and also broadcast talks on Celtic mythology. He is the author of *Myths of Babylonia and Assyria* (1915), selections of which are used in the present volume.

Sir Clements Markham
The Stolen Child; The Shepherd and the Daughter of the Sun
Sir Clements Markham K.C.B. (1830–1916) was an English geographer, writer and explorer. Serving as secretary of the Royal Geography Society from 1863 to 1888, and later the society's president for a further twelve years, Markham organized the British National Antarctic Expedition of 1901–04. He is known for spurring the nineteenth-century revival of Britain's interest in exploring the Antarctic, as well as his prolific writings on geography, travel and history. He also produced English translations of numerous Spanish works including Pedro Sarmient de Gamboa's *History of the Incas*.

Logan Marshall
The Labour of Hercules
Logan Marshall was the pen-name of Logan Howard-Smith (born in 1883). He was an American author born in Philadelphia, Pennsylvania. Marshall graduated from the University of Pennsylvania in 1905, following which he became an assistant editor at the publishing firm The John C. Winston Co. There he both edited and authored a great number of books under his pen-name. His best-known of these was *The Sinking of the Titanic and Great Sea Disasters* (1912), which grew hugely popular due to massive public interest in the tragedy.

Frederick H. Martens
The Constable; The Spirits of the Yellow River
Frederick Herman Martens (1874–1932) was an author, lyricist and translator, whose work includes a translation of Pietro Yon's 1917 Christmas carol 'Gesu Bambino', a biography of the musician A.E. Uhe (1922), *A Thousand and One Nights of Opera* (1926), *Violin Mastery (Talks with Master Violinists and Teachers)* (1919), and fairy-tale translations in *The Chinese Fairy Book* (ed. Dr. R. Wilhelm).

Minnie Martin
The Chief and the Tigers; Morena-Y-A-Letsatsi, or the Sun Chief
Minnie Martin was the wife of a government official, who arrived in South Africa in 1891 and settled in Lesotho (at that time Basutoland). In her preface to *Basutoland: Its Legends and Customs* (1903) she explains that "We both liked the country from the first, and I soon became interested in the people. To enable myself to understand them better, I began to study the language, which I can now speak fairly well." And thus she wrote this work, at the suggestion of a friend. Despite the inaccuracies pointed out by E. Sidney Hartland in his review of her book, he deemed the work "an unpretentious, popular account of a most interesting branch of the Southern Bantus and the country they live in."

William Melmoth
Letter LXXXIII to Sura
William Melmoth (*c.* 1710–1799) had a short-lived legal career before moving out of London. He translated *Letters of Pliny the Younger* and it was first published in 1746.

Elodie Lawton Mijatovich
The Dream of the King's Son
Elodie L. Mijatovich (1825–1908) was a British author. During the 1850s she lived in Boston, Massachusetts, where she advocated for the abolitionist movement. Following her marriage to a Serbian politician, she moved to Belgrade, and then to London. She was the translator of several Serbian literary works, including *Serbian Folk-Lore* (1874), *Serbian Fairy Tales* (published posthumously in 1918) and *The History of Modern Serbia* (1872). She also translated numerous Serbian national songs of the Kosovo cycle into English.

Maximilian A. Mugge
Fate
Little is known about Maximilian A. Mugge (1878–1963). He translated *Serbian Folk Songs, Fairy Tales and Proverbs* into English and it was published in 1916.

Woislav M. Petrovitch

The Ram with the Golden Fleece; He Whom God Helps No One Can Harm
Little is known about Woislav M. Petrovich (birth unknown–1934). He wrote *Hero Tales and Legends of the Serbians* and it was first published in 1914.

Katharine Pyle

The Dutiful Daughter
Katharine Pyle (1863–1938) was an American author and illustrator. She primarily wrote books for young adults, as well as works on the colonial history of her home state of Delaware. She became interested in writing and art as a child, and later attended the Philadelphia School of Design for Women. Pyle initially published poems in *St. Nicholas Magazine* and *Harper's Bazaar*, and she co-wrote the book *The Wonder Clock* (1887) with her brother Howard Pyle. She contributed to America's Golden Age of Illustration and collabourated with fellow creatives on many books as both a writer and an illustrator.

Ralph L. Roys

The Prophecy of Chilam Balam and the Story of Antonio Martinez
Ralph Loveland Roys (1879–1965) was a Research Professor of Anthropology. He was known globally for his work in Maya linguistics and translated and edited many Maya documents.

Comtesse Ségur

The Conflaguration
Sophie Rostopchine, Countess of Ségur (1799–1874) was a Russian-born French writer. She had many French-published novels. *Old French Fairy Tales* was published in 1857.

Henry Rowe Schoolcraft

Ojeeg Annung, or The Summer Maker; Tau-wau-chee-hezkaw, or The White Feather; Iosco, or The Prairie Boys' Visit to the Sun and the Moon
Henry Rowe Schoolcraft (1793–1865) devoted a significant portion of his life to interactions with Native American people. In 1822 he served as an Indian agent for the US government covering Michigan, Wisconsin and Minnesota, before later marrying Jane Johnston, who was herself the daughter of an Ojibwa war chief. From his wife Schoolcraft would learn the Ojibwa language and much about their history and way of life. He would go on to write extensively about the Native American people, with works including *The Myth of Hiawatha, and other Oral Legends, Mythologic and Allegoric, of the North American Indians* (1856) and a comprehensive six-volume series titled *Historical and Statistical Information Respecting the History, Condition, and Prospects of the Indian Tribes of the United States* that was published between 1851 and 1857.

Lewis Spence

Berossus's Account of the Deluge; The Vision of Yupanqui
James Lewis Thomas Chalmers Spence (1874–1955) was a Scottish journalist, poet, author, folklorist and occult scholar. After graduating from Edinburgh University he pursued a career in journalism, during which time his interest was sparked in the myth and folklore of Mexico and Central America. Spence was a Fellow of the Royal Anthropological Institute of Great Britain and Ireland, and vice-president of the Scottish Anthropological and Folklore Society. He also founded the Scottish National Movement. Over his long career, Spence published

more than forty books of history and mythology. He was also a published poet. He is the author of *Myths and Legends of Babylonia and Assyria* (1916), selections of which are used in the present volume.

Henry M. Stanley
The Prince Who Insisted on Possessing the Moon; How Kimyera Became King of Uganda; The Legend of the Leopardess and Her Two Servants; Dog and Jackal; The Elephant and the Lion

"Dr Livingstone, I presume?" Welshman Sir Henry Morton Stanley (1841–1904) is probably most famous for a line he may or may not have uttered on encountering the missionary and explorer he had been sent to locate in Africa. He was also an ex-soldier who fought for the Confederate Army, the Union Army and the Union Navy before becoming a journalist and explorer of Central Africa. He joined Livingstone in the search for the source of the Nile and worked for King Leopold II of Belgium in the latter's mission to conquer the Congo basin. His works include *How I Found Livingstone* (1872), *Through the Dark Continent* (1878) *The Congo and the Founding of Its Free State* (1885), and *My Dark Companions* (1893).

Capt. C.H. Stigand
The Sultan's Snake-child; The Young Thief

Chauncey Hugh Stigand (1877–1919) was a British army officer, colonial administrator and big game hunter who served in Burma, British Somaliland and British East Africa. He was in charge of the Kajo Kaji district of what is now South Sudan, and was later made governor of the Upper Nile province and then Mongalla Province before being killed during a 1919 uprising of the Aliab Dinka people. During his time in Africa he managed to write prolifically, from *Central African Game and its Spoor* (1906), through *Black Tales for White Children* (1914), to *A Nuer-English Vocabulary*, published posthumously in 1923.

Frona Eunice Wait
Tulla, the Hiding Nook of the Snake

Frona Eunice Wait (1859–1946) was an American author and journalist who published numerous books as well as articles for various newspapers and magazines. Following the death of her second child in 1880, Wait began her career in journalism. Working at the *Santa Rosa Republican* and later the *San Francisco Examiner*, she was one of just two women journalists on staff. She later became an associate editor for the *Overland Monthly*.

Alice Werner
Kwege and Bahati; The Road to Heaven; How a Girl Reached the Land of the Ghosts and Came Back; Sudika-Mbambi the Invincible; Ryangombe and Binego; King Kitamba kia Shiba (and the Kingdom of Death)

Alice Werner (1859–1935) was a writer, poet and professor of Swahili and Bantu languages. She travelled widely in her early life, but by 1894 she had focused her writing on African culture and language, and later joined the School of Oriental Studies, working her way up from lecturer to professor. *Myths and Legends of the Bantu* (1933) was her last main work, but others on African topics include *The Language Families of Africa* (1915), *Introductory Sketch of the Bantu Languages* (1919), *The Swahili Saga of Liongo Fumo* (1926) and *Swahili Tales* (1929).

W.B. Yeats

The Banshee of the Mac Carthys; The Curse of the Fires and of the Shadows

William Butler Yeats (1865–1939) was an Irish poet and is considered one of the greatest writers from the twentieth century. He played an important role in the Celtic Twilight, a revival of Irish literature focused on Gaelic heritage and Irish nationalism. Yeats was fascinated by Irish legends, including many Irish heroes in his works and focusing his poetry on Irish folklore. Alongside his poetry he is famous for writing short stories and plays. Yeats set up the Abbey Theatre in 1899 which held Irish and Celtic performances. In recognition of Yeats' important work he received a Nobel Prize in 1923.

FLAME TREE PUBLISHING
Epic, Dark, Thrilling & Gothic
New & Classic Writing

Flame Tree's Gothic Fantasy books offer a carefully curated series of new titles, each with combinations of original and classic writing:

*A Dying Planet • African Ghost • Agents & Spies • Alien Invasion • Alternate History
American Gothic • Asian Ghost • Black Sci-Fi • Bodies in the Library • Chilling Crime
Chilling Ghost • Chilling Horror • Christmas Gothic • Compelling Science Fiction • Cosy Crime
Crime & Mystery • Detective Mysteries • Detective Thrillers • Dystopia Utopia • Endless Apocalypse
Epic Fantasy • First Peoples Shared Stories • Footsteps in the Dark • Haunted House
Heroic Fantasy • Hidden Realms • Immigrant Sci-Fi • Learning to be Human
Lost Atlantis • Lost Souls • Lost Worlds • Lovecraft Mythos • Moon Falling • Murder Mayhem
Pirates & Ghosts • Robots & AI • Robots Past & Future • Science Fiction • Shadows on the Water
Spirits & Ghouls Strange Lands • Sun Rising • Supernatural Horror • Swords & Steam
Terrifying Ghosts • Time Travel • Urban Crime • Weird Horror • Were Wolf*

Also, new companion titles offer rich collections of classic fiction, myths and tales in the gothic fantasy tradition:

*Charles Dickens Supernatural • George Orwell Visions of Dystopia • H.G. Wells • Lovecraft
Sherlock Holmes • Edgar Allan Poe • Bram Stoker Horror Stories • Mary Shelley Horror Stories
Sheridan Le Fanu Horror Stories • M.R. James Ghost Stories • Algernon Blackwood Horror Stories
Arthur Machen Horror Stories • William Hope Hodgson Horror Stories • Robert Louis Stevenson
The Age of Queen Victoria • Alice's Adventures in Wonderland • The Wonderful Wizard of Oz
King Arthur & The Knights of the Round Table • Ramayana • The Odyssey and the Iliad • The Aeneid
The Divine Comedy • Paradise Lost • The Decameron • One Thousand and One Arabian Nights
Moby Dick • Don Quixote • Hans Christian Andersen Fairy Tales • Brothers Grimm Fairy Tales
Babylon & Sumer Myths & Tales • Persian Myths & Tales • African Myths & Tales
Greek Myths & Tales • Norse Myths & Tales • Chinese Myths & Tales • Japanese Myths & Tales
Native American Myths & Tales • Aztec Myths & Tales • Egyptian Myths & Tales • Viking Folk & Fairy Tales
Celtic Myths & Tales • Irish Fairy Tales • Scottish Folk & Fairy Tales • Heroes & Heroines Myths & Tales
Quests & Journeys Myths & Tales • Gods & Monsters Myths & Tales • Titans & Giants Myths & Tales
Beasts & Creatures Myths & Tales • Witches, Wizards, Seers & Healers Myths & Tales
Origins & Endings Myths & Tales • Prophecies & Oracles Myths & Tales*

Available from all good bookstores, worldwide, and online at
flametreepublishing.com

See our new fiction imprint
FLAME TREE PRESS | FICTION WITHOUT FRONTIERS
New and original writing in Horror, Crime, SF and Fantasy

And join our monthly newsletter with offers and more stories:
FLAME TREE FICTION NEWSLETTER
flametreepress.comflametreepress.com

For our books, calendars, blog
and latest special offers please see:
flametreepublishing.com